At that second I rolled to the right, yanked my stiletto out of its sheath and then braced myself as the animal leaped toward me again.

This time the razor-sharp stiletto blade caught the dog in the chest, and I pulled violently to the left, opening a huge hole in its body.

The dog howled in pain and leaped to the left and then around in circles as it snapped at its own entrails hanging from the gaping wound.

I jumped up, sheathed the stiletto, grabbed my jacket and quickly climbed the fence. At the top, I flipped the jacket on top of the barbed wire, scrambled to the other side and dropped down to the ground.

At least four of the dogs were dead and my jacket was up in the barbed wire. When all that was discovered, DeGourcy's staff would have no doubt that someone not easily discouraged had come to pay a visit. No doubt at all. . . .

## NICK CARTER IS IT!

"Nick Carter out-Bonds James Bond."

—*Buffalo Evening News*

"Nick Carter is America's #1 espionage agent."

—*Variety*

"Nick Carter is razor-sharp suspense."

—*King Features*

"Nick Carter is extraordinarily big."

—*Bestsellers*

"Nick Carter has attracted an army of addicted readers . . . the books are fast, have plenty of action and just the right degree of sex . . . Nick Carter is the American James Bond, suave, sophisticated, a killer with both the ladies and the enemy."

—*The New York Times*

## FROM THE NICK CARTER KILLMASTER SERIES

CHESSMASTER
THE COYOTE CONNECTION
THE DAMOCLES THREAT
THE DAY OF THE DINGO
DEATHLIGHT
THE DEVIL'S DOZEN
DOMINICAN AFFAIR
DOOMSDAY SPORE
DUBROVNIK MASSACRE
EARTH SHAKER
THE GOLDEN BULL
HUMAN TIME BOMB
THE ISRAELI CONNECTION
THE JUDAS SPY
KATMANDU CONTRACT
LAST SAMURAI
LIVING DEATH
THE MAN WHO SOLD DEATH
THE NICHOVEV PLOT
NORWEGIAN TYPHOON
PAMPLONA AFFAIR
THE PARISIAN AFFAIR
THE PEMEX CHART
THE PUPPET MASTER
THE Q MAN
THE REDOLMO AFFAIR
THE RED RAYS
THE SATAN TRAP
SIGN OF THE COBRA
THE SIGN OF THE PRAYER SHAWL
SIX BLOODY SUMMER DAYS
THE SNAKE FLAG CONSPIRACY
SOCIETY OF NINE
STRIKE OF THE HAWK
SUICIDE SEAT
TEMPLE OF FEAR
THUNDERSTRIKE IN SYRIA
TIME CLOCK OF DEATH
THE TREASON GAME
TRIPLE CROSS
TURKISH BLOODBATH
THE TURNCOAT
UNDER THE WALL
WAR FROM THE CLOUDS
THE WEAPON OF NIGHT

**Dedicated to the men of the
Secret Services of the
United States of America**

A Killmaster Spy Chiller

# THE HUNTER

A Division of Charter Communications Inc.
A GROSSET & DUNLAP COMPANY
51 Madison Avenue
New York, New York 10010

THE HUNTER





An Ace Charter Original.



First Ace Charter Printing May 1982
Published simultaneously in Canada
Manufactured in the United States of America

# THE HUNTER

# PROLOGUE

In a way Tom Edwards was disappointed that his wife Sarah and the children were not coming back to Moscow with him. But in another way he was happy that they would no longer have to be subjected to the harsh conditions of a correspondent's life in the Soviet Union. The next eighteen months were going to be lonely, but they would pass and he would be back home in London before he knew it.

Edwards stubbed out his cigarette in the tiny armrest ashtray as the NO SMOKING, FASTEN SEATBELT sign came on, and he tightened his seatbelt.

The 727 sank down for a landing at Moscow's Vnukovo Official Airport, as most of the passengers strained to look out the windows for their first glimpse of Russia. Edwards didn't, however. He had been here for twenty-four months; this was his first leave in that time.

The Soviet Union no longer held any personal interest for him; it only piqued his newsman's natural curiosity. Washington, D.C. and Moscow. The two most important news cities in the world. Perhaps he would luck out, and Reuters would assign him the American capital next.

Sarah had more than once chided him for not being more insistent with the powers in London.

"Why Moscow, Tom? Why not America?" she asked.

*Why not America?* he often asked himself. All in due time. All he needed was one big break, one big story, and then he could call his own shots.

The British news agency was no different than the American Associated Press, or even Tass. All of them held *the* story as God. *The* newsman who came up with *the* story, wrote his own ticket.

The jetliner touched down into the deepening Soviet afternoon with a bark of its tires, rolled to the last intersection and then powered to the terminal building as most of the passengers, Edwards included, nervously checked to make sure they had their passports and entry documents, and prepared themselves for the intimidating Soviet customs service.

"Welcome to the Union of Soviet Socialist Republics," a feminine voice came over the aircraft's loudspeakers as Edwards undid his seatbelt, stood up and retrieved his jacket and briefcase from the overhead locker.

"Please have your passports and baggage claim checks ready for inspection on deplaning."

Edwards was just ducking back into his seat, when a tall, stern-looking man brushed past him, nearly knocking him over.

"Excuse me," the British newsman started to say as he straightened up and turned around, but the words died on his lips. He knew the man.

Standing by his seat, other passengers streaming past him, Edwards watched as the tall man said something to the stewardess by the door and then stepped off the plane, giving him a profile view.

"Sonofabitch," Edwards said to himself. Leaving behind the book he had been reading, he pushed his way up the crowded aisle, barely nodded at the stewardess and hurried out the door of the plane and down the boarding tunnel after the tall man who had just turned the corner ahead of him.

By the time Edwards had reached the end of the tunnel and had hurried down the corridor and into customs, the tall man was just leaving the large room by a side door.

Edwards hurried to one of the windows and looked outside as the man came down the outside stairs and was met at the bottom by a driver and limousine.

The man turned and looked up at Edwards standing at the window, and then climbed into the long, black, Zil limousine, and the car took off.

In that brief moment, however, Edwards had gotten a perfect look at the man's face. And he *did* recognize him.

"It was Sprague DeGourcy, I'd bet my last dollar on it," Edwards told his boss later that afternoon.

He had processed through customs, had taken a shuttle into Moscow and then a bus out to his apartment in the foreigners' section of the city. After he had unpacked, he had gone immediately down to the Reuters' office in the foreign press building just off Embassy row on Tchaikovsky Street, where Tony Van Camp, the bureau chief, had been surprised to see him.

"You sure about that Tom?" Van Camp asked.

"Dead sure," Edwards said.

For a long moment Van Camp was silent, but Edwards could almost hear the veteran newsman's brain working.

"What the hell would the comptroller of the Bank of Geneva be doing in Moscow?" Van Camp mused half to himself. "And why the VIP treatment?"

"I want to run with it," Edwards said. This was his big chance. No doubt the Soviets were cooking up some kind of a deal and needed Western currency. It could be *the* story.

Van Camp looked up. "You're damned right you're going to run with it, but first let me check with Tass, very quietly, to see what they have. If DeGourcy is actually here in Moscow, he won't be going anywhere in a hurry. We've got time."

"I'm going to do some checking on my own, Tony," Edwards said. "Just to find out where DeGourcy is staying."

Van Camp shook his head. "Too dangerous, my boy. Let me sniff around a bit first."

A couple of hours later, Van Camp had left for the night, and shortly afterward Edwards left, too; but instead of returning to his apartment he went to the Metropole Hotel downtown, where at the bar he ordered himself a Scotch and soda.

The Metropole was the major hotel for foreign visitors to Moscow, and Edwards figured that it was a safe bet that DeGourcy was staying there.

A few high-ranking Soviets usually hung out at the Metropole, along with most influential foreigners to the city, and this evening was no exception; the barroom was crowded.

After Edwards had gotten his drink, he moved to a small, vacant table near the door that led into the lobby and sat as inconspicuously as possible, as he watched the goings on out in the lobby.

The hotel was busy this evening, and three times Edwards spotted men he took to be Soviet officials crossing to the elevators.

In each instance, the elevator indicator stopped on the

fourth floor. The VIP floor. DeGourcy's floor.

Edwards ordered himself a second drink a little later, and when it came and he paid the waiter, a fourth man —this one definitely a KGB type—hurried across the lobby and took the elevator up to the fourth floor.

"That's it," Edwards said to himself. He drank his Scotch down, left the bar and went across the lobby to the ground-floor restrooms.

Instead of going into the men's room, however, he hurried down the back corridor and took the stairs up, two at a time, to the fourth floor.

He waited in the stairwell for nearly forty-five minutes, watching the fourth-floor corridor until the elevator stopped again, the doors opened and another man, obviously a Soviet official, stepped off and hurried down to a room halfway down the hall.

The man knocked twice, and a moment later the door was opened and he disappeared inside.

Edwards' heart was accelerating as he stepped into the corridor and hurried down the hall to the room. Keeping one eye on the elevator he put his ear to the thin wooden door.

At first he could hear nothing, but then someone laughed, and then he was hearing voices speaking in Russian. But Russian had been his minor in college. It was one of the reasons he had been assigned to the Moscow bureau. ". . . it will be a great surprise for them, no?" a deep-throated man's voice said clearly.

Another man laughed. "A surprise that will cost your government a great deal of money. A great deal indeed."

The man who had spoken had a definite German accent to his Russian. DeGourcy?

"A fee we will gladly pay El Cazador," another Russian said.

The room was suddenly silent and Edwards' heart

nearly hammered out of his chest. El Cazador, The Hunter, the world famous assassin. A dozen Western countries wanted the man's head. For twenty years the elusive name had, in itself, been cause for abject terror in as many capitals around the world.

His name had been linked with everyone from Kennedy, to the fall of Khrushchev, and from the Bader Meinhof Gang in Germany to Colonel Quadafi in Lybia.

El Cazador. *The* story!

A muffled voice said something that Edwards couldn't quite catch, and he pressed his ear closer to the door at the same moment it was yanked open.

Nearly losing his balance, Edwards managed to jump back and straighten up in time to look into DeGourcy's cold, unyielding eyes.

Edwards held up his right hand as if to ward off a blow, as DeGourcy raised his silenced pistol and fired six times, emptying the weapon at point-blank range into the British newsman's body.

# ONE

It was mid-July and Washington, D.C., was damned near unbearable. An oppressive heatwave had descended upon the city, bringing with it temperatures in the mid-nineties and the humidity to match.

Automobile accidents were up; violent crimes were the worst they had been since the rioting in the sixties; and a thick haze hung over the entire city and its suburbs.

I had left AXE headquarters on DuPont Circle about noon for a quick lunch at a little bar and grill I knew downtown, and now, a scant forty-five minutes later, as I walked back into the Operations Center, the Foreign Desk clerk thrust a thick sheath of communications flimsies into my hand.

"These came through while you were out," he said.

"You're all heart, Smitty," I replied sarcastically, as I loosened my tie and headed across to my desk in the OD's cubicle.

I had been playing games now as Officer of the Day for the past four and a half weeks and was getting damned sick of it. I was almost beginning to wonder if David Hawk, AXE's hard-bitten director, and the one man on this earth I respected most, had forgotten I even existed.

I don't particularly thrive on trouble, and I have been in some sticky spots over the past few years, but anything—almost anything—is better than shuffling papers for a living.

Inside my little office I shut the door, dropped the flimsies on the desk, peeled off my sportcoat and draped it over the back of my chair.

Taking off my shoulder holster, a line of sweat across my back from the wide elastic band, I dropped the Luger in the OUT basket and sat down behind my desk.

The door opened and Caroline Mills, the dayside coordinator, stuck her head around the corner. "Hello, Nicky," she said in a singsong voice.

I looked up and smiled at her. "You're either trying to proposition me or you've brought trouble," I quipped. "Which is it?"

"A little of both," she said, coming all the way into my office. She was carrying a three or four page message flimsy. I groaned.

"I've got a dozen of the damned things already. Don't bring me anymore," I said.

She laid the flimsies on my desk and smiled sweetly. "These are the trouble. And now for the proposition. A couple of honest-to-God pheasants, some real wild rice, and a couple of bottles of Beaujolais—on ice."

"Ice," I said reverently.

She smiled.

"What time?"

"Eight o'clock?" she said. Caroline was my age. Her husband had been a Killmaster until two years ago when he bought it in East Berlin. She wasn't promiscuous; she still loved her husband, or his memory, but she and I spent an evening together from time to time. Tonight was as good a night as any.

"I'll be there," I said. "But now, get the hell out of here. I've got a ton of work to do."

"Don't be late," she said backing out of my office and closing the door.

I smiled to myself. Actually I had been planning on inviting her over to my place later this week.

I lit myself one of my specially made, gold-tipped cigarettes and began tackling the messages from our field stations.

AXE is not a particularly large organization, but what we lack in size, we more than make up for in efficiency.

From a couple of dozen offices worldwide, AXE agents gather material on as many unfriendly foreign governments, digest the information and include it in high speed, coded messages to headquarters here in Washington. Under the guise of the Amalgamated Press and Wire Services, our field office people are the best anywhere in the world. Recruited from the ranks of law enforcement agencies, including Interpol, the FBI and of course the CIA, they're a highly trained bunch of snoops, whose natural curiosity is only outdone by their innate distrust of nearly everything.

I had been working steadily for nearly three hours before I finally got down to the three-page flimsy Caroline had brought me. It was from our office in Moscow, and on almost any other day—a day when I was busy, my mind preoccupied with an assignment—I wouldn't have given it a second glance. But this afternoon, something in the message set off a low, warning rumble deep inside my gut. Intuition, or merely the after effects of my lunch, I don't know.

Soviet authorities had turned over the body of a Reuters' correspondent to the British Embassy early yesterday afternoon. Tom Edwards, the newsman, had been shot at least twenty-seven times by Soviet guards at Lubyanka Prison, when he had evidently attempted to gain entry to the lockup by climbing over the east wall about two in the morning.

The Soviets were apologizing all over the place—the first of several sour notes in the text of the message—but maintained that the Lubyanka guards had no other choice.

I looked up from the flimsy and took a deep drag on my cigarette. In the first place, the Soviets never apologize for anything. In the second place, what the hell was a British newsman doing trying to climb over the walls of Lubyanka Prison? And in the third, why hadn't the Soviets made more of an issue out of it? Normally, such an incident would have produced an outpouring of protests from the Russians. Imperialist spies. Plots against the Kremlin. British arrogance. Western interference. The entire gambit. But this time, nothing.

Normally, that would have been the end of the report, but our people in Moscow had dug a little deeper.

Edwards had been a small-time, but respected, correspondent in Moscow for the past two years. He had just returned from a home leave in London that same day.

The rumor around the press corps club was that Edwards had spotted a Swiss banker, Sprague DeGourcy, somewhere in Moscow and had been following the man around town that night.

This morning, an hour or two before our office had prepared this report, DeGourcy had been positively identified at Vnukovo Official Airport. *VIP treatment,* the reporting officer had written.

What was DeGourcy, a banker from a neutral country, doing in Moscow? And was there any connection between his presence in Moscow and Edwards' death?

I sat back in my chair and lit myself another cigarette

when I finished the report. I could think of a dozen explanations that would fit the facts, but none of them very satisfying.

Number one: Edwards had obviously been chasing after a story. A Swiss banker in Moscow would be news.

Number two: If Edwards was like any other newsman, he'd have been working on more than one story at a time. Perhaps DeGourcy had been a dead end for the night, and Edwards had decided to tackle another story instead . . . one having to do with Lubyanka. But climbing over the prison walls?

"Bullshit," I said half to myself.

I gathered up the message flimsies I had worked on—all but the Moscow one—left my office and went across Operations where I dropped them on Smitty's desk.

He looked up at me. "Anything you want to triple six?"

"Not in this batch," I said. "But Caroline brought me a Moscow query that I'm going to run down."

"Be my guest," the man said, and I left Operations and took the elevator down to Records, three stories below street level.

As an AXE Killmaster I enjoyed the free run of any and all sections within headquarters, so I was shown into the main computer terminal center without question.

Hal Sloacum, the chief records clerk, came out of his office when I entered the center and waved me over.

"What brings you to my domain this afternoon? No action upstairs?"

"Not much," I said. "I need some information."

Sloacum grinned. "That's the name of the game."

Quickly I explained the situation in Moscow to him, and asked for any and all information he could provide me on Sprague DeGourcy and Tom Edwards.

Sloacum ducked back into his office where he grabbed a clipboard from his desk. "I can schedule it for the swing shift tonight. Have it for you first thing in the morning."

"Right now, Hal. I can't wait."

Sloacum looked up at me, a serious expression on his face. "Is this an action order?"

"Not yet, but I've got a funny feeling about it."

Sloacum said nothing for a moment, but then nodded. "Let's get on it then," he said. He went quickly across to the main control terminal, shuffled aside the junior operators working there and began keying the complicated machine.

"Do you want just the profiles, or do you want everything?" Sloacum asked.

"The works," I said, "including whatever the Bureau and the Agency have."

Our computer was interfaced with the FBI and CIA records keeping and analysis machines. Whatever they knew, we automatically knew.

Sloacum, quickly and expertly opened the memory banks for all three computers, and began punching in his first query. Within seconds, information on DeGourcy began spitting out on one of our high-speed printers. A few seconds after that, a second printer began its readout on Edwards.

I moved over to both machines and began reading the material that was coming out of the computer at seven hundred and fifty words per minute; there wasn't much, and within a couple of minutes both printers stopped.

Beyond bare data of birthdate, parents, schooling, marriages and a brief summary of Tom Edwards' life, there was nothing of value. Edwards had been an average student in an average London school. His college days had been undistinguished, he had married a plain woman, had three children and had worked his way up to foreign correspondent status with Reuters. Nothing more. No indications that he had ever worked on a Lubyanka prison story. Nothing.

The information we had on DeGourcy was even less helpful, although it did set me to thinking.

He had been born in Hong Kong, his parents Swiss missionaries in China, and he had been schooled in the Orient, not returning to his homeland until he was eighteen and ready for the university.

He graduated from the Swiss Polytechnic (the same university that Albert Einstein had attended), with honors in mathematics, in 1961.

From there DeGourcy opened his own financial institution in Geneva, where he had remained until seven years ago when he had become chief comptroller for the Bank of Geneva.

And that was it.

Sloacum had been reading over my shoulder, and when I was finished I looked up.

"How about the limited access memories?" I asked.

"Included," he said. "I figured you'd want those too."

"This is it then?"

Sloacum nodded. "No help?"

I glanced back at the printers. "Not a bit," I said. "But thanks anyway."

"Any time," Sloacum said to my back as I turned and headed for the elevator.

It was shortly after five P.M. by the time I got back up to my office. Smitty was getting ready to leave for the day and Don Brinkerman, the nightside foreign desk clerk, was just coming in.

I nodded at both of them, then went into the OD's cubicle where I shut the door, sat down behind my desk and flipped open my private telephone index.

I've been bouncing around the service for a number of years, and during that time I've made quite a few friends, several of whom now owe me favors. Although the incident I was working on was probably not worth the effort, I decided to call in a couple of those favors. If for no one else other than Tom Edwards' wife and children, I told myself.

Finding the number I was looking for, I picked up the phone, got our special overseas operator and had her place a person-to-person call to Helmut Vanderman, head of Anti-Clandestine Operations for ININ—NATO's intelligence network, in Brussels, Belgium.

Within five minutes the call had gone through to Vanderman's home, just outside the city. It was a few minutes after eleven P.M. there when the craggy old Belgian answered.

"It sounds like your best friend ran off with your wife," I quipped.

"Worse," Vanderman snapped. "My favorite dog died. What the hell do you want at this hour, Nicholas?"

"A big favor," I said.

"Business?"

"Possibly, so keep it under your hat."

Vanderman said nothing, waiting for me to continue, and I quickly explained the situation, asking him if he had ever heard of DeGourcy.

"Swiss banker. Banque de Genève, I think."

"What else," I asked.

"Nothing off hand. Where can I reach you later tonight?"

I gave him Caroline's number, thanked him for his trouble and offered my condolences for his dead dog.

*"Sheisse,"* Vanderman growled, and he hung up.

* * *

* * *

Besides being good looking, wonderful in bed and comfortable to be with, Caroline was a good cook. The pheasant was done to a turn, the wild rice was perfect and the Beaujolais refreshingly cold.

We had eaten dinner, had made love on her living room floor in front of the television set and were sitting, our backs to the couch, when the telephone rang around one in the morning. She started to get up, but I held her back and got up instead.

"For me," I said.

She looked up and smiled sadly at me. "You're worse than Del, for Christ's sake," she said without anger. Del was her husband. Although he and I had never been close, I respected the man. He had been good at his job. Just not lucky.

I answered the phone on the second ring. It was Vanderman.

"I sincerely hope I interrupted something," he said, jovially.

"What'd you come up with, Helmut?" I asked, ignoring his remark.

"Very little more than you indicated you already know, except for rumor."

"Go ahead," I said.

"DeGourcy is indeed a legitimate banker," Vanderman said. "But there is one tiny blemish, if you could call it that, on his record."

"I'm all ears," I said.

"It was buried deep. Ten years ago. A lot of time has passed since then."

"What happened then?"

"There were rumors at the time about El Cazador—do you know the name?"

I had heard of the man. Practically everyone had

heard of him, but I knew nothing about him. "Of course."

"Well, the rumors connected DeGourcy with El Cazador. At first it was thought that they might be one and the same man. Later it was believed they at least had an intimate connection."

"But?" I asked.

"But nothing," Vanderman said. "You must understand, Nicholas, that the investigation was done very quietly. There was absolutely no hint of scandal. Simply, nothing came of it, and the investigation was dropped."

"Who instigated the original investigation?" I asked.

"The wife of Walther Brandt, a German politician who was assassinated—presumably by El Cazador. She had some reason, evidently, to believe that DeGourcy and her husband's assassin were one and the same."

"Where can I reach her?"

"Unfortunately, Nicholas, she was an old woman at the time. She has since died."

"I see," I said.

"It would seem that your investigation is at a dead end."

"Perhaps," I said. "But thanks for your help, Helmut."

"Think nothing of it, Nicholas."

# TWO

Thursday morning was a repeat of the day before. The weather was hot and sticky, and when I came into work, the flimsies from the overnight crew were stacked three inches deep on my desk.

I shoved them aside, however, and telephoned Hawk's secretary. "Is he in?" I asked when I had her on the line.

"I can fit you in after lunch," she said, but then Hawk himself broke in on the line.

"What's up, Nick?"

"I need five minutes of your time this morning, sir," I said.

"Come on up," he said, and he broke the connection.

I hung up the phone, got up and came around my desk as Caroline came in.

"Oh boy, have you got the look," she said, stepping aside from the open door to let me pass.

"All work and no play . . ." I said leaving the homily unfinished as I passed her.

She shook her head, a wan expression in her eyes, and she said something that I couldn't quite catch.

Upstairs, Hawk's secretary told me to go right in. I knocked once on his door, and then went inside where he motioned me to a chair across the desk from him.

He was speaking to someone on the telephone, the ever-present cigar firmly clenched in his teeth, and as I sat down he swiveled his chair around so that he was looking outside at the hazy Washington morning.

"I can be in your office with the reports by three this afternoon, Mr. President," he was saying. And after a moment, "No, sir. I'm stacked up until then."

I had to smile. The CIA has always been either the darling child or the whipping boy of the American public. But AXE, our most secret action service, was no one's maid servant. We were commissioned to do a job, and we did it—all bullshit aside.

Hawk hung up the phone with his goodbyes and then swiveled back to face me. There were bags under his eyes, and his thick shock of white hair was mussed up.

"If you need a pay raise or a vacation, you're out of luck," he growled.

I had to smile. "Neither, sir. I came across something I'd like to look into."

For a long moment Hawk looked deeply into my eyes. "This DeGourcy thing?"

I nodded, not in the least surprised. There was very little that escaped Hawk's attention.

"You think there's a possibility he may be El Cazador?"

Again I nodded.

"How seriously do you think so?" he asked me.

I started to shrug, but then thought better of it. "So far it's just a hunch, sir. But I'd like to follow up on it."

For a long moment he was silent. "Normally I'd say no, Nick. We've plenty to keep us busy without chasing will-o'-the-wisps. But field men should be in the field, not behind a desk. So, to save myself a lot of future trouble, I'll give you the go ahead."

I smiled. "Thank you, sir. If nothing comes of it I'll behave myself. For awhile longer."

"I sure as hell hope so," Hawk said, as I got to my feet.

He picked up his telephone, but before he spoke into it, he looked up at me. "Be careful, Nick," he said. "If DeGourcy is El Cazador, he's the best, the very best."

"Thank you, sir," I said. I left his office and went back down to my own cubicle, where over Smitty's protests I shuffled off the flimsies I was supposed to be working on today. I pulled off my jacket, loosened my tie and began.

First I called Sloacum down in Records to send up the hard copies of the computer printouts on DeGourcy and Tom Edwards, and then asked him for everything we had on the assassin El Cazador.

"We're a little tied up here this morning," Sloacum started to say.

"This is a triple six, Hal," I snapped, and before he had a chance to reply, I broke the connection then set up a pair of overseas calls; the first back to Helmut Vanderman in Brussels, and the second to Dieter Grundt, chief of operations for INTERPOL in Geneva, Switzerland.

The call to Vanderman was delayed because he was out in the field on a NATO exercise with British, French and West German troops near Trier, and it came through finally about the same time Sloacum came into my office with the information I had requested.

I motioned for him to have a seat as I got on the line with my Belgian friend.

"Still chasing hobgoblins?" Vanderman asked.

"Perhaps," I said. "But I need another big favor from you, my friend."

"You're serious about this then?"

"Very," I said.

"Then you will have my help. What can I do?"

"I need a list of every suspected El Cazador assassination. Subjects, dates and times, locations, and methods of assassination."

"There are two lists, Nicholas. One for certain, and the second for speculation."

"I want them both."

"I'll send them immediately."

"Not here," I said. "Send them under sealed cover to me in care of Grundt."

"Geneva?"

"Yes."

"You *are* serious."

"I am," I said.

"The lists will be in Geneva before you are," Vanderman said, and he hung up.

When I put down the phone and looked up, Sloacum had a glum expression on his face. "Are we working on something urgent?"

"I don't know, Hal," I said, taking the bulky hard copies from him. "But I'm going to need a lot of help on this one."

"Everything we have on El Cazador is there."

"How about the lower probability stuff? Unsolved assassinations, coup d'etats, money deals, fundings, anything."

"How low do you want to go?"

"All the way to the bottom. Anything with at least a one percent probability connection with either El Cazador or DeGourcy."

Sloacum's eyebrows rose. "That could amount to a formidable pile of material."

"Boil it all down for me. I want the information with none of the embellishments."

"It'll take time," he said.

"Not too much time, Hal. I'm leaving for Geneva this evening."

Sloacum got up from his chair, and without a word left my office. One thing about the man: when there was work to be done, he never sat around talking about it.

My call to Dieter Grundt came through just after I had called Travel Section and had them arrange my flight to Geneva, including hotel reservations at the same place where I had worked with Grundt a couple of times over the past few years. After one of my assignments, the two of us had spent an enjoyable five days on the Spanish Riviera with a couple of girls from Oslo down on winter vacation.

Grundt was a worrier of a little man, but he was damned good at what he did, and his name was highly respected within INTERPOL. He was happy to hear from me.

"Are you ready for another Spanish sojourn my old friend?" he asked jovially.

"After the heat here in D.C., I'd just as soon go up to Oslo this time."

"It can be arranged, Nick," Grundt said. "But I suspect you have not telephoned to make vacation arrangements. Business?"

"Sprague DeGourcy," I said.

"A venerable banker," Grundt said guardedly. "Comptroller for our Banque de Genève."

"If you were to be handed a list of dates, would it be possible to find out what DeGourcy was doing at those times? Where he was? Witnesses?"

"Yes," Grundt said. "But you must understand that DeGourcy is a respected name in Geneva."

"I understand that, Dieter. That's why I'm telephoning you."

There was a silence on the line for a long moment. "Is it the rumors all over again?"

"Yes," I said.

"And the list of dates. Perhaps they are the dates of El Cazador assassinations?"

"Right again."

"Then I can tell you with assurance, Nicholas, that in every instance DeGourcy was here in Geneva. When this all first came up, we looked very closely into DeGourcy's movements. He has witnesses who will testify that he was here in Geneva every time El Cazador struck. You are chasing your own tail."

I laughed. "You're probably right, but I might need your help anyway."

"Officially I can do nothing for you, Nicholas. It is a closed case. But unofficially I can hardly refuse you, although I'll tell you now that I will not like it."

There was a hard note in Grundt's voice. I was on the verge of completely using up a favor, and badly straining a friendship. The man did have his loyalties. But so did I.

"I'm sorry, Dieter, but I may be coming to Geneva to look into this matter. Vanderman is sending me some material under sealed cover, in care of you. I'd appreciate it if you'd hold it for me."

"As you wish, Nick. Is there anything else?"

"Not for now," I said, and he hung up.

I put the phone down, and sat back at my desk for a moment. If DeGourcy was El Cazador, his true identity would be well covered. And in the guise of the Swiss banker he would have made many influential friends. My investigation was going to ruffle some feathers, and if I was wrong, the entire thing could blow up in my face.

But, assuming for a moment that DeGourcy was indeed the assassin, he had made one very large mistake. There were very few people who could account for every moment of their time. The fact that DeGourcy had a rock solid alibi for *every single time* that El Cazador was active, was in itself just too much of a coincidence for me to swallow.

No matter what was said or done, I was definitely going to look a little deeper into DeGourcy's background. And if I was exposed, my excuse would be a simple one. I was an Amalgamated Press newsman who had heard through the grapevine that DeGourcy had recently been in Moscow. Why?

Geneva was in full bloom for the summer tourist season. Even from the air, as we made our approach to the city for a landing, I could see the large number of boats on the lake, Mount Blanc rising scenically behind it, with the city spread out along the west shore.

Once I had passed through customs I took a taxi from the busy airport to the Hotel du Rhône, a nice hotel though far from the best. It did have one thing going for it, however, and that was its restaurant, Le Neptune, which featured one of the finest wine lists anywhere in the country.

I turned my passport in at the desk, and then went immediately up to my room, where I unpacked a few things and took a quick shower.

All that had taken me a little more than a half an hour, and when I was drying myself off in the bathroom my telephone rang. It was Dieter Grundt.

"Your package arrived this morning, Nicholas. And knowing what was in it, I took the liberty of opening it and matching the dates for you. I will be at Le Neptune in ten minutes."

"Right," I started to say, but Grundt had already hung up, and I slowly replaced the French-styled telephone on its cradle.

Grundt had to be plenty mad to work this efficiently. Usually the local police took at least twenty-four hours to check the passports of incoming hotel guests and then report them to Interpol. This time the word had evidently gone out to every hotel to look for me. I had expected my arrival here in the city to be relatively anonymous, but that was ruined now. Every hotel clerk from here to Nyons knew that I was coming.

I went back into the bathroom where I shaved, and then got dressed in a light pair of slacks, a knit shirt and a light sport coat, my 9mm Luger, Wilhelmina, in place comfortably beneath my left armpit; my stiletto, Hugo, in its chamois sheath up my sleeve strapped to my left forearm; and the tiny, but very lethal gas bomb, Pierre, that AXE's armorer had designed for me some years ago, in its pouch, strapped high on my right thigh.

Downstairs I crossed the lobby, went through the inner restaurant and out on the terrace, requested and was given a table for two along the rail, looking down at the river and the city.

The day was lovely; the temperature warm, but the humidity low by comparison with D.C., and I sat back and relaxed with a cigarette as I studied the wine list and waited for Grundt to show up.

I had just about selected a good but relatively inexpensive Rhine wine, a Hattenheimer Mannberg, when Grundt showed up and took his place across the small table from me. He was carrying a thick manila envelope velope with him.

*"Guten Morgen, Dieter,"* I said.

Grundt nodded stiffly as he set the Manila envelope down and reached for the wine list from me. The waiter had just come to our table.

"Have you made a selection *meine Herrn?"* the man asked.

"The Hattenheimer Mannberg, 1970," I said, but Grundt cut me off.

"You are on an expense account from your press service, so let us order well," he said. He slapped the wine list shut and, without looking up at the waiter, ordered a full bottle of Hattenheimer Nussbrunnen, 1971. It was a beautiful white German wine that cost at least fifteen times as much as the wine I was going to order.

*"Sehr gut,"* the waiter said with a click of his heels and he was gone.

"Is that not the American way, Nicholas?" Grundt said, sarcasm thick in his voice. "The best money can buy, no matter the occasion?"

"Cut the bullshit, Dieter," I said softly. "I asked for a favor, but if your loyalties lie elsewhere, forget it. I'll find the information on my own."

For several seconds Grundt just stared across the table at me, not even a hint of friendliness in his expression. "There will be trouble here in Switzerland, I can smell the death around you."

I stubbed my cigarette out and started to rise, but Grundt gestured me back.

"There is no use fighting like this," he said resignedly. "I owe you a favor and I intend paying. After that?" he shrugged.

"After your performance here, I really don't give a damn," I snapped. The Swiss are a wonderful people, but at times they can be damned insufferable.

Our wine came a few minutes later, and the waiter showed the label to Grundt for his approval; but the little detective barely glanced at it, and then nodded for the waiter to continue.

The man quickly opened the bottle, poured Grundt a sample, which he tossed down, and then filled both our glasses and left us alone.

I tasted the wine; it was excellent, but then Grundt passed over the thick Manila envelope to me.

"Everything is there, including the material you requested of me, as well as the file Vanderman sent," Grundt said.

He poured himself another glass of the expensive wine, tossed it down as if it was nothing but water and then got to his feet.

"I do not wish you luck in this assignment, Nicholas. You will find nothing, but I hope that you come to that realization very quickly and then leave Switzerland."

"Thank you," I said.

"Don't get yourself into any trouble. You have no friends here."

I raised my glass in salute, as Grundt turned on his heel and stalked out of the restaurant.

A few people had turned our way, sensing that there had been some trouble between us, but when I sat back in my chair, opened the Manila envelope and began reading the material it contained, while sipping my wine, they quickly lost interest.

The first assassination in which El Cazador had been mentioned as a suspect, was the murder of a highly placed Spanish businessman in Johannesburg, South Africa in 1966. The Spanish government had hunted the assassin for nearly a year before they gave it up. And it was the Spanish press that had coined the phrase *El Cazador,* the hunter.

Three other assassinations over the next two years—another in Africa, one in Germany and one in New York City—were all credited to El Cazador, but authorities in those three countries, had come no closer than the Spaniards had to catching the elusive phantom killer.

And then the stories began, according to Vanderman's report. Any political death, any kidnapping, any midair explosion, even an earthquake, was blamed on El Cazador. For a time it became the fashionable thing to do, in certain circles, blaming El Cazador for the latest disaster.

At least three assassinations, however, were officially placed on the man's shoulders in 1970–71. Then he was quiet until 1973, when in a single year he was credited with more than nine assassinations.

Off and on it went like that until just last year when he was believed to be connected with the Bader Meinhof Gang in Germany, as well as the PLO, and with the Lybian leader Colonel Qaddafi.

Written beneath each of the assassinations credited to El Cazador, was a brief account of DeGourcy's movements at that time. In each instance DeGourcy had definitely been here in Geneva, Switzerland. And I suddenly understood why Grundt had been so angry.

In at least four instances, DeGourcy's alibi had been Grundt himself. DeGourcy and Grundt were friends! Or at least close acquaintances.

I stuffed the files back into the envelopes, finished the rest of my wine and then signed the check, leaving a healthy tip for the waiter.

Back up in my room, I lay down on my bed to get a couple of hours of sleep, but I kept thinking about DeGourcy and Grundt, and then about Tom Edwards, the Reuters correspondent who had been shot twenty-seven times.

Each seemed to be a dead end, and yet I could not shake the feeling that DeGourcy's alibis were just too pat. That, and the distrust of the Soviet's explanation about Edwards' death, worried me.

Finally, around five in the afternoon, I got up, changed clothes again, this time into dark slacks, a thin dark pullover and a Navy blue blazer, and went downstairs to the desk where I rented myself a car for the next two days.

When I had completed the forms, I went outside and got into the little Ford Cortina and headed away from the city along the scenic drive on the north shore of the lake.

DeGourcy's estate was about fifteen miles north of the center of Geneva, just above the small town of Nyon, which had been founded by Julius Caesar in 45 B.C. as a camp for war veterans.

I stopped at a tourist restaurant in the town around seven where I had a supper of sausages, cheese, dark bread and two bottles of a Swiss beer that had a slight taste of raspberry. It was well after nine-thirty P.M. and dark outside by the time I finally left the restaurant and climbed into my car.

Studying the map that Sloacum had provided me with, I pinpointed the turnoff to DeGourcy's estate and then headed north.

I had no real plan in mind, other than getting a close look at DeGourcy's home turf. From what Sloacum had provided me with from the computers, I knew that the Swiss banker lived very well. He was a rich man, by any account, from his financial dealings here in Geneva. If he was El Cazador, he certainly didn't need the money that the assassinations earned him.

But DeGourcy was an odd duck. He had never been married, although it was rumored he had had a number of affairs. He lived alone on his ten-acre estate, except for his house staff and his valet, a man by the name of Daniel Lin Yun San.

The dirt road up to DeGourcy's place was well hidden

in the trees, and I almost missed it in the darkness. But a couple of hundred yards farther up the highway, no other traffic along the stretch of the road for the moment, I flipped off the Cortina's headlights, pulled off the highway and parked down in the ditch.

I didn't plan on being very long, so it wasn't very likely that anyone would do anything about a car being parked at the side of the road in that time.

Pocketing the keys, I got out of the car and climbed up the other side of the ditch where I came to a tall wire mesh fence, barbed wire at the top, fifty feet into the woods.

DeGourcy's property sloped upward toward the northwest where his house was located. I headed north along the fence, where a few hundred yards away I came to the corner of his property, the fence angling to the west.

It was pitch black here, but every now and then I caught a glimpse of lights from deep within the property. It had to be the house, and as I continued along the fence the land began to rise sharply; at one point I could look up through a narrow clearing at the lights in the distance.

I stopped once to rest, but a minute or two later continued up the steepening slope, coming fifteen minutes later to another bend in the fence at a spot I assumed was the extreme northwestern edge of the estate. From there I could not see the house, because the trees and brush were too thick.

I was crouched next to the fence, listening for any kind of a sound but hearing nothing, and I was about ready to look for a way over the fence, when something smashed into my back, sending me sprawling.

I twisted around as I reached for my gun, but the narrow beam of a flashlight caught me in the eyes and I suddenly couldn't see a thing.

# THREE

"Very carefully remove your hand from your jacket," a man said in German.

For a long moment I lay there, blinking up at the light, my right hand inside my jacket, my fingers curled around the grip of the Luger; but then I let go of the gun and very slowly withdrew my hand.

"Hands on your head, fingers interlocked, and then get to your feet," the man barked.

I complied, and when I had gotten to my feet, someone came up behind me and reached around to pull the gun from my holster.

At that instant I spun around in the opposite direction, grabbing the arm and yanking the person in front of me as a shield.

*"Verdammt,"* the man with the flashlight swore.

I pulled my stiletto out and raised the blade to the neck of the person struggling in my grasp.

"Quiet!" I snapped. The same moment the person I was holding stopped struggling, I realized it was a woman.

She was small and dressed in a black commando outfit, wisps of her blonde hair just visible beneath her black knit cap.

"Turn out the light," I said to the man.

The light remained steady.

"Turn it off or the woman dies," I snapped. *"Now!"*

The flashlight was extinguished, and I waited for a minute or two until my night vision began to return and I was able to make out at least the outline of the man standing a few feet away from me.

"It's your turn to put your weapon down and place your hands on top of your head," I said.

Slowly the man did as I ordered, and when he had placed his hands on his head, I was able to see much better. He was a large man, and like the woman, was dressed in a black commando uniform.

"How did you know I was here?" I asked.

"We heard you coming," the man said. He was keeping his voice low. "And if you do not speak a little more softly, DeGourcy's dogs will be here."

"You don't work for DeGourcy?" I asked.

*"Das Schwein!"* the woman hissed.

"What are you two doing here, then?"

The man held his silence, but after a moment the woman said, "We came to kill him."

"Why?"

"No, Gerta, it is none of his concern," the man said in a rapid-fire, low-German dialect.

"It *is* my concern," I said in the same Plattdeutsch, the woman stiffening in my grasp. "And you will tell me why you want him dead. Now!"

The man looked toward the fence, then back at us. I could see that he wanted to try something, but I sincerely hoped that he would not. I did not want trouble with these people.

"Because DeGourcy killed our father, that is why," the woman said.

The German diplomat whom Vanderman had spoken

of. "DeGourcy," I said, "or El Cazador?"

The man gasped, and I released the woman. She nimbly skipped to one side, and as I replaced my stiletto in its sheath her brother scooped up his gun.

I looked up and smiled. "It seems as if we came here for essentially the same reason."

The man started forward, but the woman held him off. "No, Peter. This one tells the truth."

"We can't be sure," the man whispered urgently.

"Yes we can. He could have killed me. Or he could have called for help. He did not."

Again the man glanced toward the fence and seemed to be listening for something. When he looked back at me, there was an expression of indecision on his face. But then he finally holstered his weapon.

"That's better," I said, relieved. "Now just who the hell are you two, and how can you be sure DeGourcy killed your father?"

"I am Gertrude Brandt," the woman said stepping forward and offering me her hand. I shook it. "And he is my brother, Peter."

Peter stepped forward, but he did not offer me his hand. He was still suspicious.

"Who are you?" he said.

"Nick Carter."

"And what is your grudge with El Cazador?" he asked.

"Let's just say it's the same as yours. I want to settle a score. That is if DeGourcy is El Cazador."

"He is," Peter said with assurance.

"How can you be sure?"

"We saw him," Gertrude said, with feeling. "The night he killed our father. It was ten years ago. Peter and I were school children. We watched it." She glanced at her grim-lipped brother. "It is a face we will never forget."

"Why didn't you tell the authorities?" I asked.

"To do what?" Peter spat. "To bargain with the Swiss for his extradition? To let him stand trial and perhaps be found innocent?"

"How did you find out he was DeGourcy?"

"We saw his photograph in a news magazine two weeks ago. We came here to Geneva for a closer look," Gertrude said.

"And you spotted him?"

She nodded. "Downtown. In a cafe. We sat right next to him. He is El Cazador."

"So you've come out here tonight to kill him."

"Yes," Peter said softly. "The same way he killed our father, with a bullet in the brain."

Neither of them was more than twenty. They were amateurs, and so damned young. If they ever did confront DeGourcy, he would kill them without hesitation.

I made as if to turn away, and as I did I pulled out my Luger and swung back. "You two are going home," I said.

Peter started to reach again for his gun, but I shook my head.

"You both will disarm yourselves, very slowly, and place your weapons on the ground."

They both stood there staring at me, pure hate in their eyes.

"I don't want to see either one of you hurt. If—and it's still a big *if* at this point—DeGourcy is El Cazador, you'd never have a chance against him. He'd kill you before you knew what was happening."

"You work for him!" Gertrude said.

"No I don't. I'm here for the same thing you two are."

"Then let us help," the girl said with emotion.

"You'd just be in the way," I said. "Now your weapons please."

"No," Peter said.

I reached up with my left hand and snapped the ejector slide back, levering a round into the chamber, the noise loud in the still woods. They both flinched.

*"Jetzt!"* I said.

Slowly then, they both pulled out their pistols, Peter's a snub-nosed Smith & Wesson .38 and hers, a woman's purse gun, a five-shot .22. They both laid their weapons on the ground in front of them.

"How'd you get here?" I asked.

"Motorcycle," the girl said.

"Then go back to your motorcycle and return to Geneva. What hotel are you staying at?"

"Citè Universitaire," Gertrude said, naming a youth hostel.

"I'll contact you there in the morning," I told her. "Now get the hell out of here."

They hesitated a moment longer.

"If he escapes tonight because of this, I will kill you," the young man said, and then he and his sister turned, and within a second or two they were lost to the darkness of the woods.

I remained still, listening to the sounds of their departure becoming fainter and fainter until I could no longer hear a thing. Then I holstered my Luger and picked up their weapons, throwing them as far into the underbrush as I could. I turned and without waiting for anything else to happen, quickly climbed a tree near the fence.

Once I was above the level of the barbed wire, I swung out over the fence and dropped down inside DeGourcy's estate.

For several seconds I remained in a crouch where I had dropped, listening for the sounds of an alarm; none came, and I headed as quietly as I could through the dark forest in the direction of DeGourcy's estate.

Within five hundred yards I had come to the edge of the woods, which opened to a huge expanse of lawn, across which was a fairly small and somewhat plain two-story brick house.

DeGourcy may have been rich, but he certainly did not live lavishly.

The front of the house was bathed in lights, and even as I watched, a tan Mercedes sedan came up the driveway, pulled around to the back of the house, and a small man got out.

For a moment he stood by the door, looking toward the woods in my general direction, but then he went inside the house.

Unless I missed my guess the little man was Daniel Lin Yun San, DeGourcy's valet. And I had a sneaking suspicion that he had just returned from taking his boss somewhere. It would explain what the hired help was doing running around at night in such an automobile.

The lights at the front of the house went out, and a few moments later so did the downstairs lights, leaving only a couple of windows upstairs at the rear of the house lit up.

I found a wide tree and sat down beneath it, my back against the trunk, and relaxed as I waited for the house staff to settle down for the night.

DeGourcy had probably gone somewhere, and although he would not be so foolish as to leave anything at his house that would possibly be incriminating, I wanted to take a look anyway. I wanted DeGourcy to know that someone had intruded on his private domain. I wanted him to know that someone was interested in him.

It was possible that Tom Edwards had stumbled onto something and DeGourcy himself had killed him for it.

I wanted DeGourcy to come after me.

The last lights in the house went out around midnight, and although the evening had turned cool and damp, I waited a full hour before I moved away from the tree and worked my way through the concealing darkness of the forest to a position opposite the rear of the house.

There was no moon tonight, for which I was thankful, as I dashed across the back lawn, pulling up short beside the garage.

I crouched in the shadows there for a few moments, listening for the sound of an alarm; when none came I raced across the driveway to the house itself.

There was a line of shrubbery at the base of the house, and I pushed my way through it so that I could look into the first-floor windows.

At the corner was the kitchen, a large room with stainless steel appliances and a large butcher block table in the middle, copper pots and pans hanging above it.

Working my way toward the front of the house, I looked into the dining room, then into what looked like some kind of a sitting room and finally at a set of French doors that led into a small, book-lined room, the center of which was dominated by a large, leather-topped desk.

It was probably DeGourcy's study, and if there would be anything for me to find in the house, it would probably be in this room.

I took out my penlight, twisted the red lens over the bulb and flipped it on. Working inward from the hinges of the French door, I examined each pane of glass as well as the latch and lock. If the door was alarmed I was unable to detect it. DeGourcy either had nothing to hide inside, or he was so arrogant he did not believe any one would attempt to spy on him here.

I put the flashlight away, pulled out my stiletto and, using the point of the slender blade, picked the simple lock, the three tumblers softly slipping back into their recesses.

Slipping the stiletto back in its sheath, I slowly opened the door, stepped inside and softly closed it behind me.

The house was deathly still, and after a few seconds I crossed the study to the inner door and put my ear to the wood, but I couldn't hear a thing.

I tried the doorknob, but the door was locked from the outside. Satisfied that no one was going to barge in on me, I went back to the French doors and pulled the heavy drapes closed, making sure they completely covered the doors before I turned and went to the desk.

I pulled the chair out, sat down and flipped on the brass desk lamp, the room filling with a soft white light.

DeGourcy's desk was that of a typical banker. To the left was a leather tray that contained a single prospectus for a German wire mill. To the right was a telephone and at the center, a blotter. Nothing more.

The center drawer contained a few pencils, paper clips and other odds and ends, in addition to a half a pack of British Player cigarettes. The other three drawers, none of them locked, contained more business annual reports, a fairly complicated calculator, some stationery, and very little else.

His desk was too clean. There was none of the little bits of junk that cluttered most people's desks, no scraps of paper with phone numbers, in fact no telephone index; no photographs, magazines or letters. None of that. Either DeGourcy was very careful, or he had recently cleaned house.

Getting up from the desk, I let my gaze roam around the book-lined room. It would take more time than I had this night to make a proper search here. And even if I had the time, I strongly suspected I would find nothing.

If DeGourcy was the assassin El Cazador, this certainly was not his base of operations.

A dog or some other animal bayed outside in the distance, and I quickly reached out and flipped the desk lamp off, went to the French doors, flipped the drapes back and looked outside.

The same sound came again, this time much closer as I opened the doors and stepped outside. Then a second and a third dog started to howl and bark off to the southeast toward the highway.

Probably DeGourcy's dogs, I figured. I only hoped they were chasing a rabbit or some other night creature, and that Peter Brandt and his sister had not decided to come back.

I moved silently to the back of the house again, and keeping low, dashed across the parking area to the side of the garage.

At the back of the garage, I listened a moment as the dogs bayed again, and then I started across the wide expanse of lawn toward the woods.

I had gotten about halfway, when lights came on everywhere, illuminating the house and lawns around it like daytime.

A high-pitched whine sounded from the front of the house, and then an amplified voice shouted, *"Halt!"* as I raced toward the darkness of the woods.

*"Remain perfectly still and the dogs will not harm you,"* the amplified voice boomed from the other side of the house.

Two shots, and then a third and a fourth were fired, from what sounded like a very small caliber pistol, off toward the highway as I reached the edge of the lawn and ducked into the underbrush.

The dogs were barking wildly now, and as I stood there listening, trying to pick out the individual sounds,

I heard a woman screaming in terror, two more shots were fired and then a man shouted, "Gerta."

I pulled out Wilhelmina and was about to start back toward the house, when a half a dozen large dogs came around the corner of the garage, raced around in circles where I had just been, until one of them looked directly toward where I was crouched, raised its head and howled and then headed toward me in a dead run, the others right behind it.

I dropped down on one knee, held the Luger up with both hands, and squeezed off a single shot.

The lead dog leapt straight up in the air with a howl of pain, then tumbled end over end. Two of the other dogs stopped to fight around the one I had shot while the other three continued directly for me.

I fired three more shots taking out two of the dogs, and the third stopped about ten yards from me, its legs spread, its head down as it whined and barked.

Slowly, keeping my eye on the single animal, I stood up and backed deeper into the brush. If the dog came after me I would kill it, but I wasn't going to shoot the animal if it remained where it was.

Within a few feet I was deep enough into the woods so that I no longer could see the clearing or the dog, and I stood there for a moment, listening. There was a great deal of activity on the other side of the estate, but it was a safe bet that it was already too late for Gerta and her brother.

Evidently no one had heard the shots I had fired because of the commotion, but once someone discovered that several of their animals were dead on this side of the house, the search for me would be on.

I turned and headed through the woods back to the fence, stopping every now and then to listen for the sounds of pursuit.

Once, I was certain that I could hear something coming through the brush behind me, but when I stopped, it stopped, too, and after a brief pause I continued.

I reached the fence a few minutes later where I holstered my Luger and took off my jacket.

There were no overhanging trees on this side of the fence, so I was going to have to climb it. I would spread my jacket over the barbed wire at the top and then roll over it without getting snagged.

The fence was about twelve feet high, and as I was looking up at it, something crashed through the underbrush right behind me. I spun around as the lone Doberman leaped across the clearing on top of me, and we went down in a heap.

Unlike most animals fighting with an adversary, this one made absolutely no noise. Its jaws snapped at my face and throat as I struggled with the powerful beast.

Somehow I managed to get one foot up and beneath its belly, and I kicked out with as much strength as I could manage, sending the dog rolling off me to the left.

At that second I rolled to the right, yanked my stiletto out of its sheath and then braced myself as the animal leaped toward me again.

This time the razor-sharp stiletto blade caught the dog in the chest, and I pulled violently to the left, opening a huge hole in its body.

The dog howled in pain and leaped to the left and then around in circles as it snapped at its own entrails hanging from the gaping wound.

I jumped up, sheathed the stiletto, grabbed my jacket and quickly climbed the fence. At the top, I flipped the jacket on top of the barbed wire, scrambled to the other side and dropped down to the ground.

The dog was lying nearly dead now, its legs twitching, and my jacket was hung up in the barbed wire; but I didn't even bother to look back, as I hurried along the fence, down toward the highway and then around the corner to the other side of DeGourcy's estate.

I could not leave without first finding out what had happened to Gertrude Brandt and her brother, although I suspected that I would be too late to help them.

A few minutes later I had come to a spot just above where I had parked my car, when I heard the first of the sirens in the distance. Police vehicles, they sounded like, and a few seconds later an ambulance. Probably out of Nyons.

I debated hanging around to see what would happen when they showed up, but then decided against it.

There was nothing I could do for the Brandts now. I had warned them away, but they had been driven by revenge. I just hoped that they were still alive, although I doubted it.

Quickly, I crashed through the underbrush and down to my car, as the first police car screeched around the corner a hundred yards to the south and raced up DeGourcy's driveway.

In quick succession another police car, an ambulance and finally a third police car all turned up the driveway.

I climbed in my car, started the engine and eased up out of the ditch, making a U-turn on the highway and heading back to Geneva.

At least four of the dogs were dead and my jacket was up in the barbed wire. When all that was discovered, DeGourcy's staff would have no doubt that someone not easily discouraged had come to pay a visit. No doubt at all.

# FOUR

It was well after three A.M. when I finally got back to my hotel. If my scruffy, jacketless appearance bothered the desk clerk, he gave no sign of it as he handed me my key and a message that had been left for me in my slot.

I unfolded the small slip of paper as I was going up in the elevator and read it. I had received a phone call from my "brother," who wanted me to immediately return his call.

Stepping off the elevator on my floor and hurrying down to my room, I wondered what Hawk wanted. It was unusual for him to contact me while I was in the field, unless it was of extreme importance. I only hoped that he had not decided to pull me back to the States.

In my room I locked my door, pulled my Luger out from beneath my shirt and dropped it on the bed, then poured myself a drink before I picked up the phone and dialed for the hotel operator.

I had her place a call to Hawk's private number, and then while I waited for it to go through I sat back, lit myself a cigarette and took a sip of the stiff shot of brandy I had poured myself.

I was having a tough time getting Peter and Gertrude Brandt out of my mind. Peter's cry to his sister across

DeGourcy's estate was clear in my mind. It was a call I was going to hear for a long time to come. And yet when they had first confronted me at the fence, I had suspected that they would end up that way. They had had that look of desperation about them. That could only mean failure.

The telephone rang a few minutes later and I picked it up.

"Your party is on the line *Herr* Carter," the hotel operator said.

"Sir?" I said into the phone.

The operator clicked off a moment later and Hawk's gruff voice came to me over the transatlantic line.

"They want you out of Switzerland," he snapped. "What's going on over there?"

Dieter Grundt, I thought. "I think I've ruffled some feathers, sir," I said.

"To good purpose, I hope."

"I think so, sir." Quickly I explained what had happened so far, including the likelihood that Gertrude and Peter Brandt were dead.

"You say the police were there?"

"Yes, sir."

"Then DeGourcy certainly has a case. He is guilty of nothing more than defending his property against intruders."

"I don't think DeGourcy was there," I said. "His houseboy drove up the same time I was entering the estate; he was alone."

"Probably took him to the airport," Hawk said, and he was silent a moment. I could almost see him playing with the ever-present cigar. "Then you're convinced that DeGourcy and El Cazador are one and the same?"

"Not convinced yet, sir," I said. "But the Brandts' were certain. And it is a bit coincidental that this incident came up so soon after the Moscow thing. It's a possibility that Tom Edwards somehow discovered the connection and was killed for it."

"Which leaves the biggest question of all: if DeGourcy is indeed El Cazador, what was he doing in Moscow?"

"Getting his orders for another assignment."

"Right," Hawk said dryly. "I think you'd better stick with it, Nick. But you're going to have to get out of Switzerland. At least for the time being."

"If DeGourcy took a commercial airline anywhere, I'll find out about it," I said. "Meanwhile send out a code six alert to all of our stations. DeGourcy will show up somewhere."

"Unless he's already gone underground."

"Let's hope not," I said. "Otherwise it'll be too late to stop whatever he and the Russians cooked up in Moscow."

After I hung up the phone, I went in and took a long, hot shower and afterwards shaved. I dressed in clean clothes, went back into my room, poured myself another brandy, lit one of my gold tips and sat, with my feet propped up, to wait for the dawn.

I may have dozed a couple of times, but around seven I finally got up from my chair and opened the windows. The morning air smelled fresh and clean, the city of Geneva coming alive with the sun.

In the bathroom, I splashed some cold water on my face, then put on a tie and pulled on my jacket. When I had my bags packed, I called the airlines and made reservations for the ten A.M. direct flight to Washington, D.C.

If they wanted me out of Switzerland, that would at least convince them I intended to return to the States this morning.

Next, I telephoned the Interpol office downtown and left an urgent message for Dieter Grundt to call me at the hotel.

Downstairs in the coffee shop I had a quick breakfast, and just as I was finishing my meal, Grundt showed up. He didn't look very happy.

I half rose as he approached my table, but he waved me back.

"I want you to finish your breakfast," he said. "It will be the last thing you will do in Switzerland."

"My flight leaves at ten," I said.

"I know. And you will be on it."

A waiter came and Grundt ordered himself a pot of *café au lait.* The dining room was beginning to fill up, and Grundt leaned forward slightly so that he would not have to raise his voice to be heard.

"Wherever you appear, trouble follows, Nicholas," he said.

I shrugged. "It's my business, Dieter," I said. "I'm sorry that you're taking it so personally."

Grundt eyed me for a long moment. "I don't suppose you'd know anything about a young German brother and sister, Gertrude and Peter Brandt?"

I shook my head as I sipped at my coffee. The waiter came, poured Dieter's *café au lait* and then left. The detective seemed almost saddened by my answer.

"Then it would follow that you know nothing about the trouble out at DeGourcy's estate last night?"

"Trouble?" I asked innocently.

Again Grundt gave me the same sad look. "Yes, there was some trouble out there. The Germans were apparently would-be assassins. They both died in the attempt."

"Assassins. Interesting," I said. "Especially considering the fact that *Herr* DeGourcy is nothing more than an innocent banker."

"It's just as well that you decided to leave Switzerland on your own. It saves us the unpleasantness of ejecting you."

"On what grounds, Dieter?"

Grundt smiled. "Carrying a concealed weapon?"

I returned the smile and put my coffee cup down. "One question before I go," I said.

Grundt shook his head. "I have helped you all I intend helping you."

"DeGourcy is gone. He left Switzerland yesterday evening," I said, ignoring the detective's remark. "Where did he go?"

"If I knew, I would not give you that information."

"Why?" I asked. "Am I suddenly the enemy?"

"You're an uncomfortable presence in my country."

I laughed. "You could find out very easily where DeGourcy went. After that I would not bother you. I would leave Switzerland and not come back."

"You'll leave in any event."

"Perhaps not," I said evenly. I didn't want a fight with Grundt. He was a good man and we were on the same side, but I was not going to leave Switzerland until I had found out where DeGourcy had jumped to. If it meant going back out to his estate and questioning his staff, I'd do it.

Grundt evidently sensed all that from the look in my eyes, and he finally sighed deeply and sat back. "It will be as you wish," he said. "The information will be at the Swiss Air ticket counter by the time you pick up your reservations."

"Thanks," I said. I got to my feet, left enough money on the table for the bill and for a generous tip, and then went back up to my room.

I repacked my weapons in the radio/cassette recorder

I've been carrying since the airlines started their security measures, descended to the lobby, where I paid my bill, and then ordered a cab out to the airport.

Outside, as the doorman was helping me with my bags into the cab, I happened to look across the street. Two men were watching me from a nondescript dark Mercedes sedan. When I glanced their way, they didn't bother averting their gaze.

Dieter Grundt had sent them out, no doubt, to make sure I actually left the country as I promised I would.

The incident only lasted a moment as I ducked into the cab, closed the back door and ordered the driver out to the airport, but it left me somewhat unsettled.

DeGourcy was a very big name in Geneva. Was it possible that he had been leading a double life all these years? On the one hand, posing as a successful money man in a city of money men, while on the other hand, acting as one of the most effective assassins in this century?

On the surface it did not seem possible. Assassins needed the cover of darkness, of obscurity. Whereas DeGourcy was a man of the daylight, his every move made in the public's eye.

Geneva's Cointrin Airport was busy at this hour of the morning, and I was deposited at the Swiss Air section of the terminal a couple of minutes after nine A.M. by a very closed-mouth driver. It was likely, I thought as I paid the man and then bags in hand went into the building, that Grundt had also hired this man to make sure I didn't deviate from my path out of Switzerland.

Just inside the terminal, I stepped to one side of the doors and watched the cars coming and going outside. Within a couple of minutes the dark Mercedes pulled up in a no parking zone and the two men jumped out and headed across the broad sidewalk toward the terminal.

I turned and hurried across the mezzanine to the Swiss Air ticket counter where I paid for my one way ticket to Washington, D.C. The pretty young clerk handed me a small slip of paper with one word written on it.

*London,* Dieter Grundt's message read. DeGourcy had gone to London late last night.

The clerk was watching me, waiting for me to move off.

"Do you have a flight for London this morning?" I asked.

"Yes, sir," she said. She looked up at the departure board behind her. "Flight 737. Leaves at nine-forty."

"Is there room for one?"

"What about your Washington ticket, sir?"

"I've decided to go to London."

For a moment it seemed as if she didn't know what she was supposed to do; but finally she punched the proper numbers in her computer terminal, and shortly a ticket on flight 737 popped out.

I was given a refund for the difference between the price of my Washington ticket and my London reservation, and I moved off toward the proper gate.

Even if Grundt knew what I was up to, I didn't think he'd try to stop me. His first duty was to make sure I got out of Switzerland. I didn't think anyone would really give a damn where I went, as long as it was out of the country.

One of the men from the Mercedes stopped at the ticket counter while the other one followed me through the terminal to the gate for the London flight. A minute or two later his partner joined him, and they both took up positions leaning against the wall and watched me sit down, stretch my legs out and light a cigarette.

The London flight was called for boarding a few

minutes later, and I slowly got to my feet as the people at the gate began shuffling into the boarding tunnel.

I walked across to where the two men were standing and they both stood up.

"Good morning," I smiled. "I'd like you to pass a message to *Herr* Grundt for me, if you would."

The two men just stared at me.

"Tell him that I'm going to London in pursuit of what we talked about earlier, and I would consider it in very poor taste if he tried in any way to interfere."

Still neither man said a word, and I turned on my heel, crossed the boarding gate area and, handing my pass to the clerk at the entrance to the tunnel, went aboard the airplane.

I hoped that Dieter Grundt, in a fit of national pride, would not be so foolish as to communicate to DeGourcy that I was following him. If Grundt did something like that, and if DeGourcy was indeed El Cazador, my chances for survival would be markedly diminished.

El Cazador was the best. The very best. I would need every edge I could get.

It was a few minutes after ten A.M., local time, when we landed at London's Heathrow Airport, the height of the rush hour, and it was nearly an hour after touchdown before I had cleared customs and was in a cab heading into the city.

On the way over I had worried about Hawk's suggestion that DeGourcy might already have gone underground. London was a very big city; if he had changed identities already, there would be very little chance of me catching up with him.

But then I was getting ahead of myself. I still had no direct proof that DeGourcy was indeed El Cazador, except for the rumors years ago, and except for Peter and Gertrude who had given their lives for their belief.

The Newmarket Hotel on Jermyn Street, just off Piccadilly Circus, was one of those old, established Victorian hotels, that during the sixties had been completely rebuilt into a modern structure of glass and steel. Besides the fact it was comfortable now, it was in the center of the city, convenient to almost everything.

After I had checked in and had strapped Wilhelmina beneath my left arm, Hugo under my shirt sleeve on my forearm and Pierre, the specially designed gas bomb that fits in a soft leather pouch high on my thigh, I left the hotel and headed on foot up to Charing Cross.

It was a lovely, warm sunny day and the streets were alive with pedestrians and traffic. Past Piccadilly I headed up Coventry to Leicester and finally on Charing Cross itself, ducked into a small, nondescript building with a small plaque beside the front door that read: Amalgamated Press and Wire Services.

Inside, a flight of stairs led to a second floor door, beyond which was a typical, busy newsroom.

A young, good looking woman came to where I was waiting at the service counter, smiled and started to ask if she could help me, when her eyes suddenly went wide.

"Take it easy," I said softly.

"Mr. Carter . . . I . . . we didn't . . ."

"Is Joe Green in this morning?"

"Yes, sir," she said crisply, recovering, and she led me around the counter, through the newsroom and down a short corridor to a door with a frosted glass window.

She knocked once, then opened the door.

"Mr. Green?" she said.

"What manner of shit has fallen on us now?" Green's voice came from within.

I stepped past the girl, shoving the door all the way open and went inside. "Me," I said.

For a split second Green's mouth dropped open, but

then he got to his feet. "I've been half expecting you, Carter," he said.

The girl withdrew, closing the door behind her, and I crossed the room, shook hands with Green and sat down.

"Did you get Hawk's query on DeGourcy?"

Green took his seat and nodded. "It was on a world-wide twix. Figured you might be somewhere in the picture. What's DeGourcy done?"

"Nothing yet," I said. "He flew here from Geneva last night. Have you had a chance to track him down?"

"That was easy," Green said. "We just checked the Connaught, and he was there, of course. I've put him under a loose surveillance."

"I hope your people haven't been spotted, Joe. If they have been it'll blow this thing wide open."

"They're regular fixtures in the hotel. We get a lot of business over there from time to time," Green said. "Now, do you mind telling me why DeGourcy is getting all this attention?"

Joe Green was one of the better men within AXE, or at least he used to be. He had been chief of the Moscow Station for nearly five years, when the pressure inherent in that job in that city finally got to him and he began losing his nerve. He requested and received a transfer to a much quieter post—this one—and so far he had done a great job. But if he was going to help me on this one, he was going to have to know the truth.

"What do you know about El Cazador?" I asked softly.

For a moment Green just looked at me, but then his features lit up. "Sweet Jesus, you don't think DeGourcy is the assassin, do you?"

"It's a possibility, Joe," I said. "It's why I'm here."

"Sweet Jesus," he said again. There was definitely something wrong.

I sat forward. "What the hell is it?"

"DeGourcy," Green said, reaching for his phone. "He's on his way to 10 Downing Street." He picked up the phone. "Melissa, get me Inspector Health-Bailey would you. Scotland Yard."

I waved him off.

"Hold that just a minute," Green said, and he covered the mouthpiece with his right hand.

"Even if DeGourcy is El Cazador, which I'm not a hundred percent certain, he wouldn't merely walk into 10 Downing Street and assassinate Thatcher. He doesn't work that way."

"You sure?"

"Yes," I said nodding. "But if you get the Yard in on this, DeGourcy will know that he's being followed, and we'll never get him."

I could see that Green was having trouble with that, but finally he took his hand away from the mouthpiece. "Cancel that call Melissa." He hung up the phone. There definitely was worry in his eyes now. "The next move is yours then, Nick."

"Ours," I corrected. "You and I are going back to the old gumshoe days."

"You want to follow him?"

"Everywhere," I said. "But he can't have the slightest suspicion that we're behind him. If he does, he'll stop whatever it is he's doing here."

"If DeGourcy really is El Cazador, he might do more than that," Green said.

I nodded. "Yes. He would have the option of killing us."

We spent the next three hours frantically getting ready for our surveillance of Sprague DeGourcy, all the while keeping in close contact with Green's two people at the Connaught Hotel in Mayfair.

A few minutes after noon he showed up back at his hotel where he had a long, leisurely lunch with three British bankers.

Green and a couple of his technicians were set up in the room below DeGourcy's, and I became a London cabby, my out of service sign lit up, and we settled down to wait.

During the long afternoon and early evening, a parade of London's most important money men came and went from the Connaught where DeGourcy was holding court in his suite.

Green and I were in radio contact where I was parked across from the hotel, and if DeGourcy was anything other than an influential Swiss banker, his conversations with the financiers coming to see him certainly didn't give any indications.

While I waited, my black-billed cap down low over my eyes, I kept thinking about Peter and Gertrude Brandt. They had been so young and naive, and now they were dead, ironically at the hands of DeGourcy's house staff. They hadn't even been able to get close to their main objective.

"He's alone now," Green's voice came softly from the radio concealed beneath the front seat of my cab.

I reached down and picked up the mike. "Has he called for any more appointments?" I asked. It was dark out now.

"No," Green said. "And it sounds like he's running his bath now."

There was also the possibility that even if DeGourcy was the assassin, he would not make any moves for several days. They would be a very long several days, but I was going to stick with it.

"Hold on," Green's excited voice came over the radio.

"What is it?" I asked.

"The tricky bastard. His bath water is running, but he's been spotted heading down the service stairs."

"Back door?" I asked. I started the cab's engine.

"The South Audley side," Green snapped.

I put the cab in gear, eased away from the curb and snapped the Vacant sign on, turning the corner on South Audley Street a minute later and slowly cruising down the block.

A dark-jacketed figure emerged from the hotel, started down the block, but then spotting me, waved.

I was committed now; I just hoped it was DeGourcy. I pulled over to the curb, reached over the back seat and opened the rear door.

Sprague DeGourcy, a grim expression on his face, climbed in back. I turned the meter flag down and headed away from the hotel.

"Where to, Mac?" I said in my best Brooklyn accent.

# FIVE

"New York?" DeGourcy said from the back seat, a hard edge to his voice.

I glanced at him in the rear-view mirror. His right hand was in his jacket pocket. "Is it that bad, sir?" I asked.

"What are you doing in London?"

"Driving hack," I snapped. "Beats the hell out of Brooklyn."

"I suppose it does," DeGourcy said, and I could see that he was relaxing.

"Where to?" I asked again.

"Fifth and Bateman; it's in Soho," DeGourcy said.

"I know it, sir," I said and headed up Oxford Street toward the district.

I knew there would be no way for me to effectively fake a British accent—at least not effectively enough to convince a man like DeGourcy—so I had adopted the Brooklyn accent to catch him off his guard. Apparently it had worked because as I drove, DeGourcy didn't seem to be paying any attention to me.

A few minutes later I turned down Dean Street, and four blocks later turned up Bateman, pulling up and stopping on the corner of Fifth.

The district was busy with pedestrian traffic, most of them young kids in sloppy sweatshirts and patched, faded jeans.

DeGourcy paid my fare, added a generous tip and then headed up toward the Greek section of the district.

I hurried around the block and pulled into a parking lot as I grabbed the mike.

"You still with me, Joe?" I said.

"We've got him spotted on foot," Green's voice came over the radio. "He just turned up toward the Square."

"Back off now, I'll pick it up from here," I said. I shut off the cab, yanked off the black hat and dark coat, put on a dark blue sportcoat and hurriedly walked toward Soho Square.

I picked DeGourcy up as he passed Manette Street and continued toward the square. He was walking slowly, stopping from time to time to look into shop windows, once to bend down and tie his shoes, and once to light a cigarette.

DeGourcy was definitely being cautious. I only hoped that he hadn't been spooked either by me or by Green and his people.

There were enough people out on the streets, however, so that it was relatively simple for me to stick with him and not be spotted.

Up on the Square, DeGourcy suddenly sped up, and at times I had to run to stick with him until he reached Oxford Street. He hailed a passing cab, climbed in the back seat and was gone.

It was the oldest trick in the business, and I had fallen for it!

A small Vauxhall pulled up behind me and Joe Green was there. I jumped in the car and we took off in pursuit of the cab.

"You're slipping, Nick," Green said, grinning.

"It may already be too late," I said glumly. "He obviously knows he's being followed."

"Only for a little while longer," Green said. He sped up, so that he was right on the cab's tail, then suddenly turned down a side street and pulled up to the curb.

"What the hell—" I started to say, but Green had picked up the radio microphone.

"It's one-four-seven-three-eight-J," he said.

"Got it," the radio blared.

I suddenly understood that I had badly underestimated Joe Green. Moscow hadn't changed him as much as I had feared.

"You've been busy since you've been here," I said.

Green smiled. "It's easy in a friendly country," he said.

We waited twenty minutes until the radio blared again. "Surrey Commercial Docks, Number 17 Hammersly Quay."

"Thanks, Stu," Green said. He pulled away from the curb and headed across town, crossing the river near St. Paul's, continuing through Bermondsey to Southwark Park just below the shipping area.

"Actually we got lucky this time," Green admitted. "I've only got an in with two cab companies. Haven't gotten to the others yet."

"I owe you a steak dinner," I said.

Green laughed. "I'll take you up on it."

On the other side of Southwark Park, the Surrey Commercial Docks were brightly lit, and even at this hour ships were being loaded and unloaded. A great number of canals and slips had been dug south of the river, and ocean-going vessels were lined up row after row.

Many of the private wharves were fenced off, and Green skirted these until we came to a narrow street that jutted out at an odd angle through a section of ramshackle buildings that resembled warehouses. He pulled up and parked in the middle of the block, as far away from a single light at the corner as possible, and shut off the lights.

"It's the building down on the corner," he said.

"Do you know this area?" I asked, looking through the windshield at the rundown, three-story building down the block.

"Only vaguely," Green said. "A lot of shit going on in this part of town. Drugs. Murder. You name it."

"El Cazador," I said softly.

"Do you want me to come along?"

"Nope," I said. "But you can stick around as backup if you want."

"Will do," Green said, and I got out of the car, carefully closed the door and headed down the street, keeping to the deeper shadows nearer the buildings, every one of my senses alert for a lookout.

El Cazador was a cautious man. He had to have been cautious to have survived all these years. And if DeGourcy was the man, then DeGourcy would have taken some precautions before coming down here.

At the corner I flattened myself against the building and cautiously peered across to the structure with a large number seventeen painted on its side. The cab had dropped DeGourcy off here minutes ago. No matter what or who DeGourcy really was, it definitely was an odd place and an odd hour for a successful Swiss banker.

Spanning the narrow avenue, between where I stood and Number 17, was a second floor enclosed walkway about halfway down the block.

I backed away from the corner, and at the door to the building I had hidden by, I quickly picked the padlock with my stiletto and let myself in.

It was darker inside than out, but still I could see that I was in a large space filled with huge piles of crates, the ceiling three stories above me. This definitely was a warehouse. No doubt there would be a night watchman somewhere so I was going to have to be careful.

To my left, above at the second floor level, was a catwalk, and from where I stood just within the front door I could see the opening to the skywalk that spanned the avenue over to Number 17.

I worked my way along the wall to a set of metal stairs that led up to the catwalk, and crouching there for several long moments, I strained my senses trying to detect the presence of the watchman. But I could hear nothing, and finally I started up the steps, taking great pains not to make a noise.

At the top, I could see across the entire building. Near the back, in the corner diagonal from where I stood, I could make out a very dim light behind a set of windows. The night watchman's station no doubt. And even if the man was awake and alert, he would never see me up here.

Quickly then, I hurried down the catwalk and ducked into the skyway, crossing over to the building across the avenue. A thick steel fire door blocked the entrance.

I took out my small penlight, switched the filter to red and working as quickly as I could, checked the edges of the door, finally finding the tiny twisted wires near the spring and counterweight at the top. The door was alarmed.

Pocketing the penlight, I went to one of the windows in the skywalk, and using my stiletto to pry away the old paint and grime, managed to get the window open with a minimum of noise.

The outside air smelled damp and foul from the

nearby docks and river. I climbed out of the window, reached up and caught the edge of the roof above, and then swung out and up, flipping my right leg over the roof, and then rolling my body the rest of the way up and over.

Lying flat on my stomach, I hung way over the edge of the roof and just managed to reach the window with my fingertips and swing it closed. It wouldn't do for the night watchman or anyone else to come down the skywalk and find the window open.

Getting to my feet, but crouching low, I hurried the rest of the way across the skywalk and climbed up to the broad expanse of roof on Number 17. Somewhere below, DeGourcy was meeting someone.

The mostly clear roofline was broken up here and there with exhaust vents, skylights, and near the center, an entry door to a stairwell. No doubt it would be alarmed, as would the skylights, but the latter would be easier to handle.

I cautiously approached the skylight, finally getting down on my hands and knees for the last couple of feet, and eased to the edge of the dirty glass.

A few feet below were the top crates in a tall stack. It was likely that this building was the twin of the building I had entered across the avenue. If that was so, I was looking at the top of a nearly three-story high pile of boxes.

Using the penlight, I found the alarm wires near the skylight hinge. The entire building was alarmed. Not exactly usual procedure for a dockside warehouse.

Pocketing the penlight, I again took out my stiletto, and within five minutes had the putty and diamond retainers out of one of the panes of glass and was prying the pane out with the tip of the knife.

Laying the glass aside, I took out a business card from

my wallet, tore a small piece from the corner, then reaching through the opening in the skylight, wedged the thick paper between the contacts of the alarm's trip switch.

Carefully then I unlatched the skylight, eased it open, just far enough for me to slip inside atop the crates, and then closed it. Reaching back up through the opening, I managed to grab the pane of glass and carefully ease it back in place. Then making sure everything was back the way it had been, I removed the small piece of stiff paper from between the alarm's contacts.

Only the closest of examinations would reveal that anyone had come this way. Even if a watchman or a guard was patrolling the roof, I doubted very much if he would see the putty scraped away from the small pane in a skylight.

For a minute or two I lay where I was, breathing shallowly, listening to the errant sounds of the building. Somewhere far below was the sound of some kind of a motor, and from time to time I thought I could hear the sounds of laughter.

Finally, I moved away from the skylight, slowly crawling through the uneven maze of wooden packing crates. Gradually I worked my way lower down the tall stacks as I headed toward the rear of the building, toward the running motor and the sound of talk and laughter, which became more and more distinct the closer I came.

For the most part the building was in darkness, with only an occasional light here and there over the aisles through the stacks. But near the back of the building there was a soft glow of lights from a line of windows at the third floor level.

As I came around the corner of one of the crates, I found myself looking directly into the eyes of De-

Gourcy, who stood at an open window a couple of feet below me and about thirty feet away.

I froze, not daring to move a muscle. DeGourcy's eyes seemed to bore into mine, and at the first sign he saw me I was going to blow him away.

But after ten seconds or so, DeGourcy turned around. "It will have to do, gentlemen," he said, his voice clear and loud. He was not worried about being overheard here.

"We understand the timetable, sir," a voice with a deep British accent said.

I moved around the last crate, eased my way to the end of the stack so that I was less than twenty feet from the open window, and then got down on my stomach in the shadows.

I could see into the room now. It was some kind of an office. DeGourcy's back was still to the window, and I could see at least three other men. All of them in their mid-thirties, perhaps very early forties; all of them wearing crew cuts, their faces hard, almost chiseled, and their bodies obviously well conditioned. Unless I missed my guess, I was betting that they were British mercenaries.

"Colonel Lenz is already in position with fifty American PT boats," DeGourcy was saying.

One of the others laughed. "Shit, that man was magnificent in Iraq."

"I served with him in Uganda in the old days," another said.

"Good man," the third agreed. "Will you be there, sir?"

"I won't be flying out until tomorrow afternoon, but I should be in Cap Haitien no later than Thursday," DeGourcy replied.

"Then that's it," the same man said.

"Not quite," DeGourcy said. Again he turned and

looked out the open window toward where I lay. I was certain he could not see me, but it was disconcerting nevertheless to have him staring my way.

"Is something wrong?"

"Maybe," DeGourcy said thoughtfully. He turned back again. "I may have been followed."

"Here?"

"Of course not. I lost him in Soho. Still . . ."

"Our necks are all out on the chopping block on this one. If it fails, we're all dead men."

"It won't," DeGourcy said with confidence.

But I had a hunch that he was thinking about the attack on his estate by Peter and Gertrude Brandt. That, combined with the fact he suspected he had been followed through Soho, added up to trouble in his mind. He was right.

There was a silence for a long moment, and then one of the mercenaries said, "To victory."

The others repeated the phrase, and a minute later the door opened. DeGourcy stepped out onto the catwalk, looked my way again for just a second and then headed down to street level.

There was silence then from the room, and at five-minute intervals the three mercenaries followed DeGourcy, the last one out of the room extinguishing the lights and closing and locking the door.

I waited still another five minutes in the silent warehouse, then eased back from the edge of the crates and returned to the skylight through which I had entered.

I wedged the piece of paper I had used before in the alarm trip switch, opened the skylight and climbed out onto the roof.

Quickly I pulled the pane of glass out, removed the paper and then replaced the glass, smudging some dirt and loose putty around the edges.

DeGourcy was spooked. I didn't want to give him any further reason to abandon whatever mission he had been assigned in Moscow. But whatever it was, it was going to take place in Haiti and involved mercenaries. I could think of a number of unpleasant things that the Russians might want to accomplish in our backyard. But before I took any direct action against DeGourcy, I wanted to find out what they were up to, and I wanted to know for certain that DeGourcy was indeed El Cazador.

Keeping low so that I wouldn't present a silhouette on the roofline, I hurried across to the skywalk. Above the window through which I had gained entry, I got down on my stomach and, using my stiletto, managed to reach down far enough to ease the window open.

Re-sheathing the blade, I swung down off the roof and into the skywalk, closed and re-locked the window and made my way back into the warehouse, down to street level and outside, where I re-locked the padlock.

Following DeGourcy around a city like London was no easy task. But Cap Haitien, Haiti was another entirely different matter. The town was small and DeGourcy would be a very visible presence. Of course, so would I.

Green's Vauxhall was still parked in the shadows down the block from me, and as I hurried that way I was already beginning to make my plans for the Caribbean.

So far DeGourcy had not seen me. He knew nothing about me, which for the moment gave me the edge. If they were hiring mercenaries for some kind of an operation, I might be able to join them as a recruit. Failing that, I would become an ordinary tourist.

Joe Green was seated behind the wheel, lying back against the headrest, and when I was less than ten feet away from the car, I suddenly realized that something was drastically wrong, and I flattened myself against the building.

He was dead. There was a bullet hole in the middle of his forehead. A small amount of blood had trickled down into his left eye.

As I searched the buildings, rooftops and dark streets around me, I knew that DeGourcy had done this. Leaving the warehouse meeting he had evidently spotted Joe waiting in the car. He probably figured that Joe had been the one who had followed him, so he snuck up on the car and killed him.

There was a possibility that someone was still watching the car, but I doubted it. DeGourcy and the others would not have stuck around. There would be no reason for them to suspect that Green had been working with someone else.

Yet I could not move the car or disturb anything. DeGourcy would be watching the newspapers for a story about a man found shot to death in the Surrey Commercial Dock area.

Green would be identified as an Amalgamated Press bureau chief, which would tie in with Edwards, the Reuters newsman.

If there had been even the slightest chance that Joe was still alive, I would have said the hell with it and taken him to the nearest hospital. But I've seen enough gunshot wounds and bodies to know when a man is dead. And Joe Green was definitely dead.

After a while, I turned and headed down the street, still keeping to the shadows as much as possible.

Four people were dead now, and at the center of all of them was DeGourcy. It was going to give me a great deal of pleasure to finally meet him face to face. None of his victims really had much of a chance.

I wasn't going to be so easy for him.

# SIX

By the time I had cleared customs at Haiti's Port-au-Prince International Airport, my clothes were plastered to my skin. Washington's heat and humidity seemed cool and dry compared to Haiti's weather. The temperature had to be near a hundred degrees with the humidity to match, and the customs officials all had been slow, deliberate and maddeningly officious.

I had phoned David Hawk from our London office after I had broken the news to Joe Green's staff and explained what had happened.

Hawk had been raging mad. Madder than I had ever heard him. Joe Green had been a very special person to him, and I think he felt somewhat responsible.

"If it was DeGourcy, I want the bastard nailed," Hawk's angry voice came over the transatlantic line. "But you've got to be sure, Nick. Absolutely sure."

"He's on his way to Cap Haitien," I told him. "He's planning some sort of an operation there, apparently with British mercenaries."

There was a silence on the line for a few seconds, and when Hawk started to talk again he seemed more in control, certainly a lot calmer.

"You can fly directly to Port-au-Prince," he said. "I'll have one of our staff people meet you there. Someone who knows the island."

"I'd rather work alone on this, sir," I protested.

"I know you would, Nick. But unless you know your way around Haiti, you'd stick out like a sore thumb and probably get yourself into more trouble than need be."

The remark hurt, but I held my silence.

"Listen, Nick, Haiti is in a very delicate balance, politically. The entire area is like a powder keg with a very short fuse. If you go mucking around down there in the blind, there could be some uncomfortable repercussions. You're after DeGourcy, not a coup de'état."

"I can just imagine what DeGourcy is planning," I said glumly.

"I can think of a number of nasty possibilities myself. It's imperative that you stop whatever it is he's got planned."

"Yes, sir," I said. "How will I know my contact?"

"Your contact will know you. Be careful, Nick. Whether or not DeGourcy is El Cazador, I suspect he's a dangerous man."

To that I agreed, and later that morning I left on a BOAC flight that stopped in the Azores for refueling and then continued on to the Caribbean.

It was just seven P.M., when, bags in hand, I crossed the mezzanine and stepped out into the hot early evening.

Street vendors selling everything from fruit juices to woven rope figures lined the broad sidewalk in front of the building. Two tour buses were parked in front of a row of rattletrap taxis. And people were everywhere, shouting and laughing and hugging each other.

This is always my most vulnerable point. When I get off a commercial flight, my weapons are packed in my luggage. And I usually don't like to stay out in the open very long.

Evidently signals had been crossed somewhere with the man Hawk said would be meeting me here. Either that or he hadn't planned on contacting me until after I had booked into my hotel.

I shrugged, heading across the sidewalk toward the cabs, when a white Lotus Elan convertible screeched around the corner and pulled up at the end of the row of taxis.

A tall, gorgeous black woman, wearing a white wraparound skirt and a white halter top, got out of the car and came regally down the sidewalk. She looked like a high fashion model, with small breasts, long beautifully shaped legs and a delicate face.

Heads turned as she approached me, and I started to turn around to see if there was someone behind me whom she was meeting at the airport, when she stopped and held out her hand to me.

"*Monsieur* Carter, I believe," she said, her voice soft, almost liquid, with the Haitian-French creole patois.

"Don't tell me you're the one David sent," I said.

She smiled engagingly. "I hope that you are not terribly disappointed."

"On the contrary," I said, taking her hand.

"I am Maxime Genarde. But you may call me Max."

I laughed. "All right, Max, pleased to meet you. Now if you'll direct me to the nearest air-conditioned hotel where I can get a shower, a drink and something to eat—in that order—I'd be eternally grateful."

She too laughed, the sound graceful, and I went with her back to her little sportscar, where I threw my bags in the back and climbed in the passenger side.

"Tell me, Max," I said, when we had cleared the airport and were heading into the city, "are you Haitian?"

She glanced at me. "I was born here. But I attended Vassar and Harvard. A few years ago I became an American citizen, but I was sent back to work at the embassy here."

"Vassar and Harvard," I said. I'm sure she had created quite a stir in those hallowed halls. "How long have you been working with AXE?"

"Twelve hours," she said. "Before that I was with the CIA."

"Twelve hours?" I asked incredulously.

"I've worked with your David Hawk before. Liaison mostly, but I was assigned to Clandestine Operations with the Company. Some strings were pulled this morning, I was offered the job, and I took it."

I took out a cigarette and lit it as I sat back, silent for the moment. This woman was extraordinary, there was no doubt about it. But twelve hours with AXE, and Hawk had assigned her to help me? I wondered just how extraordinary she was. Hawk usually didn't make these kinds of mistakes.

"DeGourcy's yacht *Magnum* arrived in Cap Haitien two days ago. From what I've been told, DeGourcy himself will be arriving very soon."

"How much do you know about this assignment?" I asked.

She glanced at me again. "Only two things. The first is the possibility that *Monsieur* DeGourcy and the assassin El Cazador may be one and the same. And the second is that DeGourcy is evidently planning some operation on Haiti with the aid of British mercenaries. It is our job to find out what DeGourcy is up to and stop him."

"How did you find out about DeGourcy's yacht?"

"I have many friends and family here on Haiti, *Monsieur* Carter. They have eyes and ears. They listen and watch for me."

"DeGourcy is very sharp; he'll spot your people. I want you to call them off."

"No," she said simply.

I started to protest, but she held me off.

"No, *Monsieur* Carter, because my people are people of Haiti. To DeGourcy they are nothing more than the trees or the rocks. They are vendors and hotel clerks and poor farmers mostly. They *are* Haiti. DeGourcy will see them, of course, as he will see the mountains. But he will not understand."

We had come to the sprawling downtown section of the city and Maxime turned down a side street, and a half a block later pulled into an underground garage and parked in a stall marked with her name.

She shut off the little car's engine, dropped the keys into her purse and then got out. "You will stay here with me for the night. It will be better than a hotel."

"I snore," I said, climbing out of the car and retrieving my bags.

"Not tonight," she said, and she turned and strode across the garage to the elevator, leaving me to wonder what the hell she meant by that.

Maxime's apartment, on the fourth floor of the building, was very large, very lovely and air conditioned.

She mixed me a drink, showed me where the bathroom was and told me that she would fix us something to eat while I cleaned up and changed clothes.

"How far is it to Cap Haitien?" I asked, taking a sip of the very good cognac.

"About ninety miles," she said.

"Then after we eat, I'd like to drive up there. I want to be in place when DeGourcy shows up."

"It is not advisable," she said. "Luis, my brother, is

there and watching. He will not be spotted by DeGourcy, but he will listen and watch. And when the man arrives he will telephone here."

"DeGourcy may jump immediately."

"Haiti is a small country, *Monsieur* Carter. And besides, DeGourcy has not yet arrived."

I couldn't argue with that. And Hawk had sent her to help me here in Haiti. Besides, I told myself finishing the drink and then bringing my suitcase into the large, luxurious bathroom, I was still on London time where it was after midnight. I was tired and hungry.

I took a long, leisurely shower, and when I stepped out of the stall, a large bath towel was hanging on the rack for me and Maxime had poured me a fresh drink.

When I had finished drying myself, I shaved and then got dressed in a pair of slacks and a light shirt.

With drink in hand, I went back into the living room where Maxime was setting out plates in a breakfast nook on a glassed-in balcony overlooking the lovely city and boat-lined harbor beyond. A bottle of white French wine that I did not recognize was cooling in a bucket, a corkscrew lying nearby on the table.

"Open the wine," she said. "I will get our dinner."

I did as she asked, and when I had poured us both a glass, she came back bearing a platter of abalone steaks done up in a butter sauce, surrounded with a light salad and toast wedges.

She served me and then herself, and finally sat down across the small table from me, raising her wine glass in a salute.

The wine and food were excellent, and during the meal we talked a little about Haiti and the troubles the tiny island country had experienced ever since Columbus had landed on Hispaniola. The thrust of her position was that had the island been left alone, free from outside influences, most of their troubles would have never existed.

"But your governments had always been basically unstable, Max, you have to admit to that," I argued good-naturedly.

She flared. "An unstability caused by white interference in our internal affairs."

"A curious position for an American intelligence service agent to take," I said. Maybe Hawk *had* made a mistake after all.

"It makes me sick to see what has been done here," she said, somewhat subdued. There still was an intensity in her eyes, however.

"Not entirely the doing of the United States."

She looked away, out at the lights of the city. "You're right, of course. Basically my people are lazy and ignorant. There still is an eighty percent illiteracy rate here. Yet no one seems willing to do anything about it except talk. Nothing but talk."

"So you ran away in frustration," I suggested.

She looked at me. "Something like that," she said. "Although it began more idealistically. I wanted to get a decent education so that I could come back and help my people."

"And you are helping them," I said sitting forward. "Although not in the way you originally envisioned."

"I know, I know," she waved me off. "If DeGourcy or men like him have their way, Haiti would be set up as a puppet dictatorship."

"Run from Moscow," I said.

"I know that, too," she said, almost on the verge of tears. But after a time she shook herself out of her morose mood and managed a slight smile. "You must be dreadfully tired, *Monsieur* Carter."

"Nick," I corrected.

"Nick," she said. "Go in the bedroom and get some rest. I will wake you the moment Luis calls with any news."

"Promise?" I asked.

"Promise," she said.

I drank the rest of my wine, went into her bedroom where I kicked off my shoes and lay down on the wide bed falling asleep instantly. I had been going more or less steadily for the last three days, and I was dead tired.

I don't know how long I slept or what finally woke me, but when I came awake with a start, my heart racing, it took me a moment to remember where I was. But then it came back to me and I raised my left arm so that I could see the luminous dials on my watch. It was a few minutes after two in the morning.

"Did I wake you?" Maxime's soft voice came from across the room near the windows. They were open and the air conditioning had been switched off. The air was cool, but there was a heavy, humid smell of the sea and of dark, luxurious jungles.

I could see her silhouette as she looked outside. She was nude, her body lovely.

"Has your brother called yet?" I asked.

"Not yet," she said, not turning my way. "But he will as soon as DeGourcy arrives."

"Have you slept?"

"Some," she said. "I'm frightened."

"I can call David in the morning and have someone else assigned."

"Not of DeGourcy," Maxime said. "Of me." She turned to look at me, her small breasts perfectly formed, jutting out and slightly upward, her ebony skin gleaming softly in the starlight.

She came across the room and climbed on the bed next to me.

"This isn't necessary, Max," I said as gently as I could.

"Yes it is," she replied. "I hate your kind, but . . ." She sighed deeply. "Hold me, Nick, just hold me."

I took her in my arms and we lay back on the bed, one of her long legs thrown over mine, and I held her shivering body as she cried softly. It had to have been pretty bad for her in the States. The stupid nigger from voodoo infested Haiti. The easy lay.

After a long while I got up, took off my clothes, then came back to bed to her, and we made slow, gentle love during the early Haitian morning. And for a moment I had the impression that Maxime was a virgin, but then it passed as I lost myself in her incredible delicacy and tenderness.

The telephone rang shortly before dawn, and Maxime reached over me and picked it up from the nightstand on my side of the bed.

"*Oui,*" she said.

She listened for a long time, then snapped something in rapid-fire Haitian, and finally hung up.

"Luis?" I asked, sitting up as she rolled off me.

"Yes. It was Luis," she said. She flipped on the light, and with no hint of modesty got out of the bed and crossed the room to the bathroom door, where she stopped and turned back. "You were very sweet with me, Nick," she said.

I smiled.

"We must leave. Luis is waiting for us."

"Has DeGourcy shown up?" I asked, swinging my legs over the edge of the bed.

"He came aboard his yacht this morning about two hours ago. But the boat left her anchorage almost immediately."

"Damn," I swore. "I'll have to call Hawk and order a radar search."

"It is not necessary, Luis thinks," Maxime said. "At first he said he thought the boat would head straight out to sea, but he wanted to make sure, so he followed her out beyond the harbor entrance."

"And?"

"DeGourcy's yacht turned west about five miles offshore. Going very slowly. As if it was looking for something."

"What's west up the coast?" I asked.

"Le Borgne, St. Louis De Nord, Port de Paix, but then nothing until Jean Rabel, except for a long stretch of empty countryside."

"Could a mercenary base be set up there—between Port de Paix and Jean Rabel?"

"Easily."

"That's it then," I said. "Hurry and get ready. I want to get up there as fast as possible."

She was finished in the bathroom in five minutes, and by the time I had taken a quick shower and had gotten dressed, she was ready.

Together we took the elevator down to the garage.

"You can drive if you'd like," she said. "But I know the roads better."

"Go ahead," I snapped, as I jumped in the passenger side.

She climbed in behind the wheel, the Lotus' small but powerful engine came to life, and within fifteen minutes we were outside the city, racing down a narrow highway, north toward Cap Haitien as the sun just peeked up in the east.

"What else has your brother told you about the goings on at DeGourcy's yacht?" I asked. I had to shout over the noise of the wind.

"Nothing unusual," she said. "No soldiers. No weapons in sight. Nothing more than a normal crew for a luxury yacht."

The highway did not go directly to Cap Haitien, instead it led almost due east, first to the city of Lascahibas near the Dominican Republic border, then skirted Lake de Peligre, before finally heading due north to the opposite coast.

For the most part Maxime drove in silence, leaving me alone with my thoughts. Despite her outward appearance of self-assurance, her college degrees, and her CIA training, she was a vulnerable woman. Four people had died in the last few days because of Sprague DeGourcy. I did not want Maxime to become the fifth victim. Cap Haitien was going to be the end of the line for her. If she wouldn't accept my orders to that effect, I'd have to convince her brother to keep her there.

Haiti is a heavily forested country of several mountain chains, with high passes and narrow switchback roads. Maxime handled the car well, and we made good time, finally descending into Cap Haitien, which the French had once called the Paris of the Caribbean, a little past eight-thirty A.M.

Now it was a small but bustling seaport town with a mixture of private yachts and commercial vessels in the harbor.

Maxime pulled up and parked in front of a seedy-looking cafe called Alphonse's Extraordinaire, and we went inside where her brother was waiting for us.

Luis Genarde was a bull of a man, a full head taller than me with arms that looked like hydraulic pistons and shoulders that would have done well on the Dallas Cowboys' line.

He was seated behind the bar, eating his breakfast and drinking whiskey, while a half a dozen young, fairly good-looking women served him.

"Ah, Maxime," he bellowed when we came in and crossed to him.

"You did well, Luis," Maxime said, pecking him on the cheek, but he was looking up at me, his eyes suddenly narrowed.

"You're Carter?" he asked.

"That's right," I said, extending my hand. He ignored it.

"I do not think it is a good thing, involving my sister in things of this nature."

"I agree," I said. "I was hoping to convince you to make her return to Port-au-Prince, or at least remain here."

Luis looked at me for a long time, an appraising expression in his eyes. "Go back or remain here makes no difference. But you have something else for Luis?"

Without asking I sat down in the chair across from him, took an empty glass, poured myself a stiff shot of the whiskey and downed it. "I must find out where DeGourcy has gone and what he is doing there. But it must be done very quietly. The pay is good. But the work will be dangerous."

A play of emotion crossed the big man's features, and he glanced up at his sister. "You will return to Port-au-Prince, this morning."

"I will not," Maxime said, looking over to me.

I ignored her. "Ordinarily I would ask for no help of this nature, *Monsieur* Genarde, but I do not know Haiti."

"Will it pay very well?"

"Very well," I said.

He smiled. "Then we will start as soon as I finish my breakfast. Have you any idea where DeGourcy may have gone?"

"Somewhere between Port de Paix and Jean Rabel.

But I'd like to approach the area by land."

Luis was nodding. "It will be difficult, exceedingly difficult. But then, what is *Monsieur* DeGourcy up to out there?"

I shrugged. "There may be mercenaries."

"Coup?" Luis asked, bristling.

"Perhaps."

"Then I will gather many men."

I shook my head. "Only you and me. First we must find out what they are up to, and then I will kill DeGourcy."

Luis chuckled. "I am liking this man of yours more and more, Maxime," he said to his sister.

"I am coming with you," she said.

Luis shook his head. "You will return to Port-au-Prince."

For a moment it seemed as if Maxime was going to argue with her brother, but then she thought better of it. "You bastard," she swore at me, and then she swiveled on her heel, stalked out of the club, and a moment later we could hear the roar of the Lotus, and she was gone.

Luis laughed. "A firebrand girl, that one," he said. "But best left behind."

# SEVEN

We waited in Cap Haitien until dark and then took off to the west in Luis Genarde's ancient Willys Jeep. During the morning I caught up on my rest; later in the day Luis and I talked at length about Haiti and its problems.

In many respects the tiny country was still back in the eighteen hundreds, with half the population still practicing the rites of voodoo, while the other half believes in it. In other respects Haiti was being rudely dragged into the twentieth century. Pleasure yachts calling at Cap Haitien brought with them the diverse cultures of dozens of foreign countries, especially America.

We came into Port de Paix around ten P.M. where Luis took us immediately to an old shack on the beach northwest of the city. When he shut off the jeep's engine and doused the lights, the dark, humid night suddenly seemed to press down on us.

We got out of the Jeep and I followed Luis up a path through the sand dunes to the tiny, ramshackle building that leaned at a crazy angle, as if it was on the verge of collapsing.

Luis approached the porch slowly and a few feet away stopped. I was going to ask him why he wasn't knocking on the door or at least calling out, when the screen door opened and an incredibly old black woman glided out on the porch.

In the dim light from the stars, the woman's face seemed older than Haiti itself, her arms and legs sticking out of a flour sack dress. Her limbs were incredibly thin and brittle looking.

"Good evening to you, Mother," Luis said softly, with great deference in his voice.

The woman cackled, the sound dry like dead leaves underfoot. "You have brought Mother trouble. It is in the aura of this other one."

I started to step forward, around Luis, but the old woman held up her hand.

"No," she said. "You have come seeking help, Nick Carter, but there is death around you."

I was stunned. How in Christ's name had she known me? Luis seemed clearly nervous.

"We seek to stop the trouble, Mother," he said. "Shall we go back?"

Again the old woman cackled. The hair at the nape of my neck bristled.

The ocean was a hundred yards behind the tiny shack, and the old woman half turned to look that way, as she cocked her head and seemed to be listening for something.

"They are there now," she said, her voice barely audible. "To the west. Many men, some women. Hate and greed in their hearts. Bad men, some of them. Misguided men, others of them." She turned back to look directly at me and her eyes seemed to catch some chance light, and they sparkled.

"Will we be successful, Mother?" Luis asked, licking his lips.

"It is not for Mother to see," the old woman said.

"But the man you seek is there."

I could hear the waves washing up on the beach and the night insects buzzing.

"I see Havana," the old woman said, cocking her head again. "And I see a place of mountains and cold. But there is a reflection of evil in my visions. A mirror image."

Luis was clearly agitated, but I was stunned. The place of mountains and cold was obviously Switzerland. But Havana? DeGourcy could have gathered a force of mercenaries here on Haiti. Back in London, at the warehouse meeting, one of them had mentioned American PT boats. Now the woman said she saw Havana.

Cuba was less than sixty miles across the Windward Passage from the western tip of Haiti. But Cuba and the Soviet Union were allies. If DeGourcy was working for the Russians why would he be attacking there?

"It will be as it appears, not as it really is," the old woman said to me, and then she turned and glided back inside.

"What . . ." I started to call after her, but Luis took me by the arm and urged me back to the Jeep.

"We are finished here, Nick. We must go now."

I went back to the jeep with him, and as he started it, turned around and headed back out to the highway, I kept looking at the shack. How had the old woman known my name and everything else? I don't believe in spooks or the occult, but what I had just witnessed was definitely hard to explain.

"She is Haiti," Luis said, answering my unspoken question. He was still shaken up.

"You're not going to give up because of her, are you?" I asked as we reached the main road.

Luis shook his head. "No," he said, turning west and speeding up.

The small town of Jean Rabel was another twenty-five miles down the coast, but about halfway there, Luis slowed the Jeep down, and a mile later we came to a narrow, deeply rutted track that led toward the ocean which was two or three miles through the thick jungle.

He stopped on the highway, then backed about two hundred yards down the path where he flipped off the headlights and switched off the Jeep's ignition.

"We will go on foot from here," he said. "If they're back there, they'll have sentries posted and would hear the Jeep."

I got out, checked my Luger and the two extra clips.

"If there is any trouble, we will come back here, and drive immediately back to Cap Haitien where I will call the military barracks at Port-au-Prince."

"If there is a mercenary base out here, your government will know about it."

A hard edge came into Luis' voice. "Do not say that, *Monsieur* Carter. My country does not wish a war we could not possibly win."

Luis had picked up on the old woman's mention of Havana.

"You can remain here," I suggested. "For now I just want to look."

Luis grinned. "You'll do more than look, I have no doubt of that," he said. "I will go with you." He turned and pulled up the back seat of the Jeep and from beneath withdrew an old Thompson submachine gun and two thirty-round clips. This time his grin was feral, but he said nothing.

A moment later we were heading down the dirt track, deeper into the dense jungle, the darkness closing in on us.

If there was a mercenary base back there somewhere, I didn't want to get into a fight. My target was De-Gourcy.

Every hundred yards or so, we stopped and held our breath, listening for sounds of human activity. But each time there was nothing, except for the night sounds of the jungle. We continued.

It took us nearly an hour to make it all the way to the beach, and a few hundred yards before the jungle opened up we could hear the waves crashing. If there was a base anywhere near, the men on it were being extraordinarily quiet.

We finally came out of the jungle a few minutes before midnight, and Luis was about to start across the fifty yards of sand to the water's edge, when something to the west caught my eye and I pulled him back.

"You see something?" he asked looking that way.

"I thought I did," I said. I thought I had seen a flash of light through the trees, in the distance.

Then it was there again, high in the treetops, for just an instant. Luis saw it too.

"It is a boat. That's a masthead light," he said softly.

The small white light moved up and down, disappearing behind the trees, and then reappearing again.

"Is there a river down there that DeGourcy could have brought his yacht into?"

"Not that I know of," Luis said, continuing to watch the light. "But there could be a harbor. Could be something they put together."

"We've got to get closer," I said. "But I don't want any trouble."

Luis gripped the submachine gun a little tighter. "They are on Haiti illegally."

"If we get into a firefight with them, we'll lose. Do you want that?"

Luis looked down the beach toward the light, but then shook his head. "It will be as you wish—for the time being."

We started down the beach, keeping just within the

line of trees. There would be sentries posted, but I suspected they would be concentrating their lookouts toward the open sea and the highway inland, not the beach east and west. But I couldn't be one hundred percent sure of that, so until we knew for certain what security measures DeGourcy had taken, we were going to have to be extremely careful.

The beach curved gently to the left, and as we followed it around, we began to hear an occasional out-of-place sound, the kind made by a large gathering of soldiers—but highly disciplined soldiers.

There were more lights now in addition to the masthead light from DeGourcy's yacht, many lights lower to the water and others deeper into the jungle.

We finally stopped a couple of hundred yards from where a good-sized cove indented the shoreline. A portable breakwater had been sunk just offshore to protect the tiny harbor which was filled to capacity with DeGourcy's large motor yacht *Magnum* and the fifty American PT boats.

Along the beach, within the cove, were dozens of large olive drab-colored tents, stockpiles of supplies and at least two hundred and fifty men dressed in some kind of uniform.

It was definitely a strike force, the presence of the American PT boats leaving no doubt about the target or on whom the blame would be placed. It was to be another Bay of Pigs invasion. The Americans would be blamed, opening the diplomatic doors for the Soviet Union's case to arm Cuba with "defensive" missiles. Missiles with nuclear warheads just ninety miles from Florida. The thought was chilling.

We were crouched just within the jungle, looking down at the activities on the base, when there was a movement to the left. Someone was there. Coming through the jungle.

There was a soft, metallic click as Luis flipped the safety catch on his weapon, and I reached out my hand and touched him on the arm.

He looked at me, and I shook my head.

Someone was definitely coming through the jungle now. Several people, it sounded like. Hopefully it was just a routine patrol.

I started to move back, trying to pull Luis with me, but he struggled out of my grasp.

"The bastards are here in force," he hissed. "They're going to try to take over my government."

"Not Haiti, you fool," I whispered urgently. "They're planning on attacking Cuba."

The sounds of the patrol were coming much closer now. We were running out of time.

I wanted to get back to the Jeep, drive back to Cap Haitien and telephone Hawk. There was no way the two of us were going to stop such a well-equipped force by ourselves. It was going to take the Navy. But Hawk would have to be immediately informed.

"Throw down your weapons and step out to the beach where we can clearly see the two of you," a man with a deep British accent called from the left.

They either had heat sensing equipment or infrared scopes; either way we had been spotted.

I started to move back into the shadows, when Luis suddenly jumped forward, raced to the left and opened fire with his Thompson.

Fire from a dozen automatic weapons raked Luis' body, slamming him against a tree, blood spurting from dozens of wounds, and he fell in a heap.

The silence, when it came, was almost as deafening as the noise of the weapons fire, and the smell of cordite was very strong in the jungle.

I remained where I was, in a half crouch, holding my breath, not daring to move. They obviously had infrared scopes on their weapons.

"Throw down your weapon and step very slowly out onto the beach," the same voice came from straight ahead this time.

For a moment I considered using my gas bomb, but out here in the open I could not be sure of its effectiveness. And I suspected that any sudden move on my part would result in my death.

"All right," I called out, letting Wilhelmina slip out of my grasp. Raising my hands over my head, I got slowly to my feet and headed out to the beach.

A second or two later I was surrounded by a dozen men all carrying AR15 automatic rifles equipped with infrared scopes of the same type the CIA used in its night missions, and all of them were dressed in American Army camouflage uniforms.

Two of the men were obviously British, but the others were slight of build and relatively dark skinned. They looked like Cubans.

One of the Britishers handed his weapon to another of the men and cautiously approached me.

"If you make any untoward move, you will be shot down, is that clear?" he asked.

I nodded.

He stepped closer and quickly and very efficiently frisked me, coming up not only with my stiletto, but with my gas bomb as well.

When he made me drop my trousers and remove the tiny bomb, the others watched curiously.

Pocketing my weapons, the Britisher stepped back and retrieved his AR15. "Ramirez, Gomez, bring the other body and weapon, as well as this one's handgun," he snapped.

Two of his men broke away and went back into the jungle as the Britisher waved his weapon down the beach toward the mercenary base. "Move," he said.

I turned, and keeping my hands over my head, headed down the beach.

This was a slickly run operation, there was no doubt about it. Just as I was sure that the Haitian government knew of its existence, but either chose to do nothing about it, or was paid not to do anything.

In the camp, passing the piles of supplies, I noticed the markings on the crates which contained enough small arms and ammunition, along with anti-personnel mines, hand grenades and antitank weapons to supply a small army. All of the crates were marked: PROPERTY U.S. ARMY.

It was an invasion of Cuba all right. And DeGourcy was going to make absolutely sure that the Cubans knew this was American backed.

Wouldn't it be ironic, I thought as I was marched toward one of the tents at the center of the camp, if the invasion was a success. There were plenty of weapons here to supply a good-sized force of Cuban dissidents. Stranger things had happened before.

I was made to wait outside the tent while the two Britishers went inside. A moment later one of them opened the tent flap and beckoned me inside.

I stepped through the opening, blinking against the sudden light, and when I finally focused I was looking at a small man with dark, intense eyes, seated behind a folding table.

I had expected to be brought before DeGourcy, but this was a man I had never seen before, although I guessed that he was probably Russian.

The man barely nodded his head to the right, and the two Britishers seized my arms above the elbows and roughly sat me down in a sturdy chair. My arms and legs were quickly secured with heavy leather straps.

When they stepped back, the little man got up from behind his desk and nodded toward the tent flap. They left without a word.

"Your name please," the little man asked without preamble. His accent was definitely Russian.

I just looked at him and said nothing.

He smiled almost sadly as he opened a small leather case and withdrew a small hypodermic syringe. Unhurriedly he filled the needle with a drug from a tiny, rubber-stoppered bottle, then came around the table and across to me.

"You will talk," he said softly. "But this drug has been known to have some unfortunate side effects."

"Nick Carter," I said.

The man nodded. "Who do you work for?"

"The Amalgamated Press."

"Where?"

"Washington, D.C."

"What are you doing here?"

I hesitated a moment, and the little man looked into my eyes.

"Following Sprague DeGourcy," I said at last.

"I see," the little man said, as if he really didn't. "Following this man from where?"

"Geneva," I said. "Then London, and finally here. The man with me, the one your people murdered out there, was nothing more than a Haitian informant. One of many. He told me that DeGourcy's yacht had been seen along this stretch of coastline."

"And what is your business with this Mr. DeGourcy?"

Again I hesitated. "He was seen in Moscow," I said softly, and at this his lips curled into a snarl. I had hit a nerve.

The soft whump of some kind of an explosion came

from outside, and the little man looked up, consternation and a touch of fear suddenly in his eyes. He looked back at me.

"You brought more people with you?" he snapped.

There was the sound of automatic weapons fire in the distance.

"You're damned right," I said. "The U.S. Marines. Give it up while you still can."

Another explosion rolled over the sounds of the firing and the little man laid the hypodermic syringe aside and left the tent.

Two other explosions, in quick succession, lit up the night sky as I struggled in vain with the leather straps. But at that moment a knife blade jutted through the back wall of the tent, was ripped downward, and Maxime Genarde, wearing dark slacks, a dark pullover and boots, a Uzi submachine gun slung over her shoulder, stepped inside, crossed to me, and without a word quickly undid my straps.

I jumped up from the chair and went to the tent flap where I looked outside as a fifth explosion, this one toward the highway, lit up the trees.

"Incendiaries," I said, turning back.

"That was the last one," she said. "We must go now."

Together we hurried to the long cut in the rear wall of the tent, but before we stepped outside, I kissed her on the lips.

"Can you get back to Cap Haitien?" I whispered.

"Yes, together we will go—" she started, but I cut her off.

"I'm staying," I said. I still had DeGourcy to deal with. His yacht was here and I was certain he was, as well. "Return to Cap Haitien and contact Hawk. Tell him that DeGourcy and the Russians are going to invade Cuba, probably tonight, and blame it on the CIA.

American weapons and uniforms, British mercenaries and Cuban rebels."

"You can't remain here. They will kill you," she whispered urgently.

"Do as I say," I snapped. "DeGourcy is here and I must find him. Now go."

For a long second it seemed as if she was going to argue with me, but then she realized it was useless, and she handed me her knife, then stepped out of the tent.

I was right behind her.

"They killed Luis, didn't they," she said softly.

I nodded.

"The bastards," she said. "They will pay for it. All of them."

I reached out and touched her cheek. "You have to get to Cap Haitien and make contact with Hawk, otherwise they will have won."

"I know," she said. "But be careful, Nick."

"You too," I said, and she melted away into the jungle as I turned, and keeping low, raced down to the cove where DeGourcy's yacht was nestled in and among the American PT boats, as small arms fire seemed to build toward the highway.

# EIGHT

Most of the activity was away from the cove, toward where Maxime had set off the explosives, and I made it to the water's edge without seeing any of the mercenaries.

I had no real idea what I was going to do or what I could accomplish alone, but I could not allow DeGourcy's invasion plans to go ahead unchallenged.

The *Magnum* was a one-hundred-fifty-foot motor yacht, long and sleek looking, dwarfing the relatively small PT boats.

Even the guards on the boats had joined the force toward the highway, but they would not be distracted much longer. Already the small arms fire was beginning to die down as they realized that they were no longer under attack.

My primary target was still DeGourcy, so I headed along the cove toward his yacht, keeping to the shadows as much as possible.

Here, near the boats, large piles of supplies had been stacked, preparatory to being loaded. Using the knife Max had given me, I pried open one of the crates in a pile near the last row of PT boats before DeGourcy's yacht and pulled out two American hand grenades, the bare bones of a plan beginning to form in my mind.

Carefully I replaced the wooden cover on the crate

and then moved to the next box which contained AR15 rifles. As I started to pry open the cover of this crate, someone shouted something back in the camp, and then there were the sounds of several men running my way.

I quickly ducked around behind the pile of crates and raced along the beach to the far side of DeGourcy's yacht.

The ship's ladder angled down from the main deck to the water's edge. For several seconds I remained hidden behind the crates as I studied the area around the ladder on the ground and as much of the ship's deck as I could see from this angle. If there were guards on or around the ship, I could not detect their presence.

There were the sounds of more activity back in the camp. My escape had probably been discovered, and they would be fanning out now, looking for me. I was running out of time.

Gripping the knife a little tighter, I raced from the shelter of the crates, across the twenty yards of open beach, and then hurried up the ship's ladder.

At the top I crouched low and peered over the rail, left and right along the wide deck. There was no one in sight.

Above, on the bridge, the windows were illuminated by a soft red glow, but I could see no one up there either.

From this height I could see a great deal of activity back in the camp. It looked as if they were in a big hurry to leave. Tents were being torn down, and the piles of supplies were being organized, probably to bring down to the boats.

The invasion of Cuba was apparently going to take place tonight.

I slipped over the rail, down onto the deck, and hurried forward as the first of the troops carrying supplies came out of the jungle to the beach below me, several of them heading this way.

The ship was not deserted. I was reasonably certain of that. Somewhere below there had to be crewmen, and it would be virtually impossible for me to hide down there. At least for now. Yet I was going to have to get out of sight immediately.

I continued forward, around the front of the superstructure and then to the port side of the ship, which faced the sea, hiding me from discovery from anyone below on the beach.

The ship's engines came to life suddenly and the decks were bathed in a soft light. I could hear someone on the starboard side of the ship. They were getting ready to take off.

The engines on several of the PT boats started with a roar as I looked wildly around for some place to hide.

There were four lifeboats hanging on their davits above the deck. I hurried back to the second one from the bow, loosened the cover lashings and looked around one last time to make sure no one was coming. Then I heaved myself up and over the edge. Within a couple of seconds I had reached outside the canvas cover and loosely resecured the lashings.

If one of the crewmen noticed that the lashings had been tampered with I would probably be discovered. But if the invasion was on for tonight, I didn't think anyone would take the time to notice such a minor detail.

The interior of the lifeboat was pitch black. I moved carefully over one of the wide seats and settled myself down on the bottom. Beneath the forward seat I found the emergency supply locker, and after a moment or two of fumbling with the catches in the dark, managed to get it open.

The locker was filled with cans, plastic boxes and other survival equipment.

Working as quietly as I could, I fingered everything

inside the locker, finally finding a large flashlight.

Before I switched it on, I held my breath, listening for any sounds of activity directly below me on the deck. There was plenty of noise, but all of it was on the other side of the ship, and below on the beach.

I cautiously flipped on the light, the interior of the lifeboat suddenly brightly illuminated. Looking through the other lockers I came up with a survival knife, but the one thing I wanted most—a Very Pistol—was not there.

More of the PT boat engines were roaring to life, and within a half an hour, several of the boats began moving out of the cove. The invasion was definitely on for tonight.

I switched off the flashlight then and settled back, making myself as comfortable as possible as more and more of the PT boats left the cove.

It was sixty miles across the Windward Passage to Cuba, but the PT boats were capable of more than twenty knots, so it would take less than three hours for the trip, which would place DeGourcy's mercenaries ashore shortly before dawn. It was the very best time for an attack. In the pre-dawn hours, the Cuban coastal watches would be at their least alert.

A half an hour later activity aboard the *Magnum* suddenly picked up. I could hear the shore lines being pulled in and the ship's ladder coming up the side of the hull. Within minutes the yacht's engines rose in pitch and we began moving, backing out toward the portable breakwater, and turning to port.

It was hot and very stuffy in the lifeboat, and I was bathed in sweat as I reached out beneath the canvas cover on the sea side, loosened the lashing and pulled the cover back a couple of inches.

The relatively cool air was refreshing, and as I watched, we passed through the breakwater out to the open sea, and the *Magnum* surged forward, both of her engines on full speed.

Ahead of us, in the dim starlight, I could see the PT boats, the phosphorescent wakes they were leaving in the calm sea, like slashes of bright white paint against a black velvet drop cloth. They were running without lights, but the sounds of their diesels out ahead of us was loud in the still night air.

I lay back in the lifeboat and looked at my watch. It was just two-thirty, which meant we would be off the Cuban coast some time after five A.M.

DeGourcy and his Russian masters would want at least the initial element of surprise. The invasion was doomed to fail, but I was reasonably certain that the plan was for the force to actually make it ashore and then be captured. With their American equipment, they would be held up to the world as CIA invaders.

But, I thought smiling, they were not going to make it ashore undetected. I was going to make certain of that. I was also going to make sure that DeGourcy and his Russian friends were not going to escape from these waters so that they could try again.

It was just five A.M. when the *Magnum's* twin diesels suddenly slowed down. I had been dozing, and I awoke with a start and peered out from beneath the canvas on the seaward side of the lifeboat.

At first I was unable to see much of anything except for the very dark sea. Even the PT boats were lost to view. But then I was able to pick out some lights in the distance ahead. At first I thought I was looking at a string of boats, but then I realized I was seeing the lights of some town on the Cuban coast. We had made it across the Windward Passage faster than I thought we would. If I was going to stop DeGourcy's invasion plans, I was going to have to do it now.

Scrambling to the other side of the lifeboat, I reached out from beneath the canvas cover, undid the lashings and eased the edge of the cover back.

The deck was still deserted, but above in the bridge I could see the forms of several people. Their attention would be directed toward the shoreline, at least for the moment.

I had been lucky so far; I needed just a little more luck and I'd be able to pull this off.

The Cuban coast was probably less than five miles away. The night was very quiet, the sea calm. Noises would carry a long way under these conditions.

I carefully undid more of the lashings, then taking a deep breath, I flipped the cover back and slipped over the edge, dropping silently down to the deck.

No alarm was raised, and a second later I had the lifeboat's cover back in place, and keeping close to the superstructure's bulkheads so that I would not be spotted from the bridge, I worked my way forward as I slipped out one of the hand grenades from my pocket.

I stopped at the forward edge of the superstructure, the yacht's bow coming to a point twenty-five feet away. A large ventilator jutted out of the forward deck. For a moment I debated tossing one of the grenades down the shaft.

It would do a lot of damage, possibly even sink the ship. But I was less interested in that, for the moment, than I was in alerting the Cuban shore patrols of the impending attack.

I was in a strange position here. It was ironic, but as it was turning out, I was Castro's ally. I was helping the Cubans.

I took a half a step away from the bulkhead and looked up, gauging the distance to the deck above the bridge. It was about twenty feet overhead, and it bristled with lights and antennas. The masthead jutted above that and contained more lights, as well as the ship's radar antenna.

The *Magnum's* diesels were idling and the ship was nearly stopped in the water. I stepped farther away from the bulkhead as I pulled the pin, brought my right arm back and tossed the grenade up.

Quickly stepping back to the bulkhead, I flattened myself against the steel plates as the grenade clattered on the deck above the bridge.

A second later a bright flash of light and an ear-splitting explosion shattered the peaceful night, pieces of hot steel and glass splattering the sea in all directions.

Someone above me on the bridge was screaming as I stepped away from the shelter of the bulkhead again and pulled out the second grenade.

The *Magnum's* engines came to life, and the yacht shot forward, turned to starboard and then back to port as it headed out of control, directly for the shore.

Spotlights winked on just north of the town, and in the distance I could hear sirens, and then there was the sound of automatic weapons fire.

Evidently the grenade had exploded about the same time the PT boats started going ashore.

I pulled the pin from the second grenade, and keeping low, dashed forward toward the ventilator.

Something hot and very hard slammed into my right side, knocking me off my feet and slamming me up against the ship's rail, the live hand grenade slipping from my grasp and rolling across the deck.

In one smooth motion, I pulled out the knife Maxime had given me, rolled over on my back, and sitting up, threw it at one of DeGourcy's men just coming around the superstructure.

The knife buried itself in the man's chest as I leaped up and jumped over the rail.

At that moment more shots were fired, something very hard slammed into my head, and the last events I was fully conscious of were falling over the width of the boat, the grenade going off and the rushing, dark sea coming up incredibly fast at me.

Time seemed to be held in limbo then, although at vague intervals I became somewhat aware that I was no longer alone. At times I could feel hands on my body, probing and touching; at other times I thought I could hear sirens and see bright lights, and during other periods I felt as if I was lying on a bed, but I was never sure. The only thing that was clear to me, was the dark sea rushing up and the thought of the *Magnum's* huge twin screws creating a whirlpool, sucking me down into the void.

But then there was a blank period, until I woke up and opened my eyes.

I was lying on a narrow cot, a thin blanket on top of my nude body. Overhead, the rough plaster ceiling was cracked, and in places large pieces of the plaster had fallen down, revealing the bare laths.

As I lay watching, mentally exploring the hurts in my body, a large cockroach crawled out from between the laths and unhurriedly made its way across the ceiling.

I followed it with my eyes, finally turning my head as the insect made its way down the plaster wall on the other side of the very small, filthy room I was in.

It was light, although the naked lightbulb hanging from the ceiling was off. For several long seconds I tried to work out that problem, until I realized that the light was coming from a small window behind me. It was daytime.

Slowly, I managed to sit up, my side aching, and my head throbbing so badly I thought it would split apart.

Reaching up with my right hand, my fingers touched a large bandage that encircled my head, and then I began to remember the last seconds aboard DeGourcy's yacht. The first hand grenade, and then the second.

I had been shot in the side, and then again in the head. For a vivid second I could see myself falling overboard, and I winced.

Flipping the covers back, I brought my legs over the edge of the bed, and taking great care not to move my head too quickly, managed to get to my feet.

The room swam and my stomach churned, the bile bitter at the back of my throat. It seemed like I had not eaten in months.

Besides the bandage on my head and one around my middle, I was completely nude. Even my watch and ring had been taken. Nor were my things anywhere in the spartan room, which was furnished with only the small cot and a bucket in the corner. There was a window at the back and a thick wooden door at the front.

When the dizziness and nausea had subsided, I shuffled across the room to the window and looked outside. I was on the second floor of a long building that fronted on what appeared to be a military parade ground. At least five hundred armed soldiers stood at attention in formation, while fluttering on a flagpole at the center of the parade ground was a flag with five stripes, a white star in a red triangle at the left. Cuba. I was in a Cuban prison.

Somehow I had been fished out of the sea and brought here.

As I watched, two canvas-covered trucks pulled onto the parade ground through a wide gate in the tall fence, then parked side by side, their tailgates thirty feet from a tall brick wall.

The tailgates clanged open to reveal a fifty-caliber machine gun and crew in each truck. It was to be an execution, and I had a fair idea who the victims were going to be.

Moments later someone shouted an order, and from a door just below my window, a line of raggedly dressed soldiers were marched out across the parade ground toward the brick wall. Although I could not recognize any of the individual men, I did recognize the uniforms and the fact that they were all small—they were all Cubans. There were only a dozen of them, but they were clearly from DeGourcy's invasion force.

Helplessly I watched as they were marched to the brick wall, lined up, and without ceremony, executed by the machine-gunners.

It was over in seconds; the Cuban troops were dismissed, and twenty minutes later the bodies had been loaded aboard trucks and taken away, and the blood had been hosed down.

I had been standing at the window, gripping the bars with both hands, watching all of it. When I finally turned around, a Cuban soldier, lieutenant bars on his shoulders, was standing at the open door, a wary grin on his face.

We stared at each other for a long moment, and then he tossed a bundle of clothes on the floor.

"Dress," he said, and he stepped back out into the corridor, his right hand resting on the butt of a pistol at his hip.

Beyond him in the corridor, I could see two other soldiers armed with rifles.

Slowly I shuffled forward, and with a great deal of pain from my wounds, retrieved the clothing from the floor and went back to my cot where I sat down with a deep sigh.

"Dress," the officer said again. It was probably the only English word he knew.

I pulled on the one-piece coveralls, then the cotton

slippers, and I stood up, swaying as the room spun again.

The officer barked some command, and moments later the two young Cuban soldiers entered my cell, took me by the arms, and helped me out into the corridor.

I was taken down a flight of stairs, along another corridor—this one busy with soldiers—then through a set of double doors into a large room filled with civilians seated in rows on folding chairs. They were all facing a stage at the front of the room, which was illuminated with strong overhead lights.

The stage had been set up to resemble a court of law, with three judges sitting behind a tall desk.

I was dragged to the front of the room and forced to sit in a chair at one side of the tall table.

The room was hot and I was sweating profusely, my stomach churning. The civilians in the audience all avoided looking directly at me, and none of them made any noise. It was unreal.

A man in a white coat came up to where I was sitting, told the soldiers to stand back, then rolled up my sleeve, dabbed some alcohol on my arm, and gave me a shot.

"This will help clear your mind, *Señor* Carter," the doctor said in very good English.

He moved away, and a young woman came up, wiped the sweat from my forehead and then applied some makeup to my face.

"Do not touch your face or you will spoil my work, *señor,*" she said.

A camera crew entered from the back, set up a movie camera in the main aisle, and immediately began filming, panning from me to the judges, back to me, and then around to the audience who suddenly had become loud and angry.

One of the judges at the tall table banged his gavel, said something in Spanish that I could not quite catch, and a silence fell over the courtroom.

I felt light, as if I was floating about two inches off my chair, and I gripped the armrests so that I would not float away as the judges turned to me.

"It is now time, *Señor* Nicholas Carter, to enter your plea," the judge in the center said.

His little four-cornered hat was on crooked, and I could not help but grin at him. A stern expression came over his face, and he turned to look directly at the camera which hastily turned his way.

He spoke in rapid-fire Spanish, some of which I caught. I was a CIA spy who had led an abortive invasion on Cuba under the direct orders of the imperialist running dog President of the U.S. When captured, I had freely admitted everything, dooming twelve of my loyal men to certain death, in a cowardly attempt to save my own skin.

The judge turned to me again. "It is the sentence of this court that at dawn tomorrow, you shall be taken to a place of public execution, where you shall be hanged by the neck until dead."

The man's hat slipped a little lower over his right eye, and I laughed out loud, the crowd roaring its anger and hate on cue.

The camera crew packed up their equipment and left the room. The lights were shut off, and the two soldiers who had brought me down there were back again. They pulled me roughly from the chair and dragged me through the crowd which once again had fallen silent.

We went back down the corridor, up the stairs, and into my cell where I was dumped on my bed. The soldiers left and the door was closed and locked behind them.

# NINE

It was dark when I awoke again. Although my head still hurt terribly, this time I was fully awake, my mind crystal clear, the dizziness and nausea gone.

I got up from the bed and went to the door where I listened. But the corridor was quiet. Either there was no one out there, or if there was a guard at my door, he was being exceedingly quiet.

I tried the door handle, but it was locked. I walked across the room and looked out the window, down at the deserted parade ground. A truck and a couple of Jeeps were parked in the shadows across from my building and the gates in the tall fence were open. As far as I could see, there were no guards anywhere.

Beyond the fence was a residential area, and beyond that I could see the glow in the night sky of a very large city. It was Havana. There was very little doubt of it in my mind. And in the morning I would be executed as an American spy. The films that had been taken of my sentencing no doubt would be put on Cuban television for everyone to see the "proof" of the CIA plot.

If I could get out of here and steal one of the Jeeps below, I might be able to make my way down to the U.S. Marine base at Guantánamo Bay, where I would be safe. But that was completely across the length of the island. More than five hundred miles.

My only other option would be to steal a boat and make my way through the Cuban patrols to Key West, Florida, about ninety miles away.

Either would be damned near impossible. But if I just sat here, my execution in the morning was a certainty.

I turned away from the window and pulled the thin mattress off the small metal cot. Next I pulled the bare springs off the rails, and finally I disassembled the bed, the two, six-and-a-half-foot long metal angle irons that had held the springs in place, making perfect pry bars.

Back at the window, I inserted one of the rails behind the bars, and using it like a lever, put my weight into it.

Two of the bars popped out with a loud grating noise before the soft metal angle iron bent.

I turned toward the door as I quickly pulled the angle iron down, expecting soldiers to burst into my cell at any moment.

But there was nothing but silence from the corridor, and I carefully laid the now useless piece of metal down on the floor, grabbed the other one, inserted it behind the remaining bars and with all my might levered it over.

All three bars popped out this time, one of them clanging to the floor.

I dropped the angle iron, picked up one of the thick steel bars and raced to the door. Surely someone had heard the noise and would be coming in to investigate.

My heart was pounding and my breath came in ragged gasps. Even that little bit of exertion had almost completely worn me out. I had had no solid food in I don't know how many days; I had certainly lost some blood from my wounds; and I had been given drugs.

My legs felt like rubber and my stomach was churning again as I waited, straining all my senses for some sign that someone was coming.

But the corridor remained silent. And after several minutes, I tossed the steel bar down on the mattress and went back to the window, unlatched the casement and swung it open, the night air warm and very humid.

There was no movement across the parade ground and ten feet below me, on the first floor, I could see no lights from any of the windows.

Carefully I eased my body, feet first, through the open window, hung there a moment and then dropped the ten feet to the pavement, the shock of landing sending a deep pain through my entire body from the wound in my side.

I remained crouched against the side of the building for several long seconds. I tried to catch my breath and waited for the pain to subside.

Cuban security for a condemned prisoner had to be incredibly lax, either that or they wanted me to escape. But I could think of no valid reason for the latter, unless they wanted to shoot me as I tried to escape.

Crouching there in the shadows I listened to the vagrant sounds of the military installation. I could hear the hum of a small air conditioner somewhere and a radio or record player was blaring some Rasta tune. Other than that, everything was quiet. Lights shone from several windows on the second floor of a couple of the buildings to my left, but the buildings to the right, where the Jeeps and trucks were parked, were dark.

After a while I straightened up and started along the building as fast as I could go, the feeling that something was wrong here, growing.

As I neared the corner of the building, headlights flashed across the parade ground from the main gate as a Jeep came into the compound.

Ducking low, I stepped around the corner into the

deeper shadows and watched as the Jeep pulled up alongside the others. The lights and engine were shut off, and a man got out and hurried into the building.

I let out the deep breath I had been holding, and as I was about to step back around the corner, something hard touched my back.

"No noise," a man said behind me.

I tensed, ready to spin around.

"I am one of Luis Genarde's people," the man said, his Haitian accent thick.

"Luis Genarde is dead," I said softly.

"Maxime told us," the man said.

The gun was taken away from my back and I turned around slowly to face him. He was a slightly built black man, wearing a Cuban military uniform.

"Where is Maxime?"

"Port-au-Prince. She is waiting for us."

"How did you get here?" I asked, as the man stepped around me and looked across the parade ground.

"No questions now," he said. He looked back at me. "The Jeep that just came in is for us. The keys are there. It will not be missed for two hours. But we must hurry now. And no noise." He raised the rifle and pointed it at me. "You are my prisoner, if anyone stops us."

I nodded, then turned, and the both of us headed around the parade ground, keeping in the shadows of the buildings, to where the vehicles were parked.

No one came out of the buildings, nor were we challenged by any posted guards. And I suppose it was because I was still suffering from my wounds that I didn't stop to question what obviously was a set-up deal.

"What is your name?" I asked, as we reached the Jeep.

"Raoul," he said, laying his rifle in the back seat and climbing in behind the wheel. I jumped in the passenger seat.

He started the engine, flipped on the headlights, backed out of the parking slot and then headed at a normal, unhurried speed across the parade ground and out the gate, heading right, away from the military compound.

I looked back as we rounded the next corner, but no lights had come on, no alarm had been raised. It was too slick, too easy. Yet I was free for the moment and grateful for Raoul's presence. My estimation of Maxime, which had been high to begin with, went up another couple of notches. She was one hell of a woman.

We drove through the outskirts of Havana proper, going south around the city, and then Raoul turned onto a narrow but well-maintained highway past the airport and sped up.

"Where are we going?" I asked over the noise of the wind.

Raoul turned to me and grinned. "Bahia Honda," he said. "It is a small fishing village about fifty miles west of here."

"There is a boat waiting?"

He nodded. "You will be long gone before the fools realize that their little sacrificial dove has flown." He laughed.

What little traffic there was on the highway, was mostly military, but we were not stopped or challenged. There were no screaming sirens in the night. No roadblocks.

About an hour later we passed through a small town which Raoul identified as Cabañas, and a half hour after that we came into Bahia Honda, which was a small town, totally deserted at this hour of the evening except for a busy *cantina* on the edge of town.

The ocean was nearby, I could smell it. But Raoul parked the Jeep behind a ramshackle old warehouse, climbed out and retrieved his rifle.

"We will go the rest of the way on foot, *señor,"* he said, as I climbed out.

"How far?" I asked.

He looked over his shoulder as if he expected to be challenged at any moment. "Not far," he said. "A hundred yards. But there may be *policia.* We must be careful. No noise."

He turned and headed away from the Jeep, and I had to hurry to catch up to him as he turned the corner ahead of me.

"Wait," I said softly as I came around the corner, but then I stopped in mid-stride.

Raoul was with a second man and both of them were aiming their rifles at me. Beyond them, about fifty yards away, was a large timber quay, DeGourcy's yacht *Magnum* tied up there. The destroyed bridge had been repaired with what looked like plywood.

"Move," Raoul said, waving his rifle toward the yacht.

This had all been a set up. Right from the beginning. But evidently DeGourcy did not want me dead. Otherwise he would have let me stay in the prison back in Havana.

"If you do not move immediately, *Señor* Carter, we will have to kill you," the other man said.

They parted to allow me to pass between them, and I headed down the quay to the *Magnum,* then up the ship's ladder to the main deck where a half a dozen crewmen, two of them armed, were waiting for me.

Raoul and the other man did not immediately come aboard. I looked down as they headed to the bollards holding the dock lines.

"Do not give us any trouble, Mr. Carter," one of the armed crewmen said to me, and I turned to him. "We mean you no harm."

I nodded, but said nothing.

A hatch was opened and one of the crewmen motioned me toward it as the others began preparing the ship for immediate departure.

I stepped through the hatch and went below decks, the two armed crewmen right behind me. They directed me aft, down a carpeted corridor, and then into a luxuriously appointed cabin.

"The ship's doctor will be here momentarily to attend to your wounds, Mr. Carter. You may take a shower. Soap, towels and shaving gear are there for your use, and there is more suitable clothing in the closet and drawers."

I was about to ask them about DeGourcy, but they both backed out of the cabin and shut the door, leaving me alone.

For a long moment I just stood there listening to the sounds of the ship. DeGourcy had rescued me for some reason. There was no way possible that he could still believe I was a journalist. Newsmen did not carry the weapons I had been carrying. So what was he after?

I turned and went into the small bathroom where I stepped out of my cotton slippers, peeled off the coveralls, and stepped into the shower, adjusting the spray as hot as I could stand it.

Afterward, I brushed my teeth and shaved, then nude, padded back into the cabin.

A matronly woman in her late forties or early fifties, dressed in a short, white lab coat, was waiting for me.

"Come over here and sit down," she snapped, pulling a chair away from a small writing table.

I smiled, and did as she said. "Good evening, Dr. . . ."

"Dr. Ketterling," she said. She opened her medical bag, took out a pair of scissors and quickly cut away the bandages around my head wound. Next she swabbed the wound with something that stung, and I jerked.

"Hold still," she snapped.

She worked quickly and efficiently for the next ten minutes, rebandaging my head wound as well as the wound on my side.

When she was finished and was repacking her things in her medical kit, I looked up at her and smiled.

"Will I live?"

"Probably," she said tersely. "You will get dressed now. Someone will come for you."

"I was wondering when DeGourcy was going to send for me."

"Who?" she asked offhandedly.

"DeGourcy. The owner of this ship. He is aboard, isn't he?"

The woman shook her head. "I wouldn't know. I have never heard the name, DeGourcy." She seemed sincere.

"Who's running this ship, then?"

"Captain Wilhelm Leuder. You will be having a meal with him shortly," she said. She looked down at me, a stern expression on her face. "And you would be well advised not to give the captain any trouble. He is a man of very little patience."

She closed the clasp on her bag, picked it up and went to the door. Before she left, however, she turned to look back at me and shook her head.

"From what I understand, Mr. Carter, you are a lucky man, a very lucky man indeed."

"Lucky to have been shot twice, imprisoned and sentenced to death?"

She smiled. "You won't die of your wounds, and you are here," she said. Before I could say anything else, she was gone.

I remained where I was seated, for several long seconds staring at the door. DeGourcy had attempted to work a Soviet plot to implicate the American government in another Bay of Pigs disaster. Whether or not my actions aboard this ship had in any way damaged the plan, I had no way of knowing at this moment.

But what the hell did the woman mean by telling me I was a lucky man? And when I had asked her about DeGourcy, her answer that she did not know the name had seemed genuine. It didn't make much sense.

After a while I got up and rummaged around in the closet and drawers coming up with underwear, slacks, a lightweight shirt, socks and slip-on shoes that fit me reasonably well.

When I was dressed I found my wristwatch, my small diamond ring and a packet of cigarettes in a drawer in the table.

It was a few minutes after midnight, according to my watch, when I lit myself a cigarette and the door to my cabin opened.

A young man, dressed in a set of plain white coveralls, no insignia on the sleeves or collar, came in. He was smiling.

"You look much fitter than when you first came aboard, sir," he said. His voice held a British accent. "Are you in any pain?"

"Only the pain of curiosity," I said.

"Well," the young man said, stepping aside. "Captain Leuder awaits your presence in the officers' lounge, sir."

I pocketed the cigarettes, then walked past the young man, out into the corridor.

"Just up the ladder, sir, and aft," the young man said.

I ambled down the plushly carpeted corridor, unhurriedly made my way up to the main deck and outside, then headed aft.

The young man was right behind me, and as I turned the corner around the after end of the superstructure, he stepped ahead of me and opened a hatch.

"The captain is waiting, sir," he said. "Go right in."

I inclined my head, then stepped inside, the young man closing the hatch after me.

I found myself in a wonderfully decorated lounge that could have been on the Queen Elizabeth II or on any other luxury liner.

A tall, husky man, dressed in a smartly tailored blue serge Navy uniform, stood at the bar with his back to me.

"Brandy, plain or on ice?" he asked.

"On ice," I said.

I heard the tinkle of ice cubes, the man poured my drink, and then turned around, a smile on his face. He was Sprague DeGourcy.

"I'm so happy that you could join me aboard the *Magnum,* Mr. Carter," he said.

He came across the room, moving with an athletic grace despite the fact he was probably in his early to mid-fifties, and handed me my drink.

The lounge was tastefully furnished with long, low leather couches, deep leather chairs, low tables and sideboards, and book-lined shelves on two of the bulkheads.

DeGourcy motioned for me to have a seat, and I went across the lounge and sank down in one of the chairs as he poured himself a glass of white wine and then joined me, sitting in one of the other chairs.

He raised his glass. "To the hunt," he said as a toast.

I had to smile as I raised my glass. "The hunt," I said, and we both drank.

My brandy was excellent, and I told him so, but he waved the compliment off.

"You are an interesting man, Mr. Carter," he said. His voice held a definite British accent. It was soft, and mellifluous.

"I can say the same of you, DeGourcy," I said. "Except that you are interesting in a sick, psychotic sort of way."

DeGourcy's jaws tightened. "I don't know who DeGourcy is. My name is Leuder. Wilhelm Bernard Leuder."

"Right," I said dryly. "Why did you set up the phony invasion of Cuba?"

"I did not. I was merely an observer."

"I saw you at the warehouse in London."

"That is patently impossible, Mr. Carter."

"Perhaps it was your twin brother, then," I said.

DeGourcy laughed. "That's as good an explanation as any."

Suddenly the man's toast struck me. He had said, "To the hunt." El Cazador was Spanish for the hunter.

"Tell me, DeGourcy, or Leuder, or whatever the hell you're calling yourself here in the Caribbean, what is it you're hunting these days?"

For a long moment it seemed as if DeGourcy was going to lose his temper. His face seemed to mirror some kind of an inner struggle. But then he composed himself.

"What am I hunting these days, you ask?"

I nodded.

He thought about his answer a little longer. "A worthy adversary," he said softly.

"Pistols at twenty paces? Dueling sabres? Big game rifles on an enclosed course?"

"Wits."

I raised my right eyebrow. "You're more of an arrogant sonofabitch than I gave you credit for being, El Cazador."

Again there was a tightening of his jaws. But he smiled nevertheless. The man did have a certain flair for self control. I had to give him that.

"We live in a very dull, uninteresting world, Mr.

Carter," he said. "I wonder if you ever gave it much thought?"

"As a journalist, I haven't found it so."

"Come now, it's late for us to be playing games with each other."

I shrugged.

"You are a policeman. Interpol? But no, you're American. Perhaps the FBI, or maybe the CIA. But you are a policeman."

"A worthy enough adversary?"

"By itself no," he said. "But you as an individual . . . that is another story. From what I understand, you would have done a creditable job of escaping from your prison in Havana had my people not interfered when they did."

"I was giving it a shot."

"And you did manage to interfere with the invasion operation."

"That was a pretty loose organization," I said. "Actually I was quite disappointed. I had really expected a lot more out of you."

"And I of you. Had it not been for Miss Genarde, you would not have escaped."

"What have you done with her?"

DeGourcy threw back his head and laughed out loud. It took everything within my power not to leap across the coffee table and kill him then and there.

"You are gallant, Mr. Carter," he said.

I glared at him.

"Actually I haven't done a thing with or to Miss Genarde. Her own authorities have seen to it for me."

For a time then, we sat across from each other in silence, listening to the sounds of the ship's engines.

"And now what?" I asked. "Did you rescue me from Cuba merely to kill me?"

DeGourcy shook his head. "No. I mean to release you unharmed."

"Forgive me if I'm a bit skeptical."

"Believe me, I mean what I say. You believe my name is DeGourcy, and you also believe I am the assassin El Cazador, but you are a policeman. And policemen need proof. Which you don't have at the moment."

He paused, seemed to think, then continued. "But you are an interesting man. You have wits. It will be interesting if I should happen to meet you again. But that will be up to you."

He reached in the pocket of his jacket and pulled out a pistol. "Drink your drink, Mr. Carter. You are leaving the ship."

"I'm to be thrown overboard?"

"Not quite. You'll be set adrift in a rubber raft. Florida is now about seventy miles north. You will have a fifty-fifty chance of surviving. And I sincerely wish you luck, Mr. Carter. I'd like to cross paths with you again."

# TEN

The dying sun was a bright red orb low on the western horizon as I squinted my eyes in every direction, looking for any sign of land, or a ship.

It had been eighteen hours since DeGourcy had set me adrift on the flat calm gulf in the tiny rubber raft. I had been allowed to keep my clothing, but no provisions had been placed aboard. No food, no water, nor any container with which to catch rain water.

The evening and early morning hours had been no problem, but during the day, as the subtropical sun had climbed higher and higher into the clear blue sky, I had begun to suffer. Now my lips were cracked and swollen, my throat parched and my head pounding.

Tonight, in many respects would be worse. The chills would begin, and with them the cramps and headaches of dehydration and overexposure to the harsh sun.

By tomorrow afternoon, if I was not rescued or still had no water, I would be dead.

Stiffly, I reached up and pulled my shirt down off my head. I had used it as a sun shade during the day, but tonight it would provide only a scant warmth.

A shiver passed through my body, leaving me weak for a long moment after it had passed.

The Gulf Stream here in the Straits of Florida would be pushing me gradually north and east. By tomorrow afternoon, at the latest, I figured I would be off the east coast of Florida, and well within the sport fishing grounds of the wealthy Floridians.

The problem would be staying alive long enough to be discovered.

When I had my shirt rebuttoned, I laid back and closed my eyes. I believe DeGourcy wanted me to survive this. He wanted me to come after him. But he knew that my first concern once I got back, would be to somehow effect Maxime's rescue. He had read me at least that well. He wanted time to get ready for my next move. He wanted me to try for him, but on his terms.

I opened my eyes. My logic was thin, I knew it. And yet I suspected that if DeGourcy wanted me to survive to fight again, he would have stacked the odds out here in my favor. If that was so, I could think of only three things he could have done to help.

The first would have been to leave me something that would insure my survival. Such as water, fishing gear, a flare gun. But there was nothing aboard the raft. During the first hours I made sure of that.

The second would have been to drop me overboard very close to the Florida coast, so that it would only be a matter of hours before I was rescued or had drifted ashore. But I doubted he would have done that. It would have exposed him to discovery by the U.S. Coast Guard. Even DeGourcy would not have wanted to risk that.

Finally, he might have radioed my position to the Coast Guard. He could have done it anonymously, and at any time, allowing me to stew in my own juices out here for as long as he thought I was capable of surviving.

I stood up in the raft, balancing myself against the gentle ocean swells, and scanned the horizon in all directions for any sign of a ship. But there was nothing, except in the southwest, where an ominous mass of dark clouds was beginning to gather.

A storm. If it came tonight, there would be very little chance of my survival.

I sat back down in the raft. I had thought about bending my belt buckle into a fishhook. If I could catch a fish I could survive from its moisture. I had even thought about biting my finger hard enough to draw blood, then trailing it in the water to attract a fish. But these waters abounded with sharks. And finally I had thought about peeling a section of the silver coating off the raft's flotation tubes, and using it and the sun to condense some fresh water from seawater. But the amount of fresh water I could have distilled from that method would have been so miniscule that it would not have been worth the effort.

The sun finally sank below the horizon, and soon it was dark, the stars overhead bright and seemingly an arm's length away. With the loss of daylight I began to shiver, sometimes uncontrollably, my entire body wracked with muscle spasms.

For a long time I passed in and out of consciousness, as the night deepened and the wind began to pick up with the approaching storm.

I began to hallucinate too. Twice I was certain that I saw the lights of an approaching ship, and once I thought that I could hear the screws of a distant ship. But each time I sat up and tried to see what was coming, there was nothing but the building waves, and in the distance, bobbing in the sea, some small, bright orange object, a fishing buoy or a piece of flotsam.

Lying back again, I drew my knees up to my chest in an effort to conserve my body heat, and I tried to keep my mind occupied with Sprague DeGourcy. There was little doubt that once I got to Geneva and began poking around, I would find that DeGourcy had a string of unimpeachable witnesses who would swear that he had been home the entire time this Cuban thing was going on.

It made me sick to think that my old friend Dieter Grundt was a traitor, one of those providing El Cazador with his alibis. But Grundt had backed himself into that corner. I could see no way out of it for him.

My head ached as I tried to keep my mind occupied, tried to keep my thoughts away from my dehydration and hunger, but it was nearly impossible. Everything I thought about seemed to focus on food or drink. Even thinking about Dieter Grundt brought my thoughts around to the wine he had ordered at the hotel restaurant.

But then something else intruded on my thoughts. Something I knew should be very significant. For a long terrible second I fumbled with the impression that I was missing something very vital.

I sat up with a start. The orange object I had seen in the waves! The fishing buoy, or whatever it was.

I looked in the direction I had thought I had seen it, and tried to pick out the spot of orange against the rising waves.

At first I could see nothing, but then there was a flash of orange, perhaps a hundred yards away. It was gone, lost in the trough of a wave, and I waited, keeping my eyes trained on the spot I had last seen it. And then it was there again, this time lingering high on the wave top, and I knew what it was. DeGourcy had tossed an orange canopied life raft out ahead of me. The Gulf Stream currents were carrying the life raft and the raft I was in, along the same line, but evidently at a slower speed. All this time I had been trailing my means of survival, and I had not seen it.

I continued to watch the life raft bobbing out there, a hundred yards away. Tantalizingly just out of my reach. I had no paddles, no sail, no way of shortening the gap between us before the storm hit.

No way, the sudden chilling thought came to me, if I remained aboard this raft.

It was only a hundred yards. Under ordinary circumstances an easy swim. But I was weak from lack of food and water, and from my wounds. And the sea was no longer calm.

I looked over my shoulder back at the approaching storm. It was much closer now. Before long even my slight chance of survival would be totally out of my reach.

If I remained aboard this raft, I could be swamped in the storm, and I would certainly not survive.

I turned to look the other way as the orange life raft bobbed up on a wave crest again.

Remain here and most certainly not survive until morning, or jump overboard and attempt to swim the hundred yards in an almost impossible sea.

DeGourcy was a master, but he had to be stopped—at all costs.

I reached down and slipped off my shoes, and then hanging onto the edge of the raft, waited until the orange life raft bobbed up again, fixed its position in my mind, and then I slipped overboard into the warm sea and struck out, swimming as best I could.

Almost immediately, I was caught by a large wave and tossed at least ten yards away from the rubber raft I had just left.

I turned back a second later in time to see a second wave shove the raft around, and then it capsized.

There would be no going back now. I was committed to the orange life raft.

I swam then, in a slow, easy stroke, allowing the wave action and strong Gulf Stream current to do most of the work, but even so I was tiring too fast.

Every now and then I caught a glimpse of orange out ahead of me, but for a very long time the distance seemed always to stay the same.

The same waves and current that were pushing me ahead, were also pushing the life raft.

My consciousness was finally reduced to nothing more than breathing and keeping my leaden arms working. One stroke after the other. On and on. It seemed like I had been in the water forever. There had never been, nor would there ever be anything for me, other than this existence.

A flash of lightning briefly illuminated the night, and I saw the life raft just a couple of yards to my left. An instant later the heavy roar of thunder blotted out all other sounds and the heavy rains came.

I struck out blindly to the left, arm over arm. This was my last chance to reach the life raft and I knew it. The rain had reduced visibility to near zero. I would either reach the life raft in the next minute, or I would miss it and die out here.

My right hand hit something firm, and at first I tried to push it away, but then I realized that I had reached the life raft, and I grabbed the lifeline looped around the sides of the flotation tube. I pulled myself around the life raft until I found the zippered opening.

It took me a full ten minutes to manage the zipper, to crawl inside and then to re-zipper the opening. But I was safe now. I had made it.

I lay there for a long time, until I was able to muster the strength to fumble for and find the survival kit, which contained, among other things, a flashlight.

The raft was bobbing violently in the now very heavy seas, but with the light on, I found the tins of water and a small can opener. By the time I had the can open wide enough to drink, I had spilled half the water, but I drank the rest.

Almost immediately I vomited. But I did feel better. I carefully opened the second can, and slowly drank the water.

DeGourcy had put this raft here to give me a slight chance of survival. He had played with me. Used me like a piece on a game board. Suddenly my interest in the man was personal, very personal.

It was four o'clock in the afternoon the next day when the U.S. Coast Guard cutter *Windsong* picked me up twenty miles off Marathon in the Florida Keys.

The ship's doctor rebandaged my wounds, I was given some dry clothing, fed a decent meal and then was taken immediately up to Miami, where over the protests of the Coast Guard commandant, I refused to comment on how I came to be floating around in the Gulf Stream aboard a life raft until I was allowed to telephone Hawk.

Five minutes after my telephone call, which I had made from the commandant's office, the phone rang, and the Coast Guard commander answered it himself. He did little else but listen for two minutes, and when he hung up the phone there was an odd look in his eyes.

I was given some civilian clothing and flown by military aircraft up to Washington, D.C., where Hawk had a car waiting for me.

Ten hours after I had been plucked from the sea, I was in Hawk's office, seated across the desk from him. It was two in the morning.

"You had us worried, Nick," Hawk said. "When we lost contact with you, we didn't know if you had gone deep or had been taken."

Quickly I told Hawk what had happened from the moment I had left London and was contacted by Maxime Genarde in Port-au-Prince, until I was picked up by the *Windsong*. During the telling, Hawk remained silent, puffing on his cigar, his eyes flashing every now and then at some point I was making.

When I was finished, he sat back in his chair, then swiveled around so that he could look out his window at the darkness outside.

"There have been a lot of rumblings from Castro's people over the last twenty-four hours or so," he said. "We thought it might have something to do with DeGourcy and you, but we weren't sure. In any event nothing has been made public yet."

"They probably don't want to admit that their star conspirator escaped," I offered.

"Probably," Hawk said. His reaction, or lack of it, was taking me by surprise.

"What is it, sir?" I asked after a long silence.

Hawk turned back. "Three questions, Nick," he said.

I waited for him to ask them.

"What do you want to do about Miss Genarde?"

"Get her out of Haiti," I said without hesitation.

"I know that. We're working on it at the moment. What I'm asking is, do you want to participate in her release?"

"I owe her that much," I said, again without hesitation. The answer did not seem to please Hawk.

"Once Miss Genarde's safety is assured, will you be going after DeGourcy?"

It was a strange question, considering the circumstances, but I nodded. "Yes, sir."

"Why?"

"He's El Cazador. He's a murderer. He works for the Soviets. He killed Luis Genarde and damned near killed me," I said. I passed a hand across my eyes. "There are dozens of reasons, sir. At least five people are dead because of him, not counting the mercenaries he led to Cuba."

Hawk stared at me for a long moment. "How much of your desire to chase after DeGourcy is a personal vendetta?"

I started to protest, but then held it off. Truth. Hawk held that above all else. "He toyed with me. I didn't like it."

Hawk nodded his understanding. "Last question. Are you sure, Nick, absolutely sure that the man you saw aboard the yacht, the man who set you adrift in the rubber raft, was Sprague DeGourcy?"

"Yes, sir," I said evenly.

"No doubt in your mind?"

"None, sir."

Hawk sighed deeply. "Do you know Walter Haglund?"

The name rang a bell, but for a moment I wasn't sure.

"Assistant Secretary to the Treasurer," Hawk prompted.

Then I had it. He was one of the President's up and coming stars. A big name on the Washington scene. "Yes, sir, I know of him."

Hawk nodded. "He has been a house guest of Sprague DeGourcy's for the past forty-eight hours."

"Oh," I said, because I couldn't think of anything else at that instant.

"DeGourcy did go to London, where he stayed at the Connaught. That much of your story we do know for certain," Hawk said.

"I followed him to the warehouse meeting that night," I said.

Hawk shook his head. "From what our field people in

Geneva tell me, DeGourcy showed up at his home the next day."

"He didn't leave from there?"

"No. The next day Haglund arrived."

Finally it all struck me. I had it. Or at least I had reduced the possibilities to two probabilities. "Neat," I said.

"Go on."

"It's simple, sir. Either Haglund, along with Dieter Grundt, is in DeGourcy's pocket, or DeGourcy has a double."

Hawk thought about that for a moment. "Either way, you still suspect DeGourcy is behind all this?"

"Almost certainly."

Hawk turned around again to look out the window. "I'll institute a class six background check on Haglund and Grundt. I'll have to inform the President in Haglund's case. He won't like it, but he'll go along with me. You can tag along on the operation to pull Miss Genarde from Port-au-Prince, but it's not necessary. As a matter of fact it'll probably go a lot smoother if you don't go down there. We're working it as an inside job. Your face is known in Port-au-Prince. If you're spotted, it could spoil the entire operation."

So far so good, I thought. There was only one item left on the very short list. "And DeGourcy?"

"I'd like you to back off," Hawk said softly. "I'll send Stewart."

Stewart was N5. A good man. A respected Killmaster who knew his business well. "No, sir," I said.

Hawk turned back to me, his eyes liquid. "If I ordered you to cease and desist?"

This was very difficult for me. "I've never disobeyed a direct order from you, sir," I said, choosing my words with great care.

Hawk smiled. "I can think of a couple of incidents when your impertinence has come damned close."

I smiled too.

"He's nearly killed you twice."

"Yes, sir," I said.

"Interpol out of Geneva is screaming. The situation in Haiti between our governments has disintegrated. Cuba is like a powder keg with a short fuse."

"Yes, sir."

"When would you want to start?"

"Immediately."

"Haglund is due to remain with DeGourcy in Geneva through the end of the week."

"Pull him out. Have the President recall him."

"That may not be possible without blowing the whistle."

I was suddenly angry. I could feel what little self control I had, slipping away. "Goddamn it, sir, if Haglund is involved in the cover up, he'd be there to help DeGourcy. If he's innocent, and DeGourcy is operating with a double, he'd be in the way."

Outside, a police car raced by, its siren blaring in the still night air. Downstairs, the night crew was on duty, receiving, collating and evaluating field reports. Like the city of Washington which never slept, AXE was staffed and busy twenty-four hours a day.

Hawk sighed again. "Give me twenty-four hours to get Miss Genarde out of Haiti and Haglund out of Geneva."

"He'll be expecting me, sir. A fast hit might be better."

"Too much at stake. I want to give our doctors a chance to work you over."

"Yes, sir," I said. I got stiffly to my feet and walked to the door.

"DeGourcy is important, Nicholas, but so are you," Hawk said. I could not remember the last time he had used my full Christian name, and I turned around. I loved the old man at that moment.

"Thank you, sir," I said. I left his office and took the elevator down to the parking garage in the basement where I retrieved my Alpha Romeo and headed across town to my apartment.

It was dark and the streets seemed deserted. The conditions fitted my mood. I had the assignment; all I needed now was some sleep, some food and my weapons. Twenty-four hours from now, Sprague DeGourcy, El Cazador, and I would square off for the final battle. Both of us were hunters. But who was hunting whom, this time, wasn't exactly clear.

# ELEVEN

I slept for nearly eighteen hours, and when I finally woke up, I fixed myself a large steak, a half a dozen eggs and a pot of coffee. Although I was still a little light-headed and the wounds in my head and side still ached, I felt a hell of a lot better than I had for the last two days.

It was nearly two A.M. by the time I let myself out of my apartment, drove across town to the Amalgamated Press and Wire Services Building on DuPont Circle, parked in the basement garage and went upstairs to Hawk's office.

One of the nightside people was up there, seated in the outer office, and he directed me back down to Operations where he said Hawk was waiting for me.

Together we went downstairs to the dimly lit room where Hawk was sitting, drinking coffee with the night-shift OD. They both looked up when I came in.

"Did you get her out?" I asked crossing the room.

The OD jumped up and got me a cup of coffee. I lit a cigarette.

"They touched down at McCoy Air Force Base outside Orlando about five minutes ago," Hawk said.

"Is she all right?"

"They questioned her, but she doesn't seem to be

damaged. The doctors will look at her before we bring her up here."

A light blinked on the communications console. The OD picked up the handset and punched a button. "Operations," he spoke softly. He looked at Hawk. "Yes, he's here. Put her on."

The OD passed the handset to Hawk. "It's Maxime Genarde, she wants to talk to you."

"Put it on the speaker," Hawk said, taking the handset.

The OD pressed another button and Maxime's voice, sounding small and yet defiant, came from the speaker in the console.

"Mr. Hawk, is that you?"

"Yes Miss Genarde, this is David Hawk. How are you feeling?"

"Just fine, sir. But I'm glad your people came when they did. I don't know how much longer I could have held out."

"It's all right now."

"They killed Luis, my brother. It was Sprague DeGourcy and his people," she said in a rush. "Is Nick—Mr. Carter all right? He made me leave him at the mercenary base."

"He's just fine, Miss Genarde," Hawk said looking up at me. "As a matter of fact he's standing right here. I'm sure he wants to talk to you."

Hawk gave me the handset, but before I spoke into it, I flipped the loudspeaker off, and then turned away. "Hello, Max," I said softly.

"Nicholas, is that really you?" Maxime bubbled. "You're all right?"

"Just fine," I said. "But if you hadn't gotten me out of that tent when you did, I wouldn't be here."

There was a silence on the line for a long moment, and

when Maxime finally spoke, her voice had taken on a guarded tone. "Did you stop him?"

"I stopped his invasion plans, but he escaped."

"Back to Geneva?"

"Probably. I'm going over there later today."

Again there was a silence on the line. I knew what she was going to ask me.

"I want to come with you," she said.

"No," I blurted. "It will be too dangerous."

"They killed Luis. You owe me this, Nick."

"They won't let you go from down there. Hawk wants you back in Washington as soon as possible."

"They'll let me go," she said with assurance. "I'm going to Geneva with or without you."

I turned to look at Hawk, who had been watching me. There was a non-committal expression in his eyes.

I could stop her, but it would mean that she would have to be placed under arrest. I just could not do that. But if I left her to her own devices, there was little doubt in my mind that somehow she would show up in Geneva. She was an extraordinary woman.

"I'll make the arrangements here," I said at last. "We'll meet in Paris at Charles de Gaulle Airport."

"Don't lie to me, Nick. Don't put me off."

"I'm not," I said. "I'll see you in Paris."

Hawk was shaking his head as I hung up the telephone. The OD had busied himself out of earshot at the other side of the large room.

"I don't like this at all, Nick."

"Neither do I," I said. "But it was either that or place her under house arrest."

"I may still do that."

"We'd lose her."

"It would be better than having her killed," Hawk flared. "She's an amateur. Haiti is her bailiwick, not Europe."

"She saved my life down there," I said.

Hawk got to his feet. "The President spoke with Walt Haglund last night. He'll be returning to Washington later this morning."

"What if DeGourcy jumps?"

"He won't. Haglund is scheduled to return twenty-four hours later with the details of an international monetary deal. The President himself came up with the excuse for temporarily recalling Haglund."

"Will DeGourcy become suspicious?"

"I don't think so," Hawk said. He took the cigar out of his mouth and looked at the end of it. "We're way the hell out on a shaky limb, Nick."

I held my silence.

"DeGourcy won't become suspicious because the President spoke personally with him. Told him he wanted Haglund back here so that he could hand carry the details of the deal back to Geneva. The President is in on this, Nick. Keep that in mind. Before you do anything, before you make any move against DeGourcy, you damned well better make absolutely sure he is El Cazador."

"Yes, sir," I said.

The AXE doctor came in around four and checked me over from top to bottom, rebandaged my wounds and gave me several shots of vitamin concentrates to keep me going.

Spaso Kerchefski came in around five, and over his vehement protests (he wanted to supply me with new weapons) replaced my 9mm Luger, my stiletto and my gas bomb, as well as the portable radio/cassette unit in which I carry my weapons through airport security systems.

By seven I had been fully briefed on the hastily

worked out operational plan, which would get me and Maxime to DeGourcy's estate. We would not be able to operate openly anywhere in Switzerland because of Dieter Grundt who believed DeGourcy to be innocent. But once there we would have only six hours to do whatever was necessary and then get back out before it was daylight.

"You know what's at stake here," Hawk told me as I was getting ready to catch an eight-thirty flight from Washington's National Airport.

"Yes, sir," I said. "We'll be careful. But if the DeGourcy in Geneva is the same man from the London warehouse and the mercenary base on Haiti, I'm going to bring him in if I can, or kill him."

"I'd prefer the former."

"So would I," I said. "Any word on the yacht?"

"None," Hawk said. "It's disappeared."

"He probably had it scuttled out there somewhere."

For a long moment Hawk just stared at me, his eyes locked into mine. "No personal vendettas, Nicholas. You're a professional. You have a job to do. I expect nothing less than your best performance."

"Of course, sir."

"Good luck then," he said. "And keep a short rein on Miss Genarde. She definitely has a reason to see the man who killed her brother, dead. I want no mistakes made."

"I understand, sir," I said.

It was seven-thirty P.M., Paris time, when we touched down at Charles de Gaulle Airport outside the city. I was quickly passed through customs, and out in the mezzanine I was met by Henri Trebault, a staffer at the Paris Amalgamated Press office. He was a small, dapper Frenchman, who had worked with AXE for more than five years. He would be helping Max and me get to DeGourcy's estate.

"Miss Genarde arrived several hours ago," he said, taking my overnight bag and heading toward the main doors.

"How does she look?" I asked, hurrying to keep up with him.

"She is a beautiful woman, but I don't think you mean that," Trebault said, smiling. "Physically she's in good shape, but she is very agitated, if you know what I am saying."

"I understand," I said. "Is everything ready at this end?"

"*Oui,* although it is somewhat of an unusual operation. We do not generally sneak into friendly countries. Can you tell me your target?"

"No," I said.

"Just so," he said. "Forgive me for asking."

Outside, we climbed into Trebault's small Citröen, and headed immediately across the field to the general aviation hangars.

"Miss Genarde has been kept out of sight here at the airport," Trebault said. "We thought it best."

"Fine," I said offhandedly, but my thoughts were elsewhere. Before morning, this entire business would be settled one way or the other. I wanted nothing more than to come face to face with Sprague DeGourcy on his home turf. At that moment I would know without a doubt if he was the man from the London warehouse and from Haiti, or if he was nothing more than an innocent banker; the victim of a chain of circumstantial evidence engineered by a lookalike.

Trebault pulled up and parked alongside a hangar and got out. I retrieved my bag from the back seat, got out of the car and followed him inside the large, gray building.

Maxime, and a man I presumed was the pilot, were waiting by a Cessna 180 in the dimly lit hangar. When we came in, Maxime looked up, uttered a little cry and raced across to me, flinging herself into my arms.

"Oh God, Nicholas," she said breathlessly. "I was so frightened for you. I thought you were dead."

"It's all right now," I said, trying to calm her down. She was shivering.

We kissed deeply, and when we parted she looked up into my eyes. "We will kill him, you and I," she said.

"Stay here in Paris, Max," I said softly. "Please."

She shook her head. "Did you lie to me then?"

"No. I will take you with me, if you must come. But I'm asking you to stay here. Let me go alone."

Again she shook her head. "I will go with you."

Trebault had joined the pilot and together they were busy pre-flighting the airplane.

"I'm not going to kill him, just like that," I said. "I'm going to try to take him in."

Maxime stepped back away from me. "He murdered my brother."

"I know that. He's murdered others as well. Dozens, perhaps hundreds of others."

"One of them my brother. Do you understand that?"

"If we go in and simply assassinate him, we will be no better than he is."

"Don't play word games with me, Nick," she flared. "The man is a monster. A rabid dog who deserves to die."

"That is not for us to decide."

"Bastard," she swore, turning away.

"Maxime," I said gently. "Don't make me place you under arrest. I don't want to do that, but I will if I think you'll jeopardize this mission. There's more here at stake than you can possibly know."

There were tears in her eyes when she turned again to

look at me. "It's so hard. I want to crush him. I want to grind him beneath my heel. I want to make him crawl to me on his hands and knees. Luis was a kind man. He was a patriot." She stepped closer, her hands upraised as if she was a supplicant. "I left Haiti because I could no longer believe in my own country. My brother encouraged me to go. He paid for my education. But all the while he remained at home, doing the real work to make our country a better place to live."

"I understood that from the moment I met your brother. He was a good man. The best. But it does not alter the fact that if we assassinate DeGourcy, we become exactly what we have set out to destroy—murderers."

Maxime studied my face for a long time. "Promise me that you will not let him escape this time."

"I promise I will try."

She nodded. "Then I will do as you say."

I heaved a mental sigh of relief. Trebault and the pilot had finished with their pre-flight of the aircraft and were waiting at a respectful distance.

"Are we ready?" I called.

Trebault smiled. "Whenever you are, Nick."

Maxime and Trebault climbed in the back seat of the plane while the pilot opened the hangar doors and I pulled my weapons from the radio/cassette player and strapped them on.

I stuffed my overnight bag in the plane's tiny luggage locker aft of the door, then climbed in the right-hand seat.

The pilot climbed in, started the engine, and after it had warmed up for a minute, slowly taxied out of the hangar, then across the apron.

As he headed toward the runway, he radioed the tower for instructions. I turned around in my seat to Trebault.

"What's the exact plan, Henri?"

"We're flying direct to Annecy, which is in the *Department Haute-Savoie,* about four hundred and fifty kilometers to the southeast. From there we drive the fifty kilometers north to Thonon, which is on the south shore of Lake Geneva. There will be a boat waiting for us, which will take you across."

"No word has leaked out?"

"None so far as we can determine."

We had come to the double yellow lines at the intersection of the main runway, and the pilot stopped and quickly went through his checklist.

Within a minute, we were turning onto the runway, accelerating, and then lifting off, the city of Paris, the Eiffel Tower and the Arc de Triomphe, immediately rising from the horizon as we gained altitude.

It would take us two and a half hours to fly down to Annecy, another hour by car to Lake Geneva, and then perhaps an hour or less by boat across the nine miles from Thonon. A little past midnight by the time we reached the Swiss shore. Another hour to hike up to the Lake Shore Highway and across it to the fence around DeGourcy's estate, and another hour, if all went well, to make it to his house.

Two, perhaps two-thirty, and we would be there. The household would have been long settled down for the night. Everyone would be asleep.

But DeGourcy might expect I'd be coming after him. His defenses would be up. He might even suspect that Haglund's temporary recall to Washington could have something to do with my coming. He might be waiting. Might be ready.

We left Paris behind us, to the northwest, and continued above the French countryside. Two businessmen, a woman and a pilot. Holiday seekers. Assassins.

The night deepened as we flew, and so did my mood.

Could I have been mistaken about DeGourcy? Could it all have been some kind of a vast deception?

Dieter Grundt was so certain of DeGourcy's innocence, and Maxime Genarde was so convinced of his guilt. I was somewhere in the middle.

The airport at Annecy was quiet when we touched down. The pilot taxied over to the private hangars, and without a word, we climbed out of the plane. I retrieved my overnight bag from the luggage locker, and Maxime and I followed Trebault to an old, nondescript Mercedes parked in the shadows.

Trebault waved to the pilot, who headed across to the other side of the airport, and we all climbed in the car, Trebault behind the wheel, and took off.

Thonon was a town of about twenty thousand on the Dranse River which emptied into Lake Geneva. Like Annecy it was quiet at this hour of the night, and Trebault drove straight through the town to the waterfront where we parked in a tourist parking lot.

When he had the car shut off, we got out and hurried across the lot and down to the quay where he motioned Maxime and me aboard a small, sleek hydrofoil boat.

"Peter Villiers is waiting aboard for you. He's a good man. He'll get you across with no problems," Trebault said. He pulled a small walkie-talkie out of his pocket and handed it to me. "He's been instructed to stand offshore until one-half hour before dawn. You can signal him when you're ready to be picked up."

"If we are not back by then?"

"He's been instructed to return here. I'll be waiting."

I shook Trebault's hand. "Thanks for the help, Henri," I said.

"There will be some sort of trouble over there," he said. "What if you don't show up?"

"Contact David and tell him what has happened."

"No other back up?"

I shook my head. "Just return to Paris and forget you ever saw me."

For a moment it seemed as if the Frenchman wanted to argue with me, but then he let it go. "Good luck then," he said, and he shook Maxime's hand.

"Thanks," she said softly.

We climbed aboard the boat, and went inside the pilothouse where Villiers, who turned out to be an old man, was waiting for us with a toothless grin.

He started the engine, and we eased away from the dock and out into the lake.

"I was not told specifically where you wanted to be taken," he said to me in French.

A map was spread open on the control panel and I looked down at it, pointing my finger at a spot along the opposite shore near Nyons, which was very close to DeGourcy's estate.

"A rocky shoreline there," Villiers said. "You will have to take the dinghy to shore."

I nodded. "No matter what happens, whether we're back or not, I want you out of here and well away from the Swiss side before first light."

*"Oui,"* the man said. He throttled the powerful engines forward, and the boat shot ahead, gradually lifting up on the hydrofoils, and we were skimming across the lake at a tremendous speed toward DeGourcy and whatever this night would bring.

# TWELVE

It was early, barely two by the time Maxime and I reached the Swiss shoreline in the small dinghy Villiers had supplied us with off the hydrofoil. The tiny motor on the boat seemed loud in the quiet night air, but Villiers had assured us that no one would be up and about to hear anything at this hour, so we would be relatively safe from detection.

With Maxime's help, I pulled the dinghy up on the rocks and wedged it between two particularly large boulders. It would be clearly visible from the water, but not from the roadway about twenty-five feet above us.

Walter Haglund was scheduled back at DeGourcy's estate around ten this morning, a scant eight hours away. Long before he returned to Switzerland I was going to have to have this situation resolved.

I hefted the pack of equipment that had been supplied for us aboard the hydrofoil, and Maxime and I moved silently up the steep embankment to the Lake Shore Highway. Just at the guardrail we ducked back down below the level of the roadway as a large truck lumbered around a curve in the road, its headlights flashing past where we lay, and moments later it passed us and was lost to the distance.

I helped Maxime up, and together we climbed over the guardrail, hurried across the highway and entered the dark woods at a spot that was a hundred yards east of where I had entered the woods the last time I was here.

We came to the corner of the fence surrounding DeGourcy's estate, and moving carefully, so as to make as little noise as possible, followed the fence line to the spot I had crossed what seemed like years ago.

Above, on the barbed wire, I could just make out a few tatters of my jacket, but no other evidence as to what had happened here only a few days ago.

"How far?" Maxime asked, keeping her voice low.

I pointed through the fence, down the hill. "A couple of hundred yards to a clearing. His house is across that. But we have to watch for the dogs," I whispered.

I set the pack down on the ground and opened it, extracting a dart gun, which I handed to Maxime. The maximum range of the automatic was about fifteen yards, but the anesthetic tipped darts would be very silent and effective against the dogs.

Next, I pulled out a set of wire cutters and began clipping a large hole into the mesh of the fence.

The muscles in my arms and hands were shaky, and I was sweating lightly by the time I had finished cutting the opening into the fence.

I put the cutters back into the pack and scooted through the hole, Maxime coming right behind me.

Motioning for her to make absolutely no noise now, I led the way down through the woods toward the clearing where DeGourcy's house was located.

The night was cool, the moonless sky partly cloudy. The weather forecast had called for light and variable winds this morning, from the northwest, which was why I had selected to enter his property from the southeast.

The wind would be blowing into our faces, blowing our scent away from the estate where the dogs would be running free.

It was only a scant advantage, one that we would lose if we made any noise before we were ready. But if the dogs got on to us and started making a racket, our element of surprise would be lost.

Three times we stopped in the dark woods to listen for any sounds out ahead of us, and to search for the lights from DeGourcy's estate.

Twenty yards from the clearing, I finally saw the lights, and a second later so did Maxime, and she gasped softly. I knew what she was thinking about DeGourcy, about the fact that the man who had killed her brother was less than a hundred yards away from her. She was a hundred yards away from revenge. This was the critical point for her.

I hunched down, pulling her down beside me, and leaned in close to her so that I could whisper directly into her ear.

"No shooting unless we're shot at first, or unless I give the order. Clear?"

She looked at me, her eyes hard points, but she nodded after a moment.

I didn't know how much longer I would be able to control her, but it was too late now to turn around and make her go back to the boat. We were here. We had a job to do. And I was going to make sure we did it.

Working by feel, I opened the pack and pulled out a heavy, plastic-wrapped box, then handed the pack to Maxime to carry.

The two of us moved the last few yards through the woods to the edge of the wide lawn, leading to DeGourcy's house.

There were no lights in any of the windows of the

house. Only the yard lights were on, as well as the lights over the driveway and at the rear of the house, over the garage.

For several long minutes I crouched just within the darkness of the woods, watching for a sign that DeGourcy's dogs were out there somewhere. But I didn't see any of them.

I opened the heavy box and the sweet, cloying odor of meat that was beginning to turn wafted up at me.

Maxime gagged and stepped back as I hefted a large chunk of the half-spoiled meat that was heavily laced with a powerful animal anesthetic and threw it as far out into the clearing as I could.

I picked up the box and worked my way ten yards closer to the front of the house where I tossed out another chunk of the meat.

Within twenty minutes I had thrown out all of the meat, had closed the box and put it back in the pack, and had cleaned my hands on the dew-wet grass.

Maxime and I worked our way back to a spot opposite the rear of the house and settled down to wait for the dogs to investigate the smells from the meat.

Less than five minutes later two of the large Dobermans bounded around the house and raced directly to one of the chunks of meat.

We could hear their low snarls and growls as they began tearing at the meat, and within seconds one of them whimpered, they both trotted about ten feet away, and then collapsed on the lawn.

Several more dogs came around the front of the house, went directly to the meat and began eating. And within another half an hour, seven dogs lay unconscious across the clearing from us.

I had been assured that the anesthetic would not kill the animals, but would keep them unconscious for at least a half a dozen hours, leaving them none the worse for wear when they finally recovered.

From what I had been told, the servant's quarters were at the rear of the house, while DeGourcy's bedroom was probably on the second floor at the front.

We waited another ten minutes, to make absolutely sure there were no other dogs running loose, and then Maxime and I raced across the lawn, keeping low as we angled toward the front corner of the house.

Crouching behind the hedges near the front entrance, we waited until we caught our breath. No alarm had been raised as yet, but then I had already seen, first hand, DeGourcy's monumental arrogance.

I pulled out the padded grappling hook and rope from the pack, stepped back from the hedges and looked up at the balcony jutting out from the second floor. The railing was about fifteen feet above us. Across the narrow balcony were French doors leading possibly into one of the upstairs bedrooms.

Holding the coil of rope loosely in my left hand, I let out some of the line with my right, swung the grappling hook twice and flipped it up, over the balcony railing.

The padded, four-pronged hook fell onto the balcony with a dull thud, and I held my breath for a moment as I waited for someone to look out the window. But no one came to investigate, and I tugged gently on the rope, the grappling hook finally catching on the railing.

"DeGourcy, if he is El Cazador, won't want to come with you, of course," the operations planner, Phil Graham, had stated the obvious. "He'll have to be drugged, and between you and Miss Genarde, you'll have to somehow get him back to the boat."

"Why not just walk out the front door?" I had asked.

Donald Sharfenburg, our chief political analyst had shaken his head. "DeGourcy would never get a real trial in Switzerland, Nicholas," he said. "The deck would be stacked heavily in his favor. He's one of their leading money people. And you *know* what that means over there."

"So we take him out," I said.

"But we don't want his house staff involved, if at all possible," Graham said.

"I hadn't planned on involving them."

"That might be easier said than done," Graham said. He pulled a photo from his planning file and passed it across the table to me. It was of a short, stockily built oriental man.

"Cute," I quipped.

"His name is Daniel Lin Yun San. Black belts in karate, judo and a half a dozen other martial arts disciplines. Hard as a rock. World class matches under his belt," Graham said. "He's DeGourcy's personal servant, houseboy, valet, and, we presume, bodyguard."

I looked again at the photo, this time a little more critically. The man did seem as hard as a rock. He would not be easy to get around.

"He'll almost certainly be there at the house," Graham was saying. "And if you were correct when you told us that DeGourcy may expect you to make a try on him, then almost certainly Lin Yun San will be waiting for you."

"Anything on the man?"

"Nothing we can prove," Graham said. "But of course we have never had any real cause to dig very deeply into DeGourcy's background until now."

I tugged on the rope, making sure the grappling hook would hold, then quickly climbed up to the balcony. Before I swung over the rail, I listened again. But there was nothing. And then I was over.

I motioned for Maxime, and she climbed agilely up

the rope, joining me on the balcony moments later as I went to the French doors and studied the individual panes of glass, the door latch and the hinges for signs of an alarm. But there was nothing.

Laying the pack down, I pulled out the other dart gun, Maxime pulled out hers from her pocket, and I tried the door. It was unlocked.

I looked at Maxime, our eyes met, and she smiled and nodded. Taking a deep breath, I eased the door open, pushed the drapes aside and stepped into the room.

It was dark as I stepped toward the bed across the room. Maxime came in from the balcony, pushing the drapes aside.

I raised my dart gun, and at the same time there was a sudden movement behind me, near the open French doors. The lights came on and DeGourcy snapped, "Do not move."

The covers on the bed were thrown back and Lin Yun San, grinning, started to get up, but then stopped. My dart pistol was pointed directly at his chest and I began to squeeze the trigger.

"If you fire, I will kill Miss Genarde immediately," DeGourcy said from behind me.

I believed him, and I slowly lowered the dart gun as DeGourcy's bodyguard got smoothly out of the bed.

"Take his weapons," DeGourcy said.

The Oriental moved to me, took the dart gun from my hand and tossed it back on the bed, then quickly and efficiently searched me, finding and taking all of my weapons and tossing them in turn on the bed.

He stepped away, moving with a smooth, athletic grace.

Maxime stumbled into me, and DeGourcy quickly stepped around us, to the bedroom door, giving me a clear look at him. He was grinning. He was the same man from the London warehouse and the yacht. There was no doubt of it in my mind. No doubt whatsoever.

"Nice to see you again," I said, my voice calm.

DeGourcy laughed. "Whatever do you mean?"

"London. Haiti. The Straits of Florida."

"I've been to London, I must admit. Hundreds of times. But I've never been to Haiti, nor have I ever been in the Straits of Florida."

"Why lie at this late hour?" I asked, trying to goad him into making a mistake.

"I'm not lying, believe me, I'm not lying to you. There is no reason for it."

"Murderer," Maxime hissed, and she started forward, but I reached out and held her back.

"No," I said.

"Intelligent, Mr. Carter," DeGourcy said. Then he turned to Lin Yun San.

"If you've never been to Haiti, El Cazador, how did you know Miss Genarde's name?"

DeGourcy ignored me, but the smile was gone from his face. "I'll call the police on the way out," he told Lin Yun San. "I want these intruders dead before the authorities arrive."

The Oriental bowed. DeGourcy pocketed his gun, opened the door, stepped out into the corridor and then was gone.

At that moment I lunged toward his bodyguard, but the man had anticipated my sudden attack, because he stepped back away from my charge, the edge of his right hand catching me with a numbing blow to my left shoulder.

"Nick!" Maxime shouted.

I rolled over near the bed in time to see Lin Yun San snap a blow to the side of Maxime's head, at the same moment she jerked to the left. Had she not moved when she did, she would have been dead, I was sure of it. As it was, she went down, dazed for the moment as I scrambled to my feet and grabbed for the weapons on the bed.

Lin Yun San was at my back a split instant later, slamming me to the side. I crashed into the nightstand, knocking it and the lamp to the floor.

I saw his foot coming at my head and somehow managed to roll away, then leap to my feet and back off, as I dropped into the classic karate stance.

I've won every agency martial arts tournament I've been in, but compared to Lin Yun San, I was an amateur. I think he knew it, yet he gave me the respect that any intelligent fighter automatically gives his enemy.

Lin Yun San was fighting for his boss, however, while I was fighting for my life. There is a very large difference in the motivations.

The Oriental moved to the left, causing me to circle the opposite way, which placed him between me and the weapons on the bed. He was taking no chances.

"Max," I called.

Lin Yun San's right eyebrow rose, and for a brief moment he let his eyes flicker in her direction.

I moved in, kicking out with the side of my right foot toward his right leg, at the same moment I threw a classic, stiff-armed strike at his throat. He stepped aside, easily avoiding both, and swung his right hand like a piledriver toward the back of my neck.

I managed to roll to the right, his blow smashing into my left shoulder, instantly numbing my arm but shoving me toward the bed.

He saw his mistake and came after me as I somersaulted over the bed, reaching out for one of the weapons but missing them because of my numbed arm.

Suddenly I was on my feet on the other side of the bed. Lin Yun San jumped after me, presenting the back of his head to me. I swung down with the side of my right hand, with every ounce of strength I had, connecting solidly with the man's neck.

Lin Yun San shrugged off the blow and leaped to his feet as I shuffled back out of his way.

At that point I knew there was no way I could win this fight with him, and he knew that I realized it, and he smiled.

Maxime groaned from where she lay on the floor and started to sit up.

"The weapons!" I shouted. "On the bed!"

Maxime looked up, then got to her hands and knees. Lin Yun San glanced toward her and then back at the bed, the understanding that he was outnumbered now coming into his eyes, and he charged toward me.

This time I managed to step back out of the way, and I kicked him solidly in the groin as he passed.

He grunted heavily once, then spun around on his heel as Maxime got to her feet and staggered to the bed.

I stepped forward as Lin Yun San headed toward her, and I tried to shove him aside, but he swatted me away like some kind of an insect.

"Max," I shouted as Lin Yun San reached her.

At that moment she spun around and drove her right hand upward toward his face as the Oriental crashed into her, both of them falling onto the bed.

I was on my feet, and I raced to the bed, grabbed Lin Yun San by the back of his shirt and turned him over.

His body slumped loosely to the floor; he was dead. My stiletto was buried to the haft, upward from his chin into his brain. There was very little blood from the wound and only a small amount had splashed down on Maxime's shirt, but as she sat up, she tried to brush it away with revulsion. Her entire body was shaking.

I helped her up from the bed and took her into my arms. "It's all right now," I said soothingly. "It's all right."

She looked up at me, her eyes wide. "No it isn't," she said. "DeGourcy has escaped again."

"We're going after him," I said. "We'll find him."

"We must, Nick. We must!"

My head ached, my side throbbed and my left arm was still numb, but I knew there was no time to rest now. If DeGourcy had called the Swiss police before he had left the house, they would be coming soon and we would be arrested. It would take days before it was all straightened out. In that time DeGourcy would have made good his escape.

"We're going to have to get out of here now," I said to Max. "Are you all right?"

She nodded. "But where did he go?"

"I don't know, but we'll find out. First we've got to get out of here."

I scooped up our weapons from the bed, and when I had my gas bomb back in place and my Luger holstered, I pulled the stiletto out of Lin Yun San's body, wiped it off on his shirt front and resheathed it.

At the door, I listened a moment, and hearing no sounds, I opened it a crack and peered out into the silent, deserted corridor.

"What about the pack and the rope?" Maxime asked.

"Leave them," I said. They didn't matter now. The police would soon find the drugged dogs and the hole cut into the fence anyway.

I stepped out into the corridor, Maxime right behind me, and together we went to the head of the stairs. The entire house was quiet, making me wonder if DeGourcy had sent his servants away for the evening. He might have done that. He was expecting me, and he may not have wanted to involve his other household people.

We hurried down to the ground floor, then made our way to the back door unchallenged. Outside, we hurried across the back driveway and entered the large garage.

There were three cars parked there. A Rolls, an old Citröen and a Jaguar XKE. The Mercedes I had seen the last time I had been here was gone. DeGourcy was driving it.

I went immediately to the Jag and looked inside. The keys were in the ignition. For a moment I wondered. Again I got the impression that DeGourcy was taunting; leaving me the means to chase after him. First the orange life raft in the ocean and now this car. It was as if he enjoyed the challenge and wanted the game to continue.

"Get in," I snapped, and as Maxime was climbing in the passenger seat of the sports car, I opened the garage doors.

Back at the car I climbed in behind the wheel, started the engine and drove outside, stopping long enough to climb back out, re-close the garage door and then listen to the night sounds.

Faintly, in the far distance, I thought I could hear sirens. A lot of them. DeGourcy had called the police. We were going to have to get out of here before they arrived.

I jumped back in the car, slammed it in gear and raced around the house and down the long driveway to the highway, keeping the headlights off.

Past the front gate, which was open, I turned northeast and screamed up the Lake Shore Highway away from Geneva, away from the approaching police and away from the dinghy hidden in the rocks, and Villiers waiting for us out in the lake with the hydrofoil.

# THIRTEEN

Lausanne, a city of about one hundred and fifty thousand was less than twenty-five miles up the Lake Shore Highway from DeGourcy's estate, and by the time the Swiss police were just beginning their investigation back there, I was pulling up in the driveway of the Lausanne-Palace, one of the city's finest hotels.

There was no doorman on duty at this hour of the morning, so I took Maxime's passport and went into the lobby and registered with a sleepy but surprised night clerk, telling him I would park the car myself in the basement garage and manage my own bags.

The police would be by later in the morning to check passports, but by then I hoped that I would be covered by Hawk. Either that or Maxime and I would be out of here on the way to wherever DeGourcy had skipped.

DeGourcy would have to believe that Haglund's mission was legitimate because of the personal call he had received from the President. It remained to be seen if the man was arrogant enough to contact Haglund and tell the man to meet him elsewhere. If he did, we would nail him.

Maxime and I took the elevator from the basement garage to the eighth floor where we let ourselves into the lovely room we had been given.

During the short drive up here, she had not spoken a word to me. But now she turned and looked into my eyes.

"Will he get away again, Nicholas?"

"No," I said, shaking my head tiredly. "Not if I can help it, Max."

"How will we find him?"

"Leave it to me."

She started to protest, but then realized it was no use arguing and her shoulders sagged. "I will take a shower now. When I am finished I will wash our clothes." She went into the luxurious bathroom and closed the door.

I went across to the telephone on the table by the bed and dialed for the bell captain. When he came on I asked him to bring us a bottle of brandy, two glasses, some ice and a package of American cigarettes.

He said it would be ten minutes, and when he hung up I dialed for the hotel operator and asked her to place an overseas call to the United States, giving her Hawk's special operational number.

As the call was going through I could hear the shower come on in the bathroom. Maxime had saved my life once again. From the very beginning this assignment had been going sour. Although I've never been one to worry very much about my own abilities, I *was* beginning to wonder now just how good DeGourcy was. The man was one of the best I had ever come up against. It was no wonder he had been operating all these years without being caught. Half the governments in the free world were offering a price on his head, and yet for twenty years he had operated with apparent immunity from arrest, or even from detection.

AXE's nightside operator came on. "Amalgamated Press."

"I'd like to speak with Hawk," I said.

"Moment," the woman replied, and I could see the voice print analyzer at her console searching my speech patterns for recognition. It only took a few seconds; there was a distinctive click on the line, and Hawk was answering.

"Where are you calling from Nick?"

"The Lausanne-Palace Hotel."

"All went well?"

"All did *not* go well, sir," I said. "He flew the coop, Daniel had a serious accident, and Dieter and his people came out."

"You managed to get away without being spotted?"

"Yes, sir," I said. "But I'm sure Dieter is putting two and two together right now. It'll only be a matter of hours before I'll have to move again."

There was a silence on the line for a long moment as Hawk thought this latest development out.

"Any idea where our friend might be heading?"

"No, sir, but I think he might still be considering his meeting with Walter. If that's the case, he will be communicating with him, to pass on his change of plans."

"The man can't be that brash, can he?" Hawk asked.

"I think he may be, sir," I said.

Again there was a momentary silence. "Don't get yourself cornered there, Nick," he said. "Keep on the move. If you're picked up it could take a day or two for us to effect your release."

"Yes, sir," I said.

"Give me a couple of hours and then call me again. I'll see what I can dig up from this end."

"Thank you, sir."

"How is Miss Genarde?"

"Losing her illusions right and left, sir."

Hawk chuckled. "Step lightly Nick, this is a tough

one," he said, and he hung up.

The bellhop came a couple of minutes later. I paid him, adding a very generous tip, and when he was gone poured myself a stiff shot of the brandy and lit myself a cigarette.

I had been to Lausanne once a few years ago. As a tourist. It was a lovely city of parks and fine restaurants. But this time around there wasn't going to be any touring done. By daylight, Maxime and I would be gone.

Maxime came out of the bathroom, nothing on but a towel around her wet hair, as I was pouring myself a second brandy. She seemed to be in slightly better spirits. I poured her a drink and handed it to her. She drank it down in one swallow.

"I'll wash your clothes while you're taking a shower," she said.

"We've got to leave in a couple of hours."

"We'll send them out to be dried and pressed," she said.

I looked at her for a long moment. She was a beautiful woman. "When this is all over . . ." I started, but she cut me off.

"When this is all over—if it's ever over—we'll talk about it."

I finished my drink and went into the bathroom where I pulled off my clothes and stepped into the shower. Maxime came in right behind me and washed my clothes in the sink.

By now the police would be searching DeGourcy's house, and the grounds. If they had not yet discovered the hole in the fence yet, they soon would. If they were sharp, they would also soon realize that two of DeGourcy's cars were missing. His Mercedes and the Jaguar that Maxime and I had taken.

From that point their net would widen; Geneva to the south and Lausanne to the north would be the first cities they would check. We would have to be away by then.

When I was done in the shower, I dried myself off and walked back into the bedroom. The lights were off, only the light from the open bathroom door providing any illumination in the room.

"The bellman promised to have our clothes dried, pressed and back within an hour and a half," Maxime said from the bed.

The covers were thrown back and Maxime was laying there on her back, looking at me. I went across to her.

"Come to bed, Nicholas. I'm cold."

I smiled. Like before in Port-au-Prince at her apartment, I had the feeling that Maxime was going to bed with me only because she was desperately lonely and not because of any real feeling for me. But I guess I needed comfort too.

I slipped into bed next to her and she came into my arms, pressing the entire length of her incredibly soft body against mine.

For an hour we lost ourselves in each other. The nipples of her well-formed breasts were hard, her chest was heaving and her long nails raked my back as I finally entered her, and we began making slow, delicious love.

When we were finished and I tried to pull away, she held me there.

"Don't," she said. "Not yet."

Her eyes were wide and moist as she looked up at me, studying my face. I reached down and gently kissed her on the lips.

"What will happen when you're finished with DeGourcy?" she asked.

"We're going on a vacation," I said.

"No. I mean after all of that. After you return to Washington. What then?"

I didn't say anything.

"Another case? Another Sprague DeGourcy? More

killing? Another woman?"

"It's my job," I said softly.

"And you love it, don't you? The danger. The weapons. All the macho bullshit."

I started to say of course not, but I held my tongue. It was a job that someone had to do. But did I "love" it? I honestly did not know. Although I could not see myself doing anything else with my life, I couldn't say that I loved it.

"Luis was just the same as you," Maxime said, a bitterness in her voice now. "And it got him killed."

"It happens," I said.

She shook her head. "Only to those who want it to happen, which is why once this is all over with you and I will never see each other again. I don't think I could stand another loss."

Her reaction was understandable and normal. I had run into many other women who had had the same feeling. And I could not blame them.

We parted finally and I lit myself a cigarette, then picked up the telephone and gave the hotel operator Hawk's special number again.

While I was waiting for the call to go through, Maxime got up and poured us both another brandy. By the time she was back and had handed me my glass, the phone rang and I picked it up.

"Amalgamated Press," the same AXE operator said.

"I'd like to speak with Hawk."

"Moment," the woman said, and this time the delay was much shorter.

"The Alpin Hotel, at Lauterbrunnen," Hawk said without preamble.

"Why there?" I asked.

"I don't know, but Haglund was telexed hours before he reached Washington, that when he returned he was to meet DeGourcy in Lauterbrunnen."

"Even before I had arrived at his estate?"

"Yes, which means you were right, he was expecting you. And he suspected he might lose the first round at his estate."

"I don't understand, sir."

"We've been digging a little deeper into DeGourcy's background, Nick. Among other things, we've discovered that the man is an avid mountain climber. Quite good, from what we've learned."

"So he's going to Lauterbrunnen to mountain climb and to meet with Haglund—" I began but I stopped in mid-sentence, something else coming into my mind. "The bastard *did* know all along. He's planned this entire thing."

"Presumably," Hawk said.

"Lauterbrunnen is just a cogwheel train ride from Jungfraujoch."

"What are you getting at, Nick?" Hawk asked.

"Mt. Eiger. The north wall," I said.

Hawk was silent, and my mind was running far ahead, DeGourcy's twisted thinking coming clear to me.

"Eiger's north wall is probably the most treacherous, difficult climb in Europe. Yet the climbers can be watched, every step of the way through binoculars from the hotel below. Probably the Alpin Hotel."

"You're saying that DeGourcy is luring you to that mountain?"

"Yes, sir," I said. "I'm sure of it. I've become a thorn in his side. What better way than to kill me and get away with it. My death will occur in front of anyone who wants to watch. And it will be an accident. DeGourcy will be blameless. Christ, even Haglund, a U.S. government official will be there to watch."

"What condition are you in, Nicholas?" Hawk asked after a long hesitation.

"Never been better, sir, now that I've figured out

what DeGourcy is up to."

"What kind of support do you need?"

"Maxime and I will be leaving here within the next few minutes. We'll drive directly over to Lauterbrunnen. Have one of our people come down from Bern with clothing, and luggage. They can drop it off at the Alpin before we arrive and make reservations for us. It'll look a little less suspicious."

"How about your cover? Grundt will be certain to have the police up there check all the registered guests."

"Better get us new passports and other documents as well," I said. "Although it will only slow Dieter down a little. He's got to suspect that I will be going after DeGourcy up there. He'll have to come himself to snoop around, and he'll see me."

"Even a few hours' delay could be helpful," Hawk said.

My mind was still racing ahead to Eiger's north wall. "Have our man meet us in front of the hotel, then. I don't know how long it will take us to get there, but he should be in place within the next few hours."

"All right, Nick," Hawk said. "How is Miss Genarde holding up?"

I looked up at her and smiled. "Fine now, sir. Just fine."

When I hung up, Maxime was staring at me, her eyes narrowed. "Lauterbrunnen," she said. "He'll be there?"

I nodded.

"We're going there? This morning?"

Again I nodded, and she turned and went into the bathroom as someone knocked on the door.

I jumped up, grabbed my Luger and went to the door. "Yes?" I called.

"The bellman, sir. Your laundry is ready."

"Just a moment," I said. I grabbed a towel, wrapped

it around my middle, and then grabbed a twenty dollar bill, went back to the door and opened it.

The bellman came in, handed me our clothes, I paid him and he left.

Maxime came out of the bathroom a few moments later. We got dressed and I strapped my weapons on.

Normally Lauterbrunnen would be less than a two hour drive from here, but we were going to have to be very careful now. I'd take some of the backroads and circle around to the north of the Mt. Eiger area.

Once Dieter Grundt found out that DeGourcy was there, he would order a passive cordon around the area, looking for me.

It was a little past six A.M. when we left the room and took the elevator all the way down to the parking garage beneath the hotel.

The Jaguar had not been tampered with, and as far as I could determine the car had not been staked out. As we drove up the ramp to the exit, the sleepy night shift attendant waved genially at us, and then we were outside, heading slowly toward the northern edge of the city.

I drove in an apparently aimless fashion sometimes down side streets, sometimes along the main thoroughfares and sometimes switching back, in an effort to see if we had picked up a tail. But after a half an hour of that, I was satisfied that Grundt hadn't gotten this far.

Later this morning, when the local police picked up the passports at all the hotels, the word would be flashed that Maxime and I were here. Or had been. The hotel would be surrounded and Grundt would be coming up to personally arrest me.

There had been no indications after all that DeGourcy had been working with a double. The man we had confronted at the estate was the same man from

London and from Haiti. I was dead certain of it in my mind.

No matter what the ramifications were, I was convinced now that Dieter Grundt and Walter Haglund were both involved in DeGourcy's sophisticated system of alibis.

Yet I could think of no reason for Dieter to be doing such a thing. Grundt had always struck me as a man of great fairness, a man who by his very nature found crime despicable.

I shook my head as I drove. Haglund, on the other hand, was an unknown to me. For all I knew, his work with DeGourcy had been what promoted his own career.

We stopped at a gas station just north of the city where I had the Jag filled up and bought a highway map of Switzerland.

I studied the map while the attendant was filling the gas tank, and before we pulled away I made a point of asking the man the best way to get out of the Lausanne area for a drive up to Luxembourg—in the opposite direction of Lauterbrunnen.

The attendant showed me on the map, I thanked him profusely, gave him a large tip so he would be sure to remember, then drove off to the northwest, toward the highway he had recommended.

That little ploy wouldn't stop Grundt, but it might slow him down, and certainly would divert some of his people in that direction.

At Renens, a short way to the west, I turned northeast to Le Mont, then headed through the mountains straight east to the Interlaken District—toward the picturesque village of Lauterbrunnen with its world famous cogwheel train; toward Mt. Eiger and its imfamously difficult north wall which had claimed dozens of lives over the past years; and toward DeGourcy and whatever the madman had planned for this final act in our little drama.

The morning broke pink and lovely, the air crisp and very sharp this high up in the mountains. We passed through wonderful little villages, crossed over rushing mountain streams, passed above wide chasms and finally came into the town of Interlaken itself slightly more than five miles north of Lauterbrunnen.

It was a little past eight-thirty when I finally parked the Jag in the rear parking lot of a small restaurant in Interlaken, and Maxime and I got out of the car, stretched our legs and went inside.

We were given a table by the front windows from where we could see the main street and the lovely mountain peaks beyond.

This close to DeGourcy again, Maxime had become very jumpy, her eyes darting from the passing traffic on the street outside to the other customers in the restaurant.

"We're all right here," I said to her after we had ordered coffee and croissants.

"They'll be watching Lauterbrunnen. How are we going to get down there. They'll recognize DeGourcy's car."

"Yes they will. But we're not going to drive down. We're going to take a bus," I said. I pointed to the tiny bus depot across the street from us.

Maxime smiled. "The police won't be watching the buses."

"I hope not," I said.

Actually getting into the town would only be the first step. Next we would have to get to the hotel. But once in place there, I didn't think Grundt would try anything. Especially not if Walter Haglund was there. The Swiss were very internationally minded. It would be unthinkable for Grundt to create a potentially disastrous international situation, unless I made some overt move toward a Swiss citizen, namely DeGourcy.

But I wasn't going to do that. I wasn't going to barge into the hotel and gun the man down. No. I was going to play DeGourcy's little game by his rules. He didn't have Lin Yun San with him this time. And he definitely would not make an attempt on my life at the hotel.

On the contrary. He would be gracious there, in close view of all the guests.

But once on the mountain it would be a different story. For both of us.

I motioned for the waitress, and when she came to our table I asked about the bus service to the south.

"There is a tourist bus that leaves every hour on the hour, *Mein Herr,*" she said.

I looked at my watch; we had ten minutes. "Bring me the check then, if you will," I said.

The waitress immediately handed me the check. I paid it, and then sat back with my coffee.

"We're going on the next bus?" Maxime asked, looking from me to the window where we could see one of the brightly colored tour buses loading passengers.

"Right," I said. "In just a couple of minutes."

At about five minutes before nine, I suddenly got up, and taking Maxime's arm, headed out the front door. As we crossed the street I looked around but could not spot anyone paying attention to us. Grundt's efforts were still centered to the south, in Lauterbrunnen itself.

We bought tickets and were the last passengers to board the bus, which took off moments later, the driver speaking into a microphone, telling us about the fabulous Interlaken District of Switzerland.

The bus stopped four times at scenic overlooks on the

way down to Lauterbrunnen, so it was nearly ten o'clock by the time we approached the village. Parked at the side of the road were two Swiss police vehicles, a half a dozen uniformed officers watching the traffic coming into town.

I took a cigarette out of my pack. "When I drop it, bend down and pick it up off the floor. But take your time," I whispered to Maxime.

She had seen the police as well, and she immediately understood that as a black woman, she would be instantly recognizable.

As we neared the stakeout, I fumbled with my cigarette, dropped it on the floor, and Maxime bent down to grab for it, her body suddenly below the level of the windows.

I looked the other way as we passed the police, and then we were in the village, pulling up at the bus depot, the Alpin Hotel a block away in the shadow of Mt. Eiger.

# FOURTEEN

I left Maxime in the ladies' room at the bus depot and went on foot the rest of the way to the Alpin Hotel.

A short, heavyset man dressed as a typical tourist, a camera bag over his shoulder and a tourbook in his hand, crossed the street behind me, and within a block and a half had caught up.

I crossed the street to him, and he glanced over his shoulder toward the main street before he offered me any sign of recognition.

"Any trouble getting into town?" he asked.

We stood next to each other, staring in at the window display of a leather goods shop.

"We took a bus down from Interlaken. The girl is still at the depot. Will we be able to get into the hotel without being stopped?"

"It'll be difficult, but not impossible," my contact said, speaking rapidly. "Once inside they won't try anything, however, as long as you make no overt moves. But you'll be closely watched."

He passed a package over to me.

"You're Don Howard, from Cleveland. The girl is your aide, Elizabeth Barstow. She's British."

"Are we registered?"

"Separate but connecting rooms, 304 and 305. The Swiss can be damned insufferable," he said. "You'll have to drop your passports off at the front desk in order to get your keys. The rooms are prepaid."

"Is DeGourcy there?"

"Checked in a couple of hours ago. The American, Haglund, is on his way by limousine from Bern. He should be no later than eleven A.M."

I glanced toward the main street. No one was coming our way yet. "Have you seen Dieter Grundt?"

"Not yet."

I thought a moment. "I'd like to get into the hotel before he shows up."

"Right," my contact said. "I've got an automobile. A Ford Cortina. I'll pick you and the woman up at the rear door of the bus depot in ten minutes. Once in the car, you both can keep low until I pull up at the front entrance to the hotel, then you can spring out and get inside. I'll run cover for you."

"Why won't they arrest us in the lobby?" I asked. "Haglund isn't here yet."

"The hotel is packed with American businessmen. Big time businessmen. Lots of money. A climb of Eiger's north wall is scheduled for tomorrow if the weather holds."

"Is DeGourcy in on it?"

"We don't know yet." My contact looked at me. "Do you suspect he'll be making the climb?"

"I think so," I said.

"Do you want us to run backup here for you?"

"Negative," I said. "As soon as we're inside I want you and everyone else to back way off. If DeGourcy suspects this is anyone's setup but his own, he'll go deep. I don't want to lose him."

"Right . . ." my contact started to say, but then he

stiffened. "See you," he said, and he turned and nonchalantly strolled down the street as two men, wearing business suits, came up the street toward me.

I casually reached inside my jacket as if to scratch my side, but neither man paid any attention to me as they passed where I was standing and continued around the corner.

I let out the breath I had been holding and headed back downtown, around the block from the hotel, to the bus depot where Maxime was waiting.

I didn't see her when I came into the bus depot, and for a moment I thought she had been picked up. But then I spotted her through the archway that led into a small coffee shop. She was seated at a table near the rear exit.

She looked up as I came across the room to her, and the relief was clear in her eyes.

"Did you make contact?" she asked when I sat down.

I nodded and reached across the table for her hand. "This is your last chance to get out of this, Max," I said gently.

She shook her head.

"It's going to be difficult getting into the hotel. But once we've gotten in, you're going no farther."

"What are you saying to me, Nick?"

Quickly I explained to her what was going to happen, including the likelihood that in the morning DeGourcy would be climbing Eiger's north wall.

"He's luring you onto the mountain, isn't he?"

"Yes."

"Then we will kill him tonight, in his room."

"Not unless he makes a move against us," I said. "There will be police all over the place. We wouldn't be able to get him out of here, nor would we get away with assassinating him."

She was having a lot of trouble with what I was saying

to her. "It's all that macho bullshit again, isn't it?" she said.

"It may be for DeGourcy, but for me it's a practical matter of survival. If anything happens to DeGourcy in the hotel you and I will be spending a very long time in a Swiss prison. Hawk would not be able to intervene without exposing the service. And that would never happen."

"Then how—"

"On the mountain," I said. "DeGourcy wants me up there so that he can kill me and make it look like an accident. I'm going to give him the choice of voluntarily coming with me."

"He won't do that."

"No," I said after a moment. "In that case I'll turn his little game around on him."

"What if you fail? What if DeGourcy kills you?"

"Then you'll be at the hotel when he gets back. It will be up to you then."

Maxime looked away and I studied the side of her face. She was a beautiful woman, well educated, in an advantaged position by comparison to her countrymen; yet unless this DeGourcy thing was settled here and now, it would destroy her, as surely as a bullet to the brain would end her life.

"Well?" I asked after a minute.

She turned to me. "Well what?"

"Are you going to do as I ask?"

She smiled. "I don't have any choice, do I? If I say no, you'll just walk away and leave me here."

"Something like that," I said.

She hesitated. "He's very good, isn't he?"

"The best," I said.

"Then be careful on the mountain tomorrow, Nick. I want to take that vacation with you when this is all over."

"You can count on it," I said.

We got up, I paid the waitress for Maxime's coffee and we went out the back door of the bus depot. My contact from Bern was sitting behind the wheel of a cream-colored Ford Cortina in the parking lot. Maxime and I hurried across to him and climbed in the car.

Before we took off I gave Maxime her documents, including the passport that identified her as Elizabeth Barstow, pocketed mine, then nodded. "Ready when you are."

"As we approach the hotel, Miss Genarde, I want you to duck down below the level of the windows," our contact said.

Maxime took a deep breath and let it out slowly. "All right. Let's get it over with."

"Good luck," the man said. He put the car in gear, drove around the corner and headed down the block toward the front entrance of the lovely old hotel that was constructed in the Swiss alpine style.

A half a block away, the contact said, "Now," and Maxime ducked down beside me on the seat.

A tour bus had pulled up and parked in front of the hotel, and there was a great deal of activity there as we pulled up behind it.

Our contact got out of the car and came around to our side. I could see at least three men who looked like cops, scanning the crowd getting off the bus. For the moment they were paying no attention to us.

Our contact yanked the door open. "Now," he said under his breath, and as I got out, pulling Maxime with me, he stepped up on the sidewalk and went immediately to the cops, shouting something I couldn't quite catch.

Without looking right or left, Maxime and I strode across the sidewalk and entered the hotel. Someone shouted something behind us, but we didn't slow down.

Inside, we went immediately to the front desk where I handed the clerk our passports. "We have confirmed reservations," I said.

The clerk had us sign the registration cards, then handed us our room keys with a smile. "Welcome to the Alpin Hotel," he said. "We sincerely hope you enjoy your stay."

"I'm sure we will," I said. "Has our luggage arrived?"

"Yes, sir," the clerk said. "It has been brought up to your rooms."

"Very good," I said. I took Maxime by the arm and we headed across the lobby as two of the cops, looking mad, came in the front door. They spotted us, but did and said nothing as we entered the elevator.

As the doors were closing, one of them was moving toward the desk while the other had turned and walked back outside. But it didn't matter now. We were in. And I didn't think they would try anything against us as long as we kept our noses clean.

Our rooms on the third floor, which faced Eiger's north wall, were large, bright and airy. They were located directly above the patio restaurant on the first floor, and with the windows open we could hear the sounds of people eating, drinking, talking and laughing.

Atlhough it wasn't noon yet, a bottle of champagne in an ice bucket was waiting for us in my room. Maxime opened it and poured us both a glass as I telephoned down to the desk and made reservations for us this evening in the hotel's restaurant.

Next, I telephoned the bell captain and asked him to bring me up a Bern newspaper and a carton of American cigarettes.

When I hung up, Maxime was looking quizzically at me. "What was that all about?"

"If anyone knows about a scheduled climb tomorrow, the bellman will. I want to make sure that DeGourcy is actually going to make the climb and what route he'll be taking."

"And once you have that information?"

"Then I'll have less than twenty-four hours to prepare myself for the climb," I said.

The bellman came a few minutes later as Maxime was drinking her champagne out on the balcony. I paid him for the newspaper and cigarettes, and added a twenty dollar bill.

"I'm told that there's to be an assault on the north wall tomorrow," I said.

"Yes, sir," the bellman said pocketing the money. "They set it all up a week ago."

"Who's heading the climb?"

"It'll be a two-team assault. Georgi Renoir, the crazy Frenchman is heading one team, and our own Sprague DeGourcy will be heading the other."

"The classic route?"

"Yes, sir. They'll be starting at first light."

"Thanks," I said.

When the bellman left I went back to the telephone and had the hotel operator place a long distance call to the tiny town of Feldkirch just across the Austrian border from Liechtenstein.

It had been a long time since I had been down there, at least ten years; but I remembered that time as if it had happened ten days ago.

Helmut Walther, a man who had at one time been Austria's leading climber, but who was now retired from all but rescue operations, answered the phone on the third ring.

"*Guten Morgen,* Helmut," I said. "Lovely weather for a climb this week. Better than in a snowstorm."

Ten years ago, Walther and I had been caught on a mountain in the Lechtal Alps during a snowstorm. He had broken his leg and I had carried him down off the mountain. I had been on vacation and had hired him as a guide for the climb. Since that time we had become friends.

"Nicholas?" he asked incredulously. "Nicholas Carter, is that you?"

"None other," I said. "How is your wind and your legs these days?"

"Older than the last time, but still capable," he said.

"I'm calling because I need your help, Helmut, and you're the only man I know who can do the job." Walther knew that I was some kind of a policeman, but he had never questioned me about what I did.

"Where are you calling from?"

"Lauterbrunnen. I'm at the Alpin Hotel."

"The Nord Wand?"

"A climb has been scheduled for morning."

"It's been in the papers," Walther said.

"There will be a man on that climb who I must deal with. But no one can know I'm up there. Not at first."

"Who besides you and I will be going up?"

"No one else. And once I'm in position, you can back off. I don't want you involved in the actual operation."

There was a silence on the line for a moment, but then Walther was back. "I'll leave here within two hours with all the equipment we'll be needing. I'll get someone to do the driving so I can sleep on the way. We'll be there sometime early this evening."

"I'm in 304 under the name of Donald Howard. But don't ask for me, just come up. I'll be waiting for you here at ten P.M. sharp."

"Good," Walther said. "That gives me a little more time to get ready."

"Take care, Helmut," I said.

"I do everything with care, Nicholas. See you."

Maxime had been staring up at Mt. Eiger, and when I hung up she turned around to face me. "It is going to be very dangerous, isn't it?"

I nodded.

"Then we will make the best of this afternoon," she said, coming back into the room from the balcony as she began unbuttoning her blouse.

We dressed for dinner and presented ourselves downstairs in the dining room about seven-thirty P.M. Maxime had wanted to remain in our rooms until it was time for me to leave in the morning, but I had a very special reason for wanting to mingle this evening.

The dining room was crowded with well-dressed men and women, and in one large corner of the room, near the bar, a party was going on at a huge circular table. The conversations centered on and flowed around Sprague DeGourcy, who was dressed in a well-tailored tuxedo, a bright red carnation in his lapel.

Maxime and I were seated at a small table across the room from DeGourcy and his group, and after we had ordered a light meal, I called for the wine steward.

"What is Mr. DeGourcy drinking?" I asked when the man arrived, the ceremonial wine cellar key hanging around his neck from a bright red ribbon.

The man glanced over his shoulder at the party. "A moët et Chandon," he said.

"We'll have a bottle of the same, and send another bottle to Mr. DeGourcy's table with the compliments of Mr. Howard and Miss Barstow."

"Very good, sir," the steward said, and he left.

"What are you trying to do?" Maxime asked under her breath.

I smiled. "I want him to know that we're here," I said.

Our wine came first, a few minutes later, and as our glasses were being filled, the bottle was delivered to DeGourcy's table.

He said something to the wine steward, who turned and motioned our way. DeGourcy looked over at us, and smiled, then raised his glass in a salute. I did the same.

Maxime's nostrils flared and her right eyebrow arched.

"Careful, Max," I said, maintaining my smile.

"I still don't see why you did that," she snapped.

"I want DeGourcy to know that I'm accepting his challenge."

"Why?"

"It'll guarantee our safety here in the hotel. He wants to meet me on the mountain. He'll make sure nothing happens to us tonight."

Our dinner came a little later, and for a while we settled into the meal, our conversation light, Maxime's mind off DeGourcy for the time being.

Maxime was in the middle of telling me a story about her days at Harvard when Dieter Grundt came into the dining room and went directly over to DeGourcy's table.

"Hold on," I said, interrupting Maxime's story. She turned to follow my gaze.

Grundt was speaking to DeGourcy.

"Who is he?" Maxime asked.

"Dieter Grundt. Interpol from Geneva. He and DeGourcy are friends."

"Are we going to have to fight him, too?"

I shrugged. "I hope not."

Grundt straightened up a few moments later. DeGourcy said something else to him, and he glanced over at me, then left the dining room.

Maxime was asking me something, but at that moment I wasn't hearing her. I was thinking about the good times Grundt and I had had. It made me sad to think that my old friend was in on this. And yet I could draw no other conclusions.

I looked back over at the table. I did not know what Walter Haglund looked like, but I presumed he was one of the men over there. DeGourcy would have held off any discussions about the President's financial deal until after the climb. With me dead, he would have a clear mind, because if Haglund remained afterward, it would prove that he was not involved with me. DeGourcy wasn't missing a trick.

We left the dining room a half an hour later, stopped at the bar for a quick after dinner drink and were back up in our rooms a little past nine-thirty to wait for Helmut Walther to show up from Feldkirch.

Maxime was in a strangely subdued mood, and went immediately into her room to change out of her evening clothes.

I could hear her moving around in there as I lit myself a cigarette and stepped out onto the balcony to look up at the dark masses of the mountains that surrounded us.

Tomorrow, I thought. One way or the other, it would all be settled tomorrow. This part of an operation—the waiting to begin—had always been the hardest for me, and it was now. I wanted to get started, to get it over with. But it was like DeGourcy and I were in a ballet together, a deadly pas de deux.

Helmut Walther showed up with his young assistant, Albert Stern, exactly at ten P.M. Besides the climbing gear in a van parked around the corner from the hotel, Walther had brought with him a bottle of very good Austrian cognac.

He opened it, poured us all a drink and raised his glass. "To the climb," he said.

We all drank.

"Your man is going up in the classic assault?"

Walther asked without preamble.

"Yes," I said.

"Good. Then we will begin our climb in the same fashion as the rescue workers, from the Eigerwand window."

From the nearby town of Kleine Scheidegg, the Jungfrau Railway went from there to the 11,333-foot summit of the Jungfraujoch barely six miles away. But much of the trip on the famous line was through a tunnel cut into the mountains themselves. At the 9,400-foot level, a large window was cut from the tunnel to the north wall of Mt. Eiger. It was the usual starting point for any rescue operation on the mountain.

"The train will not be running that early in the morning, will it?" I asked.

Walther smiled. "I've climbed that mountain more times than you've made love to women, Nicholas. An inspection train will make the run."

"When do you want to leave?" I asked.

"We should be out of here no later than three, if you want to be in place on the mountain as DeGourcy's and Renoir's parties come up."

"Three it is," I said.

"Get some rest now, Nicholas," Walther said. He nodded toward the other room where Maxime had remained. "Go to her and make your peace. Albert and I will bunk down in here. I will wake you in plenty of time."

"Thank you, Helmut, for coming like this."

"Go get some rest, Nicholas. Tomorrow sounds like it will be a big day."

# FIFTEEN

Maxime was awake when Walther brought me a pack of mountain clothes, but she said nothing as I got up and got dressed in the long underwear, heavy slacks and sweater, and climbing boots.

When I was ready I went back to the bed, leaned down and kissed her. "Will you be here when I get back?"

"Yes," she said. Her eyes were moist.

I started to straighten up, but she reached out and grabbed my arm, pulling me back down.

"Be careful, Nick," she said.

"I'll be back," I said. We kissed again, and then I went into the other room where Walther and Stern were waiting for me.

"There's something you'd better know before we leave," Walther said pointing to a portable radio on the nightstand. "We've got some weather coming in."

"When?"

"Within the next twelve to eighteen hours."

"Bad?"

Walther shrugged. "Even a little wind on the mountain can be bad."

"We'll go to the Eigerwand window and wait. If De-

Gourcy and his party head up, we'll go ahead with the climb."

"DeGourcy," Walther said. "An important man. That important?"

I nodded.

"So be it," he said. "Albert will come back here to the hotel. We have walkie-talkies. He will call us the moment DeGourcy and his people start up."

We left the hotel by the back door and hurried up the street in the darkness to where the van was parked. The morning air was very cold and in the streetlights I could see my breath. On the mountain itself, it would be freezing, and if a storm did come in, our chances for survival would be minimal.

Stern drove the short distance over to the railway terminal at Kleine Scheidegg as Walther and I organized the gear in the back of the van.

It was a little past three-thirty when we pulled up and parked.

"Give me a moment," Walther said, and he jumped out of the van and went into the tiny station.

I lit a cigarette while I waited for him, and five minutes later he came out of the station with an old man dressed in coveralls and a down jacket. He waved for me, and I got out of the van, hefted the heavy equipment packs and went over to where they were standing.

"Bruno Hausmann, Donald Howard," Walther made the introductions. We nodded at each other. "Bruno will take us up to the Eigerwand, but we'll be on our own from there."

"Fine," I said.

We went around to the other side of the station where a tiny inspection car, open to the cold winds, was waiting on the track.

I threw the equipment packs aboard, and Walther and

I climbed in the back seats as Hausmann started the gasoline engine, then climbed in the driver's seat, and we lurched away from the station, the track angling immediately upward toward the dark opening of the tunnel far overhead.

As we rose into the night, the cold became much more intense, the wind stronger; but below us the towns nestled in the valleys seemed warm and inviting, yet distant.

"Up here," Walther had once told me, "even if you're climbing with a large party, you're still alone. It's always just you, the mountain and God."

I felt that now, strongly, and yet I recalled what the old woman in Haiti had told Luis and me. She had mentioned Havana, but she had also mentioned a place of cold and snow. Above us, there was snow on the peaks.

We passed through the quiet, sleeping Eigergletscher Station, then entered the four-and-a-half-mile long tunnel through the Eiger and Mönch mountains, climbing higher and higher.

Time seemed to drag then, until at last the train began to slow. Walther sat up in his seat and we finally stopped at a wide opening in the tunnel through which the wind howled.

Walther and I got off, grabbed the packs, and without a word Hausmann took off, and within minutes was lost to view up the tunnel.

I followed Walther down the side tunnel, the wind becoming stronger and stronger, until finally the wide tube ended at a steel fence.

We put the packs down, stepped up to the fence and looked out. From this spot it seemed as if we could see all of Europe. Above us, the nearly sheer north wall of Mt. Eiger seemed to reach all the way up to the stars, while almost directly below us, we could see the lights of

Lauterbrunnen and one side of the Alpin Hotel.

Maxime was down there, and I wondered whether she was looking this way through binoculars and if she could see us standing here.

Walther took out his walkie-talkie, extending the antenna, and spoke into it. "You there?"

"Yes," the soft reply came from the speaker.

"What's happening?"

"They're up, having their breakfast. They'll be starting within the next few minutes."

I looked up. The eastern sides of the mountaintops had a soft pink glow. The sun was coming up.

"We're in place," Walther said. "Let us know the moment they begin."

"Yes."

Walther laid the walkie-talkie down, then walked back into the tunnel where he opened his pack, pulled out a small primus stove, started it and put a small amount of water on to boil.

"We will have our breakfast as well," he said, smiling. "A little hot soup?"

"Sounds good," I called back from where I had remained by the rail.

DeGourcy wanted me up here so that he could kill me. But he would not do it in such an obvious manner. He would have to make it look like an accident in order to cover himself.

During the last twenty-four hours I had tried to put myself in his position; tried to think what he would do. Up here on the mountain it came to me.

DeGourcy would have to know that I was up here waiting for him, so he would climb this way, toward the most difficult part of the north wall.

Once he got close enough, he would separate himself from the other men in his party, work his way around the east chimney (where he would be out of sight of the hotel), then call for help.

I would be the first one down to him, of course. And at that point it would be no one else but the two of us. But there would be no gunshot wounds, no knife cuts, nothing but a battered body at the bottom of the two-thousand foot sheer drop.

DeGourcy's body. Or mine.

"They're leaving the hotel now," Stern's voice came from the walkie-talkie.

I picked it up and keyed the transmitter. "Renoir will take the western approach, DeGourcy the eastern, I think. As soon as it becomes clear, I want you to confirm that."

"Yes."

"At that point I want you to concentrate on De-Gourcy himself. If he breaks away from his group, I'll want to know immediately."

"Yes," the young man said and I put the walkie-talkie down.

Walther came to the rail a couple of minutes later with two mugs of soup. I took mine and gratefully sipped at it, the warmth a welcome relief.

"What has this DeGourcy done, Nicholas?" he asked.

I looked at him. "He is an assassin," I said.

"Why hasn't he been arrested?"

"Because he is very good, Walther. He operates under a very solid cover."

Sudden understanding dawned on his face. And he looked at me with surprise. "Then you have lured him here to this mountain in order to kill him?"

I shook my head. "He has brought me here, to try again to kill me."

"He has tried before, then?"

"Don't ask me anything else, my old friend. You are

here only to help me down the mountain, but you will not leave this tunnel if I can help it."

Walther seemed to think about that for a long moment, but then he looked out across the mountains. It was becoming much lighter out now. And snow blew in long ragged plumes off the peaks, as if it was smoke from tall chimneys.

"When the storm comes it will drive the wind and the cold down from the upper reaches. Even this tunnel will be a very unhealthy place to be."

"We all take our chances," I said.

"They're beginning," Stern's excited voice came from the walkie-talkie at our feet.

I reached down and picked it up. "Can you tell which route DeGourcy is taking?"

"The east," Stern said. "Definitely the east."

"How long before he reaches the Eigerwand?"

"By noon, I think; but wait a moment, something is happening."

Walther and I looked at each other.

"What is it?" I transmitted.

"Some of them are turning back. It must be the weather reports."

"Is DeGourcy coming back?"

"Wait," Stern said. Then a second or two later. "No, he is continuing."

"Keep a sharp watch on DeGourcy. As soon as he separates from his group and disappears from sight let me know."

"Yes."

Again I put the walkie-talkie down. Noon. "There will be tourists up here from the train by noon," I said.

Walther shook his head. "Hausmann will have found a problem below us, just past the Eigergletscher. Unfortunately for those who wish to view the climb from here, the troubles will not be repaired until this evening at the earliest."

I went back to the packs, pulled out a pair of binoculars, and once again at the rail, studied the slopes just above the Alpin Hotel. At first I could see nothing, but then, farther up than I had suspected they would be, I saw DeGourcy's party. They were climbing fast. Very fast. They knew the storm was coming, and I suppose they expected to outrun it to some point of safety where they could string out their mountain tents on pitons, either that or reach this tunnel.

"Are they coming?" Walther asked.

I nodded and handed the glasses to him. He studied the climbers below us for a long minute. "They're going to try to reach the lateral at this level to the west," he said. He lowered the binoculars and looked at me. "But if you're right, DeGourcy will take the lead, and around the east chimney he'll break one of the pitons behind him and slip the rope."

I nodded.

"That will mean the certain death of his climbing companions if the storm does hit."

I nodded again.

"The bastard," Walther swore softly. "The dirty bastard."

The wind rose with the sun as Walther and I took turns watching DeGourcy and his party in their lightning attack on the north wall.

They were moving fast, faster than I had seen any climbers work, and it had to be evident to the people below, watching them from the hotel, that there was trouble.

Twice the group stopped, to rest, but each time De-

Gourcy continued without pause, blazing a new trail far above the others.

Around ten A.M. DeGourcy himself was out of sight far below us and Stern radioed from the hotel that he had set himself free. At this point DeGourcy was free climbing. There was no link between him and his companions whom he had left far behind.

"No guile there," Walther said. "He's making his lateral well below us, so that he can be out of sight of the hotel at the earliest possible moment."

By eleven A.M., DeGourcy had finally disappeared from Stern's view down at the hotel, nearly one-thousand feet below us, and around the hump of the chimney to the east.

"Half an hour, then you go," Walther said.

I nodded.

"You'll be able to rappel only the first two hundred and fifty feet from here, where you can tie yourself off. I'll send down a second line, but at that point you'll be out of my sight as well as the hotel's. It'll be totally up to you."

I reached beneath my sweater, pulled out my Luger and handed it to Walther. "It's either going to be me or DeGourcy coming back up the line," I said. "If it's not me, shoot him, then toss the gun over the rail. They'll find both of our bodies as well as the gun and assume that I killed DeGourcy."

Walther took the gun without hesitation. "Remember what you've been taught, Nicholas. And take care." He looked again toward the wind on the peaks. "The storm is coming much faster now. Keep an eye on it."

Back in the tunnel at the packs, I strapped on my safety lines with the thick snap rings, belted a dozen pitons and a rock hammer to my side, then donned a pair of mountaineering gloves.

We went again to the rail where I looked over the edge. I heard something. At first it sounded like a bird screeching far below me. But then it came again, and I knew it was DeGourcy shouting for help.

Stern was on the walkie-talkie. "It's happening," he said. "One of DeGourcy's team members has radioed back that DeGourcy is in trouble around the east chimney. They're going to make a try for him."

"How long will it take them to get there?" Walther snapped into the walkie-talkie.

There was a silence for a long moment. "Two hours, maybe a little more," Stern said. "They've got at least five hundred feet to climb, and then the difficult lateral around the chimney. Maybe two and a half hours."

"Let us know when they reach the lateral," Walther radioed.

"Yes."

We went to the far side of the tunnel where a section of the steel fence was out of view from the hotel. Walther tied off a pair of snap rings on the steel bars, slipped a large coil of rope through the rings, then flipped it over the edge.

I looked down as the wind caught the rope and swung it wide.

"Go with God," Walther said.

I looked at him, smiled and then we hugged. "Have Stern bring the girl and our things to the Kleine Scheidegg station. I'm going to have to get out of here in a hurry."

"All right," Walther said.

I looped the rope around my left thigh and then over my right shoulder, mounted the steel railing and eased myself over the edge.

The cold bit at me immediately, but the wind was no problem until I was about fifty feet below the window, and then a gust slammed me to the right.

I had to scramble to keep my balance against the face of the cliff and my grip on the rope, but after a few anxious seconds I continued down.

Every now and then I could hear DeGourcy's cries far below me as I continued to pay out the thick line until the colored bands passed through my gloved hands, warning me that I had only twenty-five feet of rope left.

Fifteen feet farther down, I found a narrow crack in the rock face. I tied myself off, braced myself against the wind and hammered two long, hardened steel pitons into the crack, clipped on with my snap clips, then snapped at the line above me once, twice and a third time. It was my signal to Walther that I was tied off and he should send down the next coil.

DeGourcy's cries were coming more infrequently now, but they were much closer below me.

Within a couple of minutes, a second coil of rope brushed the top of my head. I unclipped it from the leader line, snapped a pair of D rings on it, set the line up for rappelling, then unclipped my safety catches and continued farther down the north wall.

The sky was becoming overcast very rapidly, and from the look of things, the weather forecasters had been way off on this one. The storm would be here long before dark tonight.

For a long time then, DeGourcy was silent, and when I reached the end of the second coil, I braced myself against the mountain, listening for him.

"DeGourcy?" I called out finally.

But there was no answer.

"DeGourcy?" I called out again, this time a little louder over the rising wind.

Suddenly there was a noise above me, and at the same moment I looked up, my line suddenly went stiff and very heavy.

DeGourcy was about eighty feet above me, clinging to

my line. He was looking down at me.

"Too bad, Carter," he called down. "But you lose."

"If you cut my rope the authorities will know what happened."

"Cut your rope?" DeGourcy laughed. "Heavens, why would I do something like that."

He turned and started climbing upward, his movements steady and very sure. For a long second I didn't know what he was trying to prove. He had to know that someone would be above in the tunnel waiting for him, but suddenly it dawned on me. DeGourcy was climbing up to my pitons. To my only link with safety at this moment. If he got there first, before I reached him, or before I could tie myself off, he would hammer them out and I would fall to my death.

I started climbing, scrambling up the line as fast as I possibly could go, as DeGourcy's laugh came down to me.

Up this portion of the cliff, the rock face was nearly smooth. What cracks there were in the rock, were mostly hairline fissures, far too small to drive a piton into them.

I redoubled my efforts to make it up the rope, while at the same time I frantically searched for a crack, a ledge, any kind of a handhold.

But there was nothing, except for the smooth rock face, the harsh wind and the penetrating cold.

What seemed like hours later I looked up as I heard the sound of steel on steel.

DeGourcy was about thirty feet above me, hammering a piton into the crack next to the two pitons I had driven earlier.

My arms were numb, and my legs seemed like hundred-pound lead weights dragging my body down as I climbed harder and faster than I ever have in my life.

The line went momentarily slack, and I looked up in time to see that DeGourcy was now tied off with his own piton and had begun hammering at mine.

Time had run out. I could feel the hammer blows on the pitons through the taut line. Then, five feet above me and slightly to the right I saw a tiny ledge. Less than an inch wide, it ran on a gentle slope for about five feet before it abruptly ended.

Hand over hand I climbed for the ledge as my line gave a lurch.

"One down, one to go," DeGourcy laughed. "Nice try, Nicholas."

Then I was at the ledge, my fingers curling over the lip, as I released my rope at the same moment it went totally slack.

The end of the line tangled in my right foot, and I kicked as hard as I could to dislodge it before the weight of the rest of the rope came down and dragged me off my precarious perch.

But then it was free; the line above whistled past my head, and then was gone below.

I looked up. DeGourcy was twenty-five feet above me now, looping a coil of rope through his piton.

"Very good, Nicholas," he said when he was ready. "But I wonder how long you can hang on down there like that."

As he talked I searched with my toes for a foothold. Anything. My arms were dead, my fingers were shaking.

DeGourcy started down, a few feet to the left of me, as I found a small hole with the toe of my right foot. I eased my weight into it and my grip held.

I eased up a little higher, taking most of the pressure off my arms, then looked up. DeGourcy was barely ten feet above me now, his line snaking down a couple of feet to my left.

If I could reach his line before he got down to me, I would have a chance of fighting him. He evidently sensed what I was going to do, because he stopped and laughed.

"Do you want the line, Nicholas?" he said to me. He was so close I could almost reach out and touch him.

I edged to the left at the same moment DeGourcy grabbed a length of his line in his free hand and whipped it at me.

"Here!" he shouted.

The heavy line hit me on the face and shoulder, nearly dislodging me from my precarious perch.

DeGourcy laughed again. "Did you miss it? Let me try again."

The line snapped at me again, catching me on the chest, and DeGourcy jerked violently outward, pulling me away from the cliff.

For a terribly long second it seemed as if I was hanging in midair and then I began to fall away from the cliff.

I twisted as far as I could to the left and shoved off with my foot, my left elbow brushing the line, and then I had it with my right hand.

Somehow I managed to wrap my left leg around the line as well, and I stopped my sickening slid down the rope.

My breath was coming in ragged gasps. The wind had picked up now and my heart was pounding nearly out of my chest.

DeGourcy was no longer laughing as I looked up. He was climbing down the rope toward me. Quickly I pulled up a large loop of rope from below me, threaded it one handed through my D rings, and just managed to tie it off as DeGourcy's booted foot caught me on the head.

I lost my grip, fell about four feet, but then came up short on the D rings.

Suddenly the advantage had turned to me and DeGourcy knew it. There was no way now he could tie himself off.

I started up toward him. Slowly. Conserving my strength.

"Straight up, DeGourcy," I said. "If you give it up, we'll take you in. You'll get a trial."

DeGourcy said nothing as he continued to climb, but now he was moving far too fast and was beginning to make mistakes, slipping at times five feet or more, the rope tearing at his palms.

"Give it up, man, while there's still time," I said, moving cautiously.

At the top, DeGourcy looped his left arm around the rope, while with his right he fumbled out another piton and his hammer. He was going to try the same trick again.

He reached up to insert the piton in the crack when he lost his grip on the hammer and it fell out away from him.

At the last second he realized that without his rock hammer he would have no way of driving the piton, and he lunged out for it.

"DeGourcy!" I shouted.

But it was too late. The man lost his grip on the rope, his body arched out away from the rock face, and he plummeted past me as we reached out for each other.

My fingertips just brushed the back of his coat, and then he was gone, falling silently, more than two thousand feet to the rocks below.

# EPILOGUE

The sun was setting on Feldkirch's famed Schattenburg Castle as Maxime and I climbed into Walther's ancient Volkswagen and headed back to the inn.

We had been here now for the past five days, relaxing and enjoying the hospitality of Walther's town.

Yesterday Hawk had telephoned to tell me about DeGourcy's funeral in Geneva. The Swiss had played it up big—DeGourcy was being treated as a national hero, dead of an accident in the Alps.

Haglund was there, of course, representing the U.S. Government, and Grundt had been in the front row at the memorial services.

It bothered me about Grundt and Haglund, because I still didn't know about them. I had no direct proof that they had been working with or for El Cazador, yet all the circumstantial evidence pointed to such a conclusion.

Hawk had given me a fifteen day leave, and although I had only used five of those days, I was already getting anxious to get back to work.

The first order of business, I told myself, but not Hawk, would be Dieter Grundt. I was going to have to return to Geneva to find out for sure about him. I don't think I could have slept nights until I knew for certain where his real loyalties lay.

"It's not over with yet, is it?" Maxime asked me as I pulled up behind the inn and parked.

I looked at her and smiled sheepishly. "DeGourcy, El Cazador, is dead," I said. "It's over."

"It's the Interpol cop. Your friend, isn't it?"

I didn't answer at first as I got out of the car, came around to her side and opened the door. "It doesn't have anything to do with you," I said gently.

Maxime got out of the car. "If Grundt was working for DeGourcy, then he is indirectly responsible for my brother's death."

"Logic is not your strong point, Max," I said.

"If you're going to Geneva, I'm coming with you," she said firmly.

"We'll see," I replied.

Inside, the desk clerk stopped us. "Mr. Carter," he said.

We crossed the lobby to him.

"Mr. Walther is here with a friend he would like you to meet," the clerk said. "He asked me to catch you before you went up. They're at the bar."

"Thanks," I said.

Maxime was smiling. "Go ahead and have a drink with your friends. I'm going up to take a bath. Later you're going to take me out dancing."

I had to smile, too. "It's a deal," I said. "If Walther keeps me down here too long, come on down and drag me away."

"You can count on it," she said, and she turned and went up the stairs.

I went into the dimly lit bar, where after a moment I spotted Walther sitting in a booth in the corner. I couldn't see the man he was with, but Walther had a strange look on his face as I crossed the room.

"I've been given instructions from Max that I'm t have only one drink with you—" I started to say whe the words died in my throat.

Seated across the booth from Walther was Spragu DeGourcy! For a split second I was totally stunned. I was impossible. I had watched DeGourcy fall to hi death off Eiger's north wall.

But then it all came to me in a rush. Haglund wa innocent. Grundt was innocent. DeGourcy did have double. Curiously what the old woman in Haiti had tol me came back crystal clear. She said she had seen "mirror image."

"Have a seat, Mr. Carter," DeGourcy said softly.

I started to back off.

"I have a gun under the table, pointed right at you friend's balls," DeGourcy said. He was grinning. "Si down."

My weapons were upstairs. I was not on an operation There had been no reason for me to go around armed

I did as DeGourcy said, sliding carefully into th booth next to Walther.

"I'm sorry, Nick. He came to the house. There wa nothing I could do."

"Don't worry about it," I said.

The waitress came up and I ordered a beer. DeGourc said nothing until the girl came back with my beer an left us alone again.

"Where is Miss Genarde?" he asked.

"She took the train to Paris this afternoon. She' going back to the Caribbean."

"You're a very poor liar," DeGourcy said.

I leaned forward and he stiffened. "Tell me some thing," I said. "Are you DeGourcy, or was the man I killed on Eiger the real DeGourcy?"

"Bastard," the man said.

"You're going to kill us anyway. At least answer that one question for me," I said.

"All right," the man said, regaining his composure. "It was DeGourcy on the mountain."

"Who are you?" I said. Maxime came to the door from the lobby. "If you're not DeGourcy, then who are you?" I said raising my voice as if in anger.

"Shut up or I'll kill you here and now," the man hissed. Maxime had heard me, and she backed quickly out the door before he had seen her.

"Who are you then?" I repeated my question, keeping my voice low.

"I'm Sprague DeGourcy, of course," he said laughing.

I smiled. "You're not his twin brother. He didn't have any brothers. So one of you was a lookalike. We'll find out from your fingerprints, of course."

"Enough," he said. "You are both going to get up very slowly and walk out the door. I'll be right behind you. If you try anything I'll shoot you down."

I started to get up.

"Slowly," DeGourcy, or whoever he was, said.

I got to my feet and Walther joined me.

"Out the door," DeGourcy said.

We walked slowly to the door, at the same time Maxime was coming down the stairs. She was carrying my Luger. I hoped the hell she knew how to use it, because she was only going to get one shot.

Walther stepped through the doorway a moment later. I reached out, grabbed him by the coat sleeve, and hauled him to the left.

DeGourcy came through the doorway raising his gun, and Maxime fired from the hip, the bullet whistling past me and striking DeGourcy in the head, just behind the right ear.

His pistol discharged harmlessly into the floor and he

crashed sideways—instantly dead.

The temperature in Miami was in the mid-nineties as Maxime and I reached the airport, and I helped her inside with her suitcases.

It had been a week since Feldkirch, and everything had been straightened out pretty fast. The man on Eiger had been Sprague DeGourcy. The man Maxime had killed at the inn was an unknown. Probably Russian, an Interpol pathologist had guessed. My guess was that DeGourcy and his double had worked together for years. But no one would ever know fur sure.

I had made my apologies to Dieter Grundt and to the completely bewildered Walter Haglund, who never had a glimmering of what was really going on, and then followed Maxime down here.

She was returning to Haiti to straighten things out with her government, to renew her Haitian citizenship, and to take up where her brother Luis had left off.

"If ever I'm in Port-au-Prince—" I said at the gate, but Maxime held a finger up to my lips.

"No," she said. "Within a year you would not know me, Nicholas my darling. By then I will have reverted to being a black Haitian woman. There is no place for you in my life."

She was correct, of course. But I had come to admire and respect her. Three times she had saved my life.

"Forget me, Nicholas. It will be for the best."

"Never," I said. "*Au revoir.*"

## DON'T MISS THE NEXT NEW NICK CARTER SPY THRILLER

### *OPERATION: McMURDO SOUND*

I pulled my flashlight out of my pocket and switched it on. In the dim light I examined the ends of the guy wires. They had been cut. The ends were not twisted and frayed. They were straight and smooth.

I looked up. Someone had come out here and cut the guy wires. Someone didn't want us communicating with the base station back at McMurdo Sound.

I put my flashlight away and pulled out my Luger, fumbling the safety catch off with my gloved hands, and I continued forward as best I could.

Tibert's body lay crumpled in a heap beneath a section of the radio tower, his face badly mangled, and frozen blood everywhere on the snow.

He had evidently gone up the tower, and while up there, someone had cut the guy wires, causing him to fall to his death.

I cursed my own stupidity for not checking to see if the others were in their rooms before I came out here. This could have happened an hour ago—giving whoever had done it time to get back to their room before I came out.

The section of tower pinning Albert's body was dug into the snow and too heavy for me to lift. His body would have to stay out here until the storm passed and I could get some help to remove the tower.

I started to edge back along the tower toward the generator building when an engine started somewhere out ahead of me, and I stopped. A moment later another engine started, and then two sets of headlights came on.

Snowcats. Someone was out there aboard snow track vehicles. The engines were revving up as I raised my Luger and fired two shots in quick succession at a point above one set of headlights. The machine seemed to lurch toward me, and then its engine died, but the headlights remained on.

The second machine was lumbering toward me as I brought my Luger around and fired two more shots.

A shot whined off the tower metal six inches away from me, and I twisted to the right as something very hot stitched across my side, knocking me off balance.

By the time I scrambled upright again, both machines had turned away and were racing into the storm, the sounds of their engines fading rapidly in the howling wind. I fired four more shots in the direction I thought they were going, and then lowered my weapon.

It hadn't been Stalnov after all, but from what Tibert had told me, I suspected it was some of Stalnov's people from their main base. The movement the lead helicopter pilot had seen below him, on the way out here yesterday, had probably been these people.

I put my Luger in my pocket and stiffly worked my

way back to the base of the tower, then back around the generator building to where the guide line was attached.

Shaking with the intense cold, my entire left side aching from where the bullet had just grazed my ribs, I grabbed the rope and headed back toward the Administration building.

If anything, the wind had risen in intensity during the time I had been out here, and, combined with my wound, the going was very rough.

Twice I stumbled and fell, but the second time I got to my feet the rope came loose in my hand. For a long moment I stood there holding the slack rope until I looked back the way I had come and pulled on the rope. It came taut. It was still connected to the generator building.

Turning back, I carefully pulled on the rope, and it was loose. It had either broken at the Administration building end, or someone had cut it.

The cold was making it almost impossible to think straight, and for several seconds longer I stood there, stupidly holding the slack rope in my hands.

But then I started forward, keeping the rope taut behind me. Unless the rope had been cut very far from the Administration building, I could still follow it to the end and then walk in an arc until I bumped into the doorway.

In ten minutes I had come to the end of the rope where it had obviously been cut, and I drew it up tight behind me so that I was at the extreme limit. I tried to peer through the darkness for a light in one of the windows, but there was nothing.

The path had been completely covered over by the snow, which was nearly hip deep by now, and I began to realize that I was completely lost.

If I let go of the rope and stumbled forward there was

a very good chance I'd miss the Administration building. And in this weather I would not last very long . . . .

—From OPERATION: McMURDO SOUND
A New Nick Carter Spy Thriller From
Ace Charter in June

**EUROPEAN HISTORICAL DICTIONARIES**
**Edited by Jon Woronoff**

1. *Portugal*, by Douglas L. Wheeler. 1993
2. *Turkey*, by Metin Heper. 1994
3. *Poland*, by George Sanford and Adriana Gozdecka-Sanford. 1994
4. *Germany*, by Wayne C. Thompson, Susan L. Thompson, and Juliet S. Thompson. 1994
5. *Greece*, by Thanos M. Veremis and Mark Dragoumis. 1995
6. *Cyprus*, by Stavros Panteli. 1995
7. *Sweden*, by Irene Scobbie. 1995
8. *Finland*, by George Maude. 1995
9. *Croatia*, by Robert Stallaerts and Jeannine Laurens. 1995
10. *Malta*, by Warren G. Berg. 1995
11. *Spain*, by Angel Smith. 1996
12. *Albania*, by Raymond Hutchings. 1996
13. *Slovenia*, by Leopoldina Plut-Pregelj and Carole Rogel. 1996
14. *Luxembourg*, by Harry C. Barteau. 1996
15. *Romania*, by Kurt W. Treptow and Marcel Popa. 1996
16. *Bulgaria*, by Raymond Detrez. 1997
17. *United Kingdom: Volume I, England and the United Kingdom; Volume 2, Scotland, Wales, and Northern Ireland*, by Kenneth J. Panton and Keith A. Cowlard. 1997; 1998
18. *Hungary*, by Steven Béla Várdy. 1997
19. *Lantia*, by Andrejs Plakans. 1997
20. *Ireland*, by Colin Thomas and Avril Thomas. 1997
21. *Lithuania*, by Saulius Suziedelis. 1997
22. *Macedonia*, by Valentina Georgieva and Sasha Konechni. 1998
23. *The Czech State*, by Jiri Hochman. 1998
24. *Iceland*, by Gubmundur Hálfdanarson. 1997
25. *Bosnia and Herzegovina*, by Ante Čuvalo. 1997
26. *Russia*, by Boris Raymond and Paul Duffy. 1998
27. *Gypsies (Romanies)*, by Donald Kenrick. 1998
28. *Belarus*, by Jan Zaprudnik. 1998
29. *Federal Republic of Yugoslavia*, by Željan Šuster. 1999
30. *France*, by Gino Raymond. 1998
31. *Slovakia*, by Stanislav J. Kirschbaum. 1998
32. *Netherlands*, by Arend H. Huussen Jr. 1998
33. *Denmark*, by Alastair H. Thomas and Stewart P. Oakley. 1998
34. *Modern Italy*, by Mark F. Gilbert and K. Robert Nilsson. 1998
35. *Belgium*, by Robert Stallaerts. 1999

# Historical Dictionary of the Federal Republic of Yugoslavia

Željan E. Šuster

*European Historical Dictionaries, No. 29*

The Scarecrow Press, Inc.
Lanham, Md., & London
1999

SCARECROW PRESS, INC.

Published in the United States of America
by Scarecrow Press, Inc.
4720 Boston Way
Lanham, Maryland 20706

4 Pleydell Gardens
Kent CT20 2DN, England



British Library Cataloguing in Publication Information Available

**Library of Congress Cataloging-in-Publication Data**

Šuster, Željan. 1958–
Historical dictionary of the Federal Republic of Yugoslavia / Željan Šuster.
p. cm. — (European historical dictionaries : no. 29)
Includes bibliographical references.
ISBN 0-8108-3466-9 (cloth : alk. paper)
1. Yugoslavia—History—Dictionaries. I. Title. II. Series.
DR1232.S87 1999
949.76—dc21 98-14337
CIP

ISBN 0-8108-3466-9 (cloth : alk. paper)

(∞)™ The paper used in this publication meets the minimum requirements of American National Standard for Information Sciences—Permanence of Paper for Printed Library Materials, ANSI Z39.48-1984.
Manufactured in the United States of America.

*To my parents, Olga and Emil*

# Contents

# List of Maps

# List of Tables

# Series Editor's Foreword

The Federal Republic of Yugoslavia is one of the more recent states in the Balkans. Emerging from political upheaval and fragmentation that have changed the face of the region, the "new" Yugoslavia holds a powerful position. While much smaller than the "old" Yugoslavia, it remains by far the largest, most populous, and strongest successor state. Its standing among and influence upon its neighbors, and the Balkans in general, is considerable; and, as has been shown repeatedly, events in the Balkans can greatly affect Europe and the international community at large.

This book must extend its scope beyond the Federal Republic's existing boundaries and encompass the various peoples and earlier entities who lived and ruled in the region as well as those who dominated it from further afield. The significant historical figures—of the present decade, the present century, and earlier ages—are presented, as are the many economic, social, cultural, and religious bodies, and the assorted political parties and institutions. The chronology clearly maps Yugoslavia's long and tortuous history while the list of abbreviations and acronyms identifies key players. The comprehensive bibliography provides sources for further research and information.

Given the inherent complexity of the subject, and the controversial nature of so many actions and events, the author's task was a difficult one. Željan Šuster has done an admirable job of portraying Yugoslavia as it is, was, and may become. His familiarity with the recent past is not surprising, since he studied at the University of Belgrade and worked at two research institutes in Belgrade before moving to the United States. He has taught economics and East European studies at various American universities and is presently at the University of New Haven. He has also lectured and written extensively on the current and previous Yugoslavias and their older predecessors. Šuster's experience culminates in the Historical Dictionary of the Federal Republic of Yugoslavia, which updates a continuing saga and anticipates the new chapters of the future.

Jon Woronoff
Series Editor

# Acknowledgments

It is not my purpose here to write a history of Serbia and Yugoslavia. That has been attempted on numerous occasions, especially since the outbreak of civil war in Croatia and Bosnia and Hercegovina, two republics of the former Yugoslavia. I have not written a narrative or a specialized study. I have tried instead to discuss, and where it seemed possible, to explain, how Serbian culture developed its various economic, social, and political strengths and weaknesses. The emphases, and omissions, reflect my own judgment of what is most interesting and important in Serbian and Yugoslav history. Thus, in many respects, this book is a personal analysis. I have tried, however, to provide a summary, or at least the common denominator, of the views held by historians, political scientists, art historians, economists, artists, and other specialists. I hope I have succeeded in distinguishing between a generally accepted fact and an inference. This proved to be a formidable endeavor since the media coverage of the civil war often created an atmosphere with little respect for basic historical facts.

I wish to thank a number of my friends and colleagues who contributed to the preparation of this book. I am particularly grateful to Dimitrije Đorđević for his continuous encouragement and advice. David Mackenzie read the entire manuscript and proposed numerous editorial and factual improvements. Suggestions of Dušan T. Bataković were of critical importance in the very last stage of writing the manuscript. Special thanks to Života Lazić, who generously allowed me to use his personal library. My discussions with Alex N. Dragnich, Dobrica Ćosić, Stephen Fisher-Galati, David Binder, Milorad Ekmečić, Slavenko Terzić, and Svetozar Stojanović were a constant source of inspiration. The numerous editorial and factual comments of William Woodger were essential enhancements of my work. Finally, the patience and understanding of Jon Woronoff, series editor, was vital and much appreciated. I remain solely responsible for any errors and factual interpretations. Funds from the University of New Haven and the

Summer Research laboratory of the University of Illinois at Urbana-Champaign greatly facilitated the completion of this book. In addition, I was fortunate to use the resources of the Serbian Academy of Sciences and Arts, Yale University, the University of Belgrade, and the University of Connecticut.

I would never have finished this book without the constant support, help, and understanding of Sanja, who stoically endured my absenteeism and selfishness during the year and a half of writing.

# Usage Notes

Today, as in the past, the official Serbian alphabet is Cyrillic. Since the formation of the first Yugoslav state in 1918, both Cyrillic and Latin alphabets have been used. The alphabetical arrangement of entries in this book follows the Latin alphabet, that is, the sequence "a,b,c...ž," rather than that of "a,b,v...š" required by the Cyrillic alphabet. The vast majority of personal names in the dictionary section are alphabetized in accordance with the customary practice of putting the last name first; however, exceptions have been made, mainly where a person is better known by her or his first name. Thus the entry for Prince Lazar, who took part in the 14th century Battle of Kosovo, is Lazar Hrebeljanović and not Hrebeljanović, Lazar. In addition, in some exceptional cases an individual's main entry is placed under a well-known nickname. Consequently, the renowned leader may be found under Tito, Josip Broz and not Broz, Josip-Tito. The entry Broz, Josip will redirect the reader to the description under Tito. Throughout the dictionary boldface is used to indicate that an entry for that word, person, or phrase also exists, while "see also" is used to indicate that the corresponding entry is directly related to the subject being sought or discussed.

Except for some well-known Anglicized forms—Belgrade, Serbia, Bosnia—proper names have been rendered in their original language. Personal names have been rendered in their original form, with the exception of rulers and prelates with names of Biblical, Greek, or Roman origin with common Western forms. Accordingly Prince Miloš, is called by his Serbian name, while King Peter is not called Petar. There are some exceptions—Prince Michael, for example, is called by his Serbian name Mihailo. In addition, Hajduks are not called *hajduci* and Uskoks are not called *uskoci*. Turkish personal names, titles, and terms are given in the Turkish alphabet, so it is Hafiz-Paşa and not Hafiz-Paša (Serbian) or Hafiz-Pasha (English). However, the Dahije are not called *dayis*, mainly because the latter term was never used in Serbia.

While they may initially perplex an average reader, Serbian diacritic marks should not create more difficulty than French accents or German umlauts. While there are variations in the way some of the common letters are pronounced (the Serbian "t" is dentalized) the guide below should help the reader with the pronunciation of Serbian names and terms.

| Letter | Pronunciation |
|---|---|
| a | like *a* in father |
| b | like *b* in boy |
| c | like *ts* in cats |
| č | like *ch* in chess |
| ć | between *t* in tune and ch in church |
| d | like *d* in dart |
| đ | like *di* in diavolo |
| dž | like *j* in jogging or g in generate |
| e | like *e* in ebony |
| f | like *f* in father |
| g | like *g* in golf (not like in gemini) |
| h | between *h* in human and ch in loch |
| i | like *i* in give |
| j | like *y* in yet |
| k | like *k* in key |
| l | like *l* lagoon |
| lj | like *li* in million or lu in revolution |
| m | like *m* in mother |
| n | like *n* in nose |
| nj | like *ny* in canyon |
| o | like *o* in shot or aw in bawl |
| p | like *p* in Peter |
| r | like *r* in Spanish *pero* (a rolled r) |
| s | like *ss* in grass |
| š | like *sh* in sheep or sch in schism or su in sure |
| t | like *t* in trap |
| u | like *oo* in doom |
| v | like *v* in void |
| z | like *z* in zebra |
| ž | like *s* in measure or pleasure |

Turkish letters ş and ç are pronounced like English sh and ch, respectively.

In giving place names every effort has been made to preserve historical and ethnic integrity. Thus, for example, Hercegovina and not Herzegovina, which is neither Serbian nor English. In the cases where ethnic usage and historical provenance contradict each other, priority has been given to the historical. Thus, the Treaty of Passarowitz is used, not the Treaty of Požarevac, and Skoplje, not Skopje.

All dates are given according to the Gregorian calendar. In Serbia the Gregorian calendar (New Style) was adopted by a decree of January 23, 1919. Prior to that the Serbs adhered to the Julian calendar (Old Style). Since the difference between the two calendars was nine days, then 11 days in the 19th century and 12 days in the 20th century, May's Assassination happens both on May 29, 1903 and June 11, 1903. The Serbian Orthodox Church still adheres to the old Julian calendar.

# Abbreviations and Acronyms

| | |
|---|---|
| AKMO | Autonomna Kosovsko-Metohijska Oblast/Autonomous Region of Kosovo-Metohija |
| ANUBiH | Akademija nauka i umetnosti Bosne i Hercegovine/Academy of Sciences and Arts of Bosnia and Hercegovina |
| AP | Autonomna pokrajina/Autonomous province |
| APZB | Autonomna pokrajina zapadna Bosna/Autonomous Province of Western Bosnia |
| ASNOBiH | Antifašistička skupština narodnog oslobođenja Bosne i Hercegovine/Antifascist Assembly of the National Liberation of Bosnia and Hercegovina |
| ASNOS | Antifašistička skupština narodnog oslobođenja Srbije/Antifascist Assembly of the National Liberation of Serbia |
| AVNOJ | Antifašističko veće narodnog oslobođenja Jugoslavije/Antifascist Council of the National Liberation of Yugoslavia |
| B-H | Bosnia and Hercegovina |
| BEMUS | Beogradske muzičke svečanosti/Belgrade's Music Festivities |
| BiH | Bosna i Hercegovina/Bosnia and Hercegovina |
| BITEF | Beogradski internacionalni pozorišni festival/Belgrade International Theater Festival |
| BSA | Bosnian Serb Army |
| CK | Centralni komitet/Central Committee |
| CNK | Centralni nacionalni komitet/Central National Committee |
| COMINFORM | Communist Information Bureau |
| CPY | Communist Party of Yugoslavia |
| CSCE | Conference on Security and Cooperation in Europe |
| DC | Demokratski centar/Democratic Center |
| DEPOS | Demokratski pokret Srbije/Democratic Movement of Serbia |
| DM | Deutsche Mark/German Mark |
| DS | Demokratska stranka/Democratic Party |

| | |
|---|---|
| DSS | Demokratska stranka Srbije/Democratic Party of Serbia |
| EC | European Community |
| EU | Evropska unija/European Union |
| FEST | Festival festivala/International Film Festival |
| FRY | Federal Republic of Yugoslavia |
| FYROM | Former Yugoslav Republic of Macedonia |
| GATT | General Agreement on Tariffs and Trade |
| GSS | Građanski savez Srbije/Civic Coalition of Serbia |
| HAZU | Hrvatska akademija nauka i umjetnosti/Croatian Acedemy of Sciences and Arts |
| HB | Herceg Bosnia |
| HDZ | Hrvatska demokratska zajednica/Croatian Democratic Union |
| HSS | Hrvatska seljačka stranka/Croatian Peasant Party |
| IBRD | International Bank for Reconstruction and Development (World Bank) |
| IFOR | Implementation Force |
| IMF | International Monetary Fund |
| IMRO | Internal Macedonian Revolutionary Organization |
| IPTF | International Police Task Force |
| JAT | Jugoslovenski aero transport/Yugoslav Airline |
| JAZU | Jugoslavenska akademija znanosti i umjetnosti/Yugoslav Academy of Sciences and Arts |
| JMO | Jugoslovenska muslimanska organizacija/Yugoslav Muslim Organization |
| JNA | Jugoslovenska narodna armija/Yugoslav Peoples' Army |
| JNS | Jugoslovenska nacionalna stranka/Yugoslav National Party |
| JRT | Jugoslovenska radio televizija/Yugoslav Radio and Television |
| JRZ | Jugoslovenska radikalna zajednica/Yugoslav Radical Union |
| JUL | Jugoslovenska levica/Yugoslav Left |
| JVO | Jugoslovenska vojska u otadžbini/Yugoslav Army in the Fatherland |
| KLA | Kosovo Liberation Army/Oslobodilačka vojska Kosova |
| KNOJ | Korpus narodne odbrane/National Defense Corps |
| KOS | Kontraobaveštajna služba/Counterintelligence Service |
| KOSMET | Kosovo i Metohija/Kosovo and Metohija |
| LCY | League of Communists of Yugoslavia/Savez komunista Jugoslavije |

| | |
|---|---|
| LDK | Democratic League of Kosovo/Demokratska Liga Kosova |
| MANU | Makedonska akademija nauka i umetnosti/Macedonian Academy of Sciences and Arts |
| MS | Matica srpska |
| MUP | Ministarstvo unutrašnjih poslova/Interior Ministry |
| NATO | North Atlantic Treaty Organization |
| NDH | Nezavisna Država Hrvatska/Independent State of Croatia |
| NF | Narodni front /National Front |
| NKOJ | Nacionalni komitet oslobođenja Jugoslavije/National Committe of Liberation of Yugoslavia |
| NRPJ | Nezavisna radnička partija Jugoslavije/Independent Workers' Party of Yugoslavia |
| OZNA | Odelenje za zaštitu naroda/Department for Protection of the People |
| RS | Republika Srpska/Serbian Republic |
| RSK | Republika Srpska Krajina/Republic of Serbian Krajina |
| RTS | Radio televizija Srbije/Serbian Radio and Television |
| SANU | Srpska akademija nauka i umetnosti/Serbian Academy of Sciences and Arts |
| SAO | Samostalna autnomna oblast/Independent Autonomous Region |
| SAZU | Slovenačka akademija nauk i umjetnosti/Slovenian Academy of Sciences and Arts |
| SDA | Stranka demokratske akcije/Party of Democratic Action |
| SDS | Srpska demokratska stranka/Serbian Democratic Party |
| SFOR | Stabilization Force |
| SFRJ | Socijalistička Federativna Republika Jugoslavija/Socialist Federal Republic of Yugoslavia |
| SHS | Kraljevina Srba, Hrvata, i Slovenaca/Kingdom of the Serbs, Croats, and Slovenes |
| SKJ | Savez komunista Jugoslavije/League of Communists of Yugoslavia |
| SLS | Srpska liberalna stranka/Serbian Liberal Party |
| SNS | Saborna narodna stranka/Congregational National Party |
| SPC | Srpska pravoslavna crkva/Serbian Orthodox Church |
| SPO | Srpski pokret obnove/Serbian Renewal Movement |
| SPS | Socijalistička partija Srbije/Socialist Party of Serbia |
| SRS | Srpska radikalna stranka/Serbian Radical Party |
| UDBA | Uprava državne bezbednosti/Department of State Security |

| | |
|---|---|
| UN | United Nations |
| UNCRO | United Nations Confidence Restoration Operation |
| UNHCR | United Nations High Commission for Refugees |
| UNMIBH | United Nations Mission in Bosnia-Hercegovina |
| UNPA | United Nations Protected Area |
| UNPREDEP | United Nations Preventive Deployment |
| UNPROFOR | United Nations Protection Force |
| UNTAES | United Nations Transitional Authority in Eastern Slavonia |
| VJ | Vojska Jugoslavije/Yugoslav Army |
| VMRO | Vnatrešna makedonska revolucionarna organizacija/Internal Macedonian Revolutionary Organization |

# Chronology

**5th century:** South Slavs begin to arrive in the Balkan Peninsula.
**Early 7th century:** Serbs and other South Slavic tribes finally settle in the peninsula.
**8th–9th century:** First Serbian princes: Višeslav, Radoslav, and Prosigoj.
**822:** First mention of Serbs in the *Frankish Annals.*
**c. 850:** Serbian prince Vlastimir, son of Prosigoj, repulses Bulgarian attack.
**c. 863:** Cyril devises Glagolitic alphabet.
**867–874:** Serbs accept Christianity.
**c. 870:** Methodius becomes Archbishop of Panonian-Srem diocese.
**878:** First usage of the Slavic name Belgrad (Belgrade) instead of the Roman Singidunum.
**892–917:** Rule of Petar Gojniković; Raška expands westward to the Cetina River in western Hercegovina and Dalmatia.
**c. 893:** Introduction of the Cyrillic alphabet.
**927–950:** Rule of Časlav Klonimirović; Časlav makes the first effort to unite numerous Serbian clans in Raška, Duklja, Travunija, and Bosnia and Hercegovina.
**c. 930:** Rise of the Bogomils in Macedonia.
**976–1014:** Rule of Samuilo, leader of Macedonian Slavs.
**993:** Date of the oldest record written in the Cyrillic alphabet: a gravestone in the village German on Lake Prespa in Macedonia.
**1018:** Death of Jovan Vladislav; the end of Samuilo's Empire; the first records of Slava.
**1020–1022:** Establishment of the archbishopric of Dubrovnik and Raška diocese.
**1037–1051:** Rule of Prince Vojislav; the expansion of Zeta.
**1054:** The Great Schism; conflict between the Orthodox Church of the East and the Roman Catholic Church of the West intensifies and leads to mutual excommunications.
**1067:** Establishment of the dioceses of Bar.

**1077:** Mihailo, a son of Vojislav, is crowned by a legate of Pope Gregory VII.
**1080:** Building of St. Mihail's church in Ston.
**1081–1101:** Rule of king Konstantin Bodin, a son of Mihailo; the Serbian state includes Raška, Zeta, Hercegovina, and Dubrovnik.
**1096–1097:** Forces of the First Crusade cross Serbia.
**c. 1100:** The building of fortresses in Skoplje, Prilep, and Kratovo in Macedonia.
**1168–1196:** Rule of Stefan Nemanja, grand župan of Serbia and the founder of the Nemanjić dynasty; Serbia becomes independent from the Byzantine Empire; persecution of Bogomils.
**1171–1172:** Building of Đurđevi Stupovi monastery, a legacy of Stefan Nemanja.
**1176:** Birth of Rastko Nemanjić, known as Saint Sava.
**1180–1204:** Ban Kulin, son-in-law of Nemanja's brother, rules in Bosnia.
**1185–1186:** Nemanja unifies Zeta, Raška, and Hercegovina.
**1189:** Crusaders cross Serbia; Nemanja and German emperor Friedrich Barbarossa meet in Niš.
**29 August 1189:** Trade treaty is signed between Bosnia and Dubrovnik; the document known as *Ban Kulin's Charter* is written in the Cyrillic alphabet and in the Serbian language.
**1190:** Building of Studenica monastery.
**c. 1191:** Rastko Nemanjić (Saint Sava) leaves Serbia and goes to Sveta Gora (Mt. Athos).
**1196:** Stefan Nemanja yields his throne to his second son Stefan Prvovenčani.
**1197:** Nemanja leaves Serbia and joins Saint Sava at Sveta Gora.
**1198:** Hilandar monastery is founded on Sveta Gora.
**1206:** St. Sava arrives back in Serbia; becomes archimandrite of Studenica.
**1207–1220:** Building of Žiča monastery, a legacy of Stefan Prvovenčani.
**1217:** Coronation of Stefan Prvovenčani; St. Sava leaves Serbia for Sveta Gora.
**1219:** Autocephalus Serbian Orthodox Church is established; St. Sava becomes the first Serbian archbishop with his seat at the Žiča monastery.
**1227–1234:** Reign of King Radoslav Nemanjić.
**1234–1243:** Rule of King Vladislav Nemanjić.
**27 January 1236:** Death of St. Sava in Bulgarian city of Trnovo.
**1241–1254:** Arrival of Saxon miners in Serbia.
**1243–1276:** Reign of King Uroš I Nemanjić; economic and cultural development of Serbia; minting of the first Serbian silver currency.

**1260–1265:** Building of Sopoćani monastery.
**1276–1282:** Rule of King Dragutin.
**1282–1321:** Rule of King Milutin, a substantial territorial expansion of Serbia.
**1284:** Serbs capture most of northern Macedonia.
**1285:** Mongols devastate Serbia.
**c. 1295:** Peć becomes the center of the Serbian archbishopric; establishment of mines in Trepča, Rudnik, and Rogozno.
**Early 14th century:** Dubrovnik begins minting silver currency; the establishment of Novo Brdo.
**1309–1316:** Sava III, close ally of King Milutin, becomes archbishop of the Serbian Orthodox Church; reconstruction of numerous monasteries and churches.
**1313:** Milutin sends 2,000-strong force to help the Byzantine Empire fighting the Turks.
**c. 1315:** Building of Gračanica monastery.
**29 October 1321:** Death of King Milutin; Stefan Dečanski becomes king of Serbia.
**1322–1353:** Rule of Stefan II Kotromanić, *ban* of Bosnia; increasing activity of Franciscan missionaries in Bosnia.
**1327–1335:** Building of Dečani monastery.
**28 July 1330:** Combined Bulgarian and Byzantine forces attack Serbia and suffer a crushing defeat at the Battle of Velbužd.
**1331:** Dušan the Mighty becomes king of Serbia.
**1335:** Dušan defeats Hungarian king Carol Robert and captures Mačva.
**1337:** Janićije becomes archbishop; the first records of Golubac.
**1342–1343:** Dušan captures Albania, southern and eastern Macedonia.
**25 September 1345:** Serbs capture Seres.
**25 December 1345:** Dušan proclaims himself emperor in Seres.
**April 1346:** Serbian archbishopric is elevated to the rank of patriarchate; Janićije becomes the first patriarch of the Serbian Orthodox Church.
**16 April 1346:** Ceremonial coronation of Dušan in Skoplje; Dušan is proclaimed as "Emperor of Serbs and Greeks."
**1348:** Serbs capture Thessaly and Epirus.
**21 May 1349:** Dušan's Code of Law is enacted during the state Sabor (gathering) in Skoplje.
**20 September 1349:** Dušan grants Dubrovnik special trading and judicial privileges.
**1350:** Wars between Bosnian Ban Stefan II Kotromanić and the Serbs.

**1353–1391:** Tvrtko I Kotromanić reigns as king of Bosnia.
**1354:** *Dušan's Code of Law* is expanded at the state gathering in Seres.
**May 1355:** Papal mission arrives in Serbia to negotiate Crusade war against the Turks.
**20 December 1355:** Emperor Dušan dies suddenly at age 46.
**1355–1371:** Rule of Uroš II, the last Serbian emperor.
**1357:** State gathering in Skoplje, feudal lords support Uroš.
**1360:** Serbian feudal lords assert their authority over parts of the empire: Vukašin and Uglješa Mrnjavčević take much of northern and eastern Macedonia; Balšići takes Zeta, Vojinovići, western Serbia; Prince Lazar Hrebeljanović, central Serbia, Vuk Branković, Kosovo, and Metohija.
**1365:** Vukašin Mrnjavčević is proclaimed king.
**26 September 1371:** Serbian army led by Vukašin and Uglješa Mrnjavčević suffers crushing defeat by the Turks at the Battle of Maritsa.
**1373:** Prince Lazar Hrebeljanović defeats Župan Nikola Altomanović; former becomes the most powerful feudal lord in Serbia.
**1377:** With the tacit support of Lazar, Tvrtko I Kotromanić proclaims himself "king of Serbs, Bosnia, Coastal and Western Lands"; the coronation takes place in the Mileševa monastery of the Serbian Orthodox Church.
**1386:** Turks capture Niš; Lazar defeats Turks at the Battle of Pločnik.
**1388:** Vlatko Vuković, Serbian Vojvoda in Bosnia, defeats Turks at Bileća.
**28 June 1389:** Battle of Kosovo; the end of the independent medieval Serbian state.
**1389–1391:** Stefan Lazarević, son of Prince Lazar, and Vuk Branković become Turkish vassals.
**1395:** Battle of Rovine; death of Kraljević Marko.
**1396:** Battle of Nicopolis; Turks defeat the Christian army led by Hungarian king Sigismund.
**1402:** Mongols defeat Turks at the Battle of Angora; Stefan Lazarević assumes the title of despot.
**1415:** First record of the use of the name Sarajevo instead of Vrhbosna.
**1421:** Death of Balša III; Stefan Lazarević extends his rule in Zeta.
**19 July 1427:** Stefan Lazarević suddenly dies.
**1427:** Hungarians occupy Mačva, Belgrade; Turks seize Niš and Golubac.
**1427–1456:** Rule of Despot Đurađ Branković.
**1430:** Building of Smederevo, new capital of the Serbian state.
**1439:** Turks capture Smederevo and the whole of Serbia; Despot Đurađ escapes to Dubrovnik and later to Hungary.
**1444:** Peace Treaty of Szegedin; Serbian state is restored within pre-1439 borders.

**24 December 1456:** Death of Despot Đurađ.
**1456–1458:** Lazar, third son of Đurađ is Serbian despot.
**1458:** Lazar dies and his older, blind brother Stefan becomes the ruler of Serbia.
**1459:** Stefan abdicates in favor of his son-in-law Stefan Tomašević, king of Bosnia.
**20 June 1459:** Stefan Tomašević allows Turks to enter Smederevo; end of the medieval Serbian state.
**1463:** Turks execute Stefan Tomašević in Jajce; end of the medieval Bosnian state; Hungarian king Mathias Corvinus establishes despotate of Srem.
**1471:** Vuk, grandson of Đurađ Branković, becomes despot of Srem.
**1481:** Turks capture Novi (Herceg Novi); the end of the medieval Hercegovina; more than 50,000 Serbs from Sarajevo and Kruševac cross Sava River and enter Srem.
**1485:** Vuk dies; he is succeeded by his cousins Đorđe and Jovan.
**c. 1516:** Đorđe dies; end of the medieval Branković family.
**29 August 1526:** Battle of Mohacs; the end of the Hungarian empire.
**1527–1535:** Struggle for the Hungarian throne between Ferdinand of Austria and John Zapolya.
**1537:** End of Serbian despotate of Srem; Turks capture Klis, the stronghold of Uskoks, who move to Senj and the mountain of Žumberak; the last Serbian despot, Pavle Bakić, dies.
**1553:** Establishment of the Austrian defense cordon in Slavonia and Croatia.
**1557:** Reestablishment of Patriarchate of Peć; Makarije Sokolović becomes patriarch.
**1579:** Death of Mehmed-Paša Sokolović; establishment of Vojna Krajina.
**27 April 1594:** Turkish commander Sinan Paşa burns the remains of St. Sava in Belgrade; insurrection of Serbs in Banat.
**1597:** First Serbian language book (primer), written and assembled by Sava Inok, is published in Venice.
**1630:** Austrian emperor grants special privileges to Serbs in Vojna Krajina—*Statuta Valachorum.*
**1683:** 250,000-strong Turkish army led by Grand Vizier Kara Mustafa passes through Serbia and besieges Vienna; Polish king defeats Turks.
**1688:** Austrians take Belgrade, Skoplje, and most of northern Macedonia.
**Mid-January 1690:** More than 30,000 Serbs led by Arsenije III Crnojević flee the advancing Turkish troops.
**28 June 1690:** Gathering in Belgrade; Arsenije demands church autonomy from the Austrians.
**1691:** Serbs elect Đorđe Branković despot; Austrians arrest Branković and

Jovan Monastirlija, an officer in the Austrian army of Serbian origin, becomes vojvoda.
**11 September 1697:** Battle of Senta (Szent); Eugen of Savoy defeats the Turks; Bishop Danilo Petrović rules in Montenegro.
**24 January 1699:** Treaty of Carlowitz.
**21 July 1718:** Treaty of Požarevac (Treaty of Passarowitz).
**1722:** Church Sabor in Petrovaradin; unification of Belgrade and Karlovci metropolitanates.
**1739:** The Austrians lose the Battle of Grocka; Treaty of Belgrade; mass exodus of the Serbs from southern Serbia.
**1747:** Establishment of the Ilirska dvorska deputacija (Illyrian Court Delegation) in Vienna, a special institution for dealing with the Serbs.
**1751–1753:** Serbian immigrants in Russia found communities called New Serbia and Slavic Serbia.
**1766:** The abolition of the Patriarchate of Peć.
**1766–1773:** Šćepan Mali (Stephen the Small) rules in Montenegro.
**1787–1791:** War between Austria and Turkey; Koča Anđelković fights Turks; Serbs in Austria are granted civil rights; Illyrian Court Delegation becomes Ilirska dvorska kancelarija (Illyrian Court Chancellory).
**February 1802:** The Dahije take over Beogradski Pašaluk.
**February 1804:** The Dahije behead 152 prominent Serbs—Seča knezova (Slaughtering of the Elders).
**14 February 1804:** Beginning of the First Serbian Insurrection; Karađorđe becomes its leader.
**5–6 August 1804:** Vojvoda Milenko Stojković captures island of Ada Kale and executes the Dahije.
**13 May 1805:** Serbs submit a petition to the Porte demanding autonomy; Turks refuse to negotiate.
**18–20 August 1805:** Serbs defeat Hafiz-Paşa in the Battle of Ivankovac.
**Late August 1805:** Establishment of the Governing Council at the assembly in Bogovađa monastery.
**Late November 1805:** Serbs liberate Smederevo.
**February 1806:** Serbs defeat the Turkish army of Pazvant-oglu.
**13 August 1806:** Serbs under direct command of Karađorđe decisively defeat the Turkish army of Bosnia.
**August 1806:** Serbian forces under Petar Dobranjac defeat Turkish southern army at Deligrad.
**30 November–27 December 1806:** Serbs liberate Belgrade.
**January 1807:** Serbs liberate Šabac; Serbian emissary Petar Ičko concludes peace with the Porte.

**7 August 1807:** Russian envoy Constantine Rodofinikin drafts and proclaims the Serbian Constitution.
**20 August 1807:** Russian emperor Alexander I rejects Rodofinikin's Constitution.
**January 1808:** Abolishment of the Republic of Dubrovnik.
**31 August 1808:** Founding of the Great School.
**7 December 1808:** Saint Clement's Day: Karađorđe is proclaimed the "hereditary Supreme leader" during an assemblage in his house.
**26 December 1808:** The Supreme Council recognizes Karađorđe as "the prime and supreme Serbian leader."
**May 1809:** Beginning of the Serbian offensive.
**May 19 1809:** Battle of Čegar, Serbs suffer crushing defeat; death of Stevan Sinđelić.
**6 September 1810:** Battle of Varvarin.
**October 1810:** Serbs aided by Russians, defeat Turks at Tičar.
**January 1811:** Enactment of several constitutional changes; the assembly confirms Karađorđe as hereditary "supreme leader" of Serbia; reorganization of the internal administrative system and the Governing Council.
**28 May 1812:** Treaty of Bucharest between Russia and Turkey; Serbia loses Russian support.
**January–July 1813:** Negotiations between the Porte and the Serbs; Serbs reject Turkish conditions.
**Mid-July 1813:** Beginning of the Turkish offensive.
**3 October 1813:** Karađorđe leaves Serbia.
**October 1813:** Turks capture Belgrade; end of the First Serbian Insurrection; Miloš Obrenović proclaimed *knez* of Rudnik.
**28 September 1814:** Rebellion of Hadži-Prodan.
**23 April 1815:** Beginning of the Second Serbian Insurrection.
**5 November 1815:** Agreement between Miloš and Maraşli Ali Paşa.
**21 November 1815:** Peace agreement between Serbs and Turks; Miloš is proclaimed supreme *knez* and leader of the Serbian people.
**February 1816:** Turks issue four decrees, Serbs achieve semi-autonomy.
**25 July 1817:** Shortly upon his return to Serbia, Karađorđe is killed by men loyal to Miloš.
**October 1817:** Miloš declares himself a hereditary Prince of Serbia.
**1821:** Local rebellion against Prince Miloš.
**25 January–4 February 1825:** Rebellion of Đak against Prince Miloš, autocratic rule.
**7 October 1825:** Akkerman Convention between Russia and the Ottoman Empire is signed: Serbs are to be granted autonomy.

**1826:** Rebellion of the Čarapić brothers against Prince Miloš.
**15–16 June 1826:** Massacre of Janissaries in Constantinople (Istanbul).
**27 April 1828:** Russia declares war on Turkey.
**14 September 1829:** Treaty of Adrianople; Russia declares itself protector of Serbian interests and demands Hatti Şerif.
**11 October 1829:** Turks complete the Hatti Şerif.
**December 1829:** Serbs officially receive Hatti Şerif.
**6 February 1830:** The great popular assembly proclaims Serbia's autonomy.
**30 October 1830:** Petar II Petrović Njegoš becomes the ruler of Montenegro.
**13 December 1830:** New Hatti Şerif; Miloš is recognized as hereditary Prince of Serbia.
**September 1831:** Patriarch of Constantinople issues a concordat and confers autonomy on the Church of Serbia.
**Late May 1833:** Turks recognize Serbia's territorial expansion.
**December 1834:** Uprising, known as Mileta's Rebellion, against Prince Miloš.
**14 February 1835:** Presentation Constitution is promulgated.
**March 1835:** Prince Miloš officially suspends the constitution.
**November 1837:** Serbia's first military academy is established in Požarevac.
**24 December 1838:** New so-called Turkish Constitution is proclaimed in the form of Hatti Şerif.
**13 June 1839:** Prince Miloš abdicates in favor of his older son Milan.
**15 June 1839:** Miloš and his younger son Mihailo Obrenović leave Serbia.
**9 July 1839:** Milan dies; a regency takes over.
**Early March 1840:** Prince Mihailo arrives in Belgrade.
**31 August–2 September 1842:** Rebellion of Toma Vučić-Perišić against Prince Mihailo.
**6–7 September 1842:** Prince Mihailo leaves Serbia.
**14 September 1842:** Alexander Karađorđević is proclaimed prince; establishment of the regime of the Constitutionalists.
**1844:** Ilija Garašanin writes Načertanije.
**4 October 1844:** The Hussar Rebellion (Katanska buna) against Prince Alexander.
**1 May 1848:** Serbian National Assembly is held in Sremski Karlovci; proclamation of Vojvodina and self-initiated restoration of Serbian patriarchate.
**12 May 1848:** Serbs in Vojvodina rebel against Hungarians.
**4 October 1853:** Turks declare war on Russia; Serbia proclaims strict neutrality.

**1855:** The first telegraph line is built in Serbia.
**30 March 1856:** Treaty of Paris; Great Powers guarantee Serbia's territorial integrity.
**13 December 1857–4 January 1858:** St. Andrew Assembly; deposition of Prince Alexander.
**5 January 1858:** Restoration of prince Miloš Obrenović.
**September 1860:** Prince Miloš dies at age of 80; Mihailo assumes the throne of Serbia.
**19 August 1861:** Transfiguration Assembly.
**15 June 1862:** Incident at Čukur česma (Kükürt Çeşme—"Sulphur Spring"), Serbian boy is killed by three Turkish soldiers.
**18 June 1862:** Turkish artillery shells Belgrade for four and a half hours.
**8 September 1862:** Conclusion of Kanlice Conference; Turks to withdraw from two of six garrisons.
**6 October 1863:** The Great School becomes the highest institution of learning in Serbia.
**27–29 August 1866:** Ujedinjena omladina srpska (United Serbian Youth) is founded.
**23 September 1866:** Secret offensive and defensive alliance between Serbia and Montenegro.
**18 April 1867:** Serbs take over the fortress of Kalemegdan.
**6 May 1867:** The last Turkish soldier leaves Serbia.
**26 August 1867:** Treaty of Voeslau between Serbia and Greece.
**1 February 1868:** Conclusion of Serbo-Romanian alliance.
**10 June 1868:** Assassination of Prince Mihailo.
**2 July 1868:** Milan Obrenović becomes prince of Serbia; regency of Jovan Ristić, General Milivoje Petrović Blaznavac, and Jovan Gavrilović takes over.
**11 July 1869:** Trinity Constitution; first Serbian bank is founded.
**22 August 1872:** Milan celebrates his 18th birthday, comes legally of age, and assumes the throne.
**June 1875:** Rebellion of Hercegovina.
**22 June 1876:** Serbian cabinet decides on war against the Ottoman Empire.
**30 June 1876:** Serbia declares war.
**29 October 1876:** Battle of Đunis; Serbs suffer great losses.
**25 January 1877:** Peace agreement between Serbia and Turkey.
**24 April 1877:** Russia declares war on Turkey, urges Serbia to join.
**13 December 1877:** Serbia declares war on Turkey; Serbs liberate Niš, Pirot, and Vranje.
**3 March 1878:** Treaty of San Stefano.

**13 June–13 July 1878:** Congress of Berlin; Serbia and Montenegro gain full independence; Bosnia and Hercegovina come under Austro-Hungarian occupation.
**22 December 1878:** Serbia establishes its own currency—silver Dinar.
**1881:** The abolition of Vojna Krajina.
**28 June 1881:** Serbia and Austria-Hungary sign the Trade Treaty: Serbia becomes economically dependent on Austria-Hungary; Prince Milan signs the Secret Convention with Austria-Hungary, limits Serbia's political independence.
**6 March 1882:** Serbia is proclaimed a kingdom.
**23 October 1882:** Attempted assassination of Prince Milan.
**1883:** Belgrade installs its first telephone lines.
**18 January 1883:** National Bank of Serbia is founded.
**19 September 1883:** First elections involving electioneering by organized parties take place; the Radical Party wins but King Milan ignores the election results.
**October 1883:** Rebellion of Timok; Nikola Pašić escapes from Serbia.
**14 November 1885:** King Milan declares war on Bulgaria.
**17 November 1885:** Battle of Slivnica; Serbian army retreats hastily.
**27 November 1885:** Bulgars capture Pirot; Austria-Hungary mediates the conflict.
**13 January 1886:** King Milan amnesties all the participants in the Timok Rebellion.
**3 March 1886:** Peace Treaty between Bulgaria and Serbia is signed.
**1887:** Serbian Academy of Sciences and Arts is founded.
**12 May 1887:** Queen Natalia and Prince Alexander Obrenović leave Serbia.
**September 1888:** General elections in Serbia; Radical Party wins.
**25 October 1888:** King Milan divorces Queen Natalia.
**5 January 1889:** Parliament promulgates the new constitution; considerable democratization and internal administrative reorganization of Serbia.
**6 March 1889:** King Milan abdicates in favor of his minor son Alexander and leaves Serbia; the Royal Regency takes over.
**19 May 1891:** Queen Natalia is expelled from Serbia; violent clashes between demonstrators and army in Belgrade.
**13 April 1893:** Alexander dismisses the regency and takes royal authority into his own hands while still under age.
**21 May 1894:** King Alexander abolishes the Constitution of 1889 and restores the Constitution of 1869.
**23 October 1897:** King Alexander establishes a personal regime: Vladan Đorđević becomes prime minister, ex-king Milan assumes the command of the Serbian army.

**6 July 1899:** Attempted assassination of ex-King Milan; heavy repression throughout Serbia.
**21 July 1900:** Despite universal opposition King Alexander marries Draga Mašin; ex-king Milan leaves the country.
**29 January 1901:** Ex-King Milan dies in Vienna.
**19 April 1901:** New constitution is promulgated by royal decree.
**4 August 1901:** General elections in Serbia: the "Old" Radicals win majority of seats in Parliament.
**5 March 1902:** Local rebellion against King Alexander in Šabac.
**5 April 1903:** Demonstrations of trade apprentices turn into a huge and violent anti-Obrenović rally.
**10–11 June 1903:** King Alexander and Queen Draga are assassinated: end of the Obrenović dynasty.
**18 June 1903:** Parliament proclaims Peter I Karađorđević king of Serbia; promulgation of the new Constitution.
**25 June 1903:** Peter I arrives in Serbia; protesting at the brutal killing of Alexander and Draga, European powers stage a diplomatic strike.
**2 August 1903:** St. Elijah Uprising (Ilinden Uprising) in western Macedonia.
**12 April 1904:** Serbia and Bulgaria sign treaties on economic and political cooperation.
**8 September 1904:** King Peter is crowned in Belgrade Cathedral.
**1905:** The Great School is reorganized into the University of Belgrade.
**11 June 1905:** Five officers implicated for their participation in the assassination of Alexander and Draga resign; Great Britain formally recognizes the dynastic change; end of the diplomatic strike.
**22 June 1905:** Customs agreement between Bulgaria and Serbia.
**7 July 1906:** Tariff War between Austria-Hungary and Serbia.
**5 July 1908:** Young Turks rebel in the Macedonian town of Resen.
**5 October 1908:** Bulgaria declares independence from the Ottoman Empire.
**6 October 1908:** Austria-Hungary proclaims the annexation of Bosnia and Hercegovina (Annexation Crisis).
**December 1908:** Narodna Odbrana (the National Defense), a Serbian patriotic organization is founded.
**12 January 1909:** Agreement between Austria-Hungary and Turkey; Turkey recognizes the annexation of Bosnia and Hercegovina in return for 2.5 million Turkish pounds.
**26 February 1909:** Turkey officially recognizes the Austro-Hungarian annexation of Bosnia-Hercegovina.
**31 March 1909:** Serbia recognizes the annexation of Bosnia-Hercegovina and promises to cease anti-Austrian propaganda.

**Early October 1909:** Conspiracy known as the Kolašin Affair against Montenegrin Prince Nikola I Petrović is revealed.
**28 August 1910:** Montenegrin Parliament passes a resolution elevating the principality to the rank of kingdom and Nikola I to the rank of king.
**9 May 1911:** Unification or Death, a secret Serbian patriotic organization, is founded.
**13 March 1912:** Conclusion of a Serbo-Bulgarian treaty; secret annex calls for the division of Macedonia.
**12 May 1912:** Serbo-Bulgarian military convention.
**12 June 1912:** Greco-Bulgarian alliance.
**June 1912:** Montenegro signs military convention with Greece.
**August 1912:** Montenegro-Bulgarian military alliance.
**14 September 1912:** Serbia and Montenegro conclude an offensive military alliance against Turkey.
**8 October 1912:** Montenegro declares war on Turkey: beginning of the Balkan Wars.
**17–18 October 1912:** Serbia, Greece, and Bulgaria declare war on Turkey.
**24 October 1912:** Serbs defeat Turks at the Battle of Kumanovo; Bulgarians defeat Turks at Kirk Kilissa.
**15–19 November 1912:** Serbs decisively defeat Turks at the Battle of Bitolj.
**3 December 1912:** Bulgaria, Serbia, and Montenegro sign an armistice with Turkey.
**3 January 1913:** Opening of the peace conference in London.
**23 January 1913:** Fighting resumes; Serbia asks for a revision of its treaty with Bulgaria.
**6 March 1913:** Greeks take Ioannina.
**26 March 1913:** Bulgarians and Serbs capture Edirne.
**10 April 1913:** Blockade of Montenegrin coast by the Great Powers to raise the siege of Shkodër.
**22 April 1913:** Montenegro captures Shkodër.
**1 May 1913:** Serbia and Greece sign an agreement and anti-Bulgarian military convention.
**30 May 1913:** Conclusion of the peace treaty in London; Serbia does not get a corridor to the Adriatic coast.
**29–30 June 1913:** Bulgarian troops attack Serbia and Greece without a declaration of war; Serbs defeat Bulgarians at the Battle of Bregalnica.
**30 July 1913:** Treaty of Bucharest.
**28 June 1914:** Assassination of Archduke Franz Ferdinand in Sarajevo (Sarajevo Assassination).
**25 July 1914:** Austria-Hungary delivers Ultimatum to Serbia.

**26 July 1914:** Serbian government accepts the ultimatum with minimal reservations; Austria-Hungary ends diplomatic relations with Serbia.
**28 July 1914:** Austria-Hungary declares war on Serbia; outbreak of World War I.
**15–24 August 1914:** Serbian army decisively defeats the Austro-Hungarian forces in the Battle of Cer.
**September 1914:** Second Austro-Hungarian offensive begins.
**16 November–15 December 1914:** Serbian army crushes the Austro-Hungarian forces at the Battle of Kolubara.
**22 November 1914:** Yugoslav Committee is founded in Florence.
**1915:** Typhus epidemic spreads over Serbia.
**6 October 1915:** Combined Austro-German offensive.
**9–11 October 1915:** Fall of Belgrade and Smederevo; Bulgarian forces attack the Serbian army.
**14 October 1915:** Bulgaria officially declares war on Serbia.
**28 November 1915:** Serbian army begins its retreat through Albania.
**13 January 1916:** Austro-Hungarians capture Montenegrin capital Cetinje; King Nikola escapes to Italy.
**15 January 1916:** Serbian army lands on Corfu island.
**August–September 1916:** Serbian army captures Kajmakčalan.
**19 November 1916:** Serbian and French forces liberate Bitolj.
**2 April–14 June 1917:** Trial of Salonika.
**26 June 1917:** Execution of Colonel Dragutin Dimitrijević Apis.
**20 July 1917:** Corfu Declaration is signed between the Yugoslav Committee and the Serbian Government.
**15 September 1918:** Allies begin an offensive on the Salonika Front.
**6 October 1918:** National Council of Slovenes, Croats, and Serbs is organized in Zagreb.
**10 October 1918:** Liberation of Niš.
**29 October 1918:** State of Slovenes, Croats, and Serbs is proclaimed in Zagreb.
**1 November 1918:** Serbian army liberates Belgrade.
**3 November 1918:** Armistice is concluded between the Allies and Austria-Hungary.
**6–9 November 1918:** Geneva Conference; signing of Geneva Declaration, founding of a common Yugoslav state.
**26 November 1918:** National assembly of Montenegro proclaims union with Serbia; end of the Petrović dynasty.
**1 December 1918:** Proclamation of the Kingdom of the Serbs, Croats, and Slovenes (SHS) in Belgrade.

**1919:** A comprehensive land reform is introduced.
**March 1919:** Establishment of a provisional parliament.
**20–23 April 1919:** Communist Party of Yugoslavia is founded.
**14 August 1920:** Treaty of alliance between the SHS and Czechoslovakia which became foundation of Little Entente.
**10 October 1920:** Klagenfurt Plebiscite; Slovene-speaking population of northern Slovenia opts for Austria.
**12 November 1920:** The Treaty of Rapallo between Italy and the SHS.
**28 November 1920:** Elections for the Constituent Assembly; Communist Party wins 59 seats.
**8 December 1920:** Croatian Peasant Party proclaims an illegal Neutral Peasant Republic of Croatia.
**30 December 1920:** Government of the SHS promulgates Obznana.
**27 June 1921:** Treaty with Romania, second link in the Little Entente.
**28 June 1921:** Proclamation of the Vidovdan Constitution.
**29 June 1921:** A young Communist attempts to assassinate Prince Regent Alexander I Karađorđević.
**21 July 1921:** Assassination of Milorad Drašković, minister of interior of the SHS.
**1 August 1921:** Government of the SHS enacts the Law Concerning the Protection of Public Security and Order in the State (Zakon o zaštiti države).
**16 August 1921:** Death of King Peter; Alexander I Karađorđević becomes king.
**18 March 1923:** General elections; the Radical Party of Nikola Pašić wins a relative majority of votes.
**8 February 1925:** Elections; Radicals confirm their supremacy.
**18 July 1925:** Croatian Peasant Party forms a coalition government with the Radicals.
**November 1925:** Stjepan Radić becomes the minister of education.
**10 December 1926:** Nikola Pašić dies after a stormy session with King Alexander.
**June 1927:** Repeated border violations by Albanian forces.
**11 September 1927:** Elections; the Radical Party wins relative majority; however, Radić and Svetozar Pribićević form the coalition government.
**8 February 1928:** Coalition government collapses.
**20 June 1928:** Puniša Račić, a deputy of the Radical Party, kills two deputies of the Croatian Peasant Party and wounds Stjepan Radić.
**27 July 1928:** Four-party coalition government is formed.
**August 1928:** Stjepan Radić dies in Zagreb; Vladko Maček becomes leader of the Croatian Peasant Party.

**2 January 1929:** Anton Korošec, prime minister, resigns.
**6 January 1929:** King Alexander imposes personal rule (Dictatorship of January 6); General Petar Živković becomes prime minister.
**27 March 1929:** Treaty of friendship between the SHS and Greece.
**June 1929:** Increased terrorist activity by Bulgarian bands in Macedonia; border between two states is sealed.
**3 October 1929:** Name of the SHS is changed to the Kingdom of Yugoslavia; thorough internal reorganization of the country.
**3 September 1931:** King Alexander proclaims the Octroyed Constitution.
**14 November 1932:** Croatian Peasant Party denounces the regime and demands autonomy.
**15 February 1933:** Reorganization of the Little Entente.
**8 February 1934:** Conclusion of the Balkan Pact between Yugoslavia, Greece, Romania, and Turkey.
**1 June 1934:** Conclusion of a trade agreement between Kingdom of Yugoslavia and Germany.
**9 October 1934:** King Alexander is assassinated by Ustaše terrorists in Marseilles; Peter II Karađorđević becomes king; royal powers are assumed by a regency headed by Pavle Karađorđević, the late Alexander's first cousin.
**3 May 1935:** General elections.
**24 May 1935:** Although the government list wins majority of votes, prime minister Jevtić resigns.
**20 June 1935:** Milan Stojadinović forms new cabinet.
**19 August 1935:** Stojadinović founds the Yugoslav Radical Union.
**1936:** Yugoslavia concludes a barter agreement with Germany: economic and political dependence on Germany increases.
**24 January 1937:** Signing of Yugoslav-Bulgarian Treaty of Friendship and Perpetual Peace.
**25 March 1937:** Conclusion of a nonaggression pact with Italy.
**July 1937:** Josip Broz, Tito, becomes general secretary of the Communist Party of Yugoslavia.
**23 July 1937:** Ratification of Concordat; friction between Serbian Orthodox Church and the government develops.
**6 October 1937:** Formation of the National Block Agreement.
**11 December 1938:** Parliamentary elections: Stojadinović wins; Maček and Croatian Peasant Party's deputies refuse to take their seats in Parliament.
**4 February 1939:** Fall from power of Stojadinović; Dragiša Cvetković becomes prime minister.
**April 1939:** Beginning of negotiations between Cvetković and Maček.

**May 1939:** Yugoslav gold reserves are shipped to Great Britain and, later, to the Federal Reserve Bank in New York.
**26 August 1939:** Cvetković-Maček Agreement; Maček becomes vice prime minister; the Croatian Banovina is created; beginning of the end of the unified Yugoslav state.
**1 September 1939:** Germany invades Poland; the beginning of World War II.
**10 June 1940:** Establishment of diplomatic relations between Yugoslavia and the Soviet Union.
**25 March 1941:** Cvetković signs Yugoslavia's adherence to the Tripartite Pact.
**26–27 March 1941:** Coup d'etat of March 27: King Peter II assumes royal power; the government of Cvetković and Maček is overthrown; General Dušan Simović forms the new government.
**6 April 1941:** Beginning of April's War, Germany invades Yugoslavia without the declaration of war; heavy bombardment of Belgrade; king and government flee to Pale and then to Nikšić.
**10 April 1941:** Germans enter Zagreb; the proclamation of the Independent State of Croatia.
**12 April 1941:** Germans capture Belgrade.
**15 April 1941:** King and government leave the country.
**16 April 1941:** Ante Pavelić become the Poglavnik-Führer of the Independent State of Croatia.
**17 April 1941:** Yugoslav army capitulates; dismemberment of Yugoslavia.
**May 1941:** Ustaše begins with the "purification" of Croatia, genocide against Serbs begins.
**12 May 1941:** Colonel Dragoljub-Draža Mihailović arrives on Ravna Gora, the beginning of the organized antifascist resistance movement known as Četniks and Jugoslovenska Vojska u Otadžbini (JVO).
**22 June 1941:** Germany invades the Soviet Union.
**4 July 1941:** Communist Party decides to launch an armed struggle against German occupation; series of insurrections: Serbia (July 7), Montenegro (July 13), Bosnia and Hercegovina (July 22), Slovenia and Croatia (July 27).
**August 1941:** Milan Nedić becomes prime minister of the German-installed government of Serbia.
**September 1941:** The JVO and the Partisans liberate Užice. Communist-led Partisans establish the "Užice republic."
**20–23 October 1941:** In a German reprisal between 5,000 and 7,000 people are executed in Kraljevo and Kragujevac.

**November–December 1941:** German offensive; first clashes between the JVO and the Partisans; Partisans' withdrawal to Sandžak and to Bosnia.
**21 December 1941:** First "shock" brigade is formed; reorganization of the Partisan units.
**January 1942:** Yugoslav government-in-exile elevates Colonel Mihailović to the rank of General (January 19) and appoints him minister of war (January 11) and chief of staff.
**26–27 November 1942:** AVNOJ is founded in Bihać.
**March 1943:** German offensive against Partisans (Battle of Neretva).
**May–June 1943:** Battle of Sutjeska: German offensive fails to destroy Partisans; severe clashes between the JVO and Partisans.
**28–29 November 1943:** Second session of AVNOJ; establishment of the founding principles of the future Yugoslav state; establishment of the Communist-led government of Yugoslavia.
**25 January–8 February 1944:** January 25–February 8, the JVO and Ravnogorski pokret hold the congress at village of Ba.
**1 June 1944:** Ivan Šubašić, former Ban of the Croatian Banovina, becomes prime minister of the government-in-exile; Šubašić meets with Tito, accepts the resolutions of AVNOJ, and agrees to the formation of a joint government with the Communists.
**1 October 1944:** Soviet Red Army enters Yugoslavia.
**20 October 1944:** Partisans and the Red Army enter Belgrade; general mobilization in Serbia; the JVO suffers decisive defeat.
**December 1944:** Germans repulse an attack by Partisans; formation of the Sremski Front.
**January 1945:** Insurrection instigated by Balisti in Kosovo and Metohija.
**7 March 1945:** Provisional government is formed; the proclamation of Democratic Federal Yugoslavia.
**8 May 1945**: End of World War II in Europe.
**15 May 1945:** German forces surrender in Yugoslavia.
**25 May 1945:** Crushing defeat of JVO forces.
**19 June 1945:** AVNOJ forms a special committee for establishing the administrative border between Vojvodina and Croatia.
**23 August 1945:** Introduction of a land reform law.
**1 September 1945:** New administrative division of Serbia is introduced.
**29 November 1945:** Yugoslavia is proclaimed a republic.
**31 January 1946:** Proclamation of the Federal People's Republic of Yugoslavia (Federativna Narodna Republika Jugoslavija); promulgation of a Soviet-style constitution.

**February 1946:** Capture of General Mihailović.

**June–July 1946:** Trial (June 10) and execution of General Mihailović (July 17).

**1947:** Tito and Bulgarian leader Georgi Dimitrov negotiate formation of a Balkan Federation that would encompass Bulgaria, Yugoslavia, and Albania.

**28 June 1948:** Cominform Resolution; break with the Soviet Union: Yugoslavia becomes completely estranged from the Communist countries.

**September 1948:** Establishment of the prison camp at island of Goli Otok.

**January 1949:** Collectivization of agriculture begins.

**June 1950:** Enactment of the Basic Law on the Management of State Economic Enterprises by Working Collectives; the introduction of Self-management.

**November 1952:** Communist Party changes its name to League of Communists of Yugoslavia (LCY).

**January 1953:** Changes to the constitution are initiated; the Chamber of Nationalities is removed and the Chamber of Producers is introduced; Tito officially becomes president of the country.

**1954:** Istria is divided between Italy and Yugoslavia; introduction of so-called Novi Sad Agreement, unification of Serbian and Croatian languages into a single language.

**April 1955:** Bandung Conference, the beginning of the Nonaligned Movement.

**May 1955:** Relations with the Soviet Union begin to normalize; Nikita Khruschev visits Yugoslavia.

**1957:** In a preface to his book *Development of the Slovenian National Issue*, Edvard Kardelj, the leading Communist ideologist, criticizes tendencies of "integral Yugoslavism" and affirmation of the nationality of Yugoslavs.

**16 March 1962:** Tito convenes an extraordinary session of the Presidium of the Central Committee of the LCY to deal exclusively with the issue of growing nationalism.

**7 April 1963:** New Constitution is promulgated; country's name is changed to the Socialist Federal Republic of Yugoslavia; thorough administrative reorganization; five chambers are introduced in Parliament.

**July 1965:** Parliament passes a series of over 30 laws that liberalize the economy and introduce "market socialism"; rapid increase of inflation, devaluation of dinar, a rapid increase in unemployment.

**1 July 1966:** Aleksandar Ranković, vice-president of Yugoslavia, and Svetislav Stefanović, federal secretary of internal affairs, are removed from all posts during a session of Central Committee of the LCY.

**16 March 1967:** Publication of "Deklaracija" (Declaration), a statement signed by leading Croat intellectuals, and high ranking officials in the LCY and cultural institutions in Croatia asserting the separate existence of a Croatian linguistic and literary tradition; the denial of the validity of Serbo-Croatian as a historic language.
**18 April 1967:** Through lobbying by Croatia, Parliament passes four constitutional amendments which restrict economic powers of the Yugoslav Federation.
**29–30 May 1968:** Dobrica Ćosić, resigns from the Central Committee of the League of Communists of Serbia in protest at the growing Albanian nationalism in Kosovo and Metohija.
**3 June 1968:** Outbreak of student demonstrations in Belgrade.
**27 November 1968:** Violent mass demonstration in Kosovo and Metohija, Albanian demonstrators demand the status of a republic for Kosovo; police and army quell the demonstrations.
**26 December 1968:** Parliament passes amendments 7–19 to the constitution: the basic principles of autonomous provinces are changed, the prerogatives of the local legal, executive, and judicial authorities are substantially increased; and the name of Kosovo and Metohija is changed into the Socialist Autonomous Province of Kosovo.
**15 March 1969:** Ninth Congress of the LCY is held in Belgrade; introduction of so-called "parity" principle in the party leadership according to which an equal number of members from each republic and a corresponding number from the provinces would constitute the Presidency of the LCY.
**31 July 1969:** The so-called "Road affair"; the visible outbreak of Slovenian nationalism and economic particularism.
**14–17 January 1970:** Tenth Session of the League of Communists of Croatia; the leadership of the party openly espouses nationalist agenda; economic and political independence and the establishment of the Croatian army discussed.
**30 June 1971:** Parliament passes amendments 20–42 to the constitution: autonomous provinces become "sovereign" administrative units; federalization of Serbia; the term "nationality" replaces the term "national minority."
**23 November–3 December 1971:** Student strike in the University of Zagreb: students' demands echo the nationalist program of the Croatian Communist leadership.
**1–2 December 1971:** Twenty-sixth session of the Presidency of the LCY is held in Karađorđevo; Tito removes the nationalist leadership of Croatia.
**26 October 1972:** Removal of the Serbian leadership because of tendencies toward "liberalism" and "technocratism."

**21 February 1974:** Promulgation of the new constitution: the independent position of the republics is strengthened, while autonomous provinces become constitutive elements of the federation; introduction of consensus in the decision-making process; serious economic and political decentralization of the country.
**25 November 1976:** Introduction of the Law of Associated Labor which hinges upon strong anti market premises; further strengthening of autarchic tendencies.
**4 May 1980:** Tito dies, Lazar Koliševski becomes president of the collective presidency of the SFRY.
**11 March 1981:** Outbreak of violent anti-Yugoslav demonstration in Priština; demonstrations spread throughout Kosovo and Metohija; numerous Serbian medieval monuments are damaged.
**2 April 1981:** SFRY Presidency declares a state of emergency and forms the Joint Police Troops of the Federal Ministry of Internal Affairs.
**1–15 April 1981:** Fifth postwar census is carried out in Yugoslavia: between 1945 and 1981 the population of Kosovo and Metohija increased from 350,000 to 1,303,000.
**July 1983:** Trial of a Muslim fundamentalist group in Bosnia and Hercegovina; Alija Izetbegović is sentenced to 14 years in prison for his authorship of the *Islamic Declaration.*
**4 July 1983:** Parliament adopts a document known as the *Long-Term Program of Economic Stabilization*.
**20 August 1983:** Aleksandar Ranković dies, his funeral is attended by nearly 100,000 people; the first mass demonstration of Serbian discontent with the situation in Kosovo and Metohija.
**24 September 1986:** The Memorandum of the Serbian Academy of Sciences and Arts is published in Belgrade's leading daily tabloid; this document on the political economy of Yugoslavia and the status of Serbia is seen by many as a prime example of Serbian nationalism.
**24 April 1987:** Slobodan Milošević, the president of the Presidency of the League of Communist of Serbia, visits Kosovo Polje in response to Serbian complaints against aggressive Albanian nationalism.
**19 June 1987:** Yugoslav Writers' Society violates its statute and fails to elect Serbian writer Miodrag Bulatović as chair and consequently dissolves—the first Yugoslav organization to be dismantled because of national antagonism.
**August 1987:** Financial scandal known as "Agrokomerc" in Bosnia and Hercegovina; Fikret Abdić is imprisoned due to his role in it; numerous

individuals and institutions are implicated, including the Bosnian Muslim representative and acting vice president of the Presidency of the SFRY, Hamdija Pozderac.

**23–24 September 1987:** Eight Session of the Central Committee of the League of Communists of Serbia is held in Belgrade, a major political victory for Slobodan Milošević, who soon becomes the undisputed leader in Serbia.

**5–6 October 1988:** Mass demonstration in Novi Sad; the leadership of the provincial Communist organization resigns.

**17 November 1988:** Removal of the Albanian Provincial Communist leadership of Kosovo; mass protest of Albanians.

**19 November 1988:** Nearly one million people attend the rally of "Brotherhood and Unity" in Belgrade.

**10–11 January 1989:** Mass rally is held in front of the Parliament in Montenegro; the resignation of the republic's leadership.

**February 1989:** Strike by 1,000 Albanian miners in Trepča; miners protest the removal of the Communist Albanian leadership.

**27 February 1989:** Slovenian leadership openly supports Albanian demonstrators.

**28 February–1 March 1989:** Mass gathering in front of the Parliament: around one million people demand the settlement of the situation in Kosovo.

**3 March 1989:** A curfew is imposed in Kosovo.

**17 March 1989:** Ante Marković becomes prime minister of the SFRY.

**28 March 1989:** Amendments to the Constitution of Serbia are promulgated; the autonomous provinces are denied a veto on constitutional changes in Serbia and stripped of legislative, juridical, and executive powers.

**May 1989:** Slobodan Milošević is elected president of the Presidency of Serbia.

**28 June 1989:** Celebration of the 600th anniversary of the Battle of Kosovo.

**July 1989:** Organized celebration of the Battle of Kosovo is banned in Croatia.

**August 1989:** Croatian Parliament passes a bill on the name of the language, thus effectively erasing Serbian as the language of the Serbian people in Croatia.

**1 December 1989:** Slovenian authorities ban a rally of Serbs and Montenegrins from Kosovo in Ljubljana; Serbia institutes a general boycott of Slovenian goods and services.

**18 December 1989:** Introduction of the Marković Reform.

**20–22 January 1990:** Slovene and Croat delegations walk out from the 14th Special Congress of the LCY.

**1–2 February 1990:** Severe clashes between police and Albanian demonstrators in Kosovo: 27 demonstrators are killed and 54 injured, 1 policeman killed and 43 injured.
**24–25 February 1990:** First general meeting of the Croatian Democratic Union (HDZ); party leader Franjo Tudjman declares "The Independent State of Croatia was not just a mere quisling creation or fascist crime, but also expression of the historical aspirations of the Croatian people."
**8 April 1990:** Parliamentary and presidential elections in Slovenia: the united opposition wins an absolute majority; Milan Kučan, the Communist candidate, wins presidential elections.
**22 April–6 May 1990:** General elections in Croatia: the HDZ wins two-thirds majority in all three houses of Parliament thanks to majority electoral system; Tudjman becomes president of Croatia.
**5 July 1990:** Serbian Parliament dissolves the Parliament of Kosovo following the illegal proclamation of a Kosovo republic (July 2); the SFRY Presidency approves of the Serbian measures (July 11).
**25 July 1990:** Constitutional changes in Croatia; introduction of the traditional Croatian insignia (chessboard) used during the existence of the Independent State of Croatia; an assembly of Serbs issues a Declaration on the Sovereignty and Independence of Serbs in Croatia and establishes the Serbian National Council.
**16 August 1990:** Serbian National Council decides to hold a referendum on the autonomy of Serbs in Croatia.
**17 August 1990:** Croatian special police units attack a local police station in Benkovac; Serbs set up barricades throughout Kninska Krajina; the beginning of Serbian uprising.
**27–30 September 1990:** Croatian special police forces arrest 360 Serbs in Petrinja; population takes refuge in the barracks of the JNA (Jugoslovenska narodna armija).
**Early November 1990:** U.S. State Department strongly advocates holding elections in the remaining four Yugoslav republics; the suspension of economic aid is threatened.
**11–25 November 1990:** Elections in Macedonia: the nationalists win the greatest number of parliamentary seats (37).
**18 November 1990:** Parliamentary elections in Bosnia and Hercegovina: the Party of Democratic Action (SDA) wins 86 seats, the Serbian Democratic Party (SDS) 72 seats, and the HDZ 44 seats.
**9 December 1990:** Elections in Serbia and Montenegro: the Socialist Party of Serbia (SPS) wins an absolute majority and Slobodan Milošević is elected

president; League of Communists wins in Montenegro, Momir Bulatović is elected president.

**22 December 1990:** Promulgation of the new Croatian Constitution; Croatia is proclaimed "the national state of the Croatian People."

**26 December 1990:** Slovenian Parliament proclaims independence of the republic.

**9 January 1991:** The SFRY Presidency issues an executive order that calls for the disbandment of all irregular armed forces and surrender of all illegal weapons; Croatia and Slovenia refuse to comply.

**10 January 1991:** In response to an unauthorized monetary issue by Serbia, the Parliament of Slovenia declares its withdrawal from the federal fiscal system; official protest by the Federal Government (January 17).

**22 January 1991:** Beginning of a series of meetings between representatives of the Federal Government and presidents of the republics; future arrangements between the republics and the federation are negotiated.

**24–25 January 1991:** Military police make numerous arrests for illegal arms trafficking in Croatia; the Military Court issues a warrant for the arrest of Croatian defense minister Martin Špegelj (January 31); the Parliament of Macedonia declares independence.

**27 January 1991:** Kiro Gligorov is appointed president of Macedonia.

**20 February 1991:** Croatia declares the precedence of the republic's laws over the SFRY Constitution.

**28 February 1991:** The Serbian National Council and the Executive Council of the Serbian Autonomous Region of Krajina decide to initiate separation from Croatia and remain in Yugoslavia.

**2 March 1991:** Croatian special police attack a local police station in Pakrac; armed clashes with the local Serbian population; JNA intervention.

**4 March 1991:** Wave of refugees from Vukovar and Osijek arrives in Serbia.

**9 March 1991:** Mass demonstrations against Serbian government in Belgrade.

**12–14 March 1991:** Supreme Command of the JNA proposes to raise the combat readiness of the troops (rejected by the Presidency of the SFRY).

**28 March 1991:** First meeting of the six presidents of the republics, known as "the summit of the six," is held in Split.

**31 March 1991:** Armed conflict between Croatian special police and members of the SAO Krajina police: the JNA intervenes.

**4 April 1991:** Second round of negotiations between presidents of the republics is held in Belgrade.

**11 April 1991:** Third "summit of the six" is held in Kranj, Slovenia; an agreement is reached that the future status of Yugoslavia (confederation or federation) should be decided by a series of referendums in May.

**17 April 1991:** U.S. Senate passes Resolution 106: warns against a military coup in Yugoslavia.

**18 April 1991:** Fourth "summit of the six" in held in Ohrid; the Croatian Parliament declares the establishment of the National Guard.

**29 April 1991:** Fifth "summit of the six" is held in Cetinje: no progress in negotiating is reported.

**2 May 1991:** Armed clashes between the Serbian population and Croatian special police in Borovo Selo.

**6 May 1991:** First open confrontation between Croatian civilians and the JNA (in Split); one JNA soldier is killed.

**9 May 1991:** SFRY Presidency orders the JNA to prevent ethnic conflict in the Serb populated areas in Croatia.

**13 May 1991:** President of the Pan-European Union, Otto von Habsburg, states that the union proposed to the European Community (EC) that they recognize the independence of Slovenia and Croatia.

**15 May 1991:** Members of the SFRY Presidency from Serbia, Montenegro, Kosovo, and Vojvodina vote against Croatian representative Stjepan Mesić, thus preventing the regular rotation of presidents.

**19 May 1991:** Referendum on separation from Yugoslavia is held in Croatia; Serbs from SAO Krajina boycott it.

**20 May 1991:** U.S. State Department suspends economic aid to Yugoslavia because of Serbian measures in Kosovo.

**21 June 1991:** U.S. Secretary of State, James Baker, visits Yugoslavia and declares that the U.S. supports a democratic and unified Yugoslavia and would not recognize unilateral secessions.

**26 June 1991:** The Croatian and Slovenian Parliaments proclaim independence and initiate secessions of Croatia and Slovenia from Yugoslavia; Slovenian and Croatian police and paramilitary units began to occupy Yugoslav border posts.

**26 June 1991:** Federal government orders the JNA and federal police to regain control over the state borders; armed clashes between the JNA and Slovenia begin.

**28 June 1991:** Prime Minister Ante Marković calls for a cease-fire; the JNA regains control of the border posts in Slovenia; the EC sends a ministerial team to Yugoslavia (Jacques Posse, Gianni de Michaelis, and Hans van den Broek).

**1 July 1991:** Stjepan Mesić is declared President of the SFRY.

**5 July 1991:** At a summit of the EC foreign ministers in The Hague, German foreign minister Hans Dietrich Genscher proposes the imposition of an arms embargo and suspension of financial aid to Yugoslavia.
**7 July 1991:** "Brioni" Conference is held under the auspices of the EC: establishment of a three-month moratorium on secessions of Croatia and Slovenia, the JNA withdrawal from Slovenia within a period of three months; Croatian paramilitary units attack JNA forces in Baranja region.
**12 August 1991:** Meeting between representatives of Serbia, Montenegro and Bosnia and Hercegovina: the so-called Belgrade Initiative is adopted.
**21 August 1991:** Siege against JNA barracks begins in Croatia; water, food, and electricity are cut off; conflict between the JNA and Croatian paramilitary intensifies.
**3 September 1991:** The EC decides to convene a conference on Yugoslavia, Lord Peter Carrington is appointed chair, the Conference opens in The Hague (September 7) and the first plenary session begins (September 12).
**7 September 1991:** Referendum is held in Macedonia; 74 percent of the voters opt for sovereignty.
**21 September 1991:** Following numerous skirmishes with Croatian paramilitary forces, the JNA begins an offensive on the Dubrovnik front.
**26 September 1991:** UN Security Council adopts Resolution 713; an arms embargo is imposed on Yugoslavia.
**4 October 1991:** First in a series of proposals for solving the Yugoslav crisis is issued: Yugoslavia is envisioned as a loose confederation of sovereign republics with a special status for the Serbs in Croatia.
**15 October 1991:** Muslim and Croatian parliamentary deputies adopt the memorandum on a Sovereign Bosnia and Hercegovina; Serbian deputies leave the session in protest.
**18 October 1991:** Second session of the conference on Yugoslavia is held; Lord Carrington offers a new proposal on the future of the Yugoslav state (October 23) which does not include special status for the Serbian population in Croatia.
**25 October 1991:** Parliament of the Serbian people in Bosnia and Hercegovina is constituted.
**30 October–5 November 1991:** Third and fourth versions of Lord Carrington's proposals are offered; Serbia and Montenegro reject them.
**7–8 November 1991:** EC Ministerial Council decides to impose economic sanctions against Yugoslavia; later decided that sanctions should be applied only against Serbia and Montenegro (December 2).
**9–10 November 1991:** Referendum of the Serbian population in Bosnia

and Hercegovina: more than 90 percent of the voters decide to remain within Yugoslavia.

**22 November 1991:** Meeting between Slobodan Milošević and Cyrus Vance, personal envoy of the UN secretary-general: the deployment of UN peacekeeping forces in Croatia is discussed.

**27 November 1991:** Security Council of the UN passes Resolution 721 on the need for deployment of peacekeeping forces in Yugoslavia; Resolution 724 (December 15) endorses the offer of the secretary general to send to Yugoslavia a small group of military personal to prepare for possible deployment.

**4 December 1991:** Germany stops all traffic and transport links with Serbia and Montenegro.

**5 December 1991:** Upon his recall from the SFRY Presidency, Stjepan Mesić asserts, "I think I have fulfilled my duty—Yugoslavia no longer exists".

**6 December 1991:** United States imposes sanctions on all Yugoslav republics.

**9 December 1991:** Serbia and Montenegro reject the findings of the EC Arbitration Commission.

**17 December 1991:** Ministerial Council of the EC adopts the Declaration on Yugoslavia and decides to recognize secessionist republics, which need to officially declare their wish for independence: deadline for international recognition is January 15, 1992.

**18 December 1991:** Presidency of the SFRY asks the United Nations for help in preserving the integrity and sovereignty of Yugoslavia.

**19 December 1991:** Republic of Serbian Krajina (RSK) is officially proclaimed.

**20 December 1991:** Croatian and Muslim members of the Presidency of Bosnia and Hercegovina decide to ask the EC for recognition of their independence.

**21 December 1991:** Parliament of the Serbian People in Bosnia and Hercegovina decides to proclaim the "Republic of the Serbian People in Bosnia and Hercegovina" before January 14.

**23 December 1991:** Germany officially recognizes the independence of Slovenia and Croatia.

**2–3 January 1992:** Warring sides accept the Vance Plan.

**8 January 1992:** UN Security Council adopts Resolution 727, deploying 50 military liaison officers to promote maintenance of the cease-fire; Resolution 740 authorizes an increase to 75 officers (February 7); General Veljko Kadijević resigns after an EC Monitoring Mission helicopter is shot down.

**9 January 1992:** Proclamation of the Republic of the Serbian People in Bosnia and Hercegovina, a federal unit of Yugoslavia.

**15 January 1992:** Contrary to the opinion of the EC Arbitration Commission that only Macedonia and Slovenia fulfill the recognition criteria, Austria, Belgium, and Great Britain recognize Croatia and Slovenia.

**31 January–9 February 1992:** SFRY (February 2), Croatia (February 6), and the RSK (February 9) officially accept the Vance Plan.

**12 February 1992:** Leaders of Serbia and Montenegro meet in Podgorica and attempt to ensure the continuity of Yugoslavia.

**24 February 1992:** Based on the report of the UN secretary-general (February 20) the Security Council adopts Resolution 743, establishing a 14,000-strong UNPROFOR (United Nations Protection Force).

**27 February 1992:** Serbian Parliament decides to form a joint state with Montenegro.

**29 February–1 March 1992:** Referendum on independence is held in Bosnia and Hercegovina; Serbian population boycotts it; Croatian army forces cross into the territory of Bosnia and Hercegovina and ceremonially enter into the city of Bosanski Brod.

**1 March 1992:** Referendum in Montenegro; 95.94 percent of the votes cast support the formation of the common state with Serbia.

**3 March 1992:** Armed clashes erupt in Bosanski Brod.

**18 March 1992:** Fifth session of International Conference on Bosnia and Hercegovina is held in Sarajevo: the leaders of the three national parties agree that Bosnia and Hercegovina should remain in its present borders as a single state with three constituent units based on the national principle.

**26 March 1992:** JNA withdraws from Macedonia.

**2–5 April 1992:** Bloody clashes erupt throughout Bosnia and Hercegovina: Bijeljina comes under the control of Serbian paramilitary forces, which commit atrocities against Muslims; Croatian paramilitary forces kill several Serbs in Kupres, the JNA intervenes, and attacks on JNA barracks in Mostar follow.

**6 April 1992:** EC Ministerial Council recommends that member states recognize the independence of Bosnia and Hercegovina on April 7; the Parliament of Serbian People in Bosnia and Hercegovina declares the independence of the Serbian Republic of Bosnia and Hercegovina (Republika Srpska); fierce clashes between JNA and Croatian paramilitary forces in western Hercegovina.

**14 April 1992:** U.S. secretary of state James Baker warns the Serbian leadership and the JNA against their "military involvement in the internal conflicts in Bosnia and Hercegovina."

**20 April 1992:** Ralph Johnson, assistant U.S. Secretary of State, warns Milošević of a possible break in diplomatic relations.
**27 April 1992:** Federal Republic of Yugoslavia (FRY) is proclaimed in Belgrade.
**2 May 1992:** Muslim forces attack a withdrawing JNA convoy in Sarajevo, killing several officers and soldiers.
**4 May 1992:** Reorganization of the JNA (officially disbanded on May 20); all citizens of the FRY-JNA in Bosnia and Hercegovina—are ordered to return to the FRY by May 19.
**6 May 1992:** Following the request of Austria, Yugoslavia is temporarily excluded from the Conference on Security and Cooperation in Europe (CSCE).
**12 May 1992:** Parliament of the Serbian Republic in Bosnia and Hercegovina is held in Banja Luka: Radovan Karadžić becomes president and Biljana Plavšić and Nikola Koljević vice-presidents; the Bosnian Serb Army (BSA) is formed and General Ratko Mladić is appointed as commander.
**15 May 1992:** Resolution 752 calls for immediate and unconditional withdrawal of the JNA and Croatian Army from Bosnia and Hercegovina; Muslim forces attack a withdrawing JNA convoy in Tuzla, more than a hundred soldiers are killed; the ambassadors of 12 western European countries and the U.S. (May 16) are withdrawn from the FRY.
**21 May 1992:** U.S. Senate passes The Yugoslavia Sanctions Act of 1992; stipulation of six points the FRY must comply with to avoid the imposition of sanctions.
**25 May 1992:** Tripartite negotiations on ethnic division of Bosnia and Hercegovina are held in Lisbon.
**27 May 1992:** After the so-called Breadline Massacre, the EC decides on the imposition of economic sanctions against Serbia and Montenegro.
**30 May 1992:** UN Resolution 757: the Security Council applies comprehensive economic and cultural sanctions against Serbia and Montenegro.
**31 May 1992:** Parliamentary elections in the FRY: opposition parties boycott the elections; mass antiwar protest in Belgrade.
**5 June 1992:** Beginning of mass student anti-government demonstrations in Belgrade.
**11 June 1992:** European Parliament adopts a resolution on Yugoslavia: the document asserts that the SFRY ceased to exist, federation of Serbia and Montenegro could not be regarded as the sole successor of the SFRY, and that the JNA should be disbanded and put under UN control.
**15 June 1992:** Dobrica Ćosić becomes president of the FRY; BSA cap-

tures documentation detailing the presence of 40,000 Croatian army troops in Bosnia and Hercegovina.

**28 June–5 July 1992:** Democratic Movement of Serbia (DEPOS) coalition organizes St. Vitus Assembly on plaza in front of the Federal Parliament.

**30 June 1992:** Security Council urges Croatia to withdraw its army from the "pink zones."

**1 July 1992:** Milan Panić, an American businessman, is given a mandate to form the government of the FRY.

**3 July 1992:** Formal proclamation of Herceg Bosna, "Croatian state" in Bosnia and Hercegovina.

**6 August 1992:** Television pictures from Omarska, a Serbian POW camp, and especially Trnopolje, a transit camp, bring calls for military action, war crimes proceedings and many comparisons to Nazi camps of WWII.

**12 August 1992:** Parliament of the Serbian republic of Bosnia and Hercegovina changes the name of the state to Republika Srpska.

**13 August 1992:** US TV producer David Kaplan of ABC is killed by sniper-fire on Sniper Alley.

**26–27 August 1992:** International conference on Yugoslavia is held in London; establishes six working groups and a steering committee under the chairmanship of Lord David Owen and Cyrus Vance.

**30 August 1992:** BSA lifts the siege of Goražde.

**3 September 1992:** Italian relief plane is shot down on a flight to Sarajevo: The missile was fired from an area where Croat and Muslim forces were contesting control.

**21–23 September 1992:** Forty-seventh session of the UN General Assembly: Yugoslavia, one of the founding states, is excluded.

**28–30 September 1992:** Negotiations between Vance, Owen, Ćosić, and Tudjman: Tudjman and Ćosić sign a declaration that confirms the fulfillment of the terms of the London conference; an agreement on Prevlaka is reached.

**1 October 1992:** U.S. calls upon the UN Security Council to adopt a new resolution prohibiting all flights over Bosnia and Hercegovina except those authorized by the UN; Resolution 781 is adopted on October 9.

**26 October 1992:** Severe clashes between Muslim and Croat forces in central Bosnia.

**16 November 1992:** UN Security Council adopts Resolution 787, further tightening sanctions against Serbia and Montenegro.

**18 November 1992:** NATO Council decides to undertake "limited military operations" in the former Yugoslavia.

**19 November 1992:** During a meeting with Cyrus Vance and David Owen, Zdravko Zečević declares that the failure to recognize the existence of the RSK would lead either to armed conflict or the exodus of Serbs from Croatia.
**11 December 1993:** UN Security Council adopts Resolution 795 on deployment of UNPROFOR in the Former Yugoslavia Republic of Macedonia.
**15 December 1992:** International Monetary Fund revokes the membership of the SFRY and declares former republics as successors to existing assets and liabilities.
**20 December 1992:** General elections in the FRY, Serbia, and Montenegro: Slobodan Milošević defeats Milan Panić and remains president of Serbia; Radoje Kontić becomes prime minister (December 29).
**3 January 1993:** Cyrus Vance and David Owen propose the peace arrangement known as the Vance-Owen Peace Plan.
**16 January 1993:** Following the withdrawal of the BSA from Goražde Muslim forces begin an offensive from Srebrenica along the left bank of the Drina River; numerous violations of FRY borders; bombardment of several villages within borders of the FRY.
**22 January–2 February 1993:** Croatian army attacks the RSK, seizes Maslenica region, Zemunik airport (January 25), and Peruća hydroelectric power station (January 29).
**10 February 1993:** U.S. announces its plan for solving the crisis in Bosnia and Hercegovina; a special envoy (Reginald Bartholomew) is appointed to work with Vance and Owen; the UN is asked to establish an international court to try war crimes committed in the former Yugoslavia.
**28 February 1993:** NATO begins airdrops over eastern Bosnia.
**Early April 1993:** Fighting around Srebrenica intensifies.
**2 April 1993:** NATO agrees to provide air-support in enforcing "no fly" zone over Bosnia and Hercegovina.
**16 April 1993:** UN Security Council adopts Resolution 819 and demands that all parties treat Srebrenica and its surroundings as a Safe Area.
**18 April 1993:** UN Security Council adopts Resolution 820 and tightens sanctions against Serbia and Montenegro.
**20 April 1993:** Clashes between Croat and Muslim forces in western and central Bosnia intensify.
**22 April 1993:** U.S. announces that unilateral airstrikes against Serb positions in Bosnia are considered.
**1–2 May 1993:** Peace Conference on Bosnia and Hercegovina is held in Athens; Radovan Karadžić signs the Vance-Owen plan, pending the final approval of the Parliament of the RS.

**5–6 May 1993:** Parliament of the RS rejects the Vance-Owen Plan and calls for a referendum to be held on May 15–16 (96 percent of the votes cast reject the peace plan).

**22 May 1993:** Foreign ministers of the U.S., Russia, Great Britain, Spain, and France propose an alternative plan for settling the Bosnian crisis: the plan advocates a gradual instead of an all-out approach; Serbs support the plan, Muslims reject it.

**25 May 1993:** U.N. Security Council adopts Resolution 825 and establishes the International Court for War Crimes in The Hague (The Hague Tribunal).

**1 June 1993:** Parliament of the FRY releases president Dobrica Ćosic from office, under the pretext of violation of the Constitution; Zoran Lilić becomes president (June 25).

**4 June 1993:** UN Security Council adopts Resolution 824 declaring Sarajevo, Bihać, Tuzla, Žepa, Srebrenica, and Goražde and their environs as Safe Areas.

**25 June 1993:** New peace plan for Bosnia is presented in Geneva; the nine point plan envisions Bosnia and Hercegovina as a confederation of three national republics.

**29 July 1993:** David Owen and Thorvald Stoltenberg suggest a new peace plan for Bosnia and Hercegovina known as the Owen-Stoltenberg Plan; Izetbegović boycotts the negotiations.

**28 August 1993:** Parliament of the RS accepts the Owen-Stoltenberg Plan.

**9 September 1993:** The Croatian Army attacks the RSK near Gospić in Lika region: the complete destruction of three villages; dozens of civilians and at least 50 Serbian soldiers are killed; in response the Serbian Army of Krajina bombards Karlovac, Sisak, Jastrebarsko, and Zagreb (September 11); Croatian forces withdraw from the area (September 17).

**27 September 1993:** Fikret Abdić, member of the Presidency of Bosnia and Hercegovina, proclaims the Autonomous Province of Western Bosnia; the Bosnian Assembly accepts the Owen-Stoltenberg Plan provided condition that Serbs return more territory.

**3 October 1993:** Severe clashes between rival Muslim forces in Bihać area.

**20 October 1993:** Slobodan Milošević dismisses the Serbian Parliament following the parliamentary crisis initiated by a conflict between the Socialists and the Radicals; new elections are scheduled for December 19.

**16 December 1993:** Despite strong Greek opposition, six Western European countries recognize Macedonia as the Former Yugoslav Republic of Macedonia (FYROM).

**19 December 1993:** Parliamentary elections in Serbia: the SPS fails to win the majority of parliamentary seats.
**9 January 1994:** Government of Serbia approves the new Economic Stabilization Package; the stabilization package is inaugurated (January 24).
**19 January 1994:** Croatia and the FRY sign a document on the normalization of mutual relations and the opening of bureaus in Belgrade and Zagreb.
**23 January 1994:** Milan Martić wins in the second round of presidential elections in the RSK.
**5 February 1994:** In what becomes known as the Marketplace Massacre, 68 people are killed and about 200 are wounded allegedly by a single mortar shell.
**9 February 1994:** U.S. recognizes the FYROM.
**28 February 1994:** Two American F-16 jets down four planes in the vicinity of Banja Luka.
**2 March 1994:** Representatives of Bosnian Croats and Muslims signed a preliminary accord on the formation of the Muslim-Croat Federation; Dragoslav Avramović, the author of stabilization program, becomes governor of the National Bank of Yugoslavia.
**17 March 1994:** Serbian Parliament elects Mirko Marjanović as prime minister.
**18 March 1994:** Bosnian-Croat Federation is officially proclaimed during a ceremony in Washington, D.C.
**Late March 1994:** Army of Bosnia and Hercegovina (Muslim) begins an offensive in eastern Bosnia.
**5 April 1994:** BSA quells the Muslim offensive and launches a counterattack in the area of Goražde.
**10 April 1994:** Two American F-16 jets bomb Serbian positions around Goražde.
**16 April 1994:** A British jet is downed around Goražde.
**25 April 1994:** First meeting of the Contact Group.
**13 May 1994:** Contact Group reveals new plan for Bosnia and Hercegovina: according to the new territorial division, the Muslim-Croat side would get 51 percent and the Serbian side 49 percent.
**6 June 1994:** Beginning of a new round of negotiations in Geneva: the warring sides sign a month-long cease-fire.
**8 June 1994:** Muslim forces continue an offensive in central Bosnia and in the Bihać pocket.
**5–6 July 1994:** Foreign ministers of the U.S., Great Britain, France, and Germany present The Plan for Territorial Division of Bosnia and Hercegovina; government-sponsored blockade of UNPROFOR in Croatia.

**21 July 1994:** Parliament of the RS fails to accept the plan of the Contact Group since it lacks several important elements (constitutional arrangements, cease-fire, status of Sarajevo).
**23 July 1994:** Yugoslav Left (JUL) is founded by a merger of 22 left-wing parties.
**30–31 July 1994:** Presidents of Serbia and Montenegro declare their unconditional support for the Contact Group plan; beginning of the rift between the FRY and the RS.
**4 August 1994:** Government of the FRY breaks off relations with the leadership of the RS; the government of the RSK severs its ties with the RS; President Milan Martić of the RSK reverses the government decision (August 20).
**9 August 1994:** Collapse of Abdić's forces; more than 20,000 refugees flee to the RSK.
**27–28 August 1994:** Referendum in the RS on the plan of the Contact Group (96.06 percent of the electorate votes against the plan).
**24 September 1994**: UN Security Council adopts Resolution 942 on tightening sanctions against the RS and Resolution 943 on relaxing sanctions against the FRY.
**23 October 1994:** Fifth Corps of the army of Bosnia and Hercegovina launches a major offensive from the Bihać region (Safe Area).
**7–8 November 1994:** The Hague Tribunal declares the name of the first person to be indicted for war crimes, Dragan Nikolić, and initiates a request to Germany to hand over Dušan Tadić.
**21 November 1994:** 39 NATO planes bomb the Udbina airfield in the RSK; attacks on Serbian positions around Bihać (November 23).
**2 December 1994:** Contact Group announces a revised version of the peace plan.
**18 December 1994:** Former President of the U.S. Jimmy Carter arrives in Sarajevo, mediates an agreement with the leadership of the RS (December 19).
**21 December 1994:** Opening of the highway between Belgrade and Zagreb.
**31 December 1994:** As a result of the peace initiative of Jimmy Carter, the warring sides in Bosnia and Hercegovina sign an agreement on cessation of hostilities: a cease-fire takes effect.
**4 January 1995:** U.S. senator Bob Dole introduces legislation to end U.S. compliance with arms embargo against Bosnia.
**12 January 1995:** Franjo Tudjman writes to Boutros Boutros-Ghali to say that the UNPROFOR mandate in Croatia will end on 31 March; the UN Security Council votes to continue the easing of sanctions on the FRY for another 100 days.

**16 January 1995:** Newspapers in London report a disagreement between the UN and NATO after General Michael Rose apparently offers to show NATO flight plans to the Bosnian Serbs as a confidence-building measure. NATO ceases to provide the UN with flight plans.
**18 January 1995:** U.S. UN representative Madeleine Albright announces eight points that require clarification in relation to the continued partial exemption to the sanctions against the FRY.
**19 January 1995:** 100 POWs exchanged, first under the terms of the current cease-fire.
**20 January 1995:** EU, meeting in Brussels, says that the fate of an economic accord with Croatia depends on Croatia's stance toward peace in the former Yugoslavia; a decision on the accord is due in March.
**24 January 1995:** Presidents Tudjman and Izetbegović meet in Zagreb.
**26 January 1995:** Zagreb and Sarajevo call for U.S. mediation on progress of the Muslim-Croat Federation; Bosnian government forces blockade of the UN contingent in Tuzla.
**31 January 1995:** Bosnian Croat and Muslim army commanders, Tihomir Blaškić and Rasim Delić, meet in central Bosnia to sign an agreement to strengthen the Muslim-Croat Federation; Bosnian Croat members of the Bosnian presidency protest Bosnian army forces wearing green Islamic headbands and carrying Islamic flags.
**5 February 1995:** Haris Silajdžić and Andrei Kozyrev meet in Moscow; Kozyrev advises the Bosnian Serbs to agree to the Contact Group plan; U.S. achieves agreement between the Croatian and Muslim parties in the federation to accept independent binding arbitration in disputes between the two parties.
**9 February 1995:** U.S. ambassador to Croatia, Peter Galbraith, is quoted as saying the U.S. will not support Croatia if new attacks are launched against Krajina; Bill Clinton and Helmut Kohl, meet in Washington, call for a strengthening of the Muslim-Croat Federation.
**13 February 1995:** UN tribunal at The Hague indicts 21 Serbs for genocide, war crimes, and crimes against humanity; U.S. representative on the Contact Group, Charles Redman, is to be replaced with a part-time appointee; Viktor Jackovich, U.S. Ambassador to Bosnia, is to be reassigned as ambassador to Slovenia.
**14 February 1995:** Deputy director of the German Foreign Ministry, Klaus-Peter Klaiber, and the Croatian ambassador to the U.S., Josip Šarčević, announce that an unspecified compromise on UNPROFOR might be possible.
**19 February 1995:** At the end of a three-day meeting with Andrei Kozyrev,

Slobodan Milošević refuses to recognize Bosnia and Croatia, a target recently set by the Contact Group as a pre-condition for lifting of sanctions against Belgrade; Robert Frasure, new U.S. representative to the Contact Group, meets Franjo Tudjman.

**20 February 1995:** Bosnian Serbs and Krajina Serbs form a joint military council at Banja Luka.

**21 February 1995:** UN reports of transport aircraft supported by jet aircraft dropping high-tech military supplies at Tuzla are been rejected by NATO. **23 February 1995:** Washington announces an international grouping, the "Friends of the Federation," through which countries, organizations, and individuals can support the Muslim-Croat Federation in Bosnia; UN special representative Yasushi Akashi meets Slobodan Milošević in Belgrade: in the prior week, Milošević is reported to have had secret meetings with members of the Contact Group.

**26 February 1995:** British media report that the U.S. is arming the Bosnian Muslims, with flights to Tuzla airport by large cargo aircraft, possibly Turkish, supported by U.S. jets while NATO was not providing radar coverage of the no fly zone.

**6 March 1995:** Croatia and Bosnia, in the form of the Muslim-Croat Federation, establish a new military alliance; Richard Holbrooke meets Tudjman; General Ratko Mladić says that if UNPROFOR leaves Croatia, it must also leave Bosnia.

**7 March 1995:** Croatian chief-of-staff General Janko Bobetko is to head the joint Croatian-Muslim-Croat Federation military command.

**8 March 1995:** Croatia, Slovenia and Macedonia to join World Bank.

**9 March 1995:** In a report leaked to the *New York Times*, the CIA claims that the Bosnian Serbs are responsible for 90 percent of the atrocities in Bosnia.

**12 March 1995:** At the UN Conference on Social Development in Copenhagen, Tudjman meets with U.S. vice president Al Gore and announces a compromise on the UNPROFOR mandate; according to Tudjman the U.S. provides pledges on the restoration of Croatian sovereignty.

**24 March 1995:** Bosnian government starts the spring offensive with attacks on communications towers near Travnik, central Bosnia, and Tuzla in the northeast.

**30 March 1995:** The day before the UNPROFOR mandate in Croatia expires, the UN announces a UN Confidence Restoration Operation in Croatia, to be known as UNCRO.

**31 March 1995:** Reorganization of UNPROFOR is announced; in addition to UNCRO (Confidence Restoration Operation), in Macedonia UNPREDEP (Preventive Deployment), in Bosnia UNPROFOR and an HQ element called UNPF (Peacekeeping Force).

**3 April 1995:** Hans Koschnik, EU leader in Mostar, criticizes the UN for not enforcing the arms embargo; China becomes the 92nd country to recognize Bosnia.

**4 April 1995:** Contact Group, meeting in London, wants to pressure the Bosnian government into extending the May 1 deadline for the end of the cease-fire in Bosnia; Croatian troops are quietly moving into the UN-controlled Sector West, around Daruvar in Slavonia.

**5 April 1995:** Mate Granić describes UN Resolution 981 as the strongest document in Croatia's favor ever approved and now wants negotiations with the international community, and later the Serbs, on extending Zagreb's sovereignty to its internationally recognized borders.

**6 April 1995:** UN fires smoke shells at BSA guns targeting the Mt. Igman road. Bosnian government advances continue near Tuzla and Travnik; Richard Holbrooke fears the cease-fire is breaking down.

**10 April 1995:** Contact Group representatives visit Belgrade to address the question of the recognition of Bosnia; Franjo Tudjman calls for the new UNCRO force to be made up solely of Western European troops.

**12 April 1995:** The *New York Times* publishes information about direct links between Serbia and the RS in war crimes; the documents, from Čedomir Mihailović, an alleged Serbian secret service agent, prove not to be authentic according to The Hague Tribunal.

**17 April 1995:** France asks for a UN Security Council meeting on Bosnia to discuss the deployment of a "rapid reaction" UN force. Croatian and Bosnian Croat forces secure positions on Mt. Dinara, in Bosnia, from where they can shell Knin.

**19 April 1995:** A French-sponsored resolution, 987, passes the UN Security Council unanimously; it asks for an extension of the cease-fire and a review of UNPROFOR operations and mandate.

**21 April 1995:** A deadline for resolving the composition of the UN forces in Croatia passes with no consensus; Germany agrees to extradite Dušan Tadić to The Hague Tribunal.

**24 April 1995:** Krajina Serbs end a brief attempt to blockade the Zagreb-Belgrade highway.

**25 April 1995:** Britain requests the rotation of its forces in Goražde.

**1 May 1995:** Cease-fire in Bosnia ends; Croatia launches a coordinated, three-pronged attack on Western Slavonia (Sector West) with tanks and heavy artillery, along with an estimated 7,000 Croatian troops and military police; only one bridge across the Sava remains open, the others are destroyed or captured; aircraft, artillery, and rockets target the bridge and Serb-held Bosanska Gradiška in Bosnia; the site of the WWII death camp at Jasenovac is captured; 15,000 Serb refugees are due to arrive in Banja Luka; about 1,000 RSK soldiers are captured and screened for war crimes; Croatia claims some 500 Serbs are killed in the fighting, including about 120 civilians killed in crossfire.

**17 May 1995:** Boutros-Ghali outlines four options for the restructuring of UNPROFOR in Bosnia.

**21 May 1995:** Karadžić threatens to take UN personnel hostage if airstrikes are ordered and to overrun the eastern enclaves, Žepa, Srebrenica and Goražde, if the UN pulls out.

**25 May 1995:** NATO aircraft bomb an ammunition dump near Pale; 71 are reported dead in Tuzla as all UN designated safe areas are reported shelled.

**26 May 1995:** NATO aircraft again bomb installations near Pale; many UN personnel are taken hostage by the BSA.

**27 May 1995:** Bosnian foreign minister Irfan Ljubijankić is killed when his helicopter is shot down by RSK forces in the Bihać pocket.

**29 May 1995:** Britain is to send 5,000 more troops to Bosnia.

**30 May 1995:** France is to send an aircraft carrier to the Adriatic.

**2 June 1995:** A U.S. F-16 aircraft is shot down by a BSA missile.

**7 June 1995:** U.S. pilot Scott O'Grady is rescued after being shot down five days previously.

**14 June 1995:** UN sources report 20,000–30,000 Bosnian troops massing outside northern Sarajevo.

**15 June 1995:** Bosnian army launches a large offensive north of Sarajevo and also a number of offensives out of Sarajevo; UN authorizes the Rapid Reaction Force in Resolution 998.

**20 June 1995:** French UN troops destroy a BSA tank after a UN observation post came under fire.

**6 July 1995:** U.S. prepares to deploy spy planes in Albania for flights over Bosnia.

**8 July 1995:** Fighting escalates near Srebrenica; after a number of raids throughout the year, the Bosnian army attempts to secure a crossroads to the south of the enclave; BSA forces are then pushed into the enclave to neutralize the movement; Dutch UN forces try to separate the parties, one Dutch soldier killed by the Bosnian government forces and 32 captured by the BSA.

**11 July 1995:** In a continuing stand-off, Dutch UN forces exchange fire with BSA forces; NATO threatens airstrikes if the attacks continue; in the evening some 15,000 males, including 4,000–10,000 fighters, leave Srebrenica in a huge column heading towards Tuzla; the remaining townspeople head towards the UN base at nearby Potočari.
**12 July 1995:** Despite air-strikes, BSA units avoid Dutch positions and enter Srebrenica, which is deserted.
**13 July 1995:** BSA units arrive at Potočari; organization begins for the evacuation of 27,000 people.
**17 July 1995:** Rebuffing French calls for Srebrenica to be recaptured, Britain announces a conference in London on July 21.
**23 July 1995:** U.S., Britain, and France promise "massive and unprecedented" airstrikes if the BSA attacks Goražde.
**24 July 1995:** Boutros-Ghali relinquishes civilian control of airstrikes; they can now be called by UN military commanders in Yugoslavia without reference to New York.
**25 July 1995:** Karadžić, Mladić and Milan Martić indicted by The Hague Tribunal; neither the Breadline Massacre nor the February 1995 Marketplace Massacre is on the list of atrocities in Sarajevo for which they are charged; the Tribunal can find no evidence of Bosnian Serb responsibility for these events.
**26 July 1995:** Glamoč and Grahovo, Serb towns in western Bosnia, fall to joint Croat and Bosnian Croat forces; U.S. Senate votes to lift arms embargo against Bosnia.
**31 July 1995:** Croatian government spurns peace talks for Krajina, only sending junior representatives to Geneva.
**1 August 1995:** Croatia launches a massive, well-coordinated attack on the Republic of Serbian Krajina (UN Sectors North and South); Knin and other population centers are heavily shelled; aircraft take part; helicopters and gunships operate behind RSK line; the exodus of 200,000 refugees begins, the biggest single population movement of the civil wars in Yugoslavia; up to 100,000 Croat troops and police are involved.
**5 August 1995:** Karadžic attempts to oust military commander Ratko Mladić, but 18 senior officers support Mladić.
**7 August 1995:** Remaining RSK forces sign a surrender agreement; refugee columns face shelling, attacks by aircraft, and attacks by civilians when allowed to use the Zagreb-Belgrade highway to flee; Croatian defence minister Gojko Šušak claims "Operation Storm" is over; Yeltsin suggests a meeting of Tudjman and Milošević in Moscow. Tudjman turns down the invita-

tion because Izetbegović is not invited; Croatia ostracizes EU negotiator Carl Bildt for calling "Operation Storm" 'ethnic cleansing.'

**22 August 1995:** UN Rapid Reaction Force on Mt. Igman returns fire at a BSA artillery position.

**27 August 1995:** Prior to attending peace talks in Paris, Richard Holbrooke, U.S. negotiator, states that force will be used against the Bosnian Serbs if a settlement is not reached shortly.

**28 August 1995:** Up to 37 people are killed in a reported mortar attack near Sarajevo's Markale Marketplace; preliminary UN investigations say there is no clear evidence of who is responsible (Cymbeline mortar-locating radar failed to track the fatal shell); the Bosnian government delegation threatens to pull out of the Paris talks unless military action is taken against the Bosnian Serbs; Radovan Karadžić, at about the time of the attack, announces acceptance of the Contact Group plan as a basis for negotiations.

**29 August 1995:** At 7 a.m. local time, the UN report on the Marketplace shelling is complete; in Paris, the Bosnian government delegation agrees to attend the talks; at 11 a.m. local time the UN announces that Bosnian Serbs are clearly responsible for the attack; the only new evidence cited is that someone heard the shell being fired from a Serb position; later, Russian, British, French, and Canadian investigators cast strong doubt on the certainty of the UN report.

**30 August 1995:** In the early hours of the morning NATO launches air attacks against Bosnian Serb positions throughout central and eastern Bosnia; around Sarajevo the UN Rapid Reaction Force fires more than 600 shells at Bosnian Serb positions, joined by Bosnian government artillery on Mt. Igman; a French Mirage jet is shot down near Pale; the pilot and navigator are captured by a WWII veteran Serb/farmer with his wartime pistol.

**7 September 1995:** In Geneva a formal agreement to seek a negotiated settlement is made between the warring parties; NATO attacks continue, as they have throughout the week only ceasing when the weather is poor.

**8 September 1995:** Bosnian Croat indicted by the UN Tribunal for the 1993 Stupni Do massacre.

**9 September 1995:** For the first time Bosnian Serb targets in Western Bosnia are attacked; in another first, cruise missiles are launched from U.S. ships in the Adriatic against targets around Banja Luka; Bosnian government, Bosnian Croat, and Croat forces launch offensives in western Bosnia.

**19 September 1995:** NATO air attacks on Bosnian Serb positions have been indefinitely suspended; in the 10 days of coincidental NATO air attacks, Bosnian government, Bosnian Croat, and Croatian advances, in western Bosnia, the towns of Jajce, Drvar, Šipovo and others have fallen. Up to 150,000 Serb civilians have fled to Banja Luka, many forced out of three or four towns successively since the end of July.

**26 September 1995:** U.S.-sponsored talks open in New York, attended by the foreign ministers of Croatia, Bosnia and the FRY.

**4 October 1995:** NATO jets bomb BSA missile sites which had locked on to them.

**5 October 1995:** Bosnia-wide cease-fire is signed, due to come into effect on 10 October.

**9 October 1995:** NATO jets bomb BSA positions near Tuzla, after a reported shelling attack on a refugee camp.

**10 October 1995:** In the countdown to the start of the cease-fire, combined Bosnian government, Bosnian Croat, and Croatian forces take the towns of Sanski Most and Mrkonjić Grad.

**12 October 1995:** The cease-fire, delayed while more advances were made against the BSA, begins.

**17 October 1995:** Site for the Bosnian peace talks is designated.

**23 October 1995:** Bosnian government objects to Bosnian Croats being eligible to vote in the forthcoming Croatian elections.

**1 November 1995:** Talks open in Dayton; Presidents Milošević, Tudjman, and Izetbegović are present.

**2 November 1995:** The first result from Dayton is an agreement on Eastern Slavonia; it will be under international administration for one year, possibly two, before coming under full Croatian control.

**12 November 1995:** Tudjman and Izetbegović sign an agreement in Dayton to strengthen the Muslim-Croat Federation.

**13 November 1995:** Six Bosnian Croats indicted by The Hague Tribunal for persecution of Bosnian Muslims in the Lašva Valley.

**21 November 1995:** "Dayton Peace Accord" deems Republika Srpska one "entity" within the internationally recognized Bosnia-Hercegovina (Dayton Agreement).

**1 December 1995:** NATO Council, meeting in Brussels, agrees on deployment of NATO troops in Bosnia.

**6 December 1995:** Advanced contingent of U.S. NATO troops arrives in Tuzla; British and French troops start to "change hats" from UN to NATO; German parliament votes to send 4,000 troops to support NATO deployment in Bosnia: they will be stationed in Croatia.

**8 December 1995:** Three-day conference on the reconstruction of Bosnia starts in London.

**10 December 1995:** Serbs start to leave suburbs and boroughs of Sarajevo due to be handed over to the Muslim-Croat Federation under the Dayton Agreement.
**12 December 1995:** Captured French airmen are released.
**13 December 1995:** Two-day conference opens in Paris.
**14 December 1995:** Dayton Peace Agreement, or the Elysee Accord, is signed in Paris.
**15 December 1995:** UN Security Council approves NATO deployment in Bosnia.
**18 December 1995:** One-day conference in Bonn on arms control in the former Yugoslavia.
**20 December 1995:** Formal handover of UN command to NATO.
**22 December 1995:** OSCE names Swiss diplomat Gret Haller human rights ombudsman for Bosnia.
**24 December 1995:** First prisoner-of-war exchange under Dayton Agreement.
**26 December 1995:** U.S. NATO forces set up checkpoints in Posavina corridor.
**28 December 1995:** Bill Clinton suspends U.S. sanctions against Belgrade; Boris Yeltsin suspends Russian compliance with UN sanctions against Belgrade.
**10 January 1996:** Mate Granić, Croatian foreign minister, visits Belgrade, meeting with Slobodan Milošević and Foreign Minister Milan Milutinović to discuss the normalization of relations.
**19 January 1996:** The ICRC deadline for the exchange of prisoners in Bosnia meets with limited success. Bosnian government, Croatian Defence Council (HVO), and BSA forces complete withdrawal from frontline position.
**22 January 1996:** Hasan Muratović replaces Haris Silajdžić as prime minister of Bosnia; in a secretive meeting in Sarajevo, Turkey signs an agreement to train the Bosnian government army; speaking afterwards, Bosnian General Rasim Delić said "we expect huge aid from Turkey."
**23 January 1996:** NATO confirms to the UN Security Council that the BSA has withdrawn, but, despite a Dayton stipulation, sanctions against Republika Srpska are not lifted.
**24 January 1996:** Yugoslav justice minister Uroš Klikovac announces that an office of the UN tribunal in The Hague would be opened in Belgrade in the near future; the World Bank, in a meeting in Sarajevo, announces $150 million emergency aid for reconstruction; the World Bank estimates that Bosnia will require $5.1 billion over three years.

**25 January 1996:** ICRC appeals for a further 645 prisoners in Bosnia to be released, also protesting the detention of "several dozen" unregistered Bosnian Serbs held in prison in Tuzla; Krešimir Zubak and Izudin Kapetanović, leaders of the Bosnian Muslim-Croatian Federation, visit Pale.
**30 January 1996:** Seven-member election commission established in Sarajevo, consisting of representatives from the United States, Canada, Britain, Germany, and the three Bosnian factions; General Atif Dudaković says that the Bosnian army will be reorganized along NATO lines.
**1 February 1996:** UN Preventative Deployment in Macedonia (UNPREDEP) becomes independent of other UN operations in the former Yugoslavia, reporting directly to UN headquarters in New York.
**6 February 1996:** NATO announces the admission by a Bosnian government representative that a number of Bosnian Serbs have been recently taken prisoner; these include General Đorđe Đukić, his deputy Colonel Aleksa Krsmanović, and their driver as well as up to eight others; all are held for alleged war crimes.
**7 February 1996:** ICRC announces that it believes 3,000 men missing from the Srebrenica enclave are dead and is seeking information on 5,000 others, including men who escaped the enclave into Bosnian government territory.
**10 February 1996:** Richard Holbrooke returns to the former Yugoslavia to try to stabilize the situation after the arrest of the BSA officers.
**12 February 1996:** General Đukić and Colonel Krsmanović are removed to The Hague, to be detained in UN prison cells.
**13 February 1996:** Holbrooke announces new procedures: suspected war criminals can now only be arrested at the request of the UN Tribunal in The Hague.
**17 February 1996:** Two-day conference in Rome; the principle that suspected war criminals can only be arrested at the UN Tribunal's request is extended to Croatia and the FRY; EU administration of Mostar to be extended by six months.
**20 February 1996:** Bosnian Serbs in suburbs and areas of Sarajevo due to be handed over to Bosnian government control start leaving in significant numbers.
**22 February 1996:** France announces diplomatic ties with the FRY; IFOR, having finally confirmed Bosnian Serb compliance with withdrawal on February 21, requests that sanctions remain on the RS until ties are restored following the arrest of the BSA officers.
**23 February 1996:** RS restores ties with IFOR; Russia announces unilateral lifting of sanctions against the RS.

**27 February 1996:** FRY lifts sanctions against the RS; the UN Tribunal in The Hague holds "Rule 61" proceedings against former RSK leader Milan Martić.

**1 March 1996:** BSA General Đorđe Đukić is indicted by the UN tribunal in The Hague; Colonel Krsmanović continues to be held as a potential witness.

**19 March 1996:** Central Sarajevo district of Grbavica is the last Bosnian Serb-held area to be turned over to Bosnian government control.

**21 March 1996:** Three Bosnian Muslims and one Bosnian Croat are charged by the UN Tribunal for war crimes against Bosnian Serbs in Čelebići detention camp, near Konjic in central Bosnia.

**26 March 1996:** Bosnian Croat and Bosnian Serbs agree to exchange all prisoners; Elisabeth Rehn, representative of the UN Commission on Human Rights (UNCHR), expresses concern about 2,000 Bosnian Serbs missing after the offensive in western Bosnia in the Fall of 1995.

**30 March 1996:** Dražen Erdemović and Radoslav Kremenović are transferred from Belgrade to the UN prison in Holland.

**1 April 1996:** Tihomir Blaškić, a senior figure in the HVO and the Croatian Army, arrives in The Hague after negotiating special conditions for his detention.

**3 April 1996:** U.S. commerce secretary Ron Brown, along with 34 business leaders, journalists and crew is killed in an air crash while attempting a landing at Dubrovnik airport; Colonel Aleksa Krsmanović is returned to the custody of the Bosnian government after the UN tribunal in The Hague finds no evidence for any charges against him; the Bosnian government still claims to have evidence of his participation in genocide.

**4 April 1996:** Authorities in Croatia arrest four Bosnian Muslims believed to have been part of a team attempting to assassinate Fikret Abdić, a Bosnian Muslim leader unpopular with the Bosnian government and former head of the APWB.

**7 April 1996:** Mutual recognition between the FRY and Macedonia.

**8 April 1996:** Details of the forensic investigation of at least 181 corpses, suspected to be Bosnian Serbs, from graves near Mrkonjić Grad, reveal that 102 appear to have been beaten to death.

**9 April 1996:** Britain announces that it will recognize the FRY.

**17 April 1996:** Germany announces that it will recognize FRY.

**21 April 1996:** Colonel Aleksa Krsmanović is released in Sarajevo in a prisoner exchange.

**22 April 1996:** OSCE issues a 12-page booklet detailing rules for the elections to be held later in the year.

**24 April 1996:** General Đorđe Đukić is released on bail from the UN Tribunal at The Hague due to terminal cancer; the tribunal refuses to drop the charges against him, despite such a request by the prosecutor.
**3 May 1996:** Bosnian government, at the request of The Hague Tribunal, arrests two Bosnian Muslims previously charged with crimes relating to the Čelebići detention camp.
**7 May 1996:** First war crimes trial starts in The Hague: Bosnian Serb Dušan Tadić, arrested in Germany in February 1994, faces over 30 charges; three charges relating to a rape are dropped, as the alleged victim refuses to testify; the trial is expected to last three months.
**14 May 1996:** Radovan Karadžić sacks Prime Minister Rajko Kasagić: various international bodies refuse to recognize the removal.
**15 May 1996:** National Bank governor Dragoslav Avramović, is sacked after a long-running dispute with the government.
**18 May 1996:** General Đorđe Đukić dies of cancer in Belgrade's military hospital.
**21 May 1996:** General Ratko Mladić attends Đukić's funeral in Belgrade.
**26 May 1996:** Nikola Koljević announces that Radovan Karadžić will "keep a low profile" in the RS.
**17 June 1996:** Bosnian Serb refugee Goran Lajić, arrested in Germany and extradited to The Hague, is released after it is established that he is a victim of mistaken identity.
**18 June 1996:** Long-standing arms embargo against states of the former Yugoslavia ends; it is replaced by an arms control regime agreed upon in Dayton.
**19 June 1996:** RS will establish its own war crimes court to try Bosnian Serbs.
**25 June 1996:** OSCE announces the date of the elections in Bosnia as 14 September.
**27 June 1996:** UN tribunal in The Hague starts "Rule 61" proceedings against Radovan Karadžić and Ratko Mladić; indictments against 17others, nine Bosnian Croats for acts against Bosnian Muslims and eight Bosnian Serbs for raping Bosnian Muslims at Foča, eastern Bosnia, are announced.
**5 July 1996:** Radovan Karadžić announces he will not stand for election on September 14, but will remain SDS head.
**11 July 1996:** At the culmination of the "Rule 61" hearing in The Hague, international arrest warrants are issued for Karadžić and Mladić.
**19 July 1996:** Karadžić gives up leadership of the SDS, under pressure that the party will be banned from the September elections.

**23 July 1996:** Bosnian vice president Ejup Ganić makes an official visit to Belgrade.

**24 July 1996:** U.S. announces the imminent arrival of 170 U.S. military instructors to train the new Bosnian Federation army.

**25 July 1996:** RS sends an official delegation to the UN Tribunal at The Hague: the delegation points out that the RS has no means of extradition under its constitution, but that after September 14, as part of Bosnia, it would have.

**7 August 1996:** Slobodan Milošević and Franjo Tudjman meet for talks in Athens.

**14 August 1996:** Announcement that elections for the lower house of the FRY parliament will be held on November 3; elections for the upper house must be held within 30 days of this date.

**15 August 1996:** Sarajevo airport reopens for commercial flights.

**22 August 1996:** UN Tribunal opens its office in Belgrade.

**23 August 1996:** Mate Granić arrives in Belgrade to sign a cooperation agreement following the meeting in Athens earlier in the month.

**26 August 1996:** FRY sends a trade delegation to Sarajevo in response to the delegation headed by Ejup Ganić that previously visited Belgrade.

**27 August 1996:** OSCE postpones the municipal elections for Bosnia scheduled for September 14; all other elections on that day will proceed as planned.

**4 September 1996:** RS and the two constituents of the federation agreed to establish a joint commission to exhume graves and trace people missing in the war.

**14 September 1996:** Elections in Bosnia and Hercegovina.

**29 September 1996:** OSCE certifies the results of the elections, despite allegations from all quarters that more people voted than were on the electoral rolls.

**30 September 1996:** First meeting of three-man Bosnian Presidency; Alija Izetbegović leads, Momčilo Krajišnik represents the RS, and Krešimir Zubak speaks for the Croats in the federation.

**1 October 1996:** UN trade sanctions against the FRY are formally lifted; the U.S. still blocks the FRY's participation in international organizations. In Serbia, the SPS and JUL form a coalition for the upcoming federal and municipal elections.

**3 October 1996:** B-H and FRY establish diplomatic relations at a meeting in Paris between Alija Izetbegović and Slobodan Milošević.

**7 October 1996:** The U.S. threatens sanctions against RS for non-cooperation in post-election joint bodies. The first training camp, run by the American private company Military Professional Resources Inc., is set up for the Federation's joint Muslim-Croat Army under the U.S.'s "train and equip" programme for the Federation.

**22 October 1996:** The U.S. Congress extends trade sanctions against FRY into 1997, an "outer wall" of sanctions which prevents access to international funding for reconstruction.

**24 October 1996:** The first delivery of arms is made under the U.S.'s "train and equip" programme for the Federation.

**31 October 1996:** Ibrahim Rugova announces a boycott by Kosovo Albanians of the forthcoming federal elections in FRY.

**3 November 1996:** Parliamentary elections in the FRY; the left coalition wins the majority of seats in the Chamber of Citizens of the Federal Parliament.

**10 November 1996:** Biljana Plavšić dismisses Ratko Mladić as the supreme comander of the BSA.

**17 November 1996:** Opposition parties make gains in municipal elections in Serbia, a surprise so soon after the positive results in the federal election for the SPS-JUL coalition.

**29 November 1996:** The UN war crimes tribunal hands down its first sentence, against Bosnian Croat Dražen Erdemović, who receives a 10 year prison sentence. There is an appeal.

**4–5 December 1996:** Two-day Peace Implementation Council meeting in London, to review the progress of post-Dayton B-H.

**17 December 1996:** The Bosnian Croat para-state of Herceg-Bosna is said to have ceased to officially exist.

**8 January 1997:** Meeting in Rome to settle the status of the northern Bosnian town of Brčko prior to 15 February deadline.

**13 January 1997:** Kosovo Liberation Army (KLA) claims responsibility for the death of Maliq Sheholli, an Albanian member of the SPS and Podujevo city council. According to the KLA, he was executed as a collaborator.

**14 January 1997:** The Democratic League of Kosovo (LDK) claims that a second Albanian shot dead in Kosovo had cooperated with Serbian police.

**21 January 1997:** The UN's special rapporteur for human rights, Elisabeth Rehn, warns of civil war in Kosovo after a visit.

**28 January 1997:** The OSCE announces a new date for the municipal elections in Bosnia, postponed from 14 September 1996. They will now be held on 12–13 July.

**29 January 1997:** Final steps taken in formation of joint Muslim-Croat army for the Federation.
**14 February 1997:** Decision on Brčko postponed until 15 March 1998. Meanwhile, the town is to come under international administration.
**28 February 1997:** RS and FRY sign an agreement on "special ties" between Belgrade and Pale.
**7 March 1997:** American Robert W. Farrand appointed Brčko supervisor.
**10 March 1997:** The trial starts at the UN war crimes tribunal in The Hague of three Bosnian Muslims and one Bosnian Croat for atrocities against Bosnian Serbs at Čelebići.
**15 March 1997:** The RS parliament ratifies the agreement on "special ties" with Belgrade.
**23 March 1997:** RS agrees to the deployment of 200 IPTF personnel in Brčko.
**5 May 1997:** Vojislav Šešelj announces he will run for president in Serbia.
**6 May 1997:** The U.S. tells Ibrahim Rugova, shadow president of Kosovo, that it "has never supported the idea of elections for a separate parliament in Kosovo".
**7 May 1997:** Dušan Tadić is found guilty on 11 of 31 charges at the UN tribunal in The Hague. He will appeal.
**8 May 1997:** Ibrahim Rugova postpones shadow elections in Kosovo.
**12 May 1997:** NATO begins a five day exercise in Macedonia.
**18 May 1997:** Rail traffic resumes between Tuzla, in the Federation, and Doboj, in RS.
**27 May 1997:** First train runs from Croat-held Vinkovci to Serb-held Vukovar in Croatia.
**5 June 1997:** Slobodan Milošević, Serbian president, is to run for the office of Yugoslav president.
**11 June 1997:** OSCE closes all election registration offices in Brčko, claiming massive fraud.
**16 June 1997:** The World Bank wants $8m in interest repayments before any more aid is distributed in B-H. RS claims it has no money to pay its part of the debt, relating to pre-war loans.
**18 June 1997:** The U.S. says that the "outer wall" of sanctions against FRY will remain until: free and fair federal elections are held; there is media freedom; co-operation with the UN war crimes tribunal; and broad autonomy for Kosovo.
**23 June 1997:** At the UN war crimes tribunal in The Hague, the trial of Bosnian Croat general Tihomir Blaškić begins.

**24 June 1997:** The UN announces that some peacekeepers will remain in Eastern Slavonia beyond the mid-July end date of the current operation.

**27 June 1997:** Croatian Serb, Slavko Dokmanović, arrested by UN war crimes tribunal investigators with UNTAES military support, after being tricked into attending a meeting.

**1 July 1997:** RS president Biljana Plavšić accuses Pale-based SDS figures of being involved in corruption. The SDS split which had begun with the dismissal of Ratko Mladić as chief of the army is now beyond repair.

**2 July 1997:** American general Jaques Klein is to move from his post as head of UN operation in Eastern Slavonia to become deputy to the UN High Representative in Bosnia, Carlos Westendorp. Prosecutors at the UN tribunal call Dušan Tadić "evil" and demand a life sentence for him.

**3 July 1997:** U.S., British, and French government, UN and OSCE in Sarajevo, all express support for Plavšić. British SFOR troops in Banja Luka step up patrols as a warning to the local police not to intervene against Plavšić.

**7 July 1997:** Mate Boban, one-time Bosnian Croat leader, dies of a stroke.

**8 July 1997:** NATO expresses strong support for Biljana Plavšić.

**10 July 1997:** British SFOR troops shoot and kill Simo Drljača and in a separate incident, pretending to deliver Red Cross supplies, arrest Dr. Milan Kovačević in the hospital he heads. Kovačević is flown to UN war crimes tribunal at The Hague, as are the son and son-in-law of Drljača, who were with him when he was shot. The latter two are released. The UN tribunal reveals that the two men were charged in "sealed", or secret, indictments alleging genocide.

**17 July 1997:** International spokesmen in Sarajevo describe RS media as "racist and dishonest".

**23 July 1997:** U.S. Ambassador to the UN, Bill Richardson, calls on all Western countries to support Biljana Plavšić.

**25 July 1997:** Elections in Serbia announced for September 21.

**2 August 1997:** Carlos Westendorp announces an international ban on contacts with Bosnian ambassadors until multi-ethnic replacements are agreed upon.

**6 August 1997:** Assistant Secretary of State Richard Holbrooke returns to the former Yugoslavia to ensure the Dayton agreement does not collapse.

**11 August 1997:** The EU ends the boycott of Bosnian ambassadors. The B-H central bank, headed by Frenchman Serge Robert, commences operation.

**12 August 1997:** Carlos Westendorp deems Biljana Plavšić's dissolution of the RS parliament as legal in the eyes of the international community.

**28 August 1997:** Biljana Plavšić founds her own political party, the Serbian National Alliance.

**1 September 1997:** Ibrahim Rugova and Slobodan Milošević agree on autonomy for Kosovo schools.
**2 September 1997:** OSCE confirms that the much-delayed municipal elections in B-H will go ahead on 12–13 September.
**6 September 1997:** Biljana Plavšić wants the U.S. to train the Bosnian Serb Army.
**8 September 1997:** NATO foils an alleged coup attempt against Biljana Plavšić in Banja Luka.
**15 September 1997:** Croatian foreign minister Mate Granić and FRY counterpart Milan Milutinović sign agreement on normalization of transport, border areas, social insurance, and legal aid, soon to be augmented on agreements on fighting crime and terrorism.
**21 September 1997:** Parliamentary election in Serbia. The SPS-JUL alliance wins 110 of the 250 seats, but needs to enter a coalition to govern. First round of presidential elections, with SPS candidate Zoran Lilić leading, but not gaining the necessary 50% of the vote. Lilić will face Vojislav Šešelj in an October 5 run-off.
**24 September 1997:** Contact Group foreign ministers express concern over Kosovo.
**27 September 1997:** Biljana Plavšić postpones RS parliament election for eight days.
**1 October 1997:** SFOR troops close down Bosnian Serb Television, based in Pale. OSCE announces first round of results from the September 13–14 elections; SDA loses control of Tuzla.
**5 October 1997:** In the second round of voting for the Serbian presidency, fewer than 50% of electorate vote, so a third round is required within 60 days.
**6 October 1997:** 10 Bosnian Croats indicted by the UN war crimes tribunal hand themselves over for trial.
**8 October 1997:** The 10 Bosnian Croats make an initial appearance in court, pleading not guilty.
**13 October 1997:** Biljana Plavšić and Momčilo Krajišnik in Belgrade agree on 23 November for RS parliamentary elections.
**24 October 1997:** Milan Milutinović, Yugoslav foreign minister, becomes the new SPS-JUL candidate for 7 December presidential election.
**28 October 1997:** 100 155mm Howitzer artillery pieces from the U.S. arrive in Bosnia.
**29 October 1997:** The U.S. says the Federation army must destroy 100 older artillery pieces before receiving the new weapons.
**31 October 1997:** Bosnian Serb TV is back on the air, but broadcast from Biljana Plavšić's Banja Luka power base, not Pale.

**11 November 1997:** Biljana Plavšić expresses the desire that the Bosnian Serb army become part of the U.S.'s "train and equip" programme.
**18 November 1997:** Banja Luka airport re-opens for the first time to commercial traffic.
**20 November 1997:** Slobodan Milošević and Albanian prime minister Fatos Nano agree to establish full diplomatic relations.
**22–23 November 1997:** Parliamentary elections in RS.
**26 November 1997:** The KLA make their first kidnap, of a high-ranking Serbian police official.
**28 November 1997:** The KLA make their first public appearance, at the funeral of one of their supporters.
**8 December 1997:** The OSCE announces the results of the RS parliamentary election. The SDS is reduced to 24 out of 83 seats. The Radicals won 15 seats, an increase, as did Biljana Plavšić's new SNS party; 18 seats were won by Muslim and Croat parties. Two seats were won by a minor SNS ally. America is to leave the "outer wall" of sanctions against FRY for a further one year period. America praises the "pluralism" of the RS parliamentary vote.
**9 December 1997:** Phone lines between FRY and B-H restored.
**16 December 1997:** UN High Representative for B-H, Carlos Westendorp, imposes citizenship law after the three-man presidency fails to agree.
**18 December 1997:** Two Bosnian Croats indicted by the UN war crimes tribunal are arrested by SFOR. One is slightly wounded in the action.
**22 December 1997:** Milan Milutinović is announced winner of the Serbian presidency, as total votes just topped the required 50% of the electorate. The OSCE is critical of the result.
**3 January 1998:** The SPS and SRS reject Biljana Plavšić's nominee for prime minister for RS.
**4 January 1998:** The KLA announces that the armed struggle to unite Kosovo and Albania has begun. They claim to control 60 sq km around Srbica.
**6 January 1998:** RS is warned to form a government quickly or Carlos Westendorp will take "appropriate measures". The UN war crimes tribunal starts its fourth trial, that of Zlatko Aleksovski, a Bosnian Croat charged with crimes against Muslims. Westendorp announces that he will appoint someone to oversee RS TV in Banja Luka.
**8 January 1998:** The Contact Group warns FRY to make "concrete progress" on Kosovo. The KLA confirms an earlier claim that they had carried out three bombings in Macedonia.
**12 January 1998:** A pro-Belgrade Albanian is killed in Kosovo and a police station is attacked. Carlos Westendorp appoints a committee of intel-

lectuals to suggest designs for a B-H flag, after the three-man presidency fails to agree. Momčilo Pereišić, chief of staff of VJ, regards the danger in Kosovo as very real, and a top priority for the army.

**13 January 1998:** The three-man B-H presidency announces an agreed list of 32 ambassadors.

**15 January 1998:** Eastern Slavonia returns to Croatian sovreignty. Robert Gelbard, special U.S. envoy, states that unless FRY accepts "international standards of behaviour and democratic processes" the "outer wall" of sanctions will remain.

**18 January 1998:** Milorad Dodik becomes RS prime minister; he was elected when Carlos Westendorp ordered the parliamentary session to continue after its formal close. No SDS or SRS members were present, and the election of Dodik had to wait for other minority members to be found and brought back to the session.

**19 January 1998:** The UN war crimes tribunal starts its fifth trial, with Croatian Serb Slavko Dokmanović as defendant.

**21 January 1998:** UN High Representative Carlos Westendorp introduces new B-H banknotes, after three-man presidency fails to agree.

**28 January 1998:** The Council of Europe condemns FRY's policy in Kosovo.

**30 January 1998:** Ibrahim Rugova calls for an international protectorate for Kosovo.

**2 February 1998**: Sarajevo Agreement on refugee return. 20,000 non-Muslims must be allowed to return to mainly-Muslim Sarajevo by the end of the year.

**3 February 1998:** Albanian president Rexhep Meidani meets UN secretary-general Kofi Annan in New York and calls for international pressure on Serbia over the situation in Kosovo.

**4 February 1998:** UN High Representative Carlos Westendorp imposes new Bosnian flag in time for the Winter Olympics, after the three-man presidency fails to agree.

**5 February 1998:** Roberts Owen, U.S. arbitrator for Brčko, begins discussion in Vienna on the much-delayed resolution of the status of the town.

**6 February 1998:** German foreign minister, Klaus Kinkel, calls for greater autonomy for Kosovo, whilst visiting Tirana, Albania.

**17 February 1998:** SFOR orders the Federation and RS army to reduce military stocks by one quarter, to make it easier for SFOR to monitor them.

**19 February 1998**: An undercover policeman is killed when a police car is ambushed near Priština.

**20 February 1998:** Ibrahim Rugova announces that secret talks with Serb representatives have been going on for "several days" to agree on implementation of the education agreement.

**22 February 1998:** U.S. envoy Robert Gelbard calls for calm in Kosovo. He condemns recent KLA activity: "I consider these to be terrorist actions and it is the strong and firm policy of the U.S. to fully oppose all terrorist actions and all terrorist organizations".

**23 February 1998:** Robert Gelbard announces an easing of some sanctions against FRY: JAT will be given landing rights in the U.S.; FRY will be allowed to join the Southeastern European Cooperation Initiative. The "outer wall" of sanctions will remain. Gelbard says Slobodan Milošević has shown "good will" and was "a significant positive influence" in helping to bring Milorad Dodik to power in RS. EU ministers call on all parties involved in Kosovo to refrain from acts of violence to achieve political goals.

**24 February 1998:** Montenegrin president Milo Đukanović states that Kosovo must receive "a certain degree of autonomy." Carlos Westendorp and Milorad Dodik sign an agreement for $8.5m of EU aid for RS public services wages and pensions. Bosnian Serb Simo Zarić gives himself up to the UN tribunal.

**25 February 1998:** The Contact Group criticises the Serbian police and the KLA for violence in Kosovo.

**26 February 1998:** With easing of sanctions on Belgrade, a pro-Western government in RS and the Brčko arbitration decision approaching, Muhamed Sacirbey, Bosnia's ambassador to the UN, claims that 50 Srebrenica survivors are being held in Kosovo by FRY for forced labor.

**1 March 1998:** 20 people are announced killed in weekend fighting in Kosovo, 16 Albanians and four Serbian police. Ibrahim Rugova calls for international pressure on Belgrade. Slobodan Milošević warns that "terrorism aimed at the internationalization of the issue will be most harmful to those who resorted to these means".

**2 March 1998:** A Kosovo Albanian demonstration in Priština is broken up by police with teargas and watercannon. The foreign ministry in Moscow says a Kosovo solution should respect the territorial integrity of FRY, and observe the rights of ethnic Albanians and other minorities according to OSCE standards, the Helsinki principles and the UN Charter. The Albanian parliament offers cooperation with any NATO or UN force to be deployed in the southeast Balkans. Xhafer Shatri, information minister of the Kosovo government in exile, warns of "terrible war" if the international community does not intervene in Kosovo. Ibrahim Rugova and the LDK leadership make similar appeals to the West.The U.S. is "appalled by the police violence in Kosovo" and demands "unconditional dialogue".

**4 March 1998:** Robert Gelbard blames FRY for the "overwhelming onus" of the problem in Kosovo. The LDK calls for NATO and UN intervention. Dragoljub Kunarac, a Bosnian Serb, gives himself up to the UN war crimes tribunal.

**5 March 1998:** British foreign secretary Robin Cook, speaking in Belgrade, says "whilst we will always back a fight against terrorism, you cannot beat terrorism alone by police action." Sali Berisha, former Albanian president, ends boycott of Albanian parliament in a display of "national unity" on the Kosovo crisis. Heavy fighting in Prekaz, in the Drenica region, leaves up to 60 Kosovo Albanians dead. The U.S. withdraws its recent easing of sanctions against FRY. UN High Representative in B-H sacks the mayor of Stolac, Hercegovina. At the UN war crimes tribunal, Dražen Erdemović's sentence reduced to five years.

**6 March 1998:** The army in Albania is put on "high alert".

**7 March 1998:** U.S. secretary of state, Madeleine Albright, holds Slobodan Milošević "personally responsible" for the situation in Kosovo and warns that the U.S. "will not tolerate violence".

**8 March 1998:** French president Jacques Chirac says "only a message of great firmness, addressed firstly to the authorities in Belgrade... can break the spiral of war and lead to a durable peace for all in Kosovo." Bujar Bukoshi, prime minister of the Kosovo government in exile, demands nothing short of independence for Kosovo: "no kind of autonomy is acceptable".

**9 March 1998:** The Contact Group meets and calls on Belgrade within 10 days to withdraw special police; meaningful dialogue without preconditions; cooperate with the Contact Group; to accept a new OSCE mission for Kosovo; implement the 1996 Education Agreement; and to cooperate with UN war crimes tribunal over Kosovo.

**15 March 1998:** Brčko arbitration leaves RS-Federation boundary unchanged, subject to further requests by either party between 15 November and 15 January 1999.

**22 March 1998:** Kosovo Albanians hold elections; Ibrahim Rugova wins.

**23 March 1998**: Implemenation of the Education Agreement in Kosovo is signed.

**24 March 1998:** New Serbian government announced; ministerial posts go to Šešelj's SRS (15) and JUL (5).

**25 March 1998:** Contact Group meets to review progress on Kosovo.

**2 April 1998:** Slobodan Milošević suggests a referendum in Serbia on international involvement in Kosovo.

**8 April 1998:** Two Bosnian Serbs indicted by the UN war crimes tribunal, Mladen Radić and Miroslav Kvočka, detained by SFOR.

**13 April 1998:** Police station in Kosovo capital Priština attacked.
**16 April 1998:** A Bosnian Serb indicted by the UN war crimes tribunal, Zoran Zigić, detained by SFOR. LDK reorganizes, lead by Rexhep Qosja with Hidayet Hyseni as deputy.
**23 April 1998:** Referendum in Serbia on international involvement in Kosovo: 73% vote, 94% vote against international involvement.
**26 April 1998:** Serbian deputy prime minister, Ratko Marković, writes to Ibrahim Rugova, offering talks. Rugova rejects the intiative.
**29 April 1998:** Contact Group meets on Kosovo. All except Russia freeze FRY funds immediately and threaten an investment freeze by 9 May if FRY does not comply with Contact Group.
**30 April 1998:** The North Atlantic Council states that NATO is considering further security measures relating to Kosovo. Charges brought against former Montenegrin president Momir Bulatović for abuse of power.
**6 May 1998:** NATO requests political guidance on range of military measures for Kosovo. RS president Biljana Plavšić temporarily detained on war crimes charges in Vienna.
**8–9 May 1998:** G8 meet in London and, except for Russia, agree to implement the Contact Group measures of 29 April.
**9–13 May 1998:** Robert Gelbard and Richard Holbrooke visit Belgrade, Priština and Bosnia.
**15 May 1998:** With Richard Holbrooke mediating, Slobodan Milošević and Ibrahim Rugova meet in Belgrade.
**16 May 1998:** During G8 meeting in Birmingham, Contact Group meets and agrees to delay investment ban on FRY.
**20 May 1998:** Momir Bulatović becomes prime minister of FRY, against the objections of the Montenegrin parliament.
**27 May 1998:** Richard Holbrooke states that Kosovo might start a wider war, with Bulgaria "grabbing off" part of Macedonia. Bulgaria protests strongly.
**28 May 1998:** NATO foreign ministers meet on Bosnia and Kosovo. Planning for post-June SFOR in Bosnia and enchanced Partnership for Peace arrangements for Albania and Macedonia. A Bosnian Serb indicted by the UN war crimes tribunal, Milojica Koš, detained by SFOR.
**31 May 1998:** Montenegrin parliamentary and municipal elections.
**1 June 1998**: Albania calls for international diplomatic intervention and the stationing of NATO troops on the border between Albania and Serbia.
**2 June 1998:** Ibrahim Rugova requests a UN "no-fly zone" for Kosovo.
**3 June 1998:** NATO secretary-general Javier Solana is keeping "all options open" for NATO action in Kosovo.

**4 June 1998:** Kosovo Albanians call off talks with Belgrade scheduled for 5 June. The IMF approves B-H's macroeconomic plan and awards a loan of $63m to reform public finances and help foreign debt repayments.
**5 June 1998:** Former Albanian president Sali Berisha sends "special greetings" to the KLA at a press conference in Tirana.
**8 June 1998:** EU condemns FRY action in Kosovo. In RS, an anti-hardline political alliance is announced, the SNS, Socialist Party and Independent Social democrats will join forces for RS presidency vote and for elections to Serb posts in the national government. In the parliamentary elections, they will stand as separate parties. Separately, UK prime minister Tony Blair, U.S. defense secretary William Cohen and French president Jaques Chirac condemn Serb action in Kosovo and warn of potential military action against it.
**9 June 1998:** Separately the U.S. and EU freeze FRY assets and ban investment in Serbia. Russia and China voice disapproval of foreign military intervention in Kosovo.
**10 June 1998:** The Contact Group meets and hints at the use of force if FRY does not comply. The UN war crimes tribunal claims jurisdiction over the current Kosovo conflict. Richard Holbrooke says that Kosovo is not like Bosnia, as Kosovo was not a republic in Yugoslavia. NATO's top military officer, Gen Klaus Naumann, warns that airstrikes would be required against both Serbian forces and the KLA to stop fighting in Kosovo.
**11 June 1998:** Sali Berisha suggests that NATO coordinate military intervention in Kosovo with the KLA. Tony Blair reassures Ibrahim Rugova that a UN resolution authorizing military intervention in Kosovo is being sought. NATO announces live ammunition air exercises near the Serbian border.
**12 June 1998:** U.S. defense secretary William Cohen says that NATO does not require UN authorization for military strikes.
**13 June 1998:** KLA claims to control one third of Kosovo.
**15 June 1998:** 84 NATO aircraft take part in exercise "Determined Falcon" in Albania and Macedonia, along the borders with Serbia.
**16 June 1998:** RS parliament sacks "hard-liners" Dragan Kalinić and Nikola Poplašen. Robin Cook states that a "great majority" of the 15-member UN Security Council are in favor of military intervention in Kosovo. Russian president Boris Yeltsin has talks with Slobodan Milošević in Moscow.
**17 June 1998:** The KLA brands Ibrahim Rugova as "an obstacle" to independence for Kosovo.
**18 June 1998:** FRY agrees to talks with Kosovo Albanians, but without international mediation. The U.S. warns the KLA that they will be playing into Slobodan Milošević's hands if they plan further offensives.
**22 June 1998:** Elisabeth Rehn, UN special representative to Bosnia, states

that the "time is ripe" for NATO military intervention in Kosovo, but that it must have a UN mandate; she suggests the 1991 Gulf War intervention as a proper model for intervention in Kosovo.

**23 June 1998:** Richard Holbrooke warns Slobodan Milošević to accept the Contact Group proposals. Greece and Macedonia oppose NATO intervention in Kosovo.

**24 June 1998:** Javier Solana says that Kosovo has the right to secede, because it was part of a country which no longer exists, but that Ibrahim Rugova should return to the negotiating table. Other NATO officials say that Serbia is facing a determined guerilla force and that NATO should not play into the hands of the KLA. Richard Holbrooke meets with two uniformed representatives of the KLA in Junik, Kosovo. Tony Blair states that NATO military action is still an option. The Council of Europe passes a resolution blaming Slobodan Milošević for the problems in Kosovo. B-H co-prime minister, Haris Silajdžić, offers military facilities for any NATO action in Kosovo. The RS parliament votes to formally move its seat from Pale to Banja Luka.

**26 June 1998:** Richard Holbrooke returns to Priština to talk with Kosovo Albanians. U.S. special envoy holds a secret meeting with the KLA with Ibrahim Rugova's approval, as revealed on 28 June by Richard Holbrooke. Albanian prime minister Fatos Nano does not support independence for Kosovo, but says it should have republican status in FRY. Nano calls for NATO airstrikes, but says they must have UN authority.

**27 June 1998:** In B-H, the HDZ splits, with supporters of Krešimir Zubak forming the New Croatian Initiative, a Christian democrat-style party. They claim the HDZ is in favor of the partition of B-H. Adem Demaçi, a rival of Ibrahim Rugova, claims that the KLA controls half of Kosovo.

**28 June 1998:** Momir Bulatović leaves the economic forum at Crans Montana, Switzerland, after a session on security in Europe was abruptly cancelled when Fatos Nano refused to attend, saying it was pointless because "they continue to massacre civilians". UN secretary-general Kofi Annan says NATO action without a UN mandate would be a dangerous precedent. In RS, Dragan Kalinić replaces Aleksa Buha as SDS party leader.

**29 June 1998:** Croatian Serb Slavko Dokmanović is found dead in his cell at the UN war crimes tribunal in The Hague, having committed suicide before the verdict in his trial, leaving questions about the running of the UN detention centre and mental health supervision. Kofi Annan urges the international community to move swiftly in Kosovo to prevent "another Bosnia", but only under UN authority. Serbian security forces launch an operation to re-take control of the Belaćevac mine from the KLA.

**1 July 1998:** Serb police and a representative of the Ministry of Telecommunications close down Radio Kontakt, a music radio station in Priština, when it rebroadcasts news from radio B-92 in Belgrade.

**2 July 1998:** Javier Solana says NATO will not permit "another Bosnia" in Kosovo. Hans Van den Broek, EU foreign affairs spokesman, says that NATO can carry out military intervention without UN authorization. Germany announces it will stop the forced extraction of funds for the KLA from Kosovo Albanians living in Germany.

**3 July 1998:** Serb security forces relieve Kijevo, freeing about 200 Serb civilians and a dozen police who had been cut off by the KLA for more than a week.

**4 July 1998:** Bulgaria protests the kidnap of a Bulgarian citizen in Kosovo, taken hostage along with three Serbs on 2 July.

**6 July 1998:** At the UN war crimes tribunal in The Hague, the first trial involving charges of genocide, against Milan Kovačević, starts. Chris Hill, U.S. ambassador to Macedonia, says that "Kosovo cannot shoot its way out of Serbia" but that the situation must be resolved in the next 14 days; ten diplomats arrive in Kosovo to monitor the situation, a further 40 military experts and 25 EU monitors are expected soon. Richard Holbrooke and Russian deputy foreign minister Nikolai Afanasevskii end three days of fruitless shuttle diplomacy on Kosovo.

**7 July 1998:** Louise Arbour, chief prosecutor at the UN war crimes tribunal, says that the "nature and scale" of the fighting in Kosovo indicate an armed conflict as recognized in international law, and she intends to bring charges of crimes against humanity, if she can find any evidence. Alush Gashi, Ibrahim Rugova's top aide, claims divisions in the international community are causing widening divisions amongst Kosovo Albanians. In B-H, Mostar airport reopens to civilian traffic.

**8 July 1998:** The Contact Group rules out independence for Kosovo, and also calls for the KLA to stop fighting. They propose measures to reduce the funding of the KLA from expatriate Kosovo Albanians. In B-H, Carlos Westendorp appoints Slovene Tomaž Petrović as the "international arbitrator" for B-H media.

**9 July 1998:** The EU and the U.S. Agency for International Development suspend $20m of aid to Sarajevo until 20,000 non-Muslims have returned to the city, as agreed earlier in the year.

**11 July 1998:** The KLA announces that it does not recognize Ibrahim Rugova's leadership of Kosovo Albanians. They also pledge that the KLA will be in Priština soon, and call for a U.S.-led protectorate for Kosovo.

**13 July 1998:** EU foreign ministers call for a ceasefire in Kosovo, and will urge the UN Security Council to take further action if this does not come about. U.S. says that Kosovo Albanians "need to understand that their independence goals are not going to be achieved."
**16 July 1998:** Kosovo Albanians convene their first shadow parliament. Serb police close it down peacefully, removing boxes of documents.
**19 July 1998:** The U.S. Senate urges the UN war crimes tribunal to charge Slobodan Milošević with "war crimes, crimes against humanity and genocide".
**20 July 1998:** Albanian prime minister Fatos Nano says that "no more time should be lost in stopping the Serb war-machine through air strikes." Serb forces defeat a three-day attempt by the KLA to take the town of Orahovac. An estimated 100 are killed in the fighting, by far the largest battle in the conflict.
**22 July 1998:** UN High Representative in B-H, Carlos Westendorp, decrees new privatization law.
**23 July 1998:** SFOR arrests a pair of Bosnian Serb twins and flies them to the UN war crimes tribunal at The Hague. They are later returned, as they are the wrong twins. The LDK in Kosovo appeals to the same tribunal, claiming a policy of "genocide against the Albanian people".
**24 July 1998:** Ibrahim Rugova calls for an international protectorate for Kosovo. Serb police and military units start offensive against KLA.
**28 July 1998:** The KLA stronghold of Mališevo falls.
**1 August 1998:** Milan Kovačević dies of natural causes in his cell in the UN war crimes tribunal at The Hague. Since he has already suffered a stroke and minor heart attacks there are questions about medical treatment in detention and his fitness to stand trial.
**7 August 1998:** The Western European Union calls on NATO to intervene "immediately" in Kosovo. Five months of conflict have left an estimated 600 dead.
**10 August 1998:** Absentee voting starts for the September 12–13 elections in B-H.
**11 August 1998:** The KLA vows to fight on, despite recent losses.They also warn NATO against stationing troops on the Albania-Serbia border which they would consider to be "the second offensive against our freedom and our national pride".
**12 August 1998:** Serb forces launch assault on KLA stronghold of Junik.
**13 August 1998:** EU condemns attack on Junik, where 1,000 KLA and 1,000 civilians are trapped. KLA announces "tactical withdrawal", and

claims to have asked Adem Demaci, a rival to Ibrahim Rugova, to represent them politically. Rugova announces negotiating team for talks with Serbian authorities. Demaci refuses an invitation to join the team.

**16 August 1998:** Junik, the last key town held by the KLA, falls.

**24 August 1998:** The UN Security Council issues a statement condemning "all violence and acts of terrorism from whatever quarter".

**1 September 1998:** B-H is to get a unified customs agreement, starting January 1999.

**2 September 1998:** U.S. ambassador to Macedonia, Christopher Hill, says that both sides in the Kosovo dispute have agreed in principle to "a certain degree of self-administration" for an interim 3–5 year period, after which the parties concerned could "review" the situation. Hill had talks with both Slobodan Milošević and Ibrahim Rugova.

**3 September 1998:** U.S. secretary of state, Madeleine Albright, says the tentative agreement is a "good procedural step forward" but threatens that "force" may still be needed.

**6 September 1998:** The EU bans flights for the FRY airline, JAT.

**13 September 1998:** Voting closes in the B-H general election.

**15 September 1998:** The U.S. House of Representatives urges the UN war crimes tribunal to charge Slobodan Milošević with "war crimes, crimes against humanity and genocide". Carlos Westendorp extends a 4 October deadline for reclaiming property in the Federation to 4 April.

**17 September 1998:** Nikola Poplašen, a "hard-liner", claims victory in the RS presidential race.

**21 September 1998:** Adem Demaçi, political representative of the KLA, withdraws from politics for health reasons.

**24 September 1998:** The U.S. and Germany warn FRY to comply with UN and NATO demands for a ceasefire soon or face an ultimatum. The Contact Group countries, excluding Russia, believe that no further UN authorization is required for military action.

**25 September 1998:** The OSCE releases the results of the 12–13 September elections in B-H.

**26 September 1998:** 18 civilian Kosovo Albanians are reported killed by Serbs at Obrinje.

**27 September 1998:** A Bosnian Serb indicted by the UN war crimes tribunal, Stevan Todorović, detained by SFOR.

**28 September 1998:** U.S. defense secretary William Cohen warns that NATO plans are ready for military action.

**30 September 1998:** The international community queues up to condemn the killings at Obrinje. Germany offers 14 aircraft and 500 troops for any NATO military action in Kosovo. The U.S. says "the clock is ticking" on NATO action.

**1 October 1998:** UK foreign secretary Robin Cook says that Britain and NATO are ready to use military force after Obrinje. The UN Security Council meets, but does not authorize military action. The U.S. advises its citizens to leave FRY.

**2 October 1998:** The Russian Duma, the parliament, passes a resolution labelling potential NATO action in Kosovo as an illegal aggression.

**3 October 1998:** Greece opposes NATO action in Kosovo.

**5 October 1998:** Albania offers all its facilities for NATO air attacks on FRY. UN secretary general Kofi Annan reports he does not have enough people in Kosovo to decide whether FRY has complied with the Security Council. Russian and Chinese diplomats say they would oppose NATO intervention. U.S. envoys Richard Holbrooke and Christopher Hill visit Belgrade.

**6 October 1998:** U.S. envoys Richard Holbrooke and Christopher Hill visit Priština. Belarus offers unconditional support to FRY. The UN issues a statement demanding "full and sustained compliance" from FRY. FRY foreign minister Živadin Jovanović invites an OSCE team to Kosovo.

**7 October 1998:** The new three-man B-H presidency meets and agrees to hold all future meetings on Federation territory, in Sarajevo, instead of previous arrangements where some meetings would be in RS. U.S. president Bill Clinton warns FRY of NATO air strikes. Richard Holbrooke meets Madeleine Albright in Brussels. Ukraine offers "material and moral support" to FRY. The OSCE says they will not send a mission to Kosovo.

**8 October 1998:** UN High Representative Carlos Westendorp sacks the deputy leader of the SDS for comments on potential NATO air strikes in Kosovo.

**24 March 1999:** With 400 aircraft and ships in the Adriatic NATO begins its attach on FRY. B52s fly from Britain and, along with naval-launches, more than 100 cruise missiles are fired by NATO at 40 targets.

**27 March 1999:** A US F117A Stealth Fighter is shot down near the village of Budjanovci in FRY. The pilot is rescued. Eleven targets in the region of Belgrade are attacked.

**1 April 1999:** The first bridge over the Danube at Novi Sad is destroyed, cutting the towns water supply. Three U.S. soldiers are captured by VJ near the FRY/FYROM border. Milośević meets Rugova in Belgrade.

**2 April 1999:** The Serbian Interior Ministry in central Belgrade is attacked. The nearby hospital complex is damaged.

**3 April 1999:** The largest heating plant in Belgrade is attacked.

**6 April 1999:** A residential district in Aleksinac is bombed, along with an oil refinery in Novi Sad.

**10 April 1999:** NATO force deployment reaches total of 700 aircraft, including 600 from the U.S. Broadcasting facilities of TV Priština attacked.

**13 April 1999:** A passenger train crossing rail bridge is attacked, killing at least 10.

**14 April 1999:** NATO claims to have hit a food plant, a hydro-electric plant, and several bridges.

**15 April 1999:** NATO bombs hit up to four civilian convoys of displaced Albanians in Kosovo, killing up to 85.

**21 April, 1999:** The Belgrade headquarters of the SPS is attacked. The 30-story building includes offices for two TV stations.

**22 April 1999:** Milošević's official residence is attacked. Russian special envoy Viktor Chernomyrdin meets Milošević in Belgrade.

**23 April 1999:** NATO bombs Serbian Television in Belgrade, killing more than 20 and cutting off service for a few hours. NATO leaders meet in Washington to celebrate the 50th anniversary of the defensive alliance.

**26 April 1999:** NATO destroys the third and last bridge over the Danube in Novi Sad.

**28 April 1999:** A civilian district in Surdulica is bombed, killing at least 16, including 11 schoolchildren.

**30 April 1999:** NATO bombs a civilian house in Bulgaria.

**1 May 1999:** NATO bombs a civilian bus on a road bridge in Kosovo, killing at least 23.

**2 May 1999:** U.S. F16 aircraft shot down. FRY releases the three captured American soldiers after intervention by Rev. Jesse Jackson.

**3 May 1999:** NATO attacks five major power supply facilities, cutting power to most residences in FRY.

**6 May 1999:** The G-8 group of nations agrees to a five-point plan for end of NATO bombing.

**7 May 1999:** NATO cluster bombs kill at least 10 people in a market and hospital in the southern city of Nis.

**8 May 1999:** Three NATO missiles hit the Chinese Embassy in Belgrade, killing three Chinese journalists.

**14 May 1999:** NATO bombs the Kosova town of Koriša, killing at least 80 displaced ethnic Albanians.

**20 May 1999:** A NATO missile hits a Belgrade hospital, killing three people.

**21 May 1999:** NATO bombs damage the home of the Swiss Ambassador in Belgrade.

**22 May 1999:** NATO bombs hit a KLA command post, killing seven.
**27 May 1999:** Milošević and four top officials are indicted for war crimes by the UN tribunal in The Hague.
**29 May 1999:** NATO aircraft taking part in campaign now total 1,089.
**30 May 1999:** A NATO attack kills a least 11 on bridge at Varvarin, central Serbia.
**31 May 1999:** NATO bombs hit a sanatorium and nursing home in Surdulica, killing at least 10.
**1 June 1999:** An apartment block in Novi Pazar is bombed, killing at least 10 people.
**3 June 1999:** Milošević accepts a plan to end the war, presented in Belgrade by EU envoy Finnish President Martti Ahtisaari.
**9 June 1999:** NATO and FRY sign agreement on FRY withdrawal from Kosovo.
**10 June 1999:** NATO attacks are suspended after confirmation of the start of the FRY withdrawal from Kosovo. UN Resolution 1244 mandates foreign troops in Kosovo.

Map 1 The Federal Republic of Yugoslavia (Serbia and Montenegro)

Map 2 Territorial Division of the Former Yugoslavia, 1991-1995

1 — Republika Srpska
2 — Republic of Serbian Krajina
3 — Muslim-Croat Federation

Map 3 Administrative Division of Kingdom of Yugoslavia, 1931

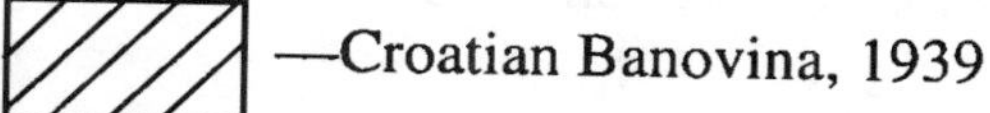

—Croatian Banovina, 1939

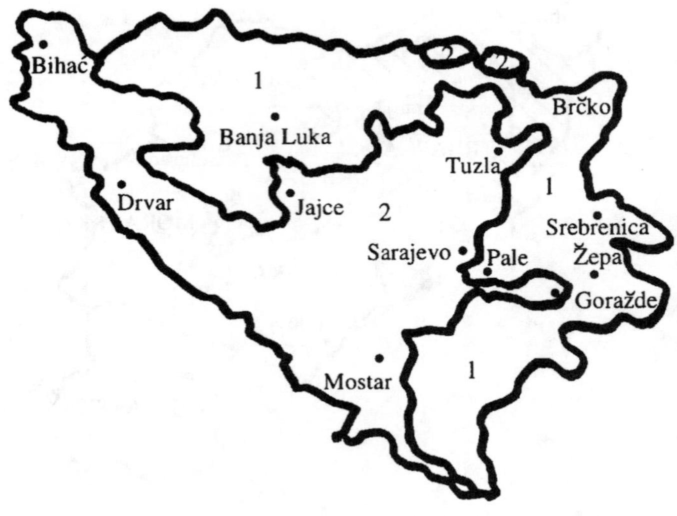


Map 4 Territorial Division of Bosnia and Hercegovina According to the Dayton Agreement, 1995

| | |
|---|---|
| 1— | Republika Srpska |
| 2— | Muslim-Croat Federation |

Map 5 Empire of Dušan the Mighty, 1331-1355

Map 6 Kosovo and Metohija

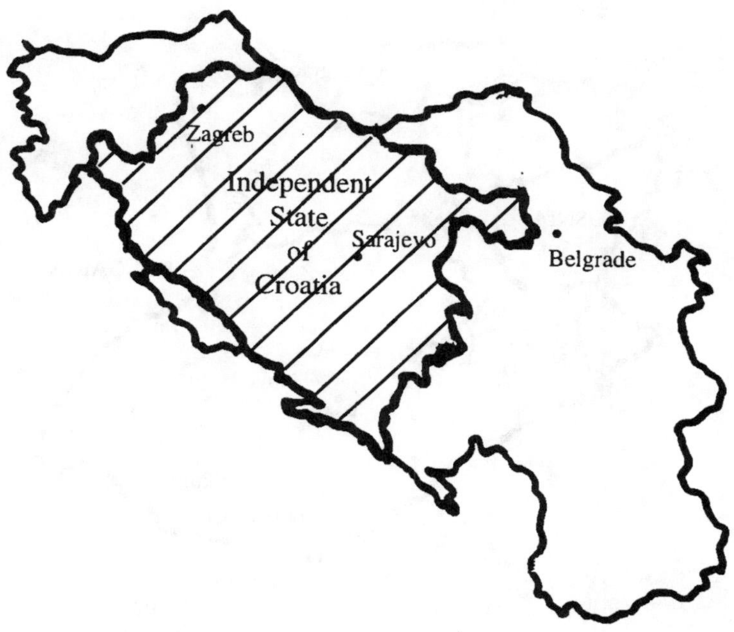


Map 7 Independent State of Croatia, 1941-1945

Map 8 Serbia during the Reign of King Milutin, 1282–1321

Map 9 Serbia during the Reign of Stefan Nemanja and Stefan Prvovenčani, the 12th and 13th Century

| | |
|---|---|
| ----- | Stefan Nemanja State |
| —— | Stefan Prvovenčani State |

Map 10 The Owen-Stoltenberg Plan, 1994

| | |
|---|---|
| Muslims— | 1 |
| Serbs— | 2 |
| Croats— | 3 |
| UN administered— | 4 |

Map 11 Jurisdiction of the Serbian Patriarchate of Peć in the 17th Century

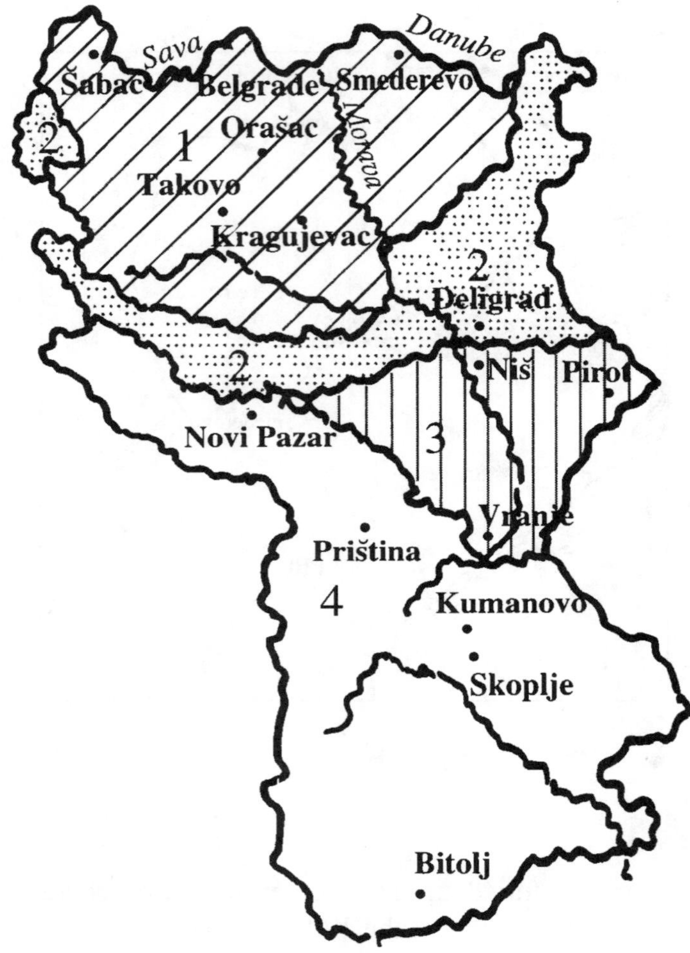


Map 12 The Expansion of Serbia, 1804–1913

| | |
|---|---|
| 1 | Beogradski Pašaluk |
| 2 | Annexed in 1833 |
| 3 | Gained at Congress of Berlin |
| 4 | Acquired in Balkan Wars 1912-1913 |

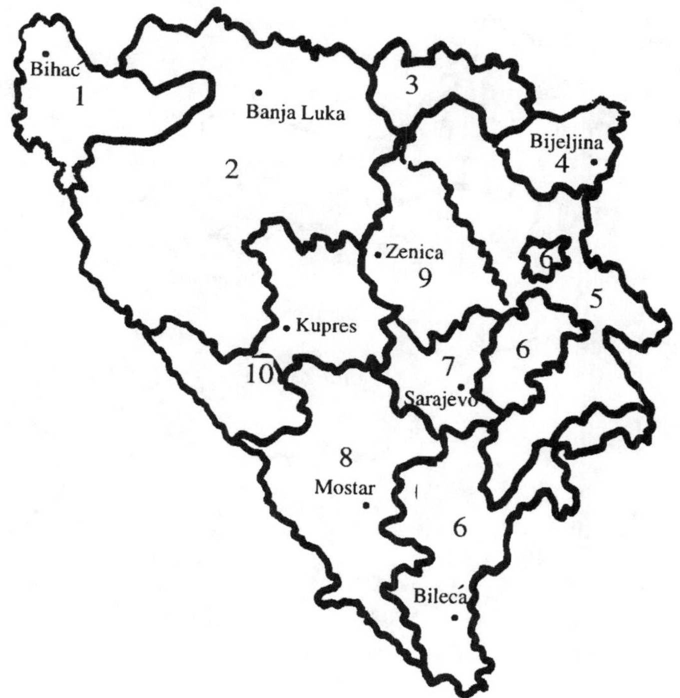


Map 13 The Vance-Owen Plan, 1993

| | |
|---|---|
| Croats — | 3, 8, 10 |
| Muslims — | 1, 5, 7, 9 |
| Serbs — | 2, 4, 6 |

Map 14 ■ Vojna Krajina, 1780

# Introduction

## GENERAL BACKGROUND

The third Yugoslav state, the Federal Republic of Yugoslavia, emerged as its predecessor, the Socialist Federal Republic of Yugoslavia, crumbled. Comprising Serbia and Montenegro, the only independent states which entered into the venture known as the Kingdom of the Serbs, Croats, and Slovenes in 1918, the new country differs substantially from the two previous Yugoslav states. The first Yugoslavia resulted from the century-long process of the Serbian struggle for national liberation that began with the First Serbian Insurrection in 1804. The Serbian national revolution, producing first an autonomous principality then an independent kingdom, paralleled the process of the establishment of national states in the 19th century; thus the concept of Greater Serbia, elaborated in Ilija Garašanin's *Načertanije*, merely echoed the rebel shout "one nation–one state" spreading throughout revolutionary Europe. With Serbs scattered throughout several regions including two different empires, and with over one third of the total number of Serbs living outside independent Serbia, the unification of traditional Serbian lands became the focus of Serbian national ideology. Creating a common state with other South Slavs played a secondary role in that ideology. The attractiveness of the Yugoslav idea directly depended upon its potential contribution toward the unification of the Serbian lands.

The absence of a national state decisively influenced the two other peoples creating the first Yugoslavia. The Croats and Slovenes pursued national identity and struggled for the acknowledgment of their "particularity" within the multinational Austro-Hungarian Empire. Unlike the Serbs, who achieved their independence through a combination of armed struggle against the Ottoman Empire and steady diplomatic advances, the national struggle of Croats and Slovenes was confined exclusively to the political framework of Austria-Hungary. Consequently, Croatian national ideology concentrated upon building a "Croat element" within that empire. Outnumbered by Czechs and Slovaks, the Croats' only hope of acquiring greater autonomy inside Austria-Hungary remained a union with the Serbs. Croatian "Yugoslavism" never perceived union with the Serbs as independence outside the Austro-Hungarian Empire. The unification of the South Slavs, under Croatian patronage, was merely an instrument in achieving greater autonomy and resisting the rapidly increasing "Magyarization" of Croatia.

The first Yugoslavia thus materialized as the second-best solution for both Serbs and Croats. The Croatian independence from Austria-Hungary simply was not possible without some sort of a union between the Serbs and Croats. On the other hand, while among Serbs the attitude toward Yugoslavia varied, the words of Nikola Pašić at the signing of the final document of the Geneva Conference where the foundation of the common state was laid, exemplified the Serbian stand the best:

> In the hardest time of my life, when the question of unification was being solved, I steeled my heart, accepted Serbia's humiliation and my own, and sacrificed them to national unification, in the firm conviction that our people, who are just judges, would quickly mend the injustice and grant recognition to the Kingdom of Serbia, which had given proof of sacrificing everything to unity.

Another dichotomy figured prominently in the respective national ideologies of the Serbs and the Croats. While Croats were marginally present in the Serbian national ideology, Serbs always played a distinctive role in that of Croats. Since the 16th century, Serbs constituted the majority of the population in the region that became known as Vojna Krajina (Military Border). The Serbs perceived Krajina as the homeland for which they fought the Ottoman invaders. Croats, on the other hand, looked upon Krajina as an integral part of their state and the Serbs as merely intruders or, at best, guests. These conceptual differences between the national ideologies of the two principal "Yugoslav" nations, as well as the absence of a primary will for the formation of a common state, warrant an explanation of why the Yugoslav state continued to exist. The answer lies in the specific combination of international and domestic factors involved in the formation of the two Yugoslav states.

Although vastly different, the two national ideologies had something in common: both Serbs and Croats claimed Krajina as their historic land. The contesting claims on and the inability to assert sole primacy over the disputed territory were dominant internal factors in constituting the first Yugoslavia. Although victorious in World War I, Serbia was not able to form Greater Serbia due to strong Allied opposition, and the formation of Yugoslavia became the most opportune way to unify Serbian lands and nation. For Croats, Yugoslavia presented an effective tool in resisting Italian territorial claims and an opportunity to advance political and economic autonomy.

The second Yugoslavia emerged from a bloody civil war, a socialist revolution, and genocidal interethnic struggle. For the victorious Communists, the federal state was a logical solution to the national question. The new administrative division of the country was supposed to eradicate contesting territorial claims, perceived by the Communists as a major source of nationalism. The specific external circumstances, the cold war, and the continuous East-West conflict, affected Yugoslavia beneficially. Internally, it mobilized the masses in resisting both Soviet and Western domination; externally it gave Yugoslavia the status of a peculiar bridge between the two blocs.

The collapse of communism in Eastern Europe and the end of the cold war removed one of these pillars supporting the second Yugoslav state. In response, internal policies in Yugoslavia resulted in the country becoming a short-lived confederation of national states with traditional national ideologies and contesting territorial claims. The formation of the first and the destruction of the second Yugoslav state had a common element: competing national ideologies and the struggle over territory. Emerging in the process of separation of the former Yugoslav republics, the third Yugoslav state lacks the contending national ideologies and territorial claims, separating it the from its predecessors.

## SERBIA AND SERBIAN LANDS FROM EARLY DEVELOPMENTS TO THE FIRST YUGOSLAV STATE

The first Slav tribes began to settle in the Balkan peninsula in the 5th century. They formed a large number of small principalities for which contemporary Byzantine writers used the common name "Sklavinia." Among the South Slav tribes, the Serbs were the most numerous. Members of the Serbian tribes established several principalities. A Serbian state was first mentioned by the Byzantine emperor Constantine VII in his *De administrando Imperio*. It stretched from the Sava River in the north to the Dinaric *massif* in the south and from the Ibar River in the east to the Vrbas River in the west. Apart from the main state, which was also called Raška (Rassa, Rascia), the

Serbian tribes settled in mountainous regions, river valleys, and the Karst (an area along the Dalmatian coast). These various tribes are known by the names Neretljani (tribes of Neretva that settled between the Cetina and Neretva Rivers), Zahumljani (tribes of Zahumlje that settled in the region between the Neretva and Dubrovnik's hinterlands), and Konavljani (tribes of the Konavli region between Dubrovnik and Boka Kotorska Bay).

Following early domination by the Avars, the Serbian principalities fell under the rule of Proto-Bulgars around 680. For two centuries the area between the Danube River and the Balkan mountains, inhabited by the Serbian tribes, was the site of a bitter rivalry between the Bulgarian and the Byzantine Empires. The unification of the Serbian tribes began after their conversion to Christianity (867–874). The Glagolitic and Cyrillic alphabets played a significant role during the unification and fostered the development of Serbian literacy.

Časlav (927–950?) was the first Serbian ruler who successfully resisted Bulgarian domination and repulsed attacks by the Magyars who settled in the Pannonian basin. The battles for primacy in the Balkans continued, however, after his death. The center of Serbian resistance moved to the south and concentrated between the Pelješac Peninsula, Dubrovnik, and Drač. This area became known as Duklja (Dioclea) and/or Zeta. The Hungarian conquest of Croatia and expansion toward the Adriatic Sea inhibited the development of the Serbian state in the littoral. The centers of the Serbian state subsequently moved to Bosnia and the fortress of Ras.

The turning point in the formation of the medieval Serbian state came during the rule of the grand župan Stefan Nemanja (1168–1196), the founder of the Nemanjić dynasty. Through a series of diplomatic negotiations and military battles, he succeeded in extending his authority to the Great Morava and South Morava Rivers, then to the region that is today known as Kosovo and Metohija, the plains of Lake Shkodër, and the bay of Boka Kotorska. After Nemanja's abdication, his oldest son Vukan established rule over the Zeta region, while his middle son Stefan inherited the main Serbian lands. A gifted politician, Stefan, although a son-in-law of the Byzantine emperor, enjoyed the support of the Pope and received a royal crown in 1217. His elevation to Serbian king brought him the title of "first crowned king" or Stefan Prvovenčani. Nemanja's youngest son, Rastko or Sava, left Serbia and became a monk at Mt. Athos. He actively participated in the political and spiritual life of Serbia and strongly opposed the growing influence of Roman Catholicism among the Serbs. After a series of diplomatic moves, he succeeded in obtaining independence for the Serbian Orthodox Church and was consecrated as the archbishop of the autocephalous Serbian Orthodox Church in 1219 in Nicaea.

The establishment and continuous strengthening of the Serbian kingdom and autocephalous church provided a solid basis for vigorous cultural development in Serbia. In a relatively short period numerous churches and monasteries were built in the particular style of the Raška School of architecture (Studenica, Žiča, Mileševa, Sopoćani, Gradac, Arilje monasteries and others.) Serbian rulers and spiritual leaders were among the most active in developing specific cultural values: both Sava and Stefan Prvovenčani wrote biographies of their father Stefan Nemanja. These texts played an important role in establishing the cult of St. Sava and the Nemanjić Dynasty. The economic development of the medieval Serbian state was characterized by rapid increase in trade with neighboring states Hungary and Byzantium. Trade with Serbian-populated areas outside the boundaries of the Serbian state—the coastal cities Dubrovnik, Kotor, Bar, Budva, and Shokdër—grew rapidly. The growth of mining prompted a strong influx of German expert miners from Saxony and Transylvania. The establishment of mining communities boosted the development of cities (Novo Brdo, Zvečan, and others).

Although the immediate successors of Stefan Prvovenčani played a secondary role in Balkan politics, they succeeded in preserving the Serbian state. The reigns of Stefan Radoslav (1227–1233) and Stefan Vladislav (1234–1243) were dominated by their personal and family ties with the Byzantine Empire and Bulgaria. Their younger brother Stefan Uroš I (1243–1276), however, expanded the boundaries of Serbia by including the Mačva region in the north and territories surrounding the city of Skoplje in the south. During his reign, the economy flourished, and Serbia became the major producer of silver, copper, and lead in the Balkans.

The Serbian state further expanded during the reign of Uroš's sons Stefan Dragutin (1276–1282) and Stefan Milutin (1282–1321). During the reign of King Milutin, Serbia extended from the Sava and Danube Rivers in the north, to the Vrbas and Cetina Rivers in the west, and from the city of Niš in the east and Demir kapija (Prosek) in the south. The northward expansion of the Serbian state, that is, the reaching of the Danube and Sava Rivers, further improved Serbia's communication links with central and western Europe and facilitated rapid economic growth. The economic expansion bolstered Serbia's cultural enrichment—during Milutin's reign more than forty churches and monasteries were built. The rule of Milutin's son Stefan Dečanski (1321–1331) was distinguished by the Serbian victory over the Bulgars in the Battle of Velbužd (July 28, 1330). This victory established an absolute Serbian supremacy in the Balkans that would last until the Turkish expansion.

Stefan Dečanski's son Stefan Dušan (1331–1355) pursued a policy of an aggressive southward expansion. As a result of several well-organized military campaigns, Dušan's territorial authority extended over all of Macedonia, Albania, Epirus, and Thessaly. Dušan elevated the Serbian archbishopric to the level of patriarchate. On April 16, 1346, he was crowned "the emperor and autocrat of the Serbs and the Greeks." His territorial expansion facilitated the economic growth of Serbia through intensive silver mining, trade and the establishment of urban centers. Serbia's growth also incited vigorous legislative activity. Dušan's empire included a wide range of territories with various legislative systems. In order to bridge the differences between Byzantine law and Serbian law, and to unify governmental structures, a special code of law known as Dušanov zakonik (Dušan's Code of Law 1349, 1354) was instituted. The code was an eclectic document that reflected the feudal structure of the Serbian and Byzantine societies at the time.

The most glorious period of Serbia's medieval history ended with Dušan's unexpected death in 1355. His son Stefan Uroš was unable to stop the dissolution of Dušan's heterogenous empire. Dušan's half-brother Simeon Paleologos proclaimed himself emperor and founded a separate state in Thessaly. Serbian nobleman followed suit and established their authority over various parts of the empire. Dejanović's family ruled in southern Macedonia, King Vukašin and Despot Jovan Uglješa Mrnjavčević in northern and eastern Macedonia, Vuk Branković in Kosovo and Metohija, Nikola Altomanović in the territory in western Serbia that stretched from the city of Užice to the Adriatic Sea, and Prince Lazar Hrebeljanović in the region around the cities of Kruševac and Novo Brdo in central Serbia.

The growing threat of Turkish expansion did not unify the divided nation. Neither did the crushing defeat of the large Serbian army led by Vukašin and Jovan Uglješa in the Battle of Maritsa (September 26, 1371), which resulted in the Turkish conquest of the whole of Macedonia and large parts of Bulgaria. Prince Lazar was the first to realize the imminent danger of the Turkish advances. However, preparation for defense was possible only after he had defeated Nikola Altomanović. Prince Lazar was helped in his struggle against Altomanović by the Bosnian ban Tvrtko I Kotromanić (1353–1391), who crowned himself king of the Serbs, Bosnia, and the Coastal and Western Lands in 1377.

Although founded by Serbian tribes, the Bosnian state developed separately from Serbia. The former was often divided between the early Croatian kingdom, Hungary, and Serbia, but at various times expanded to include the areas of neighboring Croatia and Serbia. However, the major distinction of Bosnia was neither population mix nor cultural interference: the *differentia specifica* of the medieval Bosnian state was the so-called Bosnian Church, established by the followers of Bogomilism. Serbian Bogomils moved to Bosnia following their persecution by Stefan Nemanja. Bosnian rulers often wavered between adherence to Serbian Orthodoxy, Roman Catholicism, and Bogomilism depending on the relative balance of power in the region. The lasting consequence of the confessional difference was the alienation of the two, essentially Serbian, states.

Tvrtko's coronation as the common king of the Serbs and Bosnia came too late. After a series of defeats (Pločnik, 1386; Bileća, 1388), the Turks assembled a large army in order to conquer the remaining Serbian lands. The coalition that included Prince Lazar's army, Serbian units from Bosnia and the forces of Vuk Branković collided with the Turks on June 28, 1389, in the Battle of Kosovo. Both armies withdrew after the battle, and Prince Lazar and the Turkish sultan Murad I were killed. Although the Serbian state continued to exist for the next 70 years, the Battle of Kosovo is remembered as a decisive defeat for the Serbs and the end of the medieval Serbian state.

The aftermath of the battle was characterized by the intense diplomatic activity of Lazar's wife Milica and his son, Stefan Lazarević (r. 1389–1427), who managed to unify the remnants of the Serbian state. In 1402, Stefan was proclaimed despot by the Byzantine emperor. His successor was Đurađ Branković (r. 1427–1456), a son of Vuk Branković. During the reign of these despots, Serbia was a vassal state of both Turkey and Hungary; however, it continued to flourish economically and culturally. The center of the Serbian state moved to the north toward the cities of Belgrade and Smederevo. The actual end of medieval Serbia came after the fall of Smederevo in 1459. The death of Stefan Tomašević marked the end of the medieval Bosnian state, while Hercegovina fell in 1482. In 1496 Turks conquered Montenegro (Zeta), and all of the medieval Serbian states fell under Turkish rule.

The Turkish occupation profoundly changed Serbian society. The Serbian dynasty and nobility were vanquished and secular institutions were ruined. The once prosperous Serbian economy was completely destroyed. The Serbian governmental structure was replaced by the Ottoman administrative system, mining activities almost completely ceased, and the Ottoman *čiflik* (ciftlik) system, based on an agriculture, became the subsistence basic economic unit. The heavy burdens imposed upon the non-Islamic population (disproportionate taxes and duties and *devşirme*, compulsory enlistment of Christian boys into the Turkish military and administrative service) led to the steady conversion to Islam of various groups of the Serbian population. While the extent of conversion was marginal, it did lead to the formation of a compact Muslim population, especially in Bosnia and parts of Montenegro. The Serbian Orthodox Church remained the sole institution of continuity of Serbian tradition and culture. Although greatly impoverished by losing most of its lands, the revived patriarchate of Peć extended its jurisdiction over a large territory stretching from the Adriatic Sea to the city of Budapest in Hungary. The harshness of Turkish rule caused massive migrations of the Serbian populace. In general, the Serbian population settled in the area extending from northern Dalmatia to the Transylvania mountains that separated the Habsburg and the Ottoman Empires. This area became known as the Vojna Krajina (the Military Border) and enjoyed special status within the Habsburg Empire due to the Serbian Statute (*Statuta Valachorum*, 1630) and set of privileges gained in the 1690s.

At the end of the War of Vienna (1683–1699) Montenegro became the first Serbian state to free itself from Turkish rule. Montenegro consisted of four *nahijas* (districts or boroughs) and was ruled by the Petrović dynasty. Rulers of Montenegro successfully repulsed Turkish attacks and established close connection with Russia, which from that time was considered a traditional ally of the Serbs. Despite the liberation and successful building of the Montenegrin state, most of Serbs still lived under the Turkish yoke at the end of the 18th century. Active resistance to Turkish rule came mainly from the Serbian guerilla fighters known as Hajduks and Uskosks who operated in Serbia and from the Serbian-populated Vojna Krajina. Their activities were isolated and confined to local areas.

The organized struggle for national liberation began with the First Serbian Insurrection in 1804. Following the abolition of the Patriarchate of Peć in 1766 and a prolonged period of terror exerted by the local Turkish and Muslim lords called *Dahije*, Serbs in Beogradski pašaluk (Paşalik of Belgrade) rebelled. Led by Đorđe Petrović, known as Karađorđe, the Serbs quickly defeated the Turks in several battles (Ivankovac, 1805; Mišar, 1806; Deligrad, 1806, 1807; and Varvarin, 1810) and liberated the whole of northern Serbia, including the cities of Belgrade, Smederevo, and Šabac. The Serbian military victories were followed by the establishment of an organized system of government, represented by the Governing Council, and the foundation of the Great School. Thus, the First Serbian Insurrection marked the formal beginning of the modern nation-building process among the Serbs.

The rebellion collapsed in 1813, due to the complexities of an internal power struggle among the Serbian leaders and the change in the European political arena caused by Napoleon's invasion of Russia. In 1815, the Serbs rebelled again, this time under the leadership of Miloš Obrenović. Through a series of diplomatic actions Obrenović successfully secured Serbian autonomy and was recognized as the hereditary prince (Hatti-Şerifs of 1830 and 1833). Serbia became a vassal tributary state that consisted of six *nahijas* and spread over an area of 37,511 sq km.

In 1878, after a 50-year period of dynamic state building and national cultural revival, Serbia formally acquired independence at the Congress of Berlin and reached 48,303 sq km in area. The vicious interdynastic struggle between the Karađorđević and Obrenović families, the ill-contrived war with Bulgaria in 1886, and the scandals surrounding the reign of Milan and Alexander Obrenović did not lessen the spreading of Serbia's standing in the Balkans. The growing Serbian influence was inseparable from the continuation of the struggle for national liberation. This struggle became particularly intense after the dynastic change in Serbia in 1903.

The political and economic domination of Austria-Hungary, established during the reign of King Milan Obrenović, proved to be a major obstacle in the attainment of Serbian national goals: liberation and unification of all the traditional Serbian lands (Bosnia, Macedonia, Kosovo and Metohija, Vojvodina, and the rest of the Serbian-populated Vojna Krajina). The new Serbian government was determined to end the Austro-Hungarian mastery. Poised to liberate itself from Austro-Hungarian tutelage, Serbia began to develop stronger political, economic and military ties with western European countries, especially England and France. In a relatively short period of time the Serbian government, led by the Radical party of Nikola Pašić, introduced a series of economic reforms and stabilized state finances. As its independence increased Serbia's relations with Austria-Hungary quickly deteriorated. The ensuing crisis resulted in the Tariff War, which lasted from 1906 to 1911 and became explosive with the Austro-Hungarian annexation of Bosnia and Hercegovina in 1908.

Faced with strong Austro-Hungarian opposition to the west and north and lacking the support of the Croats and Slovenes, Serbia turned to the south. After concluding a series of military alliances, the small Balkan states

(Serbia, Montenegro, Greece, and Bulgaria) attacked Turkey in 1912. The Balkan wars (1912–1913) ended Turkish rule in Macedonia and substantially reduced Turkish territory in Europe. Serbia emerged victorious from the wars and, by liberating Kosovo and Metohija and parts of Macedonia, increased its territory to 87,300 sq km. More importantly, the Serbian victories confirmed Serbia's role as the Piedmont among the South Slavs.

In the second half of the 19th century, especially after the Congress of Berlin, the Serbian struggle for national liberation became entwined with Croatian and Slovenian national desire. This in turn nurtured the Yugoslav idea, the concept that led to the establishment of the first common state of the South Slavs in 1918. Near the beginning of World War I Serbia proclaimed the unification of the Serbs, Croats, and Slovenes as its primary war objective (Declaration of Niš, 1914). The details of unification were established by the Corfu Declaration (1917) after much controversy and diplomatic maneuvering between the Serbian government and theYugoslav Committee. The victorious campaign of the Serbian army was followed by the formation of the new unified state—the Kingdom of the Serbs, Croats, and Slovenes.

## THE FIRST YUGOSLAVIA

The first Yugoslav state, the Kingdom of the Serbs, Croats, and Slovenes (SHS), was proclaimed on December 1, 1918. The new state comprised Serbia, Montenegro, Croatia-Slavonia, Dalmatia, Baranja, Vojvodina, Bosnia and Hercegovina and Slovenia. It covered an area of 247,542 sq km with a population of 12,545,000 (1921). The relative majority of the population were Serbs (46.7 percent), who together with Croats constituted 74.4 percent of the total population. The rest of the population included Slovenes (8.5 percent), Germans (4.2 percent), Hungarians (3.9 percent), Albanians (3.7 percent), Rumanians, Turks, Slovaks, Czechs, Italians, Gypsies, Vlachs, Ruthenes, and smaller groups.

### Political Developments

The SHS was organized as a parliamentary monarchy headed by the Serbian Karađorđević dynasty. After almost two years of rule by a provisional government, elections for the Constituent Assembly were held on November 28, 1920. Twenty-two political parties participated, 16 of them electing deputies. The Communist Party had a relatively strong showing at these first parliamentary elections. Although it participated in the elections, the Croatian Peasant Party (HSS) refused to participate in the constitution-making process and forbade its deputies from presenting their credentials to the Constituent Assembly. On December 8, the HSS proclaimed the Neutral Peasant Republic of Croatia, a phantom state epitomizing Croatian nationalism's aversion to a common state.

The first constitution of the new state, promulgated on St. Vitus's Day, June 28, 1921, became known as the Vidovdan Constitution. In the spirit of the Corfu Declaration, the document established a constitutional parliamentary monarchy, provided for a democratically elected unicameral parliament (Skupština), and placed Serbs, Croats, and Slovenes on an equal footing. The judiciary was made independent, and basic civil rights were extended to all citizens regardless of their nationality. In many respects the Vidovdan Constitution was centralist, mirroring the Serbian Constitution of 1903. Although its centralism equally affected all of the constituent nations, the Croats openly resisted the new constitution. The alternative proposal of the HSS (March 1921) appeared as the constitution of the Neutral Peasant Republic of Croatia, which called for the formation of a loose confederation. While the HSS joined the government in 1925, the Yugoslav political scene was dominated by the Serbo-Croat political conflict that culminated in the assassination of two Croatian deputies in the Parliament (Skupština) on June 20, 1928.

The personal dictatorship of King Alexander Karađorđević (established on January 6, 1929) represented a desperate attempt to subdue the Serbo-Croat national conflict. King Alexander initiated the administrative reorganization of the country (33 administrative districts were reduced to nine *banovinas*) and promoted "integral Yugoslavism," seeking to impose national consensus by eradicating the differences and enhancing common values among the Yugoslav peoples. The assassination of King Alexander by Ustaše terrorists on October 9, 1934, ended this experiment and further estranged Serbs and Croats. Persistent Croatian obstruction and growing separatism prompted Prince Regent Pavle Karađorđević to seek a national consensus. His initiative resulted in the Cvetković-Maček Agreement of August 26, 1939. The agreement was based on a series of concessions to the persistent Croatian secessionism and resulted in the formation of an autonomous Croatian Banovina (Hrvatska Banovina) possessing all the prerogatives of an independent state except its own army and international recognition. The territory of the Croatian Banovina embraced several areas considered traditional Serbian lands (Vojna Krajina, Hercegovina, Dubrovnik's hinterland) and included a substantial Serbian population.

The German attack on Yugoslavia on April 6, 1941, revealed the futility of the internal Serbo-Croatian arrangements instituted by the Cvetković-Maček Agreement. Croatian units of the Yugoslav army engaged in open sabotage, seriously undermining the fragile resistance of that military. On April 10, with direct German and Italian support, the Independent State of Croatia (NDH) was proclaimed, encompassing almost the entire Croatian Banovina and Bosnia and Hercegovina. By the end of World War II, Serbs living in the NDH had suffered mass killings, mass conversions to Catholicism, and mass expulsions.

### Economic Development

While agrarian reform was one of the first measures undertaken by the provisional government in 1918, the economic policies of the SHS were heavily geared toward rapid industrialization. The average annual rate of growth of the net national product between 1921 and 1939 was 3.33 percent. State interventionism and strong protectionism encouraged native capitalism. In the period 1919–1938 the establishment of over 2,000 new factories provided industrial employment for 145,000 workers. The deflationary economic policies of the 1920s stabilized the Yugoslav currency, balance of payments, and budget. With the exception of the 1930–1931 budget year, Yugoslav internal finances remained balanced throughout the 1919–1941 period. A stable Yugoslav currency attracted foreign capital, particularly concentrated in the mining industry (Trepča, Bor, and Majdanpek mines). The total share of foreign capital in Yugoslav industry in 1937 was 44.1 percent. It reached 83 percent in the electric power sector, 69.9 percent in the oil and chemical industries, and 69.2 percent in the mining industry.

While Yugoslav industrialization improved the product composition of foreign trade, the economy retained the characteristics of a colonial one. Agriculture dominated Yugoslav economy; minerals and raw materials comprised the bulk of Yugoslav exports. In 1938 the share of crops in total exports was 23.9 percent, livestock products, 12.6 percent; forestry, 14.8 percent; and minerals, 16.8 percent. The geographic composition of Yugoslav foreign trade reflected the major political developments in Europe. Italy and Germany together accounted for 42.5 percent of Yugoslav exports and 59.4 percent of imports.

### Regional Economic Development

Regional economic disparities were a major problem throughout the existence of the Yugoslav state. The nature of the problem and its consequences in the first Yugoslavia substantially differed from that in Socialist Yugoslavia. The SHS essentially comprised three distinctive economic regions: Serbia, which had embarked upon a process of rapid industrialization early in the 20th century, and the lands occupied by Austria-Hungary (Croatia-Slavonia, Dalmatia, Vojvodina, Slovenia, and Bosnia-Hercegovina), that lacked the attributes of a national economy and served as an agricultural and mineral base for that empire. The third was Macedonia, which although incorporated in Serbia during the Balkan wars, retained the specific characteristics of the Ottoman economic system. The basic obstacle to balanced regional economic development was thus not simply the different levels of development, but the widely different types of economy. Although specific sectors and businesses were economically advanced, neither Croatia or Slovenia had a national economy as such, having previously operated as a part of the Austro-Hungarian economy; Bosnia and Hercegovina and the areas liberated in the Balkan wars were grossly underdeveloped.

More critical, however, were the diverse economic objectives of Croatia and Slovenia and Serbia. Yugoslav economic policies were decisively influenced by the entire country's rapid industrialization and the reconstruction of war-ravaged Serbia. The creation of a unified market was a major objective of Yugoslav policymakers. Poised to create national economies and accustomed to easy access to the central European financial markets, Slovene and Croat politicians strenuously opposed protectionism, state interventionism, and increased reliance on domestic capital. The Yugoslav government's attempt to foster the economic transformation of the colonial economic structures of Bosnia and Hercegovina and Macedonia were labeled "exploitation" by Croatia and Slovenia. The diverse economic interests of the constituent nations represented the most significant problem for regional economic development in the first Yugoslavia.

## THE SECOND YUGOSLAVIA

The Federal People's Republic of Yugoslavia (later the Socialist Federal Republic of Yugoslavia) was formally proclaimed on November 29, 1945.

It covered an area of 255,804 sq km (after the settlement of territorial disputes with Italy in 1954) and had a population of 15,772,098 in 1948. The major ethnic groups were: Serbs (41.4 percent), Croats (23.9 percent), Slovenes (8.9 percent), Macedonians (5.1 percent), Muslims (5 percent), Albanians (4.75 percent), Montenegrins (2.6 percent), and Hungarians (3.1 percent). Minor ethnic groups included Vlachs, Turks, Slovaks, Italians, Gypsies, Rumanians, and Ruthenes.

### Political Developments and National Policy

The second Yugoslavia emerged from the remnants of the first Yugoslav state after four years of foreign occupation, civil war, and genocidal ethnic conflict. The new state incorporated traditional Yugoslav regions with the addition of the Istrian peninsula, the cities of Zadar and Rijeka, and several islands previously belonging to Italy. While the foundations of the second Yugoslavia were laid in 1943, during the second session of AVNOJ, the victorious Communists, led by Josip Broz (Tito), tightened their grip on power by promulgating the new constitution in 1946. The 1946 Constitution closely resembled the 1936 Soviet constitution. Although it guaranteed basic civil liberties, including freedom of speech and political and religious freedom, it introduced a nondemocratic single-party system. The constitution's most specific feature was Yugoslavia's new administrative division. The country was divided into six republics: Slovenia, Croatia, Bosnia and Hercegovina, Serbia, Montenegro, and Macedonia. Within Serbia two autonomous provinces were created: Vojvodina and Kosovo-Metohija. While the presence of a large Albanian-speaking population in Kosovo and Metohija and a Hungarian speaking minority in Vojvodina were used to justify such divisions, the rationale actually followed a long-standing Comintern policy of curbing Serbian "hegemonism" within Yugoslavia. The boundaries between the republics were drawn arbitrarily and inconsistently and weakened Serbia's position in the federation. While the Slovenian internal boundary respected the ethnic principle, the Croatian boundaries essentially followed "Croatian 'historic rights,'" thus including areas dominated by Serbian populations. The creation of separate Montenegrin, Macedonian, and Muslim (1971) nations pointed toward the transformation of the Yugoslav republics into national states. This strategy would have disastrous consequences for the second Yugoslavia.

The Communist national policy essentially sought to curb "Serbian hegemonism" and create a union of "equal partners" in the socialist federation. This led to appeasement of Slovene, Croat, and Albanian nationalism through the country's continuous decentralization, a trend confirmed by the Constitution of 1963. The Constitution of 1974, which came after a series of serious nationalist and secessionist outbursts in Slovenia (1969), Croatia (1967–1971), and Kosovo and Metohija (1968, 1971), transferred substantial political prerogatives to the republics and elevated the status of the autonomous provinces to a "constituent part of the federation." The confederalization of the country that ultimately resulted in the formation of the national states symbolized the complete defeat of the policy designed to contain Serbia. In the late 1980s the Yugoslav army was the only true "Yugoslav" institution in the country; the fear of Serbian domination had effectively quelled all integrative movements in Yugoslavia.

The collapse of Communism in eastern Europe and deep economic recession pressed the Yugoslav Communists to introduce economic and political reforms aimed toward democratization of the country in 1990. The political reforms included a series of multiparty elections in each of the republics. Nationalist parties that advocated further disassociation from Yugoslavia won in Slovenia and Croatia. The three major parties in Bosnia and Hercegovina were also nationally based. The institutional crisis in Yugoslavia in 1990–1991 resulted in the proclamation of the unilateral secessions of Slovenia and Croatia in 1991, and Bosnia and Hercegovina and Macedonia in1992. The international recognition of the secessionist republics (January, April 1992) and the proclamation of the Federal Republic of Yugoslavia (April 27, 1992) effectively ended the existence of the second Yugoslavia.

## Economic Development

The major feature of the economic system of the second Yugoslavia was the introduction of self-management in 1950. Self-management gave a distinctive tone toYugoslav economic development in the 1950–1991 period. The concept epitomized Yugoslavia's unique socialist experiment and the ideological break with the central planning scheme of the Soviet Union and its satellites. The pattern of development, however, continued to follow the Soviet tendency of the rapid growth of heavy industry. An inexpensive labor force and cheap energy combined with positive institutional changes facilitated rapid economic growth. During the 1950s the growth rate of the gross national product was close to 10 percent per year, while the industrial growth rate exceeded 12 percent per year. The early 1960s marked the end of the extensive expansion of the Yugoslav economy. Market-oriented economic reforms introduced in 1965 called for the liberalization of the economy: decentralization of decision making, further withdrawal of the federal government from control over investment and prices, and the reorganization of foreign trade. However, these policies failed to spur economic growth; instead, they opened both internal and external imbalances in the Yugoslav economy. The inflation and unemployment rates rapidly increased, while the foreign trade balance seriously deteriorated. Moreover, decentralization of decision making and the atomization of the banking system enhanced the autarchic tendencies in the Yugoslav economy.

The failure of the 1965 economic reforms and the growth of economic nationalism culminated in the inauguration of the system of "associated labor" promulgated by the Constitution of 1974 and the Law of Associated Labor of 1976. This concept, based on a primitive notion of communal spirit and an oversight of basic economic categories, exacerbated ever-present economic nationalism and contributed directly to the fragmentation of the Yugoslav market. Incessant budget deficits were financed by the printing of money, causing rapid inflation. Furthermore, the foreign trade deficit in the 1970s led towards an unprecedented growth of Yugoslav foreign debt. Between 1971 and 1987 the total Yugoslav hard currency debt increased from 2,350 million to 21,900 million dollars. In 1982, the Yugoslav government introduced an austerity program that curbed the current account deficit but led to economic stagnation and explosive inflation that reached 2,500 percent per year at the end of 1989.

The International Monetary Fund sponsored economic reforms, which Prime Minister Ante Marković introduced on January 1, 1990, that were supposed to curb hyperinflation and ensure a rapid transition toward a market economy. These reforms, however, adversely affected the already severe problem of uneven economic development and existing regional disparities. While certainly not part of Marković's program, the restrictive monetary policies of the reform unquestionably contributed to the overall dissatisfaction among the population and helped determine the outcome of the incoming multiparty elections. The nationalist parties effectively exploited the growing discontent caused by the falling standard of living and won elections in Slovenia and Croatia. Seriously undermined by continuous breaches of the monetary restrictions by Slovenia, Croatia, and Serbia, the stabilization program was ended in 1991 by Slovenia's and Croatia's secessions from Yugoslavia.

According to the classification of the International Bank for Reconstruction and Development (World Bank), Yugoslavia belonged to the group of Middle Income Economies. Its per capita GNP was 2,480 dollars (current prices) in 1987, while the average growth rate of per capita GNP in the 1965–1987 period was 3.7 percent. Industry was the main sector of the economy (43 percent of the total GNP), while the respective shares of the service sector and agriculture were 35 percent and 11 percent in 1987. The value of Yugoslavia's foreign trade in 1987 was 23,946 million dollars (current prices). Principal foreign trade items included machinery and manufactured goods (65 percent of exports and imports). The Soviet Union, Germany, and Italy were Yugoslavia's most important trading partners and represented 51 percent of the country's foreign trade in 1990. Life expectancy (71 years), education, and health and nutrition in Yugoslavia were comparable to that of developed western European countries.

## Regional Economic Development

The economic policies in the Socialist Yugoslavia created wide economic disparities among the constituent regions. While in the first Yugoslav state regional diversity preempted variations in economic development among the Yugoslav regions, development disparity became one of the crucial economic problems in the second Yugoslavia. Regional economic variations resulted from numerous factors, among which Serbia's containment played a distinctive role. Throughout its existence, Socialist Yugoslavia attempted to mitigate these regional differences through a centralized system of subsidies to arbitrarily defined "less developed regions" that actually widened them in the period 1945–1991 (see table 1, statistical addendum). In the late 1980s, the per capita GNPs of Slovenia and Kosovo and Metohija reached the ratio of 7.5:1. Another distinct characteristic of the regional development in the second Yugoslavia was the constant worsening of Serbia's relative position in the federation. In 1988, the per capita GNP of Serbia was below Yugoslavia's average (86.1 percent), while the national income in the Serb-populated areas in Croatia (Krajina) was 13.7 percent below the Croatian average.

The existing institutional arrangements in the second Yugoslav state ensured the privileged economic position of Croatia and Slovenia. In the period 1947–1988 these republics developed faster then any other region in Yugoslavia. In 1947, Slovenia and Croatia comprised 34.7 percent of the total population in Yugoslavia and produced 39.9 percent of Yugoslavia's GNP, while in 1988 the respective shares became 28.1 percent and 41.5

percent. In the period 1952–1987 per capita investments exceeded Yugoslavia's average by 10.7 percent in Croatia and 74.3 percent in Slovenia. In the same period investments per capita in Serbia were 10.9 percent lower than Yugoslavia's average. Regional economic disparities grew with administrative intervention that directly depended on the political balance of power. The domination of the Croatian and Slovenian Communists in the Yugoslav political arena politically and economically contained Serbia and protected Croatia and Slovenia.

## THE THIRD YUGOSLAVIA

The Federal Republic of Yugoslavia (FRY) resulted from the struggle by Serbia and Montenegro to preserve the continuity of the Yugoslav state and ensure their right of succession to the second Yugoslavia. The new state, officially proclaimed on April 27, 1992, is a federation of Montenegro and Serbia covering an area of 102,173 sq km with a population of 10,406,742 (1991 estimate). The population density is 102 per sq km. The major ethnic groups include Serbs (62.32 percent), Montenegrins (5 percent), Yugoslavs (3.3 percent), Albanians (16.6 percent), Hungarians (3.3 percent), Muslims (3.2 percent), Gypsies (1.3 percent), and Croats (1.2 percent). Minor ethnic groups include Slovaks, Rumanians, Macedonians, Vlachs, Bulgars, Turks, Ruthenes, and Slovenes (see tables 2 and 3, statistical addendum). The climate is continental in the interior and Mediterranean on the coast. The southern parts of the country are predominantly mountainous with river valleys (Morava, Zeta), lowlands (Lake Skadar), and depressions (parts of Kosovo and Metohija). The northern part of the FRY embraces the fertile plains of Vojvodina, Pomoravlje, and Mačva.

### Political Developments

Following the secessions of Croatia, Slovenia, Macedonia, and Bosnia and Hercegovina, the two remaining Yugoslav republics claimed all international functions of the SFRY and constituted a new state—the FRY—on April 27, 1992. Serbia plays a dominant role in the FRY, although constitutional provisions envision confederal arrangements within the new state. The leading political forces in the FRY are the Serbian Socialist Party and the Montenegrin Democratic Party of Socialists and the People's Socialist Party, while the major opposition parties include the Radical Party, Serbian Renewal

Movement, the Democratic Party, the Democratic Party of Serbia, and the National Party.

Political upheaval in Serbia occurred in 1992 when strong anti-government sentiment erupted in May and June. The appointment of Milan Panić, an American businessman of Serbian origin, as Yugoslav prime minister and the election of Dobrica Ćosić as president of the FRY by the Parliament represented an apparent attempt to quell both internal discontent and the external pressure that materialized with the imposition of comprehensive sanctions by the United Nations (1992–1993). The general elections held in December 1992 ensured the dominant position of Slobodan Milošević, president of Serbia, who remained the most influential politician in the FRY throughout the 1992–1996 period.

**Economic Development**

The economic development of the FRY was decisively affected by the comprehensive sanctions imposed by the United Nations in the 1992–1995 period. They repressed foreign trade and inhibited economic growth. The GNP of the FRY declined from $18.38 billion in 1991 to $9.52 billion in 1993, while the per capita GNP decreased from $1,766 to $908. The index of physical production dropped more than 40 percent. From June 1992 to 1993 industrial output declined by 35.8 percent. From January 1992 to March 1994, the unemployment-employment ratio soared by 348 percent. The sanctions spurred the rapid growth of an informal economy, and at the end of 1993 it was estimated that its contribution to the real GNP exceeded 40 percent (see tables 4, 5, 6, 7, and 8, statistical addendum).

The sanctions directly contributed to the worst hyperinflation in European history, which reached five billion percent per year in the month of December 1993 (see table 9, statistical addendum). On January 24, 1994, the Yugoslav government introduced a stabilization program designed by Dragoslav Avramović, a long-term World Bank employee who became governor of the National Bank of Yugoslavia in March 1994. The stabilization program echoed the German stabilization program of 1923 and hinged heavily on monetary discipline and international reserves and provided temporary relief to the hardships caused by deficit financing. However, continuous pressure from local cliques and the lack of sufficient foreign exchange reserves led toward the continued depreciation of the Yugoslav currency, confirmed by the depreciation of the dinar following the suspension of sanctions in December 1995.

While the FRY attempts to reintegrate itself into the world community, with the Kosovo and Metohija question still unresolved, many problems in post-Dayton Bosnia and Hercegovina still unsettled, and the complete reintegration of Eastern Slavonia into Croatia anticipated, more major changes, political and economic, are to be expected in the coming years.

# The Dictionary

## - A -

ABDIĆ, FIKRET (1937– ). Secular Muslim politician and businessman from **Velika Kladuša**. In the mid-1980s Abdić was involved in a major financial scandal in Yugoslavia, when, under his supervision, the huge agroindustrial complex "Agrokomerc" issued a large amount of promissory notes without financial backing. For his role Abdić was sentenced to prison but was released in 1990. In the first multi party elections in **Bosnia and Hercegovina** in 1990, Abdić received the majority of votes as a presidential candidate, but declined the post in favor of **Alija Izetbegović** (Abdić received 1,010,618 votes, compared to 847,386 for Izetbegović). In 1993, following prolonged disagreement with Izetbegović, Abdić proclaimed the **Autonomous Province of Western Bosnia**, which led to severe intra-Muslim clashes from September onward. In August 1994 his forces were defeated and driven out of the **Bihać Pocket**. Supported by the army of the **Republic of Serbian Krajina** (RSK) he re-entered the pocket in November 1994, sparking a major crisis among Western nations and organizations and selective **NATO** bombing of targets in the RSK and the **Republika Srpska**. In August 1995, after the collapse of his major supporter, the RSK, Abdić escaped to Croatia. He waged an unsuccessful attempt to reenter the political arena during the first post-civil war elections in Bosnia and Hercegovina in September 1996.

ADA CIGANLIJA. Small peninsula (formerly a river island) covering an area of 286 hectares. Close to **Belgrade**, Ada had strategic military value during the Austro-Turkish wars (1688–1690) and especially during **World War I**. Since the 1970s the island has connected with the right bank of the **Sava** River, creating an artificial lake. Ada is Belgrade's favorite recreational center.

ADA KALE. Island on the **Danube** River close to the Romanian city of Orşova. During the **First Serbian Insurrection,** between August 5–6, 1804, **Milenko Stojković** captured and executed the **Dahije** on the island. Ada Kale was submerged after the building of the **Đerdap** hydroelectric plant.

AGOŠTON, ANDRAŠ (1944– ). Deputy in the Serbian **Parliament** and former president of the **Democratic Union of Hungarians from Vojvodina** (DZVM). Agošton, a middle-ranking official in the regional Communist Party organization, became president of DZVM following the dissolution of the **Communist Party of Yugoslavia** in 1990. Under his leadership, the DZVM insisted on broad cultural, political, and economic autonomy for the Hungarian minority in **Vojvodina**. Serbian nationalist parties view Agošton's political platform as secessionist.

AGRICULTURAL PARTY/ZEMLJORADNIČKA STRANKA. Political party formed in 1920 through the merger of peasant parties and organizations from **Serbia, Dalmatia,** and **Bosnia and Hercegovina**. Under the leadership of **Jovan-Pižon Jovanović**, the Agricultural Party supported the concept that **Serbs**, Croats, and Slovenes are essentially various tribes of the same nation. The party promoted a strong centralized state, organized on the **Zadruga** principle, and supported the equality of men and women.

ALAVANTIĆ'S AFFAIR. Unsuccessful putsch attempt made by Rade Alavantić. In the dawn of March 5, 1902, accompanied by four associates, Alavantić crossed the **Sava** River from the Austro-Hungarian side and attempted to incite a revolt in **Šabac**, his hometown. Having failed to overcome the local gendarmerie, he was shot in a gun fight. Alavantić's affair exemplified the dissatisfaction with the regime of King **Alexander Obrenović**.

ALBANIAN RETREAT (December 1915–April 1916). The forced retreat of the Serbian army after large German forces accompanied the twice previously defeated Austrian forces. With Bulgaria attacking and cutting off retreat to the south, the retreat was forced through the Albanian mountains in harsh winter conditions. Allied ships transported the survivors to **Corfu Island**. After recuperating, the army was transferred to the **Salonika front** in the spring of 1916. 150,000 died on the retreat; of 40,000 new recruits only 8,000 survived. 150,064 soldiers and 8,500 refugees were evacuated to Corfu.

ALBANSKA SPOMENICA. Medal established in 1920 and awarded to everyone who participated in the withdrawal of the Serbian army through Albania in 1915. See also WORLD WAR I; CORFU ISLAND; ALBANIAN RETREAT.

ALEKSIĆ, MILOSAV-MIJA (1923–1994). Prominent Serbian actor and comedian. Although he acted in many movies and plays, he is best remembered for several television comedies. Aleksić was the recipient of numerous domestic and international awards.

ALEXANDER I KARAĐORĐEVIĆ, KING (1888–1934). Second son of King **Peter I Karađorđević** and King of the Serbs, Croats, and Slovenes 1921–1929 and of Yugoslavia 1929–1934. Living in exile as a boy, Alexander went to St. Petersburg, where he entered the Russian imperial corps of pages in 1904. In 1909, after his older brother Đorđe renounced his right of succession, Alexander returned to **Serbia**. After distinguishing himself as a military commander in the **Balkan wars**, Alexander was appointed regent of Serbia on June 24, 1914. During **World War I**, Alexander served as commander in chief of Serbia's armed forces. Upon the liberation of Serbia and the lands under the occupation of Austria-Hungary, Alexander proclaimed the creation of the **Kingdom of the Serbs, Croats, and Slovenes** on December 1, 1918. After the death of his father, Alexander officially became king on August 16, 1921.

The continuous friction between Serbian and Croatian politicians culminated in an incident during the **Parliament** session on June 20, 1928, when Puniša Račić, the Radical deputy, fired several shots killing and wounding two Croatian deputies. Alexander resolved the impasse that followed by introducing the rule known as the **Dictatorship of January 6, 1929**. At that time, Alexander did not accept the suggestions of several Serbian politicians who favored the separation of Serbia and **Croatia**, known as the "amputation." Instead of simply acquiring traditional Serbian lands in **Bosnia and Hercegovina** and **Vojna Krajina**, he pursued the creation of a unified state by reorganizing the administration, standardizing the legal system, and outlining school curricula. The official change of the country's name to the Kingdom of Yugoslavia on October 3, 1929, reflected the unity Alexander wanted to enforce. In 1931, he promulgated a new constitution known as the **Octroyed Constitution**, which restored Parliament and civil rights. Besides strenuous efforts to promote the country's internal consolidation, Alexander enhanced the international position of Yugoslavia by strengthening the **Little**

**Entente** and engaging in the **Balkan Pact**. Alexander was killed by **Ustaše** terrorists during an official visit to France on October 9, 1934.

ALTOMANOVIĆ, NIKOLA (?–1376). Powerful lord in medieval **Serbia**. The center of his lands was the city of Užice, and his realm extended along the valleys of the **Drina** and **Lim** Rivers all the way to the Adriatic coast. His attempts to establish himself as undisputed ruler of all Serbia ended in 1376, when his forces were decisively defeated by the combined army of Prince **Lazar Hrebeljanović** and Bosnian ruler **Tvrtko I Kotromanić**.

AMERICAN COMMITTEE FOR YUGOSLAV RELIEF. Committee that coordinated the work of several organizations of Yugoslav immigrants in the period 1945–1949. The famous Yugoslav violinist Zlatko Baloković was the President of the Committee and Eleanor Roosevelt was an honorary president.

AMFILOHIJE, RADOVIĆ RISTO (1938– ). Metropolitan of the **Serbian Orthodox Church** and professor of the School of Theology in **Belgrade**. Born in **Montenegro**, Amfilohije was educated in Belgrade, Berne, Rome, and Athens, where he obtained his doctorate in theology. He worked as a priest in Greece and later became a professor at the Spiritual Academy of St. Serge in Paris. His numerous works include *Duhovni smisao hrama Svetog Save* (*Spiritual Meaning of Saint Sava's Temple*), and *Osnovi pravoslavnog vaspitanja* (*Primer of the Orthodox Pedagogy*).

ANASTASIJEVIĆ, MIŠA (1803–1885). Influential Serbian merchant and member of the **Constitutionalists**. He was appointed *kapetan dunavski* (captain of the Danube) by Prince **Miloš Obrenović** in 1863. In the same year Anastasijević donated a building known as "Captain Miša's Building." It became a center of intellectual activity in **Serbia**, and some of the land's greatest scholars lectured in its halls. The **National Museum**, the **National Library**, and the **Great School** were located there in the 19th century. Currently, the building serves as the residence of the Rector of the **University of Belgrade**.

ANDRIĆ, IVO (1892–1974). One of the greatest Serbian and Yugoslav writers, he finished high school in **Sarajevo** and received his doctorate in history from the University of Graz in Austria. Born in **Bosnia and**

**Hercegovina** (B-H) to a Catholic family, Andrić often emphasized that he perceived himself as a Serbian writer. During **World War I** he was arrested and detained by the Austro-Hungarians on several occasions. Between the two wars Andrić was in the diplomatic service of the Kingdom of Yugoslavia. His rich narrative opus is varied both in themes and literary norms. However, his narrative is especially complex and balanced in writings on Bosnia. Andrić's work had a profound impact on the formation of the Serbian literary movement. Andrić received the Nobel Prize for Literature in 1961 for his well-known novel *The Bridge over the Drina* (*Na Drini ćuprija*). His numerous works have been translated into several languages and include *Put Alije oerzeleza* (*The Journey of Ali oerzelez*), *Travnička hronika* (*The Travnik Chronicle*), *Prokleta avlija* (*Devil's Yard*), and *Gospođica* (*The Spinster*).

ANDRIJA (?–1250). Prince of **Zahumlje** and son of Prince Miroslav. His capital was in the city of Ston in the Pelješac peninsula, and he maintained a good relationship with Split and **Dubrovnik**.

ANĐELKOVIĆ, KOČA (1755–1788). Leader of the Serbian volunteers who fought in the Austro-Turkish war (1788–1791). During February and March of 1788, Koča and his forces liberated substantial territory, including **Požarevac**, Smederevska Palanka, Bagrdan, Batočina, and **Kragujevac**. These actions cut the Turkish communication lines between **Belgrade** and **Niš** and became known as **Kočina krajina**. During the Turkish offensive in **Banat** (August-September 1788), Koča was captured and impaled.

ANNEXATION CRISIS. International crisis that developed following the annexation of **Bosnia and Hercegovina** (B-H) by Austria-Hungary in 1908. Anxious to prevent possible reinstatement of the Turkish authority over B-H and determined to suppress the national struggle of the **Serbs** from B-H, Austria-Hungary annexed B-H on October 6, 1908. Although initially approving the annexation, Russia, having failed to secure the opening of the Bosphorus and Dardanelles Straits to its warships, began to support Serbian claims for the partition of B-H. However, unable to obtain support from France, Russia advised **Serbia** to demobilize its troops and acknowledge the Austro-Hungarian annexation. Although immediate war was avoided, the annexation led to the further deterioration of relations between Austria-Hungary and Serbia.

ANNUNCIATION COUNCIL/BLAGOVEŠTANSKI SABOR. Last political convention of **Serbs** in Hungary. It took place in **Karlovci Sremski** in 1861 under the chairmanship of Patriarch **Josif Rajačić**. The Serbs considered their existing privileges to be given by international treaties and therefore demanded a separate Serbian territory—Serbian **Vojvodina**, which included **Srem**, Lower **Bačka**, **Banat**, and **Baranja**. The demands envisioned an independent Serbian administration headed by a **vojvoda** (duke). The Hungarian Parliament did not consider any of the Serbian demands.

ANTIFAŠISTIČKO VEĆE NARODNOG OSLOBOĐENJA JUGOSLAVIJE. See AVNOJ.

APIS, DRAGUTIN DIMITRIJEVIĆ (1876–1917). Colonel of the Serbian General Staff and the main organizer of the assassination of King **Alexander Obrenović** in 1903. In 1911, Apis joined the secret organization **Unification or Death**, popularly known as the Black Hand, and became its chief leader. During **World War I** Apis disagreed with **Nikola Pašić** over the policy toward Bulgaria and threatened a military coup. In 1917, after a series of Pašić intrigues Apis was arrested together with surviving leaders of the Black Hand. After a short tribunal known as the **Trial of Salonika**, he was sentenced to death and executed by firing squad on June 26, 1917. Apis was among the most controversial figures in modern Serbian history and his influence in Serbian politics extended far beyond his official positions in the Serbian army.

APRIL'S CONSTITUTION (1901). See CONSTITUTION.

APRIL'S WAR. War between the Kingdom of Yugoslavia and the Axis and its satellites between April 6 and April 17, 1941. After conquering France, Germany intensively prepared for war against the Soviet Union. In order to secure its southern flank, Germany forced several Balkan countries into submission. First Hungary, then Rumania and Bulgaria joined the Tripartite Pact, leaving only Yugoslavia and Greece out of the immediate control of Germany.

In March 1941 the German Foreign Ministry exerted increasing pressure on the Yugoslav government, led by Prime Minister **Dragiša Cvetković** and his deputy **Vladko Maček**, to join the Tripartite Pact. After negotiations Yugoslav representatives reluctantly signed the treaty on March 25, 1941. The treaty had a secret annex that gave Yugoslavia several major concessions, including some territorial gains (the port of Salonika). Despite the fact that relative to other member-countries Yugoslavia was given highly preferential treatment (the Yugoslav army was not to participate in war and Yugoslav territory was not to be used for Axis military transports), less than two days after Yugoslavia joined the pact, a group of pro-British officers executed the **Coup d'état of March 27, 1941**. The change of government was followed by popular discontent with the pro-German policy of the Cvetković-Maček government that turned into massive anti-German demonstrations.

Although the new Yugoslav government headed by General **Dušan Simović** pledged to fulfill all of the contractual obligations of the Cvetković-Maček government, including Yugoslavia's strict adherence to the stipulations of the Tripartite Pact, Germany attacked Yugoslavia without a declaration of war on April 6, 1941.

The attack, which started with the aerial bombardment of **Belgrade**, was carried out simultaneously by German, Italian, Hungarian, and Bulgarian armies. Vastly outnumbered and outgunned, and riven inside by the disastrous activities of the Croatian and German 'fifth column,' Yugoslav army resistance collapsed in two weeks. On April 15, King **Peter II Karađorđević** and the Yugoslav government left the country and went into exile in London. On April 17, Yugoslavia signed an act of unconditional surrender to German forces and was subsequently divided among Germany, Italy, Hungary, and Bulgaria.

APRILSKI RAT. See APRIL'S WAR.

ARALICA, STOJAN (1883–1980). Prominent Serbian painter born in **Croatia**. He studied at the Münich art academy from 1909 to 1914 and at Prague in 1916 and 1917. Initially, Aralica was close to impressionism, but later became a leading abstract painter in Yugoslavia. Besides Yugoslavia, he exibited in Paris, Prague, and Sweden.

ARBANASI. (i) A customary but nowadays rarely used term for Albanians living in Yugoslavia. (ii) Formerly a village in the vicinity of **Zadar**, but now a part of the city. The name of the village came from the Albanians who were brought there by the archbishop of Zadar, Vicko Zmajević.

ARCHIMANDRITE. Eastern Orthodox church dignitary ranking just below a bishop, usually the head of a monastery (similar to the Western abbot).

ARNAUTI. Turkish name for Albanians. The term was also customary for Serbs assimilated by Albanian tribes in Northern Albania and **Kosovo and Metohija**.

ARSENIJE I (?–1266). Serbian archbishop 1233–66. He succeeded **Saint Sava**, the founder of the **Serbian Orthodox Church**. After a Bulgarian attack on Serbia in 1253, he moved the church center from **Žiča** monastery to **Peć**.

ARSENIJE III CRNOJEVIĆ (1633–1706). Patriarch of the **Serbian Orthodox Church** from 1672. During the Turkish attack on Vienna in 1683, he actively recruited volunteers for the Austrian army. His continuous attempts to find allies in the struggle against the Turkish occupation led him to approach Russia, Austria, the Venetian Republic, and the Vatican. On October 27, 1689, an anti-Turkish accord between Austria and Arsenije was signed. However, the Austrian defeat in 1690 caused a massive movement of the Serbian population of the **Kosovo and Metohija** region northward away from the advancing Turks. This exodus of became known as Velika Seoba. See also SEOBA SRBA.

ARSENIJE IV JOVANOVIĆ-ŠAKABENTA (1698–1748). Patriarch of the **Serbian Orthodox Church** from 1724. During the Austro-Turkish War of 1737-1739, Arsenije cooperated with Austria and was forced by the Turks to leave **Peć** in 1737. In 1742 he went to Austria, where he became metropolitan of **Karlovci Sremski**, with the right to bear the title of patriarch.

ATANASIJE, JEVTIĆ (1938– ). Bishop of **Hercegovina** of the **Serbian Orthodox Church** (SPC). After completing studies at **Bogoslovija** and graduating from the School of Theology in **Belgrade**, Atanasije received his doctorate from the University of Athens. Prior to his appointment as episcop (bishop) of Hercegovina he was a professor at the Orthodox Spiritual Academy in Paris, dean of the School of Theology in Belgrade, and the bishop of **Banat**. Atanasije is considered as a "hard line" leader in the SPC.

AUTONOMOUS PROVINCE OF WESTERN BOSNIA/AUTONOMNA POKRAJINA ZAPADNA BOSNA (APZB). The refusal of **Alija Izetbegović** to accept the **Owen-Stoltenberg Plan** led to an internal split in the **Party of Democratic Action**. On July 18, 1993, **Fikret Abdić**, member of the rump presidency of **Bosnia and Hercegovina** (B-H), sent an open letter to Izetbegović appealing to him to accept a peaceful solution to the B-H crisis. The ensuing disagreements led to the proclamation of the Autonomous Province of Western Bosnia (APZB) on September 27, 1993, in **Velika Kladuša**. More than 400 delegates elected Fikret Abdić president of the province. The proclamation of the APZB led to intense intra-Muslim clashes between forces loyal to Izetbegović (the Fifth Corps of the B-H Army) and Abdić's supporters. In August 1994, Abdić's forces were forced to retreat into the **Republic of Serbian Krajina** (RSK) but succeeded in recapturing Velika Kladuša in November. The APZB ceased to exist in August 1995, following the Croatian army offensive against the RSK and the **Republika Srpska**.

AVAKUMOVIĆ, JOVAN (1841–1928). Serbian statesman and politician. A distinguished lawyer schooled in Germany and France, Avakumović was a member of the **Liberal Party** and occupied several important posts, including minister of justice in 1880 and prime minister and foreign minister in 1892–1893. After the assassination of King **Alexander Obrenović** in 1903, Avakumović again became prime minister of **Serbia**. He wrote the first systematic textbook on criminal law in Serbia, *Teorija kaznenog prava* (*Theory of Criminal Law*).

AVALA. Mountainous hill (511 m) located 14 km south of **Belgrade**. An ancient city called Žrnov was located at the top of the mountain until 1934, when the monument to the Unknown Soldier was erected to commemorate the 1912-1918 wars for Serbian liberation.

AVARS. Nomadic Mongol tribe of Turkish origin that came to Europe in the fifth century and conquered many South Slavic tribes in the **Balkan Peninsula**. In 626, Avars attacked Constantinople but were defeated by Byzantine forces. They remained in the Panonian basin (territory that corresponds to contemporary Hungary) until 769 when defeated by Charlemagne.

AVNOJ (Antifašističko veće narodnog oslobođenja Jugoslavije—Anti-Fascist Council of National Liberation of Yugoslavia). Main law-making body of the antifascist Yugoslav forces led by **Tito** and the **Communist Party of Yugoslavia** founded in November 1942. Although it was officially declared an assembly of all 'progressive' political parties representing all the people of Yugoslavia, AVNOJ was an instrument of the Communist Party as it worked to establish itself as the main and the only antifascist force in the occupied country.

The founding convention of AVNOJ was held between November 26 and 27, 1942, in **Bihać**. In founding AVNOJ Tito and the Communist Party attempted to gain international recognition as a major antifascist force in occupied Yugoslavia; to strengthen their position and acquire broad popular support; to discredit and delegitimize the Yugoslav government-in-exile; and to weaken Allied support to forces led by Colonel **Dragoljub-Draža Mihailović**. These objectives became apparent at the second AVNOJ convention held in **Jajce** between November 29 and 30, 1943.

During the second convention, AVNOJ was constituted as the supreme legislative and executive representative body of the peoples of Yugoslavia and the Yugoslav state. The executive functions were assigned to the NKOJ (Nacionalni komitet oslobođenja Jugoslavije—National Committee of Liberation of Yugoslavia), which effectively became the government of Yugoslavia. The second convention also declared that as a consequence of the betrayal of the interests of the Yugoslav peoples and the Yugoslav state, the government-in-exile had been stripped of all its privileges. In addition, AVNOJ declared that Yugoslavia would be constituted as a federal state. AVNOJ's declarations represented new constitutional acts and an attempt to construct a new state.

The third convention of AVNOJ was held in free **Belgrade** between March 7 and 10, 1945. According to the Yalta Convention, the representatives of other political parties also participated in this convention. However, the existing imbalance between the number of delegates of the Communist Party and its satellite organization **Narodni Front** (318) and opposition parties (50) ensured the passage of electoral laws for the Constitutional Assembly. At this third Convention AVNOJ essentially ceased to exist and was succeeded by the Provisional People's Parliament, which functioned until the general elections on November 11, 1945.

AVRAMOVIĆ, DRAGOSLAV (1919– ). Governor of the **National Bank of Yugoslavia** from March 1994 to May 1996. Previously, Avramović had worked in the World Bank, the Economic Commission of the United Nations, and in the Bank of Credit and Commerce International (BCCI). In January 1994, he implemented a stabilization program that ended the worst **hyperinflation** in European history. Due to disagreements regarding the privatization policy and strategy in ongoing negotiations between the **Federal Republic of Yugoslavia** and the International Monetary Fund, Avramović was forced to resign the post of governor in May 1996.

AVRAMOVIĆ, GAVRILO (?–1588). Metropolitan of the **Serbian Orthodox Church** and exarch of the Serbian patriarch in **Dalmatia** between 1578 and 1588. Fleeing advancing Turks, he escaped from Bosnia into **Croatia**, where he founded the Serbian monasteries of **Marča** and Gomirje.

AVRAMOVIĆ, MIHAILO (1864–1945). Founder of peasant associations (*zadruga*) in **Serbia**. He founded the first modern *zadruga* in Vranovo village in 1896 and helped spread the idea of peasant association to neighboring Bulgaria and Greece.

## - B -

BABIĆ, MILAN (1950– ). Politician from **Knin**. He joined Jovan Rašković and the **Serbian Democratic Party** and together with **Milan Martić** led the resistance to the Croatian special police attempt to seize control of Knin in 1990. In 1991 he became the first president of the **Republic of Serbian Krajina** (RSK). His opposition to the initiative of Serbian president **Slobodan Milošević** and the **Vance Plan** prompted his removal. He was defeated by Milan Martić in the 1993–1994 presidential elections. In August 1995, a few days prior to the Croatian offensive on the RSK, he left Krajina for **Belgrade**.

BAČKA. A fertile region in northern **Serbia**. It is located between the **Danube** River to the south and west, the **Tisa** River to the east and Hungary to the north. The total area of the region is 8,913 sq km with a population of 974,344 (1991 estimate). Together with **Banat** and **Srem,** it constitutes the **Vojvodina** region and represents one of the most important agricultural regions in Serbia and Yugoslavia. After **World War II** metal, machine-building, electronic, textile, and oil industries were developed. The biggest cities are **Novi Sad** and **Subotica**.

**South Slavs** (mainly Serbian tribes) inhabited Bačka in the sixth century. Hungarians appeared for the first time in the 10th century, while a massive immigration of Serbs began in the 15th century. Bačka was under Turkish occupation from the Battle of Mohacs in 1526 to the **Treaty of Carlowitz** in 1699. Under Austrian (1699–1867) and Hungarian (1867–1918) domination a systematic colonization of Hungarians and Germans to Bačka occurred. From 1849 to 1860 Bačka was a part of Serbian Vojvodina. During **World War II**, Bačka was annexed by Hungary.

BADINTER COMMISSION. Arbitration commission set up by the **European Community** in fall 1991 to work within the framework of the peace conference on the **Socialist Federal Republic of Yugoslavia** (SFRY). The commission consisted of legal experts from five member countries and was presided over by Robert Badinter. Its principal task was to work out the general criteria regarding the unilateral secessions of **Slovenia** and **Croatia**. The principal findings of the commission were that the SFRY was in the process of dissolution and that the borders among Yugoslav republics could not be changed. These findings effectively granted recognition to the unilateral secessions and reduced the group of **Serbs** outside **Serbia** from constituent nation to minority. The Yugoslav government strongly opposed the commission findings.

BAJAZID I (1360–1403). Turkish sultan from the **Battle of Kosovo** to the Battle of Angora (1389–1402). After the Battle of Kosovo he conquered the remaining parts of Bulgaria (1393) and decisively defeated a Christian army under King Sigismund at Nicopolis in 1396. He forced **Serbia** to become a vassal state of the Ottoman Empire and married Olivera, a daughter of Prince **Lazar Hrebeljanović**. He was defeated by Mongols under Timur at the Battle of Angora in 1402.

BAKALI, MAHMUT (1936– ). High official in the self-proclaimed, separatist Republic of Kosovo. He was president of the Central Committee of the Communist Party in the autonomous province of **Kosovo and Metohija** and a member of the Central Committee of the **Communist Party of Yugoslavia** until 1981, when he was removed from all posts because of Albanian separatism. In recent years, he has actively supported Kosovo's secession from Yugoslavia.

BAKIĆ, PAVLE (?–1537). Last Serbian nonhereditary **despot** in Hungary (*regni nostri Rascie*). At first, he and his five brothers accepted the Turkish feudal order and actively collected taxes for the Turks. In 1525, together with a large number of Serbs, they escaped into Hungary. Bakić participated in the Battle of Mohacs in 1526. He was killed in the Battle of Đakovo in 1537.

BALISTI. Term used for members of the Albanian nationalist organization Bali Kombëtar (National Front) formed in 1942. Despite its patriotic slogans the organization actually collaborated with the German Nazi forces. Paramilitary units of this organization were directly responsible for crimes against the Serbs in **Kosovo and Metohija**. The remnants of *balisti* bands continued their terrorist activities long after the official end of **World War II** but were subsequently destroyed by special units of the Yugoslav army.

BALKAN LEAGUE. (i) An alliance between **Serbia**, Greece, and **Montenegro**. The idea of an alliance was initiated by Serbia during the reign of Prince **Mihailo Obrenović**. The foundations of the alliance were secret agreements concluded between Serbia and Montenegro (1866) and Serbia and Greece (1867). They called for a general insurrection of the Balkan peoples against Ottoman domination. An additional, less binding, agreement was concluded between Serbia and Romania in 1868. The alliance lost practical importance with the death of Prince Mihailo in 1868.

(ii) A chain of alliances among Balkan states during 1912. On the initiative of the Russian minister **Nikolai Hartwig** in **Belgrade** and the Russian military attaché Romanovsky in Sofia, Bulgaria and Serbia signed an alliance in March 1912. Russia had sponsored the alliance to stop Austria-Hungary's *Drang nach Osten* (eastward drive) and to stop the quarrelling among the small Slavic states. By bringing Bulgaria, Serbia, and Montenegro into her orbit, Russia intended to secure her hegemony in the Balkans. The military convention that was an integral part of the treaty between the two states stipulated that Bulgaria would send 200,000 soldiers to aid Serbia in the event of Austrian aggression, while Serbia would mobilize 120,000 troops to support Bulgaria against Turkey. The two countries roughly divided their spheres of influence in **Macedonia**. There were four allotments of territory: Serbia was to receive outright all territory north and west of the **Šar Mountain**, Bulgaria was to receive all land east of the Rhodope Mountains and the river Struma. The remaining territory was to become an autonomous province. If, however, the organization of an autonomous region became impossible, Bulgaria was to receive all land up to a definitely demarcated line running from Mt. Golem on the Bulgarian frontier to Lake Ohrid. Finally, the territory between this line and the boundary of the territory granted to Serbia, i.e., Šar Mountain, was to constitute a contested zone. It was agreed that the Russian emperor as arbiter should draw the definite boundary line between the two states in this region.

In June 1912 a Greco-Bulgarian alliance was also signed. The treaty was aimed solely against Turkey and, in contrast with the Serbo-Bulgarian agreement, contained no territorial provisions. Montenegro entered into an alliance with Bulgaria in August 1912 and signed a treaty with Serbia in September 1912. With the Montenegrin agreements, the Balkan League was completed. Formal alliances existed between Bulgaria and Serbia, Bulgaria and Greece, Serbia and Montenegro, and a verbal agreement amounting to an alliance between Bulgaria and Montenegro had been made.

The league collapsed in 1913 as a result of the conflicting claims of Serbia and Bulgaria in Macedonia, which ultimately led to the outbreak of the Second Balkan War.

BALKAN MOUNTAINS. Group of mountains in eastern **Serbia** and Bulgaria with an overall length of more than 640 km and width of 48 km. The highest peaks are Botev, 2,376 m, Vezen, 2,198 m, (both in Bulgaria); and Midžor, 2,196 m (in Serbia). From a geological point of view, the Balkan mountains represent an extension of the South Carpathian mountains. In Serbia, mountains belonging to the Balkan group are rich in natural resources such as coal, copper, silver, and gold.

BALKAN PACT. Pact between the Kingdom of Yugoslavia, Romania, Greece, and Turkey signed in 1934 on the initiative of the Yugoslav king **Alexander Karađorđević**. The main goals of the pact were closer cooperation between the Balkan states and France and prevention of German and Italian penetration into the **Balkan Peninsula**. After the assassination of King Alexander in Marseilles on October 9, 1934, and after gradual weakening of France's position in European affairs, the pact lost all practical importance.

BALKAN PENINSULA. Area 520,000 sq. km. Located in southeast Europe between the **Sava** and **Danube** Rivers to the north, the Black and Aegean Seas to the east, the Mediterranean Sea to the south, and the

Adriatic and Aeonian Seas to the west. The population of the peninsula includes **Serbs**, Bulgarians, Greeks, Turks, Albanians, Croats, Rumanians, **Cincars**, **Vlachs**, and Jews. The peninsula had much strategic importance throughout history as it was a major link between Europe and Asia through Asia Minor. The major communication lines are through the basins of the **Morava** and **Vardar** Rivers and the **Morava** and Maritsa Rivers.

The Balkan peninsula was the site of the first Serbian states: **Raška, Bosnia and Hercegovina, Duklja, Zeta,** and **Montenegro**. After the Battle of Mohacs in 1526 most of the peninsula was occupied by the Ottoman Empire. The formation of national states of Serbs, Greeks, and later Bulgarians and the subsequent **Balkan wars** (1912–1913) led to the end of Turkish domination.

Currently the following states are situated in the peninsula: the **Federal Republic of Yugoslavia**, Bulgaria, Greece, Albania, Bosnia and Hercegovina (**Muslim-Croat Federation** and **Republika Srpska**), **Croatia**, the **Former Yugoslav Republic of Macedonia**, European portion of Turkey, and Romania.

BALKAN WARS. Wars among Balkan states during 1912 and 1913. During the First Balkan War, October 1912 to May 1913, member countries of the **Balkan League**, i.e., Bulgaria, **Serbia**, Greece, and **Montenegro**, fought against Turkey. The Second Balkan War, June-July 1913, resulted from the conflicting claims of Serbia, Greece, and Bulgaria to territories seized from Turkey during the First Balkan War.

**First Balkan War:** *Background of the conflict*. The **Congress of Berlin** (1878) created several acute problems in the **Balkan Peninsula**. One of the quandaries was the treaty's failure to settle conflicting interests both of the Balkan states and the Great Powers. Among the Balkan states the rival claimants for the European territories of the Ottoman Empire were **Serbia**, Greece, and Bulgaria, while the rival claimants among the Great Powers were Russia and Austria-Hungary.

The Austro-Hungarian administration of **Bosnia and Hercegovina** had been resisted fiercely since its institution by the Congress of Berlin both by the local Serbian majority and Muslim groups. In addition, the Young Turk regime began to press for the extension of the Ottoman franchise to the provinces under Austro-Hungarian military occupation. Austria-Hungary found a way out of these difficulties by declaring the annexation of Bosnia and Hercegovina on October 7, 1908. The annexation effectively repudiated the Congress of Berlin and eradicated an already very shaky *status quo* among the Great Powers as well as among Balkan states.

Russia's response to the aggressive Balkan policy of Austria-Hungary was to form an alliance of Balkan states. The alliance was intended to prevent further penetration by Austria-Hungary and to secure Russia's sway in the Balkans. Russia did not initially envision the **Balkan League** as an anti-Ottoman instrument. However, when the initiative of the Russian minister in Istanbul, Nikolai Charykov, to include Turkey in the league did not yield any result, it became obvious that an alliance among Christian states in the Balkans would be directed against the Ottoman Empire. While Austria-Hungary's annexation of Bosnia and Hercegovina imperilled Serbian national interests and delivered a serious blow to Russia's aspiration in the Balkans, it also set a course for smaller Balkan states in their dealings with Turkey. Consequently, although the national aspirations of Serbia, Bulgaria, Greece, and Montenegro clashed in various respects, these countries shared a common aim: a quick end to the Turkish occupation and presence in the peninsula. Thus, although initially envisioned to counter Austro-Hungarian expansionism in the peninsula, the Balkan League became increasingly anti-Ottoman.

While anti-Turkish movements were developing in the Balkan states, affairs in Turkey became turbulent. The Young Turks failed to carry out true reforms. Their insistence on an ultra-nationalistic Turkish policy at the expense of non-Turkish elements and their refusal to institute a decentralized administration led to revolt and insurrection in all parts of the empire. The situation was especially precarious in 1912. The Turks were still engaged in war with Italy over Tripoli while European Turkey was wrecked by mutinies against the Young Turk regime. Border incidents between Turkey and its northern neighbors occurred regularly. When pro-Bulgarian *comitadji* (guerilla fighters) set off two bombs in the market place at Kočane on July 31, 1912, Turks retaliated with a massacre of local Christians. This incident prompted Bulgaria to announce its readiness to undertake a war with Turkey unless the Great Powers could make the sultan fulfill Bulgarian demands to implement reforms under Article 23 of the Congress of Berlin. Bolstered by the Great Powers' insistence on avoiding war, Turkey made an attempt to startle the allies and mobilized its troops near the Bulgarian border on the pretext of maneuvers. The Turkish move backfired—the member states of the Balkan League replied with open mobilization on October 1, and on October 8, 1912, Montenegro declared war on Turkey.

*War Operations*. Confronted with the hostile Turkish response to their reform demands Serbia, Bulgaria, and Greece declared war on Turkey on October 17 and 18 in three separate acts. Serbia mobilized 365,000, Montenegro 33,000, Bulgaria 294,000, Greece 108,000, and Turkey 307,000 soldiers. In addition to the regular troops, Turkish forces included 104,000 Albanians who refused, however, to fight outside what they perceived as their territory. There were four theaters of war: **Macedonia** and Old Serbia, the Turko-Montenegrin border around Shkodër (Scutari), the Greek-Turkish border, and the Turko-Bulgarian boundary in Thrace.

The Allies were victorious on all fronts. The Serbian First Army decisively defeated Turkish forces at the **Battle of Kumanovo** and the **Battle of Bitolj**, leading to the cease-fire of December 3, 1912. The Serbian Second Army attacked Turkish forces in **Kosovo**, and Albania and seized Durrës on November 30. On October 22 and 23 the Bulgarians were overwhelmingly victorious at Kirk-Kilisse and on October 29, 30, and 31 at Lule-Burgas. The Greek army, facing very little opposition, captured Salonika on November 8, 1912. The Montenegrin army quickly routed Turkish forces and reached Shkodër at the end of October. Having nothing left to them in Europe except Ioannina, Shkodër, and Adrianople (Edirne), the Turks proposed peace to the Bulgarians. On December 3 the Allies, except for the Greeks, who still hoped to capture Ioannina, signed an armistice with the Turks.

The peace conference opened in London on December 16, 1912. However, the negotiations collapsed on January 23, 1913, when the Young Turks overthrew the Turkish government and resumed fighting. Their gambit had disastrous effects: the Greeks took Ioannina on March 6, Bulgarians and Serbs took Adrianople on March 26, and Montenegrin forces captured Shkodër on April 23.

*Peace Negotiations*. The peace treaty between Turkey and member states of the Balkan League was signed in London on May 30, 1913. According to the treaty, the Turks gave up all their European territory beyond the line between Enos and Midia, except for Albania which remained nominally under their control. The division of this territory was left to the six powers of Europe (France, Great Britain, Russia, Austria-Hungary, Germany, and Italy). As a result of pressure exerted by Austria-Hungary and Italy, both of which regarded Albania as their sphere of influence, Serbia and Montenegro were forced to abandon Shkodër and Durrës. Serbia lost (dead, wounded, captured) 30,000 soldiers; Turkey, 153,000; Bulgaria, 84,000; Greece, 28,600; and Montenegro, 10,000.

**The Second Balkan War:** *Background of the conflict*. Having lost an outlet to the Adriatic Sea, Serbia asked for a revision of the Serbo-Bulgarian treaty of March 1912. The Serbian government argued that while Serbia had to forgo an important acquisition with the creation of Albania, Bulgaria had received a large area in Thrace not envisioned in the original treaty. The Serbs also underscored that Bulgaria had failed to send troops to the Vardar front as stipulated by the treaty, while Serbia had sent troops to aid the Bulgars in Thrace and in capturing Adrianople. Consequently, Serbia asked for compensation-territory in Macedonia. Greece also proposed to Bulgaria a revision of their boundary on three separate occasions.

Bulgaria rejected the initiatives of both Serbia and Greece, and its relations with the former allies grew constantly worse. Faced by repeated skirmishes with the Bulgarian forces in Macedonia, Serbia and Greece signed a protocol providing for a common policy towards Bulgaria on May 5. Shortly afterwards, Romania, on June 10, and Montenegro, on June 27, declared that they would not remain neutral in the case of a new conflict in the Balkans. Anxious to prevent war, Russia invited all four premiers of the Balkan states to St. Petersburg on May 30, 1913. The Bulgarian war party headed by Tsar Ferdinand, however, pressed for conflict, and on the night of June 29–30, 1913, Bulgarian troops attacked the Serbian and Greek forces without any declaration of war. Serbia and Greece responded with formal declarations of war on July 5 and July 6.

*War operations*. Bulgaria entered the war with an army of 440,000, Serbian forces numbered 384,000 men, and Greece had an army of 101,000 soldiers. War operations began on the night of June 29 with a sudden attack by the Bulgarian Fourth Army on Serbian positions at the Bregalnica River. The following morning the Bulgarian Second Army attacked the Greeks at Salonika. The Serbian First and Second armies decisively defeated the Bulgars in the **Battle of Bregalnica**, while the Greeks overwhelmed the Bulgars and occupied Kavalla, Serrai, and Drama. Romania declared war on Bulgaria on July 10, and her troops immediately crossed the border and reached the suburbs of the Bulgarian capital, Sofia, on July 25. Turkey seized the opportunity and retook Adrianople on July 22. Faced with disastrous defeats on all fronts, Bulgaria asked for an armistice. War operations halted on July 31 and the war officially ended with the conclusion of the **Treaty of Bucharest**.

Serbia lost (dead, wounded, captured) 41,000 soldiers, while Bulgarian losses exceeded 83,000 men. Greece and Montenegro lost 21,860 and 1,200 soldiers respectively.

**The Aftermath of the Wars:** When the Balkan wars ended, Serbia's territory and populace had nearly doubled. Serbia's area increased from 48,300 sq km to 87,300 sq km, and the population increased from 2,911,701 to 4,527,992. Two Serbian states—Serbia and Montenegro achieved a common border at last, and no Serbs were left under Turkish rule.

The Balkan wars changed the European political arena. The Balkan League was dead, and the peninsula became divided into two blocs—Serbia, Greece, Montenegro, and Romania and Bulgaria and Turkey. The balance of power was upset, and the animosity between the Triple Alliance and Triple Entente had increased. The Treaty of Bucharest directly challenged the supremacy of Austria-Hungary in the Balkans. It took only one year for the rival claims of the Great Powers to the Balkans to explode and trigger **World War I**.

BALKANIZATION. Pejorative term used to describe a particular region or a country's strong tendency toward disintegration. The term originates from the late 19th century when it was used to describe the fragmentation of the **Balkan Peninsula** that resulted from the conflicting interests of the Great Powers and the Serbian, Greek, and Bulgarian struggles for national liberation.

BALŠIĆI. Serbian feudal family first mentioned around 1360. Founder of the family was Balša. He had three sons: Stracimir, Đurađ, and Balša II. At first they ruled only in the cities of **Bar** and Budva but later extended their rule to the whole of **Zeta**. The last ruler from the family was Balša III, who ruled from 1403 to 1421.

BAN (from Avars tribal chief *bajan*). High ranking feudal title in early medieval **Croatia** (the first *ban* was Pribina around 949); later this title was given to the representatives of royal power in Croatia. Rulers of Bosnia held the title of *ban* until **Tvrtko I Kotromanić** proclaimed himself a king in 1377. In 13th-century **Dubrovnik** the highest-ranking city official held the title *ban*. The administrative division of the Kingdom of Yugoslavia was organized on the **Banovine** principle: there were nine administrative units—*banovinas*—each headed by a *ban*. In 1939, after the **Cvetković-Maček Agreement**, this administrative division was changed, and the **Croatian Banovina** was established.

BAN, MATIJA (1818–1903). Serbian poet and playwright born in Petrovo Selo, a small village in the vicinity of **Dubrovnik**. From 1884 Ban lived in Belgrade, where he worked as a professor in the Lycée (**Great School**), a diplomat, and the chief of the press bureau during the reign of Prince **Alexander Karađorđević**. He founded a secret **South Slav** society that favored Serbo-Croatian cooperation. Besides numerous poems and plays Ban was known for his work on basic military principles.

BANAT. Fertile region between the Carpathian mountains and the **Danube** River. The largest part of Banat belongs to Romania: 21,800 sq km with a population of about two million. The largest city in Romanian Banat is Timisoara (pop. 350,000). Yugoslavian amounts to 9,295 sq km with a population of 719,564 (1991). The biggest cities are **Pančevo** (pop. 125,261; 1991), **Zrenjanin** (136,778; 1991), and Kikinda (69,743; 1991). Banat traditionally has been an agricultural region. However, since **World War II** considerable industries have been built in Banat, mainly in oil, chemical, and food-processing.

The first **South Slav** tribes, predominantly Serbian, arrived in Banat in the fifth and sixth centuries. The next wave of Serbian settlers came in the 15th century, escaping from the Turks. Banat was under Turkish domination from 1552 to 1717, when it became incorporated into the Austrian Empire. Between 1849 and 1860, Banat became a part of the Serbian **Vojvodina**, a region enjoying a special status within the Austrian Empire. After the Austro-Hungarian Convention and the formation of the Dual Monarchy, Banat came under a Hungarian rule that lasted until 1918. During this period a systematic policy of Hungarian and German colonization of Banat was pursued. When Vojvodina joined Serbia in 1918, Banat became part of Serbia and Yugoslavia. See also BAČKA; SREM.

BANIJA. Hilly region between the Kupa, **Sava** and **Una** Rivers. The region covers an area of 1,792 sq km with a population of 90,588 (1991 estimate). Banija is mainly an agricultural region with a food-processing industry in **Petrinja**. Banija historically belonged to **Vojna Krajina**, and the **Serbs** constituted the majority of the population. Following Croatia's secession from the **Socialist Federal Republic of Yugoslavia** and the outbreak of civil war in the summer of 1991, Banija became the site of heavy fighting between the local Serbian population and the Croatian paramilitary forces and special police units. After the Croatian army attacked the **Republic of Serbian Krajina** in August 1995, the vast majority of Serbs fled Banija. See also KORDUN; LIKA.

BANJA LUKA. Second largest city in **Bosnia and Hercegovina** (B-H) with a population of 195,139 in 1991. The ethnic composition of the population prior to the civil war was: Serbian, 54.8 percent; Muslim, 14.6 percent; Croatian 14.9 percent; and Yugoslav, 12.0 percent. The city is situated on the left bank of the **Vrbas** River. The first records of the city date from 1494. During the Turkish occupation that lasted from 1528 to 1878 the city was the center of the Bosnian **Sandžak** and the Bosnian Paşalik. The Austro-Hungarian occupation lasted from 1878 to 1918. In 1915, a large trial against 150 Serbs charged with high treason was held in Banja Luka. During **World War II Ante Pavelić** and **Ustaše** leaders designated Banja Luka as the future capital of the **Independent State of Croatia**. After the liberation in 1945, Banja Luka became the economic and cultural center of the **Bosnian Krajina**. Machine building, metal-processing, textile, electronic, and wood-processing industries are especially developed. The University of Banja Luka is the second largest university in B-H. The city was heavily damaged during an earthquake in 1970.

During the civil war, which erupted after the secession of B-H from Yugoslavia, Banja Luka became the main stronghold in the **Republika Srpska** (RS). The reported rivalry between **Pale** and Banja Luka regarding primacy within the Serbian Republic led to armed rebellion in Banja Luka in September 1993. The leadership of Banja Luka closely cooperates with Serbian President **Slobodan Milošević**. According to the **Dayton Agreement**, Banja Luka will remain in the RS.

BANJICA. Suburb of the city of **Belgrade**. From June 1941 to October 3, 1944, a detention camp controlled by the Germans and run with the help of the Special Police of the government of **Milan Nedić** was located here. The vast majority of inmates were either hostages or members of Serbian antifascist and liberation movements. A mass execution of inmates was carried out in the village of **Jajinci**, where close to 70,000 burned bodies were recovered after the liberation of **Belgrade** in October 1944.

BANJSKA. Monastery of St. Stephen in Rogozna, near Kosovska Mitrovica.

A legacy of King **Milutin** the monastery was built between 1313 and 1315. It is one of the most notable cultural monuments and representatives of medieval architecture in **Serbia** and the burial place of King Milutin. During the Turkish occupation the monastery was converted into a mosque. It was restored in 1938.

BANOVINA HRVATSKA. See CROATIAN BANOVINA.

BANOVINE. Main administrative units in the Kingdom of Yugoslavia established by the **Octroyed Constitution** after October 3, 1931. There were nine *banovinas*: Dravska (capital: **Ljubljana**), Savska (capital: **Zagreb**), Vrbaska (capital: **Banja Luka**), Drinska (capital: **Sarajevo**), Primorska (capital: Split), Dunavska (capital: **Novi Sad**), Moravska (capital: **Niš**), Zetska (capital: **Cetinje**), Vardarska (capital: **Skoplje**). Each *banovina* was headed by a *ban* appointed directly by the king. They were semi autonomous administrative units, and their budgets needed to be ratified by the State Council. The system of *banovine* was intended to be a key element in solving the national question. Although formally retained until April 1941, the system of *banovine* was substantially changed by the creation of the **Croatian Banovina** in 1939. See also ALEXANDER I KARAĐORĐEVIĆ.

BAR. Sea port in **Montenegro** with a population of 32,535 in 1991 and after the secession of **Croatia** and **Slovenia**, the largest port in the **Federal Republic of Yugoslavia**. Since 1974 it has been directly connected with **Belgrade** by railroad. Bar was founded in the seventh century. In early medieval times it became the center of an archbishopric and enjoyed considerable autonomy and protection by Serbian rulers. In the 15th and 16th centuries Bar fell under Venetian rule and then under Turkish domination. It became a part of Montenegro in 1878.

BARANJA. Very fertile region between the Drava and **Danube** Rivers. The region encompasses an area of 5,536 sq km and is divided between Hungary and **Croatia**. Croatian Baranja extends over an area of 1,147 sq km and had a population near 100,000 in 1991. The largest city is Beli Manastir. It is mainly an agricultural region known for its milk-processing industry.

South Slavs arrived in Baranja in the fifth century. Substantial Serbian immigration began in the 15th century. The relative majority of the population was Serbian even after a strong influx of Hungarians and Germans in the 18th and 19th centuries. After 1918 Baranja became a part of the **Kingdom of the Serbs, Croats, and Slovenes**. Following the internal reorganization of the Yugoslav state and proclamation of the Kingdom of Yugoslavia, Baranja became a part of Dunavska Banovina. During **World War II** it was annexed by Hungary. Finally, after the liberation in 1945 and the new administrative division of the country, Baranja became part of the Yugoslav republic of Croatia.

After the secession of Croatia from Yugoslavia Baranja became the scene of severe clashes between Croatian paramilitary units, the **JNA**, and Serbian territorial defense forces. As a part of the **Republic of Serbian Krajina** Baranja became a **United Nations Protected Area**, Sector East, after the cease-fire of December 15, 1991. The **Dayton Agreement** envisioned the reintegration of Baranja into Croatia in 1996–1997. See also SLAVONIA; SREM.

BATINA. Small city in the **Baranja** region on the right bank of the **Danube** River. Between November 1 and November 12, 1945, it was the site of a fierce battle between allied Russian and **Partisan** forces and the Germans, ending with the liberation of the entire Baranja region.

BATAKOVIĆ, DUŠAN T. (1957– ). Professor of the **University of Belgrade** and research fellow at the Institute for Balkan Studies of the **Serbian Academy of Sciences and Arts.** Educated in Belgrade and Paris, he is the leading expert on history of **Kosovo and Metohija**. One of the co-authors of the proposal that called for the cantonization of the region, Bataković served as a special advisor to the **Serbian Orthodox Church** in negotiation on future of Kosovo. His major works include *La Yougoslavie, Nations, Religions, Ideologies* (*Yugoslavia, Nations, Relgions, Ideologies*), *The Serbs of Bosnia and Hercegovina,* and *The Kosovo Chronicles.*

BEĆKOVIĆ, MATIJA (1939– ). Prominent Serbian poet, member of the **Serbian Academy of Sciences and Arts**, and member of the Crown Council of Prince **Alexander II Karađorđević**. Bećković took an active part in massive anti government demonstrations in 1992, but was less politically active after the breakup of the **Democratic Movement of Serbia** (DEPOS). His best-known poems include "Vera Pavladoljska", "Reče mi jedan čoek" ("I Have Been Told By a Man"), "Dvadeset i jedna pesma" ("Twenty One Poem").

BELA CRKVA. (i) A village in western **Serbia**, near the city of Krupanj, where on July 7, 1941, Communist activist Žikica Jovanović Španac killed two gendarmes. This day is officially designated as the beginning of the insurrection against German occupation in Serbia.

(ii) An industrial city in **Banat** (pop. 26,535 in 1991) close to the Yugoslav-Romanian border. It has well-developed food-processing and metal-processing industries.

BELA RUKA/WHITE HAND. An unofficical term used for the group of military officers who participaded in the **May's Assassination** but later split from **Unification or Death**. The group became very close to the Royal court and especially the Crown Regent **Alexander I Karađorđević**, on whom it exerted a particularly strong influence. The leader of the organization was general **Petar Živković** and other prominent members included Petar Mišić and Josif Kostić. They all took an active part in the **Trial of Salonika** with Kostić as a judge and Mišić as the president of the High Military Court.

BELGRADE. Capital city of the **Federal Republic of Yugoslavia** and **Serbia** with a population of 1,602,226. It is situated at an altitude of 150 m above sea level on a high bluff at the juncture of the **Sava** and **Danube** Rivers.

Modern Belgrade (the White City) lies on the remnants of the old Celtic fortress of Singidunum from the third century B.C. Together with Sirmium, Singidunum was one of the most important military bases of the Roman Empire in the **Balkan Peninsula**. With the arrival of South Slavs on the peninsula, it became heavily contested between them, **Avars**, and Byzantines. The first Slavic name of the city—Belgrad—is noted in 878. Belgrade became a part of the Serbian state for the first time shortly after the **Accord of Deževo** in 1282. Since then it often changed hands between Serbs and Hungarians until conquered by the Turks in 1521. Following the Turkish defeat at Vienna in 1682, Austria seized the city and controlled it on several occasions: 1688–1690, 1718–1738, 1788–1791. Liberated by the Serbs on December 27, 1806, Belgrade remained under Serbian control until the **First Serbian Insurrection** collapsed in 1813. It immediately became a center of the Serbian state; in 1808 the **Great School** was founded, followed by **Bogoslovija** in 1810. After the **Second Serbian Insurrection** gave Serbia limited autonomy within the Ottoman Empire a rapid influx of population from inner Serbia began. Belgrade became the capital city of the Principality of Serbia in 1842, although the fortress of **Kalemegdan** remained under Turkish control until 1867, when the last Turkish soldier left the city.

During **World War I**, Belgrade was occupied by Austria-Hungary on two occasions: first between December 1 and 15, 1914, and then from October 1915 to November 1, 1918, when it was liberated by the Serbian army. The **Kingdom of the Serbs, Croats, and Slovenes** was proclaimed in Belgrade on December 1, 1918. Between the two wars, it was the capital city, and political, economic, and cultural center of the Yugoslav state.

Belgrade suffered greatly during **World War II**. Despite the fact that it was proclaimed that Belgrade will not be defended ("Open City"), the German Luftwaffe bombed the city on April 6, 1941, killing 2,271 people, and completely destroying 682 buildings including the Royal Palace and the **National Library**. Prior to its liberation on October 20, 1944, Belgrade, although of little strategic importance to the Allies, was severely bombarded by the U.S. Air Force on numerous occasions.

In the period after World War II, Belgrade embarked upon an era of rapid industrialization and economic growth. In a relatively short time numerous factories and industrial complexes were constructed. In particular, textile, machine-building, pharmaceutical, electronic, food-processing, film, and publishing industries were developed. In the 1970s several international cultural initiatives were launched in Belgrade, such as BITEF (Belgrade International Theater Festival), BEMUS (Belgrade's Music Festivities), and FEST (International Film Festival). Belgrade was on a shortlist of candidates for hosting the XXth Olympic Games. The population of Belgrade was: 89,876 (1910); 111,739 (1921); 266,849 (1931); 367,816 (1953); 598,356 (1961); 1,209,361 (1971); 1,470,073 (1981); 1,602,226 (1991). Belgrade was heavily bombed in the Spring 1999, during the NATO attack on the Federal Republic of Yugoslavia. The NATO aerial campaign shut off electricity and water supply to the city and caused more than a hundred deaths in Belgrade alone.

BELGRADE INITIATIVE. Action by the Serbian leadership in the summer of 1991 that attempted to persuade the Muslim leaders of **Bosnia and Hercegovina** (B-H) to remain in Yugoslavia. The initiative was embraced by Adil Zulfikarpašić, a wealthy businessman and the leader of the Muslim Bošnjak Party. **Alija Izetbegović** embraced the proposal at the first but denounced it later as a Serbian attempt to divide the **Muslims**.

BELGRADE, TREATY OF. Peace treaty concluded between Austria and the Ottoman Empire on November 18, 1739, after the 1737–1739 war. According to the treaty, Turkey reinstated its authority over northern **Serbia** and **Bosnia and Hercegovina**, as well as the fortresses of **Belgrade** and **Šabac**.

BELI DRIM. River in the **Metohija** region rich in hydro energy. The total length of the river is 175 km. Beli Drim is very important for irrigation in Metohija.

BELIĆ, ALEKSANDAR (1876–1960). Prominent Serbian linguist and president of the **Serbian Academy of Sciences and Arts** from 1937 to 1960. One of the founders of the syntax of the modern **Serbian language**, Belić was a member of all Slavic Academies in the world and an honorary professor of the University of Moscow.

BELIMARKOVIĆ, JOVAN (1827–1906). Serbian general and war minister. His misappropriation of military funds led to a major political scandal and prompted the fall of the government of **Jovan Ristić** in 1873. During the **Serbo-Turkish Wars** he was the commander of Šumadija's army, which liberated the city of **Niš**. With Jovan Ristić and Kosta Protić, Belimarković ruled as royal regency in the name of adolescent king **Alexander Obrenović** (1889–1893).

BELOŠ. One of four sons of **Župan** Uroš I of **Raška**. After his sister Jelena married the Hungarian king, Bela the Blind (r. 1131–1141), Beloš moved to Hungary and acquired the title of *herceg* (duke). From 1142 to 1155 and in 1163 he was a Croatian **ban**. From 1158 he was *župan* of Raška as a vassal of Byzantine emperor Manuilus Comnenius.

BEOGRAD. See BELGRADE.

BEOGRADSKI MIR. See BELGRADE, TREATY OF.

BEOGRADSKI PAŠALUK (The Paşalik of Belgrade). During Turkish occupation the territory under direct authority of Belgrade's *pasha*. The area was situated between the **Drina** River to the west, the **Sava** and **Danube** Rivers to the north and east, and the cities Stalać and **Kraljevo** to the south. It succeeded the **Sandžak** of **Smederevo** after the fall of **Belgrade** in 1521. Following the war with Austria, the Turks gave limited autonomy to the *pašaluk*, including religious freedom in 1793–1794. However, all privileges granted to Serbs were revoked in 1801 when the rule of the **Dahije** began. The subsequent *Dahije* terror led directly to the outbreak of the **First Serbian Insurrection.**

BEOGRADSKO PEVAČKO DRUŠTVO (Belgrade's Singing Society). First singing ensemble in **Belgrade** founded by **Stevan Mokranjac** and **Kornelije Stanković** in 1853. The ensemble founded the Srpska muzička škola (Serbian Music Academy) in 1899.

BERLIN, CONGRESS OF. At the end of the **Serbo-Turkish Wars** of 1876–1878, Serbia's territorial claims impinged upon the interests of three empires. Its natural expansion toward Serbian-dominated **Bosnia and Hercegovina** was prevented by the southward expansion of Austria-Hungary, while Serbian territorial aspirations toward the east and south (southern Serbia, Old Serbia, northern Macedonia, and northwestern Bulgaria, including the districts of **Niš, Prizren, Skoplje, Novi Pazar,** and Vidin) clashed with Russian and Ottoman interests. The Russian negation of Serbia's territorial aspirations found vivid expression in the **Treaty of San Stefano**, which attempted to ensure Russian domination in southeast Europe.

The disappointing Treaty of San Stefano and apparent abandonment by Russia prompted Serbia to approach Austria-Hungary to secure backing for its territorial claims. Austria-Hungary agreed to support Serbia's claims to **Pirot, Vranje,** and Trun and to the general area in the southeast upon condition that Serbia renounce its claims to the **Sandžak** and promptly conclude an economic treaty between the two countries.

The Congress of Berlin, initiated by Austria-Hungary, met from June 13 to July 13, 1878. The Congress was preceded by a series of secret agreements, and its greatest effect was to modify the Treaty of San Stefano. Greater Bulgaria was divided into three parts: Bulgaria proper, north of the Balkan mountains; Eastern Rumelia, south of the mountains under Turkish government; and Macedonia, which remained entirely Ottoman but was given certain reforms. Austria-Hungary was given a mandate (June 28) to occupy Bosnia and Hercegovina, and to garrison the Sandžak. With the exception of two villages on the right bank of the **Drina** River, Serbia did not get anything to the west and southwest, while to the south and east it was able to preserve Pirot and Vranje after intense negotiations. In total, Serbia received 200 square miles (520 sq km) of territory instead of the 150 square miles (390 sq km) it received at San Stefano, stretching out over 48,303 sq km. The congress also confirmed the independence of Serbia and **Montenegro**.

Despite the territorial gains and the confirmation of independence, the overall position of Serbia did not improve after the Congress of Berlin. In order to secure her claims to the territories already liberated in the war, Serbia was forced to accept the Austro-Hungarian occupation of

Bosnia and Hercegovina. Abandoned by Russia, Serbia found itself surrounded by Austria-Hungary on three sides and became closely integrated into the Austro-Hungarian economic system.

The division of the **Balkan Peninsula** at the Congress of Berlin primarily reflected the struggle among the Great Powers, with the national interests of the Balkan peoples of secondary importance. The fragmentation and the occupation of traditional national realms, intensifying the contesting territorial claims in the Balkans, laid the foundation for future crises.

BIHAĆ. A city in western **Bosnia and Hercegovina** with a population of 70,896 in 1991. The ethnic composition of the city prior to the civil war was 66.6 percent Muslim, 17.8 percent Serbian, 7.7 percent Croatian, and 6.0 percent Yugoslav. The city is located on the banks of the **Una** River and is the main center of commercial traffic between the Adriatic coast and the interior of the former Yugoslavia. The first chronicles of the city date from 1260. The Turks captured the city in 1592, but the struggle for control over this strategic post continued until the Austro-Hungarian annexation of Bosnia and Hercegovina in 1878. During **World War II** AVNOJ was constituted in Bihać on November 26–27, 1942.

After the war Bihać became a major industrial center with well-developed textile and wood-processing industries. The mountains of Grmeč and Plješevica, close to Bihać, became an important military site with an airfield located in the Bihać valley. After the civil war in Bosnia and Hercegovina erupted in 1992, and after the withdrawal of **JNA** units, the city came under the control of **Fikret Abdić**, a local tycoon and a member of the Presidency of Bosnia and Hercegovina. Abdić's proclamation of the **Autonomous Province of Western Bosnia** in September 1993, followed by inter-Muslim struggle, put Bihać under the control of the Fifth Corps of the Army of Bosnia and Hercegovina. Bihać remained surrounded by the forces of the **Bosnian Serb Army** and the army of the **Republic of Serbian Krajina** until August 1995, when the forces of the regular Croatian army entered the city. On May 6, 1993, Bihać city was declared a UN "safe area" under UN Resolution 821, along with four other cities, including the capital, Sarajevo, after the earlier declaration of Srebrenica as a "safe area." See also SAFE AREAS.

BIHAĆ POCKET. A term used to refer to an extensive area of northwest **Bosnia and Hercegovina** during the civil war. It is bordered by **Croatia** to the west and north. The city of **Bihać** is in the south, **Velika Kladuša** in the north. The "pocket" (a simple military term denoting an area that has been cut off by opposing forces) was often assumed, erroneously, to be a UN "safe area." The actual area centered on the city of Bihać. Under control of local Muslim-led forces during the civil war, the pocket was torn by fighting in the fall of 1993 between forces loyal to the Bosnian government in the south and to the popular local leader **Fikret Abdić** in the north. When former U.S. President Jimmy Carter brokered a four-month cease-fire in December 1994, agreement could not be reached on a cessation of hostilities in the Bihać pocket, which, by that time, involved the forces of four different armies, including those of the **Republic of Serbian Krajina**. The Bihać pocket was therefore excluded from the cease-fire agreement, and fighting continued at various levels until August 1995. See also AUTONOMOUS PROVINCE OF WESTERN BOSNIA/AUTONOMNA POKRAJINA ZAPADNA BOSNA; SAFE AREAS.

BIJELJINA. City in northeast **Bosnia and Hercegovina** with a population of 96,796 in 1991. The ethnic composition of the population prior to the civil war was: 59.4 percent Serbian, 31.3 percent Muslim, 0.5 percent Croatian, and 4.4 percent Yugoslav. The first records of the city date from 1634. It is the main economic center of the **Semberija** region, with well-developed food-processing and textile industries. According to the **Dayton Agreement** the city will be in the territory of **Republika Srpska**.

BINIČKI, STANISLAV (1872–1942). Prominent Serbian composer and orchestra director. After graduating from the Münich Conservatorium he returned to **Belgrade** and performed with the Orchestra of the King's Guard. He was the first director of the Belgrade Opera and the founder of the "Stanković" Music School. He composed the opera *Rano ustajanje* (*Rising Early*), in the style of Italian veristic opera and Serbian urban folklore.

BINIČKI, STEVAN (1840–1903). Colonel in the Serbian army, a founder of the Corps of Engineers. Born in **Lika**, he studied at military academies in Italy and Austria. Binički arrived in Serbia in 1870 and became a lieutenant in the Serbian army. He participated in both the **First and Second Serbo-Turkish Wars** (1876–1878) and **Serbo-Bulgarian War** (1885).

BIRČANIN, ILIJA (1764–1804). Respected and very influential Serbian obor-**knez** in the **Valjevo** region. He was executed by Mehmed Fočić Aga on January 23, 1804, during the mass slaughter of the Serbian notables organized by the **Dahije**.

BITOLJ, BATTLE OF. Battle between the Serbian First Army and Turkish Vardar's Army in the First Balkan War. After the defeat at the **Battle of Kumanovo,** the Turkish Vardar's Army had retreated and fortified the vicinity of the city of Bitolj. The Serbian First Army attacked on November 16 and after three days of fierce fighting broke Turkish lines on November 19, 1912. The Serbian capture of Bitolj ended the Serbo-Turkish fighting in **Macedonia**. The **Serbs** lost 3,230 men in the battle, while the Turks lost 9,300 soldiers, 6,000 of whom were captured by the Serbs.

BJELANOVIĆ, SAVA (1850–1897). Leader of **Serbs** in **Dalmatia** and a member of the Dalmatian Sabor (Dalmatian Parliament) from 1883. He was educated in **Zadar** and Vienna where he graduated with a degree in law. He founded the journals *Srpski list* (*Serbian Journal*) and *Srpski glas* (*Serbian Herald*) in Zadar.

BLACK HAND. See UNIFICATION OR DEATH.

BLAGOVEŠTANSKI SABOR. See ANNUCIATION COUNCIL.

BLAZNAVAC, PETROVIĆ MILIVOJE (?–1873). General and politician. Following the murder of Prince **Mihailo Obrenović**, he carried out a military coup on the night of June 9–10, 1868, by which the Provisional Regency was overthrown and **Milan Obrenović** proclaimed prince of Serbia. Since Milan was still a minor, the Serbian Parliament named a new regency of three, including Blaznavac. A long-time minister of war, he represented the conservative views of the most prosperous merchants and landowners, high officialdom, and the military.

BLED AGREEMENT/BLEDSKI SPORAZUM. Treaty between Yugoslavia and Bulgaria signed in the city of Bled on August 1, 1947. The treaty was intended to pave the way for eventual unification of the two countries into a single South Slavic state. Pressed by the Soviet Union, Bulgaria formally renounced the treaty after the **Cominform** Resolution.

BLEDSKI SPORAZUM. See BLED AGREEMENT.

BLOOD TRIBUTE/DANAK U KRVI. A forcible enlistment of young Serbian boys into the corps of **Janissaries**. This system, called *devşirme*, began in the 15th century and was abandoned in the late 19th century.

BODIN, KONSTANTIN (?–1101). Son of **Mihailo**, the first Serbian king. He ruled in **Zeta**, although his state encompassed **Raška, Zahumlje,** some regions in Bosnia, and **Dubrovnik** where, it seems, he had a palace. During his reign the Pope elevated the bishopric of **Bar** to an archbishopric in 1089. The archbishopric of Bar encompassed all of the area that belonged to **Serbia** during the rule of **Časlav Klonimirović**. Bodin held the title *Primas de Servilia* (The Leader of Raška and Bosnia). He was buried in the Church of St. Serge in Shkodër.

BOGDANOVIĆ, RADMILO (1934– ). Deputy of the **Socialist Party of Serbia** (SPS) in the Serbian **Parliament**. A close associate of Serbian president **Slobodan Milošević**, Bogdanović occupied several important political posts including deputy minister of defense and minister of the interior. After the violent antigovernment demonstration of March 9, 1991, he was forced to resign as minister of the interior but continued to occupy prominent posts within the ranks of the SPS.

BOGIŠIĆ, BALTAZAR (1834–1908). Prominent Serb born in Cavtat near **Dubrovnik**. He was a renowned jurist, minister of justice in **Montenegro**, and professor of Slavic law at the universities of Odessa and Kiev. He was minister of justice in Montenegro in 1893. Bogišić wrote *Opšti imovinski zakonik za knjaževinu Crnu Goru* (*General Property Law for the Principality of Montenegro*) in 1888. His works also include *Songs from the Older and Mostly Coastal Manuscripts*.

BOGOMILS. Members of a religious sect among Bulgars and **Serbs** and the Slavic populace from **Macedonia**. The name Bogomils came from a priest called Bogomil from Mt. Babuna in Macedonia. Based on a strict adherence to dualism Bogomils were divided into a rigid Dragović church (Serbs and Slavs from Macedonia) and a less strict Bulgarian church. The Dragović church insisted on the primal struggle between good and evil, while the Bulgarian church believed that evil materialized as the decline of primal goodness. Like other dualistic sects, Bogomils strongly opposed central authority. Their movement in **Raška** was destroyed by **Stefan Nemanja** in the period 1172–1180. Nevertheless, Article 45 of **Dušan's Code of Laws** (1345) still explicitly calls for punishment for spreading Bogomilism ('babunska reč'). After being routed from Serbia Bogomils found a fertile ground in another Serbian state—Bosnia—where they fought against the Hungarians and the Catholic church. In Bosnia

Bogomils founded the Bosnian Church, which lost its original antifeudal character. Bogomils were very popular in medieval Europe, especially in Italy and southern France, where they were called Patarens. Bogomils disappeared during the Turkish occupation.

After **Bosnia and Hercegovina** seceded from Yugoslavia in April 1992, there were several politically motivated attempts to establish the connection between Bogomils and the "Bosnian" nation. However, the fact that Bogomils were a religious sect without a particular national identity undermined these attempts.

BOGORODICA SVETA (Holy Virgin). Name of several churches and monasteries throughout **Serbia** and Yugoslavia. The best known are monasteries Bogorodica sveta in **Toplica,** a bequest of **Stefan Nemanja** (built between 1168 and 1178); Krajinska Bogorodica sveta (Holy Virgin of Krajina), built during the reign of Jovan between the 10th and 11th centuries; and Ljeviška Bogorodica sveta (Holy Virgin of Ljeviša), built in 1307 during the rule of King **Milutin Nemanjić.**

BOGOSAVLJEVIĆ, ADAM (1844–1880). Serbian politician and member of the **Parliament**. A school friend of **Nikola Pašić** and **Svetozar Marković**, Bogosavljević was a devoted supporter of Serbian peasantry and strongly opposed the bureaucratization of **Serbia**.

BOGOSLOVIJA. Seminary of the **Serbian Orthodox Church.** Prior to the establishment of seminaries, the education of future priests was conducted in the larger monasteries. The best-known Serbian Orthodox seminaries were in **Karlovci Sremski** (1749–1941); **Pakrac** (1809–1872); Arad (1822); **Banja Luka** (1866-1875); **Zadar** (1841–1919); Bitolj (1882–1941); **Vršac** (1822–1848 and 1854–1867); Reljevo near **Sarajevo** (1883–1917); **Sarajevo** (1917–1941); and **Cetinje** (1863–1924). At the present time there are seminaries in **Belgrade** (1810–1919 and from 1949) and **Prizren** (established in 1871).

BOGOVAĐA. Serbian monastery built in 1545. The monastery was destroyed and rebuilt several times. In 1805, during the **First Serbian Insurrection,** the **Governing Council** convened in Bogovađa. The contemporary church dates from 1852.

BOJOVIĆ, PETAR (1858–1945). One of the best military commanders in

Serbian history. During the **Balkan wars** he was chief of staff of the First Army. In **World War I** he was Commander of the First Army, and later chief-of-staff of the Supreme Command of the Serbian army. Retired in 1922. In 1941, during **April's War** he was appointed a nominal deputy commander of the Yugoslav army, a ceremonial post without any impact on actual operations.

BOKA KOTORSKA. Bay of the Montenegrin coast known for its outstanding natural beauty. The bay consists of six smaller bays similar to the Norwegian fjords. The biggest cities in the bay are **Herceg Novi** and **Kotor**.

BOR. Mining city and industrial center in eastern **Serbia** with a population of 52,849 in 1991. The biggest copper mines in Europe are located in the vicinity of Bor, and the city is the main gold producer in Yugoslavia. The production in Bor was interrupted in May 1999 when NATO planes destroyed electric power stations within this metallurgical complex.

BORIĆ. First **ban** in Bosnia (1154–1163). As a Hungarian vassal, he participated in the war against the Byzantine Empire.

BOSANSKA KRAJINA. See BOSNIAN KRAJINA.

BOSNA. River in **Bosnia and Hercegovina,** 273 km long. It is a rich source of electricity, and its valley is one of the main industrial centers of Bosnia and Hercegovina.

BOSNIA AND HERCEGOVINA (B-H). Former republic of Yugoslavia, with a total area of 51,129 sq km and a total population of 4,364,574 (1991 estimate). The ethnic composition of Bosnia and Hercegovina in 1991 was: 43.7 percent Muslim, 31.4 percent Serbian, 17.3 percent Croatian, and 5.5 percent Yugoslav (see Tables 10 and 11, statistical addendum). As the name suggests, the region has historically consisted of two distinctive parts: Bosnia, a region between the rivers **Drina** and **Sava** and the mountains **Dinara** and Plješevica; and **Hercegovina,** a region that extends east and west of the **Neretva** River. B-H is a predominantly mountainous country, especially in the south. The north, however, especially **Bosnian Krajina** and **Semberija,** are very fertile plains, essentially being the southern edge of the Panonian Depression. The climate in Bosnia is continental, while Hercegovina has a distinct variant of the Mediterranean climate.

B-H was the center of heavy industry and the defense industry in Yugoslavia. Bosnia is rich in coal and lignite (Kakanj, **Zenica, Tuzla,** Banovići basins), iron ore (Vareš, Ljubija mines), bauxite, and zinc ore (**Srebrenica** mines). The centers of the defense industry were Bugojno, **Sarajevo, Mostar, Goražde,** Novi Travnik, and **Banja Luka.** B-H is also very rich in hydroelectric energy. The biggest hydroelectric plants are Jablanica on the Neretva River and Bajina Bašta on the Drina River.

The **South Slavs** came to northern parts of Bosnia in the course of the fifth and sixth centuries. Rare historical documents from the early medieval times suggest that in the ninth century Bosnia was inhabited almost exclusively by Serbian tribes. Bosnia appears as a separate political entity after the death of Serbian king **Konstantin Bodin** in 1101. Throughout the 12th century, parts of Bosnia were under Hungarian control. The local rulers, such as **Borić**, were Hungarian vassals. In 1180 **Kulin**, a brother-in-law of Miroslav, a brother of **Stefan Nemanja**, the Grand **Župan** of **Serbia**, became the ruler of Bosnia. During **Ban** Kulin's rule the **Cyrillic alphabet** and **Serbian language** were used as the official alphabet and language in Bosnia. The rule of Kulin is distinguished by the beginning of a strong influx of **Bogomils** into Bosnia.

After the death of Kulin's successor Ban Ninoslav in 1253, the struggle over control of Bosnia intensified. The situation was stabilized by Ban **Tvrtko I Kotromanić** who ruled Bosnia from 1353 to 1391. A distant relative of the Nemanjić dynasty, he nurtured close cooperation with Prince **Lazar Hrebeljanović.** With Lazar's support Tvrtko was crowned King in the Serbian monastery of **Mileševa** in 1377. The medieval Bosnian state reached its peak during the last year of King Tvrtko's rule, when the whole of **Dalmatia**, with the exception of **Dubrovnik** and the city of **Zadar**, was incorporated into it. After the **Battle of Kosovo** in June 1389, and Tvrtko's death in March 1391, the state's power began to weaken rapidly. Tvrtko's successors were engulfed in a power struggle and were not willing or able to confront the Turkish occupation. The medieval Bosnian state ended with the death of **Stefan Tomašević** in 1463. Another Serbian land, Hercegovina, ceased to exist with the fall of city of Novi (**Herceg Novi**) in 1481.

In the course of the Turkish occupation a part of the Christian population, mainly Serbian Orthodox and Bogomils, converted to Islam. Consequently, the Austro-Hungarian occupation that came after the **Rebellions of Hercegovina** and the **Congress of Berlin** in 1878 encountered a volatile ethnic mix in Bosnia. In order to pacify Orthodox Serbs, who were the majority of population, and rebellious Bosnian Muslims, the Habsburg Monarchy instituted a **Bošnjak** nation. This, however, proved futile and was rejected by all ethnic groups. The Serbian majority was hurt the most by the occupation, which openly favored the minority Catholic Croats. This became especially apparent after the Austro-Hungarian annexation of Bosnia and Hercegovina in 1908 and led to strong Serbian resistance and the formation of revolutionary organizations. On June 2, 1910, **Bogdan Žerajić,** a student from Nevesinje, attempted an assassination of General Marijan Varešanin, the governor of Bosnia, and on June 28, 1914, **Gavrilo Princip**, a member of the revolutionary organization **Mlada Bosna**, assassinated the Austrian crown prince Franz Ferdinand.

On December 1, 1918, B-H was incorporated into the **Kingdom of the Serbs, Croats, and Slovenes**. After the internal reorganization of the state and the proclamation of the Kingdom of Yugoslavia in 1931, the territory of B-H was divided among Vrbaska, Primorska, Zetska, and Drinska **Banovine**. The majority of Bosnian Muslims gathered around a conservative political party called the **Yugoslav Muslim Organization** (JMO) and liberal society known as the **Gajret**.

During **World War II,** the entire territory of B-H became a part of the **Independent State of Croatia**. The Muslim leadership of the JMO actively joined the **Ustaše** government. In 1943, the 13th SS Handžar division was founded, consisting mainly of Muslim volunteers. This division committed atrocities against the Serbian population in northern Bosnia and **Srem**. After the liberation in 1945, B-H became a federal unit in Yugoslavia. In 1971, the status of Muslims, who were already treated not as a religious group but as national minority, was changed to that of a constituent nation. Although merely an administrative act, that decision proved to have long-lasting consequences. B-H became a Muslim-dominated republic in the course of the last two decades of Yugoslavia's existence.

The national euphoria that was rapidly growing in the years following the death of **Josip Tito** did not bypass Bosnia and Hercegovina. The first multiparty elections in B-H were held on November 18, 1990. The Muslim **Party of Democratic Action** (SDA) won the greatest number of seats in Parliament (86), followed by the **Serbian Democratic Party** (72) and the **Croatian Democratic Union** (44). The results of the election and the appointment of **Alija Izetbegović** as president proved the existence of a deep ethnic division in the republic. Following the examples of Croatia and **Slovenia**, the Muslim and Croat leadership of B-H began considering secession. At the command of the **European Community** a referendum on independence was held on February 29, 1992, which the Serbian population boycotted. On April 6, 1992, the **European Community** Ministerial Council recommended that member states recognize the independence of B-H. The following day the Parliament of Serbian People in B-H declared the independence of the **Republika Srpska**. The same day severe clashes erupted in all of B-H and civil war followed.

After more than three years of brutal fighting, the civil war officially ended with the **Paris Peace Treaty**, which followed the **Dayton Agreement.** According to the United States's brokered peace treaty, B-H was essentially divided into the **Muslim-Croat Federation** (51 percent of the territory) and the **Republika Srpska** (49 percent of the territory).

Estimates of the number of victims in the civil war range from a realistic 45,000 to the widely used but unsubstantiated 200,000–292,000. As a result of fighting and ethnic cleansing, more than 1.5 million people were displaced. Industry in B-H suffered greatly during the war. Electrical output has fallen to 17 percent of normal productive capacity, while the grain yield has dropped by 25 percent. The defense industry facilities, however, continued operating throughout the war. See also BOSNIA AND HERCEGOVINA, ELECTIONS.

BOSNIA AND HERCEGOVINA, ELECTIONS. The first post-civil war elections in **Bosnia and Hercegovina** (B-H) were held on September 14, 1996. Since, under the **Dayton Agreement,** B-H continued to exist as a single country with power split between a central government and two entities, the **Muslim-Croat Federation** and the **Republika Srpska** (RS), the elections were held on both levels. Muslim, Croat, and Serbian communities each elected one member of a three-person national presidency. **Alija Izetbegović** won the most votes (724,733) to become chairman. **Momčilo Krajišnik** became representative of the RS with 698,891 votes, while Krešimir Zubak, representative of the Bosnian Croats, won 297,976 votes.

Voters elected a 42-seat federal House of Representatives, with two thirds of the seats (28) reserved for the Muslim-Croat Federation and one-third (14) for the RS. Within the Muslim Croat federation the **Party of Democratic Action** (SDA) won 16 seats, the **Croatian Democratic Union** (HDZ) seven, the Joint List of Social Democrats three, and the

Party for Bosnia and Hercegovina two. In the RS the **Serbian Democratic Party** (SDS) won nine seats, the Muslim-only SDA won three seats, and the Democratic Patriotic Front-Union for Peace and Progress won two seats.

**Biljana Plavšić** of the SDS won the RS presidential elections with 65 percent of the vote. In the elections for the 83-seat **Parliament** of the RS, the SDS won 50 seats, the Democratic Patriotic Front-Union for Peace and Progress 10 , the **Radical Party** seven, and the SDA six, while the 10 remaining seats were divided among several minor political parties. In the elections for the 140-seat House of Representatives of the Muslim-Croat Federation, the SDA won 80 seats, the HDZ 33, the Party for Bosnia and Hercegovina 11, Joint List of Social Democrats 10, and other parties six.

BOSNIAC. See BOŠNJAK.

BOSNIAN KRAJINA/BOSANSKA KRAJINA. Historic region in northwest **Bosnia and Hercegovina** in the valley of the **Una** River. During **World War II** the Serbian population of the region was decimated by the German and **Ustaše** terror. After the war the majority of the Serbian population resettled, further changing the ethnic composition of the region. The region is rich in iron ore, coal, and hydroelectric energy. The biggest cities and industrial centers in Bosnian Krajina are **Bihać** and **Banja Luka**, and a well-developed wood- processing industry is located in **Drvar** and Prijedor.

BOSNIAN SERB ARMY (BSA). Armed forces of the **Republika Srpska** (Serbian Republic). The BSA is a conscript-based force, totalling around 65,000. The bulk of its military equipment, as well as its officer corps, was acquired from the **JNA** upon its withdrawal from **Bosnia and Hercegovina** in April–May 1992 and subsequent disestablishment in June 1992. It is estimated that the BSA has around 100 modern tanks and 30 fighter jets. According to the Dayton Agreement the BSA forces should be reduced to 13,000.

BOŠKOVIĆ, RUĐER JOSIP (1711–1787). One of the most distinguished scientists of his time. Born in **Dubrovnik**, he lived and worked in Rome, Milan, Paris, and London. Unlike Newton, he considered space and time to be relative phenomena. Among his scientific contributions are: two geometric methods for determining the elements of the rotation of the Sun from the three objects perspective; a geometric method of determining the course of comets; and a method of raising infinity to any power. His major works include *Opera pertientia ad opticam et astronomiam, tomi I–V* (*Essay on Optics and Astronomy, vol. 1–4*) and *Elementarum universae matheoseos, tomi tres* (*Elements of the General Mathematics, 3 vol.*)

BOŠNJAK (Bosniac). Term used to symbolize the integral character of **Bosnia and Hercegovina** (B-H), originally devised by the Austro-Hungarian common minister of finance **Benjámin von Kállay**. Faced with a volatile ethnic and religious mix in occupied B-H, the Austro-Hungarian administration attempted the creation of a new, integral Bošnjak nationality.

BOŽOVIĆ, RADOMAN (1953– ). President of the Chamber of Citizens in the Federal **Parliament** and a deputy of the **Socialist Party of Serbia** in both the Serbian and the Federal Parliament. Božović is considered to be a close associate of Serbian President **Slobodan Milošević**.

BRANIČEVO. Historic region in eastern **Serbia** located between the **Danube, Morava,** and **Resava** Rivers.

BRANKOVIĆ, ĐORĐE (1645–1711). Controversial figure among Serbs in Austria. In his diplomatic mission to Russia in 1688 he attempted to persuade the Russian emperor to start a war for Serbian liberation against the Turks but did not succeed. Based on the testimony of Serbian Patriarch **Arsenije III** and Wallachian Prince Sherban Cantacuzene, Branković proclaimed himself a descendant of medieval Serbian lords **Vuk Branković** and **Đurađ Branković** and received the title of *graf* from the Austrian emperor Leopold I. At first Austria supported Branković, mainly because he was seen as a person who could persuade Serbs to join the Austrian army to fight the Turks. When Branković started to promote ideas of an Illyrian Empire the Austrians arrested and confined him in Bohemia in 1689. In 1691 Serbs in Hungary proclaimed him their **despot** *in absentia,* but this election was never confirmed.

BRANKOVIĆ, ĐURAĐ (1375–1456). Son of **Vuk Branković** and maternal grandson of Prince **Lazar Hrebeljanović**. He succeeded **Stefan Lazarević** as ruler of **Serbia** and received the title of **despot** from the Byzantine emperor in 1427. The same year he began building a fortress at **Smederevo** on the **Danube** River. The fortress, with its 25 towers and ten-foot thick walls, was completed in a matter of eighteen months and became the new capital city of Serbia. At the time of Despot Đurađ's rule pressure upon the Serbian state was coming both from Turkey and Hungary. He accepted a vassal position towards both empires, often changing allegiances. During his reign the Turks conquered Serbia in 1439, but the land was given back to Đurađ after the peace treaty at Szegedin in July 1444.

Đurađ Branković died on December 24, 1456, and was buried in Kriva reka church underneath Rudnik mountain.

BRANKOVIĆ, GEORGIJE (1830–1907). Cardinal of **Karlovci** and Serbian patriarch from 1890 to1907. He organized several schools throughout **Vojvodina** and built the seminary in Karlovci.

BRANKOVIĆ, VUK (?–1398). Powerful feudal lord in **Serbia**. His realm included **Kosovo** and Drenica, and his capital was in **Priština**. His role became especially important after the death of Emperor **Uroš II** in 1371. Vuk was a son-in-law of Prince **Lazar Hrebeljanović**. He commanded the right flank of the Serbian forces in the **Battle of Kosovo**. His survival of the battle is probably the main motive for portraying him in Serbian epic poems as an arch-traitor. After their victory at Nicopolis in 1396, the Turks expelled him from Serbia because of his collaboration with the Hungarians.

BRČKO. City in eastern **Bosnia and Hercegovina** located on the right bank of the **Sava** River with a population of 87,332 in 1991. The ethnic composition of the population prior to the civil war was 44.4 percent Muslim, 20.8 percent Serbian; 25.4 percent Croatian; and 6.4 percent Yugoslav. The first records of the city date from 1548. As an important crossing point over the Sava, Brčko was severely contested during numerous Austro-Turkish wars. During **World War II**, Brčko became a part of the **Independent State of Croatia.** Toward the end of the war in 1944, the 13th SS Handžar division was transferred to the region, where it committed atrocities against the Serbian population. During the 1992–1995 civil war brutal fighting erupted in and around Brčko. Although the

**Bosnian Serb Army** succeeded in capturing the city and a large portion of the adjoining area, the **Dayton Agreement** envisions that the status of Brčko will be determined by an international arbitration commission.

BREGALNICA, BATTLE OF. Biggest battle of the Second Balkan War. The battle between the Bulgarian Fourth and Fifth armies and the Serbian First and Third armies took place at the valley of the Bregalnica River on the night of June 29–30 and lasted until July 8, 1913. The nine-day battle was fought along a front of 75 km with great losses on both sides. The battle ended with a decisive victory by the Serbian forces, which broke front lines and forced the Bulgarians to retreat. Serbia lost 16,200 soldiers, while Bulgarian losses exceeded 25,000 men. See also BALKAN WARS.

BRKIĆ-JOVANOVIĆ, VASILIJE (1719–1772). Last ethnic Serb on the throne of the **patriarchate of Peć** (1763–1765). After Turks abolished the patriarchate of Peć in 1766, all Serb bishops in **Serbia** were replaced by Greek bishops.

BROZ, JOSIP. See TITO.

BUCHAREST, TREATY OF. Title held by several peace treaties signed in the capital city of Romania. (i) Peace treaty between Russia and Turkey signed on May 28, 1812, after the Turkish defeat at Rushchuk. The signing of the treaty ended the Russo-Turkish war of 1806–1812 in which **Serbia** participated on the side of Russia. The treaty called for greater Serbian autonomy within the Ottoman Empire. However, instead of granting that autonomy, the Turks seized the opportunity that arose with Napoleon's invasion of Russia and launched an offensive against Serbia in 1813.

(ii) A peace treaty between Bulgaria and Serbia signed on March 3, 1886, after the Serbian defeat at the **Battle of Slivnica**. It concluded a brief Serbo-Bulgarian war initiated by Serbian king **Milan Obrenović**. Although the peace treaty ensured the status quo and did not favor either side in the conflict, the deep mistrust generated by the war continued to dominate the relationship between the two states.

(iii) The peace treaty of August 10, 1913, that ended the Second Balkan War. As a result of the treaty Serbia acquired the **Vardar** Valley, including the cities of Štip and Kočane. The **Sandžak** of **Novi Pazar** was divided between Serbia and **Montenegro**. However, Serbia did not get a corridor to the Aegean Sea as was suggested in a military convention with Greece. Greece gained the island of Crete, Kavalla, and a northern boundary that ran just below Bitolj parallel with the coastline. Romania gained Dobrudja (Turtukaia-Balchik line), while Turkey reconquered Adrianople (Edirne) from Bulgaria. Bulgarian claims in **Macedonia** were reduced to Pirin Macedonia (region around the Struma River).

(iv) A peace treaty between Rumania and Germany signed on May 7, 1918, nullified by the **Treaty of Versailles.** See also BALKAN WARS.

BULATOVIĆ, MIODRAG (1930–1991). Serbian writer, and a major representative of the narrative genre. A writer who abruptly changes tone and makes quick transitions from the serious to the parodical, Bulatović started a new developmental stage in Serbian prose. His major work, *Crveni petao leti prema nebu* (*The Red Rooster Flies Heavenward*), was translated into most of the major world languages.

BULATOVIĆ, MOMIR (1956– ). Prime minister of the **Federal Republic of Yugoslavia** and former president of the Republic of **Montenegro** (1990–1997). Born in **Belgrade,** Bulatović graduated from the University of Podgorica in 1980 as the best student in his generation. After the completion of his undergraduate studies he became a lecturer in economics at the same university. As a lecturer he worked under the supervision of professor Boško Gluščević, a prominent economist with strong political connections. Although previously active in the Socialist Youth Organization and connected to some political circles, Bulatović's real political career began in January 1989, when, following mass demonstrations, he and a group of young, less prominent members of the Communist Party came to power in Montenegro. A moderate left-wing politician, Bulatović won the Montenegrin presidential elections in 1992, but lost to **Milo Đukanović** in 1997.

BULOVIĆ, IRINEJ (1947– ). Bishop of **Bačka** and chair of the Department of New Testament and Greek Language at the School of Theology of the **Serbian Orthodox Church**.

BUNJEVCI. Small group living in **Vojvodina,** mainly **Bačka,** and **Baranja.** They migrated there in the first part of the 17th century from the region around the **Neretva** and Buna Rivers.

BUTMIR. Suburb of **Sarajevo**; one of the richest neolithic sights in Europe. After the outbreak of the civil war in **Bosnia and Hercegovina** in 1992, Butmir became a strategically important site where Sarajevo's main airport was located.

## - C -

CARLOWITZ, TREATY OF/KARLOVAČKI MIR. Peace treaty between the Ottoman Empire and the Holy League (Austria, Poland, Venice, and Russia) concluded on January 24, 1699, in **Karlovci Sremski**. The treaty ended the war that had begun with the Turkish siege of Vienna in July 1683 and lasted sixteen years. The treaty transferred a number of Serbian-populated lands—**Banija, Lika, Slavonia, Kordun, Bačka,** and **Dalmatia**—from Turkish to Austrian and Venetian control.

CARTER MISSION. Peace mission of the former U.S. president Jimmy Carter. Carter visited **Pale** and **Sarajevo** and held a series of talks with Serb and Muslim officials December 18–19, 1994. His initiative resulted in a cease-fire in **Bosnia and Hercegovina** (with the exception of the **Bihać Pocket**) that lasted from December 31, 1994, to the end of April 1995.

CENIĆ, MITA (1851–1888). Serbian journalist and socialist revolutionary, follower of **Svetozar Marković** and bitter opponent of the **Radical Party**, which he accused of betraying the socialist ideal. After being expelled from France in 1873, Cenić was imprisoned in **Serbia** and sentenced to eight years for an alleged assassination plot against Prince **Milan Obrenović.** Following release from prison, Cenić became the publisher of socialist papers and the journals *Radnik* (*Worker*) and *Borba* (*Struggle*).

CER, BATTLE OF. Battle between the Austro-Hungarian forces and the Serbian army between August 15 and August 24, 1914. Following the declaration of war on July 28, three Austro-Hungarian armies (250,000 men), stationed in **Bosnia and Hercegovina**, crossed the **Drina** River and entered **Serbia** on August 12. The advancing Austro-Hungarian troops clashed head-on with the 180,000-strong Serbian army. The main battle took place on the slopes of Cer Mountain in northwestern Serbia and lasted four days. Serbian forces under the command of General **Stepa Stepanović** won a great victory, forcing the Austro-Hungarian expeditionary forces to withdraw across the **Drina** and **Sava** Rivers. The Austro-Hungarians lost 25,000 men (4,500 captured) while Serbia lost 259 officers and 16,045 soldiers. The Battle of Cer was the first Allied victory in **World War I** and substantially delayed the concentration of Austro-Hungarian forces on the Russian front.

CETINJE. Small historic city in central **Montenegro** with a population of 20,258 in 1991; the capital city of the Kingdom of Montenegro until 1918. It contains numerous museums and cultural monuments and the biggest refrigerator plant in the **Federal Republic of Yugoslavia.** In the monastery in Cetinje, built by Ivan Crnojević in 1484, the first printing press among **South Slavs** was founded in 1493.

CHERNIAEV, MIKHAIL GRIGOREVICH (1828–1898). Russian general, conqueror of Tashkent, hero of the Central Asian campaign and editor of the nationalistic paper *Ruskii Mir* (*The Russian World*). Cherniaev came to **Serbia** in May 1876 as an emissary of the Moscow Slav Committee. After being named a Serbian citizen by Prince **Milan Obrenović**, he assumed the command of the 68,000-strong **Morava** army in the First **Serbo-Turkish War** of 1876. After serious disagreements with Serbian officers regarding the behavior of the Russian volunteers and following a crushing defeat at the **Battle of Đunis** on October 29, 1876, Cherniaev left Serbia. He reappeared in Serbia in 1879 with an offer from Russian bankers to construct the Belgrade-Niš railway line that the Serbian government declined.

CHETNIKS. See ČETNIKS.

CINCARS. Romance language–speaking people in northern Greece, Albania, the **Former Yugoslav Republic of Macedonia,** and **Serbia**. Unlike nomadic **Vlachs**, their close ethnic kin, the majority of Cincars were Hellenized and lived in the cities, where they were known as enterprising merchants.

COMINFORM. Communist Information Bureau (Cominform) was founded at Wilcza Góra, Poland, in September 1947; from its nine members (the Soviet Union, Yugoslavia, Bulgaria, Czechoslovakia, Hungary, Poland, Romania, and the communist parties of France and Italy), Yugoslavia was chosen as the seat of the organization. The main function of the Cominform was to coordinate the exchange of information and facilitate communications among the member-parties.

However, during 1947 relations between the Soviet Union and Yugoslavia seriously deteriorated due to a series of disagreements regarding economic, military, and foreign policies. Yugoslavia's first ambitious, Five Year Plan directly challenged the scheme in which the Soviet Union would remain the sole supplier of industrial goods, while the rest of the Communist countries would primarily supply minerals and raw materials. Differences over the organization of the **JNA** and the role of Soviet military advisors created further discord. Finally, Stalin's failure to support Yugoslav claims to Trieste convinced President **Tito** to pursue a more independent foreign policy.

The negotiations between Tito and Bulgarian leader Georgi Dimitrov about the prospective union of the two countries, resulting in the **Bled Agreement** in August 1947, fueled outrage in Moscow. In the course of the next two months the relationship between the two countries deteriorated, and in June 1948, at the Cominform meeting in Bucharest, Yugoslavia was expelled from the organization. This was followed by the complete political, economic, and military blockade of Yugoslavia. Tito's reaction was quick and decisive—in a matter of weeks, a purge of "Stalinist elements" from the Communist Party began, and in the next five years more than 15,000 people ended up in the prison of **Goli Otok**. The Soviet-style command economy was abandoned, and **Self-management** was introduced, while Yugoslav foreign policy shifted toward the Third World countries and the **Nonaligned Movement.** Relations between the Soviet Union and Yugoslavia were normalized in 1956, although great reservations remained.

COMMUNE/OPŠTINA. Basic administrative unit in the **Federal Republic of Yugoslavia**, roughly corresponding to the western term county. There are 190 communes in **Serbia** and 21 communes in **Montenegro,** grouped into 29 districts (*okrugs*).

COMMUNIST PARTY OF YUGOSLAVIA (CPY)/KOMUNISTIČKA PARTIJA JUGOSLAVIJE. The Communist Party of Yugoslavia was founded on April 20–23, 1919, in **Belgrade** under the name Socialist Workers Party (Communists'). The main initiative came from the Serbian **Social Democratic Party** (SDP), which succeeded in uniting left-wing parties from all Yugoslav lands and regions. The new party adopted the program of the SDP and called for general elections in the **Kingdom of the Serbs, Croats, and Slovenes**. In June 1920, during its second congress, the party changed its name to the Communist Party of Yugoslavia (CPY). The party participated in the local elections and won in 37 **communes**, including Belgrade. In the parliamentary elections on November 28, 1921, the CPY won 59 of the 419 seats and became the third largest party in **Parliament.** After the proclamation of the **Obznana** on December 30, 1920, the party's activities were first suspended and then banned following the enactment of the Law Concerning the Protection of Public Security and Order in the State on August 1, 1921.

During the 1921–1941 period, the CPY's role in the political life of Yugoslavia was marginalized. Unable to operate within the legal framework, the CPY resorted to underground revolutionary activity. The party was organizationally and financially dependent on the Comintern, and its policy was designed to conform to the objectives of the Soviet Union. The CPY, following instructions from Moscow, adopted a platform according to which Yugoslavia was an artificial state designed to conform to the interests of the Serbian bourgeoisie. This anti-Serbian and anti-Yugoslav stand led to the elimination of the moderate Serbian communists from the CPY (**Filip Filipović, Sima Marković, Triša Kaclerović,** and many others). This trend intensified after 1937, when Josip Broz, **Tito**, became general secretary of the CPY after another major purge.

The CPY condemned the German occupation of Yugoslavia but resorted to active resistance only after Nazi Germany attacked the Soviet Union on June 22, 1941. The CPY organized rebellions throughout the country and began forming the armed units known as **Partisans.** Although having only around 12,000 members in 1941, the CPY, exploiting the genocidal terror of the **Ustaše**, succeeded in attracting large numbers of the Serbian population in B-H and parts of Croatia. Along with the struggle against German occupation, the CPY essentially carried out a Communist revolution, which in turn led to a bloody civil war between the Communist-led Partisans and nationalist forces of the **Jugoslovenska vojska u otadžbini.**

Following the end of **World War II** and the victory of the Partisans, the CPY monopolized all power in Yugoslavia. After the break with the Soviet Union and the **Cominform** blockade, the party initiated a series of internal reforms and officially changed its name to the League of Communists of Yugoslavia (LCY) in 1952. The changes effectively decentralized the LCY and transformed it into a massive organization. The executive powers were transferred to the Communist organizations of the republics and party membership soon exceeded one million people. Despite the fact that the Yugoslav socialist experiment substantially differed from that of Eastern European, the LCY, through its regional organization, held a firm grip on power in the entire post-war period.

The regionalization of the LCY and the decentralization of the Yugoslav Federation undermined the homogeneity both of the LCY and the entire country. The absence of unity became especially apparent after the death of Tito in 1980. Historically dominated by the Slovenes and Croats, ideologically spent, and organizationally debased, the LCY proved unwilling and unable to subdue the nationalist euphoria that spread over Yugoslavia in the late 1980s. After the Slovenian and Croatian delegations walked out of the 14th Special Congress of the party held in **Belgrade** on January 20–22, 1990, the LCY ceased to exist.

On November 19, 1990, an attempt was made to prolong the existence of the LCY by the formation of the Belgrade-based League of Communists-Movement for Yugoslavia. In 1994, this organization merged with several other left-wing parties in the **Federal Republic of Yugoslavia** and formed **JUL** (Yugoslav Left).

CONSERVATIVES. Term used for a leading political force in **Serbia** formed in the aftermath of the second rule of Prince **Miloš Obrenović**. Together with the Liberals, they dominated the Serbian political arena in the period 1858–1868. The leaders of the conservatives were **Ilija Garašanin, Toma Vučić-Perišić,** and **Miša Anastasijević,** all former **Constitutionalists.** The conservatives sought the establishment of a professional bureaucracy which would be independent from both the courts and **Parliament.** See also LIBERAL PARTY; PROGRESSIVE PARTY.

CONSPIRATORS. Term used for the perpetrators of **May's Assassina-**

**tion.** Also known as "irresponsible elements," they became very influential in Serbia and had a strong hold over the king in the years immediately following the assassination. The most influential were Colonel **Damjan Popović**, commander of the Danube Division; Colonel Aleksandar Mašin, acting chief of staff of the Serbian army; Colonel Leonid Solarević, head of the military academy; General Jovan Atanacković, head of the Bureau of Decorations; Colonel Jovan Mišić, military tutor to the crown prince; Colonel Luka Lazarević, commander of the **Belgrade** garrison; and Major Ljuba Kostić, commandant of the palace guard. Both domestic and foreign diplomatic pressure forced their resignation in May 1906.

CONSTITUTION. There have been 15 constitutions in **Serbia, Montenegro,** and the three Yugoslav states since the beginning Serbia's national revolution in 1804.

**Constitution of 1807** ("Rodofinikin's Constitution"). The first Serbian constitution was devised by Constantine Rodofinikin, the first Russian diplomatic representative in Serbia. Known as "Rodofinikin's constitution," it was dated August 7, 1807, and reflected the bitter power struggle between **Karađorđe,** who wished to preserve central authority for himself, and his military leaders, who resented a central government in any form. The constitution established the "Serbian Governing Senate," nominally presided over by a prince, as the supreme power. Rodofinikin suggested that Serbia be given its old borders—from the **Drina** River to Bulgaria and from the **Sava** River to **Šar Mountain,** including **Skoplje**; that in the absence of its own written laws, Serbia adopt the laws of Russia; that Turks were not to be permitted in Serbia; and that the only tie with the Ottoman Empire would be an annual tribute of 100,000 *piasters*.

After Russian tsar Alexander I rejected Rodofinikin's constitutional proposal, Karađorđe, aggravated by the constitutional arrangements that limited his supreme power, proclaimed himself "hereditary Supreme Leader," nominally sharing power with the **Governing Council**, during an informal gathering at his house in **Topola** on December 7, 1808. On December 26, the Governing Council officially approved the Topola decision in the form of a new constitutional law.

**Constitution of 1835** ("Presentation Constitution"). After two decades of self-rule and shortly following **Mileta's Rebellion**, Prince **Miloš** appointed the State Council and granted a constitution. The constitution was written by **Dimitrije Davidović,** Miloš's secretary, and promulgated by an assembly of about 10,000 deputies who met on February 14, 1835, the Feast of the Presentation of Our Lord in the Temple; it became known as the Presentation Constitution. The State Council was given broad executive, legislative, and judicial powers, and all Serbian authorities, except the prince, depended on the State Council. The constitution envisioned basic civil liberties: equality before the law, trial by due process, abolition of the **Kuluk,** and the inviolability of property. While generally conservative and more oligarchic than democratic (the State Council took primacy over the **Parliament**), the Presentation Constitution enabled Serbia to join the enlightened nations of Europe. Some of the Great Powers, especially Austria, Russia, and Turkey, opposed the constitution as overly liberal, and Prince Miloš suspended it in March 1835.

**Constitution of 1838** ("Turkish Constitution"). Following the suspension of the Presentation Constitution the constitutional struggle in Serbia continued between the despotic Prince Miloš and notables representing themselves as "the Defenders of the Constitution" or **Constitutionalists**. The position of the Great Powers, relative to the constitutional struggle in Serbia, differed. Advancing their own aims, Britain and France supported Miloš's absolutism, while Austria and Russia attempted to limit it. Unable to reach a consensus, all sides (Prince Miloš, the Constitutionalists, Russia, and Great Britain) agreed to transfer the entire issue of Serbia's constitution to Turkey in March-April 1838. After prolonged negotiations, bargaining, and bitter resentment from Prince Miloš, a new constitution was formally proclaimed on December 24, 1838, in the form of a **Hatti Șerif.**

The constitution established a council of 17 members appointed by the prince, who could be removed only if they committed crimes against the laws of the lands. The council was given broad executive and legislative powers, and cabinet ministers (chancery) were not accountable to the prince but to the council. The adoption of the "Turkish Constitution" brought the downfall of Prince Miloš, who abdicated in favor of his son Milan and left Serbia on June 15, 1839.

**Constitution of 1869** ("Trinity Constitution"). Immediately after the assassination of Prince **Mihailo Obrenović** and the appointment of the Regency, several democratic reforms were introduced in Serbia. On December 18, St. Nicholas Day, a committee consisting of 66 citizens met to discuss the new constitution. After six months of deliberation the new constitution was proclaimed on Trinity Sunday, July 11, 1869. The Trinity Constitution preserved all the powers of the prince, strengthened the position of the **Obrenović dynasty**, and ruled out the possibility of the return of the **Karađorđević dynasty**. In addition, it guaranteed the equality of all citizens, personal freedom and property rights, and freedom of religion, speech, and press. However, these rights became subject to exclusive laws, a fact that seriously undermined the credibility of the constitution. The government was given the right to impose censorship, and citizens were not allowed to sue government officials. The selective functions of the National Assembly were restored, and the prince was given the right to appoint one of his own men for every two elected deputies. Although it represented a substantial improvement over the "Turkish Constitution" the Trinity Constitution failed to institute a system of parliamentary democracy in Serbia.

**Constitution of 1888** (1889). Defeat in the **Serbo-Bulgarian War** in 1885 seriously undermined the position of King **Milan Obrenović**, who was forced to accede to the demands of the **Radical Party** that had become a major political force in the country. The new constitution was promulgated in January 1889 (December 1888, according to the Old Style calendar). Unlike the Trinity Constitution, the new constitution precisely stipulated civil liberties and made them less liable to legislative limitations. Freedom of the press was greatly enhanced by exact provisions as to what actions could not be taken against the press. The new constitution ruled out the possibility of the suspension of constitutional rights either by the king or by the Assembly, even in an emergency such as a rebellion or a war. Citizens were given the right to sue officials directly and ministers were made more responsible to the Assembly. The new constitution stipulated the right of secret elections for the first time in Serbia's history, and the prerogatives of the Assembly were greatly enhanced. The government lost the right to appoint a third of the Assembly: deputies were to be chosen exclusively by direct elections. Local self-government was fully restored. Serbia became divided into 15 circuits (*okrugs*), each divided into districts (*srezes*) and then into **communes**. The constitution of 1889 represented a considerable step forward in the democratization of Serbia. It prompted the abdication of King Milan. However, on May 21, 1894, King **Alexander Obrenović** abolished it.

**Constitution of 1901** ("April Constitution"). After several years of personal rule, confronted by a serious decline in popularity, King Alexander acquiesced to the demands of the Radical Party and promulgated a new constitution by royal decree on April 19, 1901. The main authors of the constitution were Ministers **Milovan Milovanović**, a Radical, and **Pavle Marinković**, a Liberal. The different objectives of the two political parties were heavily reflected in the constitution, which appeared as a mixture of democratic, conservative, and reactionary provisions. The April Constitution introduced a bicameral legislature consisting of an elected assembly of 130 members and a senate of 51 members, three-fifths of whom were appointed by the king. The houses were equal, with the lower house deciding the budget. Secret voting was preserved, civil rights were recognized but limited, and ministers were made directly responsible to the king.

**Constitution of 1903.** One of the first acts of the government founded immediately after the assassination of King Alexander was the promulgation of the new constitution on June 18, 1903. The new constitution strikingly resembled the Constitution of 1889. All the laws enacted by the Constitution of 1889 were put back in force. Freedom of press, religion, and assembly were assured, and censorship was eradicated. The death penalty for political offenders was abolished, and an independent judiciary was introduced. The Constitution of 1903 established a parliamentary monarchy of the English type and set up the basic conditions for the rapid political and economic transformation of Serbia in the decade 1903–1914.

**Constitution of 1905** (Montenegrin). The first Constitution of Montenegro; closely resembling the Serbian Constitution of 1869.

**Constitution of 1921** ("Vidovdan Constitution"). After 18 months of bitter political struggle and Croatian opposition, the constitution of the **Kingdom of the Serbs, Croats, and Slovenes** was officially promulgated on June 28, 1921, St. Vitus Day—Vidovdan, the Serbian national holiday. The document reflected the basic provisions of the **Corfu Declaration.** It established a constitutional parliamentary monarchy and established a unicameral parliament, with ministers responsible both to the Assembly and to the king. Parliamentary deputies needed to be at least 30 years of age. Echoing the Corfu Declaration, the constitution referred to the "three named people," the "Serb-Croatian-Slovene" language and "Serb-Croatian-Slovene" nationality. The organization of the state was made independent of any national or religious consideration. An independent judiciary was established and judges were given permanent tenure. The Vidovdan Constitution was a liberal document. Croatian opposition to the constitution did not stem from the possible lack of liberal provisions but from the fact that the Vidovdan Constitution envisioned the creation of a unified state of equal partners. Envisioning the common state with the **Serbs** as a transient venture in the process of forming the Croatian national state, Croatian politicians viewed the constitution as a serious setback to their secessionist aspirations.

**Constitution of 1931**. See OCTROYED CONSTITUTION.

**Constitution of 1946**. The 1946 constitution was modelled after the 1936 constitution of the Soviet Union. The general provisions called for the establishment of basic civil liberties including equality before the law; freedom of press, religion, and assembly; free speech; and political association. However, the establishment of the one-party system in Yugoslavia virtually annulled most of these constitutional guaranties. The most important constitutional provisions referred to the new administrative division of the country and the establishment of a federation of six republics, each given equal status. In addition to the six republics, two autonomous provinces were created within Serbia. The Constitution of 1946 was amended in 1953 by provisions that took into account the development of **Self-Management** and reforms in local government.

**Constitution of 1963.** The slowdown in economic growth and increasing pressure toward further decentralization prompted the enactment of several new legislative initiatives that resulted in the introduction of a new constitution in 1963. The new constitution proclaimed the concept of a self-managed society, thus extending workers' self-management to the populace. The Federal Assembly was reorganized, and instead of the previous two, it now had five chambers. Substantial political and economic prerogatives were transferred from the federation to the republics. The name of the country was changed to the **Socialist Federal Republic of Yugoslavia.** The trend toward decentralization continued with the incessant adoption of constitutional amendments (1967, 1971).

**Constitution of 1974.** Numerous constitutional amendments and the explosion of nationalist euphoria in **Slovenia, Croatia, Macedonia,** and **Kosovo and Metohija** led to the promulgation of a new constitution in 1974. The Constitution of 1974 was devised by **Edvard Kardelj,** the leading ideologist of the Communist Party. The constitution provided a system of elections based on delegations drawn from occupational and interest groups. The majority of the delegations were regionally formed and under tight control of the local Party organizations. The Federal Assembly was made up of two chambers: the Federal Chamber and the Chamber of Republics and Provinces. The status of the autonomous provinces was elevated to constituent parts of the federation, while the federation was stripped of almost all economic powers (except the right to collect customs revenue and turnover tax). The introduction of consensus rule seriously impeded the decision-making process and enhanced autarchic tendencies. The Constitution of 1974 came as a result of the increasing economic and political nationalism of the republics. It instituted a highly inefficient political and economic system and increased the autarchic tendencies that culminated in the unilateral secessions of Croatia and Slovenia from Yugoslavia on June 26, 1991.

**Constitution of 1992.** The Constitution of the FRY was promulgated on April 27, 1992. The constitution proclaimed the FRY a sovereign federal state, based on the principle of equality of the citizens. The constitution provides for the equality before the law, regardless of national affiliation, race, sex, language, religion, political or other convictions, education, social origin, or property status. While it envisions numerous common elements, the constitution reflects the priority of republican constitutional arrangements, thus reducing the FRY to a confederal state.

CONSTITUTIONALISTS/USTAVOBRANITELJI. Group of several influential Serbian politicians who opposed the self-rule of Prince **Miloš Obrenović** and "defended" the **Constitution** of 1838. The leaders of the movement were **Toma Vučić-Perišić** and **Avram Petronijević**, who forced Miloš and Prince **Mihailo Obrenović** to abdicate. During the reign of Prince **Alexander Karađorđević**, 1842–1858, real power was in the hands of the Constitutionalists, headed by **Ilija Garašanin.** In the late 1850s, their regime weakened due to the increasing internal disagreements between the leaders. The movement split into two factions: one supported Prince Alexander, while the other, led by Ilija Garašanin, **Miša Anastasijević**, and Toma Vučić-Perišić, strongly opposed the prince. The removal of Prince Alexander and the return of Prince Miloš ended the Constitutionalists' role in Serbian politics. At the time of the Constitutionalist rule, Serbia got its Civil Code (1844) and ***Načertanije*** (1844), the national and state program. Great attention was paid to education, and the Lycée (1838), which later became the **Great School,** and the **Srpsko učeno društvo** (Serbian Learned Society) were founded.

CONTACT GROUP. Negotiating group composed of representatives from the United States, Great Britain, France, Germany, and Russia. Although European Union mediator Lord David Owen claims to have established the group in the aftermath of the **Sarajevo** NATO ultimatum in February 1994, it did not come to light until May of 1994, followed by the dictation of the Contact Group Plan. The plan was described as a "take or leave it" proposal to three of the sides in **Bosnia and Hercegovina** (B-H) with 51–49 split between the **Muslim-Croat Federation** and the **Republika Srpska**. Bosnian Serbs initially rejected the plan in a referendum, but faced with the intense NATO bombing of the Republika Srpska accepted it on September 7, 1995, as a basis for further negotiations. In late 1996 the Contact Group still existed as an international forum to discuss developments in B-H. At various times it has been extended to include UN troop-contributing countries or NATO member-countries.

CORFU DECLARATION/KRFSKA DEKLARACIJA. Document that emerged from the conference between representatives of the Serbian government and the **Yugoslav Committee** held from June 15 to July 20, 1917, on **Corfu Island**. The Serbian delegation, led by Prime Minister **Nikola Pašić**, and the committee, consisting of six representatives (**Croatia, Dalmatia, Slovenia, Bosnia and Hercegovina,** and **Istria**) outlined the basic form of the future South Slav state. The declaration, signed by Pašić and Trumbić on July 20, 1917, consisted of a preamble and fourteen articles. The preamble pronounced that the **Serbs**, Croats, and Slovenes were the same by blood; by language, both spoken and written; by feelings of their unity; and by the common vital interests of national survival and the manifold development of their moral and material life. The main points of the Corfu Declaration were: (1) an independent, constitutional, democratic, and parliamentary monarchy, under the **Karađorđević** dynasty; (2) equality of citizens, the **Cyrillic** and Latinic alphabets, and the Orthodox, Roman Catholic, and "Muhammedan" religions; (3) local autonomy, based on social and economic conditions; (4) the adoption of the **constitution** by the numerically qualified majority.

The Corfu Declaration was the most important document in the Yugoslav movement at that time. While no party was particularly satisfied with it, the Declaration formed a framework upon which the **Kingdom of the Serbs, Croats, and Slovenes** was established in 1918.

CORFU ISLAND (Kerkira)/KRF. Greek island in the Ionian Sea. After withdrawal through Albania, a Serbian army numbering more than 120,000 was transferred by the French fleet to Corfu Island. Between January 23 and March 23, 1916, more than 4,000 Serbian soldiers died from typhus and were buried on the small nearby islet of Vido. Around 7,000 soldiers were buried in the surrounding sea for lack of space.

COUP D'ÉTAT OF MARCH 27, 1941/DVADESETSEDMI MART 1941. At the beginning of 1941, Yugoslavia found itself virtually encircled by Germany and Italy. Neighboring countries were either occupied or joined the Tripartite Pact. Anxious to attack the Soviet Union, the Nazis wanted to secure their southern flank and increased pressure on Yugoslavia to join the pact. After prolonged negotiation, the Yugoslav government signed the pact on March 25, 1941. This provoked an outburst of anti-German feelings, predominantly in **Serbia.** At dawn on March 27, 1941, a group of pro-British generals and officers overthrew the government and the regency and brought King **Peter II Karađorđević** to the throne. Cheered in Serbia, the coup d'état was not welcomed among Croats, who perceived it as a purely Serbian affair. The events of March 27, 1941, directly led to the German invasion of Yugoslavia, which started with a massive aerial bombardment of **Belgrade** on April 6, 1941. There is substantial evidence that the coup d'état of March 27, 1941, was planned by the British Special Operations Executive (SOE).

COURT RADICALS. Term used for the moderate wing of the **Radical Party.** The wing advocated cooperation with King **Alexander Obrenović** following his coup and accession to power on April 13, 1893. The opposing wing was known as "extreme Radicals" and included **Nikola Pašić, Kosta Taušanović,** and Ranko Tajsić.

CRNA GORA. See MONTENEGRO.

CRNA RUKA (Black Hand). See UNIFICATION OR DEATH.

CRNJANSKI, MILOŠ (1893–1979). Prominent Serbian poet and writer, one of the leading proponents of the so-called "modern approach" in Serbian literature after **World War I.** Crnjanski rhythmically changed Serbian verse by giving a greater role to intonation and syntax. He lived in exile in London from 1941 until 1965, when he returned to **Belgrade.** His best-known works include a book of poems *Lirika Itake* (*Lyrics of Ithaca*), the novels *Seobe* (*Migrations*) and *Roman o Londonu* (*A Novel about London*), and the essays *Knjiga o Nemačkoj* (*A Book about Germany*).

CRNOJEVIĆI. Serbian feudal family, rulers of **Zeta** from 1465 to 1498. Ivan, who ruled 1465–1490, built the Monastery in **Cetinje** in 1484; Đurađ ruled 1490–1496 and established the first printing press in Cetinje monastery in 1493; Stephen ruled 1496–1498; and Staniša, who converted to Islam, ruled 1514–1528 under the name Skenderbeg. See also MONTENEGRO.

CROATIA, REPUBLIC OF/HRVATSKA. Former constituent republic of the **Socialist Federal Republic of Yugoslavia** (SFRY) that gained independence and international recognition in 1992. Croatia is comprised of the historic provinces **Istria, Dalmatia,** and **Slavonia** with a total area of 56,538 sq km and population of 4,784,265 in 1991. The Dalmatian coast is dominated by the Dinaric mountainous massif, while Slavonia is the south end of the Panonian Basin and the most fertile region of Croatia. Dalmatia and Istria have a typical Mediterranean climate while a Continental climate dominates in interior Croatia and Slavonia. The ethnic composition of Croatia prior to the civil war was: 77.9 percent Croatian, 12.2 percent Serbian, and 2.2 percent Yugoslav and others. Croats speak the Croatian language, and the majority of them are Roman Catholics (see table 12, statistical addendum).

With the exception of **Slovenia,** Croatia was the richest republic of the SFRY, producing close to 25 percent of the country's gross national product (GNP) at the end of the 1980s. The country is relatively rich in mineral resources—coal (Istria), crude oil, and natural gas (Slavonia)—and is highly dependent on mining, quarrying, and manufacturing. The most developed industries are chemicals, metals, shipbuilding, machine-building, electronic, wood-making and wood-processing. The main industrial centers are **Zagreb,** Slavonski Brod, Split, Rijeka, and Šibenik. The fastest growing sector of the Croatian economy is tourism, generating more than 1.5 billion U.S. dollars (current prices) per year. The biggest ports in Croatia are Rijeka, Split, and Ploče. Agricultural production in Croatia in 1991 was 2,001 million metric tons with maize, wheat, and sugar beets being the principal crops.

The **South Slavs**, mostly Croats, moved into the valleys of the **Sava** and **Drava** rivers in the course of the sixth and seventh centuries. The first records about Croats and Croatian statehood date from 852 *(Dux Chroatorum–Duke of Croats)*. Medieval Croatia prospered the most during the reign of Tomislav (910–928), who proclaimed himself king in 924. His rule was characterized by Rome's domination in church affairs, a fact that would play a decisive role in the Croatian acceptance of Roman Catholicism. After the death of the last Croatian king, Petar Svačić, in the battle against Hungarians in 1097, Croatia lost its independence and was incorporated into Hungary in 1102. Croatian nationalists advance an argument about a "personal union" between the Croatian and Hungarian nobility, according to which the Croatian state continued its existence after 1102.

After the Hungarian defeat at the Battle of Mohacs in 1526, the territory of Croatia was divided between Austria and the Ottoman Empire. Following the Battle of Mohacs, and the large influx of **Serbs** into Croatia and Slavonia, Austria formed a defensive zone populated by the Serbs, known as **Vojna Krajina.** After the proclamation of Austria-Hungary in 1868, Croatia and Slavonia were restored to the Hungarian Crown. Following **World War I,** Croatia became a part of the **Kingdom of the Serbs, Croats, and Slovenes.** Croatian nationalists gathered around the **Croatian Peasant Party** that opposed the new common state, while the Fascist **Ustaše** engaged in terrorist actions. The **Cvetković-Maček Agreement** created the **Croatian Banovina** in 1939 and extended Croatian authority over **Dalmatia, Slavonia, Srem,** and parts of **Bosnia and Hercegovina** (B-H) and **Montenegro**. Following the collapse of Yugoslavia in **April's War** of 1941, the puppet **Independent State of Croatia** was formed on the territory that encompassed the Croatian Banovina and B-H. After **World War II,** Josip Broz, **Tito,** and his associates created a new administrative division of Yugoslavia that established the present day borders of Croatia and the rest of the republics. The division was done arbitrarily and was influenced by anti-Serbian Comintern policy. Dissatisfied with the status of Croatia within the Yugoslav Federation, Croatian nationalists continued to pursue a drive toward independence, which resulted in the rapid decentralization of the federation.

In April–May 1990, the nationalist **Croatian Democratic Union** (HDZ), led by dissident and former Communist general **Franjo Tudjman,** won the first multiparty elections in Croatia. The intimidating anti-Serb and anti-Yugoslav policies of the HDZ alienated Serb-dominated areas that refused to live under what they perceived as the new Ustaše regime. Thus, the Croatian drive toward secession from Yugoslavia was echoed by the Serbian push toward independence. The Croatian proclamation of independence and unilateral secession from the SFRY led to a full scale civil war that lasted until January, 1992. Following the **European Community** (EC) recognition on January 15, 1992, Croatia formally gained independence. On the other hand, Serb-dominated areas united and proclaimed the **Republic of Serbian Krajina** (RSK) in December 1991. In February 1992, according to the **Vance Plan**, a 14,000-strong **UNPROFOR** was deployed throughout front lines between Croatia and RSK, and the **United Nations Protected Areas** (UNPA) were created. The impasse persisted until 1995, when the Croatian Army, unencumbered by **NATO** and with the tacit approval of the international community, launched major offensives on two UNPA zones thus effectively ending the existence of the the RSK. According to the **Dayton Agreement,** the remaining part of Croatia under Serbian control, formerly known as Sector East, gradually reintegrated into Croatia.

The Croatian economy suffered substantial losses in the 1991–1995 period. However, access to international financial markets as well as continuous German support played a substantial role in the economic stabilization efforts of the Croatian government. The Croatian political arena is dominated by the right-wing nationalist parties: the HDZ, the Croatian Social-Liberal Party, the Croatian Party of Rights, and the Croatian People's Party take around 90 percent of the electorate.

Croatian defense forces are estimated at 173,300 (1993) with reserves of 180,000. In addition, there were 40,000 armed military police and air defense forces of 4,000. The paramilitary forces consisted of 8,000 border police and 16,000 interior police. It is estimated that the Croatian army has more than 500 modern tanks, 820 heavy artillery pieces, and around 50 fighter jets.

CROATIAN BANOVINA/BANOVINA HRVATSKA. Administrative unit in the Kingdom of Yugoslavia created by the **Cvetković-Maček Agreement** signed by Yugoslav prime minister **Dragiša Cvetković** and the Croatian leader **Vladko Maček** on August 26, 1939. The agreement came about as a result of constant and growing calls for the secession of **Croatia** from the Kingdom of Yugoslavia, mainly from the **Croatian Peasant**

**Party,** the largest Croatian party, headed by Maček. The *banovina* included Savska and Primorska **Banovine** plus **Dubrovnik, Šid,** Ilok, **Brčko,** Gradačac, Derventa, Travnik, and Fojnica Counties. The Croatian Banovina was given a great deal of autonomy, including law-making prerogatives and almost complete independence in managing its internal affairs. The Croatian Banovina *de facto* was a state within a state. The main problem surrounding its creation was that while the *banovina* was supposed to be a Croatian national state, it encompassed areas that historically never belonged to Croats. Moreover, the sizable Serbian minority within the *banovina* were inadequately represented in the administrative and legislative bodies. The Croatian Banovina effectively ceased to exist on April 10, 1941, when the **Independent State of Croatia** was proclaimed. See also CROATIA, REPUBLIC OF.

CROATIAN DEMOCRATIC UNION/HRVATSKA DEMOKRATSKA ZAJEDNICA (HDZ). Right-wing political party in the **Republic of Croatia** formally founded on February 24, 1990. Under the leadership of **Franjo Tudjman,** the HDZ won in all consecutive multiparty elections in Croatia.

CROATIAN PEASANT PARTY/HRVATSKA SELJAČKA STRANKA (HSS). Major Croatian political party (together with the Croatian Party of Rights) prior to **World War II.** The party was founded in 1904 by **Stjepan Radić** and Ante Radić as Hrvatska pučka seljačka stranka (Croatian National Peasant Party). In 1918, after the formation of the **Kingdom of the Serbs, Croats, and Slovenes,** the party changed its name to the Croatian Republican Peasant Party. This act symbolized bitter opposition to the formation of a common state and to the Serbian **Karađorđević dynasty**. After Stjepan Radić's trip to Moscow in 1924, the party joined the Communist-controlled Peasant International. However, soon after the general **elections** held in 1924, Radić changed the name of the party to Hrvatska seljačka stranka (Croatian Peasant Party) and formed a coalition government with the **Radical Party.**

From 1926 to 1928 the HSS was one of the main opposition parties that continuously obstructed parliamentary life in Yugoslavia. After the assassination in **Parliament** on June 20, 1928, the HSS boycotted parliamentary life under the leadership of **Vladko Maček,** but participated in the elections of 1935 and 1938. Following the **Cvetković-Maček Agree-**

**ment** in 1939 and the formation of the **Croatian Banovina,** the HSS formed a coalition government with the **Yugoslav Radical Union.** Maček became deputy prime minister, the post he retained after the **Coup d'état of March 27, 1941.** After the collapse of Yugoslavia in **April's War** and the proclamation of the **Independent State of Croatia** on April 10, 1941, the majority of the party membership, including the armed units of the Party known as Seljačka straža (the Peasant Guard), joined the **Ustaše**. The HSS was revived in 1989, but without notable influence in Croatian politics. See also CROATIA, REPUBLIC OF.

CVETKOVIĆ, DRAGIŠA (1893–1969). Serbian politician, member of the Yugoslav Radical Union, and prime minister of Yugoslavia 1939–1941. In August 1939, he concluded a negotiated settlement with **Vladko Maček,** known as the **Cvetković-Maček Agreement.** The agreement changed the existing administrative structure of Yugoslavia and created the **Croatian Banovina.** On April 25, 1941, as the head of the coalition government of Yugoslavia, Cvetković signed the **Tripartite Pact**. His government was overthrown by the **Coup d'etat of March 27, 1941.**

CVETKOVIĆ-MAČEK AGREEMENT/SPORAZUM CVETKOVIĆ-MAČEK. Agreement between Yugoslav prime minister **Dragiša Cvetković** and **Vladko Maček,** the leader of the **Croatian Peasant Party.** The agreement brokered by Prince **Pavle Karađorđević** was signed on August 20, and endorsed by **Parliament** on August 26, 1939. A new government was formed, with Cvetković remaining prime minister and Maček becoming a vice-premier. The new autonomous unit known as the **Croatian Banovina** was created, and **Ivan Šubašić** became **ban.** The agreement essentially introduced dualism into the Yugoslav state and became a first step to confederalization.

CVIJIĆ, JOVAN (1865–1927). Most prominent Serbian geographer, founder of scientific geography in **Serbia,** honorary doctor of the Sorbonne, and president of the **Serbian Academy of Sciences and Arts** (1921–1927). Cvijić is especially known for his work on morphology and hydrography of the Dinaric karst region as well as for anthropological and geographic analysis of the Yugoslav lands. His main works include *Antrogeografski problemi Balkanskog poluostrva* (*Antrogeographic Problems of the Balkan Peninsula*), and *Geomorfologija* (*Geomorphology*).

CYRIL (826–869) AND METHODIUS (?–885). Byzantine missionaries, brothers Cyril (Constantin) and Methodius, who were sent by emperor Michael III to Moravia in 863 to instruct Slavic people in the Christian faith through the medium of the Slavonic tongue. Cyril devised the first Slavonic alphabet, known as the **Glagolitic alphabet**. After the death of Methodius, the members of their mission were driven out of Moravia.

CYRILLIC ALPHABET. Second oldest alphabet of the Slavs, named after Cyril (Constantin, Kiril) who devised the oldest Slavic alphabet, the **Glagolithic alphabet**. The Cyrillic alphabet was created in Bulgaria at the end of the ninth century. The alphabet was based on the Greek uncial script, from which 24 letters were taken, while 13 new letters were also created. The Serbian Cyrillic alphabet was reformed in the 18th century by **Vuk Stefanović Karadžić,** while the Russian and Bulgarian Cyrillic alphabets were reformed after the October Revolution and **World War II.** The Macedonian Cyrillic alphabet was created in 1945.

## - Ć -

ĆELE KULA (Tower of Skulls). Tower located in **Niš,** built by the Turks from the skulls of dead Serbian fighters after the **Battle of Čegar** in 1809. Originally, the tower had 56 rows with around 950 skulls; today only a few are left due to prolonged neglect and decay.

ĆIRKOVIĆ, SIMA (1929– ). Prominent Serbian historian and member of the **Serbian Academy of Sciences and Arts.** Born in **Osijek,** he graduated with a degree in history from the **University of Belgrade**. His areas of expertise include a general history of the Serbian people and the history of Serbs in **Bosnia and Hercegovina** and **Montenegro.** Ćirković is a member of Academie europeanne d'histoire in Brussels. He was a member of several academies of the former Yugoslav republics. His best known works include *Istorija srednjevekovne bosanske države* (*History of the Medieval Bosnian State*), *Istorija Crne Gore* (*History of Montenegro*), *Istorija Jugoslavije* (*History of Yugoslavia*), and *Istorija srpskog naroda* (*History of Serbian People*).

ĆOPIĆ, BRANKO (1915–1984). Serbian poet and writer from **Bosnian Krajina,** especially popular among children, and member of the **Serbian Academy of Sciences and Arts.** He spent the war with the Bosnian

**Partisans,** a significant influence on many of the books he regularly published after 1944. His best works include the poems "Ratnikovo proljeće" ("Spring of the Warrior") and the novels *Gluvi barut* (*Deaf Gunpowder*), *Doživljaji Nikoletine Bursaća* (*Adventures of Nikoletina Bursać*), and *Bašta sljezove boje* (*A Mallow-colored Garden*).

ĆOROVIĆ, SVETOZAR (1875–1919). Most significant writer of **Hercegovina** and the older brother of **Vladimir Ćorović**. Together with **Aleksa Šantić** and **Jovan Dučić** he formed the periodical *Zora* (*Dawn*) in **Mostar.**

ĆOROVIĆ, VLADIMIR (1885–1941). Prominent Serbian historian from **Bosnia and Hercegovina,** sentenced to eight years in prison by the Austro-Hungarian court during the staged proceedings against prominent **Serbs** in **Banja Luka** in 1915–1916. He was secretary of the Serbian cultural society Prosvjeta (Enlightenment). He completed *Istorija Srba* (*History of the Serbs*) in 1941. Suppressed as a "nationalistic" work, the book was finally published in 1991. His numerous works include *Istorija Jugoslavije* (*History of Yugoslavia*), *Odnosi Austro-Ugarske i Srbije u XX veku* (*The Relations between Serbia and Austria-Hungary in the 20th Century*), and *Istorija Bosne* (*History of Bosnia*).

ĆOSIĆ, DOBRICA (1921– ). Prominent Serbian writer, politician, and statesman, president of the **Federal Republic of Yugoslavia** (FRY) 1992–1993, and member of the **Serbian Academy of Sciences and Arts.** Born in Velika Drenova in the valley of the **Western Morava,** Ćosić joined the **Partisans** in 1941. After the war, he held several less prominent posts in the Communist Party until 1968, when he resigned from the party in protest against **Serbia**'s status in the **Socialist Federal Republic of Yugoslavia.** On June 15, 1992, Ćosić became the first president of the FRY. After a series of disagreements with Serbia's president **Slobodan Milošević,** Ćosić was removed by a staged no-confidence vote in the Federal **Parliament** on June 1, 1993.

For more than two decades Ćosić has been considered the spiritual leader of the Serbian national awakening. His literary work is characterized by in-depth analysis of individual psychology and focuses on motifs from Serbian history. His best known works include *Vreme smrti* (*Time of Death*), *Koreni* (*Roots*), *Deobe* (*Rifts*), *Grešnik* (*Sinful Man*), *Vernik* (*Believer*), and *Vreme vlasti* (*The Time of Power*).

## - Č -

ČABRINOVIĆ, NEDELJKO (1895–1916). Serbian revolutionary from **Bosnia and Hercegovina** and member of the **Mlada Bosna.** On June 28, 1914, in the **Sarajevo Assassination,** Čabrinović was the first to attempt to assassinate the Austro-Hungarian crown prince Franz Ferdinand by throwing a hand grenade. His death sentence was changed to 20 years imprisonment. He died in the infamous Austro-Hungarian prison Teresienstadt in 1916.

ČAČAK. Industrial city and a **commune** center in western Serbia with a population of 116, 808 in 1991. Food-processing and metal-processing industries are particularly developed there.

ČANAK, NENAD (1959– ). President of the League of the Social-Democrats of **Vojvodina**/Yugoslavia, journalist and composer. Following the success of the **Zajedno** coalition in the 1996 elections, Čanak gathered several smaller political parties, formed a mini-coalition in Vojvodina and came to power in **Novi Sad**. Čanak's liberal political agenda includes stringent anti-nationalism and the territorial and political decentralization of **Serbia**.

ČARŠIJA (Çarşi). The Serbian form of the Turkish word *çarşi* meaning market. The derogatory use of the term implies gossiping and unprincipled behavior.

ČASLAV KLONIMIROVIĆ (?–c. 950). Bulgarian-born Serbian prince who ruled from 927 to c. 950. An able ruler, he expanded the territory of **Serbia** by adding **Raška, Duklja,** a large part of **Bosnia and Hercegovina,** and Travunia to the Serbian state. He expanded the borders of Serbia to the Adriatic coastline and repulsed the attack of the Magyars (Hungarians) who formed their state in the Panonian Basin.

ČEGAR, BATTLE OF. Battle between the Turkish army under Hurşid Paşa and the Serbian forces led by **Stevan Sinđelić, Vojvoda** of the **Resava** region, that took place on a hill near **Niš** on May 19, 1809. The prolonged power struggle among Serbian leaders resulted in the complete disorganization of the southeastern front of the Serbian army. After his positions were attacked and overwhelmed by a superior Turkish force, Sinđelić blew up the ammunition depot, killing a substantial number of Turks and his own troops. After the battle, Turks built **Ćele Kula** from the skulls of dead **Serbs.**

ČERNIAEV, MIKHAIL GRIGOREVICH. See CHERNIAEV, MIKHAIL GRIGOREVICH.

ČETNIKS/CHETNIKS. Traditional Serbian guerilla fighters and volunteers. While the existence of Četniks can be traced back to the times of **Hajduks,** their number grew substantially after the **Serbo-Turkish Wars** (1876–1878). Četniks were especially numerous and active in **Macedonia,** which remained under Ottoman rule until 1912. During the **Balkan Wars** Četniks were attached to regular units of the Serbian army and participated in every major battle. During **World War I,** Četniks were organized into four squadrons (2,250 soldiers) and put under the command of the Third Army. The bravery of Četniks in the **Battle of Cer** and **Battle of Kolubara** brought them fame as the best units of the Serbian army. In 1915, Četnik forces were reorganized into the 4,000-strong Dobrovoljački odred (the Volunteers Squadron), which engaged in heavy fighting against the Bulgarian army in southern **Serbia.** After the withdrawal through Albania only 400–500 Četniks reached **Corfu Island.**

After the war the Association of Četniks was formed with the primary objective of caring for the families of fallen comrades and nurturing the Četnik tradition. **Kosta Milovanović-Pećanac**, who abused the movement by engaging in dubious financial speculations, became the leader of the organization in 1929. After the collapse of Yugoslavia in April 1941, he personally began to collaborate with the Germans, completely discrediting him with the **Serbs.** In May 1941, Colonel **Dragoljub-Draža Mihailović** formed the Command of Četniks' Squadrons of the Yugoslav Army (later **Jugoslovenska vojska u otadžbini**), and his forces became popularly known as Četniks.

ČIFLIK (Çiflik). Ottoman feudal estate or farm and a basic economic unit in **Bosnia and Hercegovina** and **Macedonia** in the beginning of the 20th century. The *çifliks* were disbanded in **Serbia** in 1815.

ČOBELJIĆ, NIKOLA (1912– ). Well-known Serbian economist and member of the **Serbian Academy of Sciences and Arts.** Prior to joining the economics faculty of the **University of Belgrade** he occupied several political posts, including deputy minister for procurement in Serbia, federal deputy minister of economy, and deputy director of the Federal Planning Bureau. His area of expertise is national economic development. He is the author of *Politika i metodi privrednog razvoja* (*Policy and Methods of Economic Development*), *Privreda Jugoslavije—rast, struktura i funkcionisanje* (*The Economy of Yugoslavia—Growth, Structure, and Functioning*), and other works.

ČUBRILOVIĆ, VASA (1897–1990). Historian and member of the **Serbian Academy of Sciences and Arts**. He belonged to the **Mlada Bosna** organization, and for his role in the **Sarajevo Assassination** he was sentenced to 16 years in prison. After **World War I**, he joined the **Agricultural Party.** During **World War II** he was jailed in **Banjica** concentration camp. After the war he was a minister in several Yugoslav governments. His best-known works include *Bosanski ustanak 1875–1878* (*Bosnian Uprising 1875–1878*), *Poreklo muslimanskog plemstva u Bosni i Hercegovini* (*The Origins of the Muslim Gentry in Bosnia and Hercegovina*), and *Istorija političke misli u Srbiji XIX veka* (*The History of Political Thought in 19th Century Serbia*).

ČUBRILOVIĆ, VELJKO (1886–1915). Serbian revolutionary from **Bosnia and Hercegovina** and older brother of **Vasa Čubrilović**. He belonged to the **Mlada Bosna** and was among the main organizers of the **Sarajevo Assassination.** He was sentenced to death and executed for his participation in the assassination.

ČUKUR ČESMA (Čukur Spring). A Serbian name for the public fountain in **Belgrade,** which Turks called Kükürt Çeşme (Sulphur Spring). In 1862 at the Čukur česma Turkish soldiers killed a Serbian boy, which prompted a series of severe clashes between Serbs and **Muslims** in Belgrade. To avoid full-scale war, the Great Powers initiated negotiations in which France and Russia supported **Serbia**, while Britain and Austria supported the Turks. The negotiations resulted in the Turkish withdrawal from two out of six remaining fortresses in Serbia.

ČUPIĆ, NIKOLA (1836–1870). Educator and benefactor. A grandson of **Stojan Čupić**, he finished artillery military academy and became an officer in the Serbian army in 1856. By donating his property he helped to establish a trust known as Zadužbina Nikole Čupića (Foundation of Nikola Čupić) which was formally instituted in 1871. The trust was managed by a board consiting of 12 members. From 1871 to 1941, when it ceased to exist, the foundation published 6,013 issues of its main publication *Godišnjica* (*Yearbook*) and 838 other publications.

ČUPIĆ, STOJAN (?–1815). Serbian **Vojvoda** in the **First Serbian Insurrection**. He operated in western **Serbia** along the **Drina** River and participated in the **Battle of Mišar**. He was known for his passionate public speeches and was a fearsome duelist. After the collapse of the insurrection he remained in Serbia and hid in the **Mačva** region. While organizing the **Second Serbian Insurrection** with **Miloš Obrenović** he was captured by the Turks and executed.

## - D -

DABAR. Region in the valley of the **Lim** River, between the cities of Prijepolje and **Priboj**. In 1219, **Saint Sava** founded the diocese of Dabar with its center at Banja monastery. The name of the diocese was changed to Dabrobosanska in the 16th century, and **Sarajevo** became its center in the 17th century.

DABČEVIĆ-KUČAR, SAVKA (1923– ). Croatian politician. As the president of the Communist Party of Croatia, she was also a leader of a nationalist Croatian movement, known as Croatian Spring (Hrvatsko proljeće). In December 1971, at a meeting in Karađorđevo she was removed from all political functions. She reentered politics in 1990 and headed the bloc of opposition parties in the elections of 1992 and 1995.

DABIŠA, STEFAN (?–1395). First cousin and successor of the Bosnian king **Tvrtko I Kotromanić.** During his reign central power was substantially weakened, and Bosnia came under heavy Hungarian influence. See also BOSNIA AND HERCEGOVINA.

DAHIJE/DAYIS. The term used for four **Jannissaries** who came to power in **Beogradski pašaluk** after the execution of the Ottoman governor of **Belgrade** Haçi-Mustafa Şinik-oglu in 1801. The Dahije Mehmed Fočić Aga, Aganlija, Kučuk Alija and Mula Jusuf imposed unprecedented cruelty upon the **Serbs**. Their regime ended Serbian autonomy, and in early 1804 the Dahije executed 152 Serbian leaders. The Dahije terror further intensified Serbian preparation for the general uprising. See also FIRST SERBIAN INSURRECTION.

DALJ. Small city in western **Srem** located within the administrative borders of the **Republic of Croatia.** During the civil war several meetings of the **Parliament** of the **Republic of Serbian Krajina** were held in Dalj.

DALMATIA. Historic region in the middle and southern portion of the Croatian Adriatic coast. The total area of the region, including a number of islands, is 12,158 sq km with more than a million inhabitants. The biggest cities, industrial centers, and seaports are Split, **Zadar**, Šibenik, and Ploče. The shipbuilding, plastic, and aluminum industries are particularly developed; however, the region is best known for its tourism. Prior to the secession of **Croatia** from Yugoslavia and the subsequent civil war, **Serbs** constituted a substantial portion of the total population in Dalmatia.

DAMJANOVIĆ, VASILIJE (1734–1792). Author of the first printed mathematical book in the **Serbian language**. *Novaja serbskaja aritmetika* (*New Serbian Arithmetic*) was published in Venetia in 1776.

DANAK U KRVI. See BLOOD TRIBUTE.

*DANICA*. One of the first Serbian literary almanacs, published in Vienna between 1826 and 1834 by **Vuk Stefanović Karadžić**. *Danica* (*The Morning Star*) played an important role in acquainting Europe with Serbian culture and tradition.

*DANICA ILIRSKA*. Croatian literary magazine published and edited by **Ljudevit Gaj**. It appeared first in 1835 as the supplement of *Narodne novine* (*National Gazette*) under the name *Danica hrvatska, slavonska i dalmatinska* (*The Morning Star of Croatia, Slavonia, and Dalmatia*). The first issue was printed in a local Croatian dialect and the rest of the issues in the major Serbian and later Croatian dialect, known as Štokavian. The magazine played an important role in the process of Croatian national awakening.

DANIČIĆ, ĐURO (1825–1882). Prominent Serbian linguist and fervent follower of **Vuk Stefanović Karadžić**. He was born in **Novi Sad** and studied in Bratislava, Pest (Budapest), and Vienna. He was the first secretary of **Jugoslovenska Akademija Znanosti i Umjetnosti,** Secretary of **Društvo Srpske Slovesnosti** (Serbian Society of Letters), and professor of the **Great School** in **Belgrade.** His most valuable studies include

*Mala srpska gramatika* (*A Little Serbian Grammar*), *Srpska sintaksa* (*Serbian Syntax*), *Osnove srpskog ili hrvatskog jezika* (*Basic Principles of Serbian or Croatian Language*), and *Rječnik hrvatskog ili srpskog jezika* (*The Dictionary of Croatian or Serbian Language*).

DANIL, KONSTANTIN (1798–1873). One of the greatest Serbian painters in the 19th century and a main representative of classicism in Serbian art.

DANILO I (1826–1860). Prince and first secular ruler of **Montenegro**. He actively supported an anti-Turkish rebellion in **Hercegovina** that prompted the Turkish invasion. However, in the **Battle of Grahovo** on May 1, 1858, **Montenegrins** defeated the Turkish army. This victory resulted in the formal recognition of the independence of Montenegro in 1860.

DANILO II (1270–1337). Archbishop of the **Serbian Orthodox Church.** He wrote biographies of Serbian Kings **Uroš I, Milutin,** and **Dragutin** and several archbishops. His work is compiled in *Životi kraljeva i arhiepiskopa srpskih* (*Lives of Serbian Kings and Archbishops*).

DANILO PETROVIĆ (1670–1735). Montenegrin bishop and ruler. During his reign the mass slaughter of **Montenegrins** who had converted to Islam was carried out. This event was masterfully portrayed by Petar Petrović Njegoš in his important work *Gorski vijenac* (*The Mountain Wreath*). Danilo's struggle against the Turks (Battles of Carev Laz, 1712 and 1714) and the establishment of close relations with the Venetian Republic and Russia substantially elevated Montenegro's status in Europe. See also MONTENEGRO.

DANUBE. Second largest river in Europe and the longest in the **Federal Republic of Yugoslavia** (591 km). The Danube is a major traffic route between **Serbia** and the Black Sea and an important source of hydroenergy (hydroelectric plants at **Đerdap**).

DANUBE-TISA-DANUBE/DUNAV-TISA-DUNAV. Major irrigation system in **Vojvodina**. The system consists of a series of waterways (330 km long) that connect the **Danube** and **Tisa** Rivers. Prior to **World War II,** the official name of the irrigation system was the Canal of King Alexander and King Petar.

DARDA. Small town and water distribution center in the **Baranja** region.

Given its strategic importance for the region, Darda became a site of heavy fighting between the **JNA** and Croatian paramilitary forces during the civil war in **Croatia** in 1991.

DAVIČO, OSKAR (1909–1989). Controversial Yugoslav poet and writer, the youngest among Serbian surrealists. His collections *Pesme* (*Poems*) and *Hana* (*Hanna*) are considered among the best books of poetry written between the two world wars. Davičo's rich literary output ranged from plain revolutionary literature to surrealism. His best works also include *Višnja za zidom* (*Cherry Tree Behind the Wall*), and *Pesma* (*Poem*).

DAVIDOVIĆ, DIMITRIJE (?–1839). Close associate of Prince **Miloš Obrenović** and one of the most educated men in **Serbia** in the first half of the 19th century. A secretary to the National Chancery, minister of foreign affairs, minister of interior and education, and secretary of Prince Miloš, he wrote the **Constitution** of 1835 (Presentation Constitution). He closely cooperated with **Vuk Stefanović Karadžić.**

DAVIDOVIĆ, LJUBOMIR-LJUBA (1863–1940). Prominent Serbian and Yugoslav politician. Together with **Jaša Prodanović** he founded the **Independent Radical Party** in 1902, and after the formation of the **Kingdom of the Serbs, Croats, and Slovenes,** he became the president of the **Democratic Party.** He occupied several important posts, including minister of education (1904, 1914–1917, and 1918) and prime minister (1919, 1924). Davidović is remembered as an extremely modest man and honest politician.

DAYTON AGREEMENT. The peace agreement brokered by the United States and signed by the presidents of **Bosnia and Hercegovina** (B-H), **Croatia,** and **Serbia.** In the beginning of November 1995, after strenuous mediating activity by the U.S. envoy **Richard Holbrook**, representatives of B-H, Croatia, Serbia, **Montenegro,** and **Republika Srpska** (Serbian Republic) were summoned to Wright-Patterson Air Force Base in Dayton, Ohio. The proposed peace plan called for the division of Bosnia into two administrative units (entities): **Muslim-Croat Federation** (51 percent of the territory) and Republika Srpska (49 percent of the territory). The plan also envisioned the holding of democratic **elections** in Bosnia, return of property to all displaced persons, and barring alleged war criminals from political life. The implementation of the plan would be secured by a 60,000-strong **NATO** force under American command.

After intense negotiations, the peace agreement was initialled on November 21, 1995, despite the dissatisfaction of the RS delegation. Following the Dayton Agreement, the peace treaty was signed in Paris on December 14, 1995.

DEČANI. A monastery in the vicinity of **Peć**, built between 1327 and 1335. The monastery is a legacy of King **Stefan Dečanski** and his son, later Emperor **Dušan the Mighty**. The largest collection of decorative wall paintings, known as frescoes, and a rich collection of icons are located in the monastery.

DEČANSKI, STEFAN (?–1331). A son of King **Milutin** and Serbian king from 1322 to 1331. The rule of Dečanski was distinguished by the **Battle of Velbužd** in 1330 in which the **Serbs** decisively defeated the Bulgars.

DEDINAC, MILAN (1902–1966). A Serbian poet, the finest representative of surrealism in Serbian poetry. While some of his first poems were considered a model of pure poetry, he readily experimented with different lyric styles. He published *Od nemila do nedraga* (*Hard Times*).

DEJANOVIĆI. A feudal family in medieval **Serbia** ruling the lands in northern **Macedonia** east of the **Vardar** River. The founder of the family was **Vojvoda** Dejan, a son-in-law of the Emperor **Dušan the Mighty**. Dejan's sons, Konstantin and Jovan, became Turkish vassals after the **Battle of Maritsa** in 1371. Constantin XI Dragaš, the last Byzantine Emperor, was a son of Konstantin's daughter Jelena.

DELIGRAD. A town in **Serbia** 25 km north of **Niš.** During the **First Serbian Insurrection** several battles took place at Deligrad (1806, 1807, 1809, and 1813). A battle also occurred there during the **Serbo-Turkish War** of 1876.

DEMOCRATIC CENTER/DEMOKRATSKI CENTAR. A political party that emerged from the internal split of the **Democratic Party** following the replacement of **Dragoljub Mićunović** as the leader of the party in 1994. Mićunović's Democratic Center mainly gathers the older generation of the former Democrats and lacks substantial popular support.

DEMOCRATIC LEAGUE OF KOSOVO/DEMOKRATSKA LIGA KOSOVA/LIDHJA DEMOKRATIKE e KOSOVËS (LDK). Political organization formed by **Ibrahim Rugova** on December 24, 1989. The main body of the organization consisted of the members of the Kosovo regional **Parliament**. On July 2, 1990, a few days after the Serbian Parliament decided to dissolve the regional parliament, the LDK declared the secession of Kosovo from Serbia. On October 19, 1991, the LDK proclaimed the so-called the Republic of Kosova and formed a provisional government. On May 24, the LDK organized "parliamentary elections" and won 89 percent of the vote.

In 1996, an internal split in the LDK occurred between Rugova's group and the faction led by Adem Demaçi and Rexep Qosja. The latter criticised Rugova's policy of peaceful resistance and formed an alternative organization called the Democratic Forum in November 1997. Soon thereafter, Demaçi became the leader of the political wing of the **Kosovo Liberation Army** (KLA). Although seriously weakened by the aggressive policies of the KLA, Rugova remained president of the LDK.

DEMOCRATIC MOVEMENT OF SERBIA/DEMOKRATSKI POKRET SRBIJE (DEPOS). A coalition of 12 opposition parties formed on May 23, 1992, in Belgrade. The **Serbian Renewal Movement** (SPO), **Democratic Party of Serbia,** and **New Democracy** were the most important coalition partners and were the main organizers of the mass anti-government demonstration that took place in June 1992. In 1992 **Elections** DEPOS received 16.9 percent of votes (50 seats in the Serbian **Parliament**) while in 1993 elections DEPOS received 16.6 percent of votes (45 seats). The political platform of DEPOS mainly concentrated around severe criticism of the **Socialist Party of Serbia** (SPS) and Serbian President **Slobodan Milošević**. DEPOS lost political influence following the internal split of the SPO and the decision of New Democracy to form a coalition government with the SPS in December 1993.

DEMOCRATIC PARTY/DEMOKRATSKA STRANKA. A political party founded in May 1919. The Democratic Party materialized as a merger of the **Independent Radical Party**, the **Progressive Party**, and Narodna stranka (The National Party) from **Serbia** and the Democratic Party of **Svetozar Pribićević** from **Croatia**. **Ljubomir-Ljuba Davidović** led the Party until his death in 1940 when he was succeeded as president of the Party by **Milan Grol.** The Program of the Party was adopted in 1921. It promoted a democratic, centralist and unitary state organization and an activist economic policy. The base of the party were intellectuals and the petite bourgeoisie. The Democrats were genuine supporters of the

Yugoslav idea and enjoyed support throughout the country, especially among **Serbs** outside Serbia.

In 1924, the Independent Democrats led by Pribićević split from the Democratic Party. Like other political parties, the Democratic Party was banned during the **Dictatorship of January 6, 1929,** that lasted from 1929 to 1931. The Democrats participated in the **elections** of 1935 and 1938 in coalition with the Peasant Party and **Agricultural Party.**

After **World War II** Milan Grol, leader of the Party, headed the United Democratic coalition that challenged **Narodni Front,** the Communists' organization, in the 1945 elections. The overwhelming victory of Narodni Front signaled the beginning of the one-party system in Yugoslavia.

The Democratic Party reemerged in Serbia's political life in 1990. The president of the Party became **Dragoljub Mićunović**, who was later replaced by **Zoran Đinđić**. The base of the party is mainly in the big cities among intelligentsia, professionals, and younger people in general. In 1992, **Vojislav Koštunica** split from the Party and formed the **Democratic Party of Serbia.**

DEMOCRATIC PARTY OF SERBIA/DEMOKRATSKA STRANKA SRBIJE (DSS). A political party that emerged from the internal split of the **Democratic Party** in 1992. The main platform of this right-center party is an inflamed anti-communism which rests upon relentless criticism of the government's national and economic policies. While initially a member of the unified opposition block, the DSS left the opposition **Zajedno** due to the differences regarding policy of **Serbia** toward the **Republika Srpska** and foreign policy matters.

DEMOCRATIC PARTY OF SOCIALISTS/DEMOKRATSKA PARTIJA SOCIJALISTA (DPS). The ruling political party in **Montenegro**. Following the collapse of the League of Communists of Yugoslavia and the formation of new political parties, the leadership of the Montenegrin communists changed its name from the League of Communists of Montenegro to the Democratic Party of Socialists. The party decisively won all elections in Montenegro. In the last Montenegrin republican **elections**, the party won 45 of 71 legislative seats. Its main rival, the National Unity coalition picked up 19, while the Party of Democratic Action won three, and the Democratic League of Montenegro and the Democratic League of Albanians each won two. Following the rift between **Momir Bulatović** and **Milo Đukanović** the party split into two factions. While most of the party leadership sided with Đukanović, Đulatović's faction called the **Socialist People's Party** appeared to retain an edge amongst the membership at large. However, in the last parliamentary elections in Montenegro, the DPS decisively defeated Bulatović's PSP.

DEMOCRATIC UNION OF HUNGARIANS FROM VOJVODINA/ DEMOKRATSKI ZAJENICA VOJVOĐANSKIH MAĐARA (DZVM). Political organization of the Hungarian minority leaving in **Vojvodina.** The party advocates substantial autonomy for the Hungarians leaving in the region and is continuously represented in the **Parliament**. See also AGOŠTON ANDRAŠ.

DEMOKRATSKA STRANKA. See DEMOCRATIC PARTY.

DEMOKRATSKA STRANKA SRBIJE (DSS). See DEMOCRATIC PARTY OF SERBIA.

DEMOKRATSKI CENTAR. See DEMOCRATIC CENTER.

DEMOKRATSKI POKRET SRBIJE (DEPOS). See DEMOCRATIC MOVEMENT OF SERBIA.

DEPOS. See DEMOCRATIC MOVEMENT OF SERBIA.

DEROKO, ALEKSANDAR (1894–1990). A prominent architect, a specialist in medieval Serbian architecture, and member of the **Serbian Academy of Sciences and Arts.** He is the author of *Arhitektura u srednjevekovnoj Srbiji* (*Architecture in Medieval Serbia*).

DESNICA, VLADAN (1905–1967). A Serbian writer born in **Dalmatia**. He studied law and philosophy in **Zagreb** and Paris and graduated with a degree in law at the University of Zagreb. Desnica founded the literary-historical yearbook *Magazin sjeverne Dalmacije* (*Almanac of Northern Dalmatia*) in 1934. He was the first to use themes from the Serbian-populated parts of Dalmatia during the **World War II** period. In his later works he became preoccupied with existentialism. His best works are *Proljeća Ivana Galeba* (*The Springtimes of Ivan Galeb*), *Zimsko ljetovanje* (*The Winter Summer Holiday*), *Olupine na Suncu* (*Wreckage on Sunshine*), and *Proljeće u Badrovcu* (*Spring in Badrovac*).

DESPIĆ, ALEKSANDAR (1927– ). President of the **Serbian Academy**

**of Sciences and Arts** since 1993 and member of the European Academy of Sciences. Born in **Belgrade,** he studied in London where he graduated in chemical engineering. Author of 160 journal articles and numerous monographs in the area of chemical engineering. His best known works include *Doprinos teoriji mehanizma hemijskih reakcija* (*A Contribution to a Theory of the Mechanism of Chemical Reactions*) and *Teorija slojevitog taloženja metala* (*Theory of the Stratification of Metals' Sediments*).

DESPOT. A non-hereditary title in Byzantine and Serbian courts. The rank of the title falls between Emperor and King. Starting from 1402, Serbian rulers held this title.

DEŽEVO, ACCORD OF/DEŽEVSKI UGOVOR. An agreement between King **Dragutin** and his brother **Milutin**, the two sons of late King **Uroš I Nemanjić.** Having lost a battle against the Byzantines, King Dragutin was forced to transfer his powers to his younger brother Milutin in 1282. According to the agreement that became known as the Accord of Deževo, Milutin assumed the throne of **Serbia** while Dragutin continued to rule over a territory that included northern parts of **Šumadija** (north of **Western Morava**), **Mačva, Pomoravlje, Semberija** and Posavina, **Srem**, and the city of **Belgrade.** In addition, the accord called for Dragutin's son Vladislav to succeed Milutin as the Serbian King.

DEŽEVSKI UGOVOR. See DEŽEVO, ACCORD OF.

DICTATORSHIP OF JANUARY 6, 1929/ŠESTOJANUARSKA DIKTATURA. A pejorative term used for the personal regime of King **Alexander Karađorđević** instituted on January 6, 1929. The assassination in **Parliament,** in which after a heated debate and a series of personal insults directed at him, a deputy of the **Radical Party**, Puniša Račić, killed three and wounded two deputies of the **Croatian Peasant Party** (HSS), was followed by the complete obstruction of parliamentary life by the HSS. After the resignation of Prime Minister **Anton Korošec** in December 1928, King Alexander assumed personal rule, asserting the impossibility for life to continue under the present circumstances. He suspended the "Vidovdan" **Constitution** and dismissed the Parliament. Political parties were abolished, and the Law of Protection of the State strengthened. In addition, the King was made the wielder of all political power, censorship was instituted, local self-government was abolished, and a special court for political crimes was established. The king's rule was exercised through a cabinet headed by General **Petar Živković** and consisting of several politicians from all major parties (including dissidents from the HSS).

In late 1929, Alexander changed the name of the country from the **Kingdom of the Serbs, Croats, and Slovenes** to the Kingdom of Yugoslavia. The country's 33 administrative districts were reduced to nine, called **Banovine.** These changes were intended to enhance national unity and to reduce centralism. In September 1931, Alexander's personal rule ended and the **Octroyed Constitution** was implemented.

The personal regime of King Alexander did not solve the national problem in Yugoslavia, while the numerous arrests of political enemies led to the increased radicalization of nationalist groups.

DIMITRIJE (1846–1930). Metropolitan (1905–1920) and patriarch (1920–1930) of the **Serbian Orthodox Church**. He was the patriarch of the united Serbian Orthodox church following the formation of the **Kingdom of the Serbs, Croats, and Slovenes**.

DIMITRIJEVIĆ, DRAGUTIN-APIS. See APIS, DIMITRIJEVIĆ DRAGUTIN.

DINAR. An official currency of the **Federal Republic of Yugoslavia** (FRY). As the currency in **Serbia,** the silver dinar dates from the reign of King **Milutin**. The Serbian dinar had a lower silver content than the Venetian dinar (2.178:1.807 grams of silver), which provoked strong protests by the Venetians, who accused Milutin of counterfeiting. Dante went so far as to proclaim King Milutin a sinner in his *Divine Comedy*. During the rule of Emperor **Dušan the Mighty,** the silver content of the Serbian dinar was further reduced to 1.429 g, while in the last period of the Serbian medieval state the dinar's value fluctuated.

The dinar was re-instituted as official currency in Serbia in 1879, and after 1918 it became the official currency of Yugoslavia. Until 1965, the dinar was covered by gold at a value of 0.00071937 grams of gold per dinar. In 1966, the dinar was denominated on the basis of 100 "old" dinars per one "new" dinar, and gold coverage became 0.071035 grams. Since then the dinar was devalued several times, in 1971, 1973, and 1980. During the 1980s, a growing budget deficit created strong inflationary pressure in the Yugoslav economy. The inflation and foreign trade deficit led to the constant loss of value of the dinar. Between 1980 and 1989 the dinar depreciated relative to the dollar from 19 dinars per dollar to 80,500 dinars per dollar. On January 1, 1990, the dinar was denominated on the basis of 10,000 "old" dinars per one "new" dinar and pegged to the German mark at the then exchange rate nine of dinars for one mark.

After the outbreak of the civil war in Yugoslavia in June 1991, the dinar began to lose value rapidly since the central banks of all of the republics resorted to relentless war financing. During 1991–1992, former Yugoslav republics established their own currencies, while the **Federal Republic of Yugoslavia** (FRY) retained the dinar as its official currency. The exhaustive **sanctions** applied against the FRY in 1992 and 1993 accompanied by the continuous deficit financing of the Yugoslav government, resulted in the worst **hyperinflation** in world history. The inflation rate between October 1, 1993, and January 24, 1994, was 500 billion percent. On January 24, the stabilization program designed by **Dragoslav Avramović** was introduced, and the period of hyperinflation ended. The exchange rate was fixed at one dinar per one German mark. In December 1995, after partial lifting of sanctions, the dinar was devalued to 3.6 dinars per one German mark.

DINARA. Highest mountain in **Dalmatia,** on the border between **Croatia** and **Bosnia and Hercegovina.** The highest peaks are Troglav 1,913 m and Dinara, 1,831 m.

DIPLOMATIC STRIKE (1903–1905). Diplomatic boycott imposed by the leading European nations on **Serbia** following the **May's Assassination**. Great Britain was the last country to restore full diplomatic relations with Serbia in 1906 after the removal of the **Conspirators**.

*DNEVNI LIST* (*DAILY PAPER*). A daily newspaper published in **Belgrade** from December 1, 1887, to November 24, 1914. Since 1902, *Dnevni list* became an unofficial journal of the **Independent Radical Party.**

DOBOJ. Industrial city in **Bosnia and Hercegovina** located in the valley of the river **Bosna** (pop. 102,546; 1991). The ethnic composition of the population prior to the civil war was: 40.2 percent Muslim; 39.0 percent Serbian; 13.0 percent Croatian; and 5.5 percent Yugoslav. Production of electronic equipment and pneumatic materials are particularly well- developed industries. According to the **Dayton Agreement**, Doboj will remain in the **Republika Srpska**.

DOBOR. Fortress in the Usora region in **Bosnia** and **Hercegovina** located on the bank of the **Bosna** River. The fortress was built in the 14th century and was in the possession of the Serbian **despot** Stevan Berislavić until it fell to the Turks in 1536.

DOBRIČ. Region in Serbia, between the city of **Prokuplje** and **Jastrebac** Mountain.

DOBRINOVIĆ, PERA (1853–1923). Prominent Serbian actor and the most significant represenative of the realist phase in Serbian acting. A talented performer of the ultimate artistic level, he interpreted roles in plays of Shakespeare (Richard III, Iago), Moličre (Orgon), Goethe, Hugo, Chekov, and others.

DOBRNJAC, TODOROVIĆ PETAR. (1771–1831). Serbian **vojvoda** from the **First Serbian Insurrection.** He proved an able commander during the **Battle of Ivankovac** in 1805 and Battle of **Deligrad** in 1806. After Deligrad fell to the Turks in 1809, he left Serbia due to his opposition to **Karađorđe**. Dobrnjac returned to Serbia in 1810 but was expelled by Karađorđe the next year. He died in exile in Jassy, Romania.

DOBROTVORNE ZADRUGE SRPKINJA (Charitable Cooperatives of Serbian Women). Learning and humanitarian societies of Serbian women from the regions under Austro-Hungarian rule. The first society was founded in **Novi Sad** in 1867.

DOMANOVIĆ, RADOJE (1873–1908). Leading Serbian satirist. His stories contain elements of grotesque fantasy and depict the negative side of Serbian society. He was a strong opponent of the corrupt regime of the **Obrenović dynasty**. His best work includes *Vođa* (*The Leader)*, *Mrtvo more* (*Dead Sea*), *Stradija* (*The Suffering Land*), and *Danga*.

DOMENTIJAN. (c. 1200–1264). Monk and biographer of **Saint Sava** and **Stefan Nemanja.** His work is an important source of information about medieval **Serbia.**

DOMOVNICA. Originally a document similar to the identity card. In 1990, Croatian authorities instituted *domovnica* in the form of a certificate necessary for obtaining Croatian citizenship. The vast majority of the Serbian population in **Croatia** refused to obtain the certificate.

DRAGAČEVO. Fruit-producing region in **Serbia** southeast of the city of **Čačak.**

DRAGUTIN (?–1316). Serbian king, elder son of King **Uroš I**, and son-in-law of the Hungarian king Stephen V. He became king in 1276 after deposing his father. After suffering military defeat at the hands of the Byzantine Empire, he transferred his powers to his younger brother, King **Milutin,** in 1282. Dragutin, however, continued to rule territories in northern **Serbia, Srem,** and northeast **Bosnia and Hercegovina.** See also DEŽEVO, ACCORD OF.

DRAINAC, RADE (1899–1943). Serbian poet, the founder of "Hypnism," a literary style close to zenithism and futurism. He founded and edited *Hipnos* (*Hypnos*), a literary journal published, with interruptions, since 1922.

DRAŠKOVIĆ, DANICA (1945– ). Member of the Governing Board of the **Serbian Renewal Movement** and director of the journal *Srpska reč* (*Serbian Word*).

DRAŠKOVIĆ, MILORAD (1873–1921). Serbian politician and statesman. After 1906, he held several ministerial posts as the representative of the **Independent Radical Party.** After 1918, he joined the **Democratic Party.** As Yugoslav minister of internal affairs, he implemented **Obznana** in 1920 and effectively outlawed the **Communist Party of Yugoslavia**. He was assassinated by Alija Alijagić, a member of the terrorist organization called Crvena Pravda (Red Justice) in July 1921.

DRAŠKOVIĆ, VUK (1946– ). Serbian writer and politician, president of the **Serbian Renewal Movement** (SPO), and a deputy of the **Democratic Movement of Serbia** (DEPOS) in the Serbian **Parliament.** Drašković was born in the small town of Gacko in **Hercegovina.** He studied in Belgrade and graduated with a degree in literature. Upon his graduation he worked as a journalist for the Yugoslav news agency TANJUG and later became a staff member in the government-controlled Yugoslav Union Organization. In the early 1980s Drašković became a professional writer best known for his hardcore Serbian nationalism. In 1990, he founded and became president of the SPO. Upon establishing himself as the most charismatic leader of the opposition, he made two unsuccessful bids for the Serbian presidency, decisively defeated by **Slobodan Milošević.** In 1993, following a violent antigovernment demonstration in Belgrade, he and his wife **Danica Drašković** were arrested and beaten by police. In 1996, he became a leader of the coalition **Zajedno**.

While initially champion of the unification of the all Serbian lands, Drašković became the main proponent of the peaceful solution of the civil war in **Bosnia and Hercegovina** and actively supported various peace initiatives, including the **Vance-Owen Peace Plan, Owen-Stoltenberg Plan,** and **Dayton Agreement.** His best known-works include *Sudija* (*Judge*), *Nož* (*Knife*), *Molitva I-II* (*Prayer I-II*), and *Ruski konzul* (*Russian Consul*). In 1999, he joined the coalition government with the Socialist party of Serbia and became a deputy prime minister of the Federal government. Although supportive of the policies of Yugoslav president Slobodan Milošević, he was dismissed from his post in May 1999. Following the Yugoslavia acceptance of the G-8, Draskovic attempted to make a political comeback as the most prominent opposition leader in Serbia.

DRINA. Border river between **Serbia** and **Bosnia and Hercegovina.** The river is 346 km long (486 km with the **Tara** River) and extremely rich in hydro-energy—there are several hydroelectric plants on the river. The Drina is often looked upon, although not without controversy, as a border between Eastern (Byzantine) and Western (Rome) cultures.

DRUGI SRPSKI USTANAK. See SECOND SERBIAN INSURRECTION.

DRUŠTVO SRPSKE SLOVESNOSTI (Serbian Society of Letters). A scientific and literary society founded by **Jovan Sterija Popović** and Atanasije Nikolić in **Belgrade** in 1824. The main objective of the society was to encourage the dissemination of knowledge in **Serbia** and the cultivation of the **Serbian language** through development of a dictionary and orthography. The society published the journal *Glasnik Društva srpske slovesnosti* (*Herald of the Serbian Society of Letters*). After accepting revolutionaries Garibaldi, Chernyshevsky, and Hertzen as members, the society was disbanded in 1864 and replaced by **Srpsko Učeno Društvo** (Serbian Learned Society).

DRUŠTVO ZA UJEDINJENJENJE I OSLOBOĐENJE SRPSKO (Fellowship for the Serbian Unification and Liberation). Society of Serbs from **Vojvodina** organized by **Svetozar Miletić** in 1872. An offspring of the

**Ujedinjena omladina srpska**, the society worked actively toward raising a rebellion in **Bosnia and Hercegovina.** A number of members of the society joined the **Rebellions of Hercegovina** in 1875.

DRVAR. City in southwest **Bosnia and Hercegovina** with a population of 17,079 in 1991. The ethnic composition of the city prior to the civil war was: 97.3 percent Serbian; 0.4 percent Croatian and Muslim; and 2.2 percent Yugoslav. The strongest industry is wood-processing. On May 25, 1944, German paratroopers conducted a massive airdrop on Drvar in order to capture **Tito** and the Supreme Command of the **Partisans**, without success. The Croatian army conquered Drvar in its offensive against the **Republika Srpska** in October 1995. According to the **Dayton Agreement,** Drvar would become a part of the **Muslim-Croat Federation.**

DRŽAVNA HIPOTEKARNA BANKA (State Mortgage Bank). Bank founded in 1862 under the name Uprava fondova (Funding Department). Its operations were heavily concentrated in various equity loans. After **World War II,** the bank was first transformed into Državna investiciona banka (State Investment Bank) and then merged into the **National Bank of Yugoslavia.**

DUBLJE. Village in **Serbia** at which **Serbs** defeated Turkish forces on July 26, 1815, during the **Second Serbian Insurrection.**

DUBROVNIK. Coastal city in **Croatia** with a population of 70,676 in 1991. It is the most important tourist center on the entire Adriatic coast; it is rich in historic monuments and is protected by UNESCO. The first records of the city date from the seventh century, when refugees from the Greek-Roman city of Epidaurus established a small town, Ragusium or Ragusa. **South Slavs** founded their habitat nearby under the name of Dubrovnik. Gradually, Slavs became the dominant element, and the two towns merged into the single city of Dubrovnik in the 13th century. A mercantile city, Dubrovnik was the nexus between the **Balkan Peninsula** and Italy. Although the city acknowledged the primacy of various empires at different times (Byzantine until 1204, Venetian from 1204 to1358, Hungarian 1358–1526, and Turkish 1526–1808), it remained virtually independent. The relationship between Dubrovnik and medieval **Serbia** was particularly close, because **Serbs** constituted the majority of the population in the lands surrounding the city. Dubrovnik leased this land from Serbia, and the city was proclaimed a republic at the beginning of the 15th century. The population of the city was divided into three classes—gentry, citizenry (middle class), and peasants—governed by the Upper, Lower, and Executive councils. The splendid development of Dubrovnik was interrupted by a severe earthquake on June 6, 1667, that practically destroyed the city. French troops captured the city in 1806, and the Republic of Dubrovnik formally ceased to exist in 1808.

After **World War II,** Dubrovnik became part of the Yugoslav republic of Croatia. In the civil war that followed Croatian secession from Yugoslavia, heavy fighting erupted in the vicinity of Dubrovnik in **Konavle** in September 1991.

DUČIĆ, JOVAN (1871–1943). Serbian poet born in **Bosnia and Hercegovina**. His career ranged from elementary school teacher in Serbian schools in Austria-Hungary to celebrated Yugoslav diplomat. An admirer of **Vojislav Ilić,** he wrote symbolist poetry, using French models. His writing style was flawless and descriptions are given in perfect proportions. He died in exile in the United States. His numerous works include *Lirika* (*Lyrics*), which is considered the best of Serbian meditative lyric poetry in rhymed verse.

DUKLJA. Ancient city (Dioclea) and region in the vicinity of the Montenegrin capital, **Podgorica**. In the course of the 11th century the region became known as **Zeta**. See also MONTENEGRO.

DUNAV-TISA-DUNAV CANAL. See DANUBE-TISA-DANUBE.

DURMITOR. Mountainous region and a national park in northwest **Montenegro** known for its exceptional beauty. The region covers an area of 1,852 sq km, and the summit of Mt. Durmitor rises to 2,522 m. The earliest written record of Durmitor is found in the 12th century *Chronicles of Father Dukljanin* (*Letopisi Popa Dukljanina*). Durmitor is mainly an agricultural region with a long tradition of lumber and woodworking, with tourism and commerce recently developed.

DUŠAN THE MIGHTY, THE EMPEROR (1308–1355). Most influential ruler in the medieval Serbian state, Dušan became a king after deposing his father **Stefan Dečanski** in 1331. After conquering **Macedonia,** Thessaly, Albania, and most of the Adriatic and Ionian coasts, Dušan assumed the title of "emperor of Serbs and Greeks" in 1345, with a coronation carried out on Easter Sunday April 16, 1346, in **Skopje.**

During Dušan's rule, medieval **Serbia** reached its zenith. His empire extended from **Belgrade** in the north to the Aegean in the south and from the **Neretva** River in the west to the Gulf of Corinth in the east. The state economy was strengthened, agriculture flourished, and a number of German miners from Transylvania came to Serbia to develop copper, tin, led, silver, and gold mines. The **Serbian Orthodox Church** was elevated to a patriarchate with its center in **Peć.** Dušan the Mighty is also known as Dušan the Lawgiver because of his introduction of the legal code known as ***Dušan's Code of Laws*** on May 21, 1349. In the last years of his life Dušan actively worked on forming an alliance against the Turks. He died on December 20, 1355. His death marked the beginning of the rapid decline of medieval **Serbia.**

*DUŠAN'S CODE OF LAWS/DUŠANOV ZAKONIK*. Code of laws introduced by the Serbian emperor **Dušan the Mighty** at the assembly in **Skoplje** on May 21, 1349. The document originally consisted of 135 articles and was based on existing Serbian judicial practice but also included elements of Byzantine law. It was expanded at Serrai in 1354 when an additional 66 articles were added. The code established a principle of legality in the Serbian state, ensuring that the law had primacy over the will of a ruler. The document was the first comprehensive legal code among **South Slavs** and one of the most advanced legal texts in medieval Europe.

*DUŠANOV ZAKONIK*. See *DUŠAN'S CODE OF LAWS*.

DVADESETSEDMI MART 1941. See COUP D'ÉTAT OF MARCH 27, 1941.

## - Đ -

ĐAJA, IVAN (1884–1957). Prominent Serbian biologist and physiologist, a founder of the Department of Physiology in **Serbia** in 1910, and the author of the first textbook on physiology. He is best known for his work on hypothermia. His main works include *Od života do civilizacije* (*From Life to Civilization)* and *Pogled u život* (*A Look at Life*).

ĐAJA, JOVAN (1846–1928). Serbian politician and journalist, one of the most prominent members of the **Radical Party.** Born in **Dubrovnik** he graduated with a degree in philosophy from the University of Vienna.

He was arrested during the **Rebellion of Timok** but released shortly afterwards. Đaja advocated a compromise between the **Liberal Party** and the Radicals after the **Serbo-Bulgarian War** (1885). He was minister of interior (1890–1892) and Serbian emmisary in Athens and Sofia (1899–1905). In 1884, he founded the journal *Odjek* (*Echo*) and in 1896 became the editor of the journal *Narod (People*). He published *Savez Srbije i Bugarske* (*A Treaty Between Serbia and Bulgaria*) and translated Tacit's *Annals*.

ĐAK, REBELLION OF/ĐAKOVA BUNA. An uprising led by Milivoje Popović Đak (deacon) against the **knez** of the **Smederevo** region in January 1825. Although the insurrection lasted only ten days, it was a significant event in the history of modern **Serbia.** Unlike previous rebellions, which were struggles for national liberation, this uprising had a distinct socioeconomic dimension. Peasants frustrated by political oppression, high taxes, and the tyranny of local bureaucrats demanded the end of the absolutism of Prince **Miloš Obrenović** and the establishment of local autonomy. Inadequately organized, the uprising was quickly crushed.

ĐAKOVA BUNA. See ĐAK, REBELLION OF.

ĐAKOVIĆ, ISAIJA (?–1708). Bishop of Arad and Metropolitan of **Karlovci Sremski** after the death of **Arsenije III Crnojević.** During **Seoba Srba,** he negotiated the future status of the Serbs in the Austrian Empire. Unlike Arsenije III, whose demands focused predominantly on Serbian religious autonomy, Isaija insisted on achieving political and administrative autonomy for the Serbs. As a result of his efforts, Serbs were granted substantially larger freedom than originally demanded.

ĐAKOVICA. City in the autonomous province of **Kosovo and Metohija,** close to the Albanian border, with a population of 115,097 in 1991. The city has relatively developed tobacco and cotton industries, and a plant for the production of chrome is located in the vicinity.

ĐERDAP. Canyon of the **Danube** River between Rumania and **Serbia.** It is 100 km in length and is the longest of its kind in Europe. Numerous historical monuments are located in the canyon, including "Tabula Triana," the Table of the Roman emperor Trajan. Two hydroelectric plants were built in Đerdap. The capacity of Đerdap I plant is two million kilowatts, and it produces 11,500 million Kwh. The capacity of Đerdap II plant is 432 kilowatts with a production of 2,600 million Kwh. The construction of hydroelectric plants led to the creation of an accumulation lake. The total area of the lake is 172 sq km with an average depth of 100 m.

ĐILAS, MILOVAN (1911–1995). The best-known Yugoslav dissident. Born in **Montenegro**, he joined the **Communist Party of Yugoslavia** and in 1937 became a member of the Central Committee. During **World War II**, after the collapse of the **Partisans** in Montenegro, for which he bore a great deal of responsibility, Đilas became a leading propagandist in **Tito**'s movement. At the end of the war he was a member of the *ad hoc* group that designed the borders between the Yugoslav republics. After the war he occupied several important posts in the government and was generally considered the third most important person in the Communist hierarchy. In January 1954, after a series of articles in which he questioned the basic principles of Communist rule, Đilas was removed from all political posts and expelled from the Communist Party. The continuation of his dissident activity led to his arrest and imprisonment. He is the author of several books: *New Class*, *Land Without Justice*, *Conversations with Stalin*, *Rise and Fall*, and others.

ĐINĐIĆ, ZORAN (1952– ). President of the **Democratic Party** (DS) and a deputy in the Serbian **Parliament** since 1990. Born in Bosnia and Hercegovina, he was educated in Belgrade, graduating with a degree in philosophy. Đinđić was an organizer of the revival of the DS in 1990. He became president of the party in 1993 following an internal power struggle and the removal of the representatives of the "old" generation, mainly **Dragoljub Mićunović**. In 1996, together with **Vesna Pešić** and **Vuk Drašković**, he became a leader of the coalition **Zajedno** (Together).

ĐORĐEVIĆ, ANDRA (1854–1914). Lawyer, politician, and prominent member of the **Progressive Party.** As minister of education, he initiated several liberal reforms.

ĐORĐEVIĆ, DIMITRIJE (1922– ). Leading Serbian historian and member of the **Serbian Academy of Sciences and Arts.** He joined the forces of General **Dragoljub-Draža Mihailović** and took an active role in the Serbian nationalist movement in 1941. After being captured by the Germans in 1942, he was sent to the Mauthausen death camp. After **World**

**War II,** he was imprisoned for anti-Communist activities. Since 1970, he has lived in the United States. Đorđević is the foremost expert on the modern history of **Serbia** and the Balkan countries in general. His work includes *Carinski Rat Austro-Ugarske i Srbije 1906–1911* (*The Tariff War between Austria-Hungary and Serbia, 1906–1911*), *The Balkan Revolutionary Tradition*, *The Creation of Yugoslavia*, and *Ožiljci i opomene* (*Scars and Admonitions*).

ĐORĐEVIĆ, JOVAN (1826–1900). Writer and the founder of **Srpsko narodno pozorište** (Serbian National Theater) in **Novi Sad**. He was also one of the founders of the **National Theatre** in **Belgrade**. He is the author of *Markova sablja* (*Marko's Sabre*), and *Opšta istorija* (*General History*).

ĐORĐEVIĆ, PURIŠA (1926– ). One of the most acclaimed movie directors in Yugoslavia. A highly creative director, he pictures individual destinies in a rapidly changing environment and the specific Yugoslav cultural milieu. He directed *Jutro* (*Morning*), *Prvi građanin male varoši* (*The First Citizen of the Small Town*), *Kros Kontri* (*Cross Country*), and others.

ĐORĐEVIĆ, VLADAN (1844–1930). Serbian statesman and close associate of King **Milan Obrenović**. He was a founder of the Serbian Red Cross and **Srpsko lekarsko društvo** (Serbian Medical Society). In 1875, he founded the journal ***Otadžbina*** (*Fatherland*). During the personal regime of King **Alexander Obrenović,** Đorđević was nominally the prime minister, but his influence in political affairs was minimal. He left **Serbia** after the king's marriage with **Draga Mašin** in 1900.

ĐUKANOVIĆ, MILO (1960– ). President of **Montenegro**. A professional politician, Đukanović occupied several mediocre positions within the communist bureaucracy prior to coming to prominence in 1989. Following the overthrow of the old guard communist leadership of Montenegro, Đukanović became prime minister of Montenegro while his close associate **Momir Bulatović** was elected President. Đukanović used the post of prime minister to establish strict control over business interest groups in the region. In the course of events his relationship with Bulatović deteriorated. In order to weaken and discredit Bulatović, who openly sided with then Serbian President **Slobodan Milošević**, Đukanović embraced a "Montenegro first" policy which often bordered on open secession. The crisis climaxed in 1997 and resulted in a bitter division within the **Democratic Party of Socialists** and within the population of Montenegro. Due to his opposition to Milošević, Đukanović secured the backing of the United States and the European Union and he won the presidential elections in the second round in December 1997. Bulatović, who appeared to enjoy more popular support, contested the result of the elections on the grounds of widespread irregularities, but yielded to the pressure of international monitors and accepted the result. In May-June 1999, Đukanović met with several European leaders and the US President Clinton in order to assert himself as a viable alternative to Milošević.

ĐUKIĆ, RADIVOJE-LOLA (1927–1995). The most prominent director and scriptwriter of television movies in Yugoslavia. He is best known for a television series from the 1960s, in which he ridiculed the increasing fragmentation and social division in Yugoslav society.

ĐUNIS, BATTLE OF. A major battle of the **Serbo-Turkish Wars**. The battle took place in the vicinity of the village of Đunis on October 29, 1876. Following several indecisive encounters between the Serbian and Turkish armies both sides concentrated large forces (40,000 **Serbs** and around 54,000-strong Turkish army). Due to their superior artillery and battle plan the Turkish forces succeeded in breaking through the Serbian line of defense and captured the city of Aleksinac. However, the Turkish forces did not pursue the retreating Serbian army which limited the scope of the Turkish success. This battle ended the Serbo-Turkish war in 1876.

ĐURĐEVDAN. St. George's Day, celebrated on May 6. In the old mythology of the **South Slavs** it was celebrated as the day of spring, and fertility. In Serbian folk poetry, Đurđevdan was the first day of the **Hajduks** gathering after winter.

ĐURĐEVI STUPOVI. (i) A monastery on the hills overlooking **Novi Pazar** built by **Stefan Nemanja** after 1168. (ii) A monastery in the vicinity of Berane, **Montenegro**, built by Nemanja's first cousin Prvoslav before 1219.

ĐURETIĆ, VESELIN (1933– ). Serbian historian and research fellow of the Institute of Balkan Studies of the **Serbian Academy of Sciences and Arts.** Born in **Montenegro,** he was educated in **Sarajevo,** graduating with a degee in history. He worked in Sarajevo until 1971, when he joined the Institute for Contemporary History in **Belgrade.** In 1983 he published a controversial book, *Saveznici i jugoslovenska ratna drama* (*The Allies and the Yugoslav War Tragedy*), in which he challenged the official historiography regarding the role of the **Jugoslovenska vojska u otadžbini** and **Četniks** during **World War II.**

ĐURIĆ, JANIĆIJE (1779–1850). Personal secretary of **Karađorđe** since the beginning of the **First Serbian Insurrection.** He exerted considerable influence over Karađorđe and actively participated in diplomatic missions. He wrote *Srbska povestnica Karađorđevog vremena* (*Serbian History in the Times of Karađorđe*).

ĐURIĆ, MIHAILO (1925– ). Prominent philosopher and former professor of the **University of Belgrade**. Born in **Šabac,** he graduated with a degree in philosophy from the University of Belgrade in 1954. In 1972 he was sentenced to nine months in prison for his criticism of the draft of the **Constitution** of 1974. His best-known works include *Humanizam kao politički ideal* (*Humanism as Political Ideal*), *Utopija izmene sveta* (*Utopia of Changing the World*), and *Niče i metafizika* (*Nietzche and Metaphysics*).

ĐURIĆ, MILOŠ (1892–1967). Serbian philologist, philosopher, and translator of Homer's *Iliad* and *Odyssey* into the **Serbian language**. He was considered the foremost expert on Greek philosophy in Yugoslavia. Besides numerous translations of Plato, Aristotle, Plutarch, Jung, and Adler, he is the author of *Vidovdanska etika* (*The Ethics of St. Vitus Day*), *Istorija helenske etike* (*History of the Helenic Ethics*), and *Racionalizam u savremenoj nemačkoj filosofiji* (*Rationalism in the Contemporary German Philosophy*).

## - DŽ -

DŽUMHUR, ZUKO (1921–1991). Serbian painter, journalist, cartoonist, and globetrotter. Born to a Muslim family in **Bosnia and Hercegovina,** Džumhur studied and worked in **Belgrade**. The author of numerous political cartoons, he wrote *Nekrolog jednoj čaršiji* (*In Memoriam for an Alley*).

## - E -

EKMEČIĆ, MILORAD (1928– ). Prominent Serbian historian from **Bosnia and Hercegovina**. Born in the village of Prebilovci in **Hercegovina**, Ekmečić is among the few survivors of the **Ustaše** pogrom. Educated in **Zagreb** and **Belgrade**, he worked as a history professor at the University of **Sarajevo** until 1992. In 1992, after the outbreak of the civil war in Bosnia and Hercegovina, Ekmečić was arrested and tortured by the Muslim paramilitary forces. A member of the **Serbian Academy of Sciences and Arts,** he is a leading expert in Serbian national history. His major works include *Ratni ciljevi Srbije 1914. godine* (*War Objectives of Serbia in 1914*), *Ustanak u Bosni 1875–1878* (*The Uprising in Bosnia 1875–1878*), and *Istorija Jugoslavije* (*History of Yugoslavia*).

*EKONOMSKA POLITIKA* (*Economic Policy*). Liberal weekly published in **Belgrade** since 1952. The *Economic Policy* supports market-oriented reforms, privatization, and the rapid transformation of the economy of the **Federal Republic of Yugoslavia.**

ELECTIONS.

*Elections of 1920*. The first parliamentary elections in the **Kingdom of the Serbs, Croats, and Slovenes** were held on November 28, 1920. Twenty-two political parties participated, with 16 electing deputies. 65 percent of the eligible voters cast ballots. Of the 419 parliamentary seats, the **Democratic Party** won 92, the **Radical Party** 91, the **Communist Party of Yugoslavia** (CPY) 59 (one was subsequently declared void), the **Croatian Peasant Party** (HSS)—(then officially the Croatian Republican Peasant Party) 50, the **Agricultural Party** 39, the Slovene People's party 27, and the **Yugoslav Muslim Organization** (JMO) 24. The HSS deputies boycotted the Constituent Assembly and refused to participate in parliamentary life. The success of the CPY prompted the promulgation of **Obznana**, a decree that forbade all communist propaganda, including publications and meetings.

*Elections of 1923*.The second elections were held on March 18, 1923. Thirty-four parties participated, with 15 electing deputies. Out of 312 seats the Radical Party won 108, the HSS 70; the Democratic Party 51, the Agricultural party 10, and the JMO 18. The aftermath of the elections was characterized by increased political uncertainty and political maneuvering. Thus, in 1924 Yugoslavia had five different cabinets, four headed by **Nikola Pašić** and one by **Ljubomir-Ljuba Davidović**.

*Elections of 1925*. In the elections that were held on February 8, 1925, 45 parties participated, and 13 elected deputies. The voter turnout was exceptionally high and exceeded 77 percent. The Radicals alone won 123 seats, and together with their allies gathered 160. The HSS became the largest opposition party with 67 seats.

*Elections of 1927*. The fourth elections were held on September 11, 1927. Twenty-seven parties participated, and 13 elected deputies. Sixty-nine percent of eligible voters cast ballots. The Radicals won 112 seats, the Democrats 59, the HSS 61, the Independent Democrats of **Svetozar Pribićević** 22, the Democratic Union 11, and the JMO eight. The most important outcome of the elections was the formation of an alliance between the HSS and the Independent Democrats, former political enemies. The Peasant-Independent Democratic coalition was proclaimed on November 10, 1927.

*Elections of 1931*. The first parliamentary elections after the **Dictatorship of January 6, 1929**, were held on November 8, 1931. The **Parliament** was elected by direct and popular vote, and voting was public and oral. Due to the specifics of the new electoral law, the cabinet list of General **Petar Živković** was virtually uncontested and won the majority of seats. Following the elections the first political parties reemerged, with the **Yugoslav Radical Union** (JRZ) becoming the strongest.

*Elections of 1935*. The next elections in Yugoslavia were held in May 1935, less than a year after the assassination of King **Alexander I Karađorđević**. Voters were presented with four lists of candidates, the two most important being prime minister Bogoljub Jevtić's and the **Udružena Opozicija** (United Opposition), headed by **Vladko Maček**. Jevtić's list obtained 61 percent of the vote and the United Opposition 37.4 percent. The complicated electoral law gave Jevtić's list 303 seats and the United Opposition 67. Soon after the election, Jevtić resigned as prime minister and was replaced by **Milan Stojadinović**.

*Elections of 1938*. Three political groups participated in the elections that were held on December 11, 1938: the JRZ, headed by Stojadinović; the United Opposition, led by Vladko Maček; and the small rightist group led by **Dimitrije Ljotić**. The government (JRZ) list won 54 percent, the United Opposition received 45 percent, and the Ljotić list received slighty more than one percent. Dissatisfied with the outcome of the elections, Prince **Pavle Karađorđević** initiated Stojadinović's removal from the leadership of the JRZ. On February 4, 1939, he forced Stojadinović to resign and appointed **Dragiša Cvetković** prime minister.

*Elections of 1946*. The first post-**World War II** elections in Yugoslavia were held on Novemeber 11, 1945. After intense Communist propaganda and policies that effectively precluded the establishing of a viable political opposition, only one list was presented—that of **Narodni Front**, a communist umbrella organization. The presence of the "empty box", or the "blind box" as it was popularly called, was to ensure a multiparty and democratic outlook to the elections. The Narodni Front won decisive victories in every republic. The share of "empty box" votes varied from one region to another: **Slovenia**, 16.8 percent; **Vojvodina**, 14.6 percent; **Serbia**, 11.4 percent; and **Croatia**, 8.5 percent.

*Elections in Serbia*. The first multiparty elections in Serbia were held on December 9, 1990, with a second round taking place on December 23. The electoral turnout was 71.5 percent, and 44 political organizations took part in the elections. The **Socialist Party of Serbia** (SPS) received 2,320,587 votes (46.1 percent) and won 194 (77.6 percent) seats in the Serbian Parliament. The main opposition party, the **Serbian Renewal Movement** (SPO), received 794,786 votes (15.8 percent) and secured 19 seats (7.6 percent), while none of the remaining 12 parties that entered Parliament received more than 10 seats. What differentiated political parties and public opinion in the 1990 elections in Serbia was the attitude toward socialism and anticommunism; the national question and the future of the **Socialist Federal Republic of Yugoslavia** was of secondary importance.

The next elections in Serbia were held on December 20, 1992. Approximately 70 percent of the eligible voters took part. The SPS received 1,359,086 votes (28.8 percent) and won 101 seats (40.4 percent); the **Serbian Radical Party** (SRS) received 1,065,765 votes (22.6 percent), securing 73 seats (29.2 percent); and the **Democratic Movement of Serbia** (DEPOS), a coalition of several parties led by the SPO, received 797,831 votes (16.9 percent) and won 50 seats (20 percent). None of the other six parties in the Parliament received more than 10 seats. The major issues in the second elections were the national question and the civil war in **Bosnia and Hercegovina.** The electoral platform of the two winning parties (the SPS and the SRS) was hard-line nationalism, while the DEPOS platform featured anticommunism and vaguely defined peace.

The third elections were held on December 19, 1993. The SPS received 1,576,287 votes (36.7 percent) and won 123 seats (49.2 percent), DEPOS received 715,564 votes (16.6 percent) and secured 45 seats (18 percent), the SRS received 595,467 votes (13.8 percent) and won 39 seats (15.6 percent), and the Democratic Party (DS) received 497,582 votes (11.6 percent) and won 29 seats (11.6 percent). Three more parties entered the Parliament, securing 14 seats altogether. Although the third elections centered around ideological issues, they essentially represented a major showdown between former allies, the SPS and the SRS.

The latest parliamentary elections in Serbia were held on September 21, 1997. Yugoslav President **Slobodan Milošević**'s leftist alliance won 110 mandates in the 250-seat parliament. The SRS collected 81 mandates and Serbian Renewal Movement 46. The Vojvodina Coalition and Union of Vojvodina Hungarians won four seats each, the List of **Sandžak** three, and the Preševo-Bujanovac Coalition and the Democratic Alternative one each.

In the first presidential elections (December 9, 1990), Slobodan Milošević received 3,285,799 votes (65.34 percent) and became president of Serbia. His major opponent, **Vuk Drašković,** received 824,674 votes (16.4 percent). In the second presidential elections (December 20, 1992) Milošević won 2,515,047 votes (53.24 percent), while **Milan Panić** won 1,516,693 votes (32.11 percent).

*Elections in Montenegro*. After a decisive victory in the first multiparty elections on December 9, 1990, the Communist Party of Montenegro changed its name to the **Democratic Party of Socialists** (DPS) in 1991. In the second elections the party secured an absolute majority of seats in the Montenegrin Parliament (46), and **Momir Bulatović** was reelected president of Montenegro after receiving 158,772 votes (63.29 percent) in the second round of voting held on January 10, 1993. In the Montenegrin republican elections held on November 3, 1996, the DPS won 45 of 71 legislative seats. Its main rival, the National Unity Coalition, won 19. The **Party of Democratic Action** won three, and the Democratic League of Montenegro and Democratic League of Albanians each won two.

In the Spring of 1997, a rift between the former allies, **Milo Đukanović** and Momir Bulatović occured. After a prolonged period of intense sqaubbles the DPS split into two factions. Presidental elections were held in October 1997. Đukanović won the elections in the second round after receiving 174,475 votes (50.7 percent), while Bulatović won 169,257 votes (49.2 percent). The result of the elections was followed by unrest organized by Bulatović's supporters who claimed that elections were tainted with serious irregularities.

The newest round of parliamentary elections in Montenegro took place on May 31, 1998. Seven political parties are represented in the Montenegrin Parliament: the DPS holds 30 seats; the Socialist People's Party 29; the People's Party 7; the Liberal Alliance of Montenegro 5; the Social Democratic Party (SDP) 5; Democratic Alliance of Montenegro 1, and the Democratic League of Albanians 1. The DPS, SDP and the People's Party comprise the coalition "For a Better Life" and have a majority in the Montenegrin Parliament (42).

*Elections in the Federal Republic of Yugoslavia.* Elections for the Federal Parliament were held on May 31, 1992. The electoral turnout was only 56 percent since the major opposition parties boycotted them. In Serbia the SPS received 43.44 percent of the votes cast and the SRS 30.44 percent, while in Montenegro the DPS won 32.66 percent. The second elections for the Chamber of Citizens of the Federal Parliament were held on November 3, 1996. The left coalition consisting of the SPS, **JUL**, and **New Democracy** won 42.41 percent of the votes cast; the coalition **Zajedno** (Together), consisting of the Democratic Party, the **Democratic Party of Serbia,** the Serbian Renewal Movement, the **Democratic Center,** and the Civic Coalition won 22.55 percent; and the SRS won 17.88 percent. The left coalition won 66 seats in the Chamber of Citizens, Zajedno 22, the Montenegrin DPS 20, the SRS 16, the National Party of Montenegro eight, the Democratic Movement of Vojvodina Hungarians three, the coalition "Vojvodina" two, the Party of Democratic Action one, the Social Democratic Party of Montenegro one, and the List for Sandžak one. See also BOSNIA AND HERCEGOVINA, ELECTIONS.

ENERGOINVEST. One of the largest conglomerates in **Bosnia and Hercegovina** and Yugoslavia, founded in **Sarajevo** in 1951. The main activities of the conglomerate were building electrical machines and operating chemical, oil, and food-processing industries. In the mid-1980s Energoinvest employed more than 40,000 workers.

EPIDAUR. Old Greek-Roman city located south of modern **Dubrovnik.** After the city was destroyed by the **South Slavs** in the seventh century, the population moved north and founded the city of Ragusa. Ragusa merged into Slavic-populated Dubrovnik in the course of the 12th century.

ERIĆ, DOBRICA (1936– ). Serbian folk poet and editor of the journal *Raskovnik* (*The Book of Naturalism*). His main works include *Svet u suncokretu* (*The World in Sunflower*) and *Orfej među šljivama* (*Orfeus among Plum Trees*).

ESAD-PAŞA, TOPTANI (1856–1920). Turkish general of Albanian ancestry. During the First Balkan War, he was the commander of Shkodër. During 1913 and 1914 Esad-Paşa was a minister of interior in the newly formed government of Albania. Aided by **Serbia**, he extended his control over central Albania. In **World War I**, he supported the Allies and helped the Serbian army during its withdrawal through Albania. See also ALBANIAN RETREAT; BALKAN WARS;

ETEROVIĆ, IVO (1935– ). Celebrated Yugoslav photographer. Born in Split, he was educated in Germany and Italy. He was a special military photographer for the United Nations peacekeeping forces in the Middle East in 1957. He exhibited in several European cities.

EUGENE OF SAVOY (1663–1736). Austrian military commander and governor of the parts of northern Serbia that remained under Austrian control after the **Treaty of Passarowitz** in 1718. He defeated the Turks in several battles and liberated **Petrovaradin** in 1716 and **Belgrade** in 1717. There is a gate named after him (Eugen von Savoyen) in the fortress at **Kalemegdan.**

EUROPEAN COMMUNITY (EC). The European Community took an active role throughout the break-up of the **Socialist Federal Republic of Yugoslavia** (SFRY) and the ensuing civil wars in **Croatia** and **Bosnia and Hercegovina.** In the days immediately following Croatian and Slovenian secessions, an EC ministerial delegation arranged the controversial rotation of the SFRY Presidency. Stjepan Mesić, the Croatian representative in the Collective Presidency, became president of the country. This was followed by a series of initiatives by the various bodies of the EC. On September 3, 1991, a declaration on Yugoslavia was adopted in The Hague. It called for the Conference on Yugoslavia (The Peace Conference) to be held in The Hague on September 7 under the chairmanship of Lord Peter Carrington. The declaration also called for the establishment of an arbitration commission under the chairmanship of Robert Badinter (**Badinter Commission**).

On the recommendation of the arbitration commission, the conference issued a statement on October 4, 1991. The statement contained the main elements of the upcoming Declaration on Yugoslavia: the forming of a loose confederation of independent republics, a guarantee of human rights for minorities, and the inadmissibility of a unilateral changing of borders. On October 18, the conference proposed the Declaration on Yugoslavia that envisioned full sovereignty of the former federal units, their international recognition as states, and protection of human and minority rights. After the Yugoslav and Serbian delegation rejected a proposed settlement on the grounds that the conference precipitated the destruction of the Yugoslav state, the EC Ministerial Council decided to impose sanctions against Yugoslavia on November 7–8. On December 2, the council decided that economic sanctions should refer only to **Serbia** and **Montenegro.**

On December 9, following the recommendation of the arbitration commission, Lord Carrington organized a meeting of the presidents of all Yugoslav republics in The Hague. The underlying premise of the Badinter arbitration commission, that Yugoslavia was in the process of dissolution, was rejected by Serbia and Montenegro. Regardless of the lack of consensus among the interested parties, the EC Ministerial Council accepted the Criteria for Recognition of the New States in Eastern Europe and the USSR. The Yugoslav republics were given an ultimatum to confirm their wish for independence by December 23, 1991, while the deadline for international recognition was set for January 15, 1992.

After the process of recognition of Croatia and **Slovenia** was set in motion, the EC sponsored the international conference on Bosnia and Hercegovina on February 14. On April 6, 1992, the EC Ministerial Council recommended the recognition of the independence of Bosnia and Hercegovina. The EC placed the primary responsibility for the ensuing civil war on the **Federal Republic of Yugoslavia** (FRY) and the **JNA.** This led to the further deterioration of diplomatic relations between the FRY and the EC countries, and on May 27, 1992, the EC imposed a comprehensive trade embargo on Serbia and Montenegro.

On December 16, 1992, six European Union countries recognized the **Former Yugoslav Republic of Macedonia,** despite Greek opposition.

EUROPEAN UNION. See EUROPEAN COMMUNITY.

EVLI, ÇELEBI (1611–1682?). Renowned Turkish travel writer. He described conditions in the countries and regions belonging to the Ottoman Empire in the 17th century. He described **Serbia** and the rest of the Yugoslav lands in volumes V, VI, VII, and VIII of his ten-volume *Putopis* (*Travel Record*).

EXARCHATE. Form of church organization in Bulgaria and **Macedonia**. After the abolition of the **Patriarchate of Peć** in 1766 and the archbishopric of Ohrid in 1767, all bishoprics came under the jurisdiction of the patriarchate of Constantinople. This resulted in the increased Hellenization of the Serbian and Bulgarian population. In order to prevent the spread of growing discontent among the local non-Greek population, the **Porte** established the Bulgarian exarchate. By placing the purely Serbian districts of **Vranje, Pirot,** and **Niš** under exarchate jurisdiction, the Porte intentionally created a potential source of conflict between **Serbia** and the Bulgarian provinces. In Macedonia, the exarchate actively promoted a policy of Bulgarization. After the **Balkan Wars,** exarchate activity was confined to Bulgaria.

## - F -

FEDERAL REPUBLIC OF YUGOSLAVIA/SAVEZNA REPUBLIKA JUGOSLAVIJA (FRY). The **Federal Republic of Yugoslavia**, consisting of Serbia and Montenegro, was proclaimed on April 27, 1992, after the international recognition of unilateral secessions of other republics from the former Socialist Federal Republic of Yugoslavia (SFRY). While the formation of the FRY was challenged by the United States and western European countries, the country was officially recognized after the conclusion of the Dayton Agreement. The United States still refuses to recognize the FRY as the sole legal successor of the former SFRY.

FILIPOVIĆ, FILIP (1878–1938). Serbian politician, one of the founders and leaders of the **Communist Party of Yugoslavia**. Born in **Čačak**, Filipović graduated from the University of St. Petersburg and worked as a professor of mathematics at the Denisov Trading Academy. In Russia, he became a member of the Russian Social Democratic Party (Bolsheviks) and upon his return to **Serbia** in 1912, joined the Serbian **Social Democratic Party**. In 1919–1920 he became secretary of the Executive Board of the Socialist Workers' Party (Communists) and the Communist Party of Yugoslavia. After the general elections in 1920, Filipović became mayor of **Belgrade** and a parliamentary deputy. In 1921, after the assassination attempt on Prince Regent **Alexander Karađorđević,** Filipović was arrested and sentenced to two years in prison. After the **Independent Workers' Party,** which he founded in 1923, was banned, Filipović emigrated to the Soviet Union. He was killed during Stalin's purge.

FILM. The first movie projection in **Serbia,** and in the Balkans as well, was presented on June 6, 1896, in Belgrade. The oldest preserved film shot in Serbia was of the coronation of King **Peter I Karađorđević** in September 1904. The first permanent cinema among the Serbs opened in Sombor, **Vojvodina** in 1906. The first permanent cinema in Serbia opened in 1909, and there were about 30 cinemas in 1914. The repertoire was dominated by French movies. Movie production started in 1911, when the first Serbian movie, *Karađorđe*, was shot. Between the world wars **Belgrade** was the most important cinematic center. The movies shot at that time included *Tragedija naše dece* (*Tragedy of our Children*), *Sve za osmeh* (*Anything for a Smile*), *Rudarova sreća* (*Miner's Happiness*), and *Bezgrešni grešnik* (*Sinless Sinner*). After **World War II** Belgrade remained the center of Yugoslav cinematography. Radoš Novaković, Vladimir Pogačić, Živorad Mitrović, and Aleksandar Petrović were among the those who contributed to the further development of Yugoslav cinema. For the direction of the movie *Veliki i mali* (*Big and Small*), Pogačić won the first prize at the International Festival in Karlovy Vary.

The last three decades marked the constant advancement of film in Serbia. More than 300 movies were shot in Serbia, and new directors and styles emerged. **Puriša Đorđević** introduced distinctive war movies, Dušan Makavejev became an internationally renowned director for his original expression of the problems of contemporary life, and Živojin Pavlović portrayed life in an naturalistic way. The best-known Serbian director of the time was Aleksandar Petrović who won the Grand Prix at the International Film Festival in Cannes in 1967 for his movie *Sakupljači perja* (*I Met Some Happy Gypsies Too*). The 1970s brought a new generation of movie directors who were educated in Prague and Belgrade: Goran Paskaljević, Dejan Karaklajić, Slobodan Šijan, and Darko Bajić. Along with other prominent movie directors (Emir Kusturica, Miloš Radivojević, Živojin Pavlović, Miomir Stamenković, Dragan Kresoja, Želimir Žilnik, and Predrag Golubović) they won numerous national and international awards. The production of documentary, short, and animated movies also developed in that period.

The violent breakup of the **Socialist Federal Republic of Yugoslavia** did not halt movie production in Serbia and the **Federal Republic of**

**Yugoslavia.** In 1995, Emir Kusturica won the Grand Prix at the Cannes festival for *Bila jednom jedna zemlja* (*Underground*). Along with more experienced directors, new authors emerged. The most noticeable is Srđan Dragojević, director of *Mi nismo anđeli* (*We Are No Angels*) and *Lepa sela lepo gore* (*Pretty Villages, Pretty Flames*).

FIRST SERBIAN INSURRECTION/PRVI SRPSKI USTANAK. In his attempt to modernize the Turkish army and limit its influence, Sultan Mahmud I (1730–1754) scattered the **Janissaries** throughout the empire. As a result, of that action the number and power of Janissaries in **Serbia,** that is **Beogradski pašaluk,** significantly increased. Although Janissaries in Serbia, with the support of the Turkish warlord of Vidin, Osman Pazvant-oglu, rebelled against the Sultan on several occasions, it was the growing Serbian independence that worried the **Porte.** At the beginning of the 19th century, the semiautonomous Serbian nation possessed within its borders its own administration and tax system, national church, and well-armed and battle-trained army. The Porte's policy of appeasing Muslim rebels at the expense of Serbs resulted in the execution of Haçi-Mustafa Şinik-oglu, the Ottoman governor of **Belgrade**, and the Janissaries' seizure of Beogradski Pašaluk in 1801. In the ensuing scramble for power, by the middle of February 1802 four Janissaries, called the **Dahije,** came to the fore: Mehmed Fočić Aga (Mehmed Foça-oglu), Aganlija (Aganli Bayraktar), Mula Jusuf (Mula Yusuf), and Kučuk Alija (Kuçuk-Ali).

The Dahije regime ended Serbian autonomy and imposed unprecedented cruelty upon Serbs in Beogradski Pašaluk. The Serbian leaders were first stripped of their powers and then executed. In early 1804, under the pretext of a looming Serbian rebellion, the Dahije massacred 152 Serbian leaders (**knez**) and men of distinction. The Dahije terror that had already instigated rebellion among the Serbs culminated with the mass slaughter of Serbian leaders and notables and precipitated a general uprising of Serbs. On February 14, 1804, a gathering of Serbian notables and fighting men was held in the village of **Orašac** in central **Šumadija**. Around three hundred men decided on an organized uprising against the Dahije and elected **Karađorđe** as their leader.

At the very beginning of the uprising, the Serbs decisively defeated the Janissaries, and on the night of August 5–6, Serbian **vojvoda Milenko Stojković** beheaded the Dahije on the island of **Ada Kale.** The Serbs liberated several cities and surrounded **Belgrade**. The execution of the Dahije was the climax of the first phase of the insurrection. After that, and especially after fruitless negotiations with the vizier of Bosnia, Abu Bekir Paşa, what started as an uprising against the Janissaries became the Serbian revolutionary war of independence.

The rapid spread of the uprising prompted the Porte to send Hafiz Paşa of **Niš** to force the Serbs into submission. His army, however, suffered a severe defeat at the **Battle of Ivankovac** on August 18–20, 1805. Despite unfavorable developments on the international scene, mainly the Austro-Russian defeat at Austerlitz, the Serbs successfully repulsed the Turkish attack. Left to their own resources, the Serbs struck hard at the Turks in early 1806. After defeating the army of Pazvant-oglu, the Serbs decisively defeated the regular Turkish forces at the **Battle of Mišar** and at the **Battle of Deligrad.** By achieving control over the entire Beogradski pašaluk, the Serbs acquired an excellent bargaining position. However, despite the fact that the Turks accepted all of the Serbian requests, the outbreak of war between Russia and the Porte prompted the Serbs to cease peace negotiations and ally with Russia. After that, Serbian affairs became heavily dependent on developments in the Russo-Turkish and the Russo-French relationships. The period 1806–1812 was characterized by constant changes of fortune in the war between the Serbs and Turks. During 1809, the Turks defeated Serbian forces in the battle of Kamenica and captured **Požarevac** and **Jagodina**: the Serbs successfully routed the Turks from Serbia in 1810. However, after the conclusion of the **Treaty of Bucharest** on May 28, 1812, and the subsequent Serbian refusal of the humiliating stipulations envisioned by it, the Turks attacked Serbia in mid-July 1813. Without a consensus about the organization of defenses, Serbian forces suffered repeated defeats, despite individual acts of heroism. Negotin and later **Smederevo** fell to the advancing Turkish forces after the death of **Hajduk Veljko** Petrović on August 13, 1813. Incapable of participating actively in the campaign due to a prolonged illness, Karađorđe left Serbia on October 3, 1813, and Belgrade fell to the Turks on October 7. After receiving the news of Karađorđe's flight and of the Turkish capture of Smederevo, the remnants of the Serbian army around **Šabac** dissolved. The fall of Šabac effectively ended the First Serbian Insurrection.

Although the Serbian rebellion ended as it had begun—in a Turkish reign of terror—it generated profound and long-lasting changes for the Serbian nation. The insurrection brought political independence to the Serbs. The establishment of the **Governing Council,** the national army, a new fiscal system, and an independent judiciary marked the beginning of modern Serbian statehood. The military defeat in 1813 was only a temporary setback. The **Rebellion of Hadži-Prodan** in 1814 and the **Second Serbian Insurrection** continued the revolutionary war that started with the insurrection of 1804.

FORMER YUGOSLAV REPUBLIC OF MACEDONIA (FYROM). Official name used by the international community for the Republic of **Macedonia.** The provisional term FYROM emerged as a compromise due to strenuous Greek objection to the use of the name Macedonia.

FRESCOES. Wall paintings covering the interior of Serbian churches. A form of watercolor painted on wet plaster, frescoes feature Biblical themes. The lower parts of all walls are covered with paintings of earthly saints, kings, and warriors, while the upper parts and all ceilings portray heavenly motifs.

FRUŠKA GORA. Mountains in **Srem**, south of the **Danube** river. The mountain peeks at 539 m, with an average length of 75 km and width of 12–15 km, covering an area of 22,850 ha. A national park and a tourist resort, Fruška gora is a site of numerous Serbian monasteries.

## - G -

GAĆINOVIĆ, VLADIMIR (1890–1917). Serbian revolutionary from **Bosnia and Hercegovina,** and founder of **Mlada Bosna.** Gaćinović finished high school in **Mostar** and studied in **Belgrade**, Vienna, Lausanne, and Freiburg. During the **Annexation Crisis** he emigrated to **Montenegro** and later to **Serbia.** During **World War I** he served in the Montenegrin army and in the French navy. He died in Freiburg, and in 1934 his remains were reburied in **Sarajevo.**

GAGIĆ, JEREMIJA (1781–1859). Serbian merchant from **Zemun.** He took an active part in the **First Serbian Insurrection** as the secretary of the **Governing Council.** A strong supporter of the pro-Russian faction among the leaders of the insurrection, he entered Russian diplomatic service in 1812. In 1815, he became the Russian consul in **Dubrovnik.**

GAJ, LJUDEVIT (1809–1872). Writer from **Croatia,** the leader of the Croatian National Party ("Illyrians"). Gaj is best known for his work on language reform. He modified the latinic alphabet to conform to the rule "one sound—one letter" established in the **Cyrillic alphabet** by **Vuk**

**Stefanović Karadžić**. In 1834, he began publishing the newspaper *Narodne ilirske novine* (*National Illyrian Gazette*) and ***Danica Ilirska,*** which were written in the Štokavian dialect of the **Serbian language**. Having been led by personal material interests to become a secret agent of the Austrian government, Gaj went to Serbia in 1846 to report on the state of affairs there. Although he entertained the Yugoslav ideal (formation of a common state of Serbs and Croats), he essentially envisioned Croatian national liberation within the Habsburg Empire.

GAJRET (Self-Improvement, Aid). Muslim society founded in 1903 in **Sarajevo.** The major objectives of the society were to provide economic and educational aid to the **Muslims** of **Bosnia and Hercegovina.** The society published its journal *Gajret* from 1907 to1914 and 1921 to 1941. The journal covered a broad spectrum of cultural topics and exhibited a strong pro-Serbian orientation. Osman Đikić, the main editor, used the journal to establish closer links between Serbs and Muslims.

GAMS, ANDRIJA (1911– ). University professor and law specialist. The author of numerous books and journal articles, he is known for his criticism of the Federal Constitution of 1974. His best-known works include *Uvod u građansko pravo* (*Introduction to Civil Law*), *Društvene norme* (*Societal Norms*), and *Biblija i savremena društvena misao* (*Bible and Contemporary Thought*).

GAMZIGRAD (Romuliana). One of the most important archeological finds in Serbia, dating from the fourth century A.D. Remnants of the archaic Roman and Byzantine city are located in the vicinity of **Zaječar**, south from the **Danube** River. The fortress was built by the Roman emperor Galerius and named after his mother Romula. The city was surrounded by a rectangular shaped defensive wall that was enhanced by twenty towers. It was an important administrative and economic center of the Roman province. Excavation work began in 1953.

GANIĆ, EJUP (1949– ). Former vice president of **Bosnia and Hercegovina** (B-H) and the **Muslim-Croat Federation.** Born in the region of **Sandžak,** Ganić supported the Yugoslav option of Ante Marković in the B-H elections in 1990. Having failed in the **elections**, he joined **Alija Izetbegović** and the victorious **Party of Democratic Action** (SDA) and eventually became its vice-president. On May 2, 1992, he masterminded an attack on a **JNA** convoy in **Sarajevo** despite a previous agreement with

**UNPROFOR.** In May 1996, he visited **Belgrade**, thus becoming the first Bosnian official to visit **Serbia** since the beginning of the civil war in B-H in 1992.

GARAŠANIN, ILIJA (1812–1874). Serbian statesman and politician. Born in **Šumadija** to a well-to-do family who lived near **Kragujevac,** he was the first commander of the Serbian army under Prince **Miloš Obrenović.** During the domination of the **Constitutionalists,** he was a minister of interior and foreign minister. Garašanin is the author of **Načertanije,** a document that called for the liberation of all South Slav lands and their unification into a single state. In 1848, he helped to organize some 8,000 Serbian volunteers who fought in **Vojvodina** against Hungarian forces during the revolutions of 1848. As the prime minister of **Serbia** during the reign of the Prince **Mihailo Obrenović,** he actively worked on forming an anti-Turkish alliance between Serbia, **Montenegro,** and Greece. He retired from politics in 1867 over the disputed marriage of Prince Mihailo to Julia Hunyadi, a Hungarian-born woman whom many perceived as anti-Serbian.

GARAŠANIN, MILUTIN (1843–1898). Prominent Serbian politician and statesman. A son of **Ilija Garašanin** and the leader of the **Progressive Party,** Milutin was prime minister of Serbia, minister of the interior, and Serbian ambassador in Vienna.

GARAŠANIN, MILUTIN (1920– ). Prominent archeologist and president of the Board for Archeology of the **Serbian Academy of Sciences and Arts.** The author of over 300 books and journal articles, Garašanin is the recipient of several national and international awards. His main works include *Praistorija na tlu Srbije* (*Prehistoric Times in Serbian Lands)*, and *Umetnost na tlu Jugoslavije, Praistorija* (*Artistry in the Yugoslav Lands, Prehistoric Times*).

GAVRILO, DOŽIĆ (1881–1950). Patriarch of the **Serbian Orthodox Church** from 1938 to 1950. A member of the Great National Assembly of the Kingdom of **Montenegro**, Gavrilo led a delegation designated to complete unification with **Serbia** in 1918. In 1941, the Germans arrested him and sent him to the Dachau concentration camp.

GAVRILOVIĆ, DRAGUTIN (1882–1945). Colonel of the Serbian and

Yugoslav armies. During the siege of **Belgrade** in October 1915, he commanded the 10th Regiment and Sremski odred (Srem's Squadron) in their heroic counterattack against the German forces.

GAVRILOVIĆ, JOVAN (1796–1877). Serbian politician and educator. Born in **Vukovar**, he arrived in **Serbia** in 1831 and became director of the Royal Chancellery during the reign of Prince **Mihailo Obrenović**. In 1861, he became finance minister and, after Mihailo's death, a member of the regency. A long-time friend and supporter of **Vuk Stefanović-Karadžić**, he was president of **Srpsko učeno društvo** and **Društvo srpske slovesnosti**.

GAVRILOVIĆ, MIHAILO (1868–1924). Diplomat and historian. His research focused on19th-century Serbia, and his four volume monograph *Miloš Obrenović* is still considered one of the best studies on the reign of that prince.

GAVRILOVIĆ, SLAVKO (1924– ). Historian and member of the **Serbian Academy of Sciences and Arts.** His area of expertise includes the history of **Serbs** in **Slavonia** and **Srem**. His best-known works include *Srem u revoluciji 1848–1849* (*Srem in the Revolution 1848–1849*), *Jevreji u Sremu u XVIII i XIX veku* (*Jews in Srem in the 18th and 19th centuries*), *Iz istorije Srba u Hrvatskoj, Slavoniji, i Ugarskoj XV–XIX veka* (*History of the Serbs from Croatia, Slavonia, and Hungary 15th–19th centuries*).

GAVRILOVIĆ, ZORAN (1926– ). Literary critic and writer; his best works include *Uočavanja* (*Grasping*), a comparative analysis of American and Serbian literature in the interwar period; *Antologija srpskog ljubavnog pesništva* (*Anthology of Serbian Love Poetry)*, and *Antologija srpskog rodoljubivog pesništva* (*Anthology of Serbian Patriotic Poetry*).

GAVRILOVIĆ, ŽARKO (1933– ). President of Srpska Svetosavska stranka (Serbian Party of Saint Sava) and a former cleric of the **Serbian Orthodox Church**. The Church immediately distanced itself from Gavrilović's Party.

GENČIĆ, ĐORĐE (1861–1938). Journalist and politician, one of the leaders of the **Liberal Party.** Genčić was the interior minister in the government of **Vladan Đorđević** but resigned in 1900, protesting the marriage of King **Alexander Obrenović** and **Draga Mašin.** He was one of the most prominent **Conspirators** in the assassination of King Alexander in 1903.

GENEVA CONFERENCE. Conference among representatives of the Serbian government, the Serbian Parliament, the National Council of the Slovenes, Croats, and Serbs, and the **Yugoslav Committee** that took place in Geneva between November 6 and November 9, 1918. The Montenegrin Committee was not present. The principal issues on the agenda were the question of the organization of the future common state; recognition of the National Council in **Zagreb** as the representative and government of the State of the Slovenes, Croats, and Serbs, a joint protest against Italian occupation of Yugoslav territory; and relations with **Montenegro.** After intense negotiations and under severe pressure from France and Britain, the Serbian government recognized the National Council in Zagreb and signed the **Geneva Declaration.**

GENEVA DECLARATION. Final document of the **Geneva Conference** signed on November 9, 1918. This document was supposed to supersede the **Corfu Declaration** and called for the establishment of a common Yugoslav state. The declaration left the question of the form of government open. Dissatisfied with the basic provisions and supported by Prince Regent **Alexander I Karađorđević**, Serbian prime minister **Nikola Pašić** rejected the declaration and returned to **Serbia** on November 10.

GERASIM. Patriarch of the **Serbian Orthodox Church** 1574–1580 and 1586–1587. A close relative of **Mehmed-Paša Sokolović** and **Makarije Sokolović,** he continued the policy of cooperation with the Turkish State.

GERMAN (1899–1993). Patriarch of the **Serbian Orthodox Church** 1958–1991. Hranislav Đorić, as he was known before entering into the monastic order, studied law in Paris and graduated from the Theological Faculty in **Belgrade**. Although his tenure was troubled by severe conflicts within the Serbian Orthodox Church caused by the separation of the Macedonian Church (1967) and the break with the North American Diocese, German greatly enhanced the international position of the church.

GERŠIĆ, GLIGORIJE (1842–1918). One of the founders of the **Radical Party** and minister of justice in various Radical governments. He was a noted expert on international law and member, professor of the **Great School**, and member of the **Serbian Academy of Sciences and Arts.** His major works include *Enciklopedija prava* (*Law Encyclopedia*), *Sistem rimskog privatnog prava* (*The System of Private Roman Law*), and *Međunarodno-pravni bilans u poslednjoj balkanskoj krizi* (*International Law Settlement in the Last Balkan Crisis*).

GLAGOLITIC ALPHABET. First alphabet of Slavs, constructed by **Cyril** prior to his and Methodiu's visit to Moravia around 860. The base of the Glagolitic alphabet was a Greek minuscule. The alphabet contained forty sounds, and had a letter for each of the sounds. Bulgars, Russians, and **Serbs** replaced the Glagolitic alphabet with the simpler **Cyrillic alphabet** during the 10th century, while a variant of the Glagolitic alphabet was used in **Croatia** until the 18th century.

*GLAS CRNOGORCA* (*The Voice of the Montenegrin*). *Glas Crnogorca* was a weekly political and literary journal of the government of **Montenegro** published in **Cetinje** from 1873 to1915.

GLAS SRPSKE AKADEMIJE NAUKA I UMETNOSTI (*The Herald of the Serbian Academy of Sciences and Arts*). Chronicle of the **Serbian Academy of Sciences and Arts** published since 1887. Issues of *Glas* (Herald) are categorized by particular sciences.

*GLASNIK DRUŠTVA SRPSKE SLOVESNOSTI* (*The Herald of the Serbian Society of Letters*). *Glasnik društva srpske slovesnosti* was the official journal of **Društvo Srpske Slovesnosti** published in **Belgrade** in the period 1846–1892.

GLAVAŠ, STAMATOVIĆ STANOJE (?–1815). **Vojvoda** in Smederevska **Nahija**. Prior to the **First Serbian Insurrection**, Glavaš was a prominent leader of the Serbian guerilla fighters known as **Hajduks**. At the meeting of Serbian notables in **Orašac** in 1804, he was initially elected as the leader of the insurrection; he declined and recommended **Karađorđe** instead. Glavaš was captured and beheaded by the Turks following the **Rebellion of Hadži-Prodan** in 1814.

GLIGORIĆ, SVETOZAR (1923– ). One of the best Yugoslav grandmasters of all time and world-renowned chess referee. During the 1950s Gligorić won numerous chess tournaments and was considered the best chess player outside the Soviet Union. An excellent journalist, he is the author of numerous articles and several books, among which *Spaski protiv Fišera* (*Spassky against Fisher*), *Nimcovičeva indijska odbrana* (*Nimzovich Indian Defense*), and *Igram protiv figura* (*I Play against the Pieces*) are the most popular.

GLIGORIĆ, VELIBOR (1899–1977). Writer and president of the **Serbian Academy of Sciences and Arts** 1965–1971. His numerous works include *Srpski realisti* (*Serbian Realists*), *Kritike* (*Critics*), and *Kuća smrti* (*House of Death*).

GLIGOROV, KIRO (1917– ). President of the **Former Yugoslav Republic of Macedonia**. A professional politician Gligorov occupied numerous important posts in the former Yugoslavia: president of the National Assembly, vice-premier of the federal government, member of the Federal Presidency, member of the Presidency of the Central Committee of the Communist Party, etc. In 1990 he was elected president in the then Yugoslav republic of Macedonia. In 1994, he again won office. In October 1995, he was seriously wounded in an attempted assassination in **Skoplje.**

GLINA. City and county in **Banija** region with a population of 23,002 in 1991. Prior to the civil war in 1991, the city was a center of the region's textile industry. Serbs constituted an absolute majority of the population in Glina county, and the city was one of the political centers of the **Republic of Serbian Krajina**. Along with the rest of Serbian-controlled territory, the city fell to Croatian forces during the offensive in the first week of August 1995.

GLIŠIĆ, MILOVAN. Writer and one of the founders of literary realism in **Serbia**. His work involves accurate and often humorous depictions of the 19th-century Serbian village. His best novels are *Glava šećera* (*A Sugar Ball*), and *Redak zver* (*Rare Beast*).

GODOMIN. Region southeast of **Smederevo** in the valley of the **Morava** River. One of the biggest agricultural complexes in **Serbia** is located in Godomin.

GOLEŠ. Mountain located on the western perimeter of **Kosovo Polje**. The mountain is rich in nickel and magnesium ores.

GOLI OTOK. Small, desolate island in the Adriatic Sea, which lies three kilometers off the northern Croatian coastline. Between 1948 and 1953 around 15,000 people, accused of supporting the **Cominform**, were imprisoned on the island.

GOLUBAC. A small city in eastern **Serbia.** The city was built in the 14th century on a steep rock directly overlooking the right bank of the **Danube.** Together with **Smederevo**, the city constituted the major defensive line in Serbia under the rule of **Despot Stefan Lazarević** and Despot **Đurađ Branković.** The impressive remains of the city-fortress are considered to be the most beautiful example of medieval Serbian architecture.

GORAŽDE. City in eastern **Bosnia and Hercegovina** with a population of 37,505 in 1991. The ethnic composition of the population prior to the civil war was: 70.2 percent Muslim; 26.2 percent Serbian; 2.2 percent Yugoslav; and 0.2 percent Croatian. The beginnings of the city date from 1446, when the church of St. George was built. In the 16th century, a number of Serbian documents were printed in the church. The expansion of the city dates from the 1960s, when several chemical and metal processing factories were built. "Pobjeda" (Victory) was the biggest ammunition factory in Bosnia. During the civil war in Bosnia, Goražde was proclaimed a United Nations Safe Area (**Safe Areas**, popularly known as Safe Heavens). However, Muslim forces from inside the city often launched attacks on neighboring Serbian villages, which prompted responses by the **Bosnian Serb Army** (BSA). After the city almost surrendered to the advancing BSA units in April 1994, the United Nations yielded to NATO pressure and authorized air strikes against the Serbs. According to the **Dayton Agreement** and **Paris Peace Treaty**, Goražde will remain under full Muslim control in the **Muslim-Croat Federation.**

GORNJAK. Monastery built between 1379 and 1380 in the Gornjačka klisura—the canyon of the Mlava River.

GORNJI MILANOVAC. Industrial city south of the Rudnik mountains with a poulation of 50,087 in 1991. After **World War II**, metal-processing, food-processing, textile, and publishing industries were developed. Silver and zinc mines are located in the vicinity of the city.

GOSPIĆ. City in the **Lika** region (pop. 31,263; 1981). A cultural and economic center of the region, the city was the site of heavy fighting during the civil war in 1991. On September 9, 1993, the Croatian army launched an attack on the Medak region south of Gospić. The destruction of three Serbian villages prompted a protest from **UNPROFOR** commander Jean Cot.

GOVERNING COUNCIL/PRAVITELJSTVUJUŠČI SOVJET. Government of Serbia during the **First Serbian Insurrection**. The council was founded at the National Assembly in Borak in 1805. The main initiator of the council was **Prota Mateja Nenadović,** while the actual organization was completed by **Božidar Grujović**, a Serbian professor at the University of Kharkov in Russia. According to Grujović's design, the council consisted of 12 elected representatives from 12 regions called **nahije**. The president of the council was elected from among the representatives and served a term of one month. According to the constitutional changes of 1811, the council was divided into two sections. The first consisted of a cabinet of six ministers (**popečitelj**); the second, consisting of the remaining members, constituted a supreme court. Together these two sections formed the government. The council often changed its location. Its first location was Voljača monastery, then it moved into **Bogovađa** monastery where the seal of the council was designed, and then, after a short stay in **Smederevo**, the council finally moved to **Belgrade**. Acting as a central government, the Council was the major unifying force in the 1804–1813 Serbian revolution.

GRABEŽ, TRIFKO (1896–1916). Member of **Mlada Bosna** and one of the assassins of Franz Ferdinand on June 28, 1914, in **Sarajevo.** He died in an Austro-Hungarian prison.

GRAČANICA. Monastery in the vicinity of **Priština** built between 1313 and 1315. It is the final work of the unique complex conception of churches with multiple cupolas. The legacy of King **Milutin Nemanjić**, Gračanica represents one of the finest achievements of Serbian architecture under Byzantine influence.

GRADAC. Monastery in the valley of the **Ibar** River built in the second part of the 12th century. The monastery was built by Helen of Anjou, wife of King **Uroš I**, and represents one of the best examples of the Gothic style in medieval Serbian architecture.

GRAHOVO, BATTLE OF/GRAHOVSKA BITKA. Battle between

**Montenegrins** and Turks that started on May 1, 1858. The battle lasted eight days and ended as a great victory for the Montenegrins. The outcome of the battle led to the formal recognition of Montenegro's independence in 1860.

GREAT SCHOOL/VELIKA ŠKOLA. First post-elementary learning institution in modern **Serbia,** founded on August 31, 1808, in **Belgrade** by **Dositej Obradović.** The school had three grades, and **Vuk Stefanović Karadžić** was among the first students. The school ceased operation after the collapse of the **First Serbian Insurrection** in 1813. After continuous appeals by Vuk Karadžić, Prince **Miloš Obrenović** revived the high school in 1831. In 1835, the school was transferred to **Kragujevac** and reorganized into four grades.

In the summer of 1838, with the inauguration of the "**Turkish Constitution**," the high school was extended to six years and raised to the level of a Lycée. The following year, the Lycée was formally separated from the lower grades of the high school and expanded to two classes with five professors. In 1841, following the establishment of a gymnasium, the Lycée was transferred back to Belgrade. From its inauguration in 1838 to its demise in 1863, the Lycée had some 1,205 students, of whom only 238 received diplomas. The inadequacies of the Lycée (low level of instruction, low budgets, the lack of technical and scientific subjects, etc.) led to the reestablishment of the Great School on October 6, 1863. The Great School had three divisions: philosophy (liberal arts), law, and technology. The Great School was the highest institution of learning in Serbia, until the founding of the **University of Belgrade** in 1905. The university that had five colleges: theology, philosophy, law, medicine, and technical sciences, and two associated curricula, agriculture and pharmacy. Unlike the Great School, the university enjoyed all of the rights of autonomy.

GREATER SERBIA. Originally, the idea of a Serbian state that would include the Serbs of the surrounding lands, especially **Bosnia and Hercegovina**, **Montenegro**, and northern Albania. The idea was first elaborated in the ***Načertanije*** of **Ilija Garašanin** in 1844. Since the Serbs of the Austro-Hungarian lands were beyond practical reach at the time, the expansion was carried southward toward the Turkish-occupied provinces of Old Serbia (**Raška, Kosovo and Metohija, Pirot,** and **Vranje** region) and **Macedonia**. In its original form the concept included only traditional Serbian lands, which were occupied either by the Ottoman Empire or Austria-Hungary. The modern widely-used interpretation of the term implies the territorial expansion of **Serbia**.

GRDELIČKA KLISURA. Fifty km-long canyon of the **Southern Morava** River between **Vranje** and **Leskovac**. An integral part of the Morava-Vardar Valley, the canyon is an important commercial and traffic route. See also VARDAR.

GROL, MILAN (1876–1952). Literary critic and prominent liberal politician. A long-time general manager of the **National Theater** in **Belgrade**, Grol was a close associate of **Jovan Skerlić**. After the death of **Liubomir-Ljuba Davidović**, he became the leader of the **Democratic Party**. During **World War II,** Grol was a minister in the Yugoslav government-in-exile. He returned to Yugoslavia in 1945 and became a deputy prime minister in the coalition government. He resigned after a short period of time because of the alleged obstruction of the Communists.

GROŠ. Currency unit in Serbia until 1918. The value of the groš was 0.20 **dinar.**

GRUJIĆ, JEVREM (1826–1895). Prominent Serbian politician, career diplomat, and one of the founders of the **Liberal Party**. He held several important posts, including prime minister of **Serbia** during the **Serbo-Turkish War** (1876–1878). Grujić was among the most capable Serbian politicians in the 19th century. He wrote *Zapisi* (*Memoirs*).

GRUJIĆ, SAVA (1840–1913). General, politician, and prominent member of the **Radical Party**. Grujić held several important posts, including defense minister and prime minister of Serbia. He was prime minister in seven Serbian governments.

GRUJOVIĆ, BOŽIDAR (1778–1807). Born as Teodor Filipović in **Srem**, he changed his name to hide his identity from the Austrian authorities. A graduate of the University of Pest (Budapest) and professor of the Kharkov University, Grujović returned to **Serbia** in 1805 and became the first secretary of the **Governing Council.**

GRUJOVIĆ, MIHAILO (1780–1842). Brother of **Božidar Grujović**. He succeeded Božidar as the secretary of the **Governing Council** and together with **Mladen Milovanović** wrote the constitutional proposal of 1811.

GUBERINA, VELJKO (1925– ). Prominent defense attorney and politician. He is a member of the Presidency of the Serbian Bar Association and honorary president of the **Radical Party**. Guberina is one of the organizers of the Society against the Death Penalty. He is the author of four books and the recipient of numerous awards.

GUNDULIĆ, IVAN (1589–1638). Poet from **Dubrovnik.** In his major work, the poem "**Osman**," he foresaw the end of the Ottoman Empire and the unification of the **South Slavs**.

GUSLE. Folk musical instrument made from oak. Gusle consist of a strand or strands of horsehair played by a bow. Among the **Serbs,** the instrument is used exclusively to accompany the chanting of epic poetry.

## - H -

HADŽI-PRODAN, REBELLION OF. Short-lived and poorly organized rebellion against the Turks led by Hadži-Prodan Gligorijević, a **vojvoda** from the **First Serbian Insurrection.** The rebellion broke out spontaneously in the Požega district on September 28, 1814. The rebellion was joined by the local **Hajduks** and soon spread to neighboring **Kragujevac** and **Jagodina.** However, the most notable Serbian leaders, including **Miloš Obrenović,** not only refused to join the resistance but collaborated with the Turks in putting it down. The rebellion was followed by a period of massive Turkish terror. After a general massacre, about 300 rebels were brought to **Belgrade** and subjected to gruesome torture and death, mostly by impalement. Despite this crushing defeat, the Hadži-Prodan Rebellion precipitated the **Second Serbian Insurrection** and Serbian national liberation.

HADŽI-RUVIM (1754–1804). Archimandrite of the **Bogovađa** monastery and an organizer of the **First Serbian Insurrection**. He was caught by **Dahije** during his visit to the metropolitan of **Belgrade** and, after severe torture, executed. He was also known for his paintings and work on icons in several Serbian monasteries.

HADŽIĆ, GORAN (1953– ). Politician from western **Srem**. In 1991 he began to organize the opposition to the nationalist practices of the Croatian government of **Franjo Tudjman**. Hadžić was accused by the Croatian authorities of subversion and conspiracy against the territorial integrity of the Croatian state. He became the president of the **Republic of Serbian Krajina** after the dismissal of **Milan Babić** but was removed following the Croatian offensive in the **Gospić** region. He negotiated the reintegration of eastern **Slavonia** and western Srem into **Croatia** in 1995.

HADŽIĆ, JOVAN (1799–1869). Serbian writer, lawyer, and politician. A founder of **Matica Srpska,** he wrote the civil law of the principality of **Serbia**. He was a bitter opponent of the language reform of **Vuk Stefanović Karadžić**. His major works include numerous translations of classical poetry.

HAGUE TRIBUNAL. On May 3, 1993, the secretary-general of the United Nations submitted to the Security Council a detailed report on the establishment of the International Tribunal under Chapter VII of the UN Charter. The Tribunal was formally established by Security Council Resolution 827 (1993) on May 25, 1993, with the sole purpose of prosecuting persons responsible for serious violations of international humanitarian law committed on the territory of the former Yugoslavia, from January 1, 1991. In August 1994, Judge Richard Goldstone of South Africa was appointed chief prosecutor of the tribunal. On October 1, 1996, he returned to South Africa to take up Supreme Court duties and a university post and was replaced by a Canadian, Louise Arbour. Currently, there are 75 indicted by the tribunal: 54 are Serbs (including three former **JNA** officers from the **Federal Republic of Yugoslavia** and General Đorđe Đukić, who died while out on bail), 18 are Bosnian Croats, and three are Bosnian **Muslims**. The former president of the **Republika Srpska, Radovan Karadžić**; the supreme commander of the **Bosnian Serb Army, Ratko Mladić**; and president of the former **Republic of Serbian Krajina, Milan Martić**, are among the most prominent Serbs indicted.

The Hague Tribunal is the first international tribunal since **World War II** and epitomizes the changes in international relations following the collapse of Communism and the outbreak of regional conflicts. The first trial, of Bosnian Serb Dušan Tadić, started on May 7, 1996. A Bosnian Croat with the BSA, Dražen Erdemović pleaded guilty in the second trial on May 28, 1996, and was sentenced to 10 years in prison in December 1996.

HAJDUK VELJKO/ PETROVIĆ VELJKO (1780–1813). One of the greatest heroes of the **First Serbian Insurrection**. He was a fighter in the **Hajduks** of **Stamatović Stanoje Glavaš** and became **Vojvoda** in 1811. Under his command the Serbs defeated Turkish armies in the battles of Podgorac, Crna Reka, Varvarin and Soko Banja. He was best known for his personal bravery, lack of discipline, insubordination, and numerous mischiefs. He was killed during the Turkish siege of the city of Negotin.

HAJDUKS. Serbian guerilla fighters. Hajduks became famous for their fight against the Ottoman occupation of **Serbia, Bosnia and Hercegovina,** and **Macedonia** between the 16th and 19th centuries. Most of the actions were directed along the major communication routes, although hajduks organized and led major popular rebellions against Turkish rule. Many of the hajduks' leaders and their struggle are depicted in Serbian folk poems.

HARAČ (Haraç). Tax in the Ottoman Empire, paid by every Christian male (seven years of age and older). The tax was determined either as a lump sum or as a proportion of the yearly yield (revenue), in which case, it was set between 10 and 50 percent. The taxpayers were divided into three categories: the first paid 11 groš, the second 5.5 groš, and the third 3.75 groš per capita. The tax was collected in March. Taxpayers from the **Beogradski pašaluk** paid the lowest of the tax categories. See also GROŠ.

HARTWIG, HENRIKHOVICH NIKOLAI (1854–1914). Russian diplomat. He was Russian special envoy in **Serbia** From 1909 to 1914 and actively promoted the idea of a Balkan pact. He strongly influenced Serbian polictics and supported **Nikola Pašić** and the **Radical Party**.

HATTI ȘERIF (Decree) Personal and executive decree of the sultan of the Ottoman Empire. Three Hatti Șerifs were especially important for **Serbia.** The Hatti Șerif of 1830 created an autonomous Serbian state with its own army, granted freedom of trade and an autonomous tax system, guaranteed the people freedom of worship, proclaimed **Miloš Obrenović** hereditary prince, allowed the formation of an independent educational system, hospitals, and printing establishments, and called for **Muslims** to leave Serbia, with the exception of the city garrisons. The Hatti Șerif of 1833 regulated the evacuation of civilian Turks from Serbia and extended Serbia's jurisdiction to six additional districts. The Hatti Șerif of 1838 gave Serbia its **Constitution.**

HERCEG BOSNA. See HERCEG BOSNIA.

HERCEG BOSNIA (HB)/HERCEG BOSNA. Self-proclaimed state of Bosnian Croats that emerged after the outbreak of the civil war in **Bosnia and Hercegovina** (B-H). Proclaimed on July 3, 1992, Herceg Bosnia was dominated by the extreme wing of the **Croatian Democratic Union.** The state possessed a military force known as the Croatian Defense Council (HVO) whose troops committed numerous atrocities during the civil war in B-H. Although officially dismantled in the summer of 1996, Herceg Bosnia continued to exist through its executive branches (the HVO, police force, and local and municipal governments and administration).

HERCEG NOVI. Coastal city and major tourist resort in **Montenegro** (pop. 27,819 in 1991). The city was founded in 1382 by **Tvrtko I Kotromanić.** The remnants of the old city are protected by UNESCO.

HERCEGOVAČKI USTANCI. See HERCEGOVINA, REBELLIONS OF.

HERCEGOVINA. Historical region situated east and west of the **Neretva** River; a constituent part, although not an administrative unit, of **Bosnia and Hercegovina.** With the exception of the regional center **Mostar**, Hercegovina is predominantly an agricultural region, with tobacco production as the main activity. For the most part of the period between the 12th and 14th centuries, Hercegovina was a part of medieval **Serbia** under the **Nemanjić** dynasty. In the 14th century the region was divided between Serbia and medieval Bosnia. For a short period, between 1448 and 1466, Hercegovina became an independent country ruled by Prince Stefan Vukčić, who proclaimed himself "Herceg of Saint Sava". Following his death in 1466, the Turks exploited the internal struggle among Stefan's sons and by capturing **Herceg Novi** conquered Hercegovina in 1482. In the second part of the 19th century popular revolts against the Turks and local **Muslims**, known as the **Rebellions of Hercegovina**, became common. The Ottoman inability to deal with a massive revolt and the involvement of Serbia, **Montenegro**, and Russia led to war and the conclusion of the **Treaty of San Stefano** and the **Congress of Berlin** in 1878.

**Serbs** historically constituted the majority of the population in Hercegovina. The ethnic composition of the region substantially changed after the 16th century, due to the Turkish occupation, the conversion of the Orthodox Serbs to Roman Catholicism, and the **Ustaše** terror during **World War II**. According to the **Dayton Agreement,** the larger part of Hercegovina will become a part the **Muslim-Croat Federation**, while a portion of eastern Hercegovina will be in the **Republika Srpska.**

HERCEGOVINA, REBELLIONS OF/HERCEGOVAČKI USTANCI. Rebellions of **Serbs** from **Hercegovina** against the Turkish occupation. The first rebellion lasted from 1852 to 1862. It consisted of several successive mutinies of the local population, which were actively supported by **Montenegro**. The rebellion was organized and led by **Luka Vukalović**, a gunsmith from Trebinje, and was carried out primarily in eastern Hercegovina, where more than 90 percent of the population were Orthodox Serbs. The major Turkish defeat in the **Battle of Grahovo** in May 1858, and the increased prestige of Montenegro among Slavs under Austrian rule prompted Austria to oppose any further Serbian struggle for national liberation in Hercegovina. Supported by Austria, the Turks launched a major offensive against the insurgents and Montenegro, which led to the conclusion of peace between the two states and the end of the insurrection in August 1862.

The Turkish failure to institute political and economic reforms in Hercegovina after the end of the rebellion led to continuous dissatisfaction among the Christian population. After unsuccessfully appealing to Austria and Russia in 1872–1873, and following the Turkish use of terror in collecting excessive taxes in early 1875, insurrection erupted in the Hercegovina district of Nevesinje on June 27, 1875. The revolt was led by **Mićo Ljubibratić**, the former chief collaborator of Luka Vukalović. The rebels' demands included freedom of religion, equality before the law, the abolition of the arbitrary tax levies and, at a later stage of the insurrection, unification with Montenegro. The rebellion quickly spread and fueled nationalistic feelings in Serbia, Montenegro, and Russia. This led to the **Serbo-Turkish Wars**, ended by the **Treaty of San Stefano** and the **Congress of Berlin** in 1878, and the proclamation of Serbia's and Montenegro's independence.

The rebellions of Hercegovina, though they did not result in the liberation of the region due to the Austro-Hungarian occupation of **Bosnia and Hercegovina** in 1878, played an important role in the process of Serbian national liberation.

HILANDAR. A Serbian monastery built by **Saint Sava** and **Stefan Nemanja** in 1198 on **Sveta Gora** (Mt. Athos). The central church of the monastery built in 1293 is dedicated to the Presentation of the Mother of God and is the legacy of King **Milutin.** Prince **Lazar Hrebeljanović** built a vestibule and outer vestibule before 1389. Most of the **frescoes** in the monastery were painted between 1319 and 1320. The monastery was one of the centers of Serbian culture during the Turkish occupation. Besides being one of the finest Serbian cultural and religious relics, Hilandar has a library that holds the most important book collection on Serb-related topics (over 20,000 titles).

HOLBROOKE, RICHARD C.A. (1941– ). Holbrooke was the chief U.S. architect of the **Dayton Peace Agreement**. Widely seen as a belligerent, even unpleasant, negotiator, Holbrooke is acclaimed by many as the man to bring the war in **Bosnia and Hercegovina** to an end. He later returned to Wall Street to follow a career which has shared its time with government position, which started in the early 1960s, with foreign service posting to Vietnam and part of President Johnson's Paris peace negotiating team from 1966–1969. Under President Carter he was assistant secretary of state for Asian and Pacific affairs. In 1994, he was appointed assistant secretary of state for European and Canadian affairs. In 1998 he was nominated as the next U.S. Ambassador to the United Nations. His post-Dayton diplomatic involvement includes negotiations with Greece and Turkey over the ongoing division of Cyprus and a summer 1998 intervention in **Kosovo and Metohija**, when he met senior members of the **Kosovo Liberation Army**. In hectic shuttle diplomacy in October 1998, Holbrooke produced an initial agreement on the **Federal Republic of Yugoslavia**'s compliance with UN Resolution 1199, which was accepted by Yugoslav president **Slobodan Milošević** under threat of NATO air campaign of cruse missiles and a fleet of some 450 aircraft.

HOMOLJE. Region in eastern **Serbia**, in the valley of the Mlava River. A large concentration of **Vlachs** lives in this mainly agricultural and mining region.

HRISTIĆ, NIKOLA (1818–1911). Serbian politician and statesman, prime minister in several governments, political conservative, and a supporter of the **Obrenović dynasty**, he crushed the **Rebellion of Timok**.

HRISTIĆ, STEVAN (1888–1958). Prominent Serbian composer and conductor, impressionist, and member of the **Serbian Academy of Sciences and Arts.** Educated in Leipzig, Moscow, Rome, and Paris, Hristić was director of the Belgrade Opera and Philharmonic Orchestra. His technically sophisticated compositions were hued with folk melodies.His best-known works include the ballet *Ohridska legenda* (*The Legend of Ohrid*) and the opera *Suton (Sundown*).

HRVATSKA. See CROATIA.

HRVATSKA DEMOKRATSKA ZAJEDNICA. See CROATIAN DEMOCRATIC UNION.

HRVATSKA SELJAČKA STRANKA. See CROATIAN PEASANT PARTY.

HRVATSKO-SRPSKA KOALICIJA (Croato-Serbian Coalition). Coalition of Croatian and Serbian political parties in **Croatia, Dalmatia,** and **Istria** established by the Resolution of Rijeka on December 12, 1905. The primary objective of the coalition was to remove the influence of pro-Hungarian political constituents. The Coalition's victory in the elections for the local Croatian Assembly in 1908 prompted the Croatian **ban** to dissolve the Assembly.

HUSSAR REBELLION/KATANSKA BUNA. Short-lived rebellion against Prince **Alexander Karađorđević**. On October 4, 1844, two dozen Serbian horsemen dressed in Hungarian Hussar uniforms crossed the **Sava** River from Austria. They were led by Stojan Jovanović-Cukić, the son of a prominent **Belgrade** family and a stipendiary of the Serbian government. They took over the city of **Šabac** due to the confusion caused by their uniforms, which gave the appearance of Austria's support, but were stopped by **Prota Mateja Nenadović** in the vicinity of **Loznica.** In the meantime, **Toma Vučić-Perišić** assembled a large force in Belgrade and quelled bloodily the rebellion on October 8. This further enhanced Vučić-Perišić's personal power and the influence of the **Constitutionalists.** The rebellion was a vivid example of the deep rivalry between the **Obrenović** and **Karađorđević dynasties**.

HYPERINFLATION. Having lost access to hard currency due to international **sanctions**, the government of the **Federal Republic of Yugoslavia** resorted to inflationary financing. Operating under the assumption that sanctions would be removed after a short period of time, the government continued to finance its expenditures via a rapid increase in the money supply and monetary base. This resulted in an explosive price increase that peaked at the end of 1993 and January 1994 when the yearly inflation rate reached 5 billion percent. On January 24, 1994, the government launched a comprehensive stabilization program designed by **Dragoslav Avramović**, who became governor of the **National Bank**. The Yugoslav episode was the worst hyperinflation in European history.

## - I -

IBAR. River in **Serbia** 241 km long and a source of hydroelectric energy. The valley of the Ibar River is very fertile, being especially rich in coal and magnesium ore. The medieval Serbian state was situated mainly along the valley of the Ibar.

IČKO, PETAR (?–1808). Serbian diplomat from the **First Serbian Insurrection** who served as a Serbian emissary at the Turkish court in Istanbul. In late December 1806, Ičko brokered a peace agreement between the **Serbs** and the Ottoman Empire by which Serbia would be granted autonomous status. However, the outbreak of war between Russia and the **Porte**, and the Serbs' decision to actively support Russia, effectively annulled Ičko's peace.

IFOR (Implementation Force). Multinational, NATO-led Peace Implementation Force. IFOR succeeded **UNPROFOR** and is the military guarantor of the **Dayton Agreement.** In December 1996, the IFOR mandate was changed, becoming SFOR (Stabilization Force), and will operate until June 1998.

IGALO. Coastal town and a tourist resort, situated 2.5 km southwest of **Herceg Novi** in the bay of **Boka Kotorska,** best known for its thermal baths.

IGMAN. Mountain in **Bosnia and Hercegovina** southwest of **Sarajevo**. The mountain peaks at 1,667 m. Between January 27 and 28, 1942, during **World War II, Partisans** of the First "Shock" (Proletarian) Brigade, avoiding a direct confrontation with German and **Ustaše** forces, successfully crossed the mountain through snow drifts of over three feet at temperatures of minus 32 degrees Celsius. On August 19, 1995, three high-ranking United States diplomats on a peace mission in the former Yugoslavia died in an automobile accident on the mountain.

IGNJATOVIĆ, JAKOV (1824–1889). Serbian writer from **Szent Endre**, a suburb of Budapest. He was one of the founders of realism in Serbian literature. An intuitive observer of life, he was a powerful writer and the only among Serbian realists who was mostly story-oriented. His main works *Milan Narandžić* and *Večiti mladoženja* (*Eternal Groom*), gained him a reputation as the Serbian Balzac.

ILIĆ, VOJISLAV (1862–1894). Eminent Serbian poet close to Western postromantic trends, especially to those of the Parnassians and symbolists. Although he wrote poems about country landscapes, he gave greatest consideration to themes from the Greek and Roman periods. An artist in poetry, Ilić was the reformer of Serbian verse and master of form. His best poems include "Zimska idila" ("Winter Idyll"), "Korintska Hetera" ("Corinth's Heter"), and "Maskenbal na Rudniku" ("Masquerade on Mt. Rudnik").

ILINDEN UPRISING/ILINDENSKI USTANAK. Insurrection of the population of **Macedonia** against Turkish rule. Having completely miscalculated the actual balance of power and the contemporary international situation, the leadership of the **Internal Macedonian Revolutionary Organization** decided at its Salonika (Thesallonika) and Smiljevo Congresses to begin an armed rebellion in Macedonia on August 2, 1903. The center of the uprising was the small town of Kruševo, where rebels proclaimed the Kruševo Republic. Despite fierce resistance, the rebellion was quickly and cruelly crushed by the Turks, who captured Kruševo on August 13, 1903.

ILINDENSKI USTANAK. See ILINDEN UPRISING.

ILIRI. See ILLYRIANS.

ILIRIDA. Self-proclaimed republic of ethnic Albanians living in the western part of the **Former Yugoslav Republic of Macedonia.**

ILIRIJA. Term often used by Serbian and Croatian historians from the 19th century to describe the lands from which later Yugoslavia was formed.

ILIRSKA DVORSKA DEPUTACIJA (Illyrian Court Delegation). Special ministry at the Austrian Imperial Court founded by Empress Maria Theresa in 1747. The ministry dealt with Illyrian (Serbian) affairs and effectively replaced the Court Commission. The delegation was succeeded by the Illyrian Court Chancellory in 1791, which in turn was terminated the following year, when all Serbian affairs were transferred to the Hungarian Court Commission.

ILLYRIANS/ILIRI. Ancient group of tribes that together with Celts and Thracians inhabited the **Balkan Peninsula.** After their conquest by the Romans, they were subjected to heavy Romanization and virtually disappeared. In the 19th century it was widely believed that **South Slavs** were descendants of the Slavicized Illyrians. The Croatian movement, led by **Ljudevit Gaj**, that advocated the unification of South Slavs under the rule of Austria-Hungary was known as the Illyrian Movement.

INDEPENDENT RADICAL PARTY/SAMOSTALNA RADIKALNA STRANKA. Political organization that emerged from the internal split of the **Radical Party** in 1903. The Independent Radicals, mainly the younger members of the party, did not accept a change in party philosophy and negotiations with the **Progressive Party** on a new **constitution** in 1901. By proclaiming allegiance to the Radical Program of 1881 and refusing to recognize the Constitution of 1901, the Independent Radicals became principal supporters of the interests of small businesses and landowners in Serbia. The official party gazette was ***Odjek*** (*Echo*), and the party's leaders were Ljubomir Živković (until May 1911, 1905) and **Ljubomir Stojanović**. Following the formation of the **Democratic Party** in 1919, the party ceased to exist.

INDEPENDENT STATE OF CROATIA/NEZAVISNA DRŽAVA HRVATSKA (NDH). State proclaimed on April 10, 1941, by Slavko Kvaternik, one of the leaders of the **Ustaše**. The NDH encompassed the entire territory of the present **Bosnia and Hercegovina**, **Croatia** without **Istria** and parts of **Dalmatia**, and almost the whole region of **Srem**, with a total area of 115,135 sq km and population of 6,300,000 (1941 estimate). The state was organized on strictly fascist and authoritarian lines, and the undisputed leader of the country was **Ante Pavelić**, who held the title *poglavnik* (*führer*). Croats and **Muslims** enjoyed a privileged position and Džaferbeg Kulenović, the leader of the **Yugoslav**

**Muslim Organization,** was deputy prime minister of the NDH. The NDH enacted numerous laws that mirrored the racial laws of Nazi Germany. Immediately upon the establishment of the new regime in April 1941, a mass slaughter of the **Serbs,** who numbered more than two million in the NDH, began. No other regime under German control committed so many cruel acts; German and Italian sources estimated that in less than a year the Ustaše killed more than 300,000 Serbs. In August 1941, at **Jasenovac**, the Ustaše established the biggest concentration camp in the **Balkan Peninsula**, in which some 600,000 Serbs, Jews, and Gypsies were murdered in a four-year period. After the collapse of German resistance in Yugoslavia in April–May 1945, Pavelić and almost the entire Ustaše leadership succeeded in escaping to Latin America and Spain. Although perpetrators of crimes that were surpassed only by the mass extermination of Polish Jews, Pavelić and his associates, including the commanders of Jasenovac, were never extradited or tried. See also CROATIA; LIKA; VOJNA KRAJINA.

INDEPENDENT WORKERS' PARTY OF YUGOSLAVIA. See NEZAVISNA RADNIČKA PARTIJA JUGOSLAVIJE.

INTERNAL MACEDONIAN REVOLUTIONARY ORGANIZATION/ VNATREŠNA MAKEDONSKA REVOLUCIONARNA ORGANIZACIJA (VMRO). Secret revolutionary organization founded at the end of the 19th century in the region of **Macedonia**. The organization called for the unification of all "oppressed elements" in Macedonia and the Edirne region and the formation of an autonomous Macedonian state. The organization was led by well-educated Macedonian Slavs (Dame Gruev, Petre Pop-Arsov, Goce Delčev, Đorče Petrov, and others) centered in Salonika. After the collapse of the **Ilinden Uprising** the VMRO split into two factions: right, pro-Bulgarian, which advocated the inclusion of Macedonia into Bulgaria, and left, which remained loyal to the original objectives of the organization. Following **World War I**, the right-wing faction, sponsored by the Bulgarian government, organized numerous terrorist attacks in Yugoslav Macedonia. Although formally banned by the Bulgarian government, the VMRO continued terrorist activity until **World War II**. In 1934, together with the **Ustaše**, members of the VMRO participated in the assassination of Yugoslav king **Alexander I Karađorđević**.

In 1990, Macedonian nationalists formed a political organization called

VMRO, which eventually became the most popular political party in the **Former Yugoslav Republic of Macedonia**.

INTERNATIONAL BRIGADES. Military units consisting of volunteers who fought on the side of the Republican Government against the forces of Generalissimo Francisco Franco during the Spanish Civil War. More than 1,660 volunteers from Yugoslavia fought in international brigades between 1936 and 1938.

ISAKOVIĆ, ANTONIJE (1923– ). Serbian writer and member of the **Serbian Academy of Sciences and Arts**. His early literary work portrayed events from **World War II**; while later he concentrated on the description of individual tragedies surrounding the expulsion of Yugoslavia from the **Cominform** and the **Goli Otok** camp. After the dissolution of the **Communist Party of Yugoslavia**, he joined the **Socialist Party of Serbia** and subsequently became a vice president of the party. His works include *Velika deca* (*Grown Children*), *Paprat i vatra* (*Fern and Fire*), and *Tren* (*Moment*).

ISTRA. See ISTRIA.

ISTRIA/ISTRA. Peninsula in the former Yugoslavia, a part of the former Yugoslav republic of **Croatia**. Its area is 260,221 sq km and it has a population of 402,103 (1991). Historically, Istria was an agricultural area, mainly producing wine and olive oil, and a fishing region. However, since the late 1960s Istria has become one of the main tourist regions in the former Yugoslavia. In the latest political election in the Republic of Croatia, the Movement for Free Istria won decisively in Istria.

IVANJICA. City in southwest Serbia with a population of 36,686 in 1991. The city is the center of a very fertile region called Moravički, known for its agricultural production.

IVANJICKI, OLJA (1931– ). Prominent Yugoslav sculptor and painter, and the best representative of contemporary surrealism.

IVANKOVAC, BATTLE OF. Battle between Serbs and Turks that took place between August 18 and 20, 1805, during the **First Serbian Insurrection.** Approximately 6,000 Serbian soldiers successfully repulsed an attack by a 15,000-strong Turkish army. This was the first direct contact between Serbian forces and regular Turkish forces. The outcome of the battle considerably boosted the morale of Serbian forces and helped to spread the insurrection.

IVANOVIĆ, KATARINA (1817–1882). Serbian painter born in the then heavily Serb-populated Hungarian city of Sekesfehervar (Serbian, Stoni Beograd). She was educated in Budapest and Paris. Most of her work is located in the **National Museum** in **Belgrade**.

IVANOVIĆ, LJUBOMIR (1882–1944). Serbian painter and long-time professor of the School of Arts in **Belgrade.** He is especially known for his realistic sketches of the various regions of Yugoslavia.

IVIĆ, ALEKSA (1881–1948). Serbian historian and professor at the Law School of the University of **Subotica**. His best-known works include *Istorija Srba u Vojvodini* (*History of Serbs in Vojvodina*) and *Austrija prema ustanku Srba pod Milošem Obrenovićem* (*Austria Toward Serbian Insurrection under Miloš Obrenović*).

IVIĆ, MILKA (1924– ). Prominent Serbian linguist, professor at the University of **Novi Sad**, and member of the **Serbian Academy of Sciences and Arts,** Norwegian Academy, and Saxon Academy. She is known for her work in the field of the syntax of the **Serbian language**. Her best known works include *Pravci u lingvistici* (*Directions in Linguistics*) and *O jeziku Vukovom i vukovskom* (*On Language of Vuk*).

IVIĆ, PAVLE (1924– ). One of the best-known Serbian linguists and a member of the **Serbian Academy of Sciences and Arts**, husband of **Milka Ivić**. A member of the American Academy of Arts and Science, Austrian Academy, and Norwegian Academy, Ivić is best known for his work on the dialects of the **Serbian language**. His numerous works include *Srpski narod i njegov jezik* (*Serbian People and Their Language*), *Word and Sentence Prosody in Serbo-Croatian*, and *O jeziku nekadašanjem i sadašnjem* (*On Language of the Past and Present*).

IVKOV, BORISLAV (1933– ). One of the best Yugoslav grandmasters of all time. He became the first world junior chess champion after winning a tournament in England in 1951.

IZETBEGOVIĆ, ALIJA (1925– ). President of **Bosnia and Hercegovina** (B-H) since 1990. Born to a Muslim family from Bosanski Šamac, Izetbegović joined an illegal Muslim-only political organization known as the Young Muslims and was arrested in 1946. After serving three years in prison, he graduated with a law degree from the University of **Sarajevo** and worked as a legal consultant in B-H. In 1970 he published *Islamska Deklaracija* (*Islamic Declaration*) in which he envisioned B-H as a part of a unified Muslim state that would spread from "Indonesia to Moroco." Izetbegović was arrested in 1983 and sentenced to 14 years in prison but was released in 1988.

Soon after his release from prison, Izetbegović founded the **Party of Democratic Action** (SDA), a Muslim-only political organization. In May 1990, the SDA won a majority of the seats in the B-H **Parliament**, and Izetbegović, as party chief, became president, although **Fikret Abdić,** a secular Muslim businessman, received the majority of popular votes. In April 1992, encouraged by the United States, Izetbegović denounced a previously signed **European Community**-sponsored proposal aimed at avoiding conflict and pursued secession from Yugoslavia and open confrontation with the **JNA**. This led to a full-scale civil war in B-H that ended in November 1995, with the acceptance of the **Dayton Agreement**. Throughout the war, Izetbegović insisted on the preservation of a unitary Muslim-dominated B-H. See also BELGRADE INITIATIVE.

IZVRŠNI NARODNI ODBOR CRNE GORE (Executive National Committee of Montenegro). Provisional government of **Montenegro**, elected at the session of the National Assembly of Montenegro on November 13, 1918. The committee was formed by supporters of the unconditional unification of Montenegro and **Serbia.**

## - J -

JABLANICA. Hydroelectric plant in **Bosnia and Hercegovina** built between 1947 and 1958 on the **Neretva** River. The maximum capacity of the plant is 180,000 kilowatts, with a potential production of 750 Kwh of electrical energy. During the civil war the intense clashes between Croats and **Muslims** seriously damaged the 80 m-high river dam.

JAGODINA. City and a **commune** center in **Pomoravlje** with a population of 77,226 in 1991. Industries include electric cable, meat processing, machine-building, textiles and beer production. The city is first mentioned in the 16th century.

JAHORINA. Mountain in the vicinity of **Sarajevo**. The mountain is 30 km long and 15 km wide, with Paloševina the highest peak at 1916 m. Jahorina was the biggest ski-resort in **Bosnia and Hercegovina**. During the civil war Jahorina was a major Serbian stronghold.

JAJCE. Picturesque city in central **Bosnia and Hercegovina** with a population of 44,903 in 1991. The ethnic composition prior to the civil war was: 38.8 percent Muslim, 35.1 percent Croatian, 19.3 percent Serbian, and 5.5 percent Yugoslav. The city is known for the waterfall of the Pliva River. Two hydroelectric plants with a combined maximum capacity of 78,000 Kw are located in the vicinity. Jajce was built by the Bosnian **vojvoda** Hrvoje Vukčić in the 15th century. The city was under Hungarian control from 1463 to 1528, then it was occupied by the Turks. During **World War II**, the second session of AVNOJ was held in Jajce on November 29–30, 1943.

JAJINCI. Small village near **Avala** Mountain, a suburb of **Belgrade.** During **World War II**, massive executions of prisoners from **Banjica** camp took place in Jajinci; it is estimated that more than 70,000 people were executed in Jajinci.

JAKŠIĆ, DMITAR (?–1486). Serbian **vojvoda** during the reign of **Đurađ Branković**. After the fall of **Smederevo** in 1459 and subsequent collapse of the medieval Serbian state, he moved with his troops to **Srem**. He continued the fight against the Turks under the Hungarian king Mathias Corvinus.

JAKŠIĆ, ĐURA (1832–1878). Serbian poet and painter, and representative of romanticism. Born in Srpska Crnja in **Banat**, he studied in Szegedin, Pest (Budapest), and **Belgrade**. Much of his life was spent as a teacher throughout the interior of **Serbia**. A versatile and gifted author, painter, poet, narrator, and playwright, he followed a unique, highly subjective path in poetry. His emotional verses are characterized by rebellious, romantic patriotism and deep personal discontent with the circumstances in which he lived. His works include the poems "Otadžbina" ("Fatherland"), "Ponoć" ("Midnight"); epic poem *Prve žrtve* (*First Victims*); plays

*Seoba Srbalja* (*Migration of the Serbs*), *Stanoje Glavaš;* paintings *Devojka u plavom* (*Lady in Blue*), and *Pogibija Karađorđa* (*The Death of Karađorđe*).

JANIĆIJE/ EUSTAHIUS II (?–1354). Serbian archbishop (1337–1346) and the first Patriarch of the **Serbian Orthodox Church** (1346–1354). A trusted ally and supporter of the Serbian Emperor **Dušan the Mighty**, Janićije became Serbian patriarch at the Church Sabor held in the medieval Serbian Capital **Skoplje** on Palm Sunday in 1346. The elevation of the Serb Archbishopric to the Patriarchate of Serbia came as a result of Dušan's territorial conquests and the incorporation of three independent church organizations within the borders of the Serbian state. Since according to the Ecumenical Council of Chaledon (451) there could be only one independent Orthodox church organization within one state, the Serb Archbishopric was elevated to the Patriarchate of Serbia and Janićije became the first Serbian Patriarch. Besides his work on church reorganization, he was heavily involved in drawing up **Dušan's Code of Laws.**

JANIČARI. See JANISSARIES.

JANISSARIES/JANIČARI. Regular Turkish infantry soldiers between the 15th and 19th centuries. The soldiers were recruited from among young boys from the occupied Christian lands through a special tribute known as *devşirme* or **Blood Tribute**. Strict religious and military training, accompanied by social and economic incentives, made janissaries the best Turkish troops. The number of janissaries in the Turkish army was greatest, around 25,000, at the end of the 17th century. As the Ottoman Empire began to disintegrate in the early 18th century, the janissaries lost their privileged position. This led to several rebellions of janissaries until they were destroyed by Sultan Mahmud on June 15–16, 1826.

JANKOVIĆ, MILICA (1881–1939). One of the most prominent female writers in **Serbia** at the turn of the 19th century.

JASENOVAC. Small village located on the left bank of the **Sava** River in **Croatia**, 100 km southeast of **Zagreb**. During **World War II**, the **Ustaše** ran the largest concentration camp in southern Europe in Jasenovac. Analogous to the Nazi death camps, Jasenovac was established in August 1941 and was one of the largest sites of mass execution in the whole of

Europe. While estimates vary, numerous sources suggest that more than 600,000 **Serbs**, Jews, and Gypsies were executed there. The park monument devoted to the victims of Ustaše genocide was severely damaged by the Croatian army during its offensive in Western **Slavonia** in May 1995.

JASTREBAC. A mountain in central Serbia between the Western **Morava** and Southern Morava Rivers. The mountain is 45 km long with Zmajevac the highest peak at 1381 m.

*JAVNOST* (*The Public*). A socialist journal founded by **Svetozar Marković** on November 11, 1873. *The Public* was published three times a week and focused on practical political, economic, and social problems. As the most vocal opponent of the regime of King **Milan Obrenović**, the journal was banned on April 20, 1874, and Marković was arrested.

JEFIMIJA. Wife of the Serbian **despot** Uglješa **Mrnjavčević.** After the **Battle of Kosovo** she lived in the **Ljubostinja** monastery, where she crafted a narrative *Pohvala knezu Lazaru* (*Homage to Prince Lazar*). It is considered one of the finest examples of medieval Serbian literature.

JEFTANOVIĆ, GLIGORIJE (1840–1929). Serb from **Bosnia and Hercegovina** (B-H) known for his strenuous work toward establishing the church and educational autonomy for Serbs living in B-H. Between 1905 and 1914 he was a vice president of Veliki upravni i prosvjetni savjet (High Administrative and Educational Council) in **Sarajevo.** After **World War I** he became president of the Bosnia-Hercegovinian National Senate and the first president of the Provisional National Assembly.

JERINA (?–1458). Greek-born wife of **Đurađ Branković,** Serbian **despot**. Jerina was very unpopular among Serbian peasants, who named her Jerina the Cursed, because of her harshness towards them during the building of **Smederevo.**

JEVTIĆ ATANASIJE. See ATANASIJE, JEVTIĆ.

JIRIČEK, JOSIF KONSTANTIN (1854–1918). Czech historian who, under the influence of **Đuro Daničić**, wrote several important works on the history of medieval **Serbia**. His work includes *Istorija Srba do 1537 (History of the Serbs until 1537), and Trgovački drumovi u srednjevekovnoj Srbiji i Bosni* (*Trade Routes in Medieval Serbia and Bosnia*).

JNA (Jugoslovenska narodna armija-Yugoslav National Army). The armed forces of the **Socialist Federal Republic of Yugoslavia** (SFRY). The JNA represented the continuation of the **Partisans**. After **World War II,** the organization of the JNA followed both the organization of the Royal Yugoslav Army and the structure of the Soviet Red Army. It was a multiethnic, conscript-based force comprising land, air, and naval services. The ground forces were divided into five armies and several corps. According to Western estimates, the JNA was the fourth largest army in Europe. It was a technically well-equipped force, with more than 1,500 modern tanks and 200 Soviet and domestically made fighter jets. In 1991, at the outset of the civil war, JNA forces totalled more than 200,000 (60,000 officer corps). **Serbs** made up 36 percent of its conscripts and 42 percent of the total forces.

The role of the JNA in the civil war was highly controversial. Often seen as one of the main culprits for the civil war and destruction in the former Yugoslavia, the JNA essentially carried out its constitutional duty, that is the defense and preservation of the SFRY. In that capacity it became a major obstacle for the secessionist republics. The situation became even more complex after the unilateral secessions of **Croatia, Slovenia,** and **Bosnia and Hercegovina** were legally sanctioned by the **European Community.** The presence of the JNA in these republics led to confusion, with actions perpetrated by paramilitary units being repeatedly blamed on the JNA. As the formation of paramilitary units rapidly grew in the secessionist republics, the ethnic composition of the JNA substantially changed. In March 1992, non-Serbs comprised less than three percent of the total armed forces. The JNA was formally disbanded in June 1992 and succeeded by the **Yugoslav Army** (Vojska Jugoslavije). The officers and conscripts born in Bosnia and Hercegovina left the JNA and joined the **Bosnian Serb Army.**

JOANIKIJE (?–1354). See JANIĆIJE.

JOB, IGNJAT (1895–1935). Serbian painter born in **Dubrovnik**. In 1913, he went to Serbia and joined the Serbian army. Upon his return to

Dubrovnik he was arrested and transferred to military prison in Šibenik. Following his release from prison in 1917, he began his studies in the academy of art in **Zagreb**. Together with Jovan Bijelić, Job is considered a founder of modern Serbian painting. His best paintings are *Mlado vino* (*Young Wine*), *Portret Tina Ujevića* (*Portrait of Tin Ujevic*), *Dvorište* (*Backyard*).

JOSIMOVIĆ, EMILIJAN (1823–1897). Architect, rector of Lycée and the **Great School,** and the first expert on urbanism in **Serbia**. A native of **Banat,** he completed his higher education in Vienna. His numerous projects include the first road tunnel in Serbia and a dock on the confluence of the **Sava** and **Danube** Rivers in **Belgrade.**

JOVAN KANTUL (?–1614). Patriarch of the **Serbian Orthodox Church.** He tried to exploit the Austro-Turkish War of 1593–1606 and actively supported several Serbian rebellions against the Turks. He negotiated a Crusade war against the Turks with the Austrian Archduke Ferdinand without success. Jovan was killed by Turks in Constantinople in 1614.

JOVANOVIĆ, ANASTAS (1817–1899). First Serbian photographer. Born in Bulgaria, he studied in **Belgrade** and Vienna. Upon his return to **Serbia,** he was appointed to the ceremonial position of marshal of the court. Besides photography, he is known for several lithographs.

JOVANOVIĆ, JOVAN-PIŽON (1869–1939). A Serbian and Yugoslav politician and diplomat and leader of the **Agricultural Party.** He was the foreign minister of **Serbia** in 1912 and deputy foreign minister 1914–1915. He was the chief of the consular section of the foreign ministry 1904–1906, chief of Serbian missions in Cairo 1906–1907, **Cetinje** 1907–1909, consul general in **Skoplje** 1911–1912, envoy in Vienna 1912–1914 and London in 1919. Jovanović was the owner of ***Srpski književni glasnik***, where he occasionally published under the pseudonym Inostrani (Foreign). He is the author of numerous monographs on Serbian diplomatic history. His study into responsibility for the outbreak of **World War I** is especially important given his position as Serbian envoy in Vienna between 1912 and 1914.

JOVANOVIĆ, JOVAN-ZMAJ. See ZMAJ, JOVAN JOVANOVIĆ.

JOVANOVIĆ LJUBOMIR (1865–1928). Serbian historian and politician, a prominent member of the **Radical Party**. In various Serbian governments he held the posts of minister of interior 1909–1910 and 1914–1918 and minister of education 1911–1914. In the **Kingdom of the Serbs, Croats, and Slovenes** he was minister of religion in 1923 and president of the **Parliament** from 1923 to 1926, when he was ousted from the party due to a disagreement with **Nikola Pašić**.

JOVANOVIĆ, LJUBOMIR-ČUPA (1877–1913). Serbian politician and fervent pro-Yugoslav nationalist, one of the founders and leaders of the secret organization **Unification or Death.** Jovanović was the editor of the daily newspaper ***Pijemont*** (*Piedmont*). He also founded the student newspaper *Slovenski jug* (*Slavic South*) at the **Great School.**

JOVANOVIĆ, MIHAILO (1826–1898). Metropolitan of the **Serbian Orthodox Church** 1859–1881 and 1889–1898. A devoted Russophile, he was in constant opposition to the pro-Austrian policy of King **Milan Obrenović.** In 1881, he was forced to relinquish his leadership of the church and leave **Serbia**, but he returned after the abdication of King Milan in 1889. He wrote *Pravoslavna crkva u kneževini Srbiji* (*The Orthodox Church in the Principality of Serbia*), and *Pogled na istoriju srpske crkve* (*A Survey of History of the Serbian Church*).

JOVANOVIĆ, PETAR (1800–1864). Metropolitan of the **Serbian Orthodox Church** between 1833 and 1864. Prior to becoming metropolitan he was a professor of gymnastics in **Karlovci Sremski** 1819–1829 and secretary to Prince **Miloš Obrenović.** He actively worked on establishing an educational system in **Serbia.**

JOVANOVIĆ, SLOBODAN (1869–1958). Prominent Serbian statesman, politician, historian, member of the **Serbian Academy of Sciences and Arts**, and one of the most erudite individuals in modern Serbian history. He was a member of **Jugoslavenska akademija znanosti i umjetnosti** and the French "l'Institut." A founder of **Srpski Kulturni klub** (Serbian Cultural Club), he became a vice president in General Simović's government of March 27, 1941. After the collapse of Yugoslavia, Jovanović emigrated to London, where he became the prime minister of the government-in-exile in 1942–1943. He actively supported **Jugoslovenska vojska u otadžbini** under the command of General **Dragoljub-Draža**

**Mihailović.** He was president of Jugoslovenski odbor (Yugoslav National Board), an organization envisioned as an alternative to the Communist regime in **Belgrade**. After **World War II** he was tried by a Communist court as a "war criminal." He died in exile. His numerous works include *O suverenosti* (*On Sovereignty*), *Druga vlada Miloša i Mihaila* (*Second Rule of Miloš and Mihailo*), *Vlada Milana Obrenovića* (*The Rule of* ***Milan Obrenović***), and *Ustavno pravo Kraljevine Srbije* (*Constitutional Law of the Kingdom of Serbia*).

JOVANOVIĆ, VIĆENTIJE (?–1737). Metropolitan of **Belgrade**-Karlovci diocese of the **Serbian Orthodox Church** and the founder of the first gymnasium (high school) in **Karlovci Sremski** and the first Greek school in Belgrade.

JOVANOVIĆ, VLADIMIR (1833–1922). Prominent Serbian politician, a founder of the **Liberal Party** and **Ujedinjena omladina srpska,** and father of Slobodan Jovanović. As finance minister (1876–1880) he introduced the gold-minted **dinar** into **Serbia**. He was the editor of *Narodna Skupština* (*National Parliament*) and published the journal *Sloboda* (*Freedom*) in Geneva. For his criticism of the **Obrenović dynasty** he was imprisoned and forced into exile. He wrote *Politički rečnik* (*Political Dictionary*).

JOVANOVIĆ, VLADISLAV (1933– ). Yugoslav ambassador at the United Nations. Jovanović was foreign minister of **Serbia** 1991–93 and minister of foreign affairs of the **Federal Republic of Yugoslavia** 1993–95. He actively participated in the negotiating process regarding the civil war in **Croatia** and **Bosnia and Hercegovina.**

JOVIĆ, BORISAV (1928– ). Serbian politician and member (1990–92) and president of the collective Presidency (1990–91) of the **Socialist Federal Republic of Yugoslavia** (SFRY). Although he occupied several important political posts (Yugoslav ambassador to Italy, vice president of the Serbian **Parliament,** and member of the Presidency of the Communist Party of Serbia), Jović's role in Yugoslav politics significantly increased following his appointment to the federal Presidency and the outbreak of the civil war in June 1991. Often seen as the main exponent of the policies of Serbian president **Slobodan Milošević,** Jović actively participated in the decision-making process during the civil war in Croatia. Following the dismantling of the SFRY and the formation of the **Federal Republic of Yugoslavia,** Jović became a vice president of the **Socialist Party of Serbia**. He was removed from all political posts in December 1995.

JUGOSLAVENSKA AKADEMIJA ZNANOSTI I UMJETNOSTI (JAZU) (Yugoslav Academy of Sciences and Arts). Academy founded by Bishop **Josip Juraj Strossmayer** in 1866. Contrary to its proclaimed Yugoslavism, the academy was an important instrument in the movement for Croatian national liberation. After **World War II,** JAZU was canonized as the highest "scientific and artistic institution" in **Croatia.** In 1992, after Croatia seceded from **Socialist Federal Republic of Yugoslavia,** JAZU was renamed the Croatian Academy of Sciences and Arts.

JUGOSLOVENSKA LEVICA. See JUL.

JUGOSLOVENSKA MUSLIMANSKA ORGANIZACIJA. See YUGOSLAV MUSLIM ORGANIZATION.

JUGOSLOVENSKA NARODNA ARMIJA. See JNA.

JUGOSLOVENSKA RADIKALNA ZAJEDNICA. See YUGOSLAV RADICAL UNION.

JUGOSLOVENSKA REPUBLIKANSKA STRANKA. See YUGOSLAV REPUBLICAN PARTY.

JUGOSLOVENSKA VOJSKA U OTADŽBINI (JVO) (Yugoslav Army in the Fatherland). Official name for an antifascist, nationalist movement founded by Colonel **Dragoljub-Draža Mihailović** in May 1941. Following the collapse of Yugoslavia in **April's War,** Mihailović and 27 officers and soldiers of the Yugoslav army refused to surrender and, upon arrival in **Ravna Gora** on May 11, formed "The Command of **Četniks**' Squadrons of the Yugoslav Army." Although Mihailović's organization was not connected with the official Četnik organization, the name *četnik* was used as a traditional symbol of Serbian resistance. After the consolidation of the movement, and following Mihailović's promotion to the rank of general and appointment as minister of defense in the government-in-exile in June 1942, the name was changed to Jugoslovenska vojska u otadžbini. The official name reflected the continuation of the Yugoslav army and Yugoslav state, although the movement continued to be popularly known as Četniks.

The political wing of Mihailović's movement was known as **Ravnogorski Pokret** (Movement of Ravna Gora). The movement worked actively on the establishment of the Central National Committee (CNK) that would gather representatives of all political parties. The executive board of the committee consisted of **Dragiša Vasić,** Stevan Moljević, and Mladen Žujović. The JVO and CNK were counterparts to the Communist-led **Partisans** and **AVNOJ.** Throughout the war, the JVO and Partisans engaged in a bitter civil war. The JVO lost the initiative after being abandoned by Great Britain and the United States in 1943. Supported by the Soviet Army, **Tito**'s forces decisively defeated the JVO in October 1944.

JUGOSLOVENSKI ODBOR. See YUGOSLAV COMMITTEE.

*JUGOSLOVENSKI PREGLED* (*Yugoslav Review*). Semi-official, monthly journal that has published articles on current political, economic, and cultural developments in Yugoslavia since 1957.

JUL (Jugoslovenska levica-Yugoslav Left). Conglomerate of 22 left-wing parties in the **Federal Republic of Yugoslavia** (FRY) formed on July 23, 1994, and led by **Mirjana Marković.** The basis of the JUL is the League of Communists—Movement for Yugoslavia, the political party founded on November 19, 1990, as the continuation of the League of Communists of Yugoslavia. The JUL is considered one of the most influential political organizations in the FRY.

JUSUFSPAHIĆ, HAMDIJA (1937– ). Leader of the Islamic religious community in the **Federal Republic of Yugoslavia** and vice president of Savezna stranka jugoslovena (Federal Party of Yugoslavs).

JUŽNA MORAVA. See SOUTHERN MORAVA.

## - K -

KACLEROVIĆ, TRIŠA (1879–1964). Serbian politician, one of the founders of the Serbian **Social Democratic Party** and the **Communist Party of Yugoslavia** (CPY). During the internal struggle within the CPY in the

1920s, Kaclerović was accused of "right-wing deviation," a phrase used to label oppositionists to the bolshevization of the party, which prompted his retirement from politics in 1925. He edited leftist journals *Radnik* (*Worker*) and *Radničke novine* (*Workers' Gazette*) and published numerous books on the development of socialism in Serbia.

KAČANIČKA KLISURA. Canyon, 23 km long, between **Šar Mountain** and Skopska Crna Gora Mountain, a natural link between **Kosovo and Metohija** and the valley of the **Vardar** River. In November 1915, Bulgarian forces captured strategic hills overlooking the canyon and prevented the intended withdrawal of the Serbian army to Greece through the valley of the Vardar River. This forced the Serbian army to retreat through Albania. See also ALBANIAN RETREAT.

KADIJEVIĆ, VELJKO (1922– ). General of the **JNA** and defense minister of the **Socialist Federal Republic of Yugoslavia** during the civil war in **Croatia.** Born in Hercegovina to a Croat-Serb mixed marriage, he joined the **Partisans** during **World War II**. A devoted Titoist and Yugoslav, he proposed early disarmament and disbandment of the Croatian and Slovenian paramilitary forces as the way to prevent the civil war. His proposal was rejected in a stormy session of the federal Presidency on March 12–14, 1991. Kadijević resigned on January 8, 1992. In 1993, he published the book *Moje vipenje raspada* (*My Views on the Break-Up*) in which he essentially justifies the actions of the JNA during the civil war in Croatia.

KAJMAKČALAN. Highest peak of Nidže Mountain (2,525 m). During **World War I,** the Battle of Kajmakčalan, between the Serbian army and combined Bulgarian and German forces, took place between September 12 and October 3, 1916. The Serbian forces consisted of two infantry divisions and some light artillery, while German-Bulgarian forces, besides two infantry divisions, had several batteries of heavy artillery. After brutal, hand-to-hand fighting, the Serbian forces stormed Kajmakčalan and routed the Bulgarians from the mountain on October 3. Although Allied Command did not utilize this success, the Serbian army liberated Bitolj on November 19, 1916.

KALEMEGDAN. Large park in **Belgrade**, located on the hills overlooking the junction of the **Sava** and **Danube** Rivers. The remains of the old city fortress, as well as numerous historic monuments, are situated in Kalemegdan. The old fortress was a main strategic point at the northern borders of the Ottoman Empire.

KALENIĆ. One of the most beautiful monasteries in **Serbia**, a legacy of **Stefan Lazarević**, Serbian **despot**, built between 1407 and 1413. The monastery was restored in 1929.

KALJEVIĆ, LJUBOMIR (1842–1907). Serbian politician and journalist, one of the founders of the **Progressive Party.** Educated in Heidelberg and Paris, Kaljević was a politically ambitious man who was able to get along with all sides. He became prime minister of Serbia in 1875 but was forced to resign shortly thereafter (May 1876) due to his cabinet's inability to agree on vital issues pertaining to the looming **Serbo-Turkish War.** He published *Srbija* (*Serbia*), the only opposition journal during the reign of Prince **Mihailo Obrenović.**

KÁLLAY, BENJÁMIN (1839–1903). Austro-Hungarian diplomat, consul general in Serbia 1868–1875, and concurrently common minister of finance in **Bosnia and Hercegovina** (B-H) 1882–1903. Kállay initiated and propagated the concept of the **Bošnjak** nation, while his main efforts were concentrated on the economic and political incorporation of B-H into the Habsburg Empire. He wrote *History of the Serbs* (in Hungarian) and *History of the Serbian Insurrection 1807–1810.*

KANAZIR, DUŠAN (1921– ). Prominent Serbian and Yugoslav biologist (molecular biology) and member of the **Serbian Academy of Sciences and Arts** and its president 1981–1994. Kanazir is also member of the Indian Academy of Sciences and Athens Academy of Sciences. His numerous awards include a French Commander of the Legion of Honor. In 1996, Kanazir became a minister of science in the Serbian government. He is the author of more than 200 hundred books, monographs, and journal articles. His works include *Radiation Induced Alterations in the Structure of Deoxyribonucleic Acid and Biological Consequences*, *Steroid, Hormones, Hormone Secretion and Steroid Receptors in Carcinogenesis, Psychosocial (Emotional) Stress*, and *Steroid Hormones and the Genesis of Cancer*.

KAPOR, MOMO (1937– ). Popular Serbian writer and painter and the author of numerous books and screenplays for several movies. His work is characteristic for its undemanding style and composition. Kapor exhibited his paintings in the galleries of New York City, Harvard, Paris, and Caracas. During the civil war in **Bosnia and Hercegovina**, Kapor actively supported the leadership of the **Republika Srpska.** His best works include *Maratonci* (*Marathon Runners*), *Ada*, *Una*, and *Alo Beograde* (*Hello Belgrade*).

KARAĐORĐE, PETROVIĆ ĐORĐE (1768–1817). Leader of the **First Serbian Insurrection** and the founder of the **Karađorđević dynasty**. He was given the nickname Karageorge (Black George) for his black temper. Karađorđe's family belonged to the Montenegrin clan of Vasojevići. He migrated to Austria in 1787 and joined the army of volunteers. After the Austro-Turkish war he returned to **Serbia** and settled in **Topola**. With the resumption of trade between Austria and the Ottoman Empire, he began to deal in swine, which gave him a good income and many ties that were to be useful later.

When the **Dahije** took over in the **Beogradski pašaluk,** Karađorđe began to organize the resistance to their regime, and on February 2, 1804, he was elected the leader of the uprising. During the uprising, which soon became a war for national liberation, Karađorđe established himself as a brilliant fighter and leader. The Serbian forces under his direct command defeated the Turks in the **Battle of Mišar** and liberated **Belgrade.** After the liberation from the Turks, the first Serbian **constitution** declared Karađorđe "first and supreme Serbian hereditary ruler" in 1808. His dominant position, however, frustrated several **vojvoda** and intensified the internal power struggle. Although, Karađorđe emerged victorious, the power struggle substantially weakened Serbia. After Russia abandoned Serbia in the **Treaty of Bucharest,** an overwhelming Turkish force crushed the Serbian opposition and reoccupied Serbia in 1813. Karađorđe, ill with typhus, fled to Austria and then to Russia. He attempted to return to Serbia in 1815 but was prevented by Russia. Karađorđe secretly returned to Serbia on June 28, 1817, intending to instigate a general uprising against the Turks. Fearing his rivalry, Prince **Miloš Obrenović** ordered Karađorđe's assassination. Karađorđe was murdered in his sleep on July 25, 1817, and his severed head was sent to the sultan in Istanbul.

Karađorđe played an extremely important role in Serbia's history.

Besides his undisputed military talents, he greatly contributed to the diplomatic and political emancipation of Serbia during her war for national liberation. Despite strong autocratic tendencies, his insistence on a strong centralized state proved more appropriate than the particularism of the local chieftains.

KARAĐORĐEVIĆ, ALEXANDER I, KING. See ALEXANDER I KARAĐORĐEVIĆ.

KARAĐORĐEVIĆ, ALEXANDER, PRINCE (1806–1885). Son of **Karađorđe** and prince of **Serbia** 1842–1858. Born in **Topola**, Alexander left Serbia after the collapse of the **First Serbian Insurrection** in 1813. He spent most of his exile years in Hotin, Besarabia. Following Prince Miloš's downfall and after Prince **Mihailo Obrenović**'s emigration in 1842, Alexander returned to Serbia. Although he refused to participate in the plot against Prince Mihailo, he accepted the offer of the **Constitutionalists** and became Serbian prince on September 14, 1842. His reign is characterized by a continuous power struggle with the Constitutionalists. He was forced to abdicate at the **St. Andrew Assembly** that took place in **Belgrade** between and December 13, 1858, and January 4, 1859.

KARAĐORĐEVIĆ, ALEXANDER II, PRINCE (1945– ). Son of **Peter II Karađorđević** and heir to the Yugoslav throne. Born in London, Alexander studied at military academies in Switzerland, the United States, and Great Britain. Upon retiring from an active military service, he became a successful businessman. While he did not assume title of king of Yugoslavia after the death of his father Peter II Karađorđević, Alexander attempted to participate actively in Serbian and Yugoslav political life in 1992–1993.

KARAĐORĐEVIĆ, DYNASTY. Serbian rulers, descendants of **Karađorđe,** the leader of the **First Serbian Insurrection.** The dynasty ruled in **Serbia** and Yugoslavia 1842–1858 and 1903–1945.

KARAĐORĐEVIĆ, ĐORĐE (1887–1972). Eldest son of King **Peter I Karađorđević**. After a series of incidents he renounced his right as successor to the Serbian royal throne in favor of his younger brother **Alexander I Karađorđević**. During **World War II**, he rejected Hitler's offer to become king of occupied **Serbia**.

KARAĐORĐEVIĆ, PAVLE, PRINCE, THE (1883–1976). First cousin of **King Alexander I Karađorđević**, and Prince Regent of Yugoslavia 1934–1941. Virtually unknown in the Yugoslav political arena, Prince Pavle became the most important political figure in Yugoslavia following the assassination of King Alexander in 1934. Establishing himself as a senior member in the three-man Royal Regency, he became the driving force in changing both the internal and foreign policy of Yugoslavia. On the domestic front, Pavle pursued a policy of appeasement toward the secessionism of the **Croatian Peasant Party** and its leader **Vladko Maček**. This policy resulted in the **Cvetković-Maček Agreement** in 1939 and the creation of the **Croatian Banovina**.

Pavle's foreign policy, despite his strong pro-British inclinations, reflected the changing balance of power in Europe and led to the increased dependency of Yugoslavia on Nazi Germany. This resulted in Yugoslavia joining the **Tripartite Pact** in March 1941. Pavle was arrested and confined following the **Coup d'état of March 27, 1941**. Later, he emigrated to Great Britain, where he died in exile.

KARAĐORĐEVIĆ, PETER I, KING (1844–1921). King of **Serbia** (1903–1918) and of the **Kingdom of the Serbs, Croats, and Slovenes** (1918–1921). Born in Belgrade, the third son of Prince **Alexander I Karađorđević**, Peter spent most of his life in western Europe. He was educated largely in Geneva and Paris, and he completed his military training at Saint-Cyr and Metz. Peter served in the French Foreign Legion and received the medal of the French Legion of Honor for his distinguished service during the Franco-Prussian War of 1870. He fought as a volunteer under the name of Petar Mrkonjić in **Bosnia and Hercegovina** (B-H) during the **Rebellions of Hercegovina.** Following the Austro-Hungarian occupation of B-H, he moved to Montenegro and married Zorka, the eldest daughter of the Montenegrin prince **Nikola I Petrović**. In 1890, after Zorka's death, he and his three children, Jelena, Đorđe, and Alexander, left for Geneva where they lived until 1903. Following **May's Assassination** and his election as king he returned to Serbia on June 25, 1903. He was solemnly crowned in Belgrade on September 8, 1904.

His reign was marked by parliamentary democracy. The **Constitution** of 1888 was reinstated, political party pluralism flourished, and the economic emancipation of Serbia began. His rule marked the most dynamic period in the history of modern Serbia. Serbia withstood a difficult **Tariff War** with Austria-Hungary and emerged victorious from the **Balkan wars** and **World War I**. In June 1914, due to his age and disagreements about the role of the army in Serbian politics, he transferred much of his royal prerogatives to his younger son Prince Regent **Alexander I Karađorđević**. In 1918, he became king of the newly created Kingdom of the Serbs, Croats, and Slovenes but relinquished his day-to-day duties to Prince Regent Alexander.

Peter was an extremely modest man and popular king, known by his nickname Čika Pera (Uncle Pete). He translated John Stuart Mill's essay *On Liberty* into Serbian.

KARAĐORĐEVIĆ, PETER II, KING (1923–1970). Oldest son of **Alexander I Karađorđević**, king of Yugoslavia 1934–1945. Peter succeeded to the throne under the regency of his uncle, Prince Paul Karađorđević, after Alexander's assassination by the **Ustaše** in 1934. During the events of the **Coup d'état of March 27, 1941,** the regency was overthrown and Peter, although still a minor, was declared king. After Yugoslavia collapsed in **April's War,** Peter fled to London, where he established a government-in-exile. After **World War II,** he remained in exile. The Communist government of Yugoslavia confiscated the property of the **Karađorđević** dynasty and banned Peter and his family from returning to Yugoslavia. This decision was annulled in 1990.

KARADŽIĆ, RADOVAN (1945– ). Former president of the **Republika Srpska** (RS) and one of the founders of the **Serbian Democratic Party.** Born in **Montenegro**, Karadžić graduated in psychiatry from the University of Sarajevo. He worked in local hospitals, wrote children's poetry books, and composed Serb folk music. In 1990, Karadžić became president of the **Serbian Democratic Party** in **Bosnia and Hercegovina** (B-H). He and his party strongly opposed the Muslim- and Croat-favored policy of secession of the B-H from Yugoslavia. After the outbreak of the civil war in B-H, Karadžić became president of the Serbian Republic. Along with General **Ratko Mladić,** the commander in chief of the **Bosnian Serb Army** (BSA), Karadžić has been indicted by the war crimes tribunal in The Hague. In the beginning of 1996, following the **Dayton Agreement,** he was forced to relinquish his presidential duties to **Biljana Plavšić,** vice president of the RS. On July 19, 1996, under strong U.S. pressure, Karadžić resigned as president of the Serbian Democratic Party and agreed to cease any political activity.

KARADŽIĆ, VUK STEFANOVIĆ (1787–1864). Leading Serbian language scholar and reformer and the creator of Serbian folk literature scholarship. In reforming the **Serbian language,** Karadžić created one of the simplest, most logical, and scientific spelling systems. In 1818, he published *Srpski rječnik* (*Serbian Lexicon*), which contained 26,270 words and numerous entries relating to Serbian folklore. The second edition of the lexicon was published in 1852 and extended to 46,270 words. In Vienna he published the journal ***Danica,*** which played an important role in promoting Serbian culture and tradition in Europe. The work of Karadžić had a tremendous impact on establishing and strengthening the cultural ties between **Serbs** and Croats. As a direct result of Karadžić's reform, Serbian and Croatian language scholars signed the Literary Agreement, according to which a single literary language would be used by both nations.

KARDELJ, EDVARD (1910–1979). Slovene Communist politician and the closest associate of Josip Broz, **Tito**. An opportunist politician, Kardelj continuously worked toward the decentralization of the **Socialist Federal Republic of Yugoslavia** and greater autonomy for **Slovenia.** Kardelj is considered to be the main political force behind the introduction of **Self-management** and the **Constitution** of 1974.

KARIĆ, BOGOLJUB (1954– ). President of "Braća Karić," one of the biggest privately owned companies in the **Federal Republic of Yugoslavia.** Born in **Peć**, he finished vocational school and later graduated with a degree in economics. He founded several very successful enterprises in the Ukraine, Kazakhstan, Russia, and Uzbekistan and is an honorary member of the Ukrainian Academy of Science. While not directly involved in Serbian politics, Karić is considered one of the most influential people in **Serbia**.

KARLOVAČKI MIR. See CARLOWITZ, TREATY OF.

KARLOVCI SREMSKI. Town in **Srem** located on the right bank of the **Danube** River. The oldest Serbian high school, founded in 1791, is located in the town. Karlovci was the center of the **Serbian Orthodox Church** following the abolishment of the **patriarchate of Peć** in 1776.

KASABA. Turkish term used for a small town. The derogatory use of the term implies primitivism and backwardness. The term is often used in **Croatia** to describe the situation in **Belgrade** and **Serbia** in general.

KATUNSKA NAHIJA. Region in **Montenegro**, southwest of the **Zeta** River, a center of medieval Montenegro. The first reference to the region dates from the 14th century.

KAŽIĆ, BOŽIDAR (1921–1995). Chess referee and deputy president of the International Chess Federation (Fide) since 1974. He was referee in numerous chess tournaments and in several qualification matches for the world championship title. He is the author of a book on world chess championships.

KIKINDA. City and industrial center in **Banat,** close to the Rumanian border, with a population 69,743 in 1991. Textile, food-processing, chemical, and machine-building industries are especially developed.

KINGDOM OF THE SERBS, CROATS, AND SLOVENES/KRALJEVINA SRBA, HRVATA, I SLOVENACA (SHS). First common state of **South Slavs**, formed on December 1, 1918, by the unification of **Serbia**, **Montenegro**, and the Yugoslav lands under Austro-Hungarian rule (**Croatia**, **Slavonia**, **Vojvodina**, **Bosnia and Hercegovina**, **Dalmatia**, and **Slovenia**). The state was declared a constitutional monarchy ruled by the Serbian **Karađorđević dynasty**. The new state faced a complex religious and linguistic pattern as well as formidable administrative problems. The organizational chaos included six customs areas, five currencies, four railway networks, three banking systems, and the remnants of four legal systems.

The process of unification and standardization was seriously hampered by the open secessionism of the **Croatian Peasant Party**, the largest political organization of Croats. Croatian secessionism was often met with rigid Serbian centralism. Thus, while it emerged as the fulfillment of the "centuries old dream of the unification of South Slavs" the Kingdom of the SHS did not succeed in narrowing the differences among the constituent nations. In 1929, King **Alexander I Karađorđević** renamed the state Yugoslavia. See also CORFU DECLARATION; DICTATORSHIP OF JANUARY 6, 1929; OCTROYED CONSTITUTION; PAŠIĆ, NIKOLA; PRIBIĆEVIĆ, SVETOZAR; RADIĆ, STJEPAN.

KIŠ, DANILO (1935–1989). One of the most celebrated Yugoslav writers. Born in a Jewish family in **Subotica,** he graduated with a degree in Literature from the **University of Belgrade**. He worked as a lector in Strasbourg. He spent the last years of his life in Paris. Kiš was known for his exceptionally sophisticated writing style characterized by a close to perfect narrative technique and modern, contemplative storyline. His best works include *Grobnica za Borisa Davidoviča* (*A Tomb for Boris Davidovič*), *Mansarda* (*The Mansard*), *Bašta, pepeo* (*Garden, Ashes*), and *Peščanik* (*The Hourglass*).

KLJUČ. City in **Bosnia and Hercegovina** with a population of 37,233 in 1991. The ethnic composition prior to the civil war was: 77.6 percent Muslim, 19.5 percent Serbian, 0.9 percent Croatian, and 1.5 percent Yugoslav. The main industry is the production of construction material. The first record of the city dates from 1325, and in 1463, **Stefan Tomašević**, the last Bosnian king, surrendered to the Turks in Ključ.

KNEZ. (i) A royal title, equivalent to prince, held by Serbian rulers from the end of the **Second Serbian Insurrection** to the proclamation of the Kingdom of **Serbia** on March 6, 1882.
(ii) A title held by a village elder in Serbia during the Turkish occupation and the rule of Prince **Miloš Obrenović**. The chief *knez*, that is the elder of several villages (***knežina***) was known as *obor-knez*.

KNEŽEVIĆ, BOŽIDAR (1862–1905). Serbian philosopher close to positivism. A highly original thinker, Knežević was a unique figure among Serbia's intellectuals in the second half of the 19th century. He presented the fundamental principles of his philosophy in *Principi istorije* (*Principles of History*).

KNEŽEVIĆ, IVO (1760–1840). Folk hero and Serbian ***knez*** in **Semberija.** After ransoming 300 **Serbs**, he fought the Turkish forces in **Bosnia and Hercegovina** during the **First Serbian Insurrection.** In 1815, he went to **Serbia** and became a district judge in **Šabac.**

KNEŽINA. District combining several villages in **Serbia** during Turkish rule. The leader of a *knežina* was an obor-***knez.***

KNIN. Industrial city and a **commune** center in **Zagora**; important communication center between the interior of **Croatia** and **Dalmatia** with a population of 42,340 in 1991. The milling, bauxite, and furniture production are important industries. The first record of the city dates from the middle of the 10th century. With the establishment of **Vojna Krajina,** the population of Knin became predominantly Serbian. In 1990, Knin became the center of Serbian opposition to the newly established Croatian regime, and in 1991, after the outbreak of the civil war in **Croatia**, Knin was declared the capital of the **Republic of Serbian Krajina.** After the vast majority of the Serbian population abandoned the city, the Croatian army captured Knin during an offensive in August 1995.

KNJAŽEVAC. City and **commune** center in eastern **Serbia** with a population of 44,036 in 1991. One of the biggest shoe-making factories and several coal mines are located in the city and its vicinity.

*KNJIŽEVNE NOVINE* (*The Literary Gazette*). Influential bimonthly newspaper, published in Belgrade, and an official publication of Savez književnika Srbije (League of Writers of Serbia). The profoundly liberal *Književne novine* was often censored during one-party rule in Yugoslavia.

KOČIĆ, PETAR (1877–1916). Serbian revolutionary writer from **Bosnia and Hercegovina** (B- H), one of the best representatives of realism in Serbian literature. Born in Zmijanje, a village in **Bosnian Krajina**, he finished gymnasium (high school) in **Sarajevo** and studied in Vienna. Upon his return to B-H he founded the newspaper ***Otadžbina***. For his work on national liberation of the **Serbs** in B-H, Kočić was continuously persecuted by the Austro-Hungarian administration. His best-known work includes the satire *Jazavac pred sudom* (*Badger Before the Court*), and the novel *Jauci sa Zmijanja* (*Crying from Zmijanje*).

KOČINA KRAJINA. Term used for the actions of **Koča Anđelković** and his Serbian volunteers during the Austro-Turkish war (1788–1791). In the period between February and September 1788, Koča and his forces effectively cut Turkish communication lines between **Belgrade** and **Niš.**

KOLJEVIĆ, NIKOLA (1936–1997). Serbian writer and politician from **Bosnia and Hercegovina** and vice president of the **Republika Srpska**. Born in **Banja Luka**, Koljević studied in **Belgrade** and graduated with a degree in philosophy. A University of Sarajevo professor and known expert on Anglo-Saxon literature, he joined the **Serbian Democratic Party** in 1990. After the proclamation of the Serbian Republic in April 1992, Koljević became a vice president together with **Biljana Plavšić**. He committed suicide in January 1997. His major work is *Teorijski osnovi nove kritike* (*Foundations of the Theory of New Critique*).

KOLO. Fast-moving, popular folk-dance performed at various festive occasions. The name of the dance is derived for the Old Slavic word for "wheel." Although being performed by almost all ethnic groups in the former Yugoslavia, the dance is the most popular among the **Serbs.** The dance can take various forms, from a straight-line pattern to a full circle.

KOLUBARA, BATTLE OF/KOLUBARSKA BITKA. Biggest and the most important battle between the Serbian and Austro-Hungarian armies during **World War I.** After the humiliating defeat in the **Battle of Cer**, General Oskar Potiorek, governer of **Bosnia and Hercegovina**, assembled a 300,000-strong army and invaded **Serbia** in the beginning of September 1914. Vastly outgunned, the Serbian army, numbering 130,000 soldiers, was forced to retreat along a 200 km long frontline. The Austro-Hungarian troops, the Fifth and Sixth Armies, reached the Kolubara River on November 16. After entering an abandoned **Belgrade** on December 2, the Austro-Hungarian army paused in order to regroup.

This pause was exploited by the commander of the Serbian First Army, General **Živojin Mišić,** who consolidated his forces and ordered a counteroffensive on December 3. Caught by complete surprise, overextended and strategically outmaneuvered, the Austro-Hungarian troops were forced to withdraw hastily toward Belgrade and across the **Sava** and **Danube** Rivers. Serbian troops reentered Belgrade and liberated Serbia on December 15, 1914. During one month of fighting, the Austro-Hungarian troops lost around 100,000 men and substantial amounts of war material. The outcome of the battle effectively ended Austro-Hungarian offensive power in the Balkans. For his achievement in the battle, General Mišić was promoted to the rank of **vojvoda**. The Battle of Kolubara represents one of the finest examples of strategic warfare.

KOLUBARSKA BITKA. See KOLUBARA, BATTLE OF.

*KOMUNIST* (*The Communist*). Official paper of the Central Committee of the **Communist Party of Yugoslavia** (CPY) published, with interruptions, from 1925. The publication of *The Communist* ceased with the dissolution of the League of Communists of Yugoslavia in 1990.

KOMUNISTIČKA PARTIJA JUGOSLAVIJE. See COMMUNIST PARTY OF YUGOSLAVIA.

KONAVLE. Karst field southeast of **Dubrovnik**, an agricultural region, known for the production of vegetables, citrus fruits, and olive oil. The first records of the region date from the 950s. The region belonged to the medieval Serbian kings who leased it to Dubrovnik; from 1808 to 1918 it was under Austrian occupation. In October 1991, during the civil war in **Croatia,** heavy fighting erupted in Konavle between the **JNA** and Croatian paramilitary forces.

KONJEVIĆ, PETAR (1883–1970). One of the best Serbian opera composers and member of the **Serbian Academy of Sciences and Arts.** He was the director of the **Zagreb** opera, the manager of the **Osijek** opera, and one of the founders of the Academy of Music and the Institute of Musicology in **Belgrade**. Konjević's operas were inspired by folk music. His work includes the operas *Knez od Zete* (*Prince of Zeta*), *Koštana*, and *Seljaci* (*Peasants*).

KOPAONIK. Biggest mountain massif in **Serbia**, rising to 2,017 m. The massif extends approximately north-south from Mt. Željin to **Kosovo and Metohija**. It is the biggest mining region in Serbia, with silver, iron, zinc, copper, molybdenum, and antimony mines. It is also a modern ski resort and a center of Serbian tourism.

KORAĆ, RADIVOJE (1939–1969). Celebrated Yugoslav basketball player and one of the best European players in the 1960s. Shortly after his tragic death in an automobile accident, the European Basketball Association established the "Radivoje Korać Cup," one of the most competitive basketball tournaments in Europe.

KORAĆ, VOJISLAV (1924– ). Well-known Serbian art historian, university professor, and member of the **Serbian Academy of Sciences and Arts**. His major studies include *Graditeljska škola pomorja* (*Architectural School of Pomorje*) and *Studenica Hvostanska* (*Studenica of Hvost*).

KORDUN. Karst region between the Karlovac Valley and **Bosnian Krajina,** north of Plitivička jezera. The region encompasses an area of 1,486 sq km and had a population of 43,410 in 1991. The region embraces the former **commune** centers Slunj, Vojnić, and Vrgin most. An economically backward region whose main industry is agriculture. Kordun was the first defense line against the Turks during the existence of the **Vojna Krajina.** With an absolute majority of Serbian population, Kordun became a part of the **Republic of Serbian Krajina** in 1991. The Serbian population fled the region during the offensive of the Croatian army in August 1995.

KOROŠEC, ANTON (1872–1940). Slovenian and Yugoslav politician and the leader of Slovenska ljudska stranka (Slovene National Party). He held various ministerial posts, including minister of interior and prime minister. A conservative politician and Slovene nationalist, he advocated Slovene participation in Yugoslavia as the most opportune and temporary solution for achieving Slovenian independence.

KOSAČE. Serbian feudal family from **Bosnia and Hercegovina.** The most prominent members of the family were **Vlatko Vuković,** Sandalj Hranić, and Stefan Vukčić.

KOSOVO AND METOHIJA/KOSOVO I METOHIJA (KOSMET). Autonomous region and administrative unit in **Serbia**; total area 10,887 sq km, having a population of 1,956,196 in 1991. The ethnic composition of the province in 1991 was: 81 percent Albanians; 10 percent Serbian; 3.2 percent Muslim; 1 percent Montenegrin; and 2.3 percent Gypsy. The region consists of two parts: **Kosovo Polje** and the **Metohija** Valley and is predominantly rural and traditionally the most backward region in Serbia and Yugoslavia (illiteracy rate above 10 percent). Agriculture, mining, and energy production are the main sectors of the region's economy: several thermoelectric and hydroelectric plants have a total capacity exceeding 1000 megawatts; **Trepča is** the biggest lead and silver mine in Europe.

Serbian tribes populated Kosovo and Metohija in the seventh century. After **Stefan Nemanja**'s victory over the Byzantine Empire, first Kosovo and then Metohija became incorporated into **Raška**. After that, the region became an economic, cultural, and spiritual center of medieval Serbia. The mines Trepča, **Zvečan, Novo Brdo**; churches and monasteries **Dečani, Gračanica, patriarchate of Peć,** and cities **Prizren, Priština,** and Janjevo date from that time. The region severely decayed during the Turkish occupation 1459–1912, especially after Velika Seoba (see **Seoba Srba**) under **Arsenije III Crnojević** in 1690 and **Arsenije IV Jovanović-Šakabenta** in 1737. The Serbian exodus from Kosovo and Metohija continued up to 1912, when the region was liberated in the **Balkan wars.** Serbs were mainly replaced by Albanian tribes who moved into the valley from the surrounding mountains. This substantially changed the ethnic composition of the region.

During **World War II**, the local Albanian population joined armed units of **Balisti**, who fought for the separation of the region. The persecution and atrocities committed by the Balisti against the Serbs augmented already existing ethnic strife between the two groups. After the war, the Kosovo and Metohija region was given the administrative status of an autonomous province within Serbia. In 1966, following the removal of **Aleksandar Ranković**, the last high ranking Serb in the Communist bureaucracy, a severe Albanian nationalist euphoria erupted in Kosovo and Metohija. Although the public unrest was quelled by force in 1968 and in 1972, **Tito** decided to further extend the autonomy of the region. These measures, followed by continuous Serbian migration from the region, resulted in complete domination by the Albanian population in the region.

In 1981, destructive demonstrations erupted in several big cities throughout the region. The demonstrators, led by an underground organization called the "Marxist-Leninist Party of Kosova," demanded the status of a republic for the region and protested Serbian "domination." The unrest continued throughout the 1980s despite strong police actions in the region.

In 1988, **Slobodan Milošević**, the new leader of Serbia, initiated several changes in the status of the region. After removing the local leadership of the **Communist Party** and imposing emergency measures, the status of the autonomous province was officially changed by adopting amendments to the **Constitution** of Serbia in 1989. The changes substantially lowered the level of the province's autonomy. Following the collapse of the **Socialist Federal Republic of Yugoslavia,** Albanian secessionists proclaimed the "Republic of Kosovo" in 1992. Currently, the ethnic division in the province is almost complete. The Albanian population refuses to take part in any activities supervised by the Serbs, including medical care and education.

In February 1998, after a series of incidents and isolated attacks on Serbian police, an all-out armed rebellion led by the **Kosovo Liberation Army** (KLA) erupted in Kosovo and Metohija. The Serbian police responded quickly and forcefully, killing a number of Albanians in a village in the Drenica region. This prompted the U.S. and NATO to issue a stern warning to the Yugoslav president Slobodan Milošević against the use of force. In the following months the KLA seized the initiative and in early June, according to Albanian sources, controlled almost one third of KOSMET. However, the increased terrorist activity of the KLA and its unwillingness to accept a Western platform for peaceful negotiation, as well as Russian support for the Yugoslav government, changed the situation dramatically. In the beginning of August Serbian police launched a coordinated attack against KLA strongholds and re- opened all the major roads in the region. However, in early October 1998 NATO issued several warnings to Yugoslavia to cease its policing operations and to order the withdrawal of its forces from Kosovo and Metohija.

The Albanian political factions still refuse to actively participate in peaceful negotiations about the future status of KOSMET, despite Western opposition to their secessionist aspirations. In March 1999, following the breakdown of peace negotiations and Yugosalv rejection of the Rambulliet Accord, NATO launched a massive air-campaign against the Federal Republic of Yugoslavia. Following the Yugoslav acceptance of the G-8 accord, international forces entered the region in June 1999.

KOSOVO, BATTLE OF. (i) A historic battle between a Serbian army led by Prince **Lazar Hrebeljanović** and Turkish forces of Sultan Murad I, fought on June 28, 1389, at **Kosovo Polje**. Turkish expansion into the **Balkan Peninsula** and Southeast Europe rapidly intensified after the Serbian defeat in the **Battle of Maritsa** in 1371. The Turks conquered the lands of the **Mrnjavčević** family, and forced Bulgarian and Byzantine emperors into vassalage. Although substantially weakened, especially given the central power that disintegrated after the death of Emperor **Dušan the Mighty, Serbia** was still a major obstacle to further Turkish expansion in Europe. Following the Battle of Maritsa, Prince Lazar succeeded in solidifying his supremacy among the Serbian nobility. After several defeats in Serbia (**Paraćin,** 1381 and **Pločnik,** 1386) and in **Bosnia and Hercegovina** (Bileća, 1388), the Turkish sultan Murad I mustered a large army in Anatolia and advanced into the interior of Serbia. Prince Lazar's forces, aided by his son-in-law, **Vuk Branković**, and **Vlatko Vuković,** Hercegovina's **vojvoda,** confronted the Turks at Kosovo Polje (The Field of the Blackbirds) in the vicinity of the modern city of **Priština.**

At first, the Serbs appeared to be victorious; a Serbian noble, **Miloš Obilić**, succeeded in breaking through the Turkish lines and slew the sultan. At that moment, messengers were sent with news of a great Serbian victory. However, the confusion among the Turks was quickly quelled by **Bajazid**, the sultan's older son. He succeeded in surrounding and crushing the center of the Serbian army and taking prisoner and executing Prince Lazar. The outcome of the battle is still a matter of controversy. Although neither side had won from the strictly military point of view, Serbia lost its independence and became a vassal state to the Ottoman Empire soon after the Battle of Kosovo. The Battle of Kosovo symbolizes the end of medieval Serbia despite the fact that the Serbian state continued its existence until the fall of **Smederevo** in 1463.

(ii) A battle between the Ottoman forces and a Wallachian coalition led by the Hungarian commander János Hunyadi fought between October 17 and 20, 1448, at Kosovo. The coalition forces suffered a crushing defeat. This was the last major effort by Christian crusaders to free the Balkans and Europe from the Turks.

KOSOVO LIBERATION ARMY/OSLOBODILAČKA VOJSKA KOSOVA/ USHTRIA ÇLIRIMTARE e KOSOVËS (KLA). The name used for the Albanian guerilla fighters in **Kosovo and Metohija**. The first public appearance of KLA fighters was at the funeral of the Albanian teacher Halid Gecaj on November 28, 1997. Led by the radical elements amongst the Albanian secessionists, the KLA pursued a policy of direct military confrontation with the Serbian security forces, which led to the outbreak of the fighting in the region in February and March of 1998. The KLA forces whose initial tactics included the assassination of local Serbs and Albanians they considered "collaborators" and attacks on police posts and vehicles, received considerable funding from Kosovo Albanians working abroad. While initially successful, the KLA, which also operates from bases in neighboring Albania, suffered heavy losses during the offensive by Serbian security forces in August and September. Despite the heavy losses, the KLA gain an upper hand over the other Albanian political forces following the withdrawal of Yugoslav security forces form the region in June 1999.

KOSOVO POLJE. Valley in **Kosovo and Metohija**; 84 km-long and 14 km-wide, with a total area of 502 sq km. The biggest cities in the valley are **Priština, Kosovska Mitrovica,** Vučitrn, and Uroševac. The entire valley is very rich in minerals: coal, lignite, silver, lead, zinc, nickel, and magnesium. The metallurgical, chemical, and textile industries are well-developed. Several thermoelectric power plants are in operation. The **Battle of Kosovo** was fought in the region.

KOSOVSKA MITROVICA. City in the Serbian autonomous province of **Kosovo and Metohija** with a population of 104,805 (1991 estimate). The majority of the population is Albanian (82,837 in 1991). The city is situated at the confluence of the **Ibar** and **Sitnica** Rivers. The city was founded around the church of Saint Demetrius, whose name it also bears. The first records are from the 15th century. The Serbian population suffered big losses in 1690 in the aftermath of the Austro-Turkish war and **Seoba Srba**. A railhead of the Ottoman Empire before 1913, the city now lies on the **Belgrade-Kraljevo-Skoplje** railway. Kosovska Mitrovica has chemical and fertilizer industries and the **Trepča** mines are located in the immediate vicinity of the city.

*KOSOVSKI CIKLUS* (*Kosovo Poems*) Collection of epic folk poems on the **Battle of Kosovo** and its aftermath. Throughout the Turkish occupation, the poems played an important role in the preservation of a national identity among the **Serbs**.

KOSTIĆ, LAZA (1841–1910). Serbian poet, born in **Bačka**, one of the best representatives of romanticism in Serbian literature. Educated in **Novi Sad**, Buda, and Pest, he joined the nationalist youth movement of **Svetozar Miletić** and participated in several secret missions to **Serbia** and **Montenegro.** A controversial personality, he is considered an originator of modern Serbian poetry and the predecessor of the avant garde. Through his highly original work, he introduced several new literary modes into Serbian poetry. He translated several of Shakespeare's works into the **Serban language**. Among his poems three great ones are often singled out: "Spomen na Ruvarca" ("A Memory of Ruvarac"), "Jadranski Prometej" ("Adriatic Prometheus"), and "Santa Maria della Salute".

KOSTOLAC. Basin of lignite and a major energy center in **Serbia**, in the vicinity of **Požarevac.** The yearly coal production is above 2.5 million tons. Several thermoelectric plants operate here, with a total capacity exceeding 500 megawatts. The plants were heavily bombed during the NATO attack on Yugoslavia in the Spring 1999.

KOŠAVA. Strong, up to 100 km/h, eastern wind in northeastern Yugoslavia, especially in eastern **Serbia, Banat,** and **Pomoravlje.** The wind originates in the southern Ukraine and Carpathian mountains, while its season extends from autumn to the early spring.

KOŠTUNICA, VOJISLAV (1944– ). Serbian politician, president of the **Democratic Party of Serbia,** and a deputy in the Serbian **Parliament**. Due to his opposition to the **Constitution** of 1974 he lost his job at the Law School of the **University of Belgrade** in 1974. Although known as a principled politician Koštunica was unable to muster broad support for his party. His best known work is *Stranački pluralizam ili monizam* (*Party Pluralism or Monism*) which he co-authored with Kosta Čavoški.

KOTOR. Historic city, seaport, and resort at the south end of Kotor Bay in **Boka Kotorska** with a population of 22,496 in 1991. Kotor was founded by the Romans as Acruvium. In the 10th century it was an autonomous city ruled by Byzantium, while from 1186 to 1371 it was a free city of medieval **Serbia**. From 1395 to 1420 it was an independent republic; it subsequently came under Venetian and Austrian control until 1918. The major earthquake that hit **Montenegro** in 1979 heavily damaged the city. Kotor has been on the UNESCO list of world cultural heritage since 1979. The natural and cultural heritage of the region of Kotor comprises an area of 12,000 hectares of land and 2,600 hectares of sea. The city of Kotor has twelve town squares and the most important monuments are the Clock Tower (8th century), St. Tryphon's Church (the 12th century), St. Luke's Church (the 12th century), and the Pima Palace (the 16th century).

KOTROMANIĆI. Feudal family that ruled in **Bosnia and Hercegovina** from 1254 to 1463. The most prominent members of the family were Stefan I (r. 1290–1310), Stefan II (r. 1314–1353), and **Tvrtko I** (r. 1353–1391).

KOVAČEVIĆ, DUŠAN (1947– ). One of the most respected modern Serbian writers. He continued the comedy tradition of **Branislav Nušić**. His comedies were staged in theaters in Germany, Hungary, Poland, Great Britain, the United States, Ukraine, Czech Republic, and Slovakia. His best-known works include *Maratonci trče poslednji krug* (*The Marathoners' Victory Lap*), *Sabirni centar* (*The Collection Center*), and *Balkanski špijun* (*The Balkan Spy*).

KOZARA. Mountain in **Bosnian Krajina**, between the rivers **Sava, Una,**

**Vrbas,** and **Sana**. The mountain peaks at 920 m, with an average length of 75 km and width of 20 km, cover an area of 1,500 sq km. During **World War II**, Kozara was the **Partisans'** stronghold. In June 1942, a combined German and **Ustaše** force launched a major offensive against Kozara. While the offensive failed to achieve the desired objective—the destruction of Partisan forces—more than 60,000 mainly Serbian refugees were captured and sent to concentration camps in the **Independent State of Croatia.**

KRAGUJEVAC. City in **Serbia** on the Lepenica River, a center of the **Šumadija** region in which **Karađorđević** led the **First Serbian Insurrection** 1804–1813. The population of the city was 180,084 in 1991. Kragujevac is the center of the defense and automobile industries in the **Federal Republic of Yugoslavia.** The conglomerate Zavodi Crvena Zastava is one of the biggest European arms producers and the biggest automobile producer in the Balkans. The city also has pharmaceutical and chemical plants.

Kragujevac was founded in the 15th century and between 1818 and 1839 was the capital of Serbia. Long after the Serbian capital was moved to **Belgrade**, Kragujevac remained the cultural center of the country: the first gymnasium and printing factory were founded there in 1833; a theater in 1834; the Lycée in 1838; and a military academy in 1837. The first newspaper in Serbia, *Novine Srbska* (*Serbian Gazette*), was published in Kragujevac. During **World War II**, between October 20–23, 1941, the Germans executed several thousand people from Kragujevac between the ages 14 and 70.

KRAJINA. Literally "borderland" or "frontier," *krajina* was a term used for a territory that separated the Ottoman and Austrian Empires. See also BOSNIAN KRAJINA; VOJNA KRAJINA.

KRAJIŠNIK, MOMČILO (1937– ). Former representative of the **Republika Srpska** (RS) in the three-member Presidency of **Bosnia and Hercegovina** (B-H) after the September 1996 elections. Prior to this he was president of the **Parliament** of the RS (1991–1996) and president of the Parliament of B-H (1991–1992). Together with **Biljana Plavšić**, who later softened her stand, Krajišnik was a major proponent of a hard-line faction within the **Serbian Democratic Party** that advocates the complete territorial, political, and economic autonomy of the RS. Following the elections in September 1998, Krajišnik was replaced by Živko Radišić as the Serbian representative in the collective presidency of Bosnia and Hercegovina. See also BOSNIA AND HERCEGOVINA, ELECTIONS.

KRAJPUTAŠI (Wayside Tombstones). Tombstones erected by relatives at the place where members of their families had fallen in battle. Every tombstone bears an inscription telling a story of the life of ordinary people, often directly relating to the history of the entire Serbian nation.

KRALJEVIĆ MARKO (1335–1395). Oldest son of King Vukašin **Mrnjavčević.** After his father's death in the **Battle of Maritsa,** Prince Marko became a Turkish vassal. He was killed during the Battle of Rovine on May 17, 1395. Despite the fact that he was a Turkish vassal, Prince Marko became the greatest Serbian folk hero and a symbol of many virtues: courage, strength, honesty, etc.

KRALJEVINA SRBA, HRVATA, I SLOVENACA. See KINGDOM OF THE SERBS, CROATS, AND SLOVENES.

KRALJEVO. Industrial city in **Serbia** at the confluence of the **Ibar** with the **Western Morava** Rivers. The population of the city was 125,772 in 1991. Heavy industry includes the manufacture of railway rolling stock and fire-brick and the production of various electronic instruments and furniture. During **World War II**, as the result of the policy of retaliation according to which 100 **Serbs** were killed for one killed German soldier, the Germans executed 2,000 males from Kraljevo.

KRESTIĆ, VASILIJE (1932– ). Prominent Serbian historian, university professor, and chief archivist of the **Serbian Academy of Sciences and Arts**. He specializes in Croatian and Serbian history in the 19th and 20th centuries. His numerous works include *Srpsko-hrvatski odnosi i jugoslovenska ideja u drugoj polovini XIX veka* (*Serbo-Croatian Relations in the second half of the 19th century*) and *Istorija Srba u Hrvatskoj i Sloveniji 1848–1914 (History of the Serbs in Croatia and Slovenia 1848–1914*).

KRFSKA DECLARCIJA. See CORFU DECLARATION.

KRIŽANIĆ, PETAR-PJER (1890–1962). Prominent Yugoslav caricaturist. For most of his career he worked on ***Politika***. Križanić was best known for his work on politically inspired caricatures. He was the first president of the Union of Yugoslav Journalists. He is the author of three books on caricature *Naše muke* (*Our Sufferings*), *Kuku Todore* (*Ouch Todor*), and *Protiv fašizma* (*Against Fascism*).

KRUŠEVAC. Industrial city in **Serbia** located at the confluence of the Rasina and **Morava** Rivers. The population of the city was 138,111 in 1991. It is a prosperous agricultural center and also has strong chemical and machine-building industries. From 1371 the city was the center of Serbia during the reign of Prince **Lazar Hrebeljanović.**

KUČAN, MILAN (1941– ). President of **Slovenia** elected in 1990. Prior to Slovenia's secession from the **Socialist Federal Republic of Yugoslavia,** Kučan occupied several prominent posts in both the federal and local Communist bureaucracy, including as a member of the federal party Presidency and Presidency of the Slovenian party. As elected president of Slovenia, he actively supported the secessionist movement.

KULENOVIĆ, SKENDER (1910–1978). Serbian poet from **Bosnia and Hercegovina.** Together with Tanasije Mladenović, Čedomir Minderović, and Dušan Kostić, he was a proponent of the "social literature" in Serbian poetry after **World War II**. His best known work is an exceptionally successful poem called "Stojanka majka Knežopoljka" ("Mother Stojanka from Knežopolje").

KULIN (?–1204). **Ban** in Bosnia, ruled from 1180 to 1204, and a close ally of **Serbia**. His trade agreement with **Dubrovnik** in 1189 represents one of the oldest written records in the **Serbian language**. See also BOSNIA AND HERCEGOVINA.

KULUK. A mandatory work obligation initially introduced in **Serbia** during the Turkish occupation and usually used for public works such as road and bridge building. The obligation was abandoned during the **First Serbian Insurrection** but was re-introduced in a different form in 1864. Kuluk proved especially important during the **Balkan Wars** and **World War I** when it was extended to agricultural work. Public works continued to be used after the unification in 1918 as well as after **World War II**.

KUMANOVO, BATTLE OF. Main battle during the First Balkan War between the First, Second, and Third Serbian Armies and the Turkish Vardar Army. The battle began with a Turkish surprise attack, which was quelled by the heroic effort of the Danube Division. Following the repulse of the Turkish attack, Serbian forces launched a decisive counterattack and broke through the Turkish lines. The battle represented a major victory for the Serbian forces, which continued their advance through **Macedonia** and destroyed the Vardar Army in the **Battle of Bitolj.** See also BALKAN WARS

KUPRES. Small city in western **Hercegovina** with a population of 9,663 in 1991. The ethnic composition prior to the civil war was: 50.7 percent Serbian, 39.6 percent Croatian, and 8.4 percent Muslim. A stronghold of the **Ustaše** in **World War II**, Kupres was the site of heavy fighting during the civil war in **Bosnia and Hercegovina.**

KUREPA, ĐURO (1907–1993). Prominent Yugoslav mathematician. Born to a Serbian family in **Banija**, he graduated with a degree in mathematics from the University of **Zagreb**. In 1935, he obtained his doctorate at the Sorbonne in Paris. He taught at the University of Zagreb and **University of Belgrade**. Kurepa was a member of the **Serbian Academy of Sciences and Arts, Jugoslavenska akademija znanosti i umjetnosti**, Academy of Sciences of **Slovenia**, and Academy of Sciences of **Bosnia and Hercegovina**. He served on the editorial boards of several international journals. Kurepa published more than 140 books and 580 articles. He is particularly known for his work on the theory of partial sets.

## - L -

LAB. River in the **Kosovo Polje** region 68 km long. The valley of the Lab River, known as Little Kosovo, is a fertile agricultural region.

LADA. First art society in Serbia, founded in 1904 at the celebration of 100 years of the **First Serbian Insurrection.** The association became the Yugoslav Art League and was divided into four departments: Serbian, Croatian, Bulgarian, and Slovenian.

LALIĆ, IVAN V. (1931–1996). Serbian poet, the main representative of contemporary symbolism (neosymbolism) in Serbian poetry. His best works include poems "Bivši dečak" ("Former Boy") and "Pismo" ("The Letter").

LALIĆ, MIHAILO (1914–1992). Celebrated Yugoslav writer and member of the **Serbian Academy of Sciences and Arts.** His main motif is his native **Montenegro** during **World War II**. Lalić's work provides an exceptional account of the ethnopsychological heritage of the people of Montenegro. His work, for which he received numerous awards, includes *Lelejska gora*, (*Lelejska Mountain*), *Ratna sreća* (*Fortune of War*), *Zlo proljeće* (*Evil Spring*), and *Hajka* (*Chase*).

LANGUAGE, SERBIAN. South Slavic language spoken in **Serbia, Bosnia and Hercegovina, Croatia,** and **Montenegro**. The language has evolved from the old Church Slavonic, the creation of **Cyril and Methodius**, and can be written using both Cyrillic and Latin alphabets. Modern literary Serbian appeared in the 19th century as the result of the language reform of **Vuk Stefanović Karadžić**. He fundamentally reformed Church Slavonic to conform to the phonological and morphological structure of the Serbian language. Karadžić also reformed the Serbian **Cyrillic alphabet** and introduced an orthography in which the written word precisely reflected the spoken word. At that time, the Croats accepted the main dialect of the Serbian language, which led to the creation of the Serbo-Croatian, or Croato-Serbian, language. Since the proclamation of the *štokavski* (*stokavian*) dialect as the basis of Serbian and Croatian, the two languages have become very similar. However, since the beginning of the formation of the common state Croatian linguists have insisted on the separation of the Serbo-Croatian language. The calls for secession gained in strength after the proclamation of the *Deklaracija of imenu i mestu hrvatskog književnog jezika* (*Declaration on the Name and Position of Croatian Literary Language*) in 1967. This led to the continuous introduction of a massive number of new words so that the Croatian literary language would differ as much as possible from Serbian. The breakup of the **Socialist Federal Republic of Yugoslavia** and the ensuing civil war in Croatia and Bosnia and Hercegovina further led to the separation of the Serbo-Croatian language. Following the practice that existed in the **Independent State of Croatia,** the government of **Franjo Tudjman** introduced numerous artificially created words, idioms, and expressions.

LAPČEVIĆ, DRAGIŠA (1864–1939). Serbian journalist and politician, one of the founders and president of the Serbian **Social Democratic Party** 1903–1905, 1908–1911. At the second congress of the **Communist Party of Yugoslavia**, Lapčević supported a centrist position that opposed the radicalization of the party. He retired from political life in 1923. The author of more than fifty books including *Istorija socijalizma u Srbiji* (*History of Socialism in Serbia*), and *Rat i srpska socijalna demokratija* (*War and Serbian Social Democracy*).

LAZAR, HREBLJANOVIĆ, PRINCE (1329–1389). Serbian feudal lord and prince from 1371 to 1389. He was born in the vicinity of the medieval Serbian city of **Novo Brdo.** His father Pribac Hrebeljanović was chancellor at the Court of the Serbian emperor **Dušan the Mighty.** Lazar married **Milica,** the daughter of Serbian prince Vratko, and served at the Court of Emperor Dušan the Mighty and the last Serbian emperor, **Uroš II.** In 1370 he became a prince and lord of the lands around Rudnik; in 1371, after the **Battle of Maritsa** and the death of Emperor Uroš, he extended his realm to the valley of the **Morava** River. He cooperated closely with **Tvrtko I Kotromanić,** a **ban** of **Bosnia and Hercegovina,** whom he also helped to assume the title of king in 1377, after they defeated **Nikola Altomanović,** Lazar's chief rival in Serbia. Despite Tvrtko's coronation, Lazar remained the real ruler in **Serbia.** Prince Lazar's policy was directed toward the containing of Turkish advances into Europe. His forces defeated Turks on several occasions, including at the Battle of Dubračica and the **Battle of Pločnik** in 1386. In 1388 Lazar's army recaptured the city of **Pirot** from the Turks. Prince Lazar died in the **Battle of Kosovo** on June 28, 1389.

LAZAREVIĆ, LAZA (1851–1890). One of the best Serbian writers and one of the best educated and most sophisticated people of his time. His literary work realistically portrayed traditional Serbian life from a patriarchal perspective. An admirer of the patriarchal tradition and its values, he depicted family dramas in which the destructive forces are overcome by mutual love and unity. He is best known for his short stories which include, "On zna sve" ("He knows everything"), "Sve će to narod pozlatiti" ("The People Will Honor It All"), and "Prvi put s ocem na jutrenje" ("First Matins with My Father"). Lazarević was a prominent physician, published in world-renowned medical journals.

LAZAREVIĆ, LUKA (1774–1852). **Vojvoda** from the **First Serbian Insurrection.** His bravery was noticed at the Battle of Mišar on August 13, 1806, after which he was appointed commander of the Serbian garrison of the city of **Šabac.** He retained his post until 1813 when he went into exile after the insurrection collapsed. He returned to **Serbia** in 1832, but as a staunch opponent of the **Obrenović dynasty**, he was imprisoned by Prince **Mihailo Obrenović** during the rebellion of **Toma Vučić-Perišić** in 1842. After the dynastic change in 1842, he became a member of the State Council.

LAZARICA. Main church in the medieval city of **Kruševac** that belonged to Prince **Lazar Hrebeljanović**. The church was built shortly after 1374 and restored in 1904. It is known for its complex and unique exterior.

LAZARICE. Traditional Serbian custom. Early in the morning of the Sabbath of St. Lazarus young girls (*Lazarice*) gathered under the supervision of an older man (*Lazar*) and played **kolo** and sang traditional folk songs in front of houses, receiving various gifts.

LAZOVIĆI. Family known as makers of icons. Simeon Lazović and his son Aleksije Lazović made several icons in monasteries of the **patriarchate of Peć** and **Dečani.**

LEAGUE OF COMMUNISTS OF YUGOSLAVIA. See COMMUNIST PARTY OF YUGOSLAVIA.

LEPENSKI VIR. Prehistoric locality and an archeological site on the right bank of the **Danube** River, in the vicinity of **Đerdap.** The excavations date from 8000 B.C. and include objects that represent the first figure portrayals of humans.

LEPOGLAVA. Village close to the Croatian city of Varaždin, known for the large prison built by Austria-Hungary in 1854 and expanded in 1914. During **April's War** the government of the **Croatian Banovina** handed over the prison to the **Ustaše** forces, which summarily executed almost all of the prisoners. **Partisans** temporarily liberated the Lepoglava prison on July 13, 1943, freeing about 700 inmates. In February and March 1945, the Ustaše committed a massive slaughter of prisoners.

LESKOVAC. Economic and cultural center in south **Serbia** with a population of 161,986 in 1991. The city is situated in the fertile valley of the **Southern Morava** River and has a territory of 1250 sq km. Leskovac has major textile, chemical, and metal industries. It is the largest economic center of Southern Serbia. The first mention of the name Leskovac dates from 1300 in the charter of King **Milutin Nemanjić.** The city was captured by the Turks in 1427, given back to **Đurađ Branković,** Serbian **despot,** in 1444 and finally occupied by Turks under Sultan Mehmed II in 1454. The city remained under Turkish rule until January 1878, except during the **First Serbian Insurrection.** In April 1841, when the population of Leskovac rebelled against brutal Turkish rule, Turks brought Albanians from the town of Jablanica, who completely destroyed 104 Serbian villages and crushed the rebellion. During **World War I,** Leskovac was occupied by Bulgarians, who destroyed all private and public libraries in the city and deported more than 1,000 people into Bulgaria. During **World War II,** Leskovac was under Bulgarian and German occupation, being finally liberated on October 11, 1944.

*LETOPIS MATICE SRPSKE* (*The Annal of Serbian Literary Society*). Oldest literary journal in the Balkans, and in Europe. The first issue was published in **Novi Sad** in 1824. Until 1864, the journal was published in Buda (Budapest) under the title *Serbska Letopis* (*Serbian Annals*). Since then it has been continuously published in Novi Sad (the name changed in 1873).

*LETOPISI POPA DUKLJANINA* (*Chronicles of Father Dukljanin*). Annals written by a Catholic priest from **Bar** during the 12th century, pertaining to the history of **Dalmatia** and **Duklja** between the Sixth and 12th centuries. Based on legends and interpretations, the work is not a reliable historic source.

*LETOPISI* (*The Annals*). Historical annals of medieval Serbian literature corresponding to the Greek chronographs. *The Annals* include a general part pertaining to old world history and a specific part devoted to Serbian history. *The Annals* are divided into the older, which are longer and characterized by a superior style, and newer, which are shorter.

LIBERAL PARTY. Serbian political party founded and led by **Jevrem Grujić** in 1858. The party took an active part in removing Prince **Alexander Karađorđević** and restoring Prince **Miloš Obrenović**. In the early 1860s the party split into two factions, with the faction led by **Jovan Ristić** coming into power after the assassination of Prince **Mihailo Obrenović**. The Liberals ruled in Serbia from 1868 to 1873 and from 1875 to 1880.

The party changed its name to Narodna liberalna stranka (National Liberal Party) and was reorganized in 1881. Although the party lacked strength and remained in opposition, individual members participated in several Serbian governments. After a series of squabbles in 1904, the party was reorganized again and continued working under the name National Party (Narodna stranka) until 1922, when it disappeared from Serbian and Yugoslav politics. The party was reestablished in 1992 under the leadership of **Nikola Milošević**. The party currently lacks significant popular support.

LIKA. Region in the former Yugoslav republic of **Croatia** situated between the mountains **Velebit,** Velika and Mala Kapela, and Plješevica, and the sources of the **Una** and Zrmanja Rivers. Its area encompasses 5,563 sq km, and it had a population of 89,204 in 1991. The territory of Lika was divided into five counties: **Gospić,** Donji Lapac, Korenica, Otočac, and Gračac.

Prior to the arrival of **South Slavs** in the **Balkan Peninsula,** the region of Lika was populated or controlled by Illyrian tribes, Romans, Ostrogoths, and Byzantines. The first South Slav tribes arrived in Lika at the end of the sixth century. After the collapse of the Croatian Kingdom, Lika came under direct control of the Hungarian king, who held nominally the title of the king of Hungary and **Croatia.** After the **Battle of Kosovo** in 1389, and especially after the Turkish occupation of **Serbia,** a large number of **Serbs,** who left Serbia and **Bosnia and Hercegovina,** settled in Lika. Occasionally, Serbs were accompanied by **Vlachs**, nomadic herdsmen who also settled in Lika and northern **Dalmatia.** In 1480, Lika became a part of **Vojna Krajina,** but after the Battle of Krbava in 1493, Lika was occupied by Turks, who organized a **Sandžak** of Lika with the center in the city of **Knin.** After the Austro-Turkish War and the **Treaty of Carlowitz** Lika came under direct Austrian control. As part of **Vojna Krajina,** Lika was administratively, economically and culturally separated from Croatia. After the demise of Vojna Krajina in 1881, Lika remained under direct Austrian control, when it was administratively included into the Croatian part of the Austro-Hungarian Empire.

Serbs from Lika, who constituted the vast majority of the population in the region since the late 14th century, suffered greatly during **World War II** under the Nazi-backed regime of the **Independent State of Croatia.** During the war, Lika lost more than 20 percent of its population, 28,587 houses were burned to the ground, and more than 60,000 people lost their homes. After World War II a number of Serbs from Lika were settled in **Vojvodina,** which further decreased Lika's population.

Economically and culturally, Lika was one of the most backward regions in Croatia. In 1990, after the nationalist **Croatian Democratic Union,** headed by **Franjo Tudjman,** won multiparty elections in Croatia, Serbs from Croatia organized a plebiscite on Serbian autonomy in Croatia. The plebiscite was held between August 19 and September 2, 1990, and on September 21, the Autonomous Region of Krajina was proclaimed, consisting of the counties from Northern Dalmatia and Lika. When, after the unilateral secessions of **Slovenia** and Croatia on June 26, 1991, the civil war erupted in the former Yugoslavia, the Autonomous Region of Krajina was joined with the rest of the territories in Croatia where Serbs constituted a majority of the population, and the **Republic of Serbian Krajina** was formed. Lika was conquered by the Croatian army in an offensive that started on August 1, 1995. Fleeing the advancing Croatian troops, most of the population of Lika abandoned their homes and escaped into the **Republika Srpska** and the **Federal Republic of Yugoslavia.**

LILIĆ, ZORAN (1953– ). Vice president of the federal government, vice president of the **Socialist Party of Serbia** (SPS), and former president of the **Federal Republic of Yugoslavia** (FRY). Lilić who occupied relatively minor posts within the SPS became president of the FRY after the removal of **Dobrica Ćosić** in 1993. Essentially a subordinate to **Slobodan Milošević**, Lilić's role in Yugoslav politics was mainly confined to ceremonial duties. He was the main candidate of the SPS in the first round of the Serbian presidental election in 1997. Unable to defeat **Vojislav Šešelj** he was replaced by **Milan Milutinović** who won the second round.

LIM. River in **Montenegro,** 220 km long, longest tributary of the **Drina** River. The river is very rich in hydroenergy. Hydroelectric plants, "Kokin brod" "Bistrica," "Potpeć," are built on the Lim River.

LISBON AGREEMENT. **European Community**-brokered agreement on political and territorial arrangements in **Bosnia and Hercergovina** (B-H) between Muslim, Croat, and Serb representatives. The agreement envisioned the recognition of the external borders of B-H and endorsed the formation of national territorial units ("cantons") within B-H. The agreement was signed on February 24, 1992, but **Alija Izetbegović,** under pressure from the power brokers of the Muslim-only **Party of Democratic Action,** refused to ratify it.

LITTLE ENTENTE. Defense agreement between Yugoslavia, Romania, and Czechoslovakia 1920–1938. The primary objective of the alliance was to suppress the influence of Hungary in the **Danube** Basin and to protect each member's territory and political independence. France functioned as the coordinator with which all three countries negotiated separate treaties. Following Hitler's seizure of power in 1933, the three countries established a Permanent Secretariat and a Permanent Council to direct a common foreign policy. German economic penetration into the region, the death of King **Alexander I Karađorđević** in 1934, and the weakening of France after German occupation of the Rhineland in 1936 undermined the political value of the entente. The entente collapsed after the German annexation of the Sudeten area of Czechoslovakia in September 1938.

LONDON, TREATY OF. Treaty between the Allied countries (France, Great Britain, Russia) and Italy concluded in London on April 26, 1915. In order to persuade Italy to enter the war against Austria-Hungary, the Allies offered her considerable territorial concessions, including almost all the Adriatic islands and northern **Dalmatia.**

LOZNICA. City and **Commune** center in northwestern **Serbia** with a population of 86,875 in 1991. Production of wood pulp and viscose are major industries.

LUBARDA, PETAR (1907–1974). Serbian painter, the most prominent representative of postimpressionism and expressionism. He extensively utilized motifs from national history. Lubarda is the recipient of several prominent international awards (Sao Paolo, Tokyo, etc.).

LUKIĆ, RADOMIR (1914– ). Serbian law expert and sociologist, and a member of the **Serbian Academy of Sciences and Arts.** His works include *Politička teorija države* (*Political Theory of the State*), and *Osnovi sociologije* (*The Foundation of Sociology*).

## - LJ -

LJOČIĆ, DRAGA (1855–1937). The first woman physician in **Serbia.** She participated in all Serbian wars in the 1875–1918 period.

LJOTIĆ, DIMITRIJE (1885–1945). Serbian politician, the leader of the neo-fascist organization, **Zbor.** During **World War II,** he actively collaborated with the German occupation forces.

LJUBIBRATIĆ, MIĆO (1839–1889). Serbian **vojvoda** from **Hercegovina,** one of the leaders of the **Rebellions of Hercegovina** 1857–1862 and 1875–1878; especially active in the military training of the insurrectionists.

LJUBIĆ. Suburb of **Čačak**; the site of a battle between 1,500 Serbian rebels led by Prince **Miloš Obrenović** and 5,000 Turkish soldiers in 1815. The battle was the first big victory of the **Serbs** in the **Second Serbian Insurrection.**

LJUBLJANA. Capital city, cultural and economic center of **Slovenia,** with a population of 323,291 in 1991. Textiles, footwear, electric consumer goods, and turbines for hydroelectric stations are produced here.

LJUBOJEVIĆ, LJUBOMIR (1950– ). One of the best Yugoslav grandmasters of all times. A native of Belgrade, he became an international grandmaster in 1971. He won first place in several major international chess tournaments. An exceptionally strong tactical player, Ljubojević relies more on his intuition than on minute theoretical preparations. In 1981 he was officially ranked the third strongest player in the world.

LJUBOSTINJA. Monastery in the vicinity of Trstenik, the legacy and the burial site of **Milica**, wife of Prince **Lazar Hrebeljanović.**

LJUBOTEN. Peak of **Šar Mountain** in **Serbia** (2,496 m), overlooking the **Kačanička klisura.**

## - M -

MACEDONIA. (i) The central part of the **Balkan Peninsula,** covering about 66,000 sq km. From ancient times the entire region has been traversed by important commercial and military corridors. Consequently, various empires—the Byzantine, Serbian, Bulgarian, and Ottoman—fought relentlessly for control over it. After the **Balkan wars** in 1913, the region was divided between **Serbia,** Bulgaria, and Greece. The territorial partition essentially followed the geographic division of the region: Vardar Macedonia was acquired by Serbia, Pirin Macedonia came under Bulgarian control, and Aegean Macedonia became part of Greece. This division, with the minor changes following **World War I**, continued until the present day, the only difference being the formation of the new, independent political unit called the **Former Yugoslav Republic of Macedonia** in 1992.

(ii) A former constituent republic of the **Socialist Federal Republic of Yugoslavia** (SFRY), occupying 25,713 sq km and having a population of 2,033,964. According to the census of 1991, ethnic Macedonians accounted for 64.6 percent of the population, ethnic Albanians 21 percent, ethnic Turks 4.8 percent, and **Serbs** 2.1 percent. **Skoplje** is the capital city (pop. 563,000 in 1991).

The country is predominantly mountainous, with several depressions and the valley of the **Vardar** River. Macedonia has a mild climate resembling the Continental type with distinct seasonal contrasts. The region is rich in minerals: lead, zinc, nickel ore, iron ore, cooper, pyrite, uranium, silver, and magnesium. In 1990, coal production was 6.6 million metric tons, and, in the same year, 6,000 metric tons of aluminum were produced. Although it was one of the least-developed Yugoslav republics, the real growth rate of Macedonia's GDP between 1956 and 1989 was 5.2 percent. In 1991, the respective share of industry and agriculture in the republic's GDP were 52.9 percent and 14 percent. The principal industrial activities were metallurgy and textiles. Traditionally, dairy farming was the most important sector in Macedonia's agriculture: in 1990, milk production totalled 217,000 metric tons.

**South Slavs** moved into the ancient province of Macedonia during the sixth century. The region was continuously contested by Bulgaria, Serbia, and the Byzantine Empire. After the consolidation of the medieval Serbian state under the **Nemanjić** dynasty, Macedonia became culturally, economically, and politically incorporated into Serbia. In 1345,

Emperor **Dušan the Mighty** proclaimed Skoplje the capital of Serbia. The Turkish occupation extended from 1395 to 1912. After the abolition of the **patriarchate of Peć** in 1776, Macedonia came under the jurisdiction of the patriarchate of Constantinople, which led to the intense Hellenization of the region. This was followed by the strong Bulgarization of Macedonia after the establishment of the Bulgarian **exarchate** in 1870. In the late 1890s, there were about 1,400 Greek schools and between 600 and 700 Bulgarian schools in Macedonia. The Serbian resistance to Bulgarization and Hellenization led to the founding of more than 100 Serbian schools at the end of the 19th century. In 1912, there were more than 400 Serbian schools in northern Macedonia with 17,453 pupils. A high school, and junior high school, and merchant academy were established in Skoplje, Salonika, and Bitolj. The formation of the **Internal Macedonian Revolutionary Organization** in 1893, under Bulgarian auspices, further intensified the Serbo-Bulgarian rivalry in Macedonia. Pro-Serbian elements in Macedonia organized **Četniks** squadrons that fought both Turkish troops and Bulgarian *comitadji*. Macedonia was not able to liberate and constitute itself as an independent nation. The primary reason for this was the lack of national identity among the majority of the population and the specific economic and political circumstances created by Ottoman feudalism and Greek and Bulgarian cultural domination.

The Balkan wars (1912–1913), were followed by the division of Macedonia among Serbia, Bulgaria, and Greece. Vardar Macedonia became a part of Serbia, known as South Serbia, and after **World War I** was incorporated into the **Kingdom of the Serbs, Croats, and Slovenes**. During **World War II**, Macedonia was divided between Bulgaria and the Italian-sponsored puppet state of "Greater" Albania. The resistance movement in Macedonia was organized by the rival **Jugoslovenska vojska u otadžbini** and Communist **Partisans**, who gained the upper hand after 1943. After the war, the Communist government, led by **Tito**, granted federal status to the territory of Macedonia and created a new ethnic identity—Macedonian. Macedonians were given the status of a constituent nation of the SFRY. In the late 1940s a new language was created by replacing the northern variant (close to the **Serbian language**) with southern dialects (closer to the Bulgarian literary language). Besides the language, the federal government sponsored a process of national awakening, including the creation of the autocephalus Macedonian Orthodox Church in 1968, despite the bitter opposition of the **Serbian Orthodox Church**. The process of building the Macedonian nation was heavily influenced by fostering anti-Serbian feelings among the Slavic population of the republic, especially by perpetuating the fear of Serbian expansionism and nationalism. Anti-Serbian frenzy, the extreme expression of Macedonian nationalism, found its most vocal proponent in the Internal Macedonian Revolutionary Organization-Democratic Party for Macedonian National Unity. The party, campaigning almost exclusively on an anti-Serbian agenda, won the majority of votes in the first multiparty **elections** in Macedonia in November–December 1990. However, the elections did not give an absolute majority to any party, and a coalition administration was formed in January 1991 with **Kiro Gligorov** of the League of Communists of Macedonia-Party of Democratic Reforms as president of Macedonia.

During the civil war in Yugoslavia that followed the unilateral secessions of Croatia and **Slovenia** in June 1991, Macedonia proclaimed its "neutrality." After a referendum on the republic's sovereignty and independence was held on September 7, 1991, the new constitution was enacted, and Macedonia was declared to be an independent country on November 17, 1991. Although the **European Community** (EC) Commission acknowledged that Macedonia fulfilled the requirements for official recognition, Greek objections to the name "Macedonia" and the use of the Star of Vergina on the republic's national flag, prevented EC recognition in January 1992. Despite Greek objections and a subsequent trade embargo (February 1994), Macedonia was admitted to the United Nations (UN) under the name the **Former Yugoslav Republic of Macedonia** in April 1993. This enabled Macedonia to become a member of the International Monetary Fund (IMF) and to gain access to financial markets. The United Kingdom, Germany, France, and the Netherlands officially recognized Macedonia in December 1993. The United States officially recognized Macedonia in February 1994, despite Greece's presidency of the European Union. Macedonia faces a serious problem in respect to the substantial Albanian minority. The relationship between the Macedonian authorities and the ethnic Albanian minority has deteriorated continuously since the proclamation of the republic's independence. The referendum of the Albanian minority held in January 1992 overwhelmingly favored the establishment of **Ilirida**, an Albanian republic, in western Macedonia. After a massive Albanian demonstration in Skoplje on November 6, 1992, the UN Security Council authorized the dispatch of a UN peace keeping force (including a United States contingent). Nevertheless, the tension between the two ethnic groups continued and presented a major challenge to Macedonia's security. The problem of internal security became especially apparent after the assassination attempt on President Gligorov in October 1995.

The economic situation worsened continuously after the republic's secession from Yugoslavia in 1991. The terms of trade deteriorated due to the loss of the Serbian market, and later the Greek-imposed trade embargo; by 1993 industrial production had plummeted by 75 percent; the unemployment rate was 35 percent; and the monthly inflation rate was 15 percent. However, due to the IMF backing and restrictive monetary policies Macedonian currency (*denar*) became convertible in the June 1998.

MAČEK, VLADKO (1879–1964). Croatian and Yugoslav politician; the leader, after the death of **Stjepan Radić**, of the nationalist **Croatian Peasant Party**. After the **Cvetković-Maček Agreement** and the creation of the **Croatian Banovina**, Maček became a vice premier of the Yugoslav government. In 1941, after the formation of the **Independent State of Croatia**, Maček called upon Croats to cooperate with the **Ustaše** regime. In 1945, Maček emigrated to Paris and later to the United States, where he wrote *In the Struggle for Freedom*.

MAČVA. Fertile region in northwest **Serbia**, between the **Drina** and **Sava** Rivers. The region covers an area of 800 sq km and had a population of 339,644 in 1991. It is mainly an agricultural region, with industrial centers in **Šabac** and **Loznica**.

MAGLAJ. City and **Commune** center in **Bosnia and Hercegovina**, located on the right bank of the **Bosna** River with a population of 43,294 in 1991. The ethnic composition prior to the civil war was: 45.4 percent Muslim, 30.7 percent Serbian, 19.3 percent Croatian, and 3.4 percent Yugoslav. Production of wood pulp and paper are important industries in the city and its vicinity. The first records of the city date from 1503.

MAGLIĆ. Remnants of a medieval Serbian city, southwest of **Kraljevo**. The city, one of the finest examples of Serbian medieval architecture, was founded between the 13th and 14th centuries.

MAJDANPEK. Miners' city and **Commune** center in eastern **Serbia** with a population of 27,326 in 1991. Center of the pyrite, cooper, gold, and silver mines in the **Bor** basin. One of the oldest mines in Serbia, dating from Roman times, is located in the immediate vicinity of Majdanpek.

MAJSKA DEKLARACIJA. See MAY'S DECLARATION.

MAJSKI PREVRAT. See MAY'S ASSASSINATION.

MAKARIJE, SOKOLOVIĆ. See SOKOLOVIĆ, MAKARIJE.

MAKSIMOVIĆ, DESANKA (1898–1993). One of the most popular Serbian poets of the twentieth century and a member of the **Serbian Academy of Sciences and Arts**. She is best known for her sensitive, unpretentious, and melodic style. Her best-known works include poems "Zeleni vitez" ("Green Knight"), "Miris zemlje" ("Scent of the Earth"), "Nemam više vremena" ("I do not have anymore time"), and "Tražim pomilovanje" ("I'm Asking for Pardon").

MAKSIMOVIĆ, IVAN (1924– ). Prominent Serbian economist, professor of the Law School of the **University of Belgrade** and a member of the **Serbian Academy of Sciences and Arts**. Born and educated in Belgrade, Maksimović was president of the Association of Yugoslav Economists and the Association of Serbian Economists. His best-known works include *Osnovne karakteristike savremene ekonomske nauke* (*Main Characteristics of the Contemporary Economic Studies*), and *Teorijski osnovi društvene svojine* (*Theoretical Basis of Social Property*).

MAMULA, BRANKO (1921– ). Retired admiral of the Yugoslav navy and former federal defense minister of the **Socialist Federal Republic of Yugoslavia**. Although retired at the time of the civil war (1991), Mamula presumably had substantial leverage on the actual defense minister, General **Veljko Kadijević**.

MANASIJA. Monastery in the vicinity of Despotovac, built between 1406 and 1418, the legacy of **Stefan Lazarević**. Also known under the old name **Resava**, the monastery was a cultural center of Serbia in the 15th century.

MARA (?–1487). Daughter of **Đurađ Branković**, wife of the Turkish sultan Murad II. After Murad's death, Mara was bequeathed the regions of

**Toplica** and Dubočica. She opposed Hungarian influence in **Serbia** and was a strong proponent of Serbia's reliance on the Turks.

MARČA. Monastery in **Slavonia** built by Serbian migrants from **Serbia** and **Bosnia and Hercegovina** in 1526. In 1609, the monastery became the center of the bishopric, until it was expropriated by the Greek Catholics in 1753. See also USKOKS.

MARINKOVIĆ, JOSIF (1851–1931). One of the most celebrated Serbian composers and choir leaders. Born in **Banat**, he studied in Prague and Vienna. Marinković was the most prominent representative of Serbian national romanticism. His best works include the chorales *Junački poklič* (*Heroic Clamor*) and *Narodni zbor* (*People's Flock*).

MARINKOVIĆ, PAVLE (1866–1925). Serbian politician and journalist, one of the leaders of the **Progressive Party**. He also founded the Ethnographic Museum and the Women Teachers' School.

MARINKOVIĆ, VOJISLAV (1876–1935). Serbian politician and statesman, the leader of the **Progressive Party** after the death of **Stojan Novaković** in 1915. After **World War I**, together with **Ljubomir-Ljuba Davidović**, **Milorad Drašković**, and **Svetozar Pribićević** he founded the Demokratska zajednica (Democratic Union), which was transformed into the **Democratic Party**. He was foreign minister in various Yugoslav governments and prime minister in 1932.

MARINOVIĆ ASSEMBLY. Session of the Serbian **Parliament** (Assembly) convened on November 27, 1873. The government of **Jovan Marinović** presented several far-reaching reform laws among which a law on the subsidization of industrial enterprises and the law on six days of land were the most important. The former authorized the government to grant various privileges and concessions to new industries, while the latter protected the peasant from forfeiting his land (a "day" equalled 5,760 sq m) in order to pay a debt. In addition, the government introduced the metric system and a native silver currency.

MARINOVIĆ, JOVAN (1821–1893). Serbian politician born in **Bosnia and Hercegovina** and a leader of the **Conservatives**. Educated in Paris, he believed in enlightenment and culture in the European style. He occupied several important political posts, including prime minister of the Conservative cabinet of 1873–1874. His cabinet established, by administrative fiat, freedom of speech and the press. On December 23, 1873, the cabinet instituted the law by which corporal punishment was abolished and the prison system was reformed. Two additional laws introduced educational reforms and the **Great School** was given greater autonomy. See also MARINOVIĆ ASSEMBLY.

MARITSA, BATTLE OF. Battle between the Serbian army of King Vukašin **Mrnjavčević** and his brother **Despot** Jovan Uglješa Mrnjavčević and Turkish forces, fought on September 26, 1371, in the vicinity of the Bulgarian city Chernomen on the Maritsa River. Rulers of Serbian lands in **Macedonia** and the most powerful feudal lords in **Serbia** after the death of Emperor **Dušan the Mighty,** Vukašin and Uglješa decided to stop further Turkish penetration into the **Balkan Peninsula.** After mustering a massive army, they surrounded the Turkish forces at Chernomen. Although vastly outnumbered, the Turkish forces surprised the **Serbs** and during a stormy night completely annihilated the Serbian army. Vukašin and his brother were killed in the battle. The battle definitely ended Serbian supremacy in the Balkans and ushered in the Ottoman domination of that region.

MARJANOVIĆ, MIRKO (1937– ). Serbian politician, prime minister of the Serbian Government, and general manager (president) of "Progress," a leading trade company in **Serbia** and the **Federal Republic of Yugoslavia.** Born in **Knin**, Marjanović graduated with a degree in economics from the **University of Belgrade**. He became prime minister in 1994 and is considered a main proponent of the rapid privatization of the Serbian economy under government auspices.

MARJAŠ. Twentieth part of a **dinar**; a nickel coin of five *paras* used in **Serbia** before **World War I**.

MARKOVIĆ, JEVREM (1848–1878). Older brother of **Svetozar Marković**. An officer of Serbian army, he was a professor at the military academy. His units liberated **Pirot** and Bela Palanka during the **Serbo-Turkish wars**. He was falsely accused of participating in the **Rebellion of Topola** and executed in 1878.

MARKOVIĆ, MIHAILO (1923– ). Prominent Serbian and Yugoslav philosopher and politician, and President of the Department of Philosophy and Social Theory of the **Serbian Academy of Sciences and Arts**. Marković was removed from the **University of Belgrade** in 1975 for his criticism of the totalitarian tendencies of **Tito.** In 1990, he joined and became vice president of the **Socialist Party of Serbia.** As a representative of the "hard nationalist" line in regard to the status of the **Republic of Serbian Krajina**, Marković was removed from the Executive Board of the SPS in December 1995, following the **Dayton Agreement** and **Paris Peace Treaty**. Marković's representative work includes *From Affluence to Praxis*, *Democratic Socialism*, and *Theory and Practice*.

MARKOVIĆ, MIRJANA (1942– ). One of the founders and leaders of the **JUL** (Yugoslav Left), university professor and wife of the president of **Serbia, Slobodan Milošević**. Marković is an outspoken advocate of womens' rights and a strenuous fighter against nationalism. She is the author of several textbooks and monographs: *Sociologija* (*Sociology*), *Odgovor* (*Rejoinder*), and others. Various political observers often emphasize that, although not holding any political posts in Serbian and Yugoslav government, she exerts considerable influence in everyday political life.

MARKOVIĆ REFORM. Drastic increase in the prices of oil and international interest rates in the late 1970s and the beginning of the 1980s, forced the Yugoslav government to seek rescheduling of its foreign debt (1982). The rescheduling of debt and drastic import restrictions improved the current account balance and reduced the foreign debt by three billion U.S. dollars by 1989. However, import restrictions adversely affected and halted the growth of the Yugoslav economy. The excess of demand in domestic markets, cost-ineffective self-managed enterprises, growing budget deficits, and excessive printing of money resulted in rapid inflation which reached 2,500 percent per year by the end of 1989.

After replacing Branko Mikulić as prime minister of the **Socialist Federal Republic of Yugoslavia** (SFRY) (March 17, 1989), Ante Marković announced the implementation of a comprehensive program of radical economic reforms on December 18, 1989. The program essentially echoed the Polish experiment designed by the World Bank economist Geoffrey Sachs (who also served as a paid advisor to Marković). The key elements of the reform were (1) introduction of a new **dinar**, to exchange for the old dinar at a rate of 10,000 old to 1 new; (2) establishment of an exchange rate of seven dinars for one German mark; (3) proclaimation of the internal convertibility of the new dinar (allowing Yugoslav citizens to buy and sell unlimited amounts of foreign currency for current transaction purposes); (4) partial import liberalization (quotas were retained for a broad range of consumer goods); (5) deregulation and privatization of the economy; (6) partial price liberalization; (7) liberalization of the regulation of foreign direct investment, allowing foreigners to own 100 percent of an asset; (8) creation of a tight monetary policy.

Marković's "shock-therapy" yielded remarkable results: in less than six months the exorbitant inflation rate of 2,500 percent per year was reduced to zero, while the foreign exchange reserves grew by 80 percent, reaching 10 billion U.S. dollars. The restrictive monetary policy, however, backfired in the second half of 1990. Under the premise that the **National Bank** was going to continue monetary expansion, commercial banks engaged in interest rate speculation and became heavily exposed to loss-making enterprises. At the end of 1990, overexposure made the collapse of the commercial banking system imminent. Faced with the complete breakdown of the banking network, regional governments (a Serbian move in November 1990 was followed by the rest of the republics) rediscounted bank loans and effectively increased the money supply independently of the National Bank. The increase in money supply reignited inflationary pressure and forced Marković's government to devalue the currency in April 1991. The unilateral secessions of **Slovenia** and **Croatia** in June 1991 and the ensuing civil war effectively ended Marković's economic reform.

The populist policies of Serbian president **Slobodan Milošević** are often singled out as the primary cause of the failure of Marković's reform. While the action of the National Bank of Serbia in November 1990 did undermine the reform, it came merely as a reaction to the ominous conditions created by Marković's policies. While Marković's government liberalized the majority of prices, it retained tight control over the prices of energy, raw materials, and semifinished goods. Serbia, as the major energy producer in the SFRY, was put in an unequal position relative to Slovenia and Croatia. Furthermore, Marković's program failed to create a viable fiscal policy and did not create a safety net, necessary in the case of massive layoffs. While the absence of a rigorous and central fiscal policy favored the high income republics (Croatia and Slovenia), the absence of a safety net clearly hurt the import-dependant and labor-intensive economy of Serbia.

MARKOVIĆ, SIMA (?–1817). Serbian **Vojvoda** from the **First Serbian Insurrection** and member and president of the **Governing Council**. He was executed in 1817 for his participation in the rebellion against Prince **Miloš Obrenović.**

MARKOVIĆ, SIMA (1884–1937). Serbian and Yugoslav politician, one of the founders and secretary of the **Communist Party of Yugoslavia** (CPY). Marković belonged to the so-called "right-wing" faction, which opposed the bolshevization of the CPY. Expelled from the party in 1929 and readmitted in 1935, he was executed in the Soviet Union during Stalin's purge in 1937. A respected intellectual and talented mathematician, he wrote *Teorija relativnosti* (*Theory of Relativity*), and *Nacionalno pitanje u svetlosti marksizma* (*National Question through the Prism of Marxism*).

MARKOVIĆ, SVETOZAR (1846–1875). Founder of the socialist movement in **Serbia**. Sent to St. Petersburg, Russia, to study at the Institute of Roads and Communications, Marković fell under the influence of the Russian radical thinkers Chernyshevskii, Pisarev, and Tkachev. Upon continuation of his studies in Zürich, Marković became affiliated with the First International of Karl Marx. Marx's historical materialism and Chernyshevsky's agrarian socialism heavily influenced Marković's model. The essence of Marković's teaching was that Serbia might skip capitalism and pass directly into socialism via the **Zadruga** or cooperative communal system. Marković founded and edited several journals: ***Radenik*** (*Worker*) in 1871, ***Javnost*** (*The Public*) in 1873, and ***Oslobođenje*** (*Liberation*) in 1874. His major work is *Srbija na istoku* (*Serbia on the East*).

MARTIĆ, MILAN (1943– ). Head of the local militia station in the city of **Knin**, Martić rose to the post of interior minister of the **Republic of Serbian Krajina** (RSK) in 1991. In the 1993–1994 presidential elections he was backed by Serbian president **Slobodan Milošević** and defeated **Milan Babić**. However, his relationship with Milošević grew worse during 1994 and even more so in the beginning of 1995. Martić led a hard-line faction that refused to accept anything short of the full recognition of the political and territorial sovereignty of the RSK. He relied on the support of **Radovan Karadžić**, president of the **Republika Srpska** (RS). Martić continued his opposition to Milošević's initiative for autonomous status for the RSK even after the fall of western **Slavonia** in May 1995. Following the offensive of the Croatian army and the fall of the RSK in August 1995, Martić fled to the RS. He has been indicted for war crimes by The **Hague Tribunal.**

MASLENICA. Sea canal in **Dalmatia**; 4 km long and between 0.2 and 0.4 km wide. An impressive bridge (155 m long and 55 m high) over the canal that was the only continental connection between the northern Croatian coast and Dalmatia was destroyed during the fighting in 1991.

MAŠIN, DRAGA (1859–1903). Queen of Serbia 1900–1903. A lady-in-waiting of Queen Natalia, Draga, a young widow, became the mistress of King **Alexander Obrenović** in 1897. This led to their marriage in 1900, which in turn triggered a series of embarrassing political scandals. Draga was killed with Alexander in **May's Assassination**.

MATANOVIĆ, ALEKSANDAR (1930– ). Yugoslav grandmaster, vice president of the International Chess Federation (FIDE) and the main editor of *Šahovski informator* (*Chess Informant*), the leading chess publication in the world. He was the principal initiator and author of the *Encyclopedia of Chess Openings*, the world-renowned chess data source.

MATAVULJ, SIMO (1852–1908). Serbian writer born in Šibenik, **Dalmatia** and one of the best representatives of realism in Serbian literature. A western-type realist, Matavulj was under the influence of Italian and French prose writers and close to Maupassant. His best works include *Bakonja fra Brne* (*Bakonja of Priest Brne*), *Beogradske priče* (*Belgrade's Stories*), *S mora i planine* (*From Sea and Mountain*), and *Našljedstvo* (*The Inheritance*).

*MATICA* (*Society*). Literary journal published by **Matica Srpska** in **Novi Sad** between 1866 and 1870.

MATICA HRVATSKA (Croatian Literary Society). Oldest Croatian literary society, established in 1842 under the name Matica ilirska (Matica Hrvatska since 1874). In the mid-1960s, Matica hrvatska became a center of Croatian nationalism.

MATICA SRPSKA (MS) (Serbian Literary Society). Serbian educational and literary society founded in 1826 in Pest (Budapest) on the initiative of **Jovan Hadžić** and several other rich merchants. Matica continued to publish *Serbska Letopis* (later ***Letopis Matice Srpske***). In 1864, Matica was transferred to **Novi Sad**, where it has been located since.

MAY'S ASSASSINATION/MAJSKI PREVRAT. Term used for the last stage of conspiracy against and the assassination of King **Alexander Obrenović** and Queen **Draga Mašin** in 1903. In 1901, a group of seven young officers, brought together by Lieutenants Antonije Antić and **Dimitrijević Dragutin Apis** conspired to murder the royal leaders of **Serbia**. Besides the outrage caused by what they perceived as a shameful marriage between the king and an immoral woman, the **Conspirators**, as they became known in Serbia, were mainly motivated by the army's and Serbia's prolonged stagnation under Alexander's regime. After several unsuccessful attempts, the Conspirators, helped by several members of the king's guard, invaded the palace and killed the royal couple on the night of June 10–11 (May 28–29, Old Style). The assassination of Alexander ended the **Obrenović dynasty** and brought **Peter I Karađorđević** to power.

The dynastic change began a new period in Serbia's history. The period of political and economic subservience to Austria-Hungary had ended and rapid transformation of Serbia's economy and society had begun. The removal of the Conspirators from the political milieu in 1906 boosted the development of political democracy and allowed Serbia to reestablish ties with Great Britain and Western Europe. These changes proved to be of crucial importance for the continuation and successful conclusion of the struggle for Serbian national liberation.

MAY'S DECLARATION/MAJSKA DEKLARACIJA. Declaration of a group of Slovenian and Croat politicians made on May 18–19, 1917. Affirming their loyalty to the Habsburg crown, they called for the establishment of an autonomous Yugoslav territory within Austria-Hungary. The territory would consist of **Croatia** and **Slovenia** and would enjoy a status equal to Hungary. The declaration did not mention Serbs and undermined the efforts of the **Yugoslav Committee.**

MEDAKOVIĆ, DEJAN (1922– ). Prominent Serbian art historian and member of the **Serbian Academy of Sciences and Arts.** Born in **Zagreb,**

Medaković escaped from the **Ustaše** terror to Belgrade in 1941. An expert on Serbian baroque art, he is the recipient of numerous national and international awards. Besides a number of professional journal articles and monographs he wrote four books of poems and a five-volume autobiography, *Efemeris* (*Ephemerally*). His works include *Srpska umetnost u XVIII veku* (*Serbian Art in the 18th Century*), *Srpska umetnost u XIX veku* (*Serbian Art in th 19th Century*), and *Putevima srpskog baroka* (*On the Paths of the Serbian Baroque*).

MEŠTROVIĆ, IVAN (1883–1962). Celebrated and world-renowned Croatian and Yugoslav sculptor. At the beginning of his career most of his work was inspired by motifs from Serbian history (**Miloš Obilić,** Kosovka Devojka, **Marko Kraljević**). A strong supporter of the Yugoslav movement in his youth, Meštrović later turned to Croatian nationalism.

METHODIUS. See CYRIL AND METHODIUS.

METOHIJA. Fertile basin of the **Beli Drim** in the autonomous province of **Kosovo and Metohija** with a total area of 4,329 sq km and a population of 790, 272 (1991 estimate). The name of the region dates from medieval **Serbia** and indicates a large church estate. The fertility of the region is facilitated by a sub-Mediterranean climate, which allows two harvests per year. Metohija is rich in minerals (lignite, chrome) and in hydroenergy. The largest cities are **Peć, Prizren,** and **Đakovica**. A number of sacred monuments of medieval Serbian culture are located in Metohija, including the **patriarchate of Peć**, and **Dečani** monastery.

In the Spring of 1998 the **Kosovo Liberation Army** (KLA) began the armed attacks against Serbian police and general populace of Metohija. The intense fighting between the special units of the Serbian police and the KLA created an acute refugee problem in Metohija during the Summer 1998. In June 1999, following the withdrawal of Yugoslav security forces from the region, almost entire Serbian population was forced to leave Metohija.

MIĆUNOVIĆ, DRAGOLJUB (1930– ). Moderate Serbian and Yugoslav politician, president of the **Democratic Center** and a deputy in the federal **Parliament**. He was president of the **Democratic Party** from 1990 to 1994, when he resigned due to his disagreements with **Zoran Đinđić** and **Miodrag Perišić**. A professor at the **University of Belgrade,** he was banned from lecturing between 1970 and 1975 due to his involvement with the Praxis group. His best known works include *Nauka i filozofija* (*Science and Philosophy*), *Birokratija i javnost* (*Bureaucracy and the Public*), and *Socijalna filozofija* (*Social Philosophy*).

MIHAILO, KING (?–1081). Son of **Stefan Vojislav,** prince of **Zeta,** and the first Serbian king. Mihailo ruled as prince from 1052 to1077 and, after receiving royal insignia from Pope Gregor VII, as king from 1077 to 1081.

MIHAILO, OBRENOVIĆ PRINCE (1823–1868). Second son of Prince **Miloš Obrenović** and prince of **Serbia** 1839–1842 and 1860–1868. Mihailo became Prince after the death of Miloš's first son, Milan, in 1839. Still a minor, Mihailo was engulfed in a power struggle between the **Constitutionalists** and the supporters of the **Obrenović dynasty** and was forced to flee Serbia in 1842. He returned on his father's restoration to the throne in 1858 and became commander in chief of the army. In 1860, after Miloš's death, Mihailo was reinstated as ruling prince of Serbia.

Mihailo's reign was characterized by strong centralism. At the **Transfiguration Assembly** in 1861 he introduced several changes to the **"Turkish Constitution"** of 1838, abolished the Council, and diminished the power of the Assembly. The law on state administration of March 1862 further increased Mihailo's personal power in Serbia. Despite its lack of political freedoms, Serbia prospered during Mihailo's reign. The **Državna Hipotekarna Banka** was established (1862), the **Srpsko Učeno Društvo** was organized (1862), and the first Serbian coins since the Middle Ages were minted.

Mihailo's foreign policy, drawn up and implemented in close collaboration with foreign minister **Ilija Garašanin**, was based on an ambitious program of national liberation and the creation of a South Slavic state under his scepter. For that purpose, Mihailo instituted a 50,000-strong regular conscript army and organized the **Balkan League** by concluding treaties with **Montenegro** (1866), Greece (1867), and Romania (1868). During his rule **Serbia** greatly expanded its influence in the areas where ethnic Serbs were living and gained affirmation as the leader in the struggle against Turkey. War with Turkey was precluded by the opposition of Austria-Hungary and Russia and by the assassination of Mihailo on June 10, 1868.

MIHAILOVIĆ, DRAGOLJUB-DRAŽA (1893–1946). Colonel of the Yugoslav army and the leader of **Jugoslovenska vojska u otadžbini** (JVO). Following the collapse of Yugoslavia in **April's War** in 1941, Mihailović and a group of army officers gathered on the mountain Ravna Gora in May 1941 and organized an antifascist resistance movement known as the JVO, popularly called the **Četniks**. The government-in-exile rallied its support behind Mihailović and subsequently promoted him to general and minister of defense. During 1941, Mihailović and **Tito** discussed the possibility of joining their forces, the JVO and **Partisans**. The vast political differences between the two antifascist movements prevented such cooperation and led to a full scale civil war. Faced by the German cruelty in Serbia and genocide against the **Serbs** in the **Independent State of Croatia,** Mihailović avoided frontal clashes with the Germans and awaited a possible Allied invasion of the **Balkan Peninsula**. After the Teheran Conference and intense lobbying by the Soviet Union, Mihailović lost British and American support. In 1944, King **Peter II Karađorđević** was forced to remove Mihailović from his post of minister of defense. Although it enjoyed more support among the Serbian population, the JVO was decisively defeated by the Partisans and the Soviet Army in 1944. After the end of **World War II**, Mihailović remained in the country and tried to organize resistance against the communists. He was captured in February 1946, sentenced to death after a short trial, and executed on July 17, 1946.

MIHAILOVIĆ, DRAGOSLAV (1930– ). Serbian writer known for his simple and traditional forms of narrative. Mihailović's themes are chosen from everyday life with extensive use of jargon and local dialect. His most notable works include *Frede, laku noć* (*Good Night, Fred*), *Petrijin venac* (*Petrija's Wreath*), and *Kad su cvetale tikve* (*When the Pumpkins Blossomed*).

MIHAILOVIĆ, KOSTA (1917– ). Influential Serbian economist, member of the **Serbian Academy of Sciences and Arts** and chief of the team of economic experts of **Slobodan Milošević**. Mihailović's area of expertise is regional economics. He is considered a major opponent of the liberalization and privatization of the Serbian and Yugoslav economy. His works include *Regionalni razvoj socijalističkih zemalja* (*Regional Development of Socialist Countries*), and *Ekonomska stvarnost Jugoslavije* (*Economic Reality of Yugoslavia*).

MIHAJLOVIĆ, DUŠAN (1948– ). President of **New Democracy** and a deputy in both the Serbian and federal **Parliaments.** Mihajlović was the main architect of the alliance between the **Socialist Party of Serbia** (SPS) and New Democracy and the formation of the coalition government of these two political parties in 1994. An influential businessman, he enjoyed the full support of **Slobodan Milošević** until the split between the New Democracy and the SPS in 1997.

MIJATOVIĆ, ČEDOMILJ (1842–1932). Serbian politician and supporter of the **Obrenović dynasty**. He served as minister of finance and foreign minister in various Serbian governments. In 1881, he signed the **Secret Convention** between **Serbia** and Austria-Hungary. After 1904, he lived in London. His best-known work is *Memoirs of a Balkan Diplomat.*

MILAN, OBRENOVIĆ KING (1854–1901). Ruler of **Serbia** from 1868 to 1889. Milan, a grandson of Jevrem, a brother of Prince **Miloš Obrenović,** assumed the throne of Serbia after the assassination of Prince **Mihailo Obrenović** in 1868. Because Milan was a minor, a regency consisting of **Jovan Ristić,** General **Petrović Milivoje Blaznavac,** and **Jovan Gavrilović** ruled the country until 1872. Milan's reign can be divided into two subperiods: the first from 1872 to 1878 and second from 1878 to 1889. The first period was characterized by the **Serbo-Turkish wars** 1876–1878 and the subsequent **Treaty of San Stefano** and **Congress of Berlin.** At the Congress of Berlin, Serbia was formally proclaimed an independent state and received 200 sq miles (520 sq km) of territory. Most of the Serbian demands at the Congress were secured through Austro-Hungarian support. This prompted Milan to pursue a pro-Austrian policy, which remained the most visible feature of the second period of his rule. After the conclusion of the Trade Treaty and **Secret Convention** between the two countries in 1881, Serbia became almost totally dependent, both politically and economically, on Austria-Hungary. Soon after the Secret Convention was signed, Milan assumed the title of king, and Serbia was proclaimed a kingdom on March 6, 1882.

Already undermined by a series of scandals, Milan's rule suffered another blow during the short **Serbo-Bulgarian War** in 1885. The humiliating Serbian defeat in the war that no one wanted except Milan, marked the end of his rule. After the proclamation of a new **constitution** on January 5, 1889, Milan went into exile on March 6. Although he renounced his Serbian nationality in 1892, Milan returned to Serbia in 1897 to serve as the commander in chief of the army of his son. However, after Alexander's marriage to **Draga Mašin,** Milan returned to exile in 1900.

The reign of Milan Obrenović was highly controversial. Serbia's territorial expansion in 1878 was overshadowed by the loss of her political and economic independence to Austria-Hungary. The acquisition of the status of kingdom was followed by the embarrassing adventure in the war against Bulgaria; the development of financial markets was darkened by Milan's extravagant spending habits; and the formal founding of political parties and the adoption of the new constitution was shadowed by Milan's autocratic behavior.

MILANKOVIĆ, MILUTIN (1879–1958). Prominent physicist, vice president of the **Serbian Academy of Sciences and Arts,** and a member of the **Jugoslovenska akademija znanosti i umjetnosti.** He is best known for his work on the impact of solar radiation on climate changes. His works include *Theorie mathematique des phenomenes thermiques produits par la radiation solaire* (*A Mathematical Theory of the Solar Radiation and Climate Changes*), *Nebeska mehanika* (*Mechanics of Space*), and *Kanon der Erdbestrahlung.*

MILEŠEVA. Monastery in the vicinity of Prijepolje, built between 1234 and 1235, a legacy of King **Vladislav.** The body of **Saint Sava** was transferred from **Hilandar** to Mileševa in 1236. In 1377, **Tvrtko I Kotromanić** was crowned as king of "Bosnia, Serbia, and Coastal Lands." In the monastery, Abbot Danilo printed *Psaltir* and *Molitvenik* (*Prayer*) in 1544. **Frescoes** from Mileševa, along with those from the subsequently built **Sopoćani** monastery, constitute the most valuable wall paintings in medieval Serbia. *The Angel of the Christ's Grave* is the best representative of Mileševa's painted art.

MILETA'S REBELLION/MILETINA BUNA. Coup against Prince **Miloš Obrenović** in 1834. The leader of the rebellion was Mileta Radojković, a distinguished military commander from the **First Serbian Insurrection** and the **Second Serbian Insurrection. Avram Petronijević**; Đorđe Protić, a member of the supreme court; and Milutin Petrović, brother of the legendary **Hajduk Veljko Petrović**, were the main plotters. Caught by surprise and unable to quell the rebellion, Prince Miloš made peace with his opponents, appointed the Council, and decided to grant a constitution that became known as the **Presentation Constitution**.

MILETIĆ, SVETOZAR (1826–1901). Journalist, the leader of the **Serbs** in **Vojvodina**, founder and one of the leaders of Serbian National Progressive Party, and the first editor of the newspaper ***Zastava.*** After gymnasium (high school), he studied in **Novi Sad** and Požun (Bratislava) and obtained a law doctorate in Vienna in 1854. He was active in the Pan-Slav movement and in 1864 was elected a deputy to the Serbian Church Council. In 1865 he became a deputy in the Croato-Hungarian Council. As a devoted champion of Serbian rights in Austria-Hungary, he was imprisoned on several occasions. Besides numerous political studies, Miletić also wrote poems.

MILETINA BUNA. See MILETA'S REBELLION.

MILICA (?–1405). Serbian princess, wife of Prince **Lazar Hrebeljanović.** After the **Battle of Kosovo,** she concluded a peace with the Turks and ruled in **Serbia** until the accession of her son **Stefan Lazarević,** Serbian **despot**. She died in **Ljubostinja** Monastery.

MILITARY BORDER. See VOJNA KRAJINA.

MILJKOVIĆ, BRANKO (1934–1961). Serbian poet, one of the most influential representatives of Yugoslav literature after **World War II**. His profoundly intellectual lyrics are pervaded by the drama of existentialism. His influential works include the books *Vatra i ništa* (*Fire and Void*) and *Smrću protiv smrti* (*With the Death against Death*).

MILOŠ, OBRENOVIĆ, PRINCE (1780–1860). Ruler of **Serbia** 1815–1839 and 1858–1860; the leader of the **Second Serbian Insurrection**; founder of the **Obrenović dynasty**. Born as Teodorović, Miloš changed his patronymic to Obrenović, the family name of his half-brother Milan, a well-to-do livestock merchant and a prominent figure from the **First Serbian Insurrection.** During the First Insurrection, Miloš distinguished himself as a military commander on the front on the **Drina** River. As a result of his military successes, Miloš was made commander of the entire southwestern front. After the collapse of the insurrection in 1813, Miloš was one of the last leaders who continued to resist rather than flee abroad. However, Miloš also was one of the first who surrendered. His sense of practicality gained him Turkish trust, and the Turks appointed him chief **knez** of the districts of **Kragujevac, Čačak,** and Rudnik. In September

1814, Miloš took an active part in helping the Turks to suppress the **Rebellion of Hadži-Prodan.**

Nevertheless, Miloš's respect among the **Serbs** led to his election as leader of the Second Serbian Insurrection in 1815. After a series of military victories, Miloš negotiated a peace settlement with the Turks. As a result, Serbia gained limited autonomy, while Miloš became prince. In 1830, Miloš secured the full political and economic autonomy of Serbia, which incorporated six districts, while he was proclaimed hereditary prince of Serbia. Despite his diplomatic successes, encouragement of Serbia's modernization, and land reforms, Miloš was essentially a **despot** intolerant of opposition. He crushed several rebellions against his autocratic rule mercilessly and continuously opposed the introduction of a **constitution** in Serbia. After a mutiny that became known as **Mileta's Rebellion,** Miloš granted a constitution and appointed a State Council. The constitution was promulgated by an assembly of 4,000 deputies on February 14, 1835, the feast of the Presentation of Our Lord in the Temple, and thus the name the "Presentation Constitution." Viewed by the Great Powers as an overly liberal document, the Presentation Constitution was abolished within a month under pressure from Austria, Russia, and the Ottoman Empire.

The new constitution drafted by the Ottomans was promulgated in the form of a **Hatti Șerif** in December 1838 and became known as the "Turkish Constitution." Shortly after the establishment of a Council of 17 senators, Miloš left Serbia. Twenty years later Miloš returned triumphantly to Serbia to replace **Alexander Karađorđević** as prince of Serbia. His second rule lasted less than two years and was mostly spent in political maneuvering.

MILOŠEVIĆ, NIKOLA (1929– ). Serbian literary critic and politician, member of the **Serbian Academy of Sciences and Arts**, a founder of the Serbian **Liberal Party,** and a strong opponent of the government of **Slobodan Milošević**. His best works include *Antropološki eseji* (*Essays in Anthropology*), *Dostojevski kao mislilac* (*Dostoyevsky as Thinker*), and *Marksizam i jezuitizam* (*Marxism and Jesuitism*).

MILOŠEVIĆ, SLOBODAN (1941– ). President and the most influential politician in the **Federal Republic of Yugoslavia** (FRY), former president of **Serbia**, and president of the **Socialist Party of Serbia.** Milošević was born in **Požarevac,** a small city in eastern Serbia, where he finished his primary and secondary education. He graduated with a degree in law from the **University of Belgrade** in 1964. Milošević married **Mirjana Marković,** his high school friend and a daughter of a prominent Serbian Communist politician.

After occupying several party-appointed positions of minor importance, he became the director of **Belgrade**'s leading bank in 1978. In 1984, **Ivan Stambolić,** chief of the Communist Party of Serbia and Milošević's godfather, appointed him head of the party's Belgrade organization. After succeeding Stambolić, who became president of the Presidency of Serbia, as Communist Party chief in 1986, Milošević's influence greatly increased. In 1987, after a series of internal disagreements over the autonomous province of **Kosovo and Metohija,** Milošević removed Stambolić and became the undisputed leader in Serbia. In 1989, he became president of the Presidency, and in December 1990, in the first democratic **elections** he was elected president. He was reelected in the presidential elections in 1992.

Milošević's role in the civil war in the former Yugoslavia is highly controversial. His supposedly nationalist agenda from the late 1980s brought him the reputation of principal instigator of the civil war in 1991. Milošević, however, became the major proponent of a peaceful settlement in 1993. He sponsored the **Vance Plan** that led to a lasting cease-fire in Croatia, the **Vance-Owen Peace Plan**, that envisioned a cantonal division of **Bosnia and Hercegovina**. In November 1995, Milošević signed the **Dayton Agreement** despite the strong opposition of the delegation of the **Republika Srpska.**

Slobodan Milošević is still a very popular politician in Serbia. His internal policies are characterized by a peculiar mix of democracy and state control. Thus, the tight control of major media, the state sponsored privatization, strong police force is contrasted by wide political freedoms and continuous liberalization of the economy. The dichotomy that characterizes his rule clearly manifested itself during November 1996 elections in Serbia. The leftist coalition, embracing his Socalist Party of Serbia and the **JUL**, led by his wife Mirjana Marković, decisively won in the federal elections. However, in the municipal elections, the opposition **Zajedno** scored an outstanding victory, winning in almost every major city in Serbia. Those results reveals a widespread discontent with the day-to-day policies of Milošević's Socialist Party. In May 1999, The Hague Tribunal indicted Slobodan Milošević for the alleged crimes against the Albanian population in Kosovo and Metohija.

MILOVANOVIĆ, MILOVAN (1863–1912). Serbian statesman and diplomat, one of the leaders of the **Radical Party**, and the architect of Serbian foreign policy and the Balkan Alliance. Milovanović was the first Serb to receive a law doctorate in Paris. As a young professor at the **University of Belgrade**, he drafted the liberal **Constitution** of 1889. In 1896–1897, Milovanović served as minister of justice but was replaced in 1897 during the government's crackdown on the Radical Party. In 1899, he was sentenced to two years' imprisonment in absentia. He returned to the government in 1900 and helped to draft the Constitution of 1901. In 1908, he became foreign minister and played a prominent role in the **Annexation Crisis**. After becoming prime minister in 1911, Milovanović established the Serbo-Bulgarian Alliance that became a major force behind the Balkan alliance against Turkey.

MILOVANOVIĆ, MLADEN (1760–1823). Serbian **Vojvoda** from the **First Serbian Insurrection,** President of the **Governing Council**, and minister of defense 1811-1813. A poor military leader, Milovanović was responsible for the Serbian military defeats in 1809. He also initiated changes in defense strategy that accelerated the military collapse of the First Insurrection in 1813. Upon his return to **Serbia,** Milovanović was killed by the order of Prince **Miloš Obrenović.**

MILUTIN, NEMANJIĆ, KING (?–1321). Younger son of King **Uroš I,** and king of **Serbia** 1282–1321. Milutin became king after his older brother, King **Dragutin,** voluntarily renounced the Serbian throne in 1282 (**Accord of Deževo**). Milutin ruled Serbia for forty years, longer than any other member of the **Nemanjić** dynasty. During his reign, Serbia prospered greatly economically, politically, and culturally and became the strongest state in the **Balkan Peninsula.** Using the war between Anjous and Paleologis, Milutin extended Serbia's possessions in **Macedonia, Dalmatia,** and in the valleys of the **Danube** and **Sava** Rivers. Intense mining and trade with **Dubrovnik** allowed Milutin to keep a large army as well as to pursue dynamic building activity in Serbia. During his reign, some forty monasteries and churches were built and renovated in Serbia, including **Gračanica** and **Banjska.**

MILUTINOVIĆ, MILAN (1937– ). President of **Serbia**. Prior to rising to relative prominence within the ranks of the **Socialist Party of Serbia**, Milutinović was appointed director of the **National Library** of Serbia. Minister of Foreign Affairs of the **Federal Republic of Yugoslavia** from 1996, Milutinović became a presidential candidate of the Socialist Party of Serbia during the 1997 **elections**, after their first choice, **Zoran** Lilić, proved incapable of defeating the radical nationalist **Vojislav Šešelj**. After a strenuous, state-supported campaign Milutinović succeeded in defeating Šešelj, despite claims of numerous irregularities and a voter turnout of less than 50 percent.

MILUTINOVIĆ, SIMA-SARAJLIJA (1791–1847). Leading poet of the first half of the 19th century. His diverse opus includes a lengthy epic poem about the **First Serbian Insurrection,** *Serbijanka* (*A Serbian Woman*), three dramas (among which *Tragedija vožda Karađorđa/The Tragedy of Karađorđe* is the most important); a collection of folk songs; lyric poetry; and some historical work. Although the quality of his works varied, he left a deep impression on many of his contemporaries including **Petar Njegoš.**

MIROSLAV (?–1198). Brother of **Stefan Nemanja** and ruler of **Zahumlje.** He married a sister of **Kulin, ban** of **Bosnia and Hercegovina.** He sponsored the creation of **Miroslav's Gospel** (1192), the most important written monument of Serbian culture in the 12th century.

MIROSLAV'S GOSPEL/MIROSLAVOVO JEVANĐELJE. The oldest fully preserved Serbian manuscript book. The Gospel was written in beautiful solemn letters, in a well-formed literary language. It was hand-written and illustrated with miniatures by Deacon Gregory in the 12th century. The Gospel was written in St. Peter's Monastery near the city of Bijelo Polje in **Montenegro.**

MIROSLAVOVO JEVANĐELJE. See MIROSLAV'S GOSPEL.

MIŠAR, BATTLE OF. One of the major battles and the greatest Serbian victories of the **First Serbian Insurrection**. The battle took place on a small plateau called Mišar in the vicinity of the city of **Šabac** on August 1, 1806. Serbian forces commanded by **Petrović Karađorđe** numbering 7,000 men and four guns annihilated the Turkish army of 50,000.

MIŠIĆ, ŽIVOJIN (1855–1921). One of the most celebrated commanders of the Serbian army in **World War I.** Mišić participated in all wars for Serbia's liberation between 1876 and 1918. He was promoted to the rank of **vojvoda** after the **Battle of Kolubara** in which he ordered the counterattack on December 3, 1915, and decisively defeated the Austro-Hungarian forces as the commander of the Serbian First Army. During preparation of the Serbian offensive at the **Salonika Front** in 1918, he served as the chief of staff of the Supreme Command. After **World War I,** he became the chief of the General Staff of the Yugoslav army. He wrote *Strategija* (*Strategy*). In May 1999, Milutinović was indicted by The Hague Tribunal for his part in the allegedly planned campaign of terror against Albanian speaking population in Kosovo and Metohija.

MLADA BOSNA (Young Bosnia). Serbian revolutionary organization, mainly of students from **Bosnia and Hercegovina,** founded in 1910, with **Vladimir Gaćinović** as its chief ideologist. The chief objectives of the organization were liberation from the Austro-Hungarian occupation, unification with **Serbia,** and the eventual formation of a Yugoslav state. The members of Mlada Bosna organized the assassination of the Austro-Hungarian crown prince Franz Ferdinand in **Sarajevo** on June 28, 1914. See also SARAJEVO ASSASSINATION.

MLADENOVAC. Small industrial city, suburb of **Belgrade** with a population of 56,389 in 1991, and an important commercial and communication center. Industries include the production of asbestos, engine parts, and transformers.

MLADIĆ, RATKO (1941– ). Colonel of the **JNA** until 1992 and the supreme commander of the **Bosnian Serb Army** (BSA) until 1996. Born in Kalinovik, a village in **Bosnia and Hercegovina** (B-H), Mladić finished the military academy in **Belgrade** and served in **Skoplje, Priština,** and **Knin.** In 1991, at the outbreak of the civil war in **Croatia,** he was the commander of the JNA garrison in Knin that was engaged in heavy fighting in **Dalmatia** and **Lika.** After the withdrawal of the JNA from the **Republic of Serbian Krajina** in January 1992, Mladić was transferred to **Bihać.** Following the eruption of the civil war in B-H, the proclamation of the **Republika Srpska** (RS), and the disestablishment of the JNA, Mladić assumed the command of the BSA. After an initial period of military successes, Mladić strongly opposed the **Vance-Owen Peace Plan.** However, following the breakdown of the relationship between the **Federal Republic of Yugoslavia** and the RS, and especially after several military setbacks, Mladić essentially sided with the policy of Serbian president **Slobodan Milošević.** Along with **Radovan**

**Karadžić,** the former president of the RS, Mladić has been indicted by the war crimes tribunal of The Hague (**The Hague Tribunal**). On November 10, 1996, **Biljana Plavšić,** newly elected, president of the RS ordered Mladić's replacement as the supreme commander of the BSA.

MOKRANJAC. Music school in **Belgrade** established by **Stevan Mokranjac** and **Stanislav Binički** in 1899 under the name of the Serbian Musical School.

MOKRANJAC, STEVAN (1856–1914). One of the leading Serbian composers of all time. Mokranjac studied at the **Great School** in **Belgrade** and musical academies of Münich, Rome, and Leipzig. He was a founder of the Serbian Musical School and many other musical institutions in Serbia. His *Rukoveti* (*Fifteen Song Collections*), an a cappella choir composition based on the folk melodies of Serbia and Old Serbia and that of **Kosovo, Montenegro, Macedonia,** and **Bosnia and Hercegovina,** is one of the greatest achievements of Serbian music.

MOLER, NIKOLAJEVIĆ PETAR (?–1816). Serbian **Vojvoda** from the **First Serbian Insurrection,** he was undisciplined and often punished by **Karađorđe.** Upon his return to **Serbia** in 1815, he was engulfed in a power struggle with Prince **Miloš Obrenović** and killed by the Turks.

MONTENEGRIN CONSTITUTION (1905). See CONSTITUTION.

MONTENEGRINS. Along with the establishment of **Montenegro** as a constituent republic of the **Socialist Federal Republic of Yugoslavia,** the leadership of the **Communist Party of Yugoslavia**, introduced the category of "Montenegrin" as a distinct nationality. Although historically and traditionally the vast majority of the population of Montenegro were **Serbs**, the insistence on the estrangement between Serbia and Montenegro throughout the post–**World War II** period led to the creation of a separate national identity. Traditionally, Montenegro's populace came from 35 tribes, among which the most widely known are Kuči, Bjelopavići, Banjani, Ceklini, Njeguši, Drobnjaci, and Vasojevići. According to the 1991 census, 547,954 persons declared themselves as Montenegrins.

MONTENEGRO/CRNA GORA. Constituent republic of the **Socialist Federal Republic of Yugoslavia** until April 27, 1992, when it, together with **Serbia**, formed the **Federal Republic of Yugoslavia.** The name of the republic originates from the Venetian Monte Nero (Black Mountain; Serbian, Crna Gora). Montenegro contains an area of 13,812 sq km and had a population of 615,267 in 1991. The ethnic composition of the population in 1991 was: 61.8 percent Montenegrin, 9.2 percent Serbian, 14.6 percent Muslim, 6.6 percent Albanian, and 4.2 percent Yugoslav (see Table 13, statistical addendum). Montenegro is bordered by **Bosnia and Hercegovina** (with both the **Republika Srpska** and the **Muslim-Croat Federation**) to the north and northwest, **Croatia** to the west, Albania to the south and southeast, and the Adriatic Sea to the west. Western Montenegro is mainly a karst region of arid hills, with some cultivable areas in the **Zeta** Valley. The western parts and the area around Lake Shkodër are more fertile and have large forests and grassy lands. The climate in the coastal area is Mediterranean and moderate and in the interior of Montenegro subcontinental.

The smallest of the all republics of the SFRY, Montenegro's share in the Gross Social Product of the SFRY in 1989 was only 2.0 percent. Traditionally, the economy of Montenegro was based on agriculture and animal husbandry. Rapid industrialization of the country occurred after **World War II,** with the production of electric power, iron, steel and nonferrous metal industries. The main industrial centers are in **Nikšić** (beer, wood processing, aluminum), **Podgorica** (textiles, chemicals, tobacco, food processing, wood processing), Berane (wood processing), and **Cetinje** (electrical equipment). With a share of 46 percent, industry was the main sector of Montenegro's economy in 1989. The city of **Bar** is the largest port in Montenegro and the FRY. In the early 1970s, tourism became the most vigorous sector of the economy. However, an earthquake in 1979 substantially damaged the main tourist resorts.

The Serbs arrived in the territory of Montenegro in the course of sixth and seventh centuries. Serbian medieval records refer to the entire territory as Primorje, which included Pagany, the area around the **Neretva** River, **Zahumlje,** Travunia, and Dioclea (**Duklja**). In the 11th century the area became known as Zeta, and in 1077, **Mihailo**, the ruler of Zeta, became the first Serbian king. During the rule of the **Nemanjić** dynasty, Zeta enjoyed a special status in the Serbian state. Following the death of Emperor **Dušan the Mighty** and the weakening of central power in the Serbian state, Zeta came under the rule of the **Balšići** family, who were replaced by the **Crnojević**, who ruled from 1465–1498. The Turks occupied Montenegro in 1499, but unconquered pockets of resistance brought fame to Montenegro as the only bastion of freedom in the **Balkan Pen-**

**insula.** In the 16th and early 17th centuries Montenegro developed a substantial autonomy and was ruled by bishops (***vladika*** in Serbian) of the **Serbian Orthodox Church** from 1516. In 1697, the **Montenegrins** chose **Danilo Petrović** as bishop, and he introduced the custom that the bishop should name his successor while he was still alive. Thus, the house of Petrović was ensured the bishop's mitre and later the titles of prince and king. During the rule of Bishop Danilo Petrović, several Montenegrin tribes were united and close relations with Russia were established. Throughout the period between 17th and 19th centuries, Montenegro struggled against the Ottoman Empire. In 1798, Bishop Peter I introduced the first Code of Laws (appended in 1803), which substantially enhanced central power in Montenegro. He was succeeded by his nephew, **Petar II Petrović Njegoš,** who continued state centralization. In 1831, a Senate was introduced as the Supreme State Court, the first printing press was established, and the first elementary school was founded. The reformation process continued during the reign of **Danilo I,** who reintroduced secular rule and was proclaimed prince of Montenegro. He published a type of **constitution**, the National Code of Laws, and curtailed the separatist tendencies of local chieftains.

Danilo I was succeeded by **Nikola I Petrović,** the last ruler of independent Montenegro. Nikola's main focus was the final liberation from the Turkish and Austro-Hungarian yokes. After taking an active part in the **Rebellions of Hercegovina** and the war against Turkey (1876–1878), Montenegro's independence was formally recognized by the **Congress of Berlin** in 1878.

Following 1903 and the dynastic change in **Serbia**, increasing competition developed between Nikola and his son-in-law, **Peter I Karađorđević**, king of Serbia. The crux of the matter was a dynastic rivalry as to who should lead the struggle for Serbian national liberation. In 1910, in order to enhance his prestige, Nikola assumed the title of king. Despite these rivalries, Montenegro's army closely collaborated with the Serbian army during the **Balkan wars** and **World War I.** Montenegro was occupied by Austria-Hungary in 1916, after the Serbian army's withdrawal to Greece. Following the liberation of Serbia and collapse of Austria-Hungary, the Grand National Assembly of Montenegro dethroned Nikola and the Petrović dynasty and proclaimed unification with Serbia.

During **World War II,** Montenegro was occupied by Italy, which installed a puppet regime, known as "separatist." The majority of the population of Montenegro, however, joined either the **Jugoslovenska vojska u otadžbini** and **Četniks** or the Communist-led **Partisans.** This bitter civil war lasted until 1945, when Montenegro became a constituent republic in the second Yugoslav state.

MORAČA. (i) The biggest river in **Montenegro** (99 km long), very rich in hydroelectric energy.

(ii) A monastery in the canyon of the Morača River built in 1252 by a grandson of **Stefan Nemanja.** Deserted during the Turkish onslaughts, the monastery was revived in the 16th century. It has a large collection of icons, among which the icons of **Saint Sava** and St. Simeon are the most valuable.

MORAVA. One of the largest rivers in **Serbia,** formed by the **Western Morava** and **Southern Morava** Rivers at Stalać; the length of the river is 216.5 km, 568 km including the Southern Morava. The Morava Valley is a fertile region and, together with the **Vardar** Valley, the most important communications link between Europe and Asia Minor.

MOSTAR. City in **Bosnia and Hercegovina** on the **Neretva** River, and center of western **Hercegovina** with a population of 126,067 in 1991. The ethnic composition prior to the civil war was 34.8 percent Muslim, 33.8 percent Croatian, 19.0 percent Serbian, and 10.0 percent Yugoslav. Aviation and aluminum fabrication and the production of tobacco are important industries. It is a university center. The first records of the city date from 1452. During the 19th century Mostar was one of the centers of Serbian culture in B-H. It was, however, heavily damaged during the civil war in B-H. After the withdrawal of the **JNA** and exodus of the Serbian population, heavy fighting erupted between Croats and Muslims. In 1993, Croatian forces destroyed the Old Bridge built in 1566. After the formation of the **Muslim-Croat Federation** in 1994, Mostar came under the protection of the **European Community** for a proposed two-year period, which the European Union has the sole right to extend or end early. The city, however, remained divided between Muslims and Croats.

MRKONJIĆ GRAD. Small city and a **Commune** center in west-central Bosnia with a population of 27,379 in 1991. The ethnic structure of the population prior to the civil war was 77.3 percent Serbian, 12 percent Serbian, 7.8 percent Croatian, and 2.2 percent Yugoslav. The regular

Croatian army captured the city during its offensive in western Bosnia in September 1995. Prior to returning the area to **Republika Srpska** control, houses were looted and burned. Subsequently, 181 bodies were found in newly dug graves in the local Serbian cemetery. Forensic experts claimed that more than a hundred of the victims, including old women, had been beaten to death. Fewer than half the bodies were in military uniform. According to the **Dayton Agreement**, Mrkonjić grad will remain in the Republika Srpska.

MRNJAVČEVIĆ. Serbian feudal family that ruled in southern and western **Macedonia.** The most prominent members were King Vukašin and **Despot** Jovan Uglješa, both of whom died in the **Battle of Maritsa,** and Vukašin's son, **Marko Kraljević**.

MUHADŽIRI. Name used for **Muslims** who abandoned **Bosnia and Hercegovina** after the Austro-Hungarian occupation in 1878. They initially settled in **Kosovo and Metohija** and **Macedonia.** After the **Balkan wars,** the majority of them left for Turkey.

MURAT, MARKO (1864–1944). Painter born in **Zadar,** member of the **Serbian Academy of Sciences and Arts,** and one of the founders of **Lada.** He studied at the Munich Academy of Art. Murat was especially well known for his monumental picture *Ulazak cara Dušana u Dubrovnik* (*The Entry of Emperor Dušan into Dubrovnik*), which won him the title of officier d'Académie in Paris in 1900.

MUSLIM-CROAT FEDERATION. A political entity, which together with the **Republika Srpska** forms **Bosnia and Hercegovina** (B-H). The federation was formally established on March 2, 1994 by the Washington Agreement and comprises 51 percent of the territory in B-H. While its formation precedes the **Dayton Agreement**, it is only in the aftermath of the agreement that the entity became operational. The functioning of the federation is seriously impeded by a deep rift between Muslim and Croat political leaders in Bosnia. The entity is de facto divided between Croat controlled areas known as **Herceg-Bosna** and territory under Muslim control.

MIŠAR, BATTLE OF. One of the major battles and the greatest Serbian victories of the **First Serbian Insurrection**. The battle took place on a small plateau called Mišar in the vicinity of the city of **Šabac** on August 1, 1806. Serbian forces commanded by **Petrović Karađorđe** numbering 7,000 men and four guns annihilated the Turkish army of 50,000.

MUSLIMS. Religious and ethnic group in Yugoslavia, mainly inhabiting **Bosnia and Hercegovina** (B-H) but also **Sandžak** and **Montenegro.** The majority of Muslims from Yugoslavia are Slavs, probably of Serbian origin. They emerged as the result of the massive Islamization of the **Balkan Peninsula** during the Turkish occupation between the 16th and early 20th centuries. Their customs are a mixture of Ottoman and local, mainly Serbian, culture, and they mostly use the **Serbian** (Serbo-Croatian) **language.** The name 'Muslims' dates from the late 19th century when it appeared among the local adherents of Islam as the reaction to the Austro-Hungarian unifying terms **Bošnjak,** Turkish potur, and derogatory Serbian poturica (Turkish convert).

The foreign occupation of B-H caused much friction among the population. The Austro-Hungarian occupation favored local Croats, and Muslims looked toward Ottoman protection, while the **Serbs,** who historically constituted the majority of the population in B-H, considered **Serbia** as their natural ally. Besides being religious and political, the conflict between Muslims and Serbs had an economic dimension. Being small land owners and the rural dwellers, Serbs were the backbone of agricultural Bosnia. On the other hand, in the course of the Ottoman and the Austro-Hungarian occupations, Muslims and Croats gravitated toward cities. This historic separation became apparent during both world wars, when Croats and Muslims formally joined in fighting Serbs.

After **World War II,** especially during the 1960s, Muslims began to enjoy preferential treatment in the multiethnic B-H. This tendency resulted in the declaration of Muslims as a constituent nation of the **Socialist Federal Republic of Yugoslavia** in 1971. In the census of the same year, Muslims became a majority of the population in B-H for the first time. Although the vast majority of Muslims were secular, they overwhelmingly rallied behind the Muslim-only **Party of Democratic Action** led by **Alija Izetbegović.**

MUŠICKI, LUKIJAN (1777–1857). Archimandrite of the monastery of Šišatovac and archbishop of the **Serbian Orthodox Church.** He was the creator of classicism in Serbian poetry and a devoted follower of **Dositej Obradović** and **Vuk Stefanović Karadžić.**

MUTIMIR (?–890). Serbian prince who ruled between 860 and 890. During his rule the conversion of the **Serbs** to Christianity was completed.

## - N -

*NAČERTANIJE* (*Memorandum, The Draft*). Serbian national and state program written by **Ilija Garašanin** in 1844. The basis of *The Draft* was a program of the Polish Prince Adam Czartoryski, actually written by **Aleksandr Zah.** Zach's document, known as *The Plan*, called for the unification of the other South Slav lands (Croatia-Slavonia, **Dalmatia,** Bulgaria, **Bosnia and Hercegovina,** Slovenian lands) by Serbia and Serbian resistance to both Russian and Austrian influence. However, unlike Zach's Yugoslavist program, Garašanin's *Draft* primarily envisioned a modern reconstruction of the medieval Serbian empire and the unification of the Serbian lands (Bosnia and Hercegovina, **Montenegro,** northern Albania, parts of Dalmatia, and **Vojna Krajina**). The union with other **South Slavs**, mainly Croats and Bulgars, was foreseen under the aegis of Serbia and its dynasty. While it suggested that Serbia must conduct its foreign policy by maintaining a balance among the Great Powers, one of the main conclusions of Garašanin's *Draft* was that Serbia must free itself from Austrian influence. *The Draft* was also a guide to action—it called for the creation of a network of agents in all South Slavic lands. Garašanin himself established numerous contacts with influential people in the neighboring regions.

NAHIJA. In the Ottoman Empire, an administrative unit roughly corresponding to the western term "county."

*NAROD* (*The People*). (i) A political journal of the **Radical Party.** *The People* was published in **Belgrade** between 1896 and 1907 under the editorship of **Jovan Đaja.**
(ii) A weekly political journal of **Serbs** from **Bosnia and Hercegovina** published in **Mostar** 1907–1908, and in **Sarajevo** 1908, 1911–1914, 1920–1925, and 1927. The editors of the journal were Uroš Krulj, Risto Radulović, and Nikola Stojanović.
(iii) A journal of the **Democratic Party** in **Vojvodina,** published in **Novi Sad** between 1924 and 1929.

NARODNA BIBLIOTEKA. See NATIONAL LIBRARY.

NARODNA ODBRANA. See NATIONAL DEFENSE.

NARODNA VEĆA. See NATIONAL COUNCILS.

NARODNI FRONT/POPULAR FRONT. A leftist mass-organization that emerged in the mid-1930s in the aftermath of the rise of Fascism and Nazism in Germany, Italy, and Spain. The main objective of the organization was the mobilization of all progressive forces outside the Communist Party.

The **Communist Party of Yugoslavia** founded the Narodni front shortly before the outbreak of **World War II**. During the war the organization played an important role in mobilizing a non-communist segment of the population to join the **Partisans**. After the war, the CommunistParty used Narodni front in its accession to power, especially during the mass campaign against the opposition candidates in the 1945 **elections**. The importance of Narodni front significantly decreased following the communists' accession to power. The organization was slowly merged into the state apparatus, and in 1953 the name of the organization was changed to the Socialist Union of Working Peoples of Yugoslavia (Socijalistički savez radnog naroda Jugoslavije).

NARODNI MUZEJ. See NATIONAL MUSEUM.

NARODNO POZORIŠTE. See NATIONAL THEATER.

NASTASIJEVIĆ, MOMČILO (1894–1938). Prominent Serbian writer and poet. His often hermetic lyric poetry, narratives, and dramas are considered among the most profound in Serbian literature. Among his best-known works are *Pet lirskih krugova* (*Five Lyric Circles*), *Magnovenja i odjeci* (*Moments and Echoes*), and *Zapis o darovima moje rođake Marije* (*An Account of the Gifts of My Cousin Marija*).

NATIONAL BANK OF YUGOSLAVIA. The first attempt to create a Central Bank in **Serbia** was made by the Regency in 1869. The attempt failed because of bad investment and the European slump in 1873. The National Bank of Serbia (Narodna Banka Kraljevine Srbije) was established on January 18, 1883. Although organized as a private joint stock institution, the National Bank was granted powers of lending to other banks and the exclusive right to issue currency. The bank gradually gained independence from the government after **May's Assassination** and the **Tariff War** of 1906–1911.

After **World War I**, the new National Bank of Serbs, Croats, and Slovenes replaced the National Bank of Serbia. Following **World War II,** the National Bank of Yugoslavia was established, together with six national banks of the republics and two national banks of the Autonomous Provinces of the **Socialist Federal Republic of Yugoslavia.** Consequently, although the National Bank of Yugoslavia was given the exclusive right to issue currency, republican national banks steadily became the real financial centers in their respective regions. In 1990, the national banks of the constituent republics began to print money independently of the National Bank of Yugoslavia. Besides its diminished financial role due to decentralization, the National Bank was completely dependent on the government. This dependence was somewhat mitigated after the appointment of **Dragoslav Avramović** as governor in March 1993 and the implementation of his Stabilization Program.

NATIONAL COUNCILS/NARODNA VEĆA. Councils established in Yugoslav lands under Austro-Hungarian control in 1918 (National Council for **Dalmatia,** National Council for **Bosnia and Hercegovina,** National Council of Slovenes, Croats, and Serbs). The first council was established in **Zagreb** on October 6, 1918. The council proclaimed the unification of Slovenes, Croats, and Serbs in a single state as its primary objective. The council's intention was to become an internationally recognized government of the self-proclaimed State of Slovenes, Croats, and Serbs. However, the representatives of the nationalist **Croatian Peasant Party** and extremist Croatian Party of Rights insisted on complete Croatian autonomy. Following intense negotiations between representatives of Serbia and the council, and after **Vojvodina**'s and **Montenegro**'s proclamation of unification with Serbia on November 25–26, the delegation of the council arrived in **Belgrade** and on December 1, 1918, the **Kingdom of the Serbs, Croats, and Slovenes** was proclaimed. See also GENEVA CONFERENCE; GENEVA DECLARATION.

NATIONAL DEFENSE/NARODNA ODBRANA. Patriotic society founded in 1908 during the **Annexation Crisis.** The principal aim of the society was to protect and propagate Serbian interests in the Serbian-populated regions outside **Serbia.** Within a few weeks of the Austro-Hungarian annexation of **Bosnia and Hercegovina** (B-H), the 220 committees that had sprung up enlisted more than 5,000 volunteers ready to fight in the case of war. The National Defense formed its committees in B-H and **Macedonia** but was forced to restrict itself to cultural activities following the official Serbian recognition of the Austro-Hungarian annexation in March 1909. However, it did maintain a network of confidential agents among South Slavs of Austria-Hungary. The activities of the National Defense were a source of constant friction between Serbia and Austria-Hungary. See also ULTIMATUM.

NATIONAL LIBRARY/NARODNA BIBLIOTEKA. Largest library in the **Federal Republic of Yugoslavia.** Founded as the City Library of **Belgrade,** it became organized as the Library and the Museum of the Government in 1853. In 1858, **Đuro Daničić** changed the name of the institution to the National Library. During the directorship of **Janko Šafarik**, who succeeded Daničić, library holdings more than doubled. Šafarik also introduced a modern professional system of classification. The National Library was improved substantially by Jovan Tomić, who was the director from 1903 to 1927. He introduced a central catalogue and supervised the restoration of the heavily damaged library after **World War I.** The library suffered enormous damage from German bombardment in April 1941, and a large number of original historical documents perished. The modern building of the National Library was finally completed in 1972.

NATIONAL MUSEUM/NARODNI MUZEJ. The National Museum was founded in 1853 as the Library and Museum of the Government. The two institutions, the **National Library** and the National Museum, were separated in 1881. The growing collections prompted the opening of separate museums of natural history and ethnography. The Museum of the Serbian Land was opened in 1899, and the Ethnographic Museum in 1904.

NATIONAL THEATER/NARODNO POZORIŠTE. The beginning of the theater tradition among the Serbs can be traced to the early 12th century. The performances in the Middle Ages were secular and entertaining. The first modern play was performed in **Karlovci Sremski** in 1734. Following the work of Joakim Vujić, the first professional theater company among the Serbs was created in **Novi Sad** in 1838. After the first theater in **Belgrade** was founded under Prince **Miloš Obrenović** in 1835, the new theater was established in 1868. It was sponsored by Prince **Mihailo Obrenović,** and the first performance in the new building was in late 1869. The building was constructed in the Renaissance style by Aleksandar Bugarski. The theater was a link with Western culture, as many masterpieces of French, German, and English theater were performed (*Romeo and Juliet*, *Julius Caesar*, *Richard III*, *The Taming of the Shrew*, *William Tell*, and others). The National Theater plays the role of the theater of national culture. Besides the National Theater, numerous major theaters include Jugoslovensko dramsko pozoriste (Yugoslav Drama Theater), founded in 1947; Beogradsko dramsko pozorište (Belgrade Drama Theater), founded in 1951; Atelje 212 (Atelier 212), founded in 1956; and Narodno pozorište (National Theater) in **Subotica**.

NATO. See NORTH ATLANTIC TREATY ORGANIZATION.

NEDIĆ, LJUBOMIR (1858–1902). Prominent Serbian literary critic, among the first to introduce to Serbia the views of Western modernism. He emphasized the aesthetic side of the lyric poem. He edited the literary journal *Srpski pregled* (*Serbian Review*). His major works include *Noviji srpski pisci* (*New Serbian Writers*), and *Kritičke studije* (*Critical Studies*).

NEDIĆ, MILAN (1877–1946). General of the Serbian and Yugoslav army, chief of General Staff and minister of defense of the Kingdom of Yugoslavia. After surrendering to the Germans in **April's War,** he became president of the German-sponsored government in Serbia in August 1941. Nedić fled **Belgrade** in October 1944 but was extradited by the Allies to **Tito**'s government in 1946. According to the official version, Nedić committed suicide during the investigation.

After the introduction of multiparty democracy in Serbia, Nedić's role in **World War II** was revised. Although still a matter of controversy, Nedić's quisling position is reexamined given his efforts to mitigate the tremendous hardship that **Serbs** endured in occupied Serbia and to save the **Serbs** from the genocide in the **Independent State of Croatia.**

NEMANJA, STEFAN (1114–1200). Youngest son of **Zavida,** born in **Ribnica,** a suburb of modern **Podgorica.** After defeating his older brothers in the Battle of Pantin in 1168, Nemanja assumed the title of grand **župan** and became the supreme leader of **Raška.** During Nemanja's rule the process of unification of the Serbian lands began: **Zeta, Kosovo and Metohija, Pomoravlje,** and parts of western **Macedonia** became parts of the Serbian state. Nemanja yielded his throne to his son, **Stefan Prvovenčani,** in 1196, became a monk, with the name of Simeon, and joined his youngest son **Saint Sava** at Mount Athos. In 1199, with the help of Stefan Prvovenčani, Sava and Nemanja built **Hilandar,** the Serbian monastery at **Sveta Gora** (Mt. Athos). Besides Hilandar, Nemanja built the monasteries **Đurđevi Stupovi** and **Studenica** and numerous churches.

NEMANJIĆ. Medieval Serbian dynasty (ruled from 1168 to 1371) founded by Grand **Župan Stefan Nemanja**. After his death, the dynasty split into **Vukan**'s lineage and the main lineage of Nemanja's younger son, **Stefan Prvovenčani.** After the death of **Uroš II** in 1371, the main line ended. Another minor line extended from Simeon, a son of **Stefan Dečanski** and the Byzantine princess Maria Paleologi. They had two sons, Stefan and Jovan Uroš, also known as Monk Josaf. With the death of Monk Josaf in 1423, this line ended. During the reign of the Nemanjić dynasty, **Serbia** greatly prospered and became one of the strongest and most developed states in Europe.

NENADOVIĆ, ALEKSA (?–1804). Serbian **knez** from **Valjevo,** one of the most eminent **Serbs** prior to the **First Serbian Insurrection.** Although he fought against the Turks in the Austro-Turkish War (1788–1791), Aleksa cooperated with Mustafa Paşa of **Beogradski pašaluk.** After the **Dahije** killed Mustafa in 1801, Aleksa began to organize Serbian resistance to their terror. On January 23, 1804, he was captured and publicly beheaded in Valjevo. His death marked the beginning of the mass slaughter of Serbian notables that ultimately led to the First Serbian Insurrection.

NENADOVIĆ, JAKOV (1765–1836). Younger brother of **Aleksa Nenadović**; a Serbian **vojvoda** and one of the most prominent leaders of the **First Serbian Insurrection.** An opponent of **Karađorđe,** Jakov was one of founders of the **Governing Council.** As president of the council, in 1810 he began to cooperate closely with Karađorđe and after approving the constitutional provisions of 1811, he became the **popečitelj** of internal affairs. After the collapse of the First Insurrection in 1813, he emigrated to Austria. He returned to **Serbia** in 1831.

NENADOVIĆ, LJUBOMIR (1826–1895). Son of **Prota Mateja Nenadović,** Serbian writer, and one of the most educated **Serbs** from the 19th century. He is best known for his travel essays, which were considered among the best in European literature: *Pisma iz Italije* (*Letters from Italy*), *Pisma iz Nemačke* (*Letters from Germany*), *O Crnogorcima* (*On Montenegrins*), and others.

NENADOVIĆ, PROTA MATEJA (1777–1854). Son of Aleksa; dean, **vojvoda**, and statesman from the **First Serbian Insurrection.** The first diplomat of modern **Serbia,** Nenadović was the founder and first president of the **Governing Council**. After the **Second Serbian Insurrection,** he returned to Serbia and became **knez** of **Valjevo**. Following his conflict with Prince **Miloš Obrenović,** he was forced into retirement and expelled from the country by Prince **Mihailo Obrenović** in 1840. He returned to Serbia in 1842. His *Memoari* (*Memoirs*) is a valuable account of the people and events of the First Serbian Insurrection.

NERETLJANI. Serbian tribe which inhabited the lower stream of the **Neretva** River; known for its struggle against the Venetian Republic.

NERETVA. Main river in **Hercegovina**; the total length is 218 km. The river rises on Lebršnik Mountain (1,277 m) and flows to the Adriatic Sea. It can be navigated for 20 km from Metković to Ploče and is very rich in hydroenergy. The building of the **Jablanica** Dam in 1947–1955 created a man-made lake of 14.4 sq km. During **World War II**, combined German-Italian and **Ustaše** forces attacked the main body of the **Partisans**' army in the Neretva region. After heavy fighting in March 1943, the Partisans succeeded in crossing the river to avoid encirclement.

NERODIMLJE. Medieval **župa** and city in **Kosovo and Metohija** on the bank of the Nerodimka River; one of the centers of medieval Serbia.

NEW DEMOCRACY/NOVA DEMOKRATIJA. Political party led by **Dušan Mihajlović.** Founded in 1990, New Democracy was on the margins of the Serbian political arena until the parliamentary **elections** of 1993. Although having participated and been elected as candidates of the **Democratic Movement of Serbia,** several deputies of New Democracy broke opposition ranks and joined the efforts of the **Socialist Party of Serbia**

(SPS) in forming a coalition government. In the aftermath of the November 1996 elections in Serbia, the New Democracy attempted to distance itself from government policies toward the mass protest that spread throughout Serbia and lasted more than two months.

NEZAVISNA RADNIČKA PARTIJA JUGOSLAVIJE (NRPJ) (Independent Workers' Party of Yugoslavia). Political party that emerged from, and continued the work of, the banned **Communist Party of Yugoslavia** (CPY). The NRPJ was founded on January 13, 1923, in **Belgrade**. The party program was a modified program of the CPY and insisted on the struggle against "Serbian hegemonism" and unitarism. The party published the newspaper *Borba* (*Struggle*) and the journal *Radnik* (*Worker*). The party was banned and dissolved in July 1924.

NIKEZIĆ, MARKO (1921–1991). Serbian and Yugoslav diplomat and politician. He was foreign minister of the **Socialist Federal Republic of Yugoslavia** 1965–1968 and president of the League of Communists of Serbia 1968–1972. In 1972, he was removed from his political office as one of the leaders of the new technocratic and liberal movement in Serbia.

NIKOLA I PETROVIĆ (1841–1921). Prince (1860–1910) and king (1910–1918) of **Montenegro**; father-in-law of Serbian king **Peter I Karađorđević** and Italian king Vitorio Emanuelle III. During his long reign Montenegro was granted formal independence at the **Congress of Berlin** (1878) and achieved a substantial extension of its territory in the **Balkan wars.** Prior to the Balkan wars, his aspiration to the throne of the unified Serbian state led to continuous friction between **Serbia** and Montenegro. After the Austro-Hungarian occupation of Montenegro in 1917, Nikola went into exile. His rule formally ended with the proclamation of the unification of Montenegro with **Serbia** on November 26, 1918. He wrote poems and dramas among which the best known are *Onamo namo* (*There and Here*) and *Balkanska carica* (*Queen of the Balkans*).

NIKOLA SVETI (Saint Nicholas). Serbian monastery built between 1169 and 1172 on the banks of the **Toplica** River. The monastery represents one of the first legacies of **Stefan Nemanja.**

NIKOLAJEVIĆ, GEORGIJE (1807–1896). Metropolitan of **Dabar**; founder of the literary journal *Srpskodalmatinski Magazin* published from 1841 to 1861. The journal had strong influence on **Serbs** from **Dalmatia** and **Hercegovina.**

NIKOLAJEVIĆ, SVETOMIR (1844–1922). Founder of the **Radical Party**, professor of the **Great School**, and a member of the **Serbian Academy of Sciences and Arts**. After becoming prime minister in 1894, he suspended the liberal **Constitution** of 1888 and reintroduced the Constitution of 1869. Nikolajević was among the most prominent masons in **Serbia**.

NIKOLIĆ, FILIP (1830–1867). First professional librarian in **Serbia,** he created the first complete catalog (alphabetic and subject) of the **National Library** in 1853–1856.

NIKŠIĆ. Second largest city in **Montenegro** in the valley of the **Zeta** River with a population of 75,025 in 1991. It is an important industrial center, with production of bauxite, a major steel-making company, a brewery, woodworking factories, and a hydroelectric station. The first records of the town date from Roman times, while the Serbian name of the city dates from 1355.

NINČIĆ MOMČILO (1876–1949). Prominent Serbian and Yugoslav politician and statesman, professor at the **University of Belgrade**, and member of the **Radical Party**. After finishing gymnasium (high school) in Belgrade, Ninčić graduated in law in Paris (1889). He occupied several important posts in the Serbian government, including minister of finance, minister of justice, and minister of trade. He was the author of the first budget and the architect of the monetary unification of the **Kingdom of the Serbs, Croats, and Slovenes.** From 1921, in several governments, Ninčić served as the minister of foreign affairs of Yugoslavia. After the German occupation of Yugoslavia, he emigrated to London and served as foreign minister in the government-in-exile (1941–1942). The founder and the editor of the journal *Novi život (New Life*) 1920–1927, he is also the author of several studies: *Naše valutno pitanje* (*Our Currency Question*), and *La crise bosniaque 1908–1909 et les Grandes puissances européennes* (*The Bosnian Crisis 1908–1909 and the Great European Powers*).

NIŠ. City and industrial center in southern **Serbia** on the **Nišava** River with a population of 248,086 in 1991. The most developed industries include the production of textiles, electronic materials, beer, tobacco, and locomotives. Niš became a university center in 1965. The city is important for its strategic location and control of the Morava-Vardar corridor and the **Nišava** corridor, the two main routes between central Europe and Asia Minor. The first record of the Roman city, Naissus, dates from the second century. Before it came under Serbian control in the 12th century, the city was contested between Bulgarians and Hungarians. Several battles between Serbs and Turks were held in the vicinity of Niš (**Battle of Pločnik, Battle of Deligrad**). The Serbian army liberated Niš in 1877, and the city was reincorporated into Serbia at the **Congress of Berlin** (1878). During the NATO attack on Yugoslavia Niš was heavily bombed on numerous occasions. See also MORAVA; VARDAR.

NIŠ, DECLARATION OF. Declaration of the Serbian government made to the Serbian **Parliament** in **Niš** on December 7, 1914. The document called for the struggle for the liberation and unification of all "our captive brethren **Serbs**, Croats, and Slovenes." This was the first document that called for the unification of all Yugoslav lands.

NIŠAVA. River in southeastern **Serbia,** total length 218 km (151 km in Serbia and 67 km in Bulgaria). The Nišava corridor is the shortest route between central Europe and Istanbul.

NONALIGNED MOVEMENT. Soon after the outbreak of the cold war, several leaders of Third World countries started to popularize the idea of peaceful coexistence among nations. Prominent among these leaders were Prime Minister Jawarhalal Nehru of India, Presidents Gamal Abdel Nasser of Egypt, Kwame Nkrumah of Ghana, Sukarno of Indonesia, Sekou Touré of Guinea, and Josip Broz, **Tito**, of Yugoslavia. Together they formed the Organization of Nonaligned Countries. The founding principles of the organization were peaceful coexistence and the struggle for independence. Unlike neutral countries, nonaligned countries actively participated in international affairs and attempted to mitigate tension between East and West.

The foreign policy of the **Socialist Federal Republic of Yugoslavia** strictly followed the basic principles of nonalignment. While this orientation facilitated Yugoslavia's emancipation from the Communist bloc, it also separated Yugoslavia from the Balkans and Western Europe. The prolonged reliance on economically inferior, culturally distant, and politically unstable Third World countries prevented Yugoslavia from successfully adjusting to changes caused by the end of the cold war and the unification of Europe.

NORTH ATLANTIC TREATY ORGANIZATION (NATO). NATO involvement in the former Yugoslavia began following the outbreak of the civil war in **Bosnia and Hercegovina** (B-H) and the United States recognition of the secessionist republics on April 7, 1992. NATO actions began with imposing a naval blockade upon the Yugoslav port of **Bar** on July 11, 1992. On September 2, NATO agreed to measures making alliance resources available in support of United Nations efforts to bring peace to the former Yugoslavia. The measures included providing resources to protect humanitarian relief and support for the UN monitoring of heavy weapons. This was followed by the authorization of the use of AWACS surveillance aircraft to monitor the "no fly" zone over B-H and supplying of **UNPROFOR** with an operational headquarters, including a staff of 100 personnel, equipment, and financial support in October-November 1992.

On April 2, 1993, NATO planes began to enforce the no fly zone over B-H. Increased involvement in the civil war in B-H came after the NATO session in Athens on June 11, when it was decided that NATO would provide air support to UNPROFOR at the request of the UN. In 1994–1995 NATO initiated a series of attacks against Serbian targets in B-H and the **Republic of Serbian Krajina** (RSK). These included bombing Serbian positions around **Sarajevo, Goražde, Bihać,** and the Udbina airfield. Following the collapse of the RSK, NATO carried out intensive bombing of the **Republika Srpska** (RS), including civilian buildings, in late August and September 1995 in response to the Markale II Marketplace massacre of August 28.

In October 1998, in order to force Yugoslav President **Slobodan Milošević** to comply with UN Resolution 1199, NATO threaten to launch an air campaign of cruise missiles and a fleet of some 450 aircraft. On March 24, the NATO launched a massive air campaign against Yugoslavia which lasted till June 10.

NOVA DEMOKRATIJA. See NEW DEMOCRACY.

NOVAK, VIKTOR (1889–1977). Yugoslav historian and a member of the **Serbian Academy of Sciences and Arts**; the author of *Magnum Cri-*

*men*, an extensive and thorough account of the **Ustaše** genocide against **Serbs**, Jews, and Gypsies during **World War II.**

NOVAKOVIĆ, STOJAN (1842–1915). Prominent politician and statesman and one of the founders of the **Progressive Party** (1880). He was prime minister 1895–1896 and during the **Annexation Crisis** in 1909, minister of education (1873, 1874, 1880), minister of internal affairs (1884), and an envoy in Constantinople (1886–1891, 1897), Paris (1899–1902) and St. Petersburg (1903–1905). He was Serbian emissary at the London conference 1912–1913. As minister of education, he initiated a complete reorganization of the school system in **Serbia.** Novaković edited the journal *Vila* (*Good Fairy*), prepared ***Dušan's Code of Laws*** for publishing, and wrote extensively on Serbian history, philology, and literature. His main works include: *Vaskrs države srpske* (*Resurrection of the Serbian State*), *Balkanska pitanja* (*Balkan Questions*), *Srpska gramatika* (*Serbian Grammar*), and *Srbi i Turci u 14. veku* (*Serbs and Turks in the 14th Century*).

NOVI BEOGRAD. Largest **commune** of **Belgrade** located on the banks of the **Sava** and **Danub**e Rivers with a population of 224,424 in 1991. The building of the city began in 1947. Most of the federal administration (presidency, government) is located in Novi Beograd. Industries include electronics, agricultural machines, and textiles.

NOVI PAZAR. City in southwestern **Serbia,** the economic and cultural center of the **Sandžak** region with a population of 85,249 in 1991. Agriculture is the main economic activity, while industries include textiles, shoe making, and wood processing. The city was built by Turks in the mid-15th century seven km from the site of the ancient Serbian capital known as **Ras**. Novi Pazar was liberated in the **Balkan wars** and reincorporated into Serbia by the **Treaty of Bucharest** (1913). The monasteries **Sopoćani** and **Đurđevi Stupovi** are located in the vicinity of the city.

NOVI SAD. Cultural and economic center and capital city of **Vojvodina,** and an imortant transit port on the **Danube** River with a population of 265,464 in 1991. It is the nucleus of a fertile agricultural region, while industries include food processing, electronics, chemicals, and milling. Novi Sad was known as the Petrovaradinski Ditch (Ditch of **Petrovaradin**) before the 18th century. After the Austro-Turkish War and **Seoba Srba,** the city became a center of Serbian culture outside **Serbia**: the **Matica Srpska** (1821), and the **Srpsko narodno pozorište** (1862) were founded in Novi Sad. During **World War II**, Hungarian occupying forces killed and expelled a substantial number of **Serbs** from Novi Sad. The Novi Sad withstood the heaviest bombardment during the NATO attack on Yugoslavia in the Spring, 1999. See also BAČKA.

NOVO BRDO. Gold, silver, lead, and iron ore mine in **Kosovo and Metohija,** the main source of the economic might of the medieval Serbian state.

*NOVO VREME* (*The New Times*). A right-wing daily newspaper published in Belgrade during the German occupation 1941–1944. *Novo Vreme* was the official newspaper of the government of **Milan Nedić.**

NUŠIĆ, BRANISLAV (1864–1938). Leading Serbian comedy writer, diplomat, and member of the **Serbian Academy of Sciences and Arts.** A versatile writer, Nušić is best known for his realistic portrayal of the negative tendencies that developed during the reign of the **Obrenović dynasty** in **Serbia.** His major works include *Sumnjivo lice* (*Suspicious Person*), *Narodni poslanik* (*The People's Representative*), *Gospođa ministarka* (*Madam Wife of a Minister*), and *Pokojnik* (*The Deceased*).

## - NJ -

NJEGOŠ, PETAR II PETROVIĆ (1813–1851). **Vladika** of **Montenegro** from 1830 to 1851; one of the best Serbian poets and philosophers. After succeeding his uncle, **Petar I Petrović,** Njegoš took the title Petar II instead of his Christian name, Rade (he is also known as Vladika Rade), and in 1833 became consecrated as a bishop. An intrepid warrior against the Turks, Njegoš introduced sweeping reforms in Montenegro: the first elementary school was founded, the first printing press was installed in **Cetinje** in 1834, the office of the civil governor was eliminated, and a council consisting of 12 local chieftains was established. Njegoš was the most enlightened ruler of his time. His classical ideas were not Roman but Greek (Homer, Pindar, and the writers of tragedies), and his fundamental themes are cosmic human destiny and the historical fate of Montenegro and of the Serbian nation. His principal works are *Gorski vijenac* (*The Mountain Wreath*), *Luča mikrokozma* (*The Ray of the Microcosm*), and *Lažni car Šćepan Mali* (*The False Tsar Šćepan the Little*).

NJEGUŠI. Village in **Montenegro,** the birthplace of **Petar II Petrović Njegoš**.

## - O -

OBILIĆ. Mining town in **Kosovo and Metohija**, the center of the coal basin (pop. 31,627). Thermoelectric plants Kosovo I-V are located in Obilić.

OBILIĆ, MILOŠ (?–1389). Great Serbian hero, also known as Miloš Kobilić, who killed the Turkish sultan Murad during the **Battle of Kosovo** on June 28, 1389.

OBOD. Fortress with a monastery above the town of Rijeka Crnojevića, where the first printshop among the **South Slavs** operated as early as 1494–1494. The first book in the **Cyrillic alphabet**, titled *Oktoih za četvroglasje* (*Oktoih for Four Voices)* was printed in there. After six books were published the Obod printshop was moved to the town of **Cetinje**.

OBRADOVIĆ, DOSITEJ (1742–1811). A Serbian educator, philosopher, writer, and translator; one of the most influential and educated **Serbs** in the 18th and the beginning of the 19th centuries. Born in **Banat**, he studied languages in several European universities. Upon his arrival in **Serbia** in 1805, he founded the **Great School** (1808) and became the first minister of education. A devoted follower of the Enlightenment and rationalism, Obradović greatly contributed to Serbia's modernization.

OBRENOVAC. Suburb and **commune** of the city of **Belgrade** in the vicinity of the Kolubara River's confluence with the **Sava** River with a population of 70,234 in 1991. It is the site of several thermoelectric plants and its industries include textiles, food processing, and woodworking.

OBRENOVIĆ, ALEXANDER, KING (1876–1903). King of **Serbia** (1889–1903) and last representative of the **Obrenović dynasty**. The only son of King **Milan Obrenović**, Alexander was proclaimed king following his father's resignation in 1889. On April 13, 1893, before coming of age, he overthrew the Regency and assumed the royal authority. In October 1897, he effectively instituted a personal regime through the cabinet of **Vladan Đorđević**. Alexander's reign was accompanied by numerous constitutional and parliamentary crises, as well as crises in the royal court. His regime was autocratic and unpopular. His marriage to **Draga Mašin**, a commoner and a courtier of his mother, Queen Natalia, caused widespread discontent throughout Serbia. He and the queen were killed on June 10–11, 1903, in the event that became known as **May's Assassination**.

OBRENOVIĆ DYNASTY. Dynasty that ruled in Serbia from 1815 to 1842 and from 1858 to 1903. The founder of the dynasty was Prince **Miloš Obrenović**; other rulers include Prince **Mihailo**, King **Milan**, and King **Alexander Obrenović**.

OBZNANA. Decree of the government of the **Kingdom of the Serbs, Croats, and Slovenes** from December 30, 1920. The decree forbade the activity of the **Communist Party of Yugoslavia** until the adoption of the new **constitution**. The creator of the decree was Interior Minister **Milorad Drašković**. The rationale behind the decree was the Communist party's relative success in the elections of 1920 and its continuous destructive activity. The decree called for the banning of Communist propaganda, prohibition of a general strike, expulsion of foreigners helping the Communist Party, and registration of firearms. The Obznana led to an increase in revolutionary disorder in the state. On June 29, 1921, an attempt on the life of Prince Regent **Alexander I Karađorđević** was made and on July 21, 1921, Milorad Drašković was assassinated. This in turn hastened the enactment of the Law Concerning Public Security and Order in the State in August 1921, which broadened the Obznana and outlawed the Communist Party altogether.

OCTROYED CONSTITUTION/OKTROISANI USTAV. The Octroyed Constitution was promulgated by King **Alexander I Karađorđević** on September 3, 1931. The constitution followed the **Dictatorship of January 6, 1929,** and restored, although not entirely, parliamentary democracy in Yugoslavia. A new administrative division of the country was introduced with nine **banovine** and the district of the city of **Belgrade**. Although Alexander's intention was to strengthen the country's unity, under the Octroyed Constitution the broad prerogatives given to the *banovine* intensified decentralizing tendencies.

*ODJEK* (*The Echo*). Political, economic, and literary journal published three times a week in **Belgrade** from 1884 to 1937 (with interruptions). Initially edited by **Stojan Protić**, *The Echo* followed the policy of the **Radical Party**. Banned on several occasions, the journal regularly changed its title: *Drugi odjek* (*Second Echo*), *Treći odjek* (*Third Echo*), *Srpski odjek* (*Serbian Echo*), *Novi odjek* (*New Echo*). After the split in the Radical Party, the journal became close to the **Independent Radical Party**. After **World War I**, the journal became an official paper of the **Democratic Party**.

OKTROISANI USTAV. See OCTROYED CONSTITUTION.

OLIVER, JOVAN GRČINIĆ (c. 14th century). A Serbian **despot** who ruled from1336 to1355 in northern **Macedonia**. He built Lesnovo monastery.

OLOVO. City and **commune** center in **Bosnia and Hercegovina** with a population of 16,901 in 1991. The ethnic composition prior to the civil war was 75.0 percent Muslim, 18.9 percent Serbian, and 3.9 percent Croatian. Wood processing industry is particularly developed. A mining center in the medieval Bosnian state. The first records of the town date from 1382.

OPLENAC. A hill above **Topola** in **Šumadija** where the members of the **Karađorđević dynasty** are buried in the Church of St. George, the legacy of King **Peter I Karađorđević**.

OPŠTINA. See COMMUNE.

ORAŠAC. Village in **Serbia**, in which **Karađorđe** was elected the leader of the **First Serbian Insurrection** in February 1804.

ORFELIN-STEFANOVIĆ, ZAHARIJE (1726–1785). One of the most educated **Serbs** of the 18th century, a member of Vienna's Academy of Arts. Born in **Vukovar,** he was educated in Buda (Budapest), Vienna, and Venice. His educational work among the **Serbs** was particularly important. Orfelin initiated *Slavenoserbskij magazin*, the first journal among the **South Slavs**. He wrote numerous novels and poems including *Plač Serbie* (*Cry to Serbia)*, *Apostolsko mleko* (*Milk of Apostle*), and *Melodiju Proleću* (*A Song to the Spring*). He is the author of *Večni kalendar* (*Perpetual Calendar*), the first monograph on astronomy in **Serbia**.

OSIJEK. Industrial and agricultural center, and the largest city in **Slavonia**, located on the banks of the Drava River with a population of 164,589 in 1991. Industries include textiles, tanneries, chemicals, and agricultural machinery. Osijek is a university center. A sizeable Serbian population lived in the city and its vicinity. However, the ethnic structure of the city's population changed considerably after the Croatian unilateral secession from Yugoslavia in June 1991, and following heavy fighting between Croatian paramilitary forces and the **JNA** that erupted in Osijek's vicinity.

OSLOBODILAČKA VOJSKA KOSOVA (OVK). See KOSOVO LIBERATION ARMY.

*OSLOBOĐENJE* (*Liberation*). (i) A journal founded and published by **Svetozar Marković** in 1875 (38 issues). The *Liberation* succeeded another of Marković's journals, *Javnost*, which was banned in 1874. Highly critical of Prince **Milan Obrenović**'s regime, the *Liberation* was banned in 1875.

(ii) A daily newspaper, the official paper of the Socijalistički savez radnog naroda (Socialist Alliance) of **Bosnia and Hercegovina** (B-H), founded in 1943. After the outbreak of the civil war in B-H, two papers succeeded *Oslobođenje*: one published in the **Republika Srpska** and the other published in **Sarajevo**, close to the official policy of **Alija Izetbegović** in the early stages of the war.

OSTROGORSKI, GEORGIJE (1902–1976). Prominent Serbian Byzantologist and member of the **Serbian Academy of Sciences and Arts**. His best-known work is *History of Byzantium*.

*OTADŽBINA* (*Fatherland*). (i) An influential literary journal published monthly in **Belgrade** and edited by **Vladan Đorđević** between 1875 and 1892.

(ii) A political journal published in **Banja Luka** by **Serbs** from **Bosnia and Hercegovina**, edited by **Petar Kočić** 1907–1908. Often banned by the Austro-Hungarian administration, the journal continued to be published in **Sarajevo** 1911–1912 and 1913–1914.

OWEN-STOLTENBERG PLAN. The peace plan proposed by Lord David Owen and Thorvald Stoltenberg, cochairmen of the International

Conference on the former Yugoslavia, on July 29, 1993. The plan represented a refined version of the **Vance-Owen Peace Plan** and envisioned **Bosnia and Hercegovina** as a union of the three "constituent republics" in which three "constituent nations" and a group of "others" lived. The plan epitomized an attempt to find a compromise between a Serbo-Croat initiative for confederation and the unitary platform of the **Muslims**. The plan was accepted by all three sides. However, the Muslims' conditional acceptance hinged on substantial alterations and revisions of the plan, which amounted to its rejection. The efforts of Owen and Stoltenberg to find a consensus among the warring parties were suppressed in January 1994 by the United States initiative that called for the establishment of the **Muslim-Croat Federation** and the subsequent creation of the plan of the **Contact Group**.

OZNA (Odeljenje za zaštitu naroda—Department for Protection of the People). Secret service organization founded at the end of **World War II**. **Aleksandar Ranković**, a Serbian Communist and close associate of **Tito**, was in charge of setting up the organization. OZNA played a major role in combating the remnants of supporters of **Draža Mihailović** and the latter's capture in February 1946. In March 1946, the OZNA was replaced by the UDBA (Uprava državne bezbednosti—Department of State Security).

OZREN. (i) A mountain in eastern Serbia in the vicinity of Sokobanja (1,074 m).
(ii) A mountain in central **Bosnia and Hercegovina** (B-H). The mountain was the site of heavy fighting during the civil war. A Serbian monastery is located on the mountain in the vicinity of the city of **Maglaj**.

## - P -

PAČU, LAZAR (1855–1915). Finance minister in several cabinets of the **Radical Party** in the period 1903–1915. One of the best financial experts in **Serbia** at the time, he successfully consolidated Serbia's internal finances during the **Tariff War** with Austria-Hungary.

PAJSIJE (c. mid-16th century–1647). Serbian patriarch, 1614–1647. He bitterly resented and fought both Turkish assimilation and unification attempts of the Roman Catholic church. In his struggle for the revival of the spiritual wealth of the Serbian people, he increased the production of church books. His major works include *Život Cara Uroša* (*The Life of Tsar Uroš*) and *Liturgija Cara Uroša* (*The Liturgy of Tsar Uroš*).

PAKRA. Monastery of the **Serbian Orthodox Church** near **Pakrac**. The monastery was founded by Dositej, the archimandrite of the monastery of **Mileševa**, in 1688. The scepter of Patriarch **Arsenije III Crnojević** was kept in Pakra monastery. In 1991, the monastery was destroyed by Croatian Ministry of Interior troops and paramilitary forces.

PAKRAC. City in **Slavonia** with a population of 27, 276 in 1991. The first mention of the city dates from 1237. During the Turkish occupation, the city was a center of the **Sandžak**, which included almost the whole of Western Slavonia. In 1708, Pakrac became a center of the **Serbian Orthodox Church** in Slavonia and northwestern **Croatia**. In April 1991, Croatian Ministry of Interior troops attacked the local police station and city hall in this predominantly Serb-populated city. This, together with clashes in Borovo Selo and Plitvice, was the prelude to the civil war in the former Yugoslavia. Pakrac was a center of the Western Slavonia region of the **Republic of Serbian Krajina** (**United Nations Protected Areas**, Sector West) until occupied by the Croatian army in May 1995. Since then, most of the Serbian population either left or was expelled from Pakrac county and Western Slavonia.

PALANKA. Turkish word used to describe a small fortification. During the Turkish occupation, a number of towns on the banks of the **Danube** River were called *palanka*. Several Serbian cities and towns are called *palanka*—Smederevska palanka, Brza palanka, Bela palanka, Banatska palanka, and others.

PALAVESTRA, PREDRAG (1930– ). A prominent Serbian writer and member of the **Serbian Academy of Sciences and Arts**. Born in **Sarajevo**, he graduated from the **University of Belgrade** in 1956 and obtained his doctorate from the same university in 1964. He was an editor of the influential Belgrade weekly, ***Književne novine*** from 1958 to 1965 and the journal *Savremenik* (*The Contemporary*) from 1966 to 1973. Palavestra was a president of the Serbian PEN Center in 1985–1989 and 1992–1994. He is a member of the Crown Council of the Crown Prince

**Alexander II Karađorđević**. His major works include *Književnost Mlade Bosne* (*The Literature of the Young Bosnia*), *Kritička književnost* (*The Critical Literature*), and *Knjiga srpske fantastike* (*A Book of Serbian Fiction*).

PALE. Small city and county center in **Bosnia and Hercegovina** (B-H) with a population of 16,310 in 1991. The ethnic composition of the population prior to the civil war was 69.1 percent Serbian, 26.7 percent Muslim, 2.4 percent Yugoslav, and 0.8 Croatian. The city is located 18 km from **Sarajevo** at an altitude of 830 m. Prior to the civil war, Pale was a recreational center. In 1992, after the secession of B-H from the former Yugoslavia, Pale became a center of the **Republika Srpska**. At the end of August 1995, **NATO** planes intensely bombarded targets in and around Pale in retaliation for the Serbian shelling of targets in Sarajevo.

*PANČEVAC*. Daily newspaper published in **Pančevo**. *Pančevac* was a very liberal paper in the 19th century. The first Serbian translation of the *Communist Manifesto* was published in *Pančevac* in 1871. Later, it became an official paper of the **Independent Radical Party**.

PANČEVO. Industrial city and a county center in south **Banat** with a population of 125,261 in 1991. Prior to the creation of the Yugoslav state in 1918, Pančevo was one of the Serbian cultural centers in Austria-Hungary. After 1945, due to rapid industrialization, Pančevo became a center of the petrochemical and glass industry.

PANČIĆ, JOSIF (1814–1888). Best-known Serbian botanist, born in northern **Dalmatia**. Pančić was the first president of the **Serbian Academy of Sciences and Arts**. He was member of numerous professional societies in Serbia and also a corresponding member of Jugoslavenska akademija znanosti i umjetnosti, Hungarian Academy of Sciences, Zoological-Botanical Society and Geological Institute in Vienna, and Botanical Society of Brandenburg in Germany. He graduated with a degree in medicine from the University of Budapest and specialized in botanical studies in Vienna. After coming to **Serbia** in 1846, he worked as a physician in the glass factory "Srpska fabrika stakla" in **Paraćin**. After he became a professor at the Lycée (**Great School**) in **Belgrade** 1856, he began intensive research into the flora of Serbia, Bulgaria, and **Montenegro**. Apart from his research and teaching, he was an active leader in Serbia's cultural development. He translated the most modern textbooks in zoology, mineralogy, geology, and botany into Serbian. His major works include *Flora kneževine Srbije* (*The Flora of the Principality of Serbia*), *Ribe u Srbiji* (*Fish of Serbia*), and *Ptice u Srbiji po analitičkom metodu* (*Birds in Serbia; Analytical Method*).

PANČEVO. Petrochemical complex in Pančevo was completely destroyed during the NATO attack on Yugoslavia in the Spring of 1999.

PANDUROVIĆ, SIMA (1883–1960). Serbian poet and literary translator, one of the founders of Serbian literary modernism. His best-known works include *Dani i noći* (*Days and Nights*) and *Razgovor o književnosti* (*A Conversation about Literature*).

PANIĆ, MILAN (1927– ). American businessman of Serbian origin. A talented cyclist, Panić emigrated to the United States in the early 1950s, where he proved his business talents and became president of the large corporation ICN Pharmaceutical. In the late 1980s, with the tacit approval of Serbian President **Slobodan Milošević,** Panić acquired a majority share in "Galenika," the largest pharmaceutical company in Yugoslavia. In 1992, while still a U.S. citizen, he became prime minister of the **Federal Republic of Yugoslavia** and launched several initiatives aimed toward ending the civil war in **Bosnia and Hercegovina.** In December 1992, he waged an unsuccessful bid for the Serbian presidency but was defeated by Slobodan Milošević. Following his electoral defeat Panić returned to the United States. However, he reentered the Serbian political scene in the mid-1990s and attempted to create a unified opposition bloc.

PAPO, ISIDOR (1913–1996). Prominent surgeon and retired general of the **JNA**. During **World War II** he was the chief of the surgical team of the Supreme Command of **Partisans**. He is a member of the **Serbian Academy of Sciences and Arts** and the French Surgical Academy and is the recipient of numerous domestic and international awards.

PARAĆIN. City in the interior of **Serbia** situated on the bank of the **Morava** River with a population of 64,119 in 1991. The city is best known for the oldest glass factory in Serbia—"Srpska fabrika stakla" (Serbian Glass Factory).

PARIS PEACE TREATY. Formal peace treaty signed by the presidents of **Bosnia and Hercegovina, Croatia**, and **Serbia** on December 14, 1995, in Paris. The United States-sponsored treaty formalized the stipulations of the **Dayton Agreement.**

PARLIAMENT/SKUPŠTINA. The Parliament of the F**ederal Republic of Yugoslavia** (FRY) is composed of two chambers: the Chamber of Republics and the Chamber of Citizens. The Chamber of Republics consists of 40 members, **Serbia** and **Montenegro** each delegating 20 representatives. The distribution of seats in the Chamber of Citizens, based on the results of the December 20, 1992, **elections** was:the **Socialist Party of Serbia** (SPS) 47, **Serbian Radical Party** (SRS) 34, the **Democratic Movement of Serbia** 20, the **Democratic Party of Socialists** (DPS) 17,the **Democratic Party** (DS) five (see Tables 14 and 15, statistical addendum).

In the November 1996 elections the left coalition (SPS, **JUL**, and the **New Democracy**) won 66 seats in the Chamber of Citizens, the coalition Zajedno (SPO, DS, the **Democratic Party of Serbia**, and the Civic Coalition) 22, the Montenegrin DPS 20, the SRS 16, the National Party of Montenegro eight, the Democratic Movement of Vojvodina Hungarians three, the coalition "Vojvodina" two, the **Party of Democratic Action** one, the Social Democratic Party of Montenegro one, and the List for **Sandžak** one.

PARTISANS/PARTIZANI. Popular name of the Communist-led, antifascist movement in Yugoslavia during **World War II.** The "Chief Command of the Partisans' Squadrons for the National Liberation of Yugoslavia" was formed together with the first armed units on June 27, 1941. In July, under the leadership of Josip Broz, **Tito**, the movement initiated a series of insurrections in every region of Yugoslavia (with the exception of **Macedonia**). For most of 1941, the Partisans concentrated their activity in **Serbia**. The initial cooperation between the Partisans and the **Jugoslovenska vojska u otadžbini** (JVO) resulted in the liberation of a sizable territory in western (**Užice**) and southeastern Serbia. The split between the two movements and the German offensive in November 1941 pushed the Partisans out of Serbia. From 1942 to 1944, the Partisans concentrated their activity in **Bosnia and Hercegovina**, where the heaviest fighting took place on the **Neretva** and **Sutjeska** Rivers in 1943. Although official figures exaggerate the size of the Partisans' forces, the movement grew considerably throughout the war, whith **Serbs** constituting the largest single ethnic group (80,000 in 1941; 150,000 in 1942;

300,000 in 1943; 450,000 in 1944; and 600,000 in 1945). In 1944, the official name for the Partisans became the Army of National Liberation of Yugoslavia and in 1945 the Yugoslav Army. Finally in 1951, the name was changed to the Yugoslav People's Army (**JNA**). The main sources of the Partisans' success were to be found in their superior organization and strict discipline and in the ability to quickly accommodate British and Soviet demands, mainly to fight the Germans at all costs. Although throughout the war Partisans insisted on an active struggle against foreign occupiers and "domestic traitors" (the term used for all their opponents), under the auspices of the Communist Party, they effectively carried out a socialist revolution.

PARTIZANI. See PARTISANS.

PARTY OF DEMOCRATIC ACTION/STRANKA DEMOKRATSKE AKCIJE (SDA). Political party of **Muslims** founded in **Bosnia and Hercegovina** (B-H) in 1990. In the same year, the party was established in **Serbia** in the **Sandžak**, in **Kosovo and Metohija** and in **Montenegro**. In the **elections** held in November 1990 in B-H, the SDA won a majority of the seats in the republic's **Parliament** (86). Although it often emphasizes its European outlook and secularism, the SDA imposes religious membership requirements that specifically exclude other constituent nationalities and religions.

PASSAROWITZ, TREATY OF/POŽAREVAČKI MIR. Peace treaty between Austria and Turkey, concluded on July 21, 1718. The treaty consisted of 20 points and was supposed to last for 24 years. According to the treaty, Austria acquired Serbian lands north of the **Western Morava** River, **Banat**, and northern Bosnia. Also, Austria acquired the following Serbian cities: **Belgrade, Paraćin**, Stalać, **Šabac, Bijeljina,** and **Brčko.** The Austro-Turkish War of 1737–1739 and the subsequent **Treaty of Belgrade** substantially changed the provisions of the Treaty of Passarowitz.

PAȘA (Paša; Pasha). Title of high Ottoman dignitaries, both civil and military. The holdings of a *pasha* was called *pașalik* (*pashaluk*). See also BEOGRADSKI PAŠALUK.

PAŠIĆ, NIKOLA (1845–1926). One of the most prominent politicians in the history of modern **Serbia**. Pašić studied in Switzerland, where he became acquainted with the radical ideas of the Russian anarchists. After returning to Serbia, he founded Narodna Radikalna Stranka, popularly known as the **Radical Party**, in 1881. Although he abandoned socialist ideas, he bitterly opposed the regime of King **Milan Obrenović.** After the **Rebellion of Timok** and his death sentence, he emigrated to Bulgaria. In 1888, he returned to Serbia and after winning the **elections** inspired the adoption of one of the most liberal **constitutions** in Europe at the time. After **May's Assassination** of 1903, he became an indispensable political figure in Serbia, serving in almost all Serbian and Yugoslav governments until his death in 1926. The most crucial events in Serbia's history, including the formation of the common state—Yugoslavia—are associated with Pašić.

PATRIARCHATE OF PEĆ/PEĆKA PATRIJARŠIJA. Patriarchate of the **Serbian Orthodox Church** founded by Emperor **Dušan the Mighty** at the church congress in **Skoplje** on April 9, 1346. The congress elevated the Serbian archbishopric to a patriarchate and Archbishop Eustahius II became the first Serbian patriarch. The patriarchate ceased to exist after the fall of **Smederevo** in 1459 but was revived by the Turkish grand vizier **Mehmed-Paša Sokolović** in 1577, and his brother **Makarije Sokolović** became patriarch. During the second Patriarchate of **Peć**, the Serbian Orthodox Church succeeded in preserving its authority over Serbian lands that were severely contested by both the Roman Catholic Church and the Greek Orthodox Church. However, after the Austro-Turkish War of 1683–1699, in which the Serbs sided with the Austrians, and the great Serbian migration from **Kosovo and Metohija** under Patriarch **Arsenije III Crnojević** in 1690, the patriarchate split into two sections. One section, consisting of seven dioceses of the patriarchate, became located in Austria, while over thirty dioceses remained in the Turkish Empire. The Austrian section gained autonomous status in 1710 and became known as the metropolitanate of **Karlovci Sremski.** After that, the Austrians strenuously attempted to alienate the metropolitanate from the patriarchate.

The continuous southward expansion of Austria persistently undermined the position of the patriarchate of Peć. As Turkish territory was reduced, so was the number of dioceses under the patriarchate's jurisdiction. After the Treaty of Passarowitz in 1718 Peć controlled 22 dioceses, while after the **Treaty of Belgrade** in 1739 only 13 dioceses were left to its jurisdiction. Moreover, fighting provoked a massive migration of Serbs towards the north, which substantially reduced the number of believers in the area of the patriarchate. Territorially strangled and economically undermined, the patriarchate was abolished in 1766. The abolition of the Patriarchate reflected the weakening of the Serbs' position within the multi-national Turkish Empire.

PAVELIĆ, ANTE (1889–1959). Organizer and long-time leader of the Croatian fascist organization called **Ustaše.** Between the two world wars Pavelić lived in Italy where, under his supervision, the assassination of King **Alexander I Karađorđević** was planned and organized. In April 1941, supported by German and Italian invaders, he proclaimed a Nazi puppet state called the **Independent State of Croatia.** Under his regime, genocide against Serbs, Jews, and Gypsies was committed throughout what are now **Croatia** and **Bosnia and Hercegovina.** Although one of the biggest war criminals of World War II, Pavelić escaped to Argentina in 1945, under circumstances that involved clergy of the Catholic church and Vatican officials. After an unsuccessful assassination attempt by a rival Ustaše gang, he fled to Madrid, Spain, where he died in 1959.

PAVIĆ, MILORAD (1929– ). Famous Serbian writer, poet, and translator. He was educated at the **University of Belgrade** and University of **Zagreb,** where he acquired his Ph.D. He was director of "Prosveta," one of the biggest publishing houses in Yugoslavia. Pavić is a well-known historian of Serbian literature and the recipient of numerous national and international awards. His major works include *Hazarski rečnik* (*Dictionary of Khazars*), *Unutrašnja strana vetra* (*Wind's Inside*), and *Istorija srpske književnosti* (*History of the Serbian Literature*).

PAVLE, PATRIARCH (1914– ). Patriarch of the **Serbian Orthodox Church** (SPC) since 1992. Born Pavle Stojčević in the vicinity of **Pakrac** in **Slavonia,** he studied theology in **Belgrade, Sarajevo,** and Athens. Patriarch Pavle is the representative of a centrist line within the SPC that advocates a limited involvement of the church in secular and current political affairs. Fluent in several languages, Patriarch Pavle is the author of numerous theological studies.

PAVLICA. Small village in the vicinity of **Raška.** Two churches in the village bear the same name. The older church—Stara Pavlica—probably dates from the 11th century. The newer church—Nova Pavlica or Monastery of Vavedenje—was built by the brothers Stefan and Lazar Musić, nephews of Prince **Lazar Hrebljanović**.

PAVLOVIĆ, DRAGOLJUB (1866–1920). Serbian politician and historian. As a member of the **Radical Party** he was the first president of the National Assembly of the **Kingdom of the Serbs, Croats, and Slovenes.** His major works include *Požarevački mir 1718* (***Treaty of Passarowitz, 1718***) and *Istorizam and racionalizam* (*Historicism and Rationalism*).

PAVLOVIĆ, JOVAN (1843–1892). Liberal journalist and founder of many journals in **Serbia** and **Montenegro**, including the journal ***Pančevac***. He later became the minister of education in Montenegro where he revamped the entire educational system.

PAVLOVIĆ, MELENTIJE (1776–1833). First Serbian to became a metropolitan in **Belgrade**. As a close associate of the Prince **Miloš Obrenović,** he installed the first **constitution** of Belgrade's metropolitan.

PAVLOVIĆ, MILOJE (1887–1941). Director of the Teacher's Academy for Women in **Kragujevac** from 1932 to 1941. On October 20, 1941, he was arrested by the Germans and after rejecting clemency was executed together with his students and 7,000 citizens of **Kragujevac**.

PAVLOVIĆ, MIODRAG (1928– ). Prominent Serbian writer and literary translator. A member of the **Serbian Academy of Sciences and Arts**, Pavlović is the author of 23 books of poetry, 14 books of essays, four anthologies, four plays, and two books of short stories. His works include *Antologija srpskog pesništva XVIII-XX vek* (*An Anthology of Serbian Poetry, 18th to 20th Centuries*), *Antologija savremene engleske poezije* (*An Anthology of Modern English Poetry*), *Pesništvo evropskog romantizma* (*Poetry of European Romanticism*), *Velika Skitija* (*The Great Scythia*), *Nova Skitija* (*The New Scythia*), and *Mleko iskoni* (*The Milk of Time Immemorial*).

PAVLOVIĆ, PEKO (1830–1903). **Vojvoda** and politician from **Montenegro.** As the leader of the volunteers from Montenegro, he actively participated in the **Rebellions of Hercegovina.** After a quarrel with Prince **Nikola I Petrović,** he emigrated to **Serbia** and Bulgaria but later returned to Montenegro.

PAVLOVIĆ, RADIVOJE (1390–1441). Serbian **vojvoda** from **Bosnia and Hercegovina.** He controlled the lands around **Trebinje,** a part of Eastern Bosnia, and half of the **Konavle** region. After his unsuccessful war with **Dubrovnik** he asked for Turkish help, which provoked a war between **Serbia** and Bosnia in 1432.

PAVLOVIĆ, TODOR (1804–1854). Journalist and editor of several journals and almanacs: *Letopis* (*Annal*), *Srpski narodni list* (*Serbian National Journal*), *Dragoljub*, etc. Influenced by the ideas of the Slovak revolutionary Jan Kolar, he abandoned his law practice and dedicated his life to civic work. Under his auspices **Matica Srpska** was reestablished in 1836.

PAVLOVIĆ, VISARION (?–1756). Bishop of **Bačka** of the **Serbian Orthodox Church**. Bishop Visarion founded the first Serbian gymnasium in **Novi Sad** and the first Serbian academy of philosophy and theology. He was an intermediary between the **patriarchate of Peć** and the metropolitanate of **Karlovci Sremski.**

PAVLOVIĆ, ŽIVKO (1871–1938). General of the Serbian army and later of the Yugoslav army and a member of the **Serbian Academy of Sciences and Arts**. From 1910 to 1912 he was a professor of tactics at the Military Academy and chief of the operations department of the general staff. During **World War I** he was the deputy chief of staff of the Supreme Command 1914–1915 and then replaced **Radomir Putnik** as chief of staff in 1915–1916. On the **Salonika Front** he commanded the Šumadijska division and later became Serbian military attache in Athens. His major studies include *Bitka na Kolubari* (***Battle of Kolubara***) and *Opsada Skadra* (*The Siege of Shkodër*).

PAVLOVIĆ, ŽIVOJIN (1933– ). Serbian writer, movie director, and professor at the Academy of Film of the **University of Belgrade**. His work, which includes 10 movies and 26 books, has received many international awards.

PEĆ. City in **Metohija** with a population of 127,796 (1991 estimate). It was also the center of the **patriarchate of Peć** in medieval **Serbia.** The city has developed wood processing, textile, and leather industries. In the Spring of 1998, heavy fighting erupted between the **Kosovo Liberation Army** and Serbian police in the vicinity of Peć. During the NATO attack on Yugoslavia the Albanian population was forced to leave the city. In the aftermaths of the withdrawal of the Yugoslav forces, the entire Serbian population was expelled from the city and its vicinity.

PEĆANAC-MILOVANOVIĆ, KOSTA (1871–1944). **Četniks** commander during **World War I** and a leader of the **Rebellion of Toplica** in 1917. President of the Četniks Association, between the wars he collaborated with German forces during **World War II**. He was executed by the forces of **Dragoljub-Draža Mihailović** in 1944.

PEĆKA PATRIJARŠIJA. See PATRIARCHATE OF PEĆ.

PEKIĆ, BORISLAV (1930–1992). Serbian writer born in **Podgorica.** A political dissident, he left Yugoslavia in the early 1970s. His best-known works, often filled with political and ideological connotations, include *Vreme čuda* (*Time of Miracles*), *Kako upokojiti vampira* (*How to Mollify a Vampire)*, *Zlatno runo* (*The Golden Fleece)*, and *Sentimentalna povest britanskog carstva* (*A Sentimental History of the British Empire*).

PELAGIĆ, VASA (1833–1899). Serbian educator. He studied theology in **Belgrade** and in 1860 became a teacher in **Brčko** where he founded the first Serbian library in **Bosnia and Hercegovina**. After spending two years in Moscow, Pelagić returned to Bosnia and became a principal at the theology school in **Banja Luka.** In 1869, the Turks expelled him from Bosnia to Asia Minor, but, with Russian help, he succeeded in escaping to **Serbia** in 1871. In Serbia and **Montenegro**, he participated in activities of **Ujedinjena Omladina Srpska** and Družina za oslobođenje srpstva (Society for the Liberation of Serbia). He collaborated with many liberal and radical journals such as *Socijal-demokrat* (*Social Democrat*), *Srpski zanatlija* (*Serbian Craftsman*), and *Zanatlijski savez* (*Artisans Union*). As a bitter opponent of the **Obrenović** regime, he was expelled from Serbia on several occasions. He died in prison in 1899. His major works include *Istorija bosansko-hercegovačkog ustanka* (*History of the Bosnian-Hercegovian Insurrection*), *Pravi narodni učitelj* (*Authentic People's Guide*), *Spas Srbije i srpstva* (*The Salvation of Serbia and Serbdom*), and *Socijalizam i osnovni preporođaj društva* (*Socialism and the Basic Transformation of Society*).

PERIĆ, ŽIVOJIN (1868–1953). Serbian politician and the founder of the Conservative Party of **Serbia** in 1914. He wrote extensively in the area of civil law and political liberties. His major works include *Zadružno* *pravo* (*Guilds' Law*) and *Granice sudske vlasti* (*Limits of Judical Power*).

PERIŠIĆ, MIODRAG (1948– ). Serbian writer and literature critic, vice president of the **Democratic Party,** and a representative in the Assembly of the **Federal Republic of Yugoslavia.** Perišić was an editor of the influential weekly ***Književne novine,*** a president of the Serbian PEN Center (1990–1992), and minister of information in the government of **Milan Panić** in 1992. He published an anthology of modern Serbian poetry, *Ukus osamdesetih* (*The Taste of the 1980s*) in 1984.

PERIŠIĆ, MOMČILO (1944– ). Former chief of the General Staff of the Yugoslav Army (VJ). In 1991, he was the commander of the artillery academy of the **JNA** in **Zadar.** After the JNA withdrew from **Croatia,** he became a corps commander stationed in **Mostar.** Following the withdrawal from **Bosnia and Hercegovina** and the subsequent reorganization of the JNA into the VJ, he became commander of the Third Army in 1993 and later in the same year the chief of the General Staff of the Army of Yugoslavia.

PERKO, FRANC (1929– ). Archbishop of the Roman Catholic Church in **Belgrade** since 1986.

PEROVIĆ, LATINKA (1933– ). Political scientist and politician currently employed at the Institute of Modern History in **Belgrade**. She was a secretary of the Central Committee of the League of Communists (Communist Party) of **Serbia** from 1968 to 1972. In 1972, under charges of "liberal deviation", she was forced to resign from all functions and expelled from the Communist Party. Her major works include *Od centralizma do federalizma* (*From Centralism to Federalism*), *Srpski socijalisti XIX veka* (*Serbian Socialists of the 19th Century*), and *Zatvaranje kruga* (*Closing the Circle*).

PERUĆICA. Hydroelectric plant in **Montenegro**. It uses the water of the rivers **Zeta** and **Gračanica**. Perućica's maximum capacity is 1,350 million Kwh of electrical energy.

PEŠIĆ, VESNA (1940– ). President of the Civic Coalition of **Serbia** (Građanski savez Srbije), a represenative of the **Democratic Movement of Serbia** in the **Parliament** of Serbia, and a founder of a coalition of opposition parties known as **Zajedno**. She is one of the founders of

Udruženje za jugoslovensku demokratsku inicijativu (Yugoslav Association for a Democratic Initiative) and the weekly ***Vreme***. Since 1991 she has been employed at the Institute of Philosophy and Social Theory. Pešić is the author of *Nationalism, War and the Disintegration of Communist Federations: The Case of Yugoslavia* and a recipient of the National Endowment for Democracy award in 1993.

PETAR I PETROVIĆ (1747–1830). Metropolitan and the ruler of **Montenegro** 1782–1830. A close friend of **Karađorđe**, he fought both the Turks and the French. He established the first written Code of Laws in Montenegro in 1796–1803 and attempted to conciliate warring clans.

PETKOVIĆ, VLADISLAV-DIS (1880–1917). One of the most talented Serbian poets. His poetry, although not faultless in its language, is among the most musical in the **Serbian language.** Author of several books, he drowned in a boat sunk by a German submarine near the island of **Corfu.** His best-known work is "Utopljene duše" ("Drowned Souls").

PETRINJA. City and county center in **Banija.** The population of the city was 35,530 in 1991. The city is best known for "Gavrilović"—one of the biggest food-processing factories in the former Yugoslavia. In the period 1991–1995, the city was under Serbian control in the **Republic of Serbian Krajina** (**United Nations Protected Areas**, Sector North), but it was seized during the August 1995 offensive of the Croatian army. The Serbs, who were the majority of the population in the city and its vicinity, either fled the Croatian forces or were expelled from the city.

PETRONIJEVIĆ, AVRAM (1791–1852). Politician and statesman, a main representative of the **Constitutionalists**. Born in eastern **Serbia**, he was schooled in the Romanian town of Orşova where he learned German, Greek, Romanian, and Italian. As chief diplomat of Prince **Miloš Obrenović**, he also learned Turkish and French. A close associate of Prince Miloš, he became a leading opposition figure after **Mileta's Rebellion.** During the reign of Prince **Alexander Karađorđević** Petronijević was a minister of foreign affairs.

PETRONIJEVIĆ, BRANISLAV (1875–1954). Philosopher, mathematician, and one of the most original Serbian thinkers. A philosopher, he was a proponent of Leibnitz's methaphysical idealism. His major contributions are in mathematics (discrete geometry) and paleontology (a study on archeoptherix). His major works are *Principles of Metaphysics* (in German), *Istorija novije filosofije* (*History of the Recent Philosophy*), and *Osnovi empirijske psihologije* (*Fundamentals of the Empirical Psychology*).

PETROV, ALEKSANDAR (1938– ). Writer and literary translator. Petrov was the president of the Writers' League of **Serbia** (1985–1988) and the acting president of the Writers' League of Yugoslavia in 1988. Since 1992, he has lived in the United States, where he edits *Amerikanski Srbobran* (*American Srbobran*). His major works include *Lady in an Empty Dress*, *Slovenska škola* (*Slavic School*), and *Istočni dlan* (*East Palm*).

PETROVA CRKVA (St. Peter's Church). Church in the vicinity of **Novi Pazar** built in the ninth century. The church is the most prominent early monument in the continental Serbian territories and was the see of the bishopric of **Ras**. In this church **Stefan Nemanja** was baptized, and his son **Stefan Prvovenčani** was chosen heir to the Serbian throne.

PETROVA GORA. Mountain between the rivers Kupa, Korana, and **Glina** situated between the regions **Banija** and **Kordun.** The mountain, originally called Gvozd (Iron Mountain), was named after the last Croatian king, Petar Svačić, who died there in a battle with the Hungarians in 1097. During **World War II**, the Serbian population of Banija and Kordun found refuge from the **Ustaše** terror on Petrova gora.

PETROVARADIN. City on the right bank of the **Danube** River across from **Novi Sad.** The first reference to the city dates from the 12th century. The strategic location of the city resulted in several severe battles between Turkish and Austrian armies in the 17th and 18th centuries.

PETROVIĆ, MIHAILO MIKA ALAS (1868–1943). Prominent Serbian mathematician. The founder of the first mathematical school in **Serbia,** and a member of the **Serbian Academy of Sciences and Arts** and several foreign academies. His major contributions were in the areas, of differential equations and mathematical spectrums. He is also considered to be the founder of mathematical phenomenology. He also was a passionate explorer and fisherman.

PETROVIĆ, MIODRAG-ČKALJA (1924– ). One of the best Serbian comedians of all times. He has acted in 26 movies, more than 20 TV movies, and 32 television series.

PETROVIĆ, NADEŽDA (1873–1915). Serbian painter and public worker. She was the most significant painter of the epoch and had a profound impact on the development of contemporary art in **Serbia**. She introduced a new style in Serbian painting that included a distinctive local element and ethnographic traits.

PETROVIĆ, RASTKO (1898–1950). One of the most original Serbian poets. After retreating with the Serbian army through Albania, he completed his education in Paris, where he graduated with a degree in law and became a professional diplomat. Among the first Serbian authors who explored primitive and exotic cultures, Petrović was influenced by the psychoanalytical school. His best known works are *Otkrovenja* (*Revelations*), *Afrika* (*Africa*), and *Dan šesti* (*Sixth Day*).

PHILIKE HETAIRIA. See SOCIETY OF FRIENDS.

PIJADE, MOŠA (1890–1957). Yugoslav politician and statesman and a member of the **Communist Party of Yugoslavia** since 1920. He spent most of the interwar period in prison where he translated the major works of Karl Marx. During **World War II** he was one of the closest associates of **Tito** and occupied several influential posts, including vice president of **AVNOJ**. After the war, he was prime minister (1953–1954) and president of the National Assembly from 1954 until his death.

*PIJEMONT (Piedmont)*. Belgrade daily, published between 1911 and 1915. The first editor was **Ljubomir Čupa Jovanović**. The newspaper expressed the views of the secret organization **Ujedinjenje ili Smrt (Unification or Death)** and regularly published articles on the national question, political circumstances, and the role of the army in Serbian society.

PIROĆANAC, MILAN (1837–1897). Serbian politician and the leader of the **Progressive Party** from 1881 to 1886. As prime minister of **Serbia** he participated in the signing of the **Secret Convention** in 1881. He resigned in 1883, following the landslide election victory of the **Radical Party**.

PIROT. City and county center in southeastern **Serbia** with a population of 67,658 in 1991. The city is located on the **Nišava** River and the strategic road between Serbia and Bulgaria. The city is best known for its rubber industry ("Tigar" enterprise), textile industry, and a special type of handmade rugs.

PIROT, REBELLION OF/PIROTSKA BUNA. Insurrection in the city of Pirot in January 1843. The leader of the rebellion was Đorđe Božinović but the real organizer was Prince **Mihailo Obrenović,** who planned the assassination of Prince **Alexander Karađorđević.**

PIROTSKA BUNA. See PIROT, REBELLION OF.

PIVA. River in **Montenegro** exceptionally rich in hydroenergy. The total length of the river is 120 km. Jointly with the river **Tara**, it forms the **Drina** River.

PLAOVIĆ, RAŠA (1899–1977). Celebrated Serbian actor, among the first to modernize Serbian acting in contemporary European fashion. He was an intuitive and emotional actor who strove to bring more creativity into performances. He created the two greatest roles in Serbian acting in the period between the two world wars (Hamlet in Shakespeare's tragedy and Leone Glembaj in Miroslav Krleža's drama *Gospoda Glembajevi* [*The Noble Glembajs*]).

PLAVŠIĆ, BILJANA (1930– ). Former president of **Republika Srpska** (RS). Born in **Tuzla,** she was educated in **Sarajevo** and **Zagreb,** where she received her doctorate in biology. A botany professor of the University of Sarajevo, she became actively involved in politics in 1990 when she became a Serbian representative in the collective Presidency of **Bosnia and Hercegovina.** A hard-line representative in the leadership of the RS, Plavšić was named acting president in July 1995, following an agreement between **Radovan Karadžić** and international mediator Carl Bildt. In the September 1996 elections she won the majority of votes as the presidential candidate of the **Serbian Democratic Party** in the RS. Since then she assumed a more moderate course and tried to distance herself from Karadžić's faction in the Serbian Democratic Party. She lost the presidential elections in 1998 to **Nikola Poplašen**.

PLOČNIK, BATTLE OF. The battle between **Serbs** and the Turks that took place in the vicinity of the village of Pločnik in the **Toplica** region in 1386. While Serbian forces decisively defeated the Turkish army, they failed to stop the Turkish expansion in the **Balkan Peninsula**.

PODGORICA. Capital city and political, economic, and cultural center of **Montenegro**, with a population of 118, 059 in 1991. The city is located on the confluence of the **Morača** and **Ribnica** Rivers on the remnants of the ancient city of Dioclea. The first records of Serbian Podgorica date from the times of **Stefan Nemanja,** who was born in the city. From 1945 to 1991, the official name of the city was Titograd (**Tito**'s City). The textile, machine-building, and tobacco industries are particularly well-developed. Since 1960 Podgorica has been an university center. See also DUKLJA.

POLIT-DESANČIĆ, MIHAILO (1833–1920). Serbian journalist and politician from **Vojvodina.** A close associate of **Svetozar Miletić,** he resisted the process of Magyarization (Hungarization) of Serbs living in Vojvodina. He was the editor of the journal *Branik* (*The Defender*) and contributor to *Zastava* (*The Flag*) and *Srpski dnevnik* (*Serbian Daily*). His best known work is *Kako sam svoj vek proveo* (*The Way I Have Lived My Life*).

POLITIKA (Politics). Oldest publishing company in **Serbia** and Yugoslavia. Founded in 1904, the company started to publish the daily newspaper *Politika*, which became the most influential and popular paper in Serbia and Yugoslavia. The newspaper was always close to the official policy of the Serbian, and later Yugoslav, governments. Current daily circulation exceeds 200,000.

POMORAVLJE. Basin of the **Morava** River, which can be roughly divided into two subregions: Lower and Upper Pomoravlje. The main part of Pomoravlje is the 20 km-wide and 350 m-deep valley of the Morava River. The basin is very densely populated and several major cities are located in the area: **Vranje, Leskovac, Paraćin, Jagodina**, etc. The Morava Valley is **Serbia**'s e most important connection between Europe and Asia Minor.

POPA, VASKO (1922–1991). One of the best modern Serbian poets. Popa was a member of the **Serbian Academy of Sciences and Arts** and the most widely translated poet in Serbia. His best-known works include *Kora* (*Epidermis*), *Vučja so* (*Wolves' Salt*), *Kuća nasred druma* (*The house in the middle of a road*), and *Sporedno nebo* (*The Ancillary Sky*). Among numerous distinctions, he was the recipient of the European Literature Award of Austria in 1967.

POPEČITELJ (Minister). Title of the ministers in **Karađorđe**'s government of **Serbia** during the **First Serbian Insurrection.** From 1811 there were six ministers: **Mladen Milovanović**, war minister; **Milenko Stojković**, foreign minister; **Dositej Obradović**, minister of education; **Todorović Petar Dobrnjac**, minister of justice and chief justice of the Supreme Court; **Sima Marković**, minister of finance; and **Jakov Nenadović,** minister of interior.

POPLAŠEN, NIKOLA (1951– ). President-elect of the **Republika Srpska** (RS). Born in **Vojvodina**, Poplašen worked as a university professor in **Sarajevo** until 1992. After the outbreak of the civil was in **Bosnia and Hercegovina** he became politically active and joined the **Radical Party**. In the presidential elections in the RS in September 1998 he defeated the Western- favored incumbent **Biljana Plavšić**. A political ally of **Vojislav Šešelj**, Poplašen is critical of the **Dayton Agreement** and opposes the unification of the RS and **Muslim-Croat Federation**.

POPOVIĆ, ALEKSANDAR (1928–1996). A popular writer. His work focuses on the themes of modern life. His best-known works are *Razvojni put Bore Šnajdera* (*Development Pattern of Bora Šnajder*), *Druga vrata levo* (*Second Door to the Left*), and screenplays for the television series *Ceo život za godinu dana* (*A Lifetime in a Year*) and *Rađanje jednog naroda* (*The Creation of One Nation*).

POPOVIĆ, BOGDAN (1863–1944). Serbian writer and literary critic. One of the founders of **Srpski književni glasnik** and a member of the **Serbian Academy of Sciences and Arts**. He introduced the views of Western European, particularly French, literary modernism to **Serbia**. His major works include *Antologija novije srpske lirike* (*The Anthology of the Recent Serbian Lyric*) and *O književnosti* (*On Literature*).

POPOVIĆ, DAMNJAN (1858–1928). Serbian general, a leading figure in **May's Assassination**. Due to the **diplomatic strike** and pressure from the United Kingdom he was forced into retirement with the rest of the **Conspirators** in 1906. Reactivated in 1912 he commanded the Serbian detachment at the siege of Shkodër and in 1913 he was appointed the "Commander of the Troops in New Regions". However, due to his opposition to government policy, he was again forced into retirement in early 1914. Reactived at the beginning of **World War I** he was subsequently replaced, arrested and sentenced to 10 years in prison. In the **Trial of Salonika** the high military court changed his sentence to 20 years.

POPOVIĆ, JOVAN STERIJA. See STERIJA, POPOVIĆ JOVAN

POPOVIĆ, KOČA (1908–1993). Serbian and Yugoslav politician. Born into an affluent family in **Belgrade,** he was educated in Paris, where he graduated with a degree in philosophy from the Sorbonne. Upon his return to Belgrade, he joined the **Communist Party of Yugoslavia**. He was a volunteer in the **International Brigades** during the Spanish Civil War. During **World War II**, he was a commander of an elite **Partisan** unit. After the war he occupied several important posts, including chief of the General Staff, 1945–1953; foreign minister, 1953–1964; vice president of the **Socialist Federal Republic of Yugoslavia** (SFRY), 1966–1967; and member of the Collective Presidency of SFRY. He resigned from all posts in 1972, after **Tito**'s purge of Serbia's liberal leadership.

POPOVIĆ, MIODRAG-MIĆA (1923–1996). Celebrated Serbian painter, writer, movie director, and member of the **Serbian Academy of Sciences and Arts.** He is a leading figure among intellectuals and artists who challenged traditional forms of expression in the 1950s.

POPOVIĆ, SRĐA (1937– ). Controversial Yugoslav attorney and political dissident specializing in "political trials." The founder of the weekly ***Vreme*** and the President of the United Yugoslav Democratic Initiative for **Kosovo and Metohija**, he was also a legal representative of American Express, Chase Manhattan Bank, Coca Cola Export, and Xerox in the former Yugoslavia. In 1991 he emigrated to the United States.

POPOVO POLJE. Valley in **Hercegovina** 20 km north from the Adriatic Sea. The length of the valley is 31 km, while the average width is around 1.5 km. The total area of the valley exceeds 45.9 sq km, and it is the most fertile region in Hercegovina. Prior to the construction of a network of waterways, the valley was regularly flooded by the Trebišnjica River. Since 1993, Popovo polje has become the site of severe clashes between Croatian army troops and the **Bosnian Serb Army** (BSA).

PORTE. Widely used term for the Ottoman Court.

POŽAREVAC. City in northern **Serbia** with a population of 84,678 in 1991. The "Kostolac" thermal power plant is located in its vicinity. Coal production is 1.5 million tons per year. The peace treaty between Austria and Turkey was concluded here in 1817. See also PASSAROWITZ, TREATY OF.

POŽAREVAČKI MIR. See PASSAROWITZ, TREATY OF.

PRAVITELJSTVUJUŠČI SOVJET. See GOVERNING COUNCIL.

PREČANI. Term used for **Serbs** living outside **Serbia** (literally "across the river"). In its narrow version it applies only to the Serbs who live in **Vojvodina**, while Serbs from **Croatia** are referred to as *hrvaćani* (literally, "from Croatia") and Serbs from **Bosnia and Hercegovina** are called *bosanci* or *hercegovci*.

PREDIĆ, UROŠ (1857–1953). One of the best known Serbian painters. He finished the Academy of Arts in Vienna, where he completed 13 pieces on classical mythology in the Upper House of Vienna's **Parliament**. After returning to **Serbia** in 1885, he concentrated his works around historical composition and canvas paintings.

*PREGLED* (*The Review*). Journal founded and published by Serbian intellectuals in **Sarajevo** from February 1, 1910, to October 1, 1912. *The Review* did not belong to any of the political parties. It emphasized the importance of economic and cultural issues and bitterly opposed the notions of the "Bosnian Nation" and the "Bosnian Language" promoted by Austria-Hungary. The most prominent contributors to the journal were **Jovan Cvijić, Kosta Stojanović,** and **Slobodan Jovanović**. The journals with the same title published in Sarajevo after **World War I** and **World War II** substantially differed from the original *Pregled.*

PREOBRAŽENJSKA SKUPŠTINA. See TRANSFIGURATION ASSEMBLY.

PREPOLAC. Mountainous passage (822 m) in southern **Serbia** overlooking the valleys of the **Lab** and **Toplica** Rivers. The passage is located on the main route between **Niš** and **Priština** and was the site of heavy fighting between the Serbian army and Turkish forces during the **Balkan wars.**

PRERADOVIĆ, PETAR (1818–1872). Prominent Serbian poet born in **Vojna Krajina.** He graduated from the Austrian military academy and later became a major general in the Austrian army. Preradović was a talented poet and belonged to the **Illyrian** Movement.

PRESENTATION CONSTITUTION (1835). See CONSTITUTION.

PRESPA. (i) A lake located on the border between Greece and the **Former Yugoslav Republic of Macedonia** covering an area of 274 sq km.
(ii) A complex of Orthodox churches located on the islands Ail and Mali grad on Lake Prespa and the villages Vinena and German. The oldest churches were built during the reign of Emperor **Samuilo**, while the newest was built in 1369.

PREVLAKA. Small peninsula (length 3 km, width 200 m) in **Boka Kotorska** Bay. On Prevlaka, **Stefan Prvovenčani** built the monastery of Archangel Michael, which became the headquarters of the bishop (later metropolitan) of **Zeta**. Throughout history, Prevlaka was bitterly contested between **Serbia**, the Venetians, France, Russia, Austria-Hungary, and local clans. After **World War II**, Prevlaka became a part of administrative **Croatia** but remained under the direct control of **JNA**. Given the peculiar location and strategic importance of the peninsula, the current status of Prevlaka is a matter of negotiation between the **Federal Republic of Yugoslavia** and **Croatia**.

PRIBIĆEVIĆ, SVETOZAR (1875–1936). Controversial Serbian politician born in Kostajnica, **Banija**. At the beginning of his political career, he was a supporter of the unification of Serbs and Croats into a single centralized state. After the formation of a common state in 1918, Pribićević occupied several important posts in the government of the **Kingdom of**

**the Serbs, Croats, and Slovenes.** After his split with the **Radical Party,** he dramatically changed his political views and in 1927 entered into a coalition with the secessionist **Croatian Peasant Party** led by **Stjepan Radić.** After the **Dictatorship of January 6, 1929,** and a short period of isolation in the small town of Brus, he went into exile in Czechoslovakia.

PRIBOJ. City in southwest **Serbia** located on the **Lim** River (population 35,951 in 1991). A large automotive factory was built in Priboj in 1950.

PRINCIP, GAVRILO (1896–1918). Young Serbian revolutionary from **Bosnia and Hercegovina.** As a member of the organization **Mlada Bosna** he assassinated the Austrian archduke Franz Ferdinand in **Sarajevo** on June 28, 1914. His death sentence was commuted to 20 years imprisonment. He died in the infamous Austro-Hungarian prison Theresienstadt in 1918. See also SARAJEVO ASSASSINATION.

PRIŠTINA. City in Serbia and capital of the autonomous province of **Kosovo and Metohija** with a population of 199,654 (1991 estimate). It was a trade center in medieval **Serbia** and during the Turkish occupation. The city was liberated during the **Balkan wars** in 1912. After **World War II**, Priština rapidly developed into the industrial and cultural center of the Kosovo and Metohija region. The city has a university and major textile and mining industries. In 1981, Priština became the center of a violent demonstration organized by Albanian separatists.

PRIZREN. City in **Kosovo and Metohija** with a population of 200,584 in 1991. The population includes an Albanian majority (157,518 in 1991). The city, under the name **Višegrad**, was established by **King Milutin** on the remnants of the Roman trade center known as Theranda. Until the coronation of **Dušan the Mighty** in **Skoplje** in 1346, Prizren was the capital of the medieval Serbian state. The city was occupied by the Turks in 1455. The churches Bogorodica Ljeviška, St. George, St. Savior, and St. Nicholas as well as the ruins of the St. Archangel monastery are located in the immediate vicinity of the city.

The modern city has developed textile, metal processing, tobacco, and leather industries.

PRODANOVIĆ, JAŠA (1876–1948). Serbian politician and writer. Initially a member of the **Radical Party**, he founded the **Yugoslav Republican Party** in 1920 with **Ljubomir-Ljuba Stojanović**. After **World War II**, he became a minister in government of Josip Broz, **Tito**, and in 1946 a deputy prime minister. He wrote *Ustavne borbe u Srbiji* (*Constitutional Struggle in Serbia*) and *Istorija političkih stranaka i struja u Srbiji* (*History of Political Parties in Serbia*).

PROGRESSIVE PARTY. Political party founded in 1880, by the young Conservative group, an organization that emerged after the death of Prince **Mihailo Obrenović** and the retirement from political life of the leaders of the **Conservatives, Ilija Garašanin** and **Nikola Hristić.** Admirers of Western Enlightenment and technical achievements, the Progressives also promoted individual rights and civil liberties. However, they championed the system of elitist oligarchy based on a senate of intellectuals and prosperous men and an electorate divided into voting classes according to the amount of taxes they paid. The main figures in the party were **Milutin Garašanin, Milan Piroćanac**, Đorđe Pavlović, and **Čedomilj Mijatović.**

The party, close to King **Milan Obrenović**, was in power in 1880–1883, 1884–1887, and 1895–1896. In 1881, during the reign of the Progressives, **Serbia** concluded a trade treaty and **Secret Convention** with Austria-Hungary. The party was formally dissolved in 1896, after King **Alexander Obrenović** began to share power with the **Radical Party.** It was reestablished in 1906 by **Stojan Novaković,** and party representatives participated in various governments. After **World War I,** the party reentered political life under the leadership of Mileta St. Novaković. After failing to enter **Parliament** in the elections of 1923, the party ceased political activity in 1925.

PROKUPLJE. City in southern **Serbia**, the center of the **Toplica** region with a population of 52,969 in 1991. The first records of the city are from the 14th century. In the 16th century a strong colony of traders from **Dubrovnik** operated in Prokuplje. The modern city has asbestos, machine-building, tobacco, and textile industries.

PROTIĆ, STOJAN (1857–1923). Prominent Serbian and Yugoslav politician and statesman and a founder of the **Radical Party.** A minister of interior and minister of finance in several Serbian governments, he formed the first Yugoslav government after **World War I.** He opposed the **Vidovdan Constitution** and proposed an alternative constitutional arrangement that called for greater autonomy for Croatian and Slovenian regions. He was the first Serbian politician to propose so-called "amputation," that is the territorial division of the Yugoslav state between **Serbs** and Croats based on the ethnic principle. He was the main editor of the journals *Delo* (*Work*) and ***Odjek*** (*Echo*). He published numerous studies under the pseudonyms Balcanicus and Veritas. His best-known works include *O Makedoniji i Makedoncima* (*On Macedonia and Macedonians*), *Tajna konvencija izmepu Srbije i Austro-Ugarske* (*The Secret Convention Between Serbia and Austria-Hungary*), and *Srbi i Bugari u Balkanskom ratu* (*Serbs and Bulgars in the Balkan War*).

PRVI SRPSKI USTANAK. See FIRST SERBIAN INSURRECTION.

PRVOVENČANI, STEFAN (Stefan "the First Crowned") (c. 1170–1228). Middle son of **Stefan Nemanja** and son-in-law of the Byzantine emperor Emmanuel Comnen. After the abdication of his father, he became grand **župan** of **Serbia** but was deposed by his older brother **Vukan**. With the support of his younger brother **Saint Sava** he finally defeated Vukan in 1207. In 1217, he was proclaimed king of Serbia by the papal legate. Although considered as "the first Serbian king," the reign of Stefan was an important period in Serbian history mainly due to the activity of St. Sava. During Stefan's rule the separate Serbian archbishopric was established in 1219. The vigorous religious and cultural activity included building of numerous monasteries (**Studenica**, Arilje, **Gradac**, **Žiča**, **Mileševa**, and others) and the translation of the Byzantine code of church laws known as *Nomokanon* or *Svetosavska krmčija* (*The Code of Sveti Sava*).

PUCIĆ, MEDO (1821–1882). Serbian writer and politician from **Dubrovnik**. He was educated in Venetia, Padova, and graduated with a degree in law from the University of Vienna. A leader of the Catholic Serbs in Dubrovnik and **Dalmatia**, Pucić was a strong supporter of **Vuk Stefanović Karadžić** and a close associate of **Ilija Garašanin**, particularly in secret misssions and national propaganda. He was a member of the **Srspko učeno društvo** and **Jugoslovenska akademija znanosti i umjetnosti**. His major works include *Slavjanska antologija iz rukopisa dubrovačkih pjesnika* (*Slav Anthology in the Works of Dubrovnik's Poets*) and *Spomenici srbski* (*Serbian Monuments*).

PUPIN, MIHAJLO (1858–1935). One of the best Serbian scientists and inventors of all time. Pupin was born in Idvor, a small village in **Banat**, and finished his primary education in **Pančevo.** In 1874, at age sixteen, he came to the United States. After several manual jobs he began his studies at Columbia University in 1879. After graduating from Columbia in 1883, he went to Cambridge and Berlin, where he successfully defended his Ph.D. thesis. In 1889 he returned to the United States and became a professor of mathematical physics in the Department of Mechanical Engineering at Columbia University. Pupin patented 24 of his inventions, mainly in the area of telecommunications. His major invention is the method for transmission of telephone impulses over long distances via specially designed inductive coils, later named Pupin's coils. Pupin also discovered secondary X-rays. Pupin was very active in the Serbian diaspora in the United States. He founded the society Serbian National Defense, and he served as the consul general of the Kingdom of **Serbia** during **World War I**. In 1924, Pupin received the Pulitzer Prize in biography for his autobiographical work *From Immigrant to Inventor*.

PUTNIK, RADOMIR (1847–1917). Celebrated Serbian military commander. He participated in all Serbian wars from 1876 to 1917. He was a major in the **Serbo Turkish wars** (1876–1877) and chief of staff of the **Danube** division. He lectured at the Military Academy and in 1890 became a deputy chief of staff of the Serbian army. As a sympathazier of the **Radical Party** he was forced into retirement in 1896, but was reactivated following **May's Assassination** in 1903. During the **Balkan Wars** and **World War I,** Putnik served as a chief of staff of the Supreme Command of the Serbian army. Under his command and strategic guidance the Serbian army accomplished its greatest victories.

## - R -

*RADENIK* (*Worker*). The first socialist newspaper in the Balkans. Published three times weekly in **Belgrade** in 1871 (86 issues) and in 1872 (51 issues) when it was banned. In the first issue of *Radenik* **Svetozar Marković** published the first socialist program among the **South Slavs**.

RADICAL PARTY/RADIKALNA STRANKA The Radical Party was formed as Narodna radikalna stranka (National Radical Party) in 1881.

It was the first party in modern **Serbia** with a solid organization and clearly defined program. The party's program published in the Radicals' official paper ***Samouprava*** (*Self-government*) on January 20, 1881, called for universal male suffrage; self-government for local districts and **communes**; direct proportional taxes; complete freedom of press, assembly, and association; free public education, and closer ties with **Montenegro**. The unsuccessful attempt of Prince **Milan Obrenović** to disband the Radical Party after the **Rebellion of Timok** in 1883 was followed by a period when the party dominated in Serbia's politics. The party's political successes were due mainly to the exceptional leadership of **Nikola Pašić, Stojan Protić, Lazar Paču,** and others. During the rule of the Radical Party, Serbia went through the most dynamic period in its modern history.

In 1901, following a disagreement about the **constitution** promulgated by King **Alexander Obrenović** and in cooperation with the **Progressive Party,** the Radical Party split into two factions. While the majority of the Radicals continued to gather around Nikola Pašić, some younger members formed the **Independent Radical Party.** However, the split did not undermine the primacy of Pašić's faction, which continued to be a dominant political party in Serbia and the **Kingdom of the Serbs, Croats, and Slovenes** until the suspension of parliamentary life under the **Dictatorship of January 6, 1929.** Following the restoration of parliament in 1931, the Radical Party split into several factions, led by the **Yugoslav Radical Union** and the so-called Main Committee.

The Radical Party was reestablished in 1990. An internal power struggle split the party into Narodna radikalna stranka (National Radical Party) and Srpska radikalna stranka (**Serbian Radical Party**) led by **Vojislav Šešelj.** In September 1994, seven parliamentary deputies led by Jovan Glamočanin, split from the Serbian Radical Party and formed the Serbian Radical Party "Nikola Pašić." Šešelj's Serbian Radical Party is an extreme nationalist organization whose members actively participated in the fighting in **Croatia** and **Bosnia and Hercegovina.** The Party participated in the 1992 and 1993 **elections** in Serbia and the **Federal Republic of Yugoslavia**, establishing itself as a considerable political force in the country. In Spring 1998, the Radicals and the **Socialist Party of Serbia** formed a coalition government. Vojislav Šešelj and Tomislav Nikolić became deputy prime ministers, and Aleksandar Vučić became minister of information in the Serbian government.

RADIĆ, STJEPAN (1871–1928). Croatian politician, a founder and a leader of the **Croatian Peasant Party** (HSS). Prior to **World War I**, due to his opposition to the rule of Khuen Hédervári, **ban** of **Croatia**, Radić was expelled from several universities across Austria-Hungary. From 1902 he lived in **Zagreb** and worked as a secretary of the Croatian United Opposition. From 1902 to 1906 Radić published a monthly journal *Hrvatska misao* (*Croatian Thought*). During World War I, Radić embraced a pro-Austrian stand and opposed the Yugoslav idea.

After the end of the war and immediately following the formation of the **Kingdom of the Serbs, Croats, and Slovenes** Radić and the HSS openly pursued a secessionist policy and called for the formation of an independent Croatian republic. In 1923, Radić attempted to link the HSS with the communist-run Peasant International. After his second imprisonment in 1925 and following his subsequent renouncement of secessionism and republicanism, Radić joined the government of **Nikola Pašić** and was appointed minister of education. In 1927, however, he again joined the opposition and in 1928 became president of a newly formed Peasant-Democratic Opposition.

On June 20, 1928 Radić was wounded in a shooting during the session of **Parliament** in **Belgrade**. While he successfully recovered from the wounds, he died shortly thereafter.

The undisputed leader of the Croatian nationalist movement between the two world wars and a stringent opponent of a Yugoslav state in any form, Radić and his political agenda became a source of inspiration and a pillar of the policy of the Croatian nationalists and the **Croatian Democratic Union** in the 1990s.

RADIČEVIĆ, BRANKO (1824–1853). Serbian poet and patriot, romanticist, and devoted follower of **Vuk Stefanović Karadžić.** Radičević was the first poet who used Vuk's reformed Serbian literary language. The founder of Serbian lyrical romanticism, he introduced Serbian poetic art into European romanticism. Radičević was a poet of primordial sensitivity, aligned with animalistic and pantheistic interpretations of the world. His best known works include *Kad mlidijah umreti* (*In the Face of Death*), *Đački rastanak* (*The Pupils' Parting*), and *Tuga i opomena* (*Sadness and Remainder*).

RADIKALNA STRANKA. See RADICAL PARTY.

*RADNIČKE NOVINE* (*The Workers' News*). Weekly socialist newspaper founded in 1897. *The Workers' News*'s editors included pioneers of Serbian socialism, **Vasa Pelagić, Jovan Skerlić, Dragiša Lapčević,** and Živojin Balugdžić. Banned in 1899, the newspaper was revived in 1902 by Radovan Dragović and **Dimitrije Tucović.** Following a short ban between March and June 1903, it became the official organ of the **Social Democratic Party.** It was the first socialist newspaper published daily in Serbia from 1911 to 1915.

RADOSLAV (1192–1233). Oldest son of **Stefan Prvovenčani,** and king of **Serbia** 1227–1234. Radoslav was an unpopular ruler, mainly because he was under the strong influence of his father-in-law, Byzantine emperor Theodor I Angelus. During Radoslav's rule Serbia obtained its first currency, although with Greek insignia. Shortly after Angelus was defeated by Bulgarians in the Battle of Klokotnica (1230), Radoslav was overthrown and his brother **Vladislav** assumed the Serbian throne.

RADULOVIĆ, RISTO (1880–1915). Serbian journalist and national revolutionary from **Mostar, Bosnia and Hercegovina,** the editor of the journal ***Narod*** (*The People*). He was imprisoned for his pro-Serbian activities and sent to the infamous Austro-Hungarian prison in Arad, where he died.

RAĐEVINA. Agricultural and mining region in western **Serbia** between Sokolska Mountain and the Jadar River; the center of the region is Krupanj (population 21,878, 1991).

RAIČKOVIĆ, STEVAN (1928– ). Prominent Serbian poet and writer, his style is characterized by an ethereal perception of nature. His numerous works include *Pesma tišine* (*Poem of Silence*), *Balada o predvečerju* (*Balad of Dusk*), and *Kamena uspavanka* (*Stone Lullaby*).

RAJAČIĆ, JOSIF (1785–1861). Metropolitan (1842–1848) and patriarch of the **Serbian Orthodox Church** (1848–1861). Rajačić became patriarch of **Vojvodina** at the so-called May Assembly (May 13–15, 1848) held in **Karlovci Sremski.** The Assembly proclaimed Vojvodina a Serbian province with **Stevan Šupljikac** as **vojvoda.** As spiritual leader of the Serbs living in Vojvodina, Rajačić bitterly opposed Hungarian nationalism and assimilation practices during the Hungarian revolution of 1848. Rajačić founded several schools and established a library and printing press at the patriarchate of Vojvodina.

RAJIĆ, JOVAN (1726–1801). A Serbian historian and writer, Rajić is the author of *Istorija raznih slovenskih narodov, napače Bolgar, Horbatov, i Serbov* (*History of Different Slavic People, Mainly Bulgars, Croats, and Serbs*), the first history of the **South Slavs.**

RAJIĆ, TANASKO (?–1815). A hero from the **First** and **Second Serbian Insurrections**, he died in the Battle of ***Ljubić*** on May 25, 1815.

RAKIĆ, MILAN (1876–1939). One of the most celebrated Serbian poets, member of the **Serbian Academy of Sciences and Arts,** and a diplomat. He used motifs from medieval **Serbia,** while his style is characterized by a striving for perfection of form. Although he published only two volumes of poems he is considered as a most influential Serbian poet. His best-known poems are "Na Gazi-Mestanu" ("On Gazi-Mestan"), and "Jefimija".

RAKIJA. Serbian national drink made by the distillation of various fruits. The best-known *rakija* is made from plums (Šlivovits), but it is also made from grapes, pears, apples, and apricots. The strength of *rakija* varies from 20 to 50 percent alchohol per volume.

RAKITIĆ, SLOBODAN (1940– ). President of the Congregational National Party (SNS). In the 1990–1994 period he was a vice president of the **Serbian Renewal Movement** (SPO) and a member of both the Serbian and Federal **Parliaments**. Following an internal split in the SPO in 1994, Rakitić's group formed the SNS. A prominent poet, Rakitić is president of the Association of Writers of Serbia. His numerous works include *Svet nam nije dom* (*World is Not Our Home*), *Osnovna zemlja* (*Basic Ground*), and *Duša i sprud* (*Soul and Drift*).

RAKOVICA. (i) A suburb and **commune** of **Belgrade** with a population of 97,752 in 1991. One of the largest machine and tractor factories in **Serbia** is located in Rakovica, as is a plant producing tires. The suburb was heavily bombed during the NATO air-campaign.
(ii) A monastery built in the 17th century near Belgrade.

RANKE, LEOPOLD (1795–1886). Prominent German historian. Based on sources provided by **Vuk Stefanović Karadžić,** he wrote *Srpska revolucija* (*Serbian Revolution*).

RANKOVIĆ, ALEKSANDAR MARKO LEKA (1909–1984). Serbian and Yugoslav politician and statesman and one of the leaders of the **Communist Party of Yugoslavia** (CPY). Ranković joined the CPY in 1928 but was soon arrested and sentenced to six years in prison. Upon his release from prison, and after **Tito** was appointed general secretary of the CPY, Ranković became a member of the Politburo of the Central Committee of the party. During **World War II**, Ranković became one of Tito's closest associates. After the war, he organized the State Secret Police and was minister of internal affairs, 1946–1953. From 1953 to 1966 he was deputy prime minister and later vice president of the **Socialist Federal Republic of Yugoslavia** (SFRY). During the internal battle for power between Croatian-Slovene and Serbian Communists, Ranković was accused of threatening the undisputed leadership of Tito and removed from all political posts during the Brioni Conference in July 1966. His funeral in 1981 was attended by more than 100,000 people and was a massive demonstration against Serbia's inferior position in the SFRY.

RANKOVIĆ, SVETOLIK (1863–1899). Serbian writer from **Šumadija,** influenced by Tolstoy and Dostoyevsky and best known for his realistic portrayal of Serbian society in the second half of the 19th century. His depiction of life is dark and pessimistic. He enriched Serbian prose in the domain of the psychological story and novel. His best-known works include *Gorski car* (*Tsar of Mountains*),and *Seoska učiteljica* (*Village Teacher*).

RAPALLO, TREATY OF. Treaty between Italy and the **Kingdom of the Serbs, Croats, and Slovenes** of November 12, 1920. The treaty consisted of nine articles that regulated the borders between the two states; Italy acquired **Zadar** and the islands of Cres, Lastovo, Lošinj, and Palagruža.

RAS. City in medieval **Serbia**, capital of **Raška**, located south of **Novi Pazar.** The monasteries **Đurđevi Stupovi** and **Sopoćani**, as well as the Church of St. Peter where **Stefan Nemanja** was baptized, are located in the vicinity of Ras.

RAŠKA. (i) An ancient name for **Serbia** used until the reign of **Stefan**

**Nemanja.** The term was primarily used by the Hungarians, while Byzantine sources used Serbia instead.

(ii) A small city and **commune** center in southwestern Serbia (population 28,784, 1991); a printing press established in 1846. The wood-working industry is particularly well developed.

RAVANICA. Monastery in the vicinity of Ćuprija, a legacy of Prince **Lazar Hrebeljanović,** built between 1375 and 1377. Although damaged, the monastery's **frescoes** are the finest examples of Serbian wall painting from the second half of the 14th century.

RAVNA GORA. Mountain in western **Serbia** (881 m), stronghold of **Jugoslovenska vojska u otadžbini** and the center of **Ravnogorski pokret.**

RAVNOGORSKI POKRET (Movement of Ravna Gora). Serbian nationalist organization founded on **Ravna Gora** in 1941. The organization was the political wing of the movement of Colonel **Dragoljub-Draža Mihailović** and actively worked on the establishment of the Central National Committee (CNK) that would gather representatives of all political parties in Serbia. The executive board of the CNK consisted of **Dragiša Vasić,** Stevan Moljević, and Mladen Žujović. The members of the movement were prosecuted by the Communist government after **World War II**.

RAŽNATOVIĆ, ŽELJKO-ARKAN (1952– ). President of the Stranka srpskog jedinstva (Serbian Unity Party) and the commander of a paramilitary organization called Srpska dobrovoljačka garda (Serbian Voluntary Guard), better known in the West as "Arkan's Tigers." Although wanted as an alleged criminal in several European countries, Arkan became a popular figure among hardcore Serbian nationalists during the civil war in Croatia. A successful entrepreneur, he ran an effective political campaign and was elected a deputy in the Serbian **Parliament** in 1992–1993.

REFUGEES. According to the Report of the United Nations High Commissioner for Refugees (UNHCR), out of 15 million refugees in the world in 1993, 2.5 million were from the former Yugoslavia. Since the beginning of the civil war in 1991 more than one million persons dispersed in and through **Serbia** and **Montenegro**. The main flow of refugees into Serbia and Montenegro occurred in 1991, 1992, and 1993. The first refugees arrived in Serbia in March 1991. Following the outbreak of the full scale civil war in June 1991, more than 170,000 people fled **Croatia** and found refuge in Serbia.

The next wave of refugees began to flow into the **Federal Republic of Yugoslavia** (FRY) in April 1992, after the eruption of the civil war in **Bosnia and Hercegovina**. The total number of refugees in the FRY in 1994 was 442,121 (395,000 in Serbia and 47,121 in Montenegro). The ethnic composition of the refugees was: 77 percent Serbian,10 percent Muslim, 2 percent Croatian, and 3 percent Montenegrin. In August 1995, in the biggest exodus in the entire war, more than 150,000 refugees, mostly **Serbs**, from the **Republic of Serbian Krajina** (RSK) crossed into Serbia. Most of the refugees (94 percent) were given shelter by individual families, while the rest were accommodated institutionally throughout the FRY. This causes a great deal of confusion in UNHCR figures. Whereas it is fairly easy to provide counts for people in refugee camps, it is very difficult to count refugees scattered throughout numerous private dwellings. Thus, in the 1995 biannual UNHCR figures, hundreds of thousands of refugees in the FRY have simply vanished without any explanation. This was before the fall of the RSK in August. The fighting in **Kosovo and Metohija** that began in Spring 1998 created a new wave of refugees. It is estimated that close to 100,000 persons left their homes during the intense fighting between Serbian police and the **Kosovo Liberation Army**. The NATO air campaign created an acute refugee problem. Following the beginning of the NATO offensive almost 800,000 Albanians from Kosovo either left their homes or were forced out. After the Yugoslav security forces left the region, almost the entire Serbian population left the Kosovo.

REIS-EL-ULEMA. Position in the Muslim hierarchy in **Bosnia and Hercegovina** (B-H) similar to the posts of Catholic archbishop and Orthodox metropolitan. The position was created by the Austro-Hungarian administration following the occupation of B-H in 1878, with the intention of making Muslim clergy independent from the Ottomans and facilitating the creation of the **Bošnjak** nationality.

REMETA. (i) Velika Remeta (Great Remeta), a monastery on **Fruška Gora**, in the vicinity of Krušedol, first mentioned in the 16th century. (ii) Mala Remeta (Little Remeta), monastery on Fruška Gora, a legacy of King **Dragutin**.

REPUBLIC OF CROATIA. See CROATIA, REPUBLIC OF

REPUBLIC OF SERBIAN KRAJINA/REPUBLIKA SRPSKA KRAJINA

(RSK). Term used for the Serbian-populated and controlled territories in **Croatia** from 1991–1995.

In July 1989, the **Serbs** living in Croatia, encouraged by the change of policy under **Slobodan Milošević,** began to organize and become politically active, demanding the rights of their own culture, language, and the Cyrillic alphabet. The Croatian authorities arrested several prominent persons during this time, which increased tension between Serbs and Croats in Croatia. The relationship between the two communities further deteriorated after the nationalist **Croatian Democratic Union** (HDZ) won the first multiparty elections in Croatia and **Franjo Tudjman** became president in April-May 1990.

On July 25, 1990, the Croatian Serbs established the Serbian National Council (SNC) as their representative body in Croatia and issued a Declaration on the Sovereignty and Independence of Serbs in Croatia. This was followed by the blockade of the Serb-controlled area that became known as Krajina of **Knin**, the proclamation of the Serbian Autonomous Region (SAO) of Krajina and the establishment of the Executive Council and Ministry of Internal Affairs on January 4, 1991, and the proclaimed separation of SAO Krajina from Croatia on March 19, and with a resolution that called for Krajina to remain in Yugoslavia on April 1. Serbian determination to remain part of Yugoslavia led to civil war following Croatia's unilateral secession from Yugoslavia. After five months of heavy fighting that took place almost exclusively in Serbian-populated areas (SAO Krajina and the Autonomous Region of Eastern **Slavonia, Baranja,** and Western **Srem**), the Republic of Serbian Krajina (RSK) was proclaimed, and Knin was declared the capital city on December 19, 1991. The total area of the republic was approximately 14,000 sq km with an estimated population of 300,000 people.

According to the **Vance Plan**, following the withdrawal of the **JNA** from Croatia and deployment of the **United Nations Protection Force (UNPROFOR)**, the territory of the RSK was divided into four **United Nation Protected Areas** (UNPA): East, West, North, and South. Relations between Croatia and the RSK remained strained and extremely tense throughout 1992–1995. The lack of international recognition, hostile policies of the United States and the **European Community** (European Union), lack of unequivocal support from the **Federal Republic of Yugoslavia**, and an internal power struggle undermined the basic foundation of the RSK. In two short and swift operations in May and August 1995, the Croatian army, with the tacit approval of the international community, captured Western Slavonia (UNPA West) and Krajina of Knin (UNPA South and North), thus ending the existence of the RSK.

*REPUBLIKA* (*Republic*). (i) A weekly political journal and official paper of the **Yugoslav Republican Party**, published in **Belgrade** 1907–1908 and 1920–1928. *Republika* was edited by **Jaša Prodanović**, **Ljubomir-Ljuba Stojanović**, and Saša Milijanović. The journal continued to be published after **World War II** until 1956.

(ii) A biweekly journal published in **Belgrade** and official paper of the Civic Alliance; its editor is Nebojša Popov.

REPUBLIKA SRPSKA (Serbian Republic) (RS). Territory and administrative unit of **Bosnia and Hercegovina** (B-H) under control of the Bosnian Serbs since 1992. The first multiparty elections held in B-H, in November 1990, reflected the existing ethnic division in the republic: the Muslim **Party of Democratic Action** (SDA) acquired 86 seats in the **Parliament**, the **Serbian Democratic Party**, 72, and the **Croatian Democratic Union**, 44. Although initially they propagated the idea of B-H remaining in Yugoslavia, the president of B-H, **Alija Izetbegović**, and the SDA radically changed their policies in the second part of 1991. Following the examples of **Slovenia** and **Croatia**, the Presidency of B-H decided to follow **European Community** instructions and applied for independence on December 20, 1991. The next day, on December 21, the Parliament of the Serbian People of B-H decided to establish the Republic of the Serbian People in B-H. The republic was nominally proclaimed on January 9, 1992, and was followed by the establishment of several autonomous regions. After the collapse of the negotiations on the future of B-H and the international recognition of the republic's independence, the Bosnian Serb Parliament proclaimed the Republika Srpska on April 7, 1992.

After three years of fighting, and several unsuccessful mediation attempts, the existence and the legitimacy of the Republika Srpska was sanctioned by the **Dayton Agreement** and **Paris Peace Treaty**. The territory of the republic includes 49 percent of B-H (25,053 sq km) and has an estimated population of one million. In November 1997 parliamentary elections, the Serbian Democratic Party won the majority of votes (24 seats), followed by the Coalition for Democratic and Unified Bosnia and Hercegovina (16 seats), **Biljana Plavšić**'s Serbian National Alliance (15 seats), Serbian Radical Party of RS (15 seats), and the Socialist Party of RS with nine seats. In the latest elections in September

1998, **Nikola Poplašen**, the candidate of the Radicals, became president of the RS. The Serbian Democratic Party won 19 seats, the Serbian National Alliance 15, the Coalition for Democratic and Unified Bosnia and Hercegovina 15, the Serbian Radical Party of RS 11, the Socialist Party of RS 10, the Social Democratic Party of Bosnia and Hercegovina eight, the Serbian Social Democratic Alliance six, the **Croatian Democratic Union** one, and New Croatian Initiative one.

REPUBLIKA SRPSKA KRAJINA. See REPUBLIC OF SERBIAN KRAJINA.

RESAVA. (i) A monastery. See **Manasija**.

(ii) River in **Serbia**, 70 km long; the valley of the river is rich in high-quality brown coal.

RESAVSKA ŠKOLA. Term used to denote cultural and literary activity in the **Manasija** monastery. The activity was initiated by **Stefan Lazarević**, Serbian **despot**, who gathered the most educated monks of the time in Manasija. Most of the activity centered around rewriting books and the rules of syntax.

REŠETAR, MILAN (1860–1942). Prominent Serbian philologist, born in **Dubrovnik**, and one of the leading experts on old dialects of the Serbian and Croatian languages. He taught at the University of Vienna and University of **Zagreb**. His best works include *Štokavski dijalekat* (*Štokavian Dialect*), *Najstariji dubrovački govor* (*The Oldest Language of Dubrovnik*), and *Die serbokroatischen Kolonien Süditaliens* (*Serbo-Croatian Colonies in Southern Italy*).

RIBARAC, STOJAN (1855–1922). Serbian politician and statesman, the leader of the **Liberal Party** from 1903. He participated in several Serbian governments from 1892. As minister of justice in the government of **Stojan Novaković** in 1909, Ribarac granted a broad amnesty to political prisoners.

RIBNICA. Medieval village on the juncture of the Ribnica and **Morača** Rivers, the birthplace of **Stefan Nemanja**.

RIBNIK. A destroyed palace of the Emperors **Dušan the Mighty** and **Uroš II** near **Prizren.**

*RILINDJA*. Daily paper published in the Albanian language in **Priština,** founded in 1959 and banned in 1991, after a series of articles calling for the secession of **Kosovo and Metohija** from **Serbia.**

RISTIĆ, JOVAN (1831–1899). Renowned Serbian politician and statesman, the leader of the **Liberal Party**, one of the regents of King **Milan Obrenović** and King **Alexander Obrenović**, prime minister, and minister of foreign affairs of **Serbia**. Ristić was a strong opponent of Austro-Hungarian expansionism in the Balkans. President of the **Serbian Academy of Sciences and Arts**, he wrote *Spoljašnji odnošaji Srbije 1848–1872* (*Foreign Relations of Serbia 1848–1872*) and *Diplomatska istorija Srbije za vreme srpskih ratova za oslobođenje i nezavisnost* (*Diplomatic History of Serbia during Serbian Wars for Liberation and Independence).* Together with **Ilija Garašanin** and **Nikola Pašić**, Ristić was among the most influential Serbian politicians.

RISTIĆ, LJUBIŠA (1947– ). Prominent Yugoslav theater worker, movie director, and producer. Ristić's highly original and unconventional style is internationally recognized by several distinguished awards, including an "Obie" for the best off-Broadway performance in 1982. He is the artistic director of a multiethnic ensemble of the **National Theater** from **Subotica** and president of **JUL** (Yugoslav Left).

RUGOVA, IBRAHIM (1945– ). An Albanian writer and dissident politician. Rugova is president of the **Democratic League of Kosovo** and prime minister of an illegal government of the self-proclaimed Republic of Kosovo. Although the main exponent of the Albanian separatism, in September 1996, Rugova signed a provisional agreement with the Serbian government that called for an end of the Albanian boycott of the official school system in Kosovo. His position as an undisputed leader of the movement for the **Kosovo and Metohija** independence was seriously undermined by extremists of the **Kosovo Liberation Army**.

RUGOVSKA KLISURA. Picturesque canyon between **Peć** in **Kosovo and Metohija** and Čakor in **Montenegro.**

RUVARAC, ILARION (1832–1905). Historian, the founder of the so-called critical school of history in **Serbia**. His best-known works include *Odlomci o grofu Đorđu Brankoviću i Arseniju Crnojeviću* (*Fragments on Groff Đorđe Branković and Arsenije Crnojević)* and *O pećkim patrijarsima (On Patriarchs of Peć*).

## - S -

SAFE AREAS. Special zones that may not be attacked or threatened by any means. UN Security Council Resolution 824 declared **Sarajevo, Bihać, Goražde, Žepa, Tuzla,** and **Srebrenica** Safe Areas. The designated zones had a strategic importance for the Muslim army, which concentrated substantial forces in Bihać (Fifth Corps) and Tuzla (Second Corps).

SAINT SAVA. See SAVA, SAINT.

SALONIKA FRONT. Formed after Allied failure in the Gallipoli operation in October 1915. Allied forces were comprised of five British and four French divisions. Upon the completion of its withdrawal to **Corfu Island**, Greece, via Albania in the winter of 1915–1916, the Serbian army (6,025 officers and 124,190 soldiers) arrived on the Salonika front in early March 1916. During heavy fighting in August-September 1916, the Serbian army captured the strategic mountain ridge **Kajmakčalan,** enabling it to capture Bitolj on November 19, 1916. In September 1918, the Serbian army was at the forefront of the Allied offensive that broke through the German-Bulgarian defenses. A combined French-Serbian attack launched on September 15, 1918, led to the capitulation of Bulgaria, the first of the Central Powers to be defeated, on September 29 and opened the way to an advance on Austria's rear. The collapse of the Salonika front led to the rapid liberation of **Serbia** and the rest of the Yugoslav lands in October-November 1918.

SALONIKA, TRIAL OF. Staged trial of Colonel **Dimitrijević Dragutin Apis** and members of the secret organization **Unification or Death**, also known as the Black Hand (Crna Ruka), held from April 2, 1917, to June 14, 1917. Apis and his associates were charged with conspiracy to kill Crown Prince **Alexander I Karađorđević** and Prime Minister **Nikola Pašić** and overturn the **Karađorđević dynasty.** Apis and two close friends were sentenced to death and executed on June 26, while the rest of the accused were given prison sentences. The entire process was staged in order to remove the potential threat of the radical officers around Crna ruka, to insure Prince Regent Alexander control over the army, and, more importantly, to conform to the demands of the Austro-Hungarian emperor Karl, who sought to negotiate a separate peace with the Allies in 1917. Apis and his associates were fully rehabilitated in 1953.

SAMARDŽIĆ, RADOVAN (1922–1995). Prominent Serbian historian and member of the **Serbian Academy of Sciences and Arts** (SANU). Born in **Sarajevo**, Samardžić was educated in Paris, Meinz, and **Belgrade**, where he graduated with a degree in history. He was dean of the School of Philosophy of the **University of Belgrade**, director of the Institute for Balkan Studies of SANU, and secretary of the History Department of SANU. His best-known works include ***Mehmed-Paša Sokolović***, *Beograd pod Turcima* (*Belgrade under the Turks*), *Veliki vek Dubrovnika* (*Great Century of Dubrovnik*), and *Pisci srpske istorije I-IV* (*Writers of Serbian History I-IV*).

SAMODREŽA. Church situated at the juncture of the **Lab** and **Sitnica** Rivers in the northern part of **Kosovo Polje**, where the Serbian army under Prince **Lazar Hrebeljanović** was consecrated before the **Battle of Kosovo** on June 28, 1389.

SAMOSTALNA RADIKALNA STRANKA. See INDEPENDENT RADICAL PARTY.

*SAMOUPRAVA* (*Self-government*). Political, economic, and literary newspaper published by the **Radical Party**. *Samouprava* was founded in 1881 under the editorship of **Pera Todorović** and **Stojan Protić.** The newspaper was first banned in 1883, reinitiated in January 1886, and banned again at the end of the same year because of the role of the Radical Party in the **Rebellion of Timok.** It continued to be published in 1903–1915 and 1918 until 1929, when it was banned due to the **Dictatorship of January 6, 1929.** From 1936 to 1941 the newspaper was published under the auspices of the **Yugoslav Radical Union.**

SAMOUPRAVLJANJE. See SELF-MANAGEMENT.

SAMUILO (?–1014). Tsar of the Macedonian Slavs, 976–1014, his empire encompassed **Macedonia,** Bulgaria, Thessaly, Epirus, present Albania, **Duklja,** parts of **Dalmatia, Raška,** and **Srem.** His power declined after the loss of **Skoplje** and Durrës to the Byzantine Empire in 1004–1005. Samuilo died in 1014, after his army was crushed and prisoners were blinded by the Byzantine emperor Basil II at the Battle of Belasica.

SANA. River in **Bosnian Krajina,** 142.6 km long. The Sana is rich in hydroenergy and is used for log transportation.

SANCTIONS. Imposition of punitive measures against Yugoslavia began on May 20, 1991, when the United States suspended economic aid to Yugoslavia "because of Serbia's use of repressive measures in Kosovo." This was followed by the **European Community**'s (EC) imposition of an arms embargo and the suspension of financial aid to Yugoslavia on July 5, 1991. On September 26, the Security Council of the United Nations adopted Resolution 713 and imposed an arms embargo on Yugoslavia. As the civil war, provoked by the Croatian and Slovenian unilateral secessions, progressed, the EC imposed economic sanctions against **Serbia** and **Montenegro** on December 2, 1991.

The outbreak of civil war in **Bosnia and Hercegovina** (B-H) on April 6, 1992, was followed by the Security Council's Resolution 757, adopted on May 30, 1992. The resolution called for the implementation of comprehensive sanctions against the newly formed state of the **Federal Republic of Yugoslavia** (Serbia and Montenegro), isolated as being the main culprit for the war in B-H. The sanctions encompassed a full economic blockade and suspension of all scientific, cultural, and sports cooperation. The resolution actually echoed the "Yugoslavia Sanctions Act of 1992" of the U.S. Congress from May 21, 1992. The rationale used for justifying the implementation of the sanctions rested solely on the notion that Yugoslavia had committed an act of aggression against Croatia and B-H. Although neither international legal norms nor Yugoslav legal documents (the **Constitution** of 1974) supported the charge of aggression, the Security Council intensified the sanctions against the FRY by adopting Resolution 787 (November 16, 1992) and Resolution 820 (April 18, 1993). Sanctions were further tightened by freezing all of the assets owned or controlled by the FRY authorities and by prohibiting all commercial maritime traffic from entering territorial waters of the FRY. On September 24, 1994, following a disagreement between Serbian President **Slobodan Milošević** and the leadership of the **Republika Srpska** over the peace initiative of the Contact Group, the Security Council adopted Resolution 942 (further tightening sanctions against the RS) and Resolution 943 (relaxation of sanctions against the FRY). Following the signing of the **Dayton Agreement** and the **Paris Peace Treaty**, the Security Council adopted Resolution 1022 (December 11) and suspended sanctions against the FRY.

Sanctions had a devastating effect on the Yugoslav economy and the standard of living of its population. The GDP of the FRY declined from 18.38 billion U.S. dollars in 1991, to 9.52 billion in 1993; the index of physical production declined more than 40 percent; the standard of living of 85 percent of the population dropped to the subsistence level; and the mortality rate due to infectious diseases went up 214 percent.

SANDŽAK/SANJAK. (i) An administrative unit of the Ottoman Empire, a subdivision of a *vilayet* (province).

(ii) A historic region between **Serbia** and **Bosnia and Hercegovina,** total area 7,100 sq km with a population of 264,424 in 1991. It is a mountainous area (the mountains Zlatar, Golija, Ljubišnja) with several plateaus (Pešter, Sjenica). The main rivers of the region are the **Lim, Uvac**, and Raška and have the hydroelectric plants Kokin brod, Raška, and Potpeć. The main centers of the region are **Novi Pazar, Priboj,** Tutin, Prijepolje, and Sjenica. Agriculture is the main sector of the region's economy. Industries include automotive production, wood-processing, and textiles.

**Raška**, the first Serbian state, was located on the territory of the contemporary Sandžak. After the Turkish occupation in the 15th century, the region had a special administrative status as a part of the Bosnian *vilayet* (province). In 1790 it was established as an independent *sandžak*, but the status of the region was often changed until 1877, when it became a part of the Vilayet of Kosovo. Between 1878 and 1908 the region was under joint Austro-Turkish control. After the **Annexation Crisis,** the Sandžak was occupied solely by the Turks until 1912, when it was liberated during the **Balkan wars.** The bulk of **Muslims** in Serbia live in the Sandžak (around 150,000).

SANDŽAK, ETHNIC STRUCTURE. The ethnic structure of the **Sandžak** region (six municipalities in **Serbia** and two in **Montenegro**) is complex. The vast majority of the region's population belong to the three ethnic groups: **Muslims, Serbs,** and **Montenegrins**. Although the region is a historical Serbian land, the Serbian and Montenegrin population decreased in the 1961–1991 period, mainly due to a relatively low birth rate and economic migration. In the 1961–1971 period, the Serbian and Montenegrin population decreased by 7.52 percent, in the 1971–1981 period by 4.84 percent, and in the 1981–1991 period by 7.53 percent. At the same time, the Muslim population continuously increased due to the institutional changes of the status of Muslims, that is, the creation of a separate Muslim national identity in 1971. Thus, in the 1961–1971 period, the Muslim population increased by 49.82 percent, in the 1971–1981 period by 19.79 percent, and in the 1981–1991 period by 11.82 percent (see Table 16, statistical addendum).

SANJAK. See SANDŽAK.

SAN STEFANO, TREATY OF. Peace treaty between Russia and the Ottoman Empire concluded on March 3, 1878. The treaty ended the Russo-Turkish War of 1877–1878 and provided a new disposition of the territory of the **Balkan Peninsula.** The treaty consisted of 29 articles and envisioned the creation of a Greater Bulgaria that would include much of **Macedonia** and extend from the **Danube** to the Aegean Sea and the Black Sea. The independence of **Serbia, Montenegro,** and Romania was recognized, and reforms in **Bosnia and Hercegovina** were required. Serbia was to extend its territory by 150 square miles (390 sq km) toward **Sandžak** and **Kosovo and Metohija,** while Montenegro would gain 200 square miles (520 sq km.) of territory and acquired **Bar** sea port. However, the treaty was never implemented. The treaty was opposed by Austria-Hungary and Great Britain because of growing Russian influence in the Balkans and by Serbia, since the Serbian districts of **Niš, Pirot,** and **Vranje** were to be incorporated into Greater Bulgaria. The Treaty of San Stefano was replaced at the **Congress of Berlin,** June–July 1878, by the Treaty of Berlin.

SARAJEVO. Capital of **Bosnia and Hercegovina** (B-H) with a population of 525,980 in 1991. The ethnic composition prior to the civil war was 49.3 percent Muslim, 29.9 percent Serbian, 10.7 percent Yugoslav, and 6.6 percent Croatian. The city is the economic and cultural center of B-H and was the fifth most important industrial center in the **Socialist Federal Republic of Yugoslavia**. Industries include automobile, electronic equipment, pharmaceuticals, tobacco, wood processing, etc. The main railroad and communication center of B-H, Sarajevo has a university (1946), an academy of sciences, and numerous hospitals. In 1984, Sarajevo hosted the Winter Olympic Games.

Besides neolithic excavations in **Butmir** and the remains of Roman dwellings, the first records of the city date from 1244, as the center of the **Župa Vrhbosna** controlled by the Pavlović Serbian feudal family. The Turks conquered Vrhbosna in 1451 and changed the name of the city to Sarajevo (literally "palace in the field"). The Turkish occupation was replaced by the Austro-Hungarian in 1878, which lasted until 1918. In 1914, **Gavrilo Princip**, a young Serbian revolutionary, assassinated the Austro-Hungarian Crown Prince Franz Ferdinand in Sarajevo. Although heavily modernized after **World War II,** Sarajevo retained a strong Oriental character.

Sarajevo became the center of international attention after the eruption of the civil war in B-H. The outbreak of hostilities between Muslim-Croat forces and the **Serbs** led to the division of the city. At the beginning of the war, the **Bosnian Serb Army** (BSA) seized the strategic hills overlooking the city, while the center of Sarajevo remained under Muslim control. During heavy fighting, the BSA shelled the city, destroying several cultural monuments. Estimates from Bosnian Muslim sources state that 10,400 people died in Sarajevo in the 1992–1995 period. The stipulation of the **Dayton Agreement** that the city would come under the control of **Muslim-Croat Federation,** caused a mass exodus of the population living in the Serbian parts of Sarajevo.

SARAJEVO ASSASSINATION/SARAJEVSKI ATENTAT. Assassination of the Austro-Hungarian crown prince Franz Ferdinand on June 28, 1914 in **Sarajevo.** The assassination was planned in part by Colonel **Dimitrijević Dragutin Apis**, leader of **Unification or Death,** and executed by the members of the revolutionary organization of young **Serbs** from **Bosnia and Hercegovina** known as **Mlada Bosna.** Almost all of the participants were arrested and sentenced by the Austro-Hungarian authorities. Austria-Hungary used the assassination as a pretext for settling accounts with **Serbia.** Although Serbia positively responded to the Austro-Hungarian **Ultimatum,** the Habsburg Monarchy declared war on Serbia on July 28, 1914, triggering **World War I**. See also ČABRINOVIĆ, NEDELJKO; GRABEŽ, TRIFKO; PRINCIP GAVRILO.

SARAJEVSKI ATENTAT. See SARAJEVO ASSASSINATION.

SAVA. (i) The biggest river in the former Yugoslavia; total length 945.5 km, 592 km of which can be navigated. The valley of the river is the main communication link between **Slovenia, Croatia, Bosnia and Hercegovina,** and the Federal Republic of Yugoslavia.

(ii) Name of several patriarchs and archbishops of the **Serbian Orthodox Church**: Sava II, the fourth son of **Stefan Prvovenčani** and the third

Serbian archbishop (1263–1271); Sava III, archbishop 1309–1316, close associate of King **Milutin Nemanjić**; Sava IV, second Serbian archbishop (1354–1375); and Sava V, patriarch 1395–1409.

SAVA, INOK. Serbian monk from the **Dečani** monastery; he wrote the first Serbian primer in the Church Slavonic language in 1597.

SAVA, SAINT (1176–1236). Patronal founder of the **Serbian Orthodox Church** and the greatest Serbian educator. Born the third and youngest son of **Stefan Nemanja,** he emigrated to **Sveta Gora** (Mt. Athos) in northeast Greece to lead a monastic life in 1192. He changed his Christian name Rastko to St. Sava, and after the arrival of his father in 1197, he cofounded the Serbian monastery **Hilandar** in 1198. The monastery became the center of medieval Serbian culture and ecclesiastical leadership. After mediating a fraternal conflict between **Vukan** and **Stefan Prvovenčani**, Sava returned to **Serbia** in 1206, and became superior of the **Studenica** monastery, the religious and political center of the emerging Serbian Church, in 1208. Opposing the papal-sponsored coronation of Stefan Prvovenčani in 1217, Sava left Serbia. In 1219, he returned and proclaimed the autocephalus Serbian Orthodox Church with its center at **Žiča** monastery. Encouraged by the patriarch of Constantinople and the Byzantine emperor, Sava became the first Serbian archbishop.

The establishment of an autonomous Serbian Orthodox Church enabled Serbia to resist both papal proselytism and Greek control and had profound effects on Serbian nation building. Besides his continuous struggle for the independence of the Serbian Orthodox Church, Sava initiated a cultural and ecclesiastical renaissance in medieval Serbia by founding numerous schools and encouraging the development of literature. He wrote *Žitije Svetog Simeona* (*The Life of St. Simeon*).

SAVEZ KOMUNISTA JUGOSLAVIJE. See COMMUNIST PARTY OF YUGOSLAVIA.

SAVIĆ, PAVLE (1909– ). Serbian and Yugoslav nuclear physicist, member and president of the **Serbian Academy of Sciences and Arts** 1974–1981. He is best known for his cooperation with Irene Zolio-Kirrie in 1937–1938.

SECOND SERBIAN INSURRECTION/DRUGI SRPSKI USTANAK. After a short conciliatory period immediately following the collapse of the **First Serbian Insurrection,** Turkish rule in **Beogradski pašaluk** became a reign of terror in 1814. After the short-lived **Rebellion of Hadži-Prodan** that was followed by severe Turkish retribution, the Second Serbian Insurrection erupted. At the assembly at **Takovo** on April 23, **Miloš Obrenović**, who at age 32 had already established himself as the most influential **knez** in **Serbia**, was chosen as the leader of the uprising. Shortly after the **Serbs** defeated local Turkish forces in the Battles of **Ljubić** and **Dublje**. However, unlike the first insurrection, military operations and fighting were not the main feature of the second insurrection. International developments, mainly Napoleon's defeat and Russian eagerness to get involved in Balkan affairs, created a much more favorable situation for the Serbs than existed during the first insurrection. Miloš wisely exploited this opportunity and instead of fighting superior Turkish forces began to negotiate a peaceful settlement. The provisions of the November 5, 1815 agreement between Miloš and the Turkish commander Maraşli Ali **Paşa** gave Serbs some limited autonomy. As a result of this agreement, a national chancery was organized, and on November 21, 1815, Miloš was recognized as "supreme *knez* and leader of the Serbian people." The beginnings of Serbian autonomy were confirmed by seven Imperial decrees from 1816. The Second Serbian Insurrection had a significant impact not only on the Serbs but also upon the entire **Balkan Peninsula**. This simple uprising turned into a Serbian national revolution, whose success accelerated national and social emancipation of the Balkan peoples.

SECRET CONVENTION/TAJNA KONVENCIJA. Protocol between Prince **Milan Obrenović** and Austria-Hungary signed on June 28, 1881. The document was kept secret until 1893. Only three Serbian leaders knew about the document (**Čedomilj Mijatović, Milan Piroćanac**, and **Milutin Garašanin**), while the entire text of the convention was not published until 1920. The conclusion of the Secret Convention followed the Alliance of the Three Emperors (Dreikaiserbund): Wilhelm I of Germany, Franz Joseph of Austria-Hungary, and Alexander III of Russia. The alliance called for Russian consent to the Austro-Hungarian annexation of **Bosnia and Hercegovina** and Austro-Hungarian permission for Bulgarian unification.

The Secret Convention consisted of 10 articles. Article one was a declaration of mutual amity between Serbia and Austria-Hungary, article two precluded any intrigues against the Dual Monarchy, and articles three and four gave Austria-Hungary's promise to recognize Milan's eventual elevation to king and Serbia's expansion toward the south, with the exception of the **Sandžak.** The rest of the articles further bound Serbia to Austria-Hungary and obligated both parties to secrecy. The Secret Convention decisively put Serbia into the Austro-Hungarian sphere of influence and became a serious impediment to Serbia's political independence.

SEKULIĆ, ISIDORA (1877–1958). Prominent Serbian writer and literary critic, one of the best essayists and interpreters of literature, and member of the **Serbian Academy of Sciences and Arts.** Born in **Bačka,** Sekulić studied education in **Novi Sad** and Budapest. In 1909 she went to **Serbia** and worked as a high school teacher until her retirement in 1931. Her often introspective works include the creative essay *Pisma iz Norveške* (*Letters from Norway*);and the novels *Hronika palanačkog groblja* (*Chronicle of the Town's Graveyard*) and *Saputnici* (*Fellow Travelers*).

SELF-MANAGEMENT. The **Cominform** blockade (1948) interrupted the fulfillment of Yugoslavia's first Five-Year Plan. The cessation of political and economic relations with the Soviet Union and its satellites dictated a thorough reassessment of the strategy for the country's economic development. The leading theoreticians of the **Communist Party of Yugoslavia**, **Edvard Kardelj** and Boris Kidrič, both Slovenes, propagated the idea of the free association of workers who would manage their own affairs (Self-management). Besides ideological reasons (Yugoslav Communists claimed that the concept of Self-management was closer to authentic Marxism than the command-type Soviet economy), the introduction of the new system called for the weakening of centralism in Yugoslavia, a tendency favored by Slovene and Croat Communists.

The concept relied on steady decentralization and an ambiguously defined notion of social property, which differed from both private and state property. Although proclaimed as the sole owner of the factories and "means of production," workers' property rights were hampered because the free disposition of physical assets was not allowed. The workers, however, both directly and through their representatives in the so-called Working Council, decided issues such as distribution of income, production plans, investment, and employment plans. This dichotomy meant that the objective function of the self-managed firm differed from its capitalistic counterpart. While the main objective of the capitalist firm is to maximize long-term profit, the main objective of the self-managed enterprise was the short-term maximization of income per worker. This bias toward current consumption relative to future consumption caused a severe shortage of capital in the Yugoslav economy.

There were three stages in the development of Self-management. The first phase lasted from 1950 to 1965, the second, from the economic reform in 1965 to the introduction of the new Constitution of 1974, and the third from 1974 to the demise of the **Socialist Federal Republic of Yugoslavia** in 1991. The vigorous economic growth that followed the introduction of Self-management stalled in the early 1960s, and the Yugoslav economy began to suffer from growing inflation, unemployment, and current account deficits. The failure of the economic reform of 1965 led to a series of changes culminating in the adoption of the **Constitution** of 1974 and the Law of Associated Labor in 1976. These changes, designed by Kardelj, virtually eliminated basic market categories from the Yugoslav economy and initiated a massive decentralization of the country's economic and political structure. With the absence of market signals, local self-government led directly to a growing autarchy in the Yugoslav economy. The increasing isolationism and the growth of economic nationalism within the Yugoslav federation in the 1980s undermined the country's basic structure and facilitated its violent breakup in 1991.

SELIMOVIĆ, MEHMED-MEŠA (1910–1985). Prominent Serbian writer from **Bosnia and Hercegovina.** Born to a Muslim family in **Tuzla,** Selimović graduated with a degree in philosophy from the **University of Belgrade**. He lived and worked in **Sarajevo** until the 1970s, when he moved to Belgrade due to growing Muslim nationalism. He published his novels relatively late in life, but they brought him quick success not only among domestic readers but among a foreign public as well. His work provides an excellent portrayal of the ethical and psychological dilemmas that the individual faces in decision making. His best-known works include *Derviš i smrt* (*The Derviš and Death*), *Tvrđava* (*The Fortress*), and *Krug* (*The Circle*).

SEMBERIJA. Fertile region in northeast **Bosnia and Hercegovina** (B-H) between the **Drina** and **Sava** Rivers, total area around 300 sq km with a population of 96,796 (1991). Agriculture and mining are the main economic sectors, and **Bijeljina** is the center of the region. In the beginning of 1992, during the growing nationalist tension in B-H, the Serbian majority proclaimed a Samostalna Autonomna Oblast Semberija (Independent Autonomous Region). According to the **Dayton Agreement,** Semberija would remain in the **Republika Srpska.**

SENT ANDREJA. See SZENT ENDRE.

SEOBA SRBA (Migration of Serbs). Term used to describe several migrations of the **Serbs** starting with the Turkish expansion into **Serbia** after the **Battle of Maritsa** in 1371 and the **Battle of Kosovo** in 1389. The general direction of the Serbian migration was originally to the north (**Vojvodina,** Hungary) but also toward the west (**Slavonia, Croatia, Dalmatia**) and east (Russia).

**Migration to Vojvodina.** The Turkish expansion following the Battle of Kosovo caused the first wave of Serbian migration to **Srem, Banat,** and **Bačka.** Before the collapse of Serbia in 1459, Serbs inhabited the whole of Vojvodina, southern Hungary (Nagybánya, Baia Mare, Baia Sprie), and Transylvania (Erdely). During the Turko-Hungarian War in 1481 around 50,000 Serbs emigrated from **Kruševac** to Timisoara, Banat, and it is estimated that between 1479 and 1483 around 200,000 Serbs migrated to Vojvodina and southern Hungary. After the Hungarian defeat in the Battle of Mohacs in 1526, Serbs mainly moved into Srem and Bačka. At the end of the 17th century there were 97 Serbian boroughs in Srem, 180 in Banat, 380 in Bačka, 160 in **Baranja** and its vicinity.

The biggest migration of the Serbs, known as Velika Seoba (The Great Migration) occurred during the Austro-Turkish War of 1683–1699. Fearing Turkish reprisals, between 30,000 and 40,000 Serbs from **Sandžak** and **Kosovo and Metohija,** led by **Arsenije III Crnojević,** joined the retreating Austrian army and arrived in **Belgrade** in March 1690. After receiving guarantees from the Austrian emperor Leopold I, Serbs crossed the **Sava** River and resettled in Bačka, Baranja, and Slavonia. The next influx of Serbs into Vojvodina took place during the Austro-Turkish War of 1788–1791 when around 60,000 people resettled in Vojvodina.

**Migration to Slavonia.** The first records of Serbian migration to

Slavonia date from the beginning of the 15th century. The Turkish occupation of Slavonia pushed Serbs further west toward the interior of Croatia. They returned to Slavonia, together with a large number of Serbs from western Serbia, **Pomoravlje,** and **Bosnia and Hercegovina** (B-H), during the Austro-Turkish War of 1683–1699.

**Migration to Croatia.** Serbian migration to Croatia began after the Turkish occupation of B-H in 1463. Although most of the Serbs inhabited **Vojna Krajina**, some resettled along the present borders between Croatia and **Slovenia.** During the Austro-Turkish War of 1788–1791 around 25,000 Serbs migrated to Croatia.

**Migration to Russia.** The Serbian migration to Russia came as a result of the Austrian annulment of privileges previously granted to the Serbs in Vojvodina. The migration started in 1721 following permission being granted by the Russian emperor Peter the Great. Most of the Serbs migrated to the Ukraine, where they formed their communities Nova Srbija (New Serbia), Slavjano Serbija (Slav Serbia) etc. It is estimated that around 20,000 Serbs resettled in Russia and the Ukraine. A number of Serbian emigrants joined the Russian army (24 Generals, 17 Colonels, eight Lt. Colonels, 36 Majors, etc.).

SERBIA/SRBIJA. Largest amongst the former constituent republics of the **Socialist Federal Republic of Yugoslavia** until April 27, 1992, when, together with **Montenegro,** Serbia formed the **Federal Republic of Yugoslavia.** Serbia possesses a territory of 88,361 sq km with a population of 9,778,991 in 1991. The autonomous provinces of **Vojvodina** (21,506 sq km, pop. 2,013,889) and **Kosovo and Metohija** (10,887 sq km, 1,956,196) are constituent parts of Serbia. The ethnic composition of the republic is: 65.9 percent Serbian, 17.1 Albanian, 1.4 percent Montenegrin, 3.5 percent Hungarian, 0.7 percent Slovak, 3.3 percent Hungarian, 2.5 percent Muslim, 1.4 percent Gypsy, and Croats 1.1 percent Croatian. The official language is Serbian, and the majority of people are members of the **Serbian Orthodox Church.**

Serbia is bounded by Hungary to the north, Romania to the northeast, Bulgaria to the southeast, the **Former Yugoslav Republic of Macedonia** and Albania to the south, **Bosnia and Hercegovina (Republika Srpska)** and **Croatia** to the west. Southern Serbia is generally mountainous, with the **Kopaonik** Mountain on the west, **Šar Mountain** and Prokletije to the south, and the **Balkan Mountains** to the east. **Pomoravlje, Metohija, Mačva,** and Vojvodina are Serbia's most fertile regions. The climate varies from subcontinental in the southern parts to continental in the rest of the country.

The **Serbs,** the strongest and the most numerous amongst the **South Slavs,** populated the territory of Serbia, Bosnia and Hercegovina (**Tuzla** region and Hercegovina), Montenegro, and Croatia (**Dalmatia, Konavle** region and **Dubrovnik,** the islands Korčula, Mljet, Hvar, and Brač) in the course of the sixth and seventh centuries. The name Serb first appeared in the *Frankish Annals* in 822. Closely related clans were organized in different **župa**, each led by the **župan.** The župan **Mutimir** accepted Orthodox Christianity in 879. Prince **Mihailo** succeeded in unifying **Raška** and **Zeta** and was recognized as king by Pope Gregory VII in 1077. His success was short-lived, and the state dissolved following the death of his son, **Konstantin Bodin.**

Serbia prospered the most under the **Nemanjić** dynasty that ruled from 1168 to 1371. **Stefan Nemanja,** the founder of the dynasty, unified central Serbian lands—Raška, Zeta, Hum, and Dalmatia and northern **Macedonia.** He was succeeded by **Stefan Prvovenčani,** under whom Serbia became a kingdom in 1217. Two years later, the youngest of Nemanja's sons, **Saint Sava,** established the autocephalous Serbian Orthodox Church. Following Stefan Prvovenčani's death in 1228, Serbia was ruled by his sons **Radoslav** (r. 1228–1233), **Vladislav** (r. 1233–1243), and **Uroš I** (r. 1243–1276). Uroš's rule marked the beginning of the economic development of the Serbian state and the issuance of a Serbian silver currency. Uroš was succeeded by his sons **Dragutin** (r. 1276–1282) and **Milutin** (r. 1282–1321). During the reign of Milutin, who held the title of ruler "from the gulf of the Adriatic, from the sea to the great river **Danube**," Serbia greatly prospered and expanded territorially. The rule of Milutin's son, **Stefan Dečanski** (r. 1321–1331), was distinguished by the **Battle of Velbužd** (1330) at which the Serbian army decisively defeated the Bulgarians. Dečanski was succeeded by his son, **Dušan the Mighty** (r. 1331–1355), who proclaimed himself "the Emperor of Serbs and Greeks" in 1346. He ruled over Albania, Epirus, Macedonia, Aeolia, and Thessaly. Besides territorial expansion and economic growth, the rule of Dušan was characterized by the enactment of ***Dušan's Code of Laws*** in 1349.

The death of Dušan was followed by the continuous weakening of central authority in the Serbian empire. Dušan's son, **Uroš II** (r. 1355–1371), essentially shared power with the most prominent feudal lords, namely brothers Vukašin and Uglješa **Mrnjavčević.** Following the crushing defeat in the **Battle of Maritsa** and death of Uroš II, the advancing Turks captured the southern parts of the Serbian state. Following the **Battle of Kosovo** in 1389, Serbia became a vassal state of the Ottoman Empire. The medieval Serbian state ceased to exist with the fall of **Smederevo** in 1459. The Turkish occupation and repressive rule caused the migration of many Serbs (**Seoba Srba**) toward Austrian-held territories (Vojvodina, **Vojna Krajina**), while **Hajduks** and **Uskoks** continued the struggle for national liberation.

The drive for national liberation resulted in the Serbian rebellions known as the **First Serbian Insurrection** (1804–1813) and the **Second Serbian Insurrection** (1815). In 1830, Serbia became an internationally recognized autonomous principality under Turkish suzerainty. The continuous struggle against Turkish domination led to a series of conflicts and the Turkish withdrawal from Serbia. After the **Serbo-Turkish War** (1876–1878), Serbia gained independence at the **Congress of Berlin.** From 1815 to 1842 and 1858 to 1903 Serbia was ruled by the **Obrenović dynasty**. During the reign of Prince **Milan Obrenović,** Serbia was proclaimed a kingdom on March 6, 1882. King Milan's reliance on Austria-Hungary resulted in Serbia's complete political and economic subservience to the Dual Monarchy. Its economic dependence was ensured by trade treaties in 1881 and 1892 and the so-called Veterinary Convention of 1886, while Austro-Hungarian political dominance was rooted in the **Secret Convention** of 1881. At the end of the 19th century, the pro-Austrian policy of the Obrenović dynasty became the major impediment in the struggle for Serbian national liberation and unification of the Serbian lands under Austro-Hungarian and Turkish occupation.

The overthrow of the last Obrenović on June 10–11, 1903, and the proclamation of the rule of **Peter I Karađorđević** brought substantial political and economic changes in Serbia and intensified the struggle for national liberation. The period 1903–1914 was the most prosperous in Serbia's history. Besides complete economic emancipation from Austria-Hungary, Serbia's political life flourished. The **Constitution** of 1903 established a parliamentary regime of the British type and granted freedoms of press and religion, while the **Parliament** was given broad powers, including the approval of the annual budget. Serbia's great leap toward democracy was accompanied by a giant improvement in education: the number of elementary schools increased from 534 (1885) to 1,263 (1911) and the number of secondary schools increased from 19 (1889) to 49 (1911). In 1905 the **Great School** was transformed into the autonomous **University of Belgrade**.

Serbia's political and economic emancipation led to the deterioration of relations with Austria-Hungary. The **Tariff War** of 1906–1911, the **Annexation Crisis,** and Serbia's victories in the **Balkan wars** served as a prelude to the showdown between the two countries. Holding Serbia directly responsible for the assassination of Crown Prince Franz Ferdinand on June 28, 1914 (**Assassination of Sarajevo**), Austria-Hungary, after issuing an unacceptable **Ultimatum,** declared war on Serbia on July 28, 1914. This led to the outbreak of **World War I,** the subsequent dissolution of the Austro-Hungarian Empire, and the formation of the **Kingdom of the Serbs, Croats, and Slovenes** in 1918, which effectively ended the existence of the Kingdom of Serbia.

Historically, Serbia was an agricultural country with a dynamic livestock trade. The process of building Serbia's national economy started after the Second Serbian Insurrection in 1815. Having power to appoint his own administration and an autonomous tax system, Prince **Miloš Obrenović** steadily lessened Ottoman involvement in Serbia's economic and political affairs. During Miloš's rule, the process of transformation of Serbia's essentially natural economy to a market economy started. The long-predominant **Zadruga** began to be replaced with individual smallholdings, while expanding trade initiated the growth of towns that became centers for livestock and exports.

During the reign of the **Constitutionalists,** Serbia's economy was further modernized by the establishment of a postal (1843) and telegraph (1855) system and by building and improving the road network. In addition, merchants were allowed to deal directly with peasants, and government regulation of trade substantially decreased. The rule of Prince **Mihailo Obrenović** was characterized by increasing urbanization and a rapid growth of foreign trade. Between 1862 and 1868, the value of foreign trade soared from 33,193,000 **dinars** to 67,787,000 dinars. The rapid increase in Serbia's population was a key factor in Serbia's economy throughout the latter half of the nineteenth century and the early twentieth century. Between 1878 and 1905 the total population increased from 1,700,000 to 2,725,000 due to territorial enlargement and immigration. In addition, the urban population increased from 91,587 in 1862 to 350,682 in 1908. The decline of animal husbandry and the rapid rise of the merchant class were additional characteristics of the growth of Serbia's economy. The rapid growth of foreign trade was facilitated by the building of a railway system (1,164 km at the beginning of the 20th century) and increasing river traffic. However, both geographic and product concentration of Serbia's foreign trade were not favorable. While agricultural products accounted for 90 percent of total exports, 69 percent of Serbia's imports were manufactured goods, and Austria-Hungary accounted for 80 percent of Serbia's foreign trade between 1879 and 1900. This heavy economic and political dependence on Austria-Hungary, determined by the trade treaties of 1881 and 1891 and the Secret Convention of 1881, prevented the development of industry in Serbia. In 1898, Serbia had only 28 industrial enterprises with 1,700 workers. Although the establishment of the **National Bank** in 1884 spurred the development of Serbia's banking system, continuous budget deficits absorbed much of the capital needed for industrial development.

The dynastic change in 1903 (**May's Assassination**) marked the beginning of the rapid transformation of Serbia's economy. The stabilization of finances and reorganization of foreign trade and the introduction of a new tariff system contributed to Serbia's economic emancipation from Austria-Hungary and to the outbreak of the Tariff War between the two countries in 1906. Serbia's vigorous adaptation to the severance of economic ties with Austria-Hungary resulted in rapid industrial development and structural changes in its foreign trade. The value of its industrial production increased from 8,954,000 dinars in 1904 to 74,378,000 in 1910, and the number of enterprises increased from 93 to 428. In the same time the relative share of Austria-Hungary in Serbia's foreign trade declined from 80 percent to 18.5 percent.

The development of Serbia's national economy was interrupted by the outbreak of World War I and the formation of the Kingdom of the Serbs, Croats, and Slovenes in 1918. Serbia's incorporation into the new state effectively ended the process of independent economic development. With her economy crippled by the war, Serbia's industrialization lagged behind that of Croatia and **Slovenia**. In terms of capital equipment for various industrial installations Croatia exceeded Serbia in chemical, paper, leather, petroleum, nonmetal processing, and mineral oil and wood spirits. Between 1918 and 1938, Slovenia developed economically 2.5 times and Croatia 1.7 times faster than Serbia.

Although it failed to mitigate Serbia's relative economic underdevelopment, the rapid industrialization following the war brought substantial changes. In 1989, Serbia's share in the social product of the Socialist Federal Republic of Yugoslavia was 36.26 percent. The respective shares in agricultural production and industry were 51 percent and 35.8 percent. At the level of particular industries, Serbia's share in the production of electrical energy was 42 percent; chemicals, 38 percent; metal processing, 38.5 percent; construction materials, 38.7 percent; and textiles, 35 percent. Industrial activities also included copper ore processing (Serbia is one of Europe's major copper producers); lead, zinc, and silver-ore processing, and the manufacture of textiles, chemicals, and machinery. The biggest industrial centers were **Belgrade, Niš, Kragujevac, Šabac, Kruševac, Novi Sad, Priština,** and **Vranje.**

SERBIAN ACADEMY OF SCIENCES AND ARTS/SRPSKA AKADEMIJA NAUKA I UMETNOSTI (SANU). Most distinguished scientific institution in **Serbia**, formally established in 1886, it essentially continued and expanded the activity of the **Društvo Srpske Slovesnosti** and **Srpsko Učeno Društvo.** The academy consists of six departments: natural sciences and mathematics, technical sciences, medical sciences, literature and language, social sciences, and painting and musical arts. In 1986, several members of the academy wrote a critical analysis, known as *Memorandum*, of the position of Serbia and **Serbs** in Yugoslavia. The content of the document became a matter of various misinterpretations that resulted in the labeling of the academy as a bastion of Serbian nationalism.

SERBIAN DEMOCRATIC PARTY/SRPSKA DEMOKRATSKA STRANKA (SDS). Political organization founded on February 17, 1990, in **Knin.** The party immediately established itself as the leading political force of the **Serbs** living within administrative **Croatia.** Their leader was Jovan Rašković, a prominent psychiatrist from **Zadar** and a member of the **Serbian Academy of Sciences and Arts.** In the same year, the SDS was founded in **Bosnia and Hercegovina** under the leadership of **Radovan Karadžić.** Thus, the SDS became the principal political organization of Serbs living outside **Serbia.**

SERBIAN LANGUAGE. See LANGUAGE, SERBIAN.

SERBIAN ORTHODOX CHURCH/SRPSKA PRAVOSLAVNA CRKVA (SPC). Formal establishment of an autocephalous Serbian Orthodox Church dates from 1219 when **Saint Sava** was consecrated as the first Serbian archbishop with the permission of the Byzantine emperor and with the blessing of the Constantinople Orthodox patriarch. The Serbian Church remained nominally subordinate to the patriarchate of Constantinople until 1346, when the archbishopric of **Peć** was elevated to the rank of patriarchate (**patriarchate of Peć**). The first Serbian patriarchate, which started with the coronation of Emperor **Dušan the Mighty,** ended with the fall of **Smederevo** in 1459.

Although the Turkish administration did not ban the Serbian Church, the inability to pay newly imposed heavy taxes led to the church's dissolution. Moreover, conversion to Islam and migration of the **Serbs** toward **Banat, Bačka, Srem, Slavonia, Bosnia and Hercegovina** (B-H), and the interior of **Croatia** and **Dalmatia** substantially lowered the population in the church's dioceses, which subsequently came under the jurisdiction of the Greek-dominated archbishopric of Ohrid.

In 1557, the Serbian patriarchate was revived, and **Makarije Sokolović,** a brother of **Mehmed-Paša Sokolović**, became the patriarch. After an initial period of steady revival and the establishment of more than 40 new dioceses, the church, as the sole unifying force of the Serbian people, became embroiled in a series of Austro-Turkish wars. The struggle against the Turks led to a new wave of massive Serbian migration (**Seoba Srba**) and consequently to the abolition of the second patriarchate in 1766. The massive migration, however, led to the establishment of church organizations outside Serbia, which became known as "provincial churches." The most prominent of these provincial churches developed in **Vojvodina** with the establishment of the metropolitanate of **Karlovci Sremski** (originally the metropolitanate of Krušedol) and the patriarchate of Vojvodina (1848). The other "provincial" churches included the Serbian Orthodox Church in **Montenegro** (the old metropolitanate of **Zeta**), B-H (the metropolitanate of **Dabar**), Slavonia, Dalmatia, Croatia, and **Macedonia.** The sultan's **Hatti Şerif** of 1830 partially restored the autonomy of the Church in Prince **Miloš Obrenović**'s Serbia. After **World War I**, the Serbian Orthodox Church was united under one ecclesiastical authority, and the patriarchate was reestablished on September 9–12, 1920.

The activities of the church, both educational and cultural, were seriously impeded in the post-**World War II** period. Following the collapse of Communism, the role of the church steadily increased. While the church remained separated from the state in the **Federal Republic of Yugoslavia,** it became fully integrated into the **Republika Srpska.** The supreme authority of the Serbian Church, the Holy Synod, is composed of all its bishops, who meet once a year. There are 31 dioceses, including the American-Canadian diocese (1920), four seminaries, and a theological faculty in **Belgrade.** See also BOGOSLOVIJA.

SERBIAN RADICAL PARTY/SRPSKA RADIKALNA STRANKA (SRS). One of the major opposition parties that emerged from the split in the **Radical Party** in 1991. The armed formations of the ultranationalist and populist, the SRS actively participated in the civil war in **Croatia** and **Bosnia and Hercegovina.** The leader of the SRS is **Vojislav Šešelj.**

SERBIAN RENEWAL MOVEMENT/SRPSKI POKRET OBNOVE (SPO). One of the major opposition parties in **Serbia,** founded on January 7, 1990. Initially a champion of Serbian nationalism, from 1992 the SPO became a distinct proponent of a peaceful solution to the crisis in the former Yugoslavia. Fervent anti-communism remains one of the main characteristics of this populist party. The leader of the SPO is **Vuk Drašković.**

SERBIAN REPUBLIC. See REPUBLIKA SRPSKA.

SERBO-BULGARIAN WAR. Following the declaration of Bulgaria's unification with Eastern Rumelia on September 18, 1885, King **Milan Obrenović,** fearing the restoration of San Stefano Bulgaria, pushed **Serbia** into war by attacking Bulgaria on November 14, 1885. Ill prepared, unmotivated, outgunned, and outnumbered, the Serbian army failed to break the Bulgarian defenses at the **Battle of Slivnica** River and hastily withdrew. Bulgarian forces regrouped, entered Serbian territory, and captured **Pirot** on November 27. The war stopped after the resolute action of 'Austria-Hungary, which did not allow Serbia's defeat. The war ended formally by a peace treaty signed on March 3, 1886. The military defeat was a serious blow to Serbia's international reputation and national pride. It marked the beginning of a bitter contest between the two states over **Macedonia,** caused the downfall of the rule of the **Progressive Party**, and led to the abdication of King Milan.

SERBO-TURKISH WARS. The outbreak of the **Rebellions of Hercegovina** in 1875 aroused national feelings in **Serbia** and increased pressure on Prince **Milan Obrenović** to begin a war against the Ottoman Empire.

Although initially opposed to the idea of Serbia's direct involvement, Milan succumbed to public pressure and declared war on the Turks on June 30, 1876. Poorly armed and organized, the Serbian army (114,500), under the command of retired Russian General **Mikhail G. Cherniaev**, suffered a massive defeat at the **Battle of Đunis** on October 29, 1876, and only decisive action by the Russian government prevented a complete disaster. In less than five months of fighting, Serbia suffered 15,000 causalities (5,000 dead, 10,000 wounded and missing) and more than 200,000 people became homeless. On February 22, 1877, the Serbian **Parliament** accepted the Turkish proposal reestablishing the status quo ante bellum between the two states. The Serbian failure in the First Serbo-Turkish War was caused by a combination of external and internal factors. The Serbian army was ill-prepared, poorly armed, and disorganized, while Serbian expectations of Russian involvement and a general Balkan insurrection did not materialize.

Soon after Serbia concluded the peace treaty with Turkey, the Russian government yielded to the pressure of the Pan-Slavists and declared war on the Ottoman Empire on April 24, 1877. Following intense Russian pressure, Serbia entered the war on December 13. The Second Serbo-Turkish War lasted only six weeks. The Serbian army liberated **Niš**, **Pirot,** and **Vranje**, key cities in southeastern Serbia. Serbia suffered 5,400 casualties: 708 dead, 2,999 wounded, 159 missing, and 1,544 who died in hospitals.

The Serbo-Turkish wars were followed by the **Treaty of San Stefano** and the **Congress of Berlin.** The independence of Serbia and **Montenegro** was formally recognized along with the territorial expansion of the two states. The wars and subsequent peace treaties radically changed the foreign policy of Prince Milan. His subsequent exclusive reliance on Austria-Hungary led to Serbia's complete economic and political dependence on its northern neighbor.

SERBS. Dominant South Slavic nation, inhabiting the central and western part of the **Balkan Peninsula.** The total number of Serbs (together with **Montenegrins**) in the former Yugoslavia is 9.5 million. Serbs migrated to the Balkans with the rest of the **South Slavs** in the course of the sixth and seventh centuries. The name Serbs was first mentioned in 822, while the unification of the Serbian tribes was achieved between the ninth and 14th centuries.

*SERBSKE NARODNE NOVINE* (*Serbian National Gazette*). *Serbske narodne novine* was published in Pest (Budapest) twice a week between 1838 and 1848 and was also published under the title *Narodne novine* (*National Gazette*) in 1842 and *Sveobšte jugoslovenske serbske narodne novine* (*General Yugoslav Serbian National Gazette*) in 1848. The newspaper published articles on the political, economic, and cultural situation in the Balkans and Europe.

*SERBSKI NARODNI LIST* (*Serbian National Journal*). Serbian weekly published in Budapest from 1835 to 1848. Several prominent **Serbs** regularly wrote for the journal, including Milorad Medaković, **Vuk Stefanović Karadžić,** and Jovan Ilić.

*SERBSKIJA POVSEDNIVNIJA NOVINI* (*Serbian Daily Gazette*). Newspaper published on Thursdays and Fridays in Vienna from March 14, 1791, to December 30, 1792. The editor and publisher was a Greek patriot, Markides Pulyo. The newspaper mainly published articles translated from the Austrian press.

SIĆEVAČKA KLISURA. Canyon of the **Nišava** River (17 km long), an important communication link between **Serbia** and Bulgaria.

SIMOVIĆ, DUŠAN (1882–1962). Air force general of the Yugoslav armed forces and prime minister of Yugoslavia 1941–1942. Together with General Borivoje Mirković, Simović was a main organizer of the **Coup d'état of March 27, 1941.**

SINĐELIĆ, STEVAN (?–1809). Serbian **vojvoda** from the **Resava** region, one of the leaders of the **First Serbian Insurrection** and the greatest hero of the insurrection. He died in the **Battle of Čegar** after blowing up an ammunition depot. From the skulls of the Serbs killed in the battle the Turks built **Ćele kula** (Skull Tower) in **Niš.**

SITNICA. River in **Kosovo and Metohija**. The right tributary of the **Ibar** River, 94 km. long, the Sitnica is the biggest river in **Kosovo Polje**.

SKADARSKO JEZERO (Lake Scutari; Lake Shkodër). Biggest lake of the **Balkan Peninsula,** situated between **Montenegro** and Albania (total lake area 391 sq km: 243.1 sq km belongs to the **Federal Republic of**

**Yugoslavia** and 147.9 sq km to Albania). The lake is 43 km long and 14 km wide with an average depth of four to seven meters.

SKERLIĆ, JOVAN (1877–1914). One of the most celebrated Serbian literary critics, editor of ***Srpski književni glasnik*** (1907–1907), founder of the Udruženje književnika Srbije (Association of Writers of Serbia), and member of the executive board of **Srpska književna zadruga**. Using modern criteria, he described the interchanges between epoch, styles, and schools. The resulting image showed that the new Serbian literature developed in a way typical of European literature. His main works include *Srpska književnost u XVIII veku* (*Serbian Literature in the 18th Century*) and *Istorija nove srpske književnosti* (*History of Modern Serbian Literature*).

SKOBALJIĆ, NIKOLA (?–1454). Feudal lord from southern **Serbia**; he defeated the Turks on September 24, 1454, but suffered a defeat two months later. Captured by Turks, he was the first Serb to be executed by impalement.

SKOPJE. See SKOPLJE.

SKOPLJE/SKOPJE. Capital city, economic and cultural center of the **Former Yugoslav Republic of Macedonia** (pop. 506,932; 1981) situated on the banks of the **Vardar** River. Diverse industries produce steel, cement, electrical equipment, tobacco, agricultural machinery, refined chrome. The city is an important communication center in the Morava-Vardar Valley and a university center. The city was founded by **Illyrians** (Scupi) and later became a capital of the Roman province of Dardania. Skoplje came under Serbian control in 1189 and in 1345 became the capital city of Emperor **Dušan the Mighty.** The city was occupied by the Turks from 1391 to 1912, when it was liberated by the Serbian army during the **Balkan wars**. During **World War II,** Skoplje was occupied by the Bulgarians. In July 1963, Skoplje was partly demolished by a strong earthquake.

SKUPŠTINA. See PARLIAMENT.

SLAVA. Celebration of the family's patron saint, a religious practice unique to the Serbs. The practice is rooted in the pagan tradition of celebrating the family protector.

SLAVONIA. Region between the Drava and **Sava** Rivers, covering an area of 14,543 sq km, with a population of around 2 million. Slavonia is a fertile agricultural region with several industrial centers: **Osijek,** Slavonski brod, **Pakrac**, Daruvar, and Vinkovci. Most of Slavonia was a part of **Vojna Krajina** and heavily populated by Serbs. The region can be divided into two, a western and an eastern part. During the civil war in Croatia in 1991, both parts of Slavonia (Pakrac, Daruvar, Slavonska Požega, Bilogora Mountain, Osijek) were scenes of heavy fighting between the local Serbian population, the **JNA,** and Croatian paramilitary forces. The ethnic structure of the region dramatically changed following the Croatian offensive in 1991 and collapse of the **Republic of Serbian Krajina** in 1995.

SLIVNICA, BATTLE OF. Main battle of the **Serbo-Bulgarian War** held November 17–19, 1885. The Serbian Supreme Command, led by King **Milan Obrenović**, underestimated the strength of the Bulgarian forces and failed to capture the village of Slivnica after two days of heavy fighting. Bulgarian forces, exploiting a hasty Serbian retreat, launched a counterattack, crossed the Serbian border, and captured **Pirot. Serbs** lost 3,000 men and the Bulgarians 2,500.

SLOVENIA. Former constituent republic of the **Socialist Federal Republic of Yugoslavia** (SFRY), which gained independence and international recognition in January 1992. Slovenia is bounded to the west by Italy, to the north by Austria, to the northeast by Hungary and to the southeast by **Croatia**, with an area of 20,251 sq km and population of 1,965,986 (1991 estimate). The vast majority of the population are ethnic Slovenes (87.8 percent), while Croats (2.4 percent) and **Serbs** (2.2 percent) are the largest minorities. The official language is Slovene and the majority of the population is Roman Catholic. Slovenia is mountainous and wooded, with deep valleys and numerous rivers. The climate is Mediterranean on the coast and continental inland. Slovenia was the richest amongst the republics of the SFRY, producing 20 percent of Yugoslavia's gross domestic product, and its per capita income was approximately double the Yugoslav average. Slovenia dominated Yugoslav glass production (60 percent) and the manufacture of industrial machinery (36 percent) and paper products (32 percent). In addition, Slovenia's share in total exports and imports in Yugoslavia was 26 and 22 percent.

Slovenian tribes arrived in the **Balkan Peninsula** in the fifth century.

After failing to established an autonomous state, Slovenes fell under foreign rule in 745 and remained subdued until 1918. Slovenes, although not entirely, were liberated following **World War I** and the formation of the **Kingdom of the Serbs, Croats, and Slovenes** on December 1, 1918. After **World War II,** and the victory of the Communist-led **Partisans,** the Slovenian republic was established in 1945. Slovenia quickly achieved a privileged position within the Yugoslav Federation due to the substantial influence of Slovenes in the **Communist Party of Yugoslavia**. The continuous decentralization of the Yugoslav Federation that came as a direct result of the economic policies and constitutional changes designed by **Edvard Kardelj** facilitated Slovenia's drive toward secession from Yugoslavia.

The relationship between **Serbia** and Slovenia especially deteriorated in the 1980s over the issue of the Serbian autonomous province of **Kosovo and Metohija.** Fearing that the reinstatement of Serbia's authority over autonomous provinces might preclude its intended secession from the Yugoslav Federation, Slovenian politicians openly supported Albanian separatists in Kosovo and Metohija.

In June 1991, Slovenia and Croatia unilaterally seceded from the SFRY. After several days of minor clashes between Slovene paramilitary forces and the **JNA**, the **European Community** (EC) brokered a cease-fire and arranged the JNA withdrawal from Slovenia. On January 15, 1992, the EC officially recognized Slovenia as an independent country.

SMEDEREVO. River port and industrial city in **Serbia** at the confluence of the **Danube** and **Morava** Rivers with a population of 115,617 in 1991. Industries include the production of steel, railway trucks, and machinery in addition to the production of wine and canned fruits and vegetables. The first records of the city date from the ninth century. The magnificent fortress of Smederevo was built between 1428–1430 by **Đurađ Branković**, Serbian **despot.** It was the capital of Serbia in 1429–1459 until captured by the Turks. The city was heavily damaged by Allied bombing in **World War II.**

SOCIAL DEMOCRATIC PARTY/SOCIJADEMOKRATSKA STRANKA. First socialist party in **Serbia**, founded on August 2, 1903, under the leadership of Radovan Dragović, **Dragiša Lapčević,** and **Dimitrije Tucović.** The party closely followed the program of the German Social Democrats until 1914. It participated in all elections held 1903–1914 and had deputies in **Parliament.** After **World War I,** the party initiated the merger of all socialist parties in the newly created **Kingdom of the Serbs, Croats, and Slovenes** and founded the Socialist Workers' Party (Communists) in 1919, which changed its name to the **Communist Party of Yugoslavia** in 1920.

SOCIAL PRODUCT. National accounts concept previously used in all socialist countries to measure the output of goods and services. It roughly corresponds to the commonly used concept of gross domestic product (GDP) but does not include activities that do not generate "value" as defined by classical economics (administration, health, culture, defense, banking, housing, etc.)

SOCIALIST FEDERAL REPUBLIC OF YUGOSLAVIA/SOCIJALISTIČKA FEDERATIVNA REPUBLIKA JUGOSLAVIJA (SFRJ). Official name for the former Yugoslav Federation 1963–1992. Prior to the SFRJ, the official name was Demokratska Federativna Jugoslavija—DFJ (Democratic Federal Yugoslavia) in 1945 and Federativna Narodna Republika Jugoslavija—FNRJ (Federal People's Republic of Yugoslavia) 1945–1963.

SOCIALIST PARTY OF SERBIA/SOCIJALISTIČKA PARTIJA SRBIJE (SPS). Most powerful political party in **Serbia,** consistently winning the majority of votes in all multiparty **elections.** The SPS was formally established by the merger of the League of Communists of Serbia and the Socialist Alliance on July 16, 1990. In the second round of the municipal elections in Serbia candidates of the SPS lost in 14 large cities. The attempt to invalidate the election results led to major popular protest throughout Serbia. The opposition challenge led to discord in the SPS, and a number of high-ranking officials distanced themselves from the party hard-liners.

SOCIALIST PEOPLE'S PARTY/SOCIJALISTIČKA NARODNA PARTIJA. Faction of the **Democratic Party of Socialists** that emerged after the split between **Momir Bulatović** and **Milo Đukanović** in 1997. The party platform advocates the strong ties between **Serbia** and **Montenegro** and supports the Yugoslav president **Slobodan Milošević**.

SOCIETY OF FRIENDS/PHILIKE HETAIRIA. Greek Secret Society.

Alexander Ypsilanti, the leader of the society, persuaded **Karađorđe Petrović** to join the society and promised him military leadership in a general Balkan uprising against the Turks. Karađorđe returned to **Serbia** but was soon executed by **Vujica Vulićević** at the orders of Prince **Miloš Obrenović** on July 25, 1817.

SOCIJALDEMOKRATSKA STRANKA. See SOCIAL DEMOCRATIC PARTY.

SOCIJALISTIČKA FEDERATIVNA REPUBLIKA JUGOSLAVIJA. See SOCIALIST FEDERAL REPUBLIC OF YUGOSLAVIA.

SOCIJALISTIČKA PARTIJA SRBIJE. See SOCIALIST PARTY OF SERBIA.

SOKOLOVIĆ, MAKARIJE (?–1574). Brother of **Mehmed-Paša Sokolović** and the first patriarch of the revived **patriarchate of Peć** (1557–1571). The jurisdiction of the revived Serbian patriarchate extended from Budapest in the north to the Adriatic Sea in the south and from the Bulgarian capital Sofia in the east to **Zagreb** in the west. He is credited with the thorough internal reorganization of the church and the rebuilding of several monasteries and churches. After Makarije, three other members of the Sokolović family became patriarchs: Antonije (1571–1575), Gerasim (1575–1586), and Savatije (1586–1589).

SOKOLOVIĆ, MEHMED-PAŠA (1505–1579). Grand vizier of the Ottoman Empire, born to a Serbian family from **Bosnia and Hercegovina.** As a young child he was taken from his parents, and his Christian name Bajica was changed to Mehmed in accordance with the Ottoman-imposed **Blood Tribute.** In Edirne he was converted to Islam and educated as *janisser* (**Janisseries**). Due to his extraordinary talents he rapidly progressed in the Ottoman administration and in 1566 became a grand vizier. After the death of Sultan Suleyman II, he effectively ruled the Ottoman Empire (1566-1574).

The rule of Mehmed-Paša was a period of consolation for the **Serbs**. In 1557, he reestablished the **patriarchate of Peć** and installed his Serbian Orthodox brother, **Makarije Sokolović,** as patriarch of the **Serbian Orthodox Church.** The **Serbian language** became a diplomatic language at the Ottoman court. The stone bridge over the **Drina** River in

**Višegrad** that served as the main motif for **Ivo Andrić**'s Nobel Prize winning novel is the legacy of Mehmed-Paša.

SOMBOR. City and **commune** center in western **Bačka** with a population of 96,105 in 1991, one of the centers of Serbian dissent from Austro-Hungarian rule in **Vojvodina.** Industries include chemicals and food processing.

SOPOĆANI. Monastery in the vicinity of **Novi Pazar,** built around 1265, the mausoleum of King **Uroš I.** Sopoćani is included in the UNESCO list of cultural heritage in 1979. **Frescoes** in Sopoćani are magnificent examples of 13th century Byzantine art and European painting of the time.

SOUTH SLAVS. Tribes that moved toward the south during the great migration of Slavs in the fifth and sixth centuries. Originally, the category comprised **Serbs**, Croats, Slovenes, and later Bulgars, an Avarian tribe that mixed with the local Slavic population. After **World War II**, not without controversy, three new South Slavic nations were formed in Yugoslavia: Montenegrin, Macedonian, and Muslim.

SOUTHERN MORAVA/JUŽNA MORAVA. River in southern **Serbia,** 352 km long. Together with the **Western Morava**, it forms the **Morava** River near the town of Stalać. The valley of the river is an integral part of the Morava-**Vardar** Valley, a major communication link between Europe and Asia Minor.

SPAHO, MEHMED (1883–1939). Muslim politician from **Bosnia and Hercegovina**, one of the founders and the long-time leader of the **Yugoslav Muslim Organization.** Member of several Yugoslav governments, Spaho built his political career exploiting the Serbo-Croatian conflict in Yugoslavia.

SPORAZUM CVETKOVIĆ-MAČEK. See CVETKOVIĆ-MAČEK AGREEMENT.

SRBIJA. (i) see SERBIA.

(ii) A liberal journal on political economy, one of the best in **Serbia**. The official paper of the **Liberal Party**, *Srbija* was published three times a week by **Ljubomir Kaljević** 1867–1870.

*SRBSKO-DALMATINSKI MAGAZIN* (*Serbo-Dalmatian Almanac*). A Serbian annual published in **Zagreb**, Vienna, and **Zadar** from 1836 to 1873. The almanac focused on literary, educational, and religious issues concerning the **Serbs** living in **Dalmatia** and **Hercegovina**.

*SRĐ*. A literary journal published in **Dubrovnik** from 1902 to 1908. The main contributors were the Serbian intellectuals and writers **Svetozar Ćorović**, **Simo Matavulj**, and **Ivo Vojnović**. The journal focused on the current literary developments in Slavic lands and had a strong Yugoslav orientation.

SREBRENICA. Town and **commune** center in eastern **Bosnia and Hercegovina** (B-H), with a population 37,211 in 1991. The ethnic composition prior to the civil war was 72.9 percent Muslim and 25.2 percent Serbian. Srebrenica was an old mining town (zinc, silver, and lead) in the medieval Serbian state. Srebrenica came to the center of international media attention during the civil war in B-H after being designated a United Nations **Safe Area** on May 6, 1993. Protected by **NATO** and **UNPROFOR**, Muslim forces launched attacks from the city, destroying several neighboring Serbian villages. After several attempts, the **Bosnian Serb Army** captured the city in July 1995. Several places around Srebrenica are regarded as sites of an alleged mass execution of Muslim prisoners.

SREM. Historic region in **Vojvodina**, between the **Danube** and **Sava** Rivers, total area 6,865 sq km, of which 4,420 sq km belongs to the **Federal Republic of Yugoslavia** and 2,445 to **Croatia** (western Srem); estimated population close to 500,000 (1991). In the northwest-southeast direction Srem is 160 km long, while its width varies from 70 km on the west to the 25 km on the east. Srem is a very fertile region, agriculture being the main economic sector. After **World War II**, several industries were developed in **Zemun** (metals, chemicals, textiles, food processing), **Vukovar** (textiles) **Sremska Mitrovica** (food processing), **Šid** (chemicals, food processing), and Vinkovci (wood production).

The first inhabitants of Srem were **Illyrians** and Celts. The Romans captured Srem between 15 and 9 B.C. and founded Sirmium (Sremska Mitrovica), which together with **Belgrade** became a major center of the Illyric province. After the split of the Roman Empire, Srem was continuously contested among Huns, the Byzantine Empire, and **Avars**, who captured Sirmium in 579. The first Slavic tribes arrived in Srem approximately at that time. After the collapse of the Avarian state in 769, Srem became a borderland of the Frankish Empire and was called Marachia. Between 882 and 927 Srem was under Bulgarian occupation and then later Hungarian domination.

The major influx of **Serbs** occurred in the 14th century, especially after the **Battle of Kosovo.** Serbs became the major element in Srem and established, under Hungarian suzerainty, a Serbian despotate. Srem fell to the Turks in 1526 and remained under Turkish control until the **Treaty of Passarowitz** in 1718. After the **Treaty of Belgrade**, Srem became part of **Vojna Krajina.** Between 1849 and 1860 Srem was a part of Srbska Vojvodina, an Austrian autonomous province. Srem became part of Kingdom of SHS in 1918. During **World War II** Srem was a part of the **Independent State of Croatia**, and the **Ustaše** committed terrible atrocities against local Serbs, Jews, and Gypsies.

Historically, Serbs constituted the majority of the population in Srem. However, in 1945 Srem was administratively divided between **Serbia** and Croatia. During the civil war in Croatia in 1991, heavy fighting took place in western Srem between the local Serbian population, the **JNA**, and Croatian paramilitary forces.

SREMAC, STEVAN (1855–1906). Writer, one of the masters of realism in Serbian literature, especially known for his authentic portrayal of 19th century **Niš** just liberated from the Turks. His best-known works are *Zona Zamfirova*, *Ivkova Slava* (*Ivko's Patron Saint)* and *Pop Ćira i pop Spira* (*Priest Cyril and Priest Spiro*).

SREMSKA MITROVICA. Biggest city and the cultural and economic center of **Srem**, with a population of 85,326 in 1991. Textile, food-processing, and wood-processing industries are particularly developed in the city and its vicinity. Founded as ancient Sirmium, the city became the most important center of the eastern part of the Roman Empire and capital of Panonia Segunda. Several Roman emperors were born in Sirmium (Aurelian, Decius, Claudius II, and Probus).

SREMSKI FRONT (Srem Front). Frontline established by the retreating German forces following the liberation of **Belgrade** in October 1944. The **Partisans** broke the German defenses on April 12, 1945, after almost six months of heavy fighting. It is estimated that more than 30,000

**Serbs,** mainly teenagers, were killed during the fighting on the Sremski front.

SREMSKI KARLOVCI. See KARLOVCI SREMSKI.

SRPSKA AKADEMIJA NAUKA I UMETNOSTI. See SERBIAN ACADEMY OF SCIENCES AND ARTS.

SRPSKA DEMOKRATSKA STRANKA. See SERBIAN DEMOCRATIC PARTY.

SRPSKA KNJIŽEVNA ZADRUGA (SKZ) (Serbian Literary Cooperative). Literary organization founded in 1892 by 17 prominent Serbian writers and poets. The main objectives of the organization were to publish distinguished literary works and further develop Serbian literature.

SRPSKA NARODNA ORGANIZACIJA (Serbian National Organization). First political organization of Bosnian Serbs that encompassed all Serbian factions in **Bosnia and Hercegovina**, from radical to moderate. The organization was founded in 1907 with the principal objective of promoting the right of self-determination of the Bosnian Serbs.

SRPSKA PRAVOSLAVNA CRKVA. See SERBIAN ORTHODOX CHURCH.

SRPSKA RADIKALNA STRANKA. See SERBIAN RADICAL PARTY.

*SRPSKA VOJSKA* (*Serbian Army*). Independent military journal, published weekly in **Belgrade** from 1908 to 1912. The main editor of the journal was **Živojin Mišić**. Besides articles on military issues the journal was publishing current political essays and was considered an unofficial voice of the Serbian military.

*SRPSKE NOVINE* (*Serbian Newspapers*). The first newspaper was published in **Serbia** during the reign of **Miloš Obrenović**. The newspaper was published from 1834 to 1919, first in **Kragujevac** and then in **Belgrade**. It was an official paper of the Serbian government. From 1916 to 1918 the newspaper was published on **Corfu Island** with the literary supplement ***Zabavnik***. In February 1919, the *Srpske Novine* were replaced by the *Službene novine* (*Official Gazette*).

*SRPSKI DNEVNIK* (*Serbian Daily*). A daily newspaper published in New York from 1917 to 1938. The founder-owner of the newspaper was **Mihajlo Pupin**.

*SRPSKI GLAS* (*Serbian Voice*). (i) The official paper of the Serbian National Party in **Dalmatia**. The main Serbian paper in Dalmatia, the journal was published weekly between 1888 and 1900 in **Zadar** under the name *Srpski list—glasilo za srpske interese na Primorju* (*Serbian Paper—a Voice of the Serbian Interest on the Coast*).

(ii) The official paper of the **Srpski kulturni klub** (Serbian Cultural Club) published in **Belgrade** from 1939 to 1940, when it was banned. The main editor was **Dragiša Vasić**.

*SRPSKI KNJIŽEVNI GLASNIK* (*Serbian Literary Herald*). One of the most important Serbian literary journals that had a profound impact on the development of literature in **Serbia**. The *Serbian Literary Herald* was founded in 1901 and **Bogdan Popović, Jovan Skerlić,** and **Slobodan Jovanović** served as editors. The journal ceased publication in 1941, but it resumed in 1991.

SRPSKI KULTURNI KLUB/SERBIAN CULTURAL CLUB. An organization of prominent Serbian intellectuals founded in 1939 in the immediate aftermath of the constitutional changes in Yugoslavia and the formation of the **Croatian Banovina**. The Club vehemently defended Serbian political, cultural, economic and historical interests in Yugoslavia. The motto of the club was "Strong **Serbia**—Strong Yugoslavia", which was in direct opposition to Croatian claims. The Yugoslav coalition government led by **Dragiša Cvetković** and **Vladko Maček** banned ***Srpski glas***, an official paper of the club, in 1940. The most prominent members of the club included **Slobodan Jovanović**, Slobodan Drašković, Vladimir Đorđević, Gojko Grđić, Bogdan Prica, **Dragiša Vasić**, and others.

SRPSKI POKRET OBNOVE. See SERBIAN RENEWAL MOVEMENT.

*SRPSKO KOLO* (*Serbian Ring*). (i) Journal published twice a week from 1881 to 1885 in **Novi Sad**. Under the editorship of **Jaša Tomić** the journal became close to the policy of the **Radical Party**.

(ii) Weekly published in **Zagreb** from 1903 to 1914 and from 1919 to 1928.

The journal advocated the policy of the **Independent Radical Party**. From 1929 the journal was published in **Belgrade**.

SRPSKO LEKARSKO DRUŠTVO (Serbian Medical Society). Professional society of physicians in **Serbia,** founded by **Vladan Đorđević** in 1882; regularly publishes *Srpski arhiv za celokupno lekarstvo* (*Serbian Archive for All Physicians*), which is among the oldest professional journals in Yugoslavia.

SRPSKO NARODNO POZORIŠTE (Serbian National Theater). First professional Serbian theater founded in **Novi Sad** in 1861, it influenced the founding of the **National Theater** in **Belgrade** in 1868. Several young producers gathered in the theater in the mid-1950s and initiated new ways of dramatic expression.

SRPSKO UČENO DRUŠTVO (Serbian Learned Society). Scientific society founded in 1864, continued the work of the **Društvo Srpske Slovesnosti.** After constant struggle with Prince **Milan Obrenović,** who opposed the active social role of the society, it merged with the **Serbian Academy of Sciences and Arts** in 1886.

ST. ANDREW ASSEMBLY/SVETOANDREJSKA SKUPŠTINA. Session of the Serbian **Parliament** held between December 13, 1858, and January 4, 1859. The Parliament was convened on the insistence of the **Constitutionalists.** It led to the overthrow of Prince **Alexander Karađorđević** and return of Prince **Miloš Obrenović**. The status of the Parliament was changed from a law-making institution to a mere advisory board.

STAMBOLIĆ, IVAN (1936– ). Serbian politician, former president of the Central Commitee of the League of Communist of Serbia and president of the collective Presidency of **Serbia**. Stambolić's political career hinged upon the heavy support of his influential uncle Petar Stambolić. He became president of Serbia after his nomination to the post of prime minister of the Yugoslav federation was blocked by **Slovenia** and **Croatia**. During his rule the problem of **Kosovo and Metohija** intensified. The growing discontent with his timid policies was exploited by **Slobodan Milosević** who staged Stambolić's removal from Serbian politics in 1987. Until recently, Stambolić was director of the Yugoslav Bank for International Cooperation.

STANKOVIĆ, BORISAV BORA (1876–1927). One of the best Serbian novelists, known for his authentic portrayal of the patriarchal life in **Vranje,** southern **Serbia**. His characters are complex, with strong internal conflict between conflicting motives. His best-known works include *Nečista krv* (*Tainted Blood*), *Koštana*, and *Gazda Mladen* (*Master Mladen*).

STANKOVIĆ, KORNELIJE (1831–1865). Serbian composer and pianist. He was among the first formally educated Serbian pianists. A founder of the national style in Serbian classical music, Stanković is especially known for his work on harmonization of Serbian church music. His best-known work is *Pravoslavno crkveno pojanje u srpskog naroda* (*Orthodox Church Singing among the Serbian Peoples*).

STARA GRADIŠKA. Village in **Slavonia** on the left bank of the **Sava** River. A large concentration camp, part of the death camp complex of **Jasenovac,** run by the **Ustaše** was located in **Stara Gradiška** 1941–1945.

STARČEVIĆ, ANTE (1823–1896). Croatian politician and founder of the Croatian Party of the Right, especially prejudicial toward the **Serbs,** whom he labelled "the inferior race." His teachings became the basis of Croatian nationalism and of **Ustaše** genocidal policies against the Serbs during **World War II**.

STEFAN LAZAREVIĆ (1371?–1427). Son of Prince **Lazar Hrebljanović** and Serbian prince 1389–1402 and **despot** 1402–1427. A Turkish vassal, he became independent in 1402 and extended the territory of Serbia by incorporating **Mačva, Zeta,** and **Belgrade**, which became Serbia's capital. His achievements include reforming the army, reorganizing the state administration, and building **Manasija** monastery. He wrote *Slovo Ljubve* (*Word of Love*).

STEFAN TOMAŠ (?–1461). King of Bosnia (r. 1443–1461), the successor of of **Tvrtko II Kotromanić**. In order to secure the backing of the Pope and the Venetians, Stefan Tomaš persecuted **Bogomils** and severed his relations with the Serbian **Despot Đurađ Branković**. During his rule central authority in Bosnia was further eroded due to Turkish expansion and his rivalry with the powerful **Kosače** family.

STEFAN TOMAŠEVIĆ (?–1463). The last king of Bosnia, son of **Stefan Tomaš**. Crowned by legate of Pope Pius XII in the city of **Jajce** in 1461, Stefan was soon abandoned by his Venetian and Hungarian allies. Following the Turkish onslaught on Bosnia in 1463 and the fall of several Bosnian strongholds, he surrendered to the Turkish army commander in the city of **Ključ** in exchange for his life. He was executed in early June of 1463 in Jajce at the order of the Turkish Sultan Muhammed the Conqueror.

STEPANOVIĆ, STEPA (1856–1929). **Vojvoda** and one of the most celebrated commanders of the Serbian army during **World War I**. He commanded the Second Army, which defeated the Austro-Hungarian forces at the **Battle of Cer**. Stepanović commanded the Serbian units that broke through the **Salonika front**. He edited the official journal *Vojni list* (*Army Journal*) and *Ratnik* (*The Warrior*).

STERIJA, POPOVIĆ JOVAN (1806–1856). Serbian playwright from **Vojvodina.** He was a professor in the Lycée (**Great School**) and a supervisor in Serbia's ministry of education. Sterija was the first Serbian author to espouse realism in literature and the theater. He is best known for his comedies, in which he ridiculed the newly created Serbian bourgeoisie. His work includes *Laža i paralaža* (*Lies and More Lies*), *Pokondirena tikva* (*The Obnoxious Blockhead*), *Kir-Janja* (*The Miser*), and *Rodoljupci* (*Patriots*).

STOJADINOVIĆ, MILAN (1888–1961). Prominent Serbian politician, statesman, and economist, the founder and president of the **Yugoslav Radical Union,** and prime minister of Yugoslavia 1935–1939. His restrictive monetary policy in the 1920s strengthened the international position of the Yugoslav **dinar** and stabilized the Yugoslav economy. As prime minister, he changed the course of Yugoslav foreign policy by strengthening Yugoslav economic and political dependence on Germany. After his removal from the post of prime minister in 1939, he was arrested and interned in April 1940. On March 18, 1941, Stojadinović was extradited to the British authorities in Greece, who interned him on the island of Mauritius. He died in Buenos Aires where *Ni rat ni pakt* (*Neither War nor Pact*) was published posthumously.

STOJANČEVIĆ, VLADIMIR (1923– ). Prominent Serbian historian and member of the **Serbian Academy of Sciences and Arts** (SANU). Born in **Skoplje,** he graduated from the **University of Belgrade** where he worked in the Historical Institute of the SANU until his retirement. He specialized in the history of Serbia in the 19th and 20th centuries, especially Serbo-Bulgarian and Serbo-Albanian relations. His numerous works include *Srbija i Bugari* (*Serbia and Bulgars*), *Srbija u vreme Prvog ustanka 1804–1813* (*Serbia in the First Insurrection 1804–1813*), and *Srbi i Arbanasi* (*Serbs and Arbanasi*).

STOJANOVIĆ, KOSTA (1867–1921). Serbian politician, statesman, and economist. He was a minister of national economy in Serbia and held the post of minister of finance in the first government of the **Kingdom of the Serbs, Croats, and Slovenes**. His best known works include *Osnovi teorije ekonomskih vrednosti* (*The Basic Principles of the Theory of Value*) and *Govori i političko-ekonomske rasprave* (*Speeches and Political-Economic Issues*).

STOJANOVIĆ, LJUBOMIR-LJUBA (1860–1929). Prominent Serbian politician and philologist. A member of the **Serbian Academy of Sciences and Arts**, he was professor at the **Great School** and the **University of Belgrade**. After **May's Assassination**, he became minister of education. After **World War I,** he and **Jaša Prodanović** formed the **Yugoslav Republican Party**.

STOJANOVIĆ, NIKOLA (1880–1964). Journalist and politician. He edited the journals *Dubrovnik* and ***Narod*** (*The People*) and formed the Serbian national organization in 1905. In 1910 he became a member of the Bosnian **Parliament** and in 1914 he approached Ante Trumbić to form the **Yugoslav Committee**. He advocated closer cooperation with the Serbian government and acted as a mediator between the Serbian and Croatian sides.

STOJKOVIĆ, MILENKO (?–1831). Serbian **vojvoda** from the **First Serbian Insurrection.** A strong opponent of **Karađorđe**, he was removed from the army command and expelled from **Serbia** in 1811.

STOKIĆ, ŽANKA (1887–1947). Serbian actress, a representative of realist expression in Serbian acting, known for her serenity. Her greatest theater successes were roles in the comedies of **Branislav Nušić.**

STRANKA DEMOKRATSKE AKCIJE. See PARTY OF DEMOCRATIC ACTION.

STROSSMAYER, JOSIP JURAJ (1815–1905). Croatian politician and educator, the leader of the National Party 1860–1873. Born to a German family in **Osijek,** Strossmayer was educated in Đakovo and Budapest, where he graduated with a degree in theology. In 1849, he was elevated to the post of Bishop of Bosnia and **Srem.** As a politician, he favored the unification of the **South Slavs** and the incorporation of their lands into Austria.

STUDENICA. Monastery in Serbia, located in the valley of the **Ibar** River, built 1186–1193; a legacy of **Stefan Nemanja** and an archetype of the so-called **Raška** style. The Studenica monastery complex is included in the UNESCO list of world cultural heritage. The complex includes the Church of the Mother of God (12th century); the Memorial Church of Stefan Nemanja, considered as the most valuable monument of the Raška School; St. Nicholas Church (12th century), and King's Church (14th century). Here the first **frescoes** with Serbian inscriptions were painted and the first original literary works were written.

SUBOTICA. Cultural and economic center of northern **Vojvodina**, close to the Hungarian border with a population of 150,534 in 1991. Industries include food processing, motorcycle and bicycle assembly, production of electrical equipment, and shoe-making. Subotica is also a university center. The city was founded by Subota Vrlić, a Serbian **vojvoda.** A sizable Hungarian minority lives in Subotica (64,277; 1991).

SUTJESKA. River in eastern **Hercegovina** 36 km long.

SUTJESKA, BATTLE OF. Battle between the **Partisans** and German forces May 15–June 15, 1943, in the valley of **Sutjeska** River, close to the border of **Hercegovina** and **Montenegro**. After an unsuccessful attempt to destroy the Partisans in the Battle of **Neretva**, a combined German-Italian and **Ustaše** force (125,000) launched a major offensive in May 1943, aiming to encircle and destroy **Tito**'s forces (15,000 plus 4,000 wounded). After more than a month of heavy fighting and severe losses (8,000), the bulk of the Partisans' army was able to break through the German lines.

SVETA GORA. Mt. Athos, a peninsula in northeast Greece where the Serbian monastery **Hilandar** was founded in 1198 by **Saint Sava** and **Stefan Nemanja**. The entire peninsula was under Serbian rule from 1345 to 1371, and the monastery enjoys complete autonomy from civil affairs.

SVETI STEFAN. Hotel town and an exclusive tourist resort in **Montenegro**. The resort is located on a rocky islet connected to the mainland by a narrow isthmus.

SVETOANDREJSKA SKUPŠTINA. See St. ANDREW ASSEMBLY.

SZENT ENDRE/SENT ANDREJA. Town on the banks of the **Danube** River in the vicinity of Budapest, formerly the residence of the Serbian patriarch and the center of Serbian culture in Hungary. Although Serbian settlers in Szent Endre were mentioned as early as 1428, the massive arrival of **Serbs** started during Velika Seoba (see **Seoba Srba**) under **Arsenije III Crnojević** in 1690. Several **Serbian Orthodox Church**es were built in the town during the 18th century. In the course of the 19th and 20th centuries, nearly the entire Serbian population of Szent Endre was either assimilated or returned to **Serbia.**

## - Š -

ŠABAC. City and cultural and economic center of the fertile **Mačva** region in northwestern **Serbia** with a population of 123,633 in 1991. The chemical and wood-processing industries are especially developed. Although archeological sites suggest that the city's surroundings were populated as early as the neolithic period, the modern city was founded in the 14th century as a part of the medieval Serbian state. During the Turkish occupation a strong fortress was built on the **Sava** bank as a stronghold in the border region with Austria. After the **First Serbian Insurrection** Šabac rapidly developed and became the county seat. Several cultural institutions were established, including a high school (1837), a national theater (1847), choral society (1865), and printing firm (1881). Prior to **World War I** it was the major export center of Serbia.

ŠAFARIK, JANKO (1814–1876). Serbian historian of Slovak origin. He was a professor of the Lyceé (**Great School**) in **Belgrade** and the founder of the **National Museum**. He is also the author of numerous works on Serbian history: *Srbski spomenici mletačkog arhiva* (*Serbian Legacies* *of the Venetian Archives*), *Život despota Stefana Lazarevića* (*Life of the Despot Stefan Lazarević*), and others.

ŠAINOVIĆ, NIKOLA (1948– ). Deputy prime minister of the government of the **Federal Republic of Yugoslavia.** He was educated in **Belgrade** and **Ljubljana,** where he received his Masters degree in chemical engineering. Since 1989 Šainović has occupied several highly visible political posts, including minister of energy and mining and Serbian deputy prime minister (1991), minister for economy (1992) in the government of **Milan Panić** (1992), and president of the Serbian government. In May 1999 Šainović along with Yugoslav president Slobodan Milošević, Serbian President Milutin Milutinović, and Chief of Staff of the Yugoslav Army general Dragoljub Ojdanić was indicted by the Hague Tribunal for the alleged crimes against Albanian population in Kosovo and Metohija.

ŠAJKAŠI. Force of Serbian fighters on the **Danube** River, named after their boats (šajka). Among the first were fighters who in 1439 founded the town known as Serbian Kovin on the river island Čepelj. After the Battle of Mohacs in 1526, they resettled in Komoran. Operating in the area between the **Tisa** and Danube Rivers, they played an important role as auxiliary troops in the Austrian army during the Austro-Turkish wars. Their battalion was divided into six companies, and the city of Titel was their organizational center.

ŠANTIĆ, ALEKSA (1868–1924). One of the most popular Serbian poets from **Bosnia and Hercegovina** (B-H). He was born and spent his entire life in **Mostar**. Together with **Jovan Dučić** and **Svetozar Ćorović**, Šantić founded **Zora**, the cultural society of Serbs from B-H. He is best known for his impressionistic style and patriotic poems such as "Ostajte ovdje" ("Stay Here") and "Boka."

ŠAR MOUNTAIN/ŠAR PLANINA. Massive mountain between Serbia and Macedonia; 80 km long, 20-30 km wide, with several peaks exceeding 2,000 m. It has chromium mines and is a tourist attraction.

ŠAR PLANINA. See ŠAR MOUNTAIN.

ŠĆEPAN MALI. Ruler of **Montenegro** 1766–1774, who claimed to be the Russian emperor Peter III and became known as Lažni car (the phony emperor).

ŠEJKA, LEONID (1932–1970). One of the most prominent modern Serbian painters. He revived the idea of "integral painting." Esoteric and illogical visions were "realistically" and logically painted. Besides his numerous masterpieces, he is known for his text *Tractate on Painting*.

ŠEŠELJ, VOJISLAV (1954– ). Leader of the **Serbian Radical Party** (SRS) and a deputy in the Serbian **Parliament**. Šešelj was born and educated in **Sarajevo**, where he received his doctorate. Upon his graduation, he taught at the University of Sarajevo from 1981 to 1984, when he became a victim of political intrigue and was sentenced to eight years in prison. Upon his release in 1986 he became one of the most vocal dissidents in Yugoslavia. In 1989 he worked actively to restore the **Četniks** movement and became the leader of the SRS. After the split between the SRS and the **Socialist Party of Serbia** (SPS) Šešelj was imprisoned on several occasions because of his vitriolic criticism of Serbian president **Slobodan Milošević**. However, he became a deputy prime minister of Serbia after the SPS and the SRS formed a coalition government in 1998. He is the most vocal and radical representative of extreme nationalism in Serbia. His numerous books include *Demokratija i dogma* (*Democracy and Dogmatism*), and *Aktuelni politički izazovi* (*Actual Political Challenges*).

ŠESTOJANUARSKA DIKTATURA. See DICTATORSHIP OF JANUARY 6, 1929.

ŠID. City and **commune** center in **Srem**, close to the border with **Croatia,** with a population of 36,317 in 1991. The largest concentration of the Croatian minority in Srem lives in the territory of Šid. Food-processing and chemical industries are particularly developed in the city.

ŠIPTARI. Term traditionally used in **Serbia** for the Albanian minority (1,727,541; 1991). Most of the Albanian minority emigrated to **Kosovo and Metohija** between the 17th and 19th centuries, when the Albanian tribes populated areas abandoned by **Seoba Srba**. The next wave of migration from Albania to Kosovo and Metohija started in the mid 1960s. It was estimated that during the next 20 years more than 300,000 Albanians migrated from Albania to Yugoslavia.

*ŠKOLSKI LIST* (*The School Journal*). First Serbian pedagogical journal.

*Školski list* was published in **Novi Sad, Sombor,** and Budapest from 1858 to 1907.

STARA PAZOVA. City in **Srem** with a population of 57,291 in 1991 and an important railway center and one of the cultural centers of the Slovak minority in the **Federal Republic of Yugoslavia.** A gymnasium (high school) and a high school of economics in the Slovak language are located in Stara Pazova. The city is known for its artisans and craftsmen.

ŠTURM, JURIŠIĆ PAVLE (1842–1922). Serbian general of German origin. He arrived in **Serbia** in 1876 as a Prussian lieutenant. From 1907 to 1917 he was the king's first military secretary. During the **Balkan wars** he commanded the **Drina** and **Danube** divisions. During **World War I** he was the commander of the 3rd Serbian Army until 1916 when he was sent to Russia as a special emissary. From 1917 to his retirement in 1921 he held the ceremonial post of the Chancellor of the Kings Medals.

ŠUBAŠIĆ, IVAN (1892–1955). Croatian and Yugoslav politician, member of the **Croatian Peasant Party**. He was **ban** of the **Croatian Banovina** 1939–1941 and prime minister of the government-in-exile 1944–1945. As the prime minister in 1944, he signed the British-sponsored agreement about the formation of a joint government with Josip Broz, **Tito**, and the **Partisans**. The agreement effectively excluded the majority of Serbian politicians and statesmen who supported General **Dragoljub-Draža Mihailović** and the **Jugoslovenska vojska u otadžbini**. After the formation of the joint government on March 7, 1945, Šubašić became the minister of foreign affairs, retiring after the war.

ŠUCKOR. Originally Schutzkorps; the Austro-Hungarian irregular militia units in **Bosnia and Hercegovina** during **World War I**. The units were staffed by local **Muslims** and were known for their terror against the Serbian population.

ŠUMADIJA. Central region in **Serbia** located between the rivers **Sava** and **Danube** to the north, Kolubara to the west, **Western Morava** to the south, and **Velika Morava** to the East. The terrain is mainly hilly with the **Rudnik** Mountain being the highest at 1,132 m. The name Šumadija suggests that the region once was covered by dense forests which gradually disappeared in the 18th and 19th centuries. The major influx of population in the region occured after the **Second Serbian Insurrection** when the Serbian population from **Montenegro**, **Kosovo and Metohija**, and **Hercegovina** moved to Šumadija. The biggest cities are **Belgrade** and **Smederevo**, while **Kragujevac** is central to the region. Agriculture is well developed, and the bulk of Serbian industry is located in the region. The biggest industrial capacities include a large metalurgical complex in Smederevo, a military complex and automobile industry in Kragujevac, thermoelectric power plants in Lazarevac, machine building in Železnik and others.

ŠUMANOVIĆ, SAVA (1896–1942). Celebrated Serbian painter, one of the most prominent representatives of cubism in Serbian painting. He often changed directions in painting, as well as his whereabouts. After achieving fame in Paris and **Belgrade** he returned to his native **Šid**, where he produced one of his most significant paintings. He was arrested without charge and executed by the **Ustaše**.

ŠUPLJIKAC, STEVAN (1786–1848). Born in **Petrinja,** Šupljikac served in the Austrian military until 1809, when, after the formation of the Illyrian Provinces, he joined the French army and became an adjutant to Marshal Marmont. In 1814, he re-joined the Austrian army and served in various garrisons in **Lika** and **Banat**. In 1848, the assembly of Serbian **Vojvodina** elected him **vojvoda**.

## - T -

TAJNA KONVENCIJA. See SECRET CONVENTION.

TAKOVO. Village in the vicinity of **Gornji Milanovac** in which the decision to begin the **Second Serbian Insurrection** was made on April 11, 1815.

TAMIŠ. River in **Banat,** a tributary of the **Danube** River; total length 339.7 km (121.7 km in the **Federal Republic of Yugoslavia**).

TANKOSIĆ, VOJISLAV (1881–1915). Major of the Serbian army, a founder of **Unification or Death**, and the founder and commander of **Četnik** forces, volunteer guerilla units that fought in **Macedonia** and eastern

**Bosnia and Hercegovina**. In July 1914, following a request of Austria-Hungary, he was arrested for his alleged participation in the **Sarajevo Assassination**, but was released after the outbreak of the war.

TARA. (i) A river in **Montenegro**, which together with the **Piva** forms the **Drina** River; rich in hydroenergy energy, total length 140.5 km. The depth of its outstanding canyon exceeds 1,000 m.
(ii) A mountain in western **Serbia**, covering an area of 183 sq km with an average altitude of 1,200 m.

TARIFF WAR 1906–1911. Serbia's economic and political dependence on Austria-Hungary became a major impediment for its further development at the beginning of the 20th century. While the economic domination of Austria-Hungary prevented the modernization and industrialization of Serbia's economy, Austro-Hungarian political control obstructed the Serbian national struggle. At the time of the dynastic change (**May's Assassination**), Austria-Hungary's share in Serbia's total imports exceeded 60 percent; it reached 95 percent for lumber and wood commodities, 84 percent for paper, 83 percent for metals, and 81 percent for textiles. Serbian exports followed a similar pattern—the Austro-Hungarian share in Serbia's total exports was 89 percent, and in the same year 98 percent of Serbia's livestock exports went to Austria-Hungary.

The dynastic and government change in Serbia in 1903 was followed by comprehensive economic reform that included stabilization of finances, reorganization of foreign trade, a new tariff system, and conclusion of new and more favorable trade treaties with several European countries. These profound changes in Serbia's economic policy, the conclusion of a customs union between Serbia and neighboring Bulgaria, and the refusal of the Serbian government to purchase guns from Austria-Hungary fueled outrage in Vienna. Austria-Hungary perceived Serbia's actions as a direct challenge to its vital interests and closed its border to Serbia's exports on July 7, 1906.

Contrary to Austro-Hungarian expectations, Serbia greatly benefited from the Tariff War, which became known as the Pig War (live hogs were the principal item in Serbia's exports). In the course of the war, which lasted from 1906 to 1911, Austria-Hungary's share in Serbia's foreign trade fell to less than 20 percent. Both the product and regional composition of Serbia's foreign trade changed, while the presence of French and British capital in the economy of Serbia substantially increased. The availability of capital spurred economic growth and industrialization. The Tariff War and **Annexation Crisis** (1908) came as the result of the expansionist policy of Austria-Hungary and its determination to control Serbia. The economic and political emancipation of Serbia that emerged as a direct consequence of the tariff war prompted Austria-Hungary to resort to more belligerent ways of settling the Balkan Question.

TAUŠANOVIĆ, KOSTA (1854–1902). Serbian politician, one of the most prominent members of the **Radical Party** and a creator of the liberal **Constitution** of 1888. As a minister in several governments, he attempted to modernize and develop Serbia's rural economy.

TEKELIJA, SAVA (1761–1842). Serbian politician and benefactor from Hungary, president of **Matica srpska**. In 1838, he founded "Tekelianum," the special residential dormitory for needy Serbian students at the University of Budapest, to which he entrusted all of his property (150,000 Hungarian forints). Shortly before **World War II**, Matica srpska transferred the library of Tekelianum from Budapest to **Novi Sad.**

TEMIŠVARSKI SABOR (Assembly of Timisoara). Congregation of **Serbs** from **Vojvodina** and Hungary held in 1790 in Timisoara, **Banat**. The assembly was initiated by Vienna in order to counterbalance Hungarian separatism. The principal Serbian demands—the creation of an autonomous territory in Banat and further advancement of religious freedoms—were only partially satisfied by the election of Stevan Stratimirović as Metropolitan and the establishment of the Ilirska dvorska kancelarija (Illyrian Court Chancellory) in 1791.

TEMNIČKI NATPIS. One of the oldest fragments of Serbian writing, written in the **Cyrillic alphabet**. Six and a half rows of text were engraved onto a square stone, probably between the late 10th and the early 11th centuries.

TENKA'S PLOT/TENKINA ZAVERA. Plot organized by Stefan Stefanović-Tenka, a politician and prominent **Constitutionalist**, in 1857. Although he occupied several important posts, including minister of education, minister of finance, and minister of justice, and held the highest title in **Serbia** below that of prince, Tenka is best remembered as a conspirator who plotted against both the Obrenović and Karađorđević princes. In 1857, he plotted the assassination of Prince **Alexander Karađorđević** in order to restore **Miloš Obrenović**. The plot was discovered and the ringleaders arrested after the would-be assassin changed his mind and attempted to blackmail his employers.

TENKINA ZAVERA. See TENKA'S PLOT.

TEPIĆ, MILAN (1957–1991). Major in the **JNA**, a national hero of the civil war of 1991. Tepić was chief officer for technical equipment in the JNA garrison in Bjelovar. On September 29, 1991, during an attack by Croatian paramilitary forces , Tepić, in order to prevent the enemy seizing valuable military equipment, blew up a huge munitions depot containing more than 170 tonnes of explosives.

TESLA, NIKOLA (1856–1943). Great Serbian physicist and inventor; he discovered the rotating magnetic field. Tesla was born in Smiljan, a village in **Lika**. His father was Orthodox priest; his mother was unschooled but highly intelligent. Tesla finished elementary school in Smiljan in 1866 and high school in Karlovac in 1875. In 1877 he began his studies at the High Technical School in Graz, Austria, and he continued them at the University of Prague. After spending a year in Budapest, Tesla went to work in Paris for the Continental Edison Company. In 1883, working after hours, he constructed his first induction motor.

In 1884, virtually penniless, Tesla arrived in the United States. After brief employment with Thomas Edison, Tesla began to work with George Westinghouse in May 1885. Their cooperation triggered a gigantic conflict between Edison's direct current systems and Tesla's alternating current approach, which ultimately won. After establishing his own laboratory, Tesla invented the Tesla coil in 1891 and experimented with shadowgraphs that were later used in discovering X-rays. In 1893, Tesla won the contract to install the first hydroelectric power machinery at Niagara Falls, and in 1898 in Madison Square Garden he demonstrated his invention of a "teleautomatic" boat guided by remote control.

In the period between May 1899 and January 1900 Tesla discovered terrestrial stationary waves. Considering this his most important achievement, Tesla returned to New York, and with the financial help of J.P. Morgan, he began construction of a "worldwide wireless" broadcasting tower. The project, however, was not concluded due to a financial panic and Morgan's withdrawal of support. Disappointed and tired by the continuous legal fighting over his patents, Tesla shifted his attention to less demanding projects: turbines, obtaining ozone. In the 1930s, Tesla withdrew from public life into solitude. After his death, Tesla's belongings were transferred and housed in the Nikola Tesla Museum in **Belgrade**.

TIMOČKA BUNA. See TIMOK, REBELLION OF.

TIMOK. River in eastern **Serbia**, a tributary of the **Danube**. A natural border between Bulgaria and the **Federal Republic of Yugoslavia** (FRY), its total length is 183 km (167 km in the FRY). The valley of the river is the center of the Timok region, which is very rich in coal; the mines Rtanj, Vrška Čuka, and Dobra Sreća are located nearby.

TIMOK, REBELLION OF/TIMOČKA BUNA. Rebellion in the **Timok** region that erupted at the end of October 1883, when the local population refused to comply with a government decree calling for the confiscation of private weapons. The rebellion was organized and incited by the members of the **Radical Party**, many of whom were either arrested or went into exile after the rebellion was crushed. Although superior government forces quelled the revolt within a week, the Timok Rebellion was the most serious peasant uprising in Serbia's modern history.

TISA. River in **Vojvodina**, the longest tributary of the **Danube**. Its total length is 966 km (158 km in the **Federal Republic of Yugoslavia**). The average width of the river is 240 m, and the average depth is between 3.9 and 4.4 m. The river is connected with the Danube at Bezdan and Banatska Palanka by the **Danube-Tisa-Danube** canal. The Tisa is the major irrigation source in Vojvodina.

TITO, JOSIP BROZ (1892–1980). Long-time president and leader of Yugoslavia. Josip Broz was born on May 7, in Kumrovec of a Slovene mother and a Croatian peasant father. After working throughout Austria-Hungary, Broz served as a noncommissioned officer in the Austro-Hungarian army during **World War I**. He was wounded and taken prisoner by the Russians in 1916. In Russia, he joined the Bolshevik Party, and upon his return to the **Kingdom of the Serbs, Croats, and Slovenes**, he became an illegal Communist party organizer. In 1934, after serving six years in prison and taking the name Tito as an alias, he went to Moscow to work for the Communist International. He returned to Yugoslavia in 1937, and after a purge, became the general secretary of the **Communist Party of Yugoslavia** in 1937.

Following the German occupation of Yugoslavia in April and the attack on the Soviet Union in June 1941, Tito, who closely followed instructions from the Communist International, formed an all-national, although initially predominantly Serbian, movement. Tito's forces, known as **Partisans**, successfully resisted the Germans and **Ustaše** and outmaneuvered and discredited the rival antifascist movement **Jugoslovenska vojska u otadžbini.** In 1945, Tito, representing the only real power in Yugoslavia, set up a one-party dictatorship. His policies, internal and foreign, caused a quick deterioration of Yugoslavia's relations with the West. In 1946 the nationalization law established the full Yugoslav control of the Western firms that operated in Yugoslavia. The dispute concerning the city of Trieste and the Yugoslav-Italian border resulted in numerous incidents and downing of several American planes. Moreover, Tito overtly supported the Greek Communist-led partisans. The newly created Yugoslav republic of **Macedonia** became a safe haven for the Greek partisans, where they received arms and supplies. It is estimated that more than 100,000 people found a refuge in Yugoslav Macedonia after the Greek civil war ended in 1948.

After the split with Stalin and the **Cominform** blockade in 1948, Tito and his associates introduced wide social and economic reforms in the country. The introduction of **Self-management** was followed by a rapid change in Yugoslav foreign policy and the establishment of the **Nonaligned Movement** in the early 1960s. While Tito's foreign policy enabled Yugoslavia to effectively exploit the cold war and to remain independent, it also, by relying on Third World countries, distanced the country from Europe and the Balkans. While the Yugoslav standard of living greatly exceeded that of the rest of the socialist countries, it was mainly achieved through intensive foreign borrowing, to which Yugoslavia had almost unlimited access due to the personal charisma of Tito. After Tito's death, however, heavy indebtedness proved to be a leading cause of the severe economic crisis that followed. The matter of ongoing controversy, internal policies during the Tito era, mainly the creating of the two autonomous provinces; founding of the Montenegrin, Macedonian, and Muslim nations; and appeasing of Croatian and Albanian nationalism and separatism contributed to the disintegration of Yugoslavia.

TITOGRAD. See PODGORICA.

TODOROVIĆ, PERA (1852–1907). Serbian politician and journalist, one of the founders of the **Radical Party**. Todorović was an early supporter of the socialist ideas of **Svetozar Marković**. He was the editor of *Rad* (*Labor*), the first socialist literary journal in **Serbia**, and the journal *Straža* (*The Guard*). Upon his return from exile in 1880, he joined **Nikola Pašić** and founded the Radical Party. Following the **Rebellion of Timok** in 1883, disappointed with the posture of many radical leaders, Todorović urged reconciliation between the party and King **Milan Obrenović.** When his initiative was rejected by party leaders, Todorović left the Radical Party. He initiated and edited several journals: *Radikal* (*Radical*), *Ogledalo* (*Mirror*), and *Male Novine* (*Little Newspaper*).

TOMIĆ, JAŠA (1856–1922). Serbian politician from **Vojvodina**. After the retirement of **Svetozar Miletić**, he became editor of the journal *Zastave* (*Banners*). In 1881, he founded the Srpska radikalna stranka (**Serbian Radical Party**) in Vojvodina. Tomić played a decisive role in Vojvodina's unification with **Serbia** in 1918.

TOPLICA. River in southern **Serbia**. The valley of this 130 km-long river is the center of the Toplica region. **Prokuplje** and Kuršumlija are centers of a predominantly agricultural region.

TOPLICA, REBELLION OF/TOPLIČKI USTANAK. Insurrection in the **Toplica** region against the Austro-Bulgarian occupation in February-April 1917. The immediate cause of the insurrection was the Bulgarian decision to draft Serbs into the Bulgarian army. Encouraged by **Četnik** forces, the local population revolted against Bulgarians in Kuršumlija on February 26, 1917. Soon after Kuršumlija, several other cities were liberated, including **Prokuplje**, Blace, Lebane, and Crna Trava. However, given the strategic importance of the region as a communications link between **Serbia** and Bulgaria and Serbia and **Macedonia**, the Germans, Bulgarians, and Austro-Hungarians assembled strong forces and crushed the rebellion in late March 1917. An international commission confirmed that during the occupiers' reprisals 20,000 people were killed, while more than 50,000 homes were burned to the ground.

TOPLIČKI USTANAK. See TOPLICA, REBELLION OF.

TOPOLA. Small town in **Šumadija**, the political center of **Serbia** during the **First Serbian Insurrection.**

TOPOLA, REBELLION OF/TOPOLSKA BUNA. Army mutiny that took place in **Topola** on December 7, 1877. One of five battalions refused to take an oath to Prince **Milan Obrenović** and attempted to raise a rebellion against the dynasty and restore Karađorđević's rule. The mutiny was quickly subdued.

TOPOLSKA BUNA. See TOPOLA, REBELLION OF.

TRANSFIGURATION ASSEMBLY/PREOBRAŽENJSKA SKUPŠTINA. Extraordinary session of the Serbian **Parliament** held between August 19 and August 29, 1861. Convened by Prince **Mihailo Obrenović**, the assembly enacted several new laws that substantially enhanced the power of the prince and considerably changed the **Constitution** of 1838 (designed by Turkey). In addition to the strengthening of Prince Mihailo's power, the Assembly envisioned the establishment of a 100,000-strong national army. The Turks perceived these changes as extremely hostile and requested their suspension until additional evaluation by the Turkish government.

TREBINJE. Small city and the **commune** center in eastern **Hercegovina** with a population of 30, 879 in 1991. The ethnic composition prior to the civil war was 69.3 percent Serbian, 17.9 percent Muslim, 4 percent Croatian, and 5.3 percent Yugoslav. Metal-processing, wood-processing, and tobacco industries are especially developed in the city and its surroundings. During the civil war in **Bosnia and Hercegovina**, Trebinje was a site of heavy fighting between the **Bosnian Serb Army** and regular Croatian army forces.

TREPČA. Biggest lead, zinc, and silver ore mine in Europe, located in the vicinity of **Kosovska Mitrovica, Kosovo and Metohija**. The yearly production of ore is close to two million tonnes.

TRESKAVAC. Monastery in the vicinity of the city of Prilep in **Macedonia**, originally built by the Byzantines and renovated by the Serbian king **Milutin Nemanjić** and Emperor **Dušan the Mighty.**

*TRGOVAČKE NOVINE* (*Commercial News*) Weekly newspaper inaugurated by the influential **Belgrade** merchant Jovan Kumanudi in 1861. Although required to confine itself to economic and cultural topics, the *Trgovačke novine* became a major opposition paper. In 1863, the publishing of the paper stopped on the personal order of Prince **Mihailo Obrenović.**

TRINITY CONSTITUTION. See CONSTITUTION.

TRIPARTITE PACT. The pact signed between Germany, Italy, and Japan on September 27, 1940. Preceded by the proclamation of an "axis" binding Rome and Berlin (October 25, 1936) and the German-Japanese Anti-Comintern Pact (November 25, 1936), the Tripartite Pact envisioned a full political and military alliance of member countries. Hungary, Romania, and Bulgaria became member states at the beginning of 1941.

After prolonged political maneuvering the Yugoslav government was forced to yield to substantial pressure from Germany and joined the pact on March 25, 1941. This provoked massive demonstrations throughout the country and lead to the **Coup d'etat of March 27, 1941**.

TUCOVIĆ, DIMITRIJE (1881–1914). Leader of the socialist movement and one of the founders of the **Social Democratic Party** (SDP) in **Serbia**. Tucović joined the socialist movement very early in his life while still attending high school. During his studies in **Belgrade** (1901–1906), he actively participated in establishing various socialist organizations. In 1908, he became the leader of the SDP, and until the outbreak of **World War I** passionately worked on uniting social democratic parties of the Yugoslav lands. A bitter opponent of nationalism, Tucović criticized both the Austro-Hungarian colonization of **Bosnia and Hercegovina** and **Nikola Pašić**'s expansionist policy toward Albania. He is the author of numerous monographs, journal articles, and essays: *Srbija i Albanija* (*Serbia and Albania*), *Za socijalnu politiku* (*For a Social Policy*), and others. He regularly collaborated with the major European social-democratic journals and papers *Vorwärts*, *Der Kampf,* and *Die Neue Zeit*.

TUDJMAN, FRANJO (1922– ). President of **Croatia** (1990– ). Born in Veliko Trgovišće in the Croatian Zagorje, Tudjman joined the Communist-led **Partisans** during **World War II**. After the war, he was promoted to the rank of general and held several influential posts in the **JNA.** In 1961, he left active military service and became a political historian and the director of the Institute of the Workers' Movement in **Zagreb.**

After a series of nationalist writings, Tudjman was expelled from the Communist Party in 1967 and arrested in 1972. A hard-line Croatian nationalist and open advocate of Croatia's secession from Yugoslavia, Tudjman was imprisoned again in 1981 and given a three-year sentence.

In 1989, with the help of nationalist Croatian émigrés, many of whom belonged to the **Ustaše** movement, Tudjman founded a political party known as the **Croatian Democratic Union** (HDZ). In April-May 1990, Tudjman's party won multiparty elections in Croatia, and he became the president. Tudjman was the main architect of Croatia's unilateral secession from the **Socialist Federal Republic of Yugoslavia**, and his policies directly led to the outbreak of civil war in Croatia. His main work is a highly controversial book *Bespuća povijesne zbiljnosti* (*Wastelands of Historical Truth*).

TURKISH CONSTITUTION. See CONSTITUTION.

TUZLA. City and industrial center in northeastern **Bosnia and Hercegovina** with a population of 131,861 in 1991. The ethnic composition prior to the civil war was 47.6 percent Muslim, 16.6 percent Yugoslav, 15.6 percent Croatian, and 15.5 percent Serbian. The city is the center of the largest mining-chemical complex in the former Yugoslavia and the site of a salt factory, an airport, and several schools of the University of Sarajevo. Originally one of the **Safe Areas**, Tuzla became the base for the American contingent of the NATO-led international force in December 1995.

TVRTKO I KOTROMANIĆ (1338–1391). Ban (1353–1377) and King of Bosnia. Tvrtko I assumed the Bosnian throne from his father, Stefan II Kotromanić. He was the most influential ruler in the medieval Bosnian state. During Tvrtko I's rule, Bosnia reached its zenith. After defeating Hungary in 1363 and consolidating his power, Tvrtko substantially strengthened the state economy. Following the defeat of Župan **Nikola Altomanović**, Tvrtko extended Bosnia's borders by seizing Konavle and the lands along **Lim, Tara,** and **Drina** Rivers. In 1377, with the support of **Prince Lazar Hrebeljanović**, Tvrtko proclaimed himself "king of Serbs, Bosnia, Coastal, and Western lands." The coronation took place in the **Mileševa** monastery.

TVRTKO II KOTROMANIĆ (r. 1404–1409 and 1421–1443). Bosnian king, son of Tvrtko I Kotromanić. Supported by Bosnian lords, he won the battle for the Bosnian throne over the Hungarian supported king Ostoja. A weak ruler with little central authority, Tvrtko II was a vassal to both Hungary and the Ottoman Turks. In 1423 he unsuccessfully fought the Serbian despot Stefan Lazarević over the mining town of **Srebrenica.**

## - U -

UBAVKIĆ, PETAR (1850–1910). First sculptor in modern **Serbia**; best known for his busts of **Vuk Stefanović Karadžić**, Prince **Miloš Obrenović**, and King **Alexander Obrenović**.

UDRUŽENA OPOZICIJA (United Opposition). Opposition bloc formed before the general elections in May 1935. The bloc was initially established by the **Democratic Party**, **Yugoslav Muslim Organization**, Savez zemljoradnika (Agricultural Union), and Samostalna demokratska stranka (Independent Democratic Party). However, since it lacked a joint political program and platform, alliances often changed; it joined the government of General **Dušan Simović** on March 27, 1941.

UJEDINJENA OMLADINA SRPSKA (United Serbian Youth). Cultural organization founded by 16 various Serbian learning and singing societies in **Novi Sad** on August 27–29, 1866. It was the Serbian equivalent of Mazzini's Young Italy or the German Tugendbund. The organization soon became a major political force of **Serbs** in **Vojvodina**; it opposed traditional romanticism and fostered the modern, liberal approach to the question of Serbian national liberation. The organization was banned by the Hungarian authorities in 1872.

UJEDINJENJE ILI SMRT. See UNIFICATION OR DEATH.

ULTIMATUM. Delivered by Austria-Hungary to the Serbian government on July 23, 1914, regarding the assassination of Crown Prince Franz Ferdinand on June 28, 1914 (**Sarajevo Assassination**). The ultimatum consisted of 10 points that Serbia had to accept to prevent war. The Serbian government was given 48 hours to answer the Austro-Hungarian demands, which called for (1) the suppression of every anti-Austro-Hungarian publication; (2) the dissolution of the nationalist organization National

Defense; (3) the cessation of all propaganda against the Dual Monarchy and the revision of school curricula; (4) the removal of army officers involved in anti-Austro-Hungarian activities; (5) the cooperation of Austro-Hungarian and Serbian police to suppress subversive movements in Serbia; (6) the permission for Austro-Hungarian police to investigate the Sarajevo Assassination in Serbia's territory; (7) the arrest of Major **Vojislav Tankosić** and Milan Ciganović; (8) the prevention of the smuggling of weapons and explosives to **Bosnia and Hercegovina** and the severe punishment members of the Frontier Service at **Šabac** and **Loznica** as accomplices to the assassination; (9) the accepting of responsibility for the anti-Austro-Hungarian statements made by the Serbian officials following June 28; (10) the reporting to the Austro-Hungarian government of the execution of the stipulated measures.

Although the ultimatum violated Serbia's independence in several respects, the Serbian government complied with nearly all Austro-Hungarian demands. The only reservation was over Austria-Hungary's fifth demand: the cooperation of Austro-Hungarian officials was allowed if not in violation of international law and Serbian judicial procedures. However, despite this Serbian compliance, Austria-Hungary broke diplomatic relations and declared war on Serbia on July 28, 1914.

UNA. River in **Bosnian Krajina**; 212.5 km-long tributary of the **Sava** River, rich in hydroenergy.

UNIFICATION OR DEATH/UJEDINJENJE ILI SMRT. Secret Serbian organization formed on May 9, 1911, by a group of officers and a few civilians, some of whom had participated in the assassination of the King **Alexander Obrenović** (**May's Assassination**). The secret aims of the society were defined in a constitution of 37 articles and rules. The organization opposed what was perceived as the compromising policy of the government and opposition and advocated the unification of Serbian lands by all available means. The founders of the organization were **Ljubomir-Čupa Jovanović**, Bogdan Radenković, **Dimitrijević Dragutin Apis**, Ilija Radivojević, and **Vojislav Tankosić**. Although the organization cooperated with the Serbian government between 1911 and 1913, the constant friction between the organization, also known as Crna ruka (Black Hand), and the government escalated over **Macedonia** in 1914. During the withdrawal of the Serbian army to Greece in 1915, Apis allegedly threatened to execute another coup d'état. In 1917, after the Austro-Hungarian emperor Karl requested the punishment of members of anti-Austrian organizations for their alleged involvement in the assassination of Crown Prince Franz Ferdinand on June 28, 1914, (**Sarajevo Assassination**), **Nikola Pašić** and Prince Regent **Alexander I Karađorđević** seized this opportunity, had leaders arrested, and after a staged trial, executed Apis and two of his associates in June 1917 (**Trial of Salonika**).

UNITED NATIONS PROTECTED AREAS (UNPA). Territories encompassing the **Republic of Serbian Krajina** and Western **Slavonia** controlled by **UNPROFOR.** The UNPA consisted of four sectors: Sector East (also known as Eastern Slavonia) included **Baranja**, Eastern Slavonia, and western **Srem**; Sector West included Western Slavonia, Sector North included **Banija** and **Kordun**; while Sector South included Kninska Krajina (**Lika** and parts of **Dalmatia**). In early 1995, UNPROFOR was renamed UNCRO (United Nations Confidence Restoration Operation). After the Croatian army attack on the RSK in May and August 1995 the former Sector East remained the only area under United Nations supervision.

UNITED NATIONS PROTECTION FORCE. See UNPROFOR.

UNIVERSITY OF BELGRADE. Founded in 1863 as the **Great School**. It changed its name to university in 1905, and today encompasses 17 independent schools with more than 60,000 students. Besides the University of Belgrade and University of Arts in Belgrade, there are five additional state universities in the **Federal Republic of Yugoslavia** (**Novi Sad, Niš, Podgorica, Kragujevac, Priština**) and one in the **Republika Srpska** (**Banja Luka**). During the existence of the **Republic of Serbian Krajina**, the University of **Nikola Tesla** operated in **Knin** 1991–1995. Braća Karić University is the only private university in Serbia.

UNPA. See UNITED NATIONS PROTECTED AREAS.

UNPROFOR (United Nations Protection Force). Following the acceptance of the **Vance Plan** and United Nations Security Council Resolution 743, a 14,000-strong force called UNPROFOR was created and deployed on the territory of the **Republic of Serbian Krajina** and in the UNPA (**United Nations Protected Areas**). In 1992, the mission of UNPROFOR extended to **Bosnia and Hercegovina** (B-H) and to **Macedonia,** numbering 26,360 soldiers. UNPROFOR failed to protect UNPA zones in **Croatia,** and in B-H it was replaced by the NATO-led Implementation Force (IFOR) following the **Dayton Agreement.**

UROŠ I NEMANJIĆ (?–1276) Third son of **Stefan Prvovenčani** and Serbian king 1243–1276. The main feature of his reign was the economic expansion of **Serbia**, especially in mining and coin mintage, as well as in strengthening of mercantile trade. He built the **Sopoćani** monastery, which later became his burial place.

UROŠ II NEMANJIĆ (1336–1371). Son of **Dušan the Mighty** and Serbian emperor 1355–1371. During his rule, noblemen who were appointed to certain regions grew more powerful and gradually became independent lords. A weak ruler, he allowed the complete collapse of the central organization of the Serbian Empire.

USHTRIA ÇLIRIMTARE E KOSOVËS (UÇK). See KOSOVO LIBERATION ARMY.

USKOKS. Term used for Orthodox Christian, mainly Serbian, refugees from **Bosnia and Hercegovina**, who continued their resistance to the Turks with border raids and guerilla attacks. After the Turks captured their stronghold fortress Klis in 1537, the Uskoks moved into Senj. Following continuous Venetian protests, Austria resettled the Uskoks to **Žumberak** Mountain, where the majority of them eventually converted to Greek Catholicism.

USTAŠE. Fascist and terrorist organization of Croatian nationalists founded in the late 1920s. The leader of the organization was **Ante Pavelić**, a member of the Croatian Party of Rights, who left Yugoslavia after the **Dictatorship of January 6, 1929**. With the help of fascist Italy and Hungary, which had territorial aspirations against Yugoslavia, Pavelić and his associates established several training camps for Ustaše terrorists (Bovegno in Italy and Janka Puszta in Hungary). On October 9, 1934, the Ustaše, aided by Bulgarian terrorists of the IMRO, assassinated the Yugoslav king **Alexander I Karađorđević** in Marseilles. During **April's War**, Ustaše leaders entered **Zagreb** and proclaimed the **Independent**

**State of Croatia** on April 10, 1941. While the establishment of a separate Croatian state was the main goal of the movement, the termination of the **Serbs** proved to be the real objective of the Ustaše. Between 1941 and 1945, the Ustaše and their associates killed, expelled, and converted to Catholicism more than 600,000 Serbs.

After **World War II**, aided by the Vatican, the Ustaše leaders, including Pavelić, escaped from Yugoslavia and continued low-level terrorist activity. Between 1945 and 1990, Ustaše agents assassinated many Yugoslav diplomats and organized several terrorist attacks against civilians around the world. Although widely condemned as members of a terrorist and fascist organization, the Ustaše were fully rehabilitated by the current regime in Croatia, with the commemorations of anti-fascist heroes (street names, etc.) being changed to applaud leading Ustaše figures and the ceremonial reburials of World War II Ustaše dead alongside the bodies of their victims.

USTAVOBRANITELJI. See CONSTITUTIONALISTS.

UVAC. River in southwestern **Serbia** 106 km long, one of the largest tributaries of the **Lim** River. Uvac is rich in hydroelectric energy, and two hydroelectric plants, Kokin brod and Bistrica, are stationed on it.

UZUNOVIĆ, NIKOLA (1873–1954). Serbian and Yugoslav politician, member of the Main Committee of the **Radical Party**. He was a minister in the governments of **Nikola Pašić** and **Petar Živković**, and prime minister in 1926/27 and again in 1934. During the **Dictatorship of January 6, 1929**, he founded Jugoslovenska radikalna seljačka demokratija (Yugoslav Radical Peasant Democracy) which changed its name to Jugoslovenska nacionalna stranka (Yugoslav National Party) in 1933.

UŽICE. City and industrial center in western **Serbia** with a population of 82,723 in 1991. Metal, milling, and leather industries are especially well developed. In medieval Serbia, the city was a center of the realm of **Nikola Altomanović**. In October 1941, the joint forces of the **Partisans** and the **Jugoslovenska vojska u otadžbini** liberated Užice, and the Partisans proclaimed the "Republic of Užice." In November 1941, Germans recaptured the city, which remained under their control until October 1944.

## - V -

VAJFERT, ĐORĐE (1850–1937). Leading industrialist in **Serbia** and the Kingdom of Yugoslavia. He founded a brewery in **Belgrade** in 1872, while his brother Ignjat managed a brewery in the neighboring city of **Pančevo.** In 1873, Vajfert acquired concessions for explorations of mineral ores throughout Serbia. He also participated in founding major financial institutions in Serbia. Vajfert was a president of the Industrial Chamber, governor and vice governor of the **National Bank**, director of Beogradske zadruge (Belgrade's Cooperatives), etc. Vajfert also was a president of the Grand Masonic Lodge "Jugoslavija" in Belgrade.

VALJEVO. Economic and cultural center of the Kolubara region, with a population of 98,226 in 1991. Agriculture and the food-processing industry are important economic factors. The surroundings of the city were inhabited in prehistoric times; the modern city is first mentioned in 1019, under the name of Gradac, and in 1398 as Valjevo.

VALTROVIĆ, MIHAILO (1839–1915). Serbian archeologist; a member of the **Serbian Academy of Sciences and Arts** and professor at the **Great School**. He was the first to study Serbian medieval architecture and relics. He is a founder of the Serbian Archeological Society in **Belgrade**.

VANCE PLAN. Peace plan designed by United Nations mediator Cyrus Vance. The plan, officially announced on January 2, 1992, called for the withdrawal of the **JNA** from **Croatia**, the demilitarization of war-affected areas in Croatia, the establishment of four **United Nations Protected Areas** (UNPA), and the deployment of a 14,000-strong special peace force known as **UNPROFOR**. The plan was annulled by a Croatian offensive against UNPA and the **Republic of Serbian Krajina** in May and August of 1995.

VANCE-OWEN PEACE PLAN (VOPP). Peace plan devised by Cyrus Vance and Lord David Owen, chief mediators of the United Nations and **European Community**. The peace plan envisioned a division of **Bosnia and Hercegovina** (B-H) into ten cantons: four would be under Serbian control, while six would remain under the control of **Muslims** and Croats. The **Serbs** would receive 43 percent of the total territory, Muslims 39, and Croats 18 percent. Foreign affairs, defense, foreign trade, and citizenship would remain under the jurisdiction of the central government, while everything else would be under regional jurisdiction. The VOPP envisioned the presence of a 60,000-strong international peace keeping force in B-H. During intense negotiation in Athens on May 1–2, **Radovan Karadžić**, president of the **Republika Srpska**, signed the agreement pending the approval of the Assembly. In a stormy session held in Pale on May 5–6, 1993, the Assembly rejected the peace plan (52 against, 2 for, and 12 abstentions) despite the pressure exerted by Serbian president **Slobodan Milošević** and Greek prime minister Constantin Mitsotakis. The Assembly confirmed its previous decision to hold a referendum on the VOPP on May 15 and 16. The referendum overwhelmingly rejected the plan (92 percent of the eligible electorate participated in the referendum, 96 percent of whom voted against the VOPP).

VARADI, TIBOR (1939– ). Director of the Law Program of the Central European University in Budapest, professor of the University of **Novi Sad**, member of the Permanent Court of Arbitrage in The Hague, and member of the **Serbian Academy of Sciences and Arts**. A deputy in the Serbian and Federal **Parliament**, Varadi became minister of justice in the government of **Milan Panić** in 1992–1993. His works include *Međunoradno privatno pravo* (*International Civil Law*), and *Socialist Law in a Period of Change*.

VARDAR. Largest river in **Macedonia**. The Vardar is 420 kilometers long (300.5 km in Macedonia and 119.5 km in Greece) and is rich in hydroenergy. The valley of the river is very fertile and is a center of the region's agricultural production. Together with the **Morava** Valley, it forms the Morava-Vardar Valley, which is a major communication route between Central Europe and Asia Minor.

VARVARIN, BATTLE OF/VARVARINSKI BOJ. Battle between combined Serbian and Russian forces against the Turks on a field near the small city of Varvarin on September 6, 1810. Although vastly outnumbered, the Serbian forces (around 4,000 soldiers) decisively defeated the Turkish army (20,000 soldiers) under the command of Kurşid-Paşa. The victory enabled the **Serbs** to liberate southern and eastern **Serbia**, while Turkish forces in western Serbia were forced to withdraw across the **Drina** River into **Bosnia and Hercegovina**. See also FIRST SERBIAN INSURRECTION.

VARVARINSKI BOJ. See VARVARIN, BATTLE OF.

VASIĆ, DRAGIŠA (1885–1945). Serbian writer and politician. Born in **Gornji Milanovac**, he finished his secondary education in **Belgrade**, where he graduated with a degree in law. During **World War II**, he joined the forces of **Dragoljub-Draža Mihailović** and became his chief ideologist and a leader of the **Ravnogorski pokret**. He was killed by the **Ustaše** in April 1945. His main works include *Crvene magle* (*Red Fog*), *Pad s građevine* (*Fall from the Building*), and *Devedstotreća* (*1903*).

VASIĆ, MILOJE (1869–1956). One of the founders of archeological research in **Serbia**. A member of the **Serbian Academy of Sciences and Arts**, he administered the excavation of Vinča, a prehistoric site (around 4000 B.C.) in the vicinity of **Belgrade.**

VASILIJE OSTROŠKI (?–1671). Bishop in **Zahumlje**. His residence was first in **Trebinje** monastery and later in Ostrog monastery near the city of **Nikšić**. He worked persistently on the struggle for liberation from the Turks.

VASILIJE PETROVIĆ (1709–1766) Bishop and ruler of **Montenegro**. He strenuously worked to improve relations between Montenegro and Russia, which he visited on several occasions in 1752, 1758, and 1762. His Russophile policy caused diplomatic troubles with the Venetian Republic and conflict with the Turks. His memoirs, *A History of Montenegro* (*Istorija o Crnoj Gori*) is the first work in that field in Montenegro.

VELBUŽD, BATTLE OF. Battle between Serbs and Bulgars in 1330 in the vicinity of Velbužd (modern name, Kjustendil). Worried by the constant strengthening of **Serbia**, Bulgaria and the Byzantine Empire joined their forces in 1328. The principal objective of the Bulgarian emperor Mihailo Šišman was to eliminate rival Serbia in the struggle for the Byzantine succession. After two years of preparations, a Bulgarian army of 15,000 soldiers and more than 3,000 mercenaries entered Serbian **Macedonia** from the east, while the Byzantine emperor Andronikus Paleologus seized several cities in southern Serbia. The Serbian king, **Stefan Dečanski**, mustered an army of 15,000 soldiers and 1,000 German mercenaries, and on July 28, 1330, in a surprise attack, defeated the Bulgarian forces at Velbužd. The Bulgarian emperor Mihailo was killed in the battle, while the bulk of Bulgarian troops surrendered to Serbian forces under the command of Stefan's son, Prince **Dušan the Mighty**, near the city of Radomir in Bulgaria. The Byzantines left Serbian territory immediately after the Bulgarian defeat. The Battle of Velbužd confirmed Serbia's primacy in the Balkans.

VELEBIT. Mountainous massif in **Croatia**. It separates **Lika** from the Adriatic coast. The length of Velebit, which extends northwest-southeast, is 165 km; its width is between 15 and 20 km. The highest points of Velebit are Vaganjski vrh (1,758 m) and Sveto brdo (1,753 m).

VELEIZDAJNIČKI PROCESI. Staged mass trials of **Serbs** conducted throughout 1915, mostly in **Banja Luka**, Travnik, **Sarajevo**, and **Mostar**. In order to quell the Serbian struggle for national liberation in **Croatia** and **Bosnia and Hercegovina**, the Austro-Hungarian administration staged two trials of prominent Serbian leaders. They involved Serbian professors, teachers, and students who were accused of forming secret and subversive pro-Serbian societies. The first trial was held in **Zagreb** in 1908–1909, when 53 Serbs were sentenced to prison; the second trial was held in Banja Luka in 1915–1916, when 159 Serbs were sentenced (16 were sentenced to death, and the rest received lengthy prison sentences).

VELIKA KLADUŠA. City in northwestern Bosnia with a population of 52,921 in 1991. The ethnic composition of the city prior to the civil war was 91.8 percent Muslim; 4.3 percent Serbian; 1.7 percent Yugoslav; and 1.3 percent Croatian. Between 1993 and 1995, it was the capital city of the former **Autonomous Province of Western Bosnia** under the leadership of **Fikret Abdić.** The city is first mentioned in the 13th century. "Agrokomerc," a huge agroindustrial and trade conglomerate, had its headquarters in Velika Kladuša. See also BIHAĆ POCKET.

VELIKA ŠKOLA. See GREAT SCHOOL.

VELIKA SRBIJA. See GREATER SERBIA.

VELIMIROVIĆ, NIKOLAJ (1880–1956). Bishop of the **Serbian Orthodox Church** and one of the most vocal champions of Serbian nationalism. During **World War I** he lived in the United Kingdom and the United States where he was active in the Serbian diaspora. In 1941, the Germans confined Velimirović to Vojlovica monastery, and then sent him to Dachau concentration camp. After the war, Velimirović lived in exile in the United States.

VELJKOVIĆ, VOJISLAV (1865–1931). Serbian politician and financier, member of of the **Liberal Party**. He was minister of finance in 1903 but resigned after a disagreement with the **Conspirators**. From 1903 to 1914 he was continuosly elected as a member of **Parliament** where he was a leader of the National Party. In the **Kingdom of the Serbs, Croats, and Slovenes** he was minster of industry and trade in the government of **Stojan Protić** and minister of finance in the government of **Ljubomir-Ljuba Davidović** in 1919.

VERSAILLES, TREATY OF. Peace treaty between the Entente Powers and defeated Germany that emerged from the Paris Peace Conference that took place between January 18, 1919, and June 28, 1920. Several separate treaties were concluded in various suburbs of Paris with each of the defeated Central Powers. These treaties recognized the formation of several new states: Poland, Hungary, Czechoslovakia, Estonia, Lithuania, Latvia, Finland, and the **Kingdom of the Serbs, Croats, and Slovenes** (SHS). Treaties regulated the border issues between the Kingdom of the SHS and Italy in regard to the partition of the Adriatic coast.

VESNIĆ, MILENKO (1863–1921). Politician and university professor. Born in **Sandžak**, Vesnić was educated in Berlin, Munich, and Leipzig, where he graduated with a degree in law. After 1891 he worked for the ministry of foreign affairs. He was the main editor of the journal *Pravnik* (*The Lawyer*). In 1921, he formed two short-lived coalition governments.

VIDOVDAN CONSTITUTION. See CONSTITUTIONS.

VIŠEGRAD. City in the former Yugoslav republic of **Bosnia and Hercegovina** with a population of 21,202 in 1991. The ethnic composition of the city prior to the civil war was 62.8 percent Muslim, 32.8 percent Serbian, 1.5 percent Yugoslav, and 0.2 percent Croatian. The first mention of the city was in 1407. Višegrad was a part of the realm of the Pavlović's, a Serbian feudal family, until 1462 when it came under Turkish occupation. A famous stone bridge, the main motif of **Ivo Andrić**'s Nobel Prize winning novel *Na Drini Ćuprija* (*The Bridge over the Drina*), was built in Višegrad by **Mehmed-Paša Sokolović.**

VIŠNJIĆ, FILIP (1767–1834). Famous Serbian folk poet. In 1809, he went to **Serbia** and created songs about the **First Serbian Insurrection**, thus greatly boosting the morale of the Serbian population in its struggle against Turkish occupation. His best-known folk poems are "Početak bune protiv dahija" ("The Beginning of the Uprising against the Dahije") and "Boj na Mišaru" ("The Battle of Mišar").

VLACHS. Term that **South Slavs** used for the native tribes which inhabited the **Balkan Peninsula** (Celts, Dacians, Illyrians, etc.). Some Serbian sources from the 13th century used the term when referring to the population of **Dubrovnik** and other coastal cities. The name Vlach is used most frequently in reference to the cattle-breeding population of Roman origin inhabiting the Balkan Peninsula. In **Croatia** the term Vlach has a derogatory meaning and is used in reference to Serbs.

VLADIKA. Rank in the hierarchical structure of the **Serbian Orthodox Church**. The term is used interchangeably with that of episcop and it is equivalent to the rank of bishop.

VLADISLAV (?–1264?). As younger son of **Stefan Prvovenčani**, Vladislav became the Serbian king in 1234 after his older brother **Radoslav** was overthrown in 1233. His uncle **Saint Sava** arranged his marriage with Boleslava, a daughter of the Bulgarian emperor Ivan Asen II. Vladislav founded **Mileševa** monastery, where St. Sava was buried until the Turks exhumed and burned his body in 1594. Following the death of Asen II and after a Mongolian raid in 1242, Vladislav was forced to abdicate in favor of his younger brother **Uroš I** in 1243. Uroš I gave the region of **Zeta** to Vladislav.

VLADISLAV II (?–1326?). Son of the Serbian king **Dragutin**. After the death of King **Milutin,** according to the **Accord of Deževo**, the Serbian king was to be either Dragutin's son Vladislav or the oldest of Milutin's sons, Konstantin. However, the younger of Milutin's sons, Stefan Uroš III **(Stefan Dečanski**), became the new king. This initiated a struggle for the Serbian throne in which Konstantin, who ruled **Zeta**, was soon killed. Vladislav II continued to rule over a part of Dragutin's lands in northern **Serbia** but soon entered into conflict with Stefan over Rudnik in 1324. Having lost Rudnik in 1324, Vladislav left Serbia and went to Hungary, where he died in 1326.

VLADISLAV, GRAMATIK (c. 15th century). One of the best Serbian biographers in the 15th century.

VLADISLAV, JOVAN (?–1018). Son-in-law of **Samuilo**, Emperor of Macedonian Slavs, and ruler of **Zeta**. Killed in the church where he was ordained a saint of the **Serbian Orthodox Church**, Vladislav is worshipped mostly in **Montenegro** and northern Albania.

VLASTIMIR (ca. 850). Serbian prince, son of Prosigoj, one of the founders of the first Serbian state. The principality was located among the **Lim, Tara, Drina,** and **Western Morava** Rivers. He successfully resisted Bulgarian attack and later seized the **Trebinje** (Travunia) region.

VNATREŠNA MAKEDONSKA REVOLUCIONARNA ORGANIZACIJA. See INTERNAL MACEDONIAN REVOLUTIONARY ORGANIZATION.

VOJINOVIĆI. Serbian feudal family from the 14th century. The founder was Vojin, whose son Vojislav was prince of **Zahumlje**. Between 1359 and 1362, Vojislav struggled with **Dubrovnik** for the control of Ston, a small city on the Pelješac peninsula. **Nikola Altomanović** was a grandson of Vojin.

VOJISLAV, STEFAN (?–1050). Prince of the Serbian land **Zeta** from 1037 to 1051, father of **Mihailo**. After the expulsion of the Byzantine administration in 1036, he defeated the Byzantine army in 1040 and in 1042. He extended his realm to the **Trebinje** (Travunia) and **Zahumlje** regions. During his reign, Zeta spread from the Bojana River to the **Neretva** River and included all lands previously controlled by **Časlav Klonimirović.**

VOJNA KRAJINA (Military Border). Region established by Austria and Hungary to prevent further advances by the Turks in the 15th century. Vojna Krajina extended along the **Sava** River from the Kupa and Drava Rivers in the west to Transylvania in the east. The beginning of Vojna Krajina dates from 1435, when the Hungarian king Sigismund established special military units, *tabors*, in regions bordering Bosnia and Venetia. Later, in 1464, the Hungarian king Mathias Corvinus organized a defensive line along the **Vrbas** River and the cities of **Jajce** and

**Srebrenica** toward **Šabac** and **Belgrade**. In 1469, he established Senjska kapetanija (The Garrison of Senj) in the lands around the Zrmanja River in order to secure **Croatia**, then a part of the Hungarian kingdom. From 1480, the borderlands between Hungary and the Ottoman Empire along the **Una** River began to be called *krajina* or *granica* (**confinia** or **loca et castra finitima**). After the Hungarian defeat at the Battle of Mohacs, the border region that extended from Senj to the Drava River was divided into two parts: the southern part with its center in Karlovac and the northern with its center in Varaždin.

Although **Serbs** inhabited Vojna Krajina from the very beginning, they became a majority of the population after the Austro-Turkish War of 1593–1605. In 1630, Serbs were given certain privileges by *Statuta Valachorum* (Serbian Statute), thus marking a new stage in the history of Vojna Krajina. The process of separation between Vojna Krajina and Croatia then began and was completed in 1744. In 1850, the Habsburg Monarchy adopted *Krajiški temeljni zakon* (Basic Law of Krajina) according to which Vojna Krajina was organized like modern Western European states. However, after the **Congress of Berlin** in 1878, the demilitarization and incorporation of Vojna Krajina into Croatia began. The main reason behind Austria-Hungary's dismantling Vojna Krajina was the fear of strengthening the movement for Serbian and South Slav unification outside the Dual Monarchy. Consequently, on August 1, 1881, Vojna Krajina officially ceased to exist and was incorporated into Croatia, which was under the direct control of Hungary. During **World War II**, the Croatian **Ustaše** regime committed genocide against the Serbian population in the regions that belonged to Vojna Krajina: **Lika, Kordun, Banija, Srem, Slavonia, Bosnian Krajina.**

In 1990, after the elections in Croatia that brought to power the nationalist party of the **Croatian Democratic Union**, which rehabilitated the Ustaše regime, the Serbian population declared its intention not to live under such a regime. Following the unilateral secession of Croatia from Yugoslavia on June 25, 1991, Serbs proclaimed the **Republic of Serbian Krajina** (RSK) and seceded from Croatia. The ensuing civil war led to United Nations intervention and the cease-fire in December, 1991. According to a brokered agreement, the RSK was divided into four **United Nations Protected Areas** (UNPA). On May 1, 1995, Croatian forces invaded and overran the Serbian enclave in Western Slavonia (UNPA, Sector West) and in an offensive that began on August 1, routed Serbs from Sectors North and South.

VOJNOVIĆ, IVO (1857–1929). Serbian poet from **Dubrovnik**. Educated in private schools in Split and Dubrovnik, Vojnović graduated with a law degree from the university in **Zagreb**. He worked as a magistrate in Croatia and in civil administration in **Dalmatia** from 1885 to 1907. In 1907 he joined the Croatian Theater in Zagreb. In 1914, being a prominent Serbian poet, he was arrested by the Austro-Hungarian authorities. In 1915, after losing an eye in prison, he was transfered to hospital in Zagreb. Vojnović, besides **Branislav Nušić**, was the most productive Serbian playwrite. His numerous works include *Dubrovačka trilogija*, *Gospođa sa suncokretom* (*Lady With Sunflower*) and *Lazarevo vaskresenje* (*Rising of Lazar*).

VOJSKA JUGOSLAVIJE. See YUGOSLAV ARMY.

VOJVODA. Term with several different meanings in the Slavic languages. In medieval Serbian lands, the term *vojvoda* was reserved for commanders of several squadrons formed in different administrative units, known as **župa.** In the Serbian and Yugoslav army before **World War II**, *vojvoda* was the highest rank (established in 1904) corresponding to the rank of fieldmarshal. There were only four *vojvodas* in the Serbian army: **Radomir Putnik, Živojin Mišić, Stepa Stepanović,** and **Petar Bojović.** The title *vojvoda* was also held by commanders of **Četniks** both in **World War I** and in World War II.

VOJVODINA. Autonomous province in the **Federal Republic of Yugoslavia.** The area of the region is 21,506 sq km having a population of 2,030,419 (1991). The ethnic composition of the population, according to the census of 1991 was 56.3 percent Serbian, 16.7 percent Hungarian, 8.5 percent Yugoslav, 5 percent Croatian, 16.9 percent Hungarian, 3.6 percent Croats, 3.1 percent Slovak, 2.2 percent Montenegrin, and 1.9 percent Romanian (see Table 17, statistical addendum). Vojvodina is situated between Hungary to the north, **Croatia** (**Baranja** and western **Srem**) to the west, Romania to the east, and the **Sava** and **Danube** Rivers to the south. Vojvodina consists of **Bačka, Banat,** and Srem, which are not administrative units, but geographic and historic regions. There are several prehistoric sites in Vojvodina. The best known is neolithic Starčevo, near **Pančevo**. The first modern inhabitants were Dacians, **Illyrians**, and Celts. Slavs came to Vojvodina during the fifth and sixth centuries and were known by the names Severi and Bodrići (Banat and Bačka, as well as names of the cities such as **Vršac, Zemun, Subotica,** are Slavic).

VRANJE. City in southern **Serbia** with a population of 86,518 in 1991. The first records of the city date from 1093. The city was known for the making of arms and various iron tools. After 1878 and the establishment of the new border between Serbia and the Ottoman Empire, Vranje became a major trading center. Industry developed after **World War II**, particularly in the production of textiles, tobacco, and furniture-making.

VRBAS. (i) River in western **Bosnia and Hercegovina**. The river is 240 km long, and the river valley is a major route to central Bosnia.
(ii) City in central **Vojvodina** with a population of 46,405 in 1991. The first records date from the first half of the 4th century. **Serbs** were the majority population until the late 17th century when the planned colonization of the Germans began. After **World War II** a strong influx of **Montenegrins** from **Nikšić** once again changed the demographic structure of the city. The cooking-oil industry and the textile industry are particularly developed.

*VREME* (*The Times*). A conservative daily newspaper established in 1921 in **Belgrade**. During the German occupation 1941–1944, published as ***Novo Vreme***. Since 1990 one of the major opposition papers in **Serbia** and the **Federal Republic of Yugoslavia.** *The Times* promotes ideas of liberal capitalism and strenuously supports the United States peace initiative in the former Yugoslavia.

VRHBOSNA. Medieval **župa** in **Bosnia and Hercegovina**. The first records of the region date from 1244. Until 1435 the *župa* belonged to the Serbian family of Pavlović-Radinović. Following the Turkish occupation, the center of the region was renamed **Sarajevo.**

VRŠAC. City in southeastern **Banat** in the immediate vicinity of the Yugoslav-Romanian border with a population of 58,228 in 1991. The first records of the city date from the 15th century. From 1552 to 1718 the city was occupied by the Turks, and from 1718 to 1918 it was under Austrian control. Initially the center of a wine-producing region, Vršac became an industrial center of the region after **World War II**. Food-processing, metal-processing, chemical, and beer industries are particularly well-developed.

VUČIĆ-PERIŠIĆ, TOMA (1790–1859). Serbian politician, a leader of the **First Serbian Insurrection** and the **Second Serbian Insurrection.** A close associate of Prince **Miloš Obrenović** he occupied very influential governmental posts including that of defense minister. He was a leading figure in bringing down the Rebellion of Đak and **Mileta's Rebellion**. As the movement of the **Constitutionalists** was gaining strength so was the rift between Prince Miloš and Vučić-Perišić. Following Prince **Mihailo Obrenović's** accession to power he emigrated, but in September of 1842 he returned to Serbia and overthrew Mihailo.

During the reign of Prince **Alexander Karađorđević**, Vučić-Perišić continued to pursue his personal agenda. This led to his retirement in 1852. However, he re-entered the political arena in 1858 as the president of the Council. While at odds with the leadership of the **Consitutionalists**, he played a major role in **St. Andrew's Assembly**. However, shortly upon his return to **Serbia**, Prince Miloš ordered the arrest of Vučić-Perišić.

VUJAKLIJA, MILAN (1891–1955). Serbian translator and lexicographer. Born in **Kordun**, he was educated in **Zagreb**, **Karlovci Sremski**, and **Belgrade** where he graduated with a degree in philology and philosophy. He was a volunteer in the Serbian army during **World War I**. After the war he was a senior advisor at the ministry of education. His best-known work is *Rečnik stranih reči i izraza* (*Dictionary of Foreign Words and Idioms*).

VUKALOVIĆ, LUKA (1823–1873). Leader of the **Rebellions of Hercegovina**. He worked as a gunsmith in **Herceg-Novi** until 1852 when, during the war between **Montenegro** and Ottoman Turkey, he returned to Hercegovina and organized the rebellion. Although Montenegro's independence was confirmed after the Turkish defeat at the **Battle of Grahovo**, Vukalović continued to fight since the large territories of Eastern Hercegovina remained under Turkish occupation. The rebellion spread all the way to northern Bosnia which prompted Austria to intervene. Afraid that the rebellion might spread to its territories Austria undermined Vukalović's actions and supported Turkey. Following the Montenegrin defeat in August 1862, left alone, Vukalović entered into an agreement with the Turkish commander Omer-Paša Latas who promised him the title of **Vojvoda**. In 1865, Vukalović attempted to raise another rebellion against the Turkish occupation but without success. He emigrated to Odessa in Russia.

VUKAN (1160–1209). Oldest son of **Stefan Nemanja**; Serbian grand **župan**. When he abandoned secular affairs in 1196, Stefan Nemanja left the throne to his younger son, **Stefan Prvovenčani**, contrary to the prevailing custom, according to which Vukan was first in line to succeed Nemanja. The main reason behind Nemanja's decision was that Vukan was a devout Roman Catholic. After Nemanja's death in 1200, the conflict between the brothers exploded, and Vukan, aided by the Hungarian king, temporarily succeeded in overcoming Stefan in 1202. However, left without Hungarian support, Vukan lost the Serbian throne to Stefan in 1205. See also SERBIA; VUKAN'S GOSPEL.

VUKAN'S GOSPEL/VUKANOVO JEVANĐELJE. Text written between 1201 and 1208, one of the most important Serbian cultural symbols from the beginning of the 13th century. Also known as Simeon's Gospel, the text provides a graphic description of conditions in the medieval Serbian state. Unlike **Miroslav's Gospel**, which has elements of the romanesque style, the figures in Vukan's Gospel show Byzantine traits.

VUKČIĆ-KOSAČA, VLATKO (?–1489). Feudal lord in medieval Bosnia. He resisted Turkish expansion using Venetian support. In 1481 he attempted to reconquer the whole of Bosnia from the Turks but was defeated.

VUKOTIĆ, DUŠAN (1921–1998). A prominent Yugoslav cartoonist and movie director, a founder of the so-called Zagreb School of Animated Movies. He was awarded an Oscar in 1962 for his animated movie *Surogat* (*Leftover*).

VUKOTIĆ, JANKO (1866–1927). Last chief of staff and celebrated commander of the Montenegrin army in the **World War I**, and later a general in the Yugoslav army.

VUKOVAR. City in the region of western **Srem** in the former Yugoslav republic of **Croatia,** situated on the bank of the **Danube** River with a population of 84,036 in 1991. Its old Slavic name, Vukovo, was replaced by the Hungarian Vukovar in the 17th century. After **World War II**, Vukovar became the region's center of textile and food-processing industries. After the unilateral secession of Croatia from the **Socialist Federal Republic of Yugoslavia** in June 1991, the city became the site of severe clashes between Croatian interior ministry troops, backed by paramilitary groups, and **JNA** and territorial defense forces mainly consisting of the local Serbian population. Later, after more than two months of heavy fighting, the JNA and territorial defence forces took the city, reduced to rubble, on November 18, 1991. In 1997, Vukovar as the center of the **United Nations Protected Area** Sector East was reintegrated into Croatia.

VUKOVIĆ, VLATKO (?–1392). Grand **vojvoda** in **Hercegovina**. He defeated theTurks in a battle near the city of Bileća in 1388. In the **Battle of Kosovo** in 1389, he was commander of the left wing of the Serbian army. In 1391, his forces took the **Konavle** region from **Dubrovnik.**

VULIĆEVIĆ, VUJICA (1773–1828). Serbian **vojvoda** from the **Smederevo** region. In the **First Serbian Insurrection** he commanded the forces that captured several strategic points in the **Belgrade** fortress during the battle for the city on December 12, 1806. After the collapse of the rebellion in 1813, he left **Serbia** together with **Karađorđe**. He returned to Serbia and became **knez** of Smederevo **Nahija** under Prince **Miloš Obrenović**. When Karađorđe returned to Serbia in 1817, Vulićević organized his murder on Miloš's orders.

## - W -

WESTERN MORAVA/ZAPADNA MORAVA. River in **Serbia**, together with the **Southern Morava** it forms the **Morava** River. The river is 298 km long and is potentially rich in hydroelectric energy. The level of the river, however, fluctuates substantially, limiting the exploitation of this energy resource. The main tributaries of the river are the **Ibar**, Đetinja, and Gruža Rivers. The basin of the Western Morava is rich in coal, chrome, magnesium, and antimony. The main population centers are **Kruševac, Kraljevo, Užice,** and **Čačak.**

WORLD WAR I. The relationship between **Serbia** and Austria-Hungary deteriorated continuously after the dynastic change in Serbia in 1903 (**May's Assassination**). Austro-Hungarian attempts to prevent Serbia's economic emancipation, the **Tariff War** and the **Annexation Crisis**, were only partially successful. Moreover, Serbia's victories in the **Balkan**

**wars** further incited national feelings among the **Serbs** in Austria-Hungary. Anxious to settle accounts with Serbia, the "war party" in Vienna was poised to use the first opportunity to attack Serbia. The Serbian government, led by **Nikola Pašić,** desperately wanted to avoid confrontation, given the exhaustion following the two Balkan wars. However, nationalist organizations, in particular the secret society **Unification or Death,** continued subversive activity against Austria-Hungary. Supported and encouraged by Unification or Death, a group of young Serbs, members of the revolutionary organization **Mlada Bosna,** assassinated the Austrian crown prince Franz Ferdinand on June 28, 1914, in **Sarajevo**.

Although the Serbian ambassador to Vienna warned Austria-Hungary about the plot, and despite the fact that the Serbian government had not been involved in the assassination, Austria-Hungary saw the crime as an occasion to humiliate Serbia and to enhance its own prestige. On July 25, Austria-Hungary presented to Serbia with an unacceptable **ultimatum** that contained 10 points. Serbia replied to the ultimatum on July 26, and Pašić's government accepted all the Austro-Hungarian demands, except a provision that would violate international law and the Serbian constitution. Austria-Hungary instantaneously rejected Serbia's reply as unsatisfactory. On July 28, Austria-Hungary declared war on Serbia, and the same night **Belgrade** was subjected to an artillery bombardment.

*Military Operations*. The first Austro-Hungarian invasion of Serbia was launched on August 12, 1914. The Austro-Hungarian forces were decisively defeated in the **Battle of Cer** and pushed back across the **Sava** and **Drina** Rivers. After Austria-Hungary's next defeat in the **Battle of Kolubara,** Germany took over the command of Balkan operations. The German offensive began on October 6, 1915, under the command of General August von Mackensen. The German and Austro-Hungarian forces, joined by the Bulgarian army, which attacked Serbia without declaration of war on October 9, numbered more than 600,000 soldiers. The armies of Serbia and **Montenegro**, cut down by typhus, had less than half that number and lacked equipment. In order to prevent encirclement, the Serbian army, after a month and a half of heavy fighting, began a mass withdrawal from **Kosovo and Metohija** via Albania to the Adriatic coast. In the dramatic retreat, only 150,000 Serbian soldiers reached the Albanian coast and Shkodër. After the Italian command refused to provide transport, Serbian troops continued the exodus toward Durrës and Vlöne (Valona) where, after a plea from the Russian emperor, the French fleet transported the survivors to **Corfu Island**. The revived

Serbian army took an active part in the fighting on the **Salonika front** in 1916–1918. In 1918, the Serbian army led the Allied attack that broke the German and Bulgarian defenses and liberated Serbia and the rest of the Yugoslav lands.

*Occupation and Wartime Losses.* Serbia and Montenegro suffered greatly under the Austro-Hungarian and Bulgarian occupation. Serbia's 13 western districts were under Austro-Hungarian occupation, while the territory east of the **Morava** River was occupied by Bulgaria. The Austro-Hungarian authorities interned 150,000 persons, many of whom died in concentration camps. Factories were stripped of machines and tools, forests cut down, and mines frantically exploited. The Bulgarian occupation was equally harsh. Entire villages disappeared, and the entire male population of **Niš** was deported. In 1917, after the **Rebellion of Toplica**, Bulgarian forces burned 50,000 homes and completely destroyed 36 villages. Twenty thousand persons perished. Serbia lost 25 percent of its total population and 62.5 percent of the male population between the ages of 15 and 55.

*Political Developments.* Immediately following the outbreak of the war, on August 4, 1914, the Serbian government proclaimed the liberation of all the South Slav lands as its main objective. This determination was reiterated in a secret session of the **Parliament**, held in Niš on August 10, 1915. The prior formation of the **Yugoslav Committee** in November 1914 added a new dimension to the process of unification. While both insisted on the necessity of liberation and unification, the Yugoslav Committee and the Serbian government differed in respect to three large issues: which South Slavic territories were to be liberated and united, how their unification would take place, and how the future state would be organized. The position of the Serbian government was that of immediate liberation and unification only of traditional Serbian lands (territories where Serbs constituted absolute or relative majorities of the population), that is, the formation of **Greater Serbia**. The Yugoslav Committee, however, expected that all Yugoslav lands would be liberated and joined into one state at the same time. The Serbian government favored a centralist organization of the new state; the committee insisted on a federalist organization. Although several diplomatic attempts were made to mitigate the discord, and the **Corfu Declaration** was adopted, the differences persisted long after the proclamation of the common state—the **Kingdom of the Serbs, Croats, and Slovenes**—on December 1, 1918.

WORLD WAR II. The international position of Yugoslavia in 1940 became increasingly difficult. After the fall of France, its strongest ally, Yugoslavia's neutral position was further compromised by the acceptance of the **Tripartite Pact** by neighboring Hungary, Romania, and Bulgaria. The Yugoslav government, led by **Dragiša Cvetković** and **Vladimir Maček**, signed the pact on March 25, 1941, under severe German diplomatic pressure. However, two days later, on March 27, a group of pro-British Yugoslav army officers led by General Bora Mirković and General **Dušan Simović** executed a coup d'état in **Belgrade**, overthrowing the regency in favor of king **Peter II Karađorđević** and reversing the government's policy.

On April 6, the Germans, anxious to secure their south flank before the invasion of the Soviet Union, attacked Yugoslavia (and Greece) with 24 divisions and 1,200 tanks. The German forces were joined by 22 Italian and five Hungarian divisions. Overpowered and broken by Croatian and German Fifth Column activity, the Yugoslav army resistance collapsed, and the capitulation was signed on April 17. The territory of Yugoslavia was divided among Germany, which annexed parts of **Slovenia** and put central **Serbia** and **Banat** under its direct control; Italy, which occupied parts of Slovenia, most of **Dalmatia**, and parts of **Montenegro**; Hungary, which annexed **Bačka** and parts of Slovenia; and Bulgaria, which occupied southern Serbia and eastern **Macedonia**. In addition, the **Independent State of Croatia** (NDH) and Greater Albania were formed.

*Resistance and Civil War*. The first organized resistance to the occupation, known as the **Jugoslovenska vojska u otadžbini** (JVO) or **Četniks** was formed by Colonel **Dragoljub-Draža Mihailović** in May 1941. Following the German attack on the Soviet Union on June 22, 1941, the **Communist Party of Yugoslavia** incited a series of uprisings and began to organize armed units known as **Partisans** throughout Yugoslavia. Although they cooperated initially, the two groups soon began fighting each other and became engaged in a bitter civil war. Confronted with the **Ustaše** genocide against the **Serbs** in the NDH (encompassing modern Croatia and Bosnia and Hercegovina) and with the exceptionally harsh German occupation of Serbia, where for one dead German soldier 100 Serbs were killed, the nationalist JVO avoided direct confrontation with German forces. On the other hand, anxious to relieve the pressure on the Soviet Union, the Communist-led Partisans insisted on active resistance.

Moreover, while the JVO fought for the unification of the Serbian lands, the Partisans carried out a Communist revolution.

Although initially favored, the JVO lost Allied support to the Partisans after the Teheran Conference in November 1943. While numerous factors chiefly British initiative, influenced this, the Partisans' ability to link their revolutionary struggle with the immediate interests of the Allies, mainly fighting Germany by all means and all costs, was crucial. On June 1, 1944, the new government-in-exile was formed with a Croat, **Ivan Šubašić**, as prime minister, but without General Mihailović as minister of defense. Finally, on September 12, King Peter II, under British pressure, called for all forces to rally behind Josip Broz, **Tito**. Intense British- sponsored negotiations between Šubašić and Tito resulted in the effective dissolution of the government-in-exile and formation of the provisional government with Tito as prime minister and Šubašić as foreign minister on March 7, 1945. In addition to diplomatic successes, the Partisans, with the support of the Soviet Army, routed the Germans from Serbia in 1944. Following the German collapse in May 1945, Partisans decisively defeated the JVO in Serbia and Bosnia and Hercegovina. Numerous members and sympathizers of the JVO were executed or imprisoned. Mihailović was captured, and after a short trial executed in July 1946. The new, Communist-led Yugoslav state was officially proclaimed on November 29, 1945.

*Occupation and Wartime Losses*. Besides the Soviet Union, Yugoslavia suffered the most during World War II. The most conservative estimates put the number of dead above one million, while the official historiography claims 1.7 million deaths. Most of the victims were Serbs, and most of the destruction took place in Bosnia and Hercegovina and Serbia. More than 36.5 percent of industrial facilities was completely destroyed. The chemical, metal, and textile industries were particularly hard hit, with 57, 49.8, and 53.4 percent of their fixed assets being obliterated. Moreover, 50 percent of railway lines were destroyed, 80 percent of agricultural equipment lost, 822,000 buildings were destroyed, and more the 3,500,000 people lost their homes. In addition, the occupiers and Ustaše destroyed two-thirds of all telephone stations, 80 percent of hospitals, and the entire public transportation system, including air transport. The occupying forces took all of the Yugoslav minted coinage, 10,425 kg of gold and 82,133 kg of silver. The total value of the destruction that Yugoslavia suffered during the war, expressed in 1946 U.S. dollars, was estimated at $9,144,889,000.

## -Y-

YOUNG BOSNIA. See MLADA BOSNA.

YUGOSLAV ARMY/VOJSKA JUGOSLAVIJE (VJ). The armed forces of the **Federal Republic of Yugoslavia**. The VJ was formed following the disestablishment of the **JNA** in May 1992. The VJ is a conscript based force and it follows the JNA's organizational structure. The ground forces are estimated at approximately 103,000 with more than 1,500 modern tanks and a substantial number of artillery pieces. The air force is estimated to have 230 planes with more than a hundred Russian-made fighter jets. The naval forces include several submarines and close to a hundred small torpedo-boats.

YUGOSLAV COMMITTEE/JUGOSLOVENSKI ODBOR. Organization formed by Croatian exiles and Serbian politicians from **Bosnia and Hercegovina** in Florence, Italy, on November 22, 1914. The main function of the Yugoslav Committee was to represent the interests of the **South Slavs** under Austro-Hungarian rule. The committee essentially represented a sort of government-in-exile for the South Slavs of the Dual Monarchy and in that capacity cooperated with the Serbian government on a broad spectrum of issues. However, apart from their common goal—the destruction of Austria-Hungary—serious differences existed between the committee and the Serbian government in respect to basic questions pertaining to the future common state. Dominated by Croats, the committee advocated the idea of unification of all Yugoslav lands, while the view of Serbian prime minister **Nikola Pašić** was that the formation of Yugoslavia should be preceded by the unification of the traditional Serbian lands, that is Bosnia and Hercegovina and **Montenegro**. Disagreements also existed with respect to the organization of the future state: while the leader of the Yugoslav Committee looked to a federal system, Pašić envisioned the extension of Serbia's centralism. These differences and generally poor relations between the committee and the Serbian government were temporarily mitigated by the **Corfu Declaration,** signed on July 20, 1917.

The disagreements continued throughout 1918 because of committee president Ante Trumbić's decision to pursue official Allied recognition of the committee as the representative of the Habsburg Monarchy's South Slavs. Pašić's stubborn opposition defeated this idea, and the struggle continued until the formal proclamation of the **Kingdom of the Serbs, Croats, and Slovenes** on December 1, 1918. The committee formally ceased its activities in 1919. As a political organization, the Yugoslav Committee primarily represented the interests of Croats and Slovenes, who feared that after the collapse of Austria-Hungary their lands would fall under Italian domination.

YUGOSLAV LEFT. See JUL.

YUGOSLAV MUSLIM ORGANIZATION/JUGOSLOVENSKA MUSLIMANSKA ORGANIZACIJA (JMO). Political organization of **Muslims** from **Bosnia and Hercegovina** (B-H) between the two world wars. Founded in 1918, the JMO protected the interests of well-to-do Muslim landlords and merchants. Under the long-time leadership of **Mehmed Spaho**, party orientation wavered from a pronounced pro-Serbianism to the demanding of the establishment of B-H as a separate Muslim-dominated unit of a federal Yugoslav state. After Spaho's death, Džaferbeg Kulenović became the leader of the JMO. In 1941 he joined the **Ustaše** government and became vice premier of the **Independent State of Croatia.**

YUGOSLAV RADICAL UNION/JUGOSLOVENSKA RADIKALNA ZAJEDNICA (JRZ). Political party formed in 1935 from a section of the **Radical Party**, the Slovenian National Party, and the **Yugoslav Muslim Organization** (JMO). The real force behind this coalition was **Milan Stojadinović,** who was the prime minister of Yugoslavia, 1935–1939. After his fall, **Dragiša Cvetković** became the leader of the JRZ. The party lost its rationale after the **Cvetković-Maček Agreement** in August 1939.

YUGOSLAV REPUBLICAN PARTY/JUGOSLOVENSKA REPUBLIKANSKA STRANKA. Left-wing political party founded in January 1920 under the name Republikanska demokratska stranka (Republican Democratic Party). The leader of the party was **Ljubomir-Ljuba Stojanović**, who was succeeded by **Jaša Prodanović**. The party published its paper ***Republika***. The party cooperated in the formation of **Narodni Front**, which it formally joined after **World War II**.

YUGOSLAVS. Census category introduced in Yugoslavia in 1953. The number of people who declared themselves as "Yugoslavs" grew rapidly in the early 1980s but halted after the outbreak of nationalist euphoria in 1990s. There were 317,124 Yugoslavs in 1961, 273,077 in 1971, 1,219,045 in 1981, and 700,735 in 1991. The category of Yugoslavs most rapidly increased in Serbia—from 20,079 in 1961 to 441,941 persons in 1981 and 317,739 persons in 1991. The increase was considerable in multinational **Vojvodina**, while the number of Yugoslavs in **Kosovo and Metohija** was insignificant (see Tables 18 and 19, statistical addendum).

## - Z -

*ZABAVNIK* (*The Almanac*). (i) The first Serbian almanac published by **Dimitrije Davidović** in Vienna 1815–1816 and 1818–1821. From 1833 to 1836, the almanac was published in Serbia.
(ii) A newspaper published as a supplement of ***Srpske Novine*** on **Corfu Island** between April 1917 and November 1918. It published articles on Serbian history, ethnography, and international politics.

ZADAR. Port city, cultural and industrial center of northern **Dalmatia** (pop. 134,669; 1991 estimate). The city has shipbuilding, machine-building, and textile industries. It was founded by ancient Liburnians in the 10th century B.C. Throughout medieval times Zadar was under Venetian control. From 1797 to 1918 the city was occupied by Austria. Under Austro-Hungarian domination, Zadar was the capital of all of Dalmatia. Between 1918 and 1943, Zadar was under Italian occupation and in 1947 was finally incorporated into Yugoslavia. During the civil war in **Croatia** in 1991, Zadar was a site of heavy battles between Croatian paramilitary forces and the **JNA**.

ZADARSKA REZOLUCIJA (Resolution of Zadar). Resolution carried by Serbian representatives in the Carevinsko veće (Imperial Council) and Dalmatinski sabor (Dalmatian Parliament) by representatives of Serbian parties in **Dalmatia** and Croatia-Slavonia on October 17, 1905. The resolution led to the formation of the **Hrvatsko-srpska koalicija** within Austria-Hungary.

ZADRUGA. Large, complex family or multiple-family communal household in **Serbia**. Founded upon patriarchal kinship, authority, and division of labor, the Zadruga system hinged upon the peasants' self-sufficiency. The introduction of a money economy following the **First Serbian Insurrection** led to the dissolution of the Zadruga system. At the end of Prince **Miloš Obrenović**'s rule, only one quarter of Serbian families lived in *zadrugas*. The *zadrugas* entirely disappeared from Serbia by the end of the 19th century.

ZAGORA. Locality in **Dalmatia** rich in bauxite, coal, and hydroenergy. The main cities are **Knin,** Sinj, Drniš, Skradin, and Benkovac. During the Croatian offensive in August 1995, the majority of the Serbian population was forced to leave the area.

ZAGREB. Capital city, cultural and industrial center of **Croatia**, with a population of 930,753 in 1991. The first records of the city date from 1094, when the bishopric was established. Since the 17th century Zagreb figures as a capital, first of Croatia-Slavonia and later of Croatia as a whole.

ZAH, FRANTIŠEK ALEKSANDR (1807–1892). Emissary of the Polish prince Czartoryski to the Serbian government. Zah's close cooperation with **Ilija Garašanin** led to the creation of ***Načertanije***, the first national program of **Serbia**. Zah became a general in the Serbian army, the first head of the artillery school (later military academy), and chief of the General Staff.

ZAHUMLJE. Region between the cities of **Mostar** and **Dubrovnik.** During medieval times, the region was contested between Serbian kings and local chieftains. The Turks conquered Zahumlje in 1490.

ZAJEČAR. City in eastern **Serbia** and industrial center of the **Timok** basin, with a population of 72,763 in 1991. Metal fabrication, machine-building, textile, and beer industries are especially well-developed. Several coal mines,Vrška čuka, Rtanj, Zvezda, are located in the vicinity of Zaječar. The city is first mentioned during **Kočina krajina**. Following the liberation from the Turks (1833), Zaječar became a major communication link between Turkish-held Bulgaria, Vallachia, and Serbia.

ZAJEDNO (Together). A coalition of opposition parties formed in the fall of 1996. The major political forces in the coalition were the **Serbian Renewal Movement** (SPO), the **Democratic Party** (DS), and the Civic

Coalition of Serbia (GSS). In the November 1996 **elections** in **Serbia**, the coalition won in 18 major cities in Serbia. The ruling coalition consisting of the **Socialist Party of Serbia** and **JUL** contested the outcome of the elections which led to massive three-month long demonstrations in almost every major city in Serbia.

Despite an unprecedented electoral success, the coalition Zajedno collapsed during the summer of 1997. The main reasons for the collapse were differences in the political platforms of the SPO and DS as well as strong personal animosity between coalition leaders.

ZAPADNA MORAVA. See WESTERN MORAVA.

*ZASTAVA* (*Flag*). Serbian newspaper published in Budapest in 1866. From 1866 until 1929, when it ceased publication, the newspaper was edited and published in **Novi Sad**. Until 1884, the newspaper was under the editorship of **Svetozar Miletić** and after that **Jaša Tomić**. Initially, the newspaper was the main voice of the Serbian liberal intelligentsia in Hungary and later became the voice of the **Radical Party**.

ZAVIDA. (ca. 11th and 12th centuries). Founder of the Serbian **Nemanjić** dynasty and the father of **Stefan Nemanja.**

ZBOR (Rally). Right-wing political party founded in 1935 by the unification of Jugoslovenska akcija (Yugoslav Action) from **Croatia**, Boja (Color) from **Slovenia**, and a group organized around **Belgrade**-based journals ***Otadžbina*** (*Fatherland*) and *Zbor* (*Rally*). The organization, also known as Jugoslovenski narodni pokret (Yugoslav National Movement), propagated the concept of integral Yugoslavism, negating the national differences between the **Serbs**, Croats, and Slovenes. The party base was in **Serbia**, and its leader was **Dimitrije Ljotić**. Banned because of its extremism in 1940, the party was revived after the German occupation in 1941, when it formed armed units known as Srpski dobrovoljački korpus (Serbian Corps of Volunteers). These units actively collaborated with the Germans and fought against both the **Jugoslovenska vojska u otadžbini** and the **Partisans.**

ZEBIĆ, JOVAN (1939– ). Deputy prime minister of the **Federal Republic of Yugoslavia** since 1993 and minister of finance since 1994. Prior to his appointment in the Yugoslav government, Zebić occupied several political posts, which included vice governor of the Serbian National Bank (1985–1986) and deputy prime minister and minister of finance of the Serbian government (1991–1993).

ZEKA BULJUBAŠA (1785–1813). Serbian hero born in **Hercegovina**, a company commander on the **Drina** River in the **First Serbian Insurrection.** His company consisted of poor people known as *golaći* (impoverished).

ZELENAŠI. Political movement in **Montenegro** originating at the beginning of the 20th century. Unlike the Bjelaši (Whites), the movement strenuously opposed unification between **Serbia** and Montenegro. The term *zelenaši* (greens) comes from the petitions that they printed on green paper.

ZELENGORA. Mountain in **Hercegovina**, a site of several heavy battles in **World War II**. In 1943, the worst clashes in the **Battle of Sutjeska** took place on Zelengora. The **Partisans** destroyed substantial forces of **Jugoslovenska vojska u otadžbini** on Zelengora in May 1945. This defeat marked the end of organized forces loyal to General **Dragoljub-Draža Mihailović.**

ZELIĆ, GERASIM (1752–1828). Archimandrite of the **Serbian Orthodox Church** from **Dalmatia** and **Boka Kotorska**. He was a strenuous opponent of Greek Catholicism. His autobiography *Žitije Gerasima Zelića* (*The Life of Gerasim Zelić*) is a valuable source for the history of **Serbs** living in Dalmatia between the 18th and the 19th centuries.

ZEMALJSKO ANTIFAŠISTIČKO VIJEĆE (Antifascist Council). A title assumed by the regional parliaments ("Supreme political body") organized by the **Partisans** after the foundation of AVNOJ in 1942. A presidium of these organizations served as the government of the region. In total, four regional organizations were founded: in **Croatia**, Zavnoh on June 13, 1943, in **Bosnia and Hercegovina** (B-H), Zavno B-H on November 26, 1943, in the **Sandžak,** Zavno Sandžaka on November 20, 1943, and in **Montenegro**, Zavno Crne Gore i Boke on November 15, 1943. See also AVNOJ.

ZEMLJORADNIČKA STRANKA. See AGRICULTURAL PARTY.

ZEMUN. City and industrial center located on the right bank of the **Danube** River, administratively a district of **Belgrade** with a population of 181,692 in 1991. A pharmaceutical factory ("Galenika"), aviation plant ("Ikarus"), the optical works ("Teleoptik"), several research institutes, and the School of Agriculture are located in Zemun. The city dates from Roman times, while the slavic name, Zemlen, was recorded in the ninth century. In the 15th century Zemun belonged to the Serbian **despot Đurađ Branković**.

ZENICA. City and industrial center in **Bosnia and Hercegovina** with a population of 145,577 in 1991. The ethnic composition prior to the civil war was 55.2 percent Muslim, 15.6 Croatian percent; 15.5 percent Serbian, and 10.8 percent Yugoslav. The city was the center of heavy industry, producing 80 percent of Yugoslavia's iron. The reserves of iron ore located in the vicinity of Zenica constituted 75 percent of the total reserves in Yugoslavia and 2.5 percent of European reserves.

ZETA. (i) A medieval Serbian state and first Serbian kingdom, originally located around the ancient region called **Duklja** (Dioclea). The state emerged after the successful Serbian uprising against the Byzantine Empire under the leadership of **Vojislav.** Vojislav's son, **Mihailo**, who ruled Zeta between 1050 and 1082, is considered the first Serbian king, as Pope Gregory VII labeled him so in a letter from 1077. During the reign of Mihailo's son **Konstantin Bodin**, the bishopric of **Bar** was elevated to the status of an archbishopric in 1089. After the death of Bodin around 1101, Zeta weakened, and in 1183 **Stefan Nemanja** incorporated Zeta into **Raška**. The name Zeta was consistently replaced by **Montenegro** at the end of the 14th century.

(ii) A river in Montenegro, 90 kilometers long, a tributary of the **Morača**. The hydroelectric plant "Perućica" produces one billion Kwh of electrical energy per year.

ZMAJ, JOVAN JOVANOVIĆ (1833–1904). One of the most popular and celebrated Serbian poets from **Vojvodina**. Born in **Novi Sad**, he studied law in Prague, Vienna, and Pest (Budapest), where he graduated from medical school. His works are exceptionally varied, including everything from patriotic poems to deeply intimate and emotional verses. He initiated and edited numerous literary and satirical journals and translated and adapted the poetry of a variety of eastern and western nations. His best-known works are *Đulići* (*Roses*) and *Đulići uveoci* (*Faded Roses*).

ZORA (Dawn). Society of Serbian students in Vienna founded in 1863. Prior to its demise, the society published the journal *Zora* (*Dawn*) between 1910 and 1912.

ZORKA. Chemical industry founded in 1938 in the city of **Šabac**. It is one of the main producers of plastic and various types of fertilizers in **Serbia.**

ZRENJANIN. City and regional economic center in **Banat** with a population of 136,778 in 1991. Various industries are located in the city including chemical, shipbuilding, metal, machine-building, and wood-processing plants. The city was founded in the 14th century.

ZVEČAN. Small city in **Kosovo and Metohija** in the valley of the **Ibar** River (pop. 10,030 in 1991). The city is located in the vicinity of the lead, zinc, and silver mines of **Trepča**. Zvečan is one of the few cities regularly mentioned throughout the existence of the medieval Serbian state.

ZVEČKA. Small town in **Serbia** near **Belgrade.** One of the strongest radio stations in Europe (2,000 kilowatts) is located there.

ZVIJEZDA. Mineral-rich mountain in **Bosnia and Hercegovina**, located north of the Sarajevo valley. The mountain is especially rich in iron ore, chrome, manganese, lead, zinc, and silver.

ZVORNIK. City in **Bosnia and Hercegovina**, located on the left bank of the **Drina** River with a population of 81,111 in 1991. The ethnic composition prior to the civil war 59.4 percent Muslim, 38 percent Serbian. Wood processing and the production of construction materials are important industries. The hydroelectric plant "Zvornik" has a capacity of 86,000 kilowatts, with a potential electrical energy production of 406 Kwh per year. Prior to the Turkish occupation in the second half of the 15th century, the city belonged to the Serbian **despot Đurađ Branković**. According to the **Dayton Agreement**, Zvornik will remain in the **Republika Srpska**.

## - Ž -

ŽERAJIĆ, BOGDAN (1886–1910). Young Serbian revolutionary from **Bosnia and Hercegovina** (B-H). On June 15, 1910, at the opening session of the Bosnian Parliament he attempted to assassinate General Marijan Varešanin, the Austro-Hungarian governor of B-H. Having failed, he committed suicide. His act inspired several members of the revolutionary organization **Mlada Bosna**, who assassinated Archduke Franz Ferdinand on June 28, 1914, in **Sarajevo** (**Sarajevo Assassination**).

ŽIČA. Monastery in the vicinity of **Kraljevo**, the legacy of the Serbian king **Stefan Prvovenčani** and **Saint Sava**, built between 1207 and 1220. In 1219, Žiča became the first Archbishopric center of the **Serbian Orthodox Church**. The monastery is of great importance to the history of the Serbian people and its church; several Serbian kings and bishops were crowned and inaugurated in Žiča. Architecturally, the church belongs to the **Raška** school of architecture. Often destroyed, Žiča was restored between 1925–1935 as well as in 1989–1990.

ŽIVALJEVIĆ, DANILO (1862–1942). Serbian writer and journalist, one of the founders of **Srpska književna zadruga.** Between 1889 and 1903, he was the editor of the journal, *Kolo* (*The Ring*). He also analyzed the literature of **Dalmatia** and **Dubrovnik**. His major works include *O Marinu Držiću* (*On Marin Držić*), and *Srpsko-hrvatska bibliografija* (*Serbo-Croatian Bibliography*).

ŽIVANOVIĆ, JOVAN (1892–1914). Serbian revolutionary from **Bosnia and Hercegovina**, one of the leading members of the revolutionary organization **Mlada Bosna**. After the outbreak of **World War I,** he left Switzerland and joined the Serbian army as a volunteer. He was captured and burned alive by Austro-Hungarian troops.

ŽIVANOVIĆ, MILIVOJE (1900–1976). Leading Serbian actor, one of the last representatives of actors who were bards, heroes, and missionaries. He was characterized by a powerful temperament, distinctive stature, and expressive voice. Živanović interpreted characters from all kinds of genres (title role in W. Shakespeare's *King Lear*, Father in *Prisoners of Altona* by J.P. Sartre, etc.).

ŽIVANOVIĆ, ŽIVAN (1852–1931). Serbian politician and historian, one of the founders of the **Liberal Party**. He held several important posts, including minister of economy and minister of education. His best-known work is *Politička istorija Srbije u drugoj polovini XIX veka* (*A Political History of Serbia in the Second Half of the 19th Century*).

ŽIVKOVIĆ, NIKOLA (1792–1870). First architect and developer in modern **Serbia**. He drafted construction plans for several buildings in **Belgrade**, such as Konak Knjeginje Ljubice (The Quarters of Princess Ljubica), and Knežev konak (Prince's Quarters).

ŽIVKOVIĆ, PETAR (1879–1953). General and politician in the Kingdom of Yugoslavia, the founder of the royalist organization called Bela Ruka (White Hand) and an architect of the **Trial of Salonika**. After the establishment of the personal regime of King **Alexander I Karađorđević** on January 6, 1929, he became the prime minister and minister of defense. In 1936, he founded Jugoslovenska nacionalna organizacija (Yugoslav National Organization), an organization that lacked popular support. After the German invasion of Yugoslavia, he emigrated to London, where he became a minister in the Yugoslav government-in-exile. A fervent anticommunist, he actively supported the forces of General **Dragoljub-Draža Mihailović**. In 1946, at the trial of General Mihailović, Živković was accused as a war criminal and sentenced to death in absentia.

ŽIVOJINOVIĆ, VELIMIR-MASSUKA (1886–1974). Serbian poet, one of the best representatives of late romanticism in Serbia's literature. He translated Shakespeare into the **Serbian language.** His best works are: *Odblesci u vodi* (*Reflections in the Water*), *Stihovi* (*Verses*), and *Pesme* (*Poems*).

ŽRNOVICA. **Župa** of **Trebinje** bequested to **Dubrovnik** by Serbian emperor **Uroš II** in 1357.

ŽUJOVIĆ, SRETEN (1899–1976). Yugoslav politician and Communist revolutionary. Žujović joined the **Communist Party** of Yugoslavia in 1924, and in 1933 he emigrated to the Soviet Union. One of the leading organizers of the **Partisans**' uprising in **Serbia** in 1941, after **World War II**, he became a minister of finance. In 1948, during the **Cominform** crisis, Žujović disapproved of **Tito**'s policies, leading to his arrest and removal from all political posts.

ŽUJOVIĆ, ŽIVOJIN (1838–1870). First propagator of socialist ideas in **Serbia**. He studied theology in Kiev and philosophy in St. Petersburg and Munich. In Russia he fell under the influence of the Russian radical thinkers Chernyshevskii, Belinskii, and Pisarev and the French philosopher Proudhon. He published in Chernyshevskii's journal *Sovremenik* (*Contemporary*) and in *Letopis Matice Srpske* (*Annals of the Serbian Literary Society*).

ŽUMBERAK. Mountainous region in **Croatia**. During the existance of the **Vojna Krajina**, it was heavily colonized by the Serbian **Uskoks**, who were later converted to Greek Catholicism.

ŽUPA. (i) A small area surrounded by mountains, characterized by moderate temperatures and lack of cold winds.
(ii) Among **South Slavs**, *župa* represented a territory and administrative unit of a particular tribe. The center of these administrative units was a city, called *župski grad*, while *župa* was ruled by a **župan.**

ŽUPAN. Title held by the ruler of a **župa**. Rulers of medieval **Serbia** held the title of *veliki župan* (great or grand župan) until the coronation of King **Stefan Prvovenčani.** In **Croatia** and some parts of **Vojvodina**, the title *župan* was held by the districts' supervisors.

# Bibliography



## INTRODUCTION

With the exception of the former Soviet Union, the Yugoslav bibliography is perhaps the richest among those of Eastern European countries. The specific geopolitical position of the country and its peculiar domestic and foreign policies (Self-management and nonalignment) generated considerable interest among western scholars. The breakup of the former Yugoslavia and civil war in Croatia and Bosnia and Hercegovina dramatically increased interest in the region and led to an increase in the production of general and specialized studies on the former Yugoslavia. The majority of the studies produced since the outbreak of the civil war are unfortunately partisan and heavily influenced by recent events. A number of these studies are written by nonspecialists, with very little respect for the facts. The situation is even worse with studies produced within the newly created states, where nationalisms of all kinds have taken precedence over historical facts. This bibliography is a representative selection of books and articles, with special emphasis on materials in English. Despite reservations, several newly produced studies are listed, given their popularity and widespread quotations.

## Bibliographies and Dictionaries

There are several excellent bibliographies, published in Britain and the United States, which are readily available and include works in English, Serbo-Croatian, Slovene, Macedonian, and other European languages. Although some of these bibliographies are becoming dated, they are still invaluable sources. Special mention should include Horton, John J. *Yugoslavia.* World Bibliographical Series, Vol. 1. Second revised and expanded edition, Santa Barbara, Calif.: Clio Press, 1990, and Terry, Garth M. *Yugoslav History. A Bibliographic Index to English-Language Articles*. Nottingham: Astra Press, 1990 (Second revised edition). In addition, readers may wish to consult Michael B. Petrovich's *Yugoslavia: A Bibliographical Guide.* Washington, D.C.: U.S. Government Printing Office, 1974, and Joel M. Halpern's *Bibliography of English Language Sources on Yugoslavia.* Amherst, Mass.: 1969, as they contain most of the classical works on Yugoslavia.

Each of the former Yugoslav republics has its own bibliographical publications. In addition, Scarecrow Press (Lanham, Md.) is publishing volumes on all of the successor states that include comprehensive bibliographies. For example: Robert Stallaerts and Jeannine Laurens, *Historical Dictionary of the Republic of Croatia* (1995); Leopoldina Plut-Pregelj and Carole Rogel, *Historical Dictionary of Slovenia* (1996); Ante Čuvalo, *Historical Dictionary of Bosnia and Hercegovina* (1997); and Valentina Georgieva and Sasha Konechni, *Historical Dictionary of Macedonia* (1997).

Readers should also consult Scarecrow volumes on neighboring countries: Raymond Detrez, *Historical Dictionary of Bulgaria* (1996); Kurt W.

Treptow and Marcel Popa, *Historical Dictionary of Romania* (1996); Raymond Hutchings, *Historical Dictionary of Albania* (1996); and Steven Bela Várdy, *Historical Dictionary of Hungary* (1997).

**Statistical Abstracts**

There is a rich body of statistical material available on both the former Yugoslavia and the Federal Republic of Yugoslavia. Representative sources include the *Statistical Yearbook of the Socialist Federal Republic of Yugoslavia*. Belgrade: Federal Statistical Office, 1991, and the *Statistical Yearbook of Yugoslavia*. Belgrade: Federal Statistical Office, 1996. Specialized research institutions publish their own statistical data using specialized methodologies. The best-known sources available in English include *Monthly Analysis and Prognosis*. Belgrade: Institute of Economic Sciences, 1994– and *Human Development Report*. Belgrade: Economics Institute, 1996.

**Cultural**

The most comprehensive list of Yugoslav literature in the English language includes Mihailovich, Vasa D., and Mateja Matejic, *A Comprehensive Bibliography of Yugoslav Literature in the English Language 1953–1980*. Columbus, Ohio: Slavica Publishers, 1984 and Mihailovich, Vasa D., *First Supplement to a Comprehensive Bibliography of Yugoslav Literature in English, 1981–1985*. Columbus, Ohio: Slavica Publishers, 1988. The recently published *The History of Serbian Culture*. Edgware: Porthill, 1995 provides an excellent overview of the development of Serbian culture. The most popular literary and cultural journals and magazines in Yugoslavia include *Književne novine* (*Literary Gazette*), *Književna reč* (*Literary Word*), *Gledišta* (*Standpoints*), and *Srpski književni glasnik* (*Serbian Literary Herald*). The relevant academic journals published in the United Kingdom, United States, and Canada include *Serbian Studies*, *Slavic Studies*, *Slavic Review, Canadian-American Slavic Studies, Oxford Slavonic Papers*, and *Slavonic and East European Review*.

**Economic**

Susan Woodward's *Socialist Unemployment: The Political Economy of Yugoslavia 1945–1990*. Princeton, N.J.: Princeton University Press, 1995 is the most comprehensive among the recent studies. The classical studies include Mihailović, Kosta. *Ekonomska stvarnost Jugoslavije* (*Economic Reality of Yugoslavia*). Belgrade: Ekonomika, 1982 and Horvat, Branko. *Business Cycles in Yugoslavia*. White Plains, N.Y.: International Arts and Sciences Press, 1971. Thorough economic history of the Yugoslav lands is given in Lampe, John R., and Marvin R. Jackson. *Balkan Economic History, 1550–1950*. Bloomington: Indiana University Press, 1982. The best-known Serbian and Yugoslav economic journals include *Economic Analysis and Workers' Self-Management*, *Ekonomska misao* (*Economic Thought*), and *Ekonomski Anali* (*Economic Annals*). The weekly *Ekonomska politika* (*Economic Policy*) is a major source on trends in the Yugoslav economy.

## History

The recently published *The History of Serbian Culture*. Edgeware: Porthill Publishers, 1995, provides a short review of Serbian history. John Lampe's *Yugoslavia as History: Twice There Was a Country*. Cambridge: Cambridge University Press, 1996, provides a general overview of the history of the region and follows the model of Fred Singleton's *A Short History of the Yugoslav Peoples*. Cambridge: Cambridge University Press, 1985. A collection of essays edited by Dimitrije Djordjevic, *The Creation of Yugoslavia*. Santa Barbara, Calif.: Clio Books, 1980, Stevan K. Pawlovitch's, *The Improbable Survivor: Yugoslavia and Its Problems, 1918–1988*. London: Hurst, 1989, and Dušan T. Bataković's, *Yougoslavie, Nations, Religions, Ideologies*. Laussanne: L'Age d'Homme, 1994, are highly recommended readings on the creation of Yugoslavia and its internal problems. Alex N. Dragnich's *The First Yugoslavia: Search for a Viable Political System*. Stanford, Calif.: Hoover Institution Press, 1983 and Ivo Banac's *The National Question in Yugoslavia: Origins, History, Politics*. Ithaca: Cornell University Press, 1984, provide numerous insights in to the Yugoslav political arena between the two world wars. Michael B. Petrovich's *History of Modern Serbia*. London: Harcourt Brace Jovanovich, 1976 provides a detailed history of Serbia since the First Serbian Insurrection.

Academic journals published in Yugoslavia include *Balcanica* and *Istorijski časopis* (*Historical Journal*).

## Civil War

While the books on Yugoslavia published since the violent breakup of the country might fall into one of the above categories, these should be classified separately since the focus in the vast majority of the studies is specifically on developments surrounding Yugoslavia's demise. The most comprehensive study on the Yugoslav civil war is Susan L. Woodward's *Balkan Tragedy: Chaos and Dissolution After the Cold War*. Washington, D.C.: The Brookings Institution, 1995. Misha Glenny's *The Fall of Yugoslavia: The Third Balkan War*. New York: Penguin books, 1992 is an objective journalist's account of the beginning of the civil war in Yugoslavia. Laura Silber and Allan Little's *Yugoslavia Death of A Nation*. New York: TV Books, 1995, is less objective but a very informative account of the breakup of Yugoslavia.

## 1. GENERAL

### Bibliographies and Dictionaries

Akademiia nauk SSSR, Institut slavianovedeniia. *Istoriia Iugoslavii* [History of Yugoslavia]. Edited by Iu.V. Bromlei et. al. Moscow: Izdatel'stvo Akademii nauk SSR, 1963. Vol. II, pp. 333–389.

American Historical Association. *The American Historical Association's Guide to Historical Literature*. Edited by George Frederick Howe, et al. New York: Macmillan, 1961.

———. *A Guide to Historical Literature*. Edited by George Matthew Dutcher et al. New York: Peter Smith, 1949.

Badali, Josip. *Jugoslavica usque ad annum MDC: Bibliographie der südslawischen Frühdrücke. Mit 65 Faksimilien*. Heitz: Aureliae Aquensis, 1959.

Carter, F.W. *A Bibliography of the Geography of Yugoslavia*. London: King's College, 1965.

Đorđević, Dimitrije V. *Istoria tes Servias 1800-1918*. Thessaloniki: Institute for Balkan Studies, 1970. Pp. 419–458.

Friedman, Francine, ed. Yugoslavia: A Comprehensive English Language Bibliography. Wilmington, Del.: Scholarly Resources, Inc., 1993.

Halpern, J. M. *Bibliography of English Language Sources on Yugoslavia*. Amherst, Mass.: 1969.

Horecky, Paul L. *Southeastern Europe: A Guide to Basic Publications*. Chicago: The University of Chicago Press, 1969. Part Six, Yugoslavia, Chapter 47, by Charles and Barbara Jelavich. pp. 501–515.

Horton, J. J. *Yugoslavia. World Bibliographic Series*. Oxford: Oxford University Press, 1977. Revised and expanded edition published in 1990.

Janićijević, Jovan, *Jugoslovenska retrospektivna bibliografska građa: knjige, brošure i muzikalije, 1945–1967* [*The Yugoslav Retrospective Bibliography: Books, Pamphlets, and Music Studies*]. Belgrade: Jugoslovenski bibliografski institut, 1969.

*Jugoslovenska retrospektivna bibliografska građa* [*TheYugoslav Retrospective Bibliography*]. Belgrade: Jugoslovenski bibliografski institut, 1968.

Kerner, Robert J. *Slavic Europe: A Selected Bibliography in Western European Languages*. Cambridge, Mass.: Harvard University Press, 1918.

Krivokapić, Radovan, V. *Bibliografija vojnih izdanja 1945–1968* [*Bibliography of Military Publications 1945–1968*]. Belgrade: Vojnoizdavački zavod, 1969.
Leskovsek, V. *Yugoslavia: A Bibliography*. New York: Studia Slovenica, 1974.
Matulic, Rusko. *Bibliography of Sources on Yugoslavia*. Palo Alto, Calif.: Ragusan Press, 1981.
Mihailović, Georgije. *Prilozi srpskoj bibliografiji osamnaestoga veka* [Contributions to the *Serbian Bibliography of the Eighteen Century*]. Inđija: Narodna biblioteka "Dr. Đorđe Natašević," 1983.
Milivojević, Dragan, and Vasa Mihailovich. *Yugoslav Linguistics in English: A Bibliography*. Columbus, Ohio: Slavica Publishers, Inc., 1990.
Pajović, Borivoj. *Bibliografija o ratu i revoluciji u Jugoslaviji. Posebna izdanja 1945–1965* [*Bibliography on War and the Revolution in Yugoslavia. Special Editions 1945–1965*]. Belgrade: Vojnoizdavački zavod, 1969.
Petrovich, Michael B. *Yugoslavia: A Bibliographic Guide*. Washington, D.C.: U.S. Government Printing Office, 1974.
Savadjian, Léon. *Bibliographie balkanique, 1920–1938*. 8 vols. Paris: Société d'imprimerie & d'édition, 1931–1939.
Savez društava istoričara Jugoslavije. *Historiographie yougoslave, 1955–1965*. Jorjo Tadić, editor. Belgrade: Fédération des Sociétés historiques de Yougoslavie, 1965.
Stavrianos, Leften S. *The Balkans since 1453*. New York: Reinhart, 1958. Bibliography, pp. 873–946.
Stokes, Gale. *Nationalism in the Balkans: An Annotated Bibliography*. New York: Garland, 1984.
Südost-Institut München. *Südosteuropa-Bibliographie*. Munich: R.Oldenbourg, 1945– .
Terry, Garth. M. *Yugoslav History: A Bibliographic Index to English-Language Articles*. Nottingham: Astra Press, 1990.
———. *A Bibliography of Macedonian Studies*. Nottingham: Astra Press, 1975.
Yugoslav National Committee for Historical Studies. *Ten Years of Yugoslav Historiography, 1945–1955*. Edired by Jorjo Tadić. Belgrade: "Jugoslavija," 1955.

## General Information and Surveys

Akademiia nauk SSSR, Institut slavianovedenia. *Istoriia Iugoslavii*. 2 vols. Edited by Iu.V. Bromlei and others. Moscow: Izdatel'stvo Akademii nauk SSSR, 1963. 2 vols.
Authy, Phyllis. *Yugoslavia*. New York: Walker, 1965.
Clissold, Stephen. *Short History of Yugoslavia from Early Times to 1966*. Cambridge: Cambridge University Press, 1968.
Čuvalo, Ante. *Historical Dictionary of Bosnia and Hercegovina*. Lanham, Md.: Scarecrow Press, 1997.
Denis, Ernest. *La grande Serbie*. Paris: Delagrave, 1915.
Devas, Georges Y. [Đurđe Jelenić]. *La nouvelle Serbie; origines et bases sociales et politiques, renaissance de l'état et son développement historique, dynastie nationale et revendications libératrices*. Paris: Berger-Levrault, 1918.
*Directory of Yugoslav Officials*. Washington, D.C.: National Technical Information Service, microfiche.

Đorđević, Dimitrije V. *Istoria tēs Servias 1800–1918*. Thessaloniki: Institute for Balkan Studies, 1970.
*Enciklopedija Jugoslavije* [*Encyclopedia of Yugoslavia*]. Zagreb: Svjetlost, 1970.
Georgieva, Valentina, and Sasha Konechni. *Historical Dictionary of Macedonia*. Lanham, Md.: Scarecrow Press, 1997.
Haumant, Émile. *La formation de la Yougoslavie (XVe–XXe sičcles)*. Institut d'études slaves de l'Université de paris. Collection historique, 5. Paris: Bossard, 1930.
*The History of Serbian Culture*. Edgeware, Middlesex: Porthill, 1995.
Jireček, Konstantin. *Geschichte der Serben. Vol. I* (to 1371). Gotha: Allgemeine staatengeschichte, 1911. Vol. II (1371–1537). Gotha: 1918.
Kállay, Bénjamin. *Geschichte der Serben von den ältesten Zeiten bis 1815*. Budapest: W. Lauffer, 1878.
Kanitz, Feliz P. *Das Königreich Serben und das Serbenvolk, von der Römerzeit bis zur Gegenwart*. 3 vols. Leipzig: B. Mayer, 1909–1914.
*Ko je ko u Jugoslaviji; bibliografski podaci o jugoslovenskim savremenicima* [*Who is Who in Yugoslavia; Biographical Data of Yugoslav Contemporaries*]. Belgrade: Sedma sila, 1957.
*Ko je ko u Srbiji*. Beograd: Mrlješ, 1995.
Lazarovitch-Hrebelianovich, Stephen L. E., prince, and Eleanor Calhoun Lazarovich-Hrebelianovich. *The Servian People, Their Past Glory and Their Destiny*. 2 vols. New York: C. Scribner's Sons, 1910. 2 vols.
*Mala enciklopedija* [*Little Encyclopedia*]. 3 vols. Belgrade: Prosveta 1989. 3 vols.
Mijatović, Elodie Lawton. *The History of Modern Serbia*. London: W. Tweedie, 1872.
Petrovich, Michael B. *A History of Modern Serbia, 1804–1918*. 2 vols. New York: Harcourt Brace Jovanovich, 1976.
Plut-Pregelj, Leopoldina, and Carole Rogel. *Historical Dictionary of Slovenia*. Lanham, Md.: Scarecrow Press, 1996.
Pogodin, A. L. *Istoriia Serbii*. St. Petersburg: Brokquaz-Efron, 1909.
Ranke, Leopold von. *Serbien und die Türkei im neunzehnten Jahrhundert*. Sämmtliche Werke, 2. Leipzig: Duncker & Humbolt, 1879.
Singleton, Fred. *A Short History of the Yugoslav Peoples*. Cambridge: Cambridge University Press, 1985.
Stallaerts, Robert and Jeannine Laurens. *Historical Dictionary of the Republic of Croatia*. Metuchen, NJ: Scarecrow Press, 1995.
Temperley, Harold W. V. *History of Serbia*. London: G. Bell, 1917.
*Vojna enciklopedija* [*Military Encyclopedia*]. Belgrade: Vojno delo, 1978.
*Yugoslavia*. New York: Praeger, 1957.

## Guides and Yearbooks, Travel and Description

Adamic, Louis. *The Native's Return: An American Immigrant visits Yugoslavia and Discovers His Old Country*. New York: Harper & Brothers, 1934.
Alexander, Nora. *Wanderings in Yugoslavia*. London: Skeffington & Son, Ltd., 1936.
Bici, Marin. *Iskušenja na putu: po crnogorskom primorju Albaniji i Srbiji, 1610*

godine [*Challenges on the Road: Along the Montenegirn Coast, Albania, and Serbia, 1610*]. Budva: Opštinski arhiv-Budva, 1985.
Blanchard, Paul. *Yugoslavia*. London: Black & Norton, 1989.
Curtis, Glenn E. *Yugoslavia, A Country Study*. Washington, D.C.: Headquarters, Department of the Army, 1992.
Denton, William. *Servia and the Servians*. London: Bell & Daldy, 1862.
Edwards, Lovett Fielding. *Profane Pilgrimage; Wanderings Through Yugoslavia*. London: Duckworth, 1938.
*Facts about the Socialist Federal Republic of Yugoslavia*. Belgrade: Federal Secretariat for Information, 1985.
Footman, David. *Balkan Holiday*. London: W. Heinemann, 1935.
Galbraith, John K. *Journey to Poland and Yugoslavia*. Cambridge, Mass.: Harvard University Press, 1958.
Levinsohn, Florence H. *Belgrade: Among the Serbs*. Chicago: I.R. Dee, 1994.
Marjanovic, Petar, ed. *1000 Facts about Yugoslavia*. Belgrade: Federal Secretariat for Information, 1963.
Mićunović, Vukašin, et al. *Handbook on Yugoslavia*. Belgrade: Federal Secretariat for Information, 1987.
Nyrop, Richard F., ed. *Yugoslavia, A Country study*. Washington, D.C.: Headquarters, Department of the Army, 1982.
Rakić, Kosta. *Socialist Republic of Serbia*. Belgrade: Jugoslovenska Revija, 1985.
Reifsnyder, William E. *Adventuring in the Alps: The Sierra Club Travel Guide to the Alpine regions of France, Switzerland, Germany, Austria, Liechtenstein, Italy, and Yugoslavia*. San Francisco: Sierra Club Books, 1986.
*Tips for Travelers to Eastern Europe and Yugoslavia*. Washington, D.C.: United States Department of State, 1987.
*Yugoslavia*. Geneva: Nagel Publishers, 1974.
*Yugoslavia. Background notes*. Washington, D.C.: United States Department of State, 1989.
*Yugoslavia, Post Report*. Washington, D.C.: U.S. Department of State, 1981.

## Statistical Abstracts

*Annuaire statistique 1929–40*. Herts: Bishops Stortford, Chadwyck-Healey, Herts, 1975.
*Annual Reports of the National Bank*. Belgrade: NBJ, 1946– .
*MAP (Monthly Analysis and Prognosis)*. Belgrade: Institute of Economic Sciences, 1994– .
OECD. *Yugoslavia, annual reports*. Paris: OECD, 1963–1990.
Sündhaussen, Holm. *Historische Statistik Serbiens, 1834–1914: mit europäschen Vergleichsdaten*. München: R. Oldenburg, 1989.
*Statistički godišnjak Jugoslavije* [*Statistical Yearbook of Yugoslavia*]. Belgrade: Savezni zavod za statistiku, 1954–1991.
*Statistički godišnjak Jugoslavije* [*Statistical Yearbook of Yugoslavia*]. Belgrade: Savezni zavod za statistiku, 1992– .
*Statistički godišnjak Jugoslavije 1918–1988* [*Statistical Yearbook of Yugoslavia, 1918–1988*]. Belgrade: Savezni zavod za statistiku, 1989.

*Statistički godišnjak Kraljevine Srbije* [*Statistical Yearbook of the Kingdom of Serbia*]. Belgrade: Uprava državne statistike, 1903–1910.

*Statistika spoljne trgovine SFRJ* [*Statistical Yearbook of Foreign Trade of the SFRJ*]. Belgrade: Savezni zavod za statistiku, 1946–1991.

*Yugoslavia—Quarterly Economic Review*. London: Economist Intelligence Unit.

United Nations Economic Commission for Europe. *Yugoslavia, Annual Reports*. Europe; ECE.

## 2. CULTURAL

Andrić, Ivo. *The Bridge on the Drina*. New York: Macmillan, 1959.

Bogdanovic, D. and Dejan Medakovic. *Chilandar*. Belgrade: Republički zavod za zaštitu spomenika kulture, 1978.

Butler, Thomas. *Monumenta Serbocroatica*. Ann Arbor, Mich.: Michigan Slavic Publications, 1980.

Castellan, Yvonne. *La culture serbe au seuil de l'indépendence (1800–1840) essai d'analyse psychologique d'une culture a distance temporelle*. Paris: Press universitaires de France, 1967.

Cvijić, Jovan. *Psihičke osobine Južnih Slovena* [*Psychological Characteristics of the South Slavs*]. Beograd: Geca Kon, 1931.

Ćurčić, Slobodan. *Gračanica: King Milutin's Church and Its Place in Late Byzantine Architecture*. University Park: Pennsylvania State University Press, 1979.

Ćurčija-Prodanović, Nada. *Heros of Serbia: Folk Ballads*. New York: H.Z. Walck, 1963.

Čajkanović, Veselin. *O srspkom vrhovnom bogu* [*On Serbian Supreme God*], Srpska Kraljevska Akademija, "Posebna izdanja", knj. cxxxii. Belgrade: Štamparija "Mlada Srbija", 1941.

Djilas, Milovan. *Njegoš*. Translated by Michael B. Petrovich. New York: Harcourt, Brace & World, 1966.

Edwards, Lovett F., trans. and ed. *The Memoirs of Prota Mateja Nenadović*. Oxford: Oxford University Press, 1969.

French, Reginald Michael. *Serbian Church Life*. New York: MacMillan, 1942.

Goulding, Daniel J. *Liberated Cinema: The Yugoslav Experience*. Bloomington: Indiana University Press, 1985.

Halpern, Joel M. *A Serbian Village*. New York: Harper & Row, 1967.

Halpern, Joel M., and Barbara Halpern Kerewsky. *A Serbian Village in Historical Perspective*. New York: Harper & Row, 1972.

*The History of Serbian Culture*. Edgware: Porthill Publishers, 1995.

Holton, Milne and Vasa Mihailovich. *Serbian Poetry from the Beginnings to the Present*. New Haven, Conn.: Yale Center for International and Area Studies, 1988.

Kandić, Olivera. *The Monastery of Gradac*. Belgrade: Institute for Protection of Cultural Monuments, 1987.

Kindersley, Anne. *The Mountains of Serbia*. London: J. Murray, 1976.

Koljević, Svetozar. *The Epic in the Making*. New York: Oxford University Press, 1980.

Labon, Joanna. *Balkan Blues: Writing out of Yugoslavia*. Evanston, Ill.: Northwestern University Press, 1995.

Lord, Albert B., ed. "The Multinational Literature of Yugoslavia." *Review of National Literature*, V, no. 1 (Spring 1974).

Low, David H. *The Ballads of Marko Kraljevich*. New York: Greenwood Press, 1968.

Lukić, Sveta. *Contemporary Yugoslav Literature: A Sociopolitical Approach*. Urbana: University of Illinois Press, 1972.

Majstorovic, Stevan. *Cultural Policy in Yugoslavia: Self-management and Culture*. Paris: UNESCO, 1980.

Matejić, Mateja, and Dragan Milivojević. *An Anthology of Medieval Serbian Literature in English*. Columbus, Ohio: Slavica Publishers, 1978.

Medakovic, D., and D. Milosevic. *Serbs in the History of Trieste*. Belgrade: Republički zavod za zaštitu kulture, 1987.

Mihailovich, Vasa D., and Mateja Matejic, eds. *Yugoslav Literature in English: A Bibliography of Translations and Criticism 1821–1975*. Cambridge, Mass.: Slavica Publishers, 1976.

Mijatovich, Chedomille. *The Memoirs of a Balkan Diplomatist*. London: Cassell & Company, 1917.

Mikasinovich, Branko, ed. *Yugoslav Fantastic Prose*. Belgrade: Vajat, 1991.

———. *Modern Yugoslav Satire*. Merrik, N.Y.: Cross Cultural Communications, 1979.

Milich, Zorka. *A Stranger's Supper: An Oral History of Centenarian Women in Montenegro*. New York: Twayne Publishers-Prentice Hall, 1995.

Milivojevic, Dragan, and Vasa Mihailovic, eds. *Yugoslav Linguistics in English 1900–1980:* A *Bibliography*. Columbus, Ohio: Slavica Publishers, 1980.

Milojkovic-Đuric, Jelena. *Tradition and Avant-Garde: Literature and Art in Serbian Culture, 1900–1918*. Boulder, Colo.: East European Monographs; New York: Distributed by Columbia University Press, 1988.

Morison, Walter A. *The Revolt of the Serbs against the Turks (1804–1813)* [*Translation of Ballads*]. Cambridge: Cambridge University Press, 1942.

Mugge, Maximilian August. *Serbian Folk Songs, Fairy Tales and Proverbs*. London: Drane's, 1916.

Nenadović, Matija. *The Memoirs of Prota Matija Nenadović*. Edited and translated Lovett F. Edwards. Oxford: Clarendon Press, 1969.

Nicholai, Bishop. *The Life of St. Sava*. Collected Works, Book XII. Grayslake, IL: Western European Diocese, 1984.

Njegos, P. P. *The Mountain Wreath*. Irvine, Calif.: C.Sh; acks, Jr., 1986.

Noyes, George R., trans. and ed. *The Life and Adventures of Dimitrije Obradović*. Berkeley: University of California Press, 1953.

Noyes, George Rapall, and Leonard Bacon. *Heroic Ballads of Serbia*. Boston: Sherman, French & Company, 1913.

Palavestra, Predrag. *Kritika i avangarda u modernoj srpskoj književnosti: književne teme VI* [*Critic and Avant-garde in Modern Serbian Literature: Literary Themes VI*]. Belgrade: Prosveta, 1979.

Perović, Sreten. *Darovi scene* [*Gifts of Stage*]. Titograd: Pobjeda, 1986.

Petkovich, Sreten. *The Patriarchate of Peć*. Belgrade: Zavod za zaštitu spomenika kulture, 1982.
Petrovich, W. M. *Hero Tales and Legends of the Serbians*. London: George Harrap & Company, 1915.
Popovich, Tanya. *Prince Marko: The Hero of South Slavic Epics*. Syracuse, N.Y.: Syracuse University Press, 1988.
Pupin, Mihailo, ed. *Serbian Orthodox Church*. London: John Murray, 1918.
Ramet, Sabrina P. *Balkan Babel: Politics, Culture, and Religion in Yugoslavia*. Boulder, Colo.: Westview Press, 1992.
Rašić, Mirko R. *The Postal History and Postage Stamps of Serbia*. New York: Theodore E. Steinway Memorial Publication Fund, 1979.
*Serbian Orthodox Church—Its Past & Present*. Belgrade: 1965. 6 vols.
Slater, Thomas J. *Handbook of Soviet and East European Films and Filmmakers*. New York: Greenwood Press, 1992.
Slijepčević, Dr. Đoko. *Istorija Srpske pravoslavne crkve* [*History of the Serbian Orthodox Church*]. 3 vols. Munich, Hümelstir: Iskra, 1962–1986.
Srejović, Dragoslav. *Europe's First Monumental Sculpture: New Discoveries at Lepenski Vir*. New York: Stein and Day, 1973.
Stewart, Cecil. *Serbian Legacy*. New York: George Allen and Unwin, 1959.
Stoianovich, Traian. *Balkan Worlds: The First and Last Europe*. New York: M.E. Sharpe, 1994.
Todorovich, Slavko. *The Chilandarians: Serbian Monks on the Green Mountain*. Boulder, Colo.: East European Monographs. 1989.
Tringham, R., and D. Krstić. *Selevac: A Neolithic Village in Yugoslavia*. Los Angeles: Institute of Archeology, University of California, Los Angeles, 1990.
Velimirovich, Bishop Nicholai D. *The Serbian People as a Servant of God*. Grayslake, IL: 1988.
Voich, D., Jr., and L. P. Stepina, eds. *Cross-Cultural Analysis of Values and Political Economy Issues*. Westport, Conn.: Praeger, 1994.
Vucinich, Wayne, and Thomas Emmert, eds. *Kosovo: Legacy of a Medieval Battle*. Minneapolis: University of Minnesota, 1991.
West, Rebecca. *Black Lamb and Grey Falcon: A Journey through Yugoslavia*. 2 vols. New York: Viking Press, 1941. 2 vols.
Wiles, James, trans. *The Mountain Wreath of Nyegosh, Prince Bishop of Montenegro*. New York: Greenwood Reprint, 1970.
Wilson, Duncan. *The Life and Times of Vuk Stefanović Karadžić 1787–1864*. Oxford: Oxford University Press, 1970.
Wolff, Robert Lee. *The Balkans in Our Time*. New York: W.W. Norton & Co., 1967.
Yelen, Anne. *En Yougoslavie orthodoxe*. Paris: J. Grassin, 1970.
Zotović, Ljubica. *Les cultes orientaux sur le territoire de la Mesie suprieure*. Leiden: E. J. Brill, 1966.

## 3. ECONOMIC

Allock, John, B. *The Collectivization of Yugoslav Agriculture and the Myth of Peasant Resistance*. Bradford: University of Bradford, 1981.
———. "The Development of Capitalism in Yugoslavia," In *An Historical*

*Geography of the Balkans*, edited by F. W. Carter. London: Academic Press, 1977.

Arisien, Patrick F. R. *Joint Ventures in Yugoslav Industry*. Brookfield, Vt.: Gower, 1985.

Bajt, Aleksander. "Investment Cycles in European Socialist Economies: A Review Article." *Journal of Economic Literature* 9 (1971): 53–63.

Bauwens, Jan G. *Industrial Co-operation and Investment in Yugoslavia*. Washington, D.C.: European Community Information Service, 1986.

Berend, Iván T., and Ránki György. *The European Periphery and Industrialization 1780–1914*. Budapest: Akadémiai Kiadó, 1989.

———. *Economic Development in East-Central Europe in the 19th and 20th Centuries*. New York: Columbia University Press, 1974.

Bonin, John. *Economics of Cooperation and the Labor Managed Economy*. New York: Harwood Academic Publishers, 1987.

Bookman-Zarkovic, Milica. *The Political Economy of Discontinuous Development*. New York: Praeger, 1991.

Bošković, Blagoje, and David Dašić. *Socialist Self-Management in Yugoslavia, 1950–1980*. Belgrade: Savremena administracija, 1980.

Calic, Marie-Janine. *Sozialgeschichte Serbiens, 1915–1941: der aufhaltsame Fortschritt während der Industrialisierung*. Munich: R. Oldenburg, 1994.

Canapa, Marie Paule. *Réformé économique et socialisme en Yougoslavie*. Paris: A. Colin, 1970.

Chittle, Charles R. *Industrialization and Manufactured Export Expansion in a Worker-Managed Economy: The Yugoslav Experience*. Tübingen, Germany: Mohr, 1979.

Cochrane, Nancy. *Trade Liberalization in Yugoslavia and Poland*. Washington, D.C.: U.S. Dept. of Agriculture, 1990.

Čobeljić, Nikola. *Privreda Jugoslavije: rast, struktura i funkcionisanje* [*The Economy of Yugoslavia: Growth, Structure, and Functioning*]. 2 vols. Belgrade: Savremena administracija, 1974.

Dimitrijević, Sergije. *Strani kapital u privredi Bivše Jugoslavije* [*Foreign Capital in the Economy of the Former Yugoslavia*]. Belgrade: Društvo ekonomista Srbije, 1958.

Dirlam, J., and J. Plummer. *An Introduction to the Yugoslav Economy*. Columbus, Ohio: Charles E. Merrill, 1972.

Dyker, David. *Yugoslavia: Socialism, Development, and Debt*. New York: Routledge, 1990.

Đorđević, Dimitrije. *Carinski rat Austro-Ugarske i Srbije 1906–1911* [*Tariff War between Austria-Hungary and Serbia 1906–1911*]. Belgrade: Istorijski institut, 1962.

Estrin, Saul. *Self-management: Economic Theory and Yugoslav Practice*. New York: Cambridge University Press, 1983.

Flakiersky, Henryk. *The Economic System and Income Distribution in Yugoslavia*. Armonk, N.Y.: M.E. Sharpe, 1989.

Grđić, Gojko. *Razvoj privrede Srbije i Vojvodine* [*Development of Economy of Serbia and Vojvodina*]. Belgrade: Ekonomski institut NR Srbije, 1953.

Hamilton, F. E. Ian. *Yugoslavia: Patterns of Economic Activity*. New York: Praeger, 1968.

Horvat, Branko. *The Yugoslav Economic System*. White Plains, N.Y.: International Arts and Sciences Press, 1976.

———. *Business Cycles in Yugoslavia*. White Plains, N.Y.: International Arts and Sciences Press, 1971.

Jancar, Barbara Wolfe. *Environmental Management in the Soviet Union and Yugoslavia: Structure and Regulation in Federal Communist States*. Durham, N.C.: Duke University Press, 1987.

Kaser, M. C., and E. A. Radice. *The Economic History of Eastern Europe 1919–1975*. 2 vols. Oxford: Clarendon Press, 1986.

Lampe, R. John, and Marvin R. Jackson. *Balkan Economic History, 1550–1950*. Bloomington: Indiana University Press, 1982.

Lydall, Harold, *Yugoslavia in Crisis*. New York: Oxford University Press, 1989.

Macesich, George. *Yugoslavia: The Theory and Practice of Development Planning*. Charlottesville: University Press of Virginia, 1964.

Macura, Miloš. *Stanovništvo kao činilac privrednog razvoja Jugoslavije*. Belgrade: Nolit, 1958.

Mihailović, Kosta. *Ekonomska stvarnost Jugoslavije* [*Economic Reality of Yugoslavia*]. Belgrade: Ekonomika, 1982.

———. *Proizvodne snage NR Srbije* [Production Forces of Serbia]. Belgrade: Ekonomski institut, 1953.

Mihailović, Kosta, and Vasilije Krestić. *Memorandum SANU; Odgovori na kritike* [*Memorandum SANU; Responses to Criticism*]. Belgrade: SANU, 1995.

Milenkovitch, Deborah D. *Plan and Market in Yugoslav Economic Thought*. New Haven, Conn.: Yale University Press, 1971.

Milić, Danica. *Strani kapital u rudarstvu Srbije do 1918* [*Foreign Capital in Serbian Mining Sector until 1918*]. Belgrade: Istorijski institut, 1970.

Miller, Robert F. *External Factors in Yugoslav Political Development*. Occasional Paper no. 14. Canberra: Department of Political Science, Research School of Social Sciences, Australian National University, 1977.

Milovanović, Milovan. *Naši trgovinski ugovori* [*Our Trade Agreements*]. Belgrade: Parna radikalna štamparija, 1895.

Mirković, Mijo. *Ekonomska historija Jugoslavije* [*Economic History of Yugoslavia*]. Zagreb: Informator, 1968.

Mladek, J.V., E. Šturc, and M. Wyczalkowski. "The Change in the Yugoslav Economic System." *International Monetary Fund Staff Papers* 2, no. 3 (November 1952): 407–38.

Monthias, John Michael. "Economic Reform and Retreat in Yugoslavia." *Foreign Affairs* 37, no. 2 (January 1959): 293–305.

Moore, John H. *Growth with Self-Management: Yugoslav Industrialization* 1952–1975. Stanford, Calif.: Hoover Institution Press, 1980.

Mulina, T., M. Macura, and M. Rašević. *Stanovništvo i zaposlenost u dugoročnom razvoju Jugoslavije* [*Population and Employment in the Long-Term Development of Yugoslavia*]. Belgrade: Ekonomski institut, 1981.

Nedeljković, Milorad. *Istorija srpskih državnih dugova* [*History of Serbian Public Debt*]. Belgrade: Štampa, 1909.

Ocić, Časlav. *Ekonomika regionalnog razvoja Jugoslavije*. [*Economics of Regional Development of Yugoslavia*]. Belgrade: Ekonomika, 1998.

OECD Economic Surveys. *Yugoslavia, 1962–90*. Paris: Organization for Economic Cooperation and Development, 1963–1990.

Pejković-Aleksić, Ljiljana. *Odnosi Srbije sa Francuskom i Engleskom 1903–1914* [*Relations between Serbia, France, and England, 1903–1914*]. Belgrade: Istorijski institut, 1965.

Popović, Tomislav. *Osnove tranzicije i program privatizacije* [*The Basics of Transition and Program of Privatization*]. Belgrade: Institut ekonomskih nauka, 1996.

Sacks, Stephen R. *Self-Management and Efficiency: Large Corporations in Yugoslavia*. London: Allen and Unwin, 1983.

———. *Entry of New Competitors in Yugoslav Market Socialism*. Berkeley: Institute of International Studies, University of California, 1973.

Sapir, André. "Economic Reform and Migration in Yugoslavia: An Econometric Model." *Journal of Development Economics* 9 (1981): 149–187.

Savezni društveni savet. *Dugoročni program stabilizacije* [*Long-Term Stabilization Program*]. Belgrade: Privredni pregled, 1984.

Schrenk, Martin, Cyrus Ardalan, and N. El Tatawy. *Yugoslavia: Self-Management Socialism and the Challenges of Development*. Baltimore: Johns Hopkins University Press for the World Bank, 1979.

Singleton, F., and B. Carter. *The Economy of Yugoslavia*. New York: St. Martins Press, 1982.

Sirc, Ljubo. *Yugoslav Economy under Self-Management*. New York: St. Martins Press, 1979.

Stamenković, Stojan, and Aleksandra Pošarac, eds. *Makroekonomska stabilizacija: alternativni pristup* [*Macroeconomic Stabilization: An Alternative Approach*]. Belgrade: Institut ekonomskih nauka, 1994.

Stojanovic, Radmila. *The Functioning of the Yugoslav Economy*. Armonk, N.Y.: M.E. Sharpe, 1982.

———. *Yugoslav Economists on Problems of a Socialist Economy*. New York: International Arts and Sciences Press, 1964.

Sugar, Peter. *The Industrialization of Bosnia-Hercegovina, 1878–1918*. Seattle: University of Washington, 1963.

Šuster, Željan E. "Serbia's Economic Relations with the West in the Decade before World War I." *Serbian Studies*, 7, no. 2, (Fall 1993):

Todorović, Milan. *Naša ekonomna politika* [*Our Economic Policy*]. Belgrade: Geca Kon, 1925.

Tyson, Laura D'Andrea. *The Yugoslav Economic System and Its Performance in the 1970s*. Berkeley, Calif.: Institute for International Studies, University of California, 1980.

Tyson, Laura D'Andrea, and Egon Neurberger. "The Transmission of International Disturbances to Yugoslavia." In *The Impact of International Economic Disturbances on the Soviet Union and Eastern Europe*, edited by Egon Neurberger and Laura D'Andrea Tyson. New York: Pergamon Press, 1980.

Uvalic, Milica. *Investment and Property Rights in Yugoslavia: The Long Transition to a Market Economy*. New York: Cambridge University Press, 1992.

Vanek, Jaroslav. *The Economics of Workers' Management: A Yugoslav Case*. London: Allen and Unwin, 1972.

Vučo, Nikola. "Yugoslavia: Economic Development 1919–1944." In *St Antony's Papers on East European Economics* 31. Oxford: St Antony's College, 1973.

———. *Agrarna kriza u Jugoslaviji 1930–1934* [*Agricultural Crisis in Yugoslavia 1930–1934*]. Belgrade: Prosveta, 1968.

———. *Privredna istorija Srbije do prvog svetskog rata* [*Economic History of Serbia until World War* I]. Belgrade: Naučna knjiga, 1955.

———. *Privredna istorija naroda FNRJ—do prvog svetskog rata* [*Economic History of the Peoples of Yugoslavia Until World War I*]. Belgrade: Naučna knjiga, 1948.

Wachtel, Howard. *Workers' Management and Wages in Yugoslavia*. Ithaca, N.Y.: Cornell University Press, 1973.

Woodward, Susan L. *Socialist Unemployment: The Political Economy of Yugoslavia* 1945–1990. Princeton, N.J.: Princeton University Press, 1995.

World Bank. *Yugoslavia: Development with Decentralization*. London: Johns Hopkins University Press, 1975.

## 4. FOREIGN RELATIONS

Armacost, Michael H. *U.S.-Yugoslav Relations*. Washington, D.C.: U.S. Department of State, Editorial Division, 1986.

Armstrong, Hamilton F. *Tito and Goliath*. New York: Macmillan, 1951.

Dedijer, Vladimir. *The Battle Stalin Lost: Memoirs of Yugoslavia, 1948–1953*. New York: Viking Press, 1971.

Halperin, Ernst. *The Triumphant Heretic; Tito's Struggle Against Stalin*. London: Heinemann, 1958.

Hoptner, Jacob B. *Yugoslavia in Crisis, 1934–1941*. New York: Columbia University Press, 1962.

Hunter, Brian. *Soviet-Yugoslav Relations, 1948–1972: A Bibliography of Soviet, Western, and Yugoslav Comment and Analysis*. New York: Garland Publishing, 1976.

Lampe, John R., Russel O. Prickett, and Ljubiša Adamović. *Yugoslav-American Economic Relations since World War II*. Durham, N.C.: Duke University Press, 1990.

Littlefield, Frank C. *Germany and Yugoslavia, 1933–1941: The German Conquest of Yugoslavia*. Boulder, Colo.: East European Monographs, 1988.

Pupo, Raoul. *Fra Italia e Iugoslavia: saggi sulla questione di Trieste (1945–1954)*. Udine: Del Bianco Editore, 1989.

Rubinstein, Alvin Z. *Yugoslavia and the Nonaligned World*. Princeton, N.J.: Princeton University Press, 1970.

Tihany, Leslie C. *The Baranya Dispute, 1918–1921: Diplomacy in the Vortex of Ideologies*. Boulder, Colo.: East European Quarterly, 1978.

Wheeler, Mark C. *Britain and the War for Yugoslavia, 1940–1943*. Boulder, Colo.: East European Monographs, 1980.

Woodhouse, Edward. *Italy and the Yugoslavs*. Boston: Richard Badger, 1920.

## 5. HISTORY

### General

Bataković, Dušan T. *The Serbs of Bosnia & Herzegovina: History and Politics*. Paris: Dialogue, 1996.

———. *La Yougoslavie: Nations, Religions, Ideologies*. Lausanne: L'Age d'Homme, 1994.

———. *The Kosovo Chronicles*. Belgrade: Plato Books, 1992.

———. *Načertanije Ilije Garašanina 1844*. Belgrade: MJV, 1991.

Djordjevic, Dimitrije, ed. *The Creation of Yugoslavia, 1914–1918*. Santa Barbara, Calif.: Clio Press, 1980.

Donia, Robert J., John V.A. Fine, Jr. *Bosnia and Hercegovina: A Tradition Betrayed*. New York: Columbia University Press, 1994.

Dragnich, Alex N. *Serbs and Croats: The Promise and the Failure of Yugoslavia*. New York: Harcourt Brace Jovanovich, 1992.

Friedman, Francine. *The Bosnian Muslims: Denial of a Nation*. Boulder, colo.: Westview Press, 1996.

*Istorija Srpskog naroda* [*History of the Serbian Peoples*]. 10 vols. Belgrade: SKZ, 1988.

Kanitz, Feliz P. *Das Königreich der Serben von den altesten Zeiten bis 1815*. Leipzig: W. Laufer, 1878.

Kazimirović, Vasa. *Srbija i Jugoslavija 1914–1945*. 4 vols. [*Serbia and Yugoslavia 1914–1945*]. Kragujevac: Prizma, 1995.

Lampe, John R. *Yugoslavia as History: Twice There Was a Country*. Cambridge: Cambridge University Press, 1996.

Malcolm, Noel. *Bosnia: A Short History*. New York: New York University Press, 1996.

Mitrović, Jeremija. *Istorija Srba* [*History of the Serbs*]. Belgrade: CURO, 1994.

Ostrogorski, Georgije. *History of the Byzantine State*. New Brunswick, N.J.: Rutgers University Press, 1969.

Pinson, Mark, ed. *The Muslims of Bosnia-Herzegovina: Their Historic Development From the Middle Ages to the Dissolution of Yugoslavia*. Cambridge, Mass: Distributed for the Center for Middle Eastern Studies of Harvard University by Harvard University Press, 1994.

Pogodin, A. L. *Istoriia Serbii*. St. Petersburg: Brokquaz-Efron, 1909.

Ranke, Leopold. *The History of Servia and the Servian Revolution*. London: Henry H. Bann, 1853.

Singleton, F.B. *Twentieth-Century Yugoslavia*. London: Macmillan, 1976.

Stanojević, Stanoje. *Istorija srpskog naroda* [*History of the Serbian People*]. Belgrade: Napredak, 1925.

Temperley, Harold W. V. *History of Serbia*. London: G.Bell, 1917.

Wilson, Sir Duncan. *Tito's Yugoslavia*. Cambridge: Cambridge University Press, 1979.

### From the Arrival on the Balkan Penninsula to the Turkish Occupation, the 5th–15th Century

Emmert, Thomas A. *Serbian Golghota: Kosovo, 1389*. Boulder, Colo.: East European Monographs, 1990.

Fine, John V. A., Jr. *The Early Medieval Balkans*. Ann Arbor: University of Michigan Press, 1983.

Jagić, Vatroslav. "Ein Kapitel aus der Geschihte der Südslavichen Sprächen." *Archiv für slavische Philologie* 17 (1895): 47–87.

Jiriček, Konstantin. *Geschichte der Serben*. Vol. I (to 1371). Gottha: Allgemeine staatengeschichte, 1911. Vol. II (1371–1537). Gotha: 1918.

Jovanović, Lj. *Iz prošlosti Bosne i Hercegovine* [*From the Past of Bosnia and Hercegovina*]. Belgrade: Izdanje uredništva "Narodnih novina," 1909.

Kovačević, Lj. "Despot Stefan Lazarević za vreme turskih mepusobica (1402–1413)." [*Despot Stefan Lazarević in Times of a Struggle Among the Turks*]. *Otadžbina 4 and 5* (1880):

Miklosich, F. *Monumenta Serbica*. Viennae: Apud Guilemum Braumüler, 1858.

Novaković, Stojan. *Zakonik Stefan Dušana cara srpskog 1349 i 1354* [*Code of Laws of Serbian Tsar Dušan* 1349–1354]. Belgrade: Državna štamparija, 1898.

———. *Prvi osnovi slovenske književnosti među balkanskim Slovenima* [*The Beginnings of the Slavic Literature among the Balkan Slavs*]. Belgrade: Srpska kraljevska akademija, 1893.

———. *Srbi i Turci XIV i XV veka* [*Serbs and Turks of 14th and 15th Centuries*]. Belgrade: Štamparija "Prosveta" 1893.

Obolensky, Dimitri. *The Byzantine Commonwealth—Eastern Europe 500–1453*. London: Oxford University Press, 1971.

Peisker, T. "The Expansion of the Slavs." *The Cambridge Medieval History II*. 1913.

Rački, Franjo. *Documenta historiae Chroaticae periodum antiquam illustrantia*. Zagreb: Jugoslavenska akademija znanosti i umjetnosti, 1877.

Ruvarac, I. "*Tri dodatka k raspravi Banovanje Tvrtka bana* [*Three Contributions to the Study of the Rule of Ban Tvrtko*]." *Glasnik Zemaljskog Muzeja 6* (1894): 611–620.

———. *O knezu Lazaru* [*On Prince Lazar*]. Novi Sad: Štamparija Dr. Svetozara Miletića, 1887.

Smičiklas, T. *Codex Diplomaticus regni Croatiae, Dalmatiae et Slavoniae*. vols II–XIV. Zagreb: Jugoslavenska akademija znanosti i umjetnosti, 1904.

Soulis, George C. *The Serbs and Byzantium during the Reign of Tsar Stephen Dušan (1331–1355) and His Successors*. Washington, D.C.: Dumbarton Oaks Library and Collection, 1984.

Stanojević, Stanoje. *Vizantija i Srbi. II Kolonizacija Slovena na Balkanskom poluostrvu* [*Byzantium and the Serbs. Colonization of Slavs on the Balkan Peninsula*]. Novi Sad: Matica Srpska, 1906.

———. *Vizantija i Srbi. I Balkansko poluostrvo do VII veka* [*Byzantium and the Serbs. Balkan Peninsula until the Seventh Century*]. Novi Sad: Matica srpska, 1903.

———. "Die Biographie Stefan Lazarević's on Konstantin dem Philosophen als Geschichtsquelle." *Archiv für Slavische Philologie* 18 (1896).

Stoianovich, Traian. *Balkan Worlds: The First and Last Europe*. Armonk, N.Y.: M. E. Sharpe, 1994.

Thaloczy, Layosz et al. *Acta ce diplomata res Albanie mediae aetatis illustrantia I*. Vindobonae: Typ. Adolphi Holzhauzen, 1913.

## From the Turkish Occupation to the National Revolution, the 15th Century–1804

Agatonović, R., and P. Spasić. *Srpski ustanci protiv Turaka u vezi s narodnim seobama u tuđinu od 1459–1814 god.* [*Serbian Rebellions against the Turks and Migrations 1459–1814*]. 2 vols. Belgrade: Štamparija Svetozara Markovića 1895–1896.

Dragnich, Alex N. (ed.) *Serbia's Historical Heritage*. Boulder, Colo.: East European Monographs, 1994.

Đurđev, Branislav. *Turska vlast u Crnoj Gori u XVI i XVII veku* [*Turkish Rule in Montenegro in the 16th and 17th Centuries*]. Sarajevo: Akademija nauka BiH, 1964.

Fine, John V. A., Jr. *The Late Medieval Balkans*. Ann Arbor: University of Michigan Press, 1987.

Ivić, A. *Iz prošlosti Srba Žumberčana* [*From the Past of the Serbs from Žumeberak*]. Belgrade: SKA, 1923.

———. *Seoba Srba u Hrvatsku i Slavoniju* [*Migration of the Serbs to Slavonia*]. Sremski Karlovci: Manastirska štamparija,1909.

Jelavich, Barbara. *History of the Balkans*. Cambridge: Cambridge University Press, 1983.

Maticki, Miodrag. *Srpskohrvatska graničarska epika* [*Serbo-Croatian Epic of the Borderlands*]. Belgrade: Rad, 1974.

Mijatović, Čed. "Šta je želeo i radio srpski narod u XVI veku." [What Serbian People Wanted to Do and What They Did in the 16th Century]. *Godišnjica* 1 (1877): 51–89.

———. "Pre trista godina."[Before Three Hundred Years]. *Glasnik* 36 (1872): 155–220.

Ninčić, Momčilo. *Istorija agrarno-pravnih odnosa srpskih težaka pod Turcima* [*History of Legal Status of Serbian Peasants Under the Turkish Rule*]. Belgrade: Geca Kon, 1903.

Novaković, S. *Tursko carstvo pred srpski ustanak 1780–1804* [*Turkish Empire on the Eve of Serbian Rebellion 1780–1804*]. Belgrade: Srpska književna zadruga, 1906.

———. *Srpska baština u starim turskim izvorima* [*Serbian Heritage in Old Turkish Sources*]. Belgrade: Državna štamparija, 1893.

Pavlović, D. "Prilog istoriji Kočine krajine i Mihaljevićevog frajkora." [A Contribution to the History of Kočina krajina and Mihaljević's Volunteers]. *Glas* 68 (1904): 109–158.

Popović, Dušan J. *Velika seoba Srba 1690* [*Great Migration of Serbs 1690*]. Belgrade: SKZ, 1954.

———. *O Hajducima* [*On Hadjuks*]. 2 vols. Belgrade: Narodna štamparija, 1931.

Radonić, J. *Graf Đorđe Branković i njegovo vreme* [*Đorđe Branković and His Times*]. Belgrade: Srpska kraljevska akademija, 1911.
Rothenburg, Gunter E. *The Austrian Military Border In Croatia, 1740–1881*. Chicago: University of Chicago Press, 1966.
———. *The Austrian Military Border in Croatia, 1522–1747*. Chicago: University of Chicago Press, 1960.
Ruvarac, I. *Montenegrina*. Zemun: Štamparija Jovana Puljo, 1899.
———. *O Pećkim patrijarsima od 1557 do 1690* [*On the Patriarchs of Peć From 1557 to 1690*]. Zadar: I. Radicke, 1888.
Samardžić, R. *Mehmed Sokolović i njegovo vreme* [*Mehmed Sokolović and His Times*]. Belgrade: Srpska književna zadruga, 1971.
Stanojević, Gligor. *Crna Gora pred stvaranje države 1773–1796* [*Montenegro on the Eve of Statehood 1773–1796*]. Belgrade: Istorijski institut, 1962.
Sugar, Peter F. *Southeastern Europe under Ottoman Rule 1453–1803*. Seattle: University of Washington Press, 1977.
Tomić, J. *Iz istorije senjskih uskoka 1604–1607*. [*From History of Uskoks of Senj*]. Novi Sad: Štamparija srpske knjižare braće M. Popovića, 1907.
———. "Politički odnos Crne Gore prema Turskoj 1528–1684 [Policy of Montenegro toward Turkey 1528–1684]" *Glas* LXVIII (1904): 1–107.
———. Danak u krvi [*Blood Tribute*]. Belgrade: Štamparija Đure Stanojeva, 1898.
Vucinich, Wayne S. *The Ottoman Empire: Its Record and Legacy*. New York: 1965.
Vucinich, Wayne S., and T. Emmert, eds. *Kosovo: Legacy of a Medieval Battle*. Minneapolis: University of Minnesota Press, 1991.
Vukićević, M. *Znameniti Srbi—Muslimani* [*Prominent Serbs—Muslims*]. Belgrade: Srpska književna zadruga, 1906.
———. *Srpski narod, crkva i sveštenstvo u turskom carstvu od 1459–1557 god* [*Serbian People, Church and Ministry in the Turkish Empire From 1459–1557*]. Belgrade: Parna radikalna štamparija, 1896.
Waniček, F. *Specialgeschichte der Militärgränze*. 1883.
Winnifrith, Tom J. *The Vlachs: The History of a Balkan People*. London: Duckworth, 1987.

## From the First Serbian Insurrection to the Creation of the First Yugoslav State, 1804–1918

Avakumović, I. "Literature on the First Serbian Insurrection (1804–1813)." *Journal of Central European Affairs* XIII (October 1953): 256–260.
Barby, Henry. *La Guerre Serbo-Bulgare Brégalnitsa 1913* [Bregalnica; Serbo-Bulgarian War 1913]. Paris: Bernard Grasset, 1914.
Cvijić, Jovan. *Balkanski rat i Srbija* [*Balkan War and Serbia*]. Belgrade: Državna štamparija Kraljevine Srbije, 1912.
Ćorović, Vladimir. *Odnosi između Srbije i Austro-Ugarske u XX veku* [*Relations Between Serbia and Austria-Hungary in the 20th Century*]. Belgrade: Državna štamparija, 1936.
Ćosić, Dobrica. *A Time of Death*. 2 vols. New York: Harcourt Brace Jovanovich, 1978.

Čubrilović, Vasa. *Srbija od 1858 do 1878 godine* [*Serbia From 1858 to 1878*]. Belgrade: Geca Kon, 1938.

Despalatović, Elinor Murray. *Ljudevit Gaj and the Illyrian Movement*. Boulder, Colo.: East European Monographs, 1975.

Djordjevic, Dimitrije, and Stephen Fisher-Galati. *The Balkan Revolutionary Tradition*. Boulder, Colo.: East European Monographs, 1981.

Djordjević, Vladan. *Das Ende der Obrenovitch; Beiträge zur Geschichte Serbiens, 1897–1900*. Leipzig: S. Hirzel, 1905.

Donia, Robert J. *Islam under the Double Eagle: The Muslims of Bosnia and Hercegovina, 1878–1914*. Boulder, Colo.: East European Monographs, 1981.

Dragnich, Alex N. *The Development of Parliamentary Government in Serbia*. Boulder, Colo.: East European Monographs, 1978.

———. *Serbia, Nikola Pašić, and Yugoslavia*. New Brunswick, N.J.: Rutgers University Press, 1974.

Đorđević, Dimitrije. "The 1883 Peasant Uprising in Serbia," *Balkan Studies* 20 (1979): 235–255.

Đorđević, Dimitrije. *Carinski rat Austro-Ugarske i Srbije 1906–1911* [*Tariff War Between Austro-Hungary and Serbia 1906–1911*]. Belgrade: Istorijski institut, 1962.

———. *Milovan Milovanović*. Belgrade: Istorijski institut, 1962.

Đorđević, Tihomir R. Iz *Srbije Kneza Miloša* [*From Prince Miloš's Serbia*]. 2 vols. Belgrade: geca Kon, 1922, 1924.

Edwards, Lovett. F., ed. & trans. *The Memoirs of Prota Matija Nenadović*. Oxford: Oxford University Press, 1969.

Ekmečić, Milorad. *Srbija između srednje Evrope i Evrop*e [*Serbia between Central Europe and Europe*]. Belgrade: Politika, 1992.

———. *Ratni ciljevi Srbije 1914* [*Serbian War Aims in 1914*]. Belgrade: Srpska književna zadruga, 1973.

Feurlicht, R. S. *The Desperate Act: The Assassination of Franz Ferdinand in Sarajevo*. New York: McGraw-Hill, 1968.

Gavrilović, Mihailo. *Miloš Obrenović*. 3 vols. Belgrade: 1908, 1909, 1912.

Gopčević, Spiridon. *Serbien und die Serben*. Leipzig: B. Elisher, 1888.

Grol, Milan. *Iz predratne Srbije: utisci i sećanja o vremenu i ljudima* [*From Serbia before the War: Reflections and Memoirs about the Times and the People*]. Belgrade: Štamparija Drag. Gregorić, 1939.

Helmreich, E. *The Diplomacy of the Balkan Wars*. Cambridge: Harvard University Press, 1938.

Jakšić, Grgur. *Evropa i vaskrs Srbije 1804–1834* [*Europe and Serbia's Resurrection*]. Belgrade: Za narodnu štampariju Mirko Drobac, 1933.

Jakšić, Grgur, Stranjaković, Dragoslav. *Srbija od 1813 do 1858 godine* [*Serbia from 1813 to 1858*]. Belgrade: Geca Kon, 1936.

Jelavich, Charles. *South Slav Nationalisms, Textbooks, and Yugoslav Union before 1914*. Columbus, Ohio: Ohio State University Press, 1990.

Jones, Fortier. *With Serbia into Exile*. New York: Century Co., 1916.

Jovanović, Slobodan. *Moji savremenici* [*My Contemporaries*]. Windsor, Ont.: Avala, 1961.

———. *Vlada Milana Obrenovića* [*Rule of Milan Obrenović*]. 3 vols. Belgrade: Geca Kon, 1926.

———. *Druga vlada Miloša i Mihaila, 1858–1868* [*The Second Rule of Miloš and Mihailo 1858–1868*]. Belgrade: Geca Kon, 1923.

———. *Vlada Aleksandra Obrenovića* [*The Rule of Aleksandar Obrenović*]. 2 vols. Belgrade: Geca Kon, 1922.

———. *Ustavobranitelji i njihova vlada, 1838–1858* [*Constitutionalists and Their Rule 1838–1858*]. Belgrade: Srpska kraljevska akademija, 1912.

———. *Političke i pravne rasprave* [Political and Legal Treatise]. 2 vols. Belgrade: Geca Kon, 1908.

Krestić, Vasilije and Radoš Ljušić. *Programi i statuti srpskih političkih partija do 1918* [*Programs of Serbian Political Parties until 1918*]. Belgrade: Književne novine, 1991.

Laffan, R. G. D. *The Guardians of the Gate*. Oxford: Clarendon Press, 1918.

Lončarević, Dušan A. *Jugoslaviens Entstehung*. Zürich: Amalthea-Verlag, 1929.

MacKenzie, David. *Violent Solutions: Revolutions, Nationalism, and Secret Societies in Europe to 1918*. Lanham, Md.: University Press of America, 1996.

———. *The "Black Hand" on Trial*. Boulder, Colo.: East European Monographs, 1995.

———. *Apis, the Congenial Conspirator: The Life of Colonel Dragutin T. Dimitrijević*. Boulder, Colo.: East European Monographs, 1989.

———. *Ilija Garašanin, Balkan Bismark*. Boulder, Colo.: East European Monographs, 1985.

———. *The Serbs and Russian Pan-Slavism 1875–1878*. Ithaca, N.Y.: Cornell University Press, 1967.

Marković, Svetozar. *Srbija na Istoku* [*Serbia on the East*]. Belgrade: Ujedinjena omladina, 1892.

McClellan, Woodford D. *Svetozar Markovic and Origins of Balkan Socialism*. Princeton, N.J.: Princeton University Press, 1964.

Mijatović, Čedomilj. *The Memoirs of a Balkan Diplomatist*. London: 1917.

———. *A Royal Tragedy: Being the Story of the Assassination of King Alexander and Queen Draga of Serbia*. New York: Dodd, Mead, 1907.

Miller, Nicholas J. *Between Nation and State: Serbian Politics in Croatia Before the First World War*. Pittsburgh, Pa.: University of Pittsburgh Press, 1997.

Nikić, Fedor. *Lokalna uprava Srbije u XIX i XX veku* [*Local Government of Serbia in the 19th and 20th Centuries*]. Belgrade: Geca Kon, 1927.

Ninčić, Momčilo [Momtchilo Nintchitch]. *La crise bosniaque (1908–1909) et les puissances européennes*. 2 vols. Paris: A. Costes, 1937.

Pawlovitch, Stevan K. *Anglo-Russian Rivalry in Serbia, 1837–1839; The Mission of Colonel Hodges*. Paris: Mouton, 1961.

Petrovich, Michael Boro. *A History of Modern Serbia 1804–1918*. 2 vols. New York: Harcourt Brace Jovanovich, 1976.

Popović, Vasilj. *Evropa i srpsko pitanje u periodu oslobođenja* [*Europe and the Serbian Question in the Liberation Period*]. Belgrade: Geca Kon, 1938.

Princip, Gavrilo. *The Sarajevo Trial*. Chapel Hill, N.C.: Documentary Publications, 1984.

Prodanović, Jaša. *Ustavni razvitak i ustavne borbe u Srbiji* [*Constitutional Development and Constitutional Struggle in Serbia*]. Belgrade: Geca Kon, 1936.

Protić, Milan, St. *Radikali u Srbiji, 1881–1903* [*Radicals in Serbia, 1881–1903*]. Belgrade: Balkanološki institut, 1990.

*Report of the International Commission to Inquire into the Causes and Conduct of the Balkan Wars*. Washington, D.C.: Carnegie Endowment for International Peace, 1914.

Schmitt, Bernadotte E. *The Annexation of Bosnia, 1908–1909*. Cambridge, England: The University Press, 1937.

Sforza, Carlo. *Pachitch et l'union des Yugoslaves*. Paris: Gallimard, 1938.

Stojančević, Vladimir. *Srbija 1908–1918* [*Serbia 1908–1918*]. Belgrade: Srpska književna zadruga, 1995.

Stokes, Gale. *Politics as Development: The Emergence of Political Parties in Nineteenth Century Serbia*. Durham, NC: Duke University Press, 1990.

———. *Legitimacy through Liberalism: Vladimir Jovanović and the Transformation of Serbian Politics*. Seattle: University of Washington Press, 1975.

Stranjaković, Dragoslav. *Vučićeva buna* [*Vučić's Rebellion*]. Belgrade: Srpska kraljevska akademija, 1936.

———. *Vlada ustavobranitelja, 1842–1858: unutrašnja i spoljna politika* [*The Rule of the Constitutionalists, 1842–1858: Internal and External Policies*]. Belgrade: Za narodnu štampariju Mirko Drobac, 1932.

Šuster, Željan E. "The Development of Serbian Parliamentary Democracy and Political Party Pluralism 1903–1914." *East European Quarterly*, 1997 (forthcoming).

Treadway, John D. *The Falcon and the Eagle: Montenegro and Austria Hungary, 1908–1914*. West Lafayette, Indiana: Purdue University Press, 1983.

Vojvodić, Mihailo. *Srbija u medjunarodnim odnosima krajem XIX i početkom XX veka* [*Serbia in International Relations at the End of the 19th and the Beginning of the 20th Centuries*]. Belgrade: SANU, 1988.

Vucinich, Wayne S., ed. *The First Serbian Uprising 1804–1913*. Boulder: East European Monographs, 1982.

———. *Serbia between East and West: The Events 1903–1908*. Stanford: Stanford University Press, 1954.

West, Rebecca. *Black Lamb and Grey Falcon: A Journey through Yugoslavia*. 2 vols. New York: Viking Press, 1941.

Wilson, Duncan. *The Life and Times of Vuk Stefanović Karadžić, 1787–1864*. Oxford: Clarendon Press, 1970.

Živanović, Živan. *Politička istorija Srbije u drugoj polovini devetnaestog veka* [*Political History of Serbia in the Second Half of the 19th Century*]. 4 vols. Belgrade: Geca Kon, 1923–1925.

Živojinović, Dragoljub R. *Petar I Karađorđević: Život i delo: U otadžbini: 1903–1914* [*Petar I Karađorđević: Life and Works: In the Fatherland: 1903–1914*]. Belgrade: BIGZ, 1990.

———. *Petar I Karađorđević: Život i delo: U izgnanstvu: 1844–1903* [*Petar I Karađorđević: Life and Works: In Exile; 1844–1903*]. Belgrade: BIGZ, 1988.

## The First Yugoslavia, 1918-1941

Avakumović, Ivan. *History of the Communist Party of Yugoslavia*. Aberdeen: Aberdeen University Press, 1964.

Banac, Ivo. *The Effects of World War I: The Class War After the Great War: The Rise of Communist Parties in East Central Europe, 1918–1921*. Boulder, Colo.: Social Sciences Monograph, 1984.

———. *The National Question in Yugoslavia: Origins, History, Politics*. Ithaca, N.Y.: Cornell University Press, 1984.

Beard, Charles A., and George Radin. *The Balkan Pivot: Yugoslavia*. New York: Macmillan, 1929.

Boban, Ljubo. *Sporazum Cvetković-Maček* [*The Cvetoković and Maček Agreement*]. Belgrade: Institut društvenih nauka, 1965.

Ćorović, Vladimir. *Istorija Jugoslavije* [*History of Yugoslavia*]. Belgrade: Narodno delo, 1933.

Čulinović, Ferdo. *Jugoslavija između dva rata* [*Yugoslavia Between the Two Wars*]. Zagreb: JAZU, 1961.

Djordjevic, Dimitrije. *The Creation of Yugoslavia, 1914–1918*. Santa Barbara, Calif.: Clio Books, 1980.

Dragnich, Alex N. *The First Yugoslavia: Search for Viable Political System*. Stanford: Hoover Institution Press, 1983.

Đurđev, Branislav, Bogo Grafenauer, and Jorjo Tadić, eds. *Historija naroda Jugoslavije* [*History of Yugoslav Peoples*]. Zagreb: Školska knjiga, 1959.

Ekmečić, Milorad. *Stvaranje Jugoslavije 1790–1918* [*Creation of Yugoslavia 1790–1918*]. 2 vols. Belgrade: Prosveta, 1989.

Faure-Biguet, J.-N. *Le roi Alexandre Ier de Yougoslavie*. Paris: Plon, 1936.

Graham, Stephen. *Alexander of Yugoslavia: The Story of the King Who Was Murdered at Marseilles*. New Haven, Conn.: Yale University Press, 1939.

Hoptner, J.B. *Yugoslavia in Crisis, 1934–1941*. New York: Columbia University Press, 1962.

Janković, Dragoslav, and Bogdan Krizman, eds. *Građa o stvaranju Jugoslovenske države* [*Materials on the Creation of the Yugoslav State*]. Belgrade: Institut društvenih nauka, 1964.

Jovanović, Dragoljub. *Ljudi, ljudi... (Medaljoni 56 umrlih savremenika)* [*People, People...Portraits of 56 Dead Contemporaries*]. 2 vols. Belgrade: Author, 1973–1975.

Jukić, Ilija. *The Fall of Yugoslavia*. New York: Harcourt Brace Jovanovich, 1974.

Krizman, Bogdan. *Ante Pavelić i Ustaše* [*Ante Pavelić and Ustaše*]. Zagreb: Globus, 1978.

Lederer, Ivo. *Yugoslavia at the Paris Peace Conference*. New Haven, Conn.: Yale University Press, 1963.

Marković, Lazar. *Jugoslovenska država i Hrvatsko pitanje (1914–1929)* [*Yugoslav State and the Croatian Question*]. Belgrade: Geca Kon A.D., 1935.

Mitrović, Andrej. *Jugoslavija na konferenciji mira: 1919–1920* [*Yugoslavia at the Peace Conference 1919–1920*]. Belgrade: Zavod za izdavanje udžbenika SR Srbije, 1969.

Nikolić, Kosta. *Boljševizacija KPJ 1919–1929: istorijske posledice* [*Bolshevization of the CPY 1919–1929*]. Belgrade: Institut za savremenu istoriju, 1994.

Pavković, Aleksandar. *Slobodan Jovanović, An Unsentimental Approach to Politics*. Boulder, Colo.: East European Monographs, 1993.

Petranović, Branko. *Istorija Jugoslavije, 1918–1978* [*History of Yugoslavia 1918–1978*]. Belgrade: Nolit, 1980.
Ristić, D.N. *Yugoslavia's Revolution of 1941*. University Park, PA: Pennsylvania State University Press, 1962.
Stojadinović, Milan M. *Ni rat ni pakt: Jugoslavija između dva rata* [*Against the War and the Pact: Yugoslavia between the Two Wars*]. Buenos Aires: El Economista, 1963.
Šišić, Ferdo. *Dokumenti o postanku Kraljevine Srba, Hrvata, i Slovenaca, 1914–1919* [*Documents on the Creation of the Kingdom of the Serbs, Croats, and Slovenes 1914–1919*]. Zagreb: Matica Hrvatska, 1920.
Živančević, Mihailo M. *Jugoslavija i federacija* [*Yugoslavia and the Federation*]. Belgrade: Privredni pregled, 1938.
Živojinović, Dragoljub. *America, Italy, and the Birth of Yugoslavia, 1917–1919*. Boulder, Colo.: East European Monographs, 1972.

## World War II, 1941–1945

Butić-Jelić, Fikreta. *Ustaše i Nezavisna Država Hrvatska, 1941–1945* [*Ustaše and the Independent State of Croatia 1941–1945*]. Zagreb: Školska knjiga, 1977.
Čulinović, Ferdo. *Okupatorska podjela Jugoslavije* [*Division of Yugoslavia by the Occupiers*]. Belgrade: Vojnoizdavački zavod, 1970.
Deakin, F. W. D. *The Embattled Mountain*. London: Oxford University Press, 1971.
Dedijer, Vladimir. *The Yugoslav Auschwitz and the Vatican*. Buffalo, N.Y.: Prometheus Books, 1992.
———. *The War Diaries of Vladimir Dedijer*. Ann Arbor, Mich.: University of Michigan Press, 1990.
Deroc, M. *British Special Operations Explored: Yugoslavia in Turmoil, 1941–1943, and the British Response*. Boulder, Colo.: East European Monographs, 1988.
Djilas, Milovan. *Wartime*. New York: Harcourt Brace Jovanovich, 1977.
Ford, Kirk. *OSS and the Yugoslav Resistance, 1943–1945*. College Station, Tex.: Texas A&M University Press, 1992.
Fotitch, Constantin. *The War We Lost*. New York: Viking Press, 1948.
Jukić, Ilija. *The Fall of Yugoslavia*. New York: Harcourt Brace Jovanovich, 1974.
Kazimirović, Vasa. *NDH u svetlu nemačkih dokumenata i dnevnika Gleza fon Horstenau, 1941–1944* [*Independent State of Croatia in German Documents and the Diary of Glaise fon Horstenau 1941–1944*]. Belgrade: 1987.
Kočović, Bogoljub. *Žrtve drugog svetskog rata u Jugoslaviji* [*Victims of the Second World War in Yugoslavia*]. London: Naše delo, 1985.
Konjhodzic, Alija. "Serbians of the Moslem Faith in Chetnik Ranks." in *Draža Mihailović Memorial Book*. Chicago: Organization of Serbian Chetniks "Ravna Gora," 1981.
Krizman, Bogdan. *Pavelić između Hitlera i Musolinija* [*Pavelić Between Hitler and Mussolini*]. Zagreb: Globus, 1980.
Lees, Michael. *The Rape of Serbia: The British Role in Tito's Grab for Power*. New York: Harcourt Brace Jovanovich, 1977.
Lindsay, Franklin. *Beacons in the Night: With the OSS and Tito's Partisan's in Wartime Yugoslavia*. Stanford, Calif.: Stanford University Press, 1993.

Maclean, Fitzroy. *Eastern Approaches*. New York: Time, 1964.

———. *Disputed Barricade*. London: J. Cape 1957.

Martić, Miloš. "Dimitrije Ljotić and the Yugoslav National Movement Zbor 1939–1945," *East European Quarterly* 14, 2, (1980): 219–239.

Martin, David. *Patriot or Traitor: The Case of General Mihailovich*. Stanford, Calif.: Hoover Institution Press, 1978.

———. *Ally Betrayed: The Uncensored Story of Tito and Mihailovich*. New York: Prentice Hall, 1946.

Mather, Carol. *Aftermath of War: Everyone Must Go Home*. London; Washington: Brassey's (UK); Riverside, NJ: Orders, Macmillan Pub. Co., 1992.

Milazzo, Matteo J. *The Chetnick Movement and the Yugoslav Resistance*. Baltimore and London: Johns Hopkins University Press, 1975.

Novak, Viktor. *Magnum Crimen*. Zagreb: TNZ Hrvatska, 1948.

Roberts, Walter R. *Tito, Mihailovich, and the Allies*. New Brunswick, N.J.: Rutgers University Press, 1973.

Stranjaković, Dragoslav. *Najveći zločin sadašnjice: Patnja i stradanje srpskog naroda u Nezavisnoj Državi Hrvatskoj* [*The Biggest Crime of the Present Times: Suffering and Agony of the Serbian People in the Independent State of Croatia*]. Gornji Milanovac: Dečije novine, 1991.

Terzić, Velimir. *Jugoslavija u aprilskom ratu* [*Yugoslavia in April's War*]. 2 vols. Belgrade: Partizanska knjiga, 1981.

Tomashevich, Jozo. *The Chetniks*. Stanford, Calif.: Stanford University Press, 1975.

Trgo, Fabijan. *The National Liberation War and Revolution in Yugoslavia, 1941–45: Selected Documents*. Belgrade: Military History Institute, 1982.

## The Second Yugoslavia, 1945–1991

Alexander, Stella. *Church and State in Yugoslavia since 1945*. Cambridge: Cambridge University Press, 1979.

Auty, Phyllis. *Tito: A Biography*. London: Longman, 1970.

Banac, Ivo. *With Stalin Against Tito: Cominform Splits in Yugoslav Communism*. Ithaca, N.Y.: Cornell University Press, 1988.

Bellof, Nora. *Tito's Flawed Legacy*. London: Gollonz, 1985.

Burg, Steven L. *Conflict and Cohesion in Socialist Yugoslavia*. Princeton, N.J.: Princeton University Press, 1983.

Carter, April. *Democratic Reform in Yugoslavia: The Changing Role of the Party*. Princeton: Princeton University Press, 1982.

Clissold, Stephen. *A Short Story of Yugoslavia from Early Times to 1966*. Cambridge, England: Cambridge University Press, 1968.

Dedijer, V., et al., eds. *History of Yugoslavia*. New York: McGraw-Hill, 1974.

Djordjevic, Dimitrije. "Three Yugoslavias—A Case for Survival." *East European Quarterly* 19/4 (1986).

Doder, Dušan. *The Yugoslavs*. New York: Random House, 1978.

Grothusen, Klaus-Detlev. *Jugoslawien=Yugoslavia*. Göttingen, Germany: Vandenhoech & Ruprecht, 1975.

Hondius, F. W. *The Yugoslav Community of Nations*. The Hague: Mouton, 1968.

Lydall, Harold. *Yugoslavia in Crisis*. Oxford: Clarendon Press, 1989.

Moorthy, Krishna K. *After Tito What?* Atlantic Highlands, N.J.: Humanities Press, 1980.

Pawlovitch, Stevan K. *The Improbable Survivor: Yugoslavia and its Problems 1918–1988*. Columbus, Ohio: Ohio State University Press, 1988.

———. *Yugoslavia*. New York: Preager, 1971.

Ramet, Pedro, ed. *Yugoslavia in the 1980s*. Boulder, Colo.: Westview Press, 1985.

Rusinow, Dennison. *The Yugoslav Experiment, 1948–1974*. London: C. Hurst & Company, 1977.

Shoup, Paul. *Communism and the Yugoslav National Question*. New York: Columbia University Press, 1968.

Singleton, Fred. *A Short History of Yugoslav Peoples*. Cambridge, England: Cambridge University Press, 1985.

Vucinich, Wayne S., ed. *The Tito-Stalin Split in a Historical Perspective*. East European Monographs 24. New York: Brooklyn College Press, 1982.

——— ed. *Contemporary Yugoslavia: Twenty Years of Socialist Experiment*. Berkeley and Los Angeles, Calif.: University of California Press, 1969.

Wolff, Robert Lee. *The Balkans in Our Time*. New York: W. W. Norton, 1967.

Zukin, Sharon. *Beyond Marx and Tito. Theory and Practice in Yugoslav Socialism*. Cambridge, England: Cambridge University Press, 1975.

## Civil War, 1991–1995

Agnes, Mario. *Le Crise en Yougoslavie: Position et Action du Saint-Sičge (1991–1992)*. Vatican City: Libraria Čditrice Vaticana, 1992.

Akhavan, Payam, and Robert Howse, eds. *Yugoslavia, the Former and Future: Reflections by Scholars from the Region*. Washington, D.C.: The Brookings Institution, 1995.

Bennet, Christopher. *Yugoslavia's Bloody Collapse: Causes, Course, and Consequences*. New York: New York University Press, 1995.

Binder, David. "Anatomy of a Massacre." *Foreign Policy*, (Winter 1994–95): 70–78.

Cohen, Leonard J. *Broken Bonds: The Disintegration of Yugoslavia*. Boulder: Westview Press, 1993.

Cvetković ,Vladimir N. *Strah i poniženje. Jugoslovenski rat i izbeglice u Srbiji 1991–1995*. [*Fear and Humiliation. Yugoslav War and Refugees in Serbia 1991–1995*]. Beograd: Institut za evropske studije, 1998.

Denich, Bette. "Dismembering Yugoslavia: Nationalist Ideologies and the Symbolic Revival of Genocide," *American Ethnologist* ( May 1994): 367–390.

Dragnich, Alex N. *Yugoslavia's Disintegration and the Struggle for Truth*. Boulder, Colo.: East European Monographs, 1995.

Drakulić, Slavenka. *The Balkan Express: Fragments from the Other Side of War*. New York: W. W. Norton, 1993.

Garde, Paul. *Vie et mort de la Yougoslavie*. Paris: Fayard, 1992.

Glenny, Misha. *The Fall of Yugoslavia: The Third Balkan War*. 3d ed. London: Penguin Books, 1996.

Gompert, David. "How to Defeat Serbia." *Foreign Policy 73* ( July-August 1994): 30–42.

Hall, Brian. *The Impossible Country: A Journey through the Last Days of Yugoslavia*. Boston: David Godine, 1994.

Holbrooke, Richard. *To End a War*. New York: Random House, 1998.

Ignatieff, Michael. *Blood and Belonging: Journeys into the New Nationalism*. New York: Ferrar Straus, and Giroux, 1994.

Jović, Borisav. *Poslednji dani SFRJ* [*The Last Days of SFRY*]. 2nd ed. Belgrade:Author, 1998.

Kadijević, Veljko. *Moje viđenje raspada: vojska bez države* [*My Views of the Breakup: Army Without the Country*]. Belgrade: Politika, 1993.

Mackenzie, Lewis. *Peacekeeper: The Road to Sarajevo*. Toronto, Ont.: Douglas and McIntyre, 1993.

Magaš, Branka. *The Destruction of Yugoslavia: Tracking the Break-up, 1980–92*. London: Verso, 1993.

Mesić, Stipe. *Kako smo srušili Jugoslaviju: politički memomari posljednjeg predsjednika Predsjedništva SFRJ* [*How We Destroyed Yugoslavia: Political Memoirs of the Last President of Yugoslavia*]. Zagreb: Globus International, 1992.

Mikasinovich, Branko. *Yugoslavia: Crisis and Disintegration*. Milwaukee, Wisc.: Plyroma, 1994.

Owen, David. *Balkan Odyssey*. New York: Harcourt Brace, 1995.

Ramet, Sabrina Petra, and Ljubiša Adamović, eds. *Beyond Yugoslavia: Politics, Economic, and Culture in a Shattered Community*. Boulder, Colo.: Westview Press, 1995.

Silber, Laura and Allan Little. *The Death of Yugoslavia*. London: Penguin Books, 1995.

Stojanović, Svetozar. *Propast komunizma i razbijanje Jugoslavije* [*The Collapse of Communism and the Destruction of Yugoslavia*]. Belgrade: Filip Višnjić, Institut za filozofiju i društvenu teoriju, 1995.

Sündhaussen, Holm. *Experiment Jugoslawien: von der Staatsgrundrung bis zum Staatzzerfall*. Mannheim: B.I.-Taschenbuchverlag, 1993.

Thompson, Mark. *Forging War: The Media in Serbia, Croatia, and Bosnia and Hercegovina*. Avon: The Bath Press, 1994.

Troebst, Stefan. *Conflict in Kosovo: Failure of Prevention? An Analytical Documentation, 1992–1998*. Working Paper, No. 1. Flensburg: ECMI, 1998.

Udovički, Jasmina, and James Ridgeway, eds. *Yugoslavia's Ethnic Nightmare*. New York: Lawrence Hill Books, 1995.

Woodward, Susan L. *Balkan Tragedy: Chaos and Dissolution after the Cold War*. Washington, D.C.: The Brookings Institution Press, 1995.

## 6. POLITICS AND GOVERNMENT

Behschnitt, Wolf D. *Nationalismus bei Serben und Kroaten, 1830–1914: Analyse und Typologie der National Ideologie*. München: Oldenburg, 1980.

Borowiec, Andrew. *Yugoslavia after Tito*. New York: Praeger, 1977.

Burg, Steven L. "Elite Conflict in Post-Tito Yugoslavia." *Soviet Studies* 38 (April 1986): 170–93.

———. *Conflict and Cohesion in Socialist Yugoslavia: Political Decision Making Since 1966*. Princeton, N.J.: Princeton University Press, 1983.

Cohen, Leonard J. *The Socialist Pyramid: Elites and Power in Yugoslavia*. Oakville, Ontario; New York: Mosaic Press, 1989.

Cohen, Leonard J., and Paul Warwick. *Political Cohesion in a Fragile Mosaic: The Yugoslav Experience*. Boulder, Colo.: Westview Press, 1983.

Denitch, Bogdan D. *Limits and Possibilities: The Crisis of Yugoslav Socialism and State Socialist Systems*. Minneapolis: University of Minnesota Press, 1990.

———. *The Legitimation of a Revolution: The Yugoslav Case*. New Haven: Yale University Press, 1976.

Djilas, Aleksa. *The Contested Country: Yugoslav Unity and Communist Revolution, 1919–1953*. Cambridge, Mass.: Harvard University Press, 1991.

Fisher, Jack C. *Yugoslavia, A Multinational State: Regional Differences and Administrative Response*. San Francisco: Chandler Publishing Co., 1966.

Gow, James. *Legitimacy and the Military: The Yugoslav Crisis*. New York: St. Martin's Press, 1992.

Hammel, E. A. *The Yugoslav Labyrinth*. Berkeley, Calif.: Institute for International Studies, University of California at Berkeley, 1992.

Hondius, Frits W. *The Yugoslav Community of Nations*. The Hague: Mouton, 1968.

Koštunica, Vojislav. *Party Pluralism or Monism: Social Movements and the Political System in Yugoslavia, 1944–1949*. Boulder, Colo.: East European Monographs, 1985.

Lederer, Ivo J. *Yugoslavia at the Paris Peace Conference: A Study in Frontiermaking*. New Haven, Conn.: Yale University Press, 1993.

Libal, Wolgang. *Das Ende Jugoslawiens: Chronik einer Selbsterz*. Wien: Europaverlag, 1991.

McFarlane, Bruce J. *Yugoslavia: Politics, Economics, and Society*. London: Pinter, 1988.

Mirić, Jovan. *Sistem i kriza: Prilog kritičkoj analizi ustavnog i političkog sistema Jugoslavije*. [*System and Crisis: A Contribution to the Critical Analysis of the Constitutional and Political System of Yugoslavia*]. Zagreb: CeKaDe, 1984.

Pawlovitch, Stevan K. *Tito—Yugoslavia's Great Dictator: A Reassessment*. Columbus, Ohio: Ohio State University, 1992.

Roberts, Adam. *Nations in Arms: The Theory and Practice of Territorial Defense*. New York: St. Martins Press, 1986.

Rusinow, Dennison. "Yugoslavia: Balkan Breakup?" *Foreign Policy* 83 (Summer 1991):

Rusinow, Dennison (ed.) *Yugoslavia: A Fractured Federalism*. Washington, D.C.: The Wilson Center Press, 1988.

Seroka, Jim, and Vukasin Pavlovic (eds.) *The Tragedy of Yugoslavia: The Failure of Democratic Transformation*. Armonk, N.Y.: M. E. Sharpe, 1992.

Shoup, Paul. *Communism and the Yugoslav National Question*. New York: Columbia University Press, 1968.

Stokes, Gale. *The Walls Came Tumbling Down: The Collapse of Communism in Eastern Europe*. New York: Oxford University Press, 1993.
Vulliamy, Edward. *Seasons in Hell: Understanding Bosnia's War*. New York: Simon & Schuster, 1994.
West, Richard. *Tito and the Rise and Fall of Yugoslavia*. London: Sinclair-Stevenson, 1994.
Williams, Paul, and Michael Scharf, eds. *U.N. Peacekeeping and the War in Former Yugoslavia*. London: Media East West, 1995.
Wolf, Hans. *Jugoslawien mellan ost och vast*. Stockholm: Forlag, 1991.
*Yugoslavia at the Brink—Prospect for Stability or Disintegration*. Washington, D.C.: U.S. Institute of Peace, 1991.
Zimmerman, Warren. *Origins of a Catastrophe*. New York: Times Books, 1996.
Zimmerman, William. *Open Borders, Nonalignment, and the Political Evolution of Yugoslavia*. Princeton, N.J.: Princeton University Press, 1987.

# Statistical Addendum

Table 1. Share of the Republics in the Socialist Federal Republic of Yugoslavia (Percentage)

| | Year | SFRJ | B-H | Mon | Cro | Mac | Slo | Ser | SeC | K-M | Voj |
|---|---|---|---|---|---|---|---|---|---|---|---|
| Terr | 1990 | 100 | 20.1 | 3.4 | 22.1 | 10.1 | 7.9 | 34.5 | 21.9 | 4.2 | 8.4 |
| Pop | 1953<br>1990 | 100<br>100 | 16.7<br>19.0 | 2.5<br>2.7 | 23.2<br>19.7 | 7.7<br>8.9 | 8.8<br>8.2 | 41.1<br>41.5 | 26.3<br>24.6 | 4.8<br>8.3 | 10.0<br>8.6 |
| Capt | 1953<br>1989 | 100<br>100 | 13.6<br>15.2 | 0.9<br>3.2 | 28.2<br>25.8 | 4.2<br>5.8 | 20.1<br>17.0 | 33.0<br>33.0 | 22.7<br>20.6 | 1.7<br>2.8 | 8.6<br>9.6 |
| Invst | 1953<br>1989 | 100<br>100 | 20.1<br>14.2 | 5.1<br>2.3 | 20.6<br>22.2 | 8.7<br>4.9 | 16.0<br>18.4 | 29.3<br>38.0 | 24.5<br>27.0 | 1.2<br>2.1 | 3.6<br>8.9 |
| AgAr | 1953<br>1990 | 100<br>100 | 17.7<br>17.8 | 3.6<br>3.6 | 24.2<br>22.7 | 9.1<br>9.3 | 6.9<br>6.1 | 38.5<br>40.4 | 21.8<br>23.7 | 3.6<br>4.1 | 13.1<br>12.6 |
| SP | 1953<br>1989 | 100<br>100 | 14.4<br>12.9 | 1.8<br>2.0 | 26.7<br>25.0 | 5.2<br>5.8 | 14.3<br>16.5 | 37.6<br>38.0 | 25.5<br>25.6 | 2.2<br>2.1 | 9.9<br>10.3 |
| SPI | 1953<br>1989 | 100<br>100 | 11.9<br>14.5 | 0.7<br>1.7 | 29.2<br>21.6 | 3.7<br>6.7 | 25.0<br>17.7 | 29.5<br>37.8 | 19.2<br>25.7 | 2.0<br>2.1 | 8.3<br>10.0 |
| SPA | 1953<br>1989 | 100<br>100 | 13.5<br>12.0 | 1.6<br>1.8 | 23.7<br>22.5 | 6.1<br>6.6 | 7.4<br>8.7 | 47.7<br>48.4 | 29.5<br>26.2 | 3.1<br>4.0 | 15.1<br>18.2 |
| Exp | 1973<br>1990 | 100<br>100 | 11.2<br>14.4 | 2.0<br>1.6 | 36.3<br>20.4 | 5.5<br>4.0 | 19.5<br>28.8 | 37.1<br>30.2 | 26.7<br>20.7 | 1.6<br>1.2 | 8.8<br>8.3 |
| Imp | 1973<br>1990 | 100<br>100 | 8.5<br>10.0 | 1.3<br>1.0 | 24.5<br>23.5 | 4.1<br>5.6 | 20.5<br>25.0 | 28.9<br>33.4 | 22.1<br>21.0 | 1.2<br>1.0 | 5.6<br>11.4 |

Terr- Territory
Pop- Population
Capt- Capital Structure
Invst- Investment, current prices
AgAr- Agricultural Area
SP- Social Product
SPI- Social Product of Industry Sector
SPA- Social Product of Agriculture
Exp- Export
Imp- Import

B-H- Bosnia and Hercegovina
Mon- Montenegro
Cro- Croatia
Mac- Macedonia
Slo- Slovenia
Ser- Serbia, Total
SEC- SERBIA, Central
K-M- Kosovo and Metohija
Voj- Vojvodina

Source: *Statistički godišnjak Jugoslavije 1991*. Belgrade: Savezni zavod za statistiku, 1991.

Table 2. The Ethnic Structure of the Federal Republic of Yugoslavia, 1948–1991

| | 1948 | 1953 | 1961 | 1971 | 1981 | 1991 |
|---|---|---|---|---|---|---|
| Serbs | 4,830,437 | 5,166,803 | 5,718,773 | 6,056,323 | 6,201,562 | 6,485,596 |
| Montenegrins | 416,869 | 449,747 | 488,741 | 480,892 | 547,954 | 520,508 |
| Yugoslavs | | | 21,638 | 134,767 | 473,184 | 343,593 |
| Albanians | 551,436 | 588,973 | 725,575 | 1,020,432 | 1,340,769 | 1,727,541 |
| Hungarians | 433,763 | 442,098 | 449,857 | 430,610 | 390,706 | 345,376 |
| Muslims | 17,702 | 87,505 | 124,132 | 224,566 | 293,246 | 327,290 |
| Croats | 176,672 | 183,060 | 207,073 | 194,105 | 156,272 | 115,463 |
| Romanies | 52,343 | 59,030 | 10,009 | 50,390 | 112,430 | 137,265 |
| Slovaks | 73,144 | 75,035 | 77,844 | 76,764 | 73,240 | 67,234 |
| Rumanians | 63,133 | 59,711 | 59,513 | 57,441 | 53,852 | 42,386 |
| Macedonians | 18,050 | 27,639 | 36,881 | 43,398 | 49,861 | 48,437 |
| Bulgarians | 59,485 | 60,167 | 58,533 | 54,194 | 33,479 | 25,214 |
| Valachians | 93,440 | 28,047 | 1,369 | 14,730 | 25,597 | 17,557 |
| Ruthenians | 22,690 | 23,727 | 25,685 | 20,646 | 19,776 | 18,339 |
| Turks | 1,916 | 54,818 | 46,826 | 18,617 | 13,957 | 11,501 |
| Slovaks | 21,482 | 21,359 | 20,776 | 16,615 | 12,570 | 8,747 |
| Other | 72,593 | 71,308 | 40,896 | 81,805 | 99,531 | 164,695 |
| Total | 6,905,155 | 7,399,027 | 8,114,121 | 8,976,295 | 9,897,986 | 10,406,742 |

Source: *Statistical Yearbook of Yugoslavia 1992.* Belgrade: Savezni zavod za statistiku, 1992.

Table 3. Population Growth in the Federal Republic of Yugoslavia, 1921–1991

| Year | Population | Population per sq km |
|---|---|---|
| 1921 | 5,130,771 | 50.2 |
| 1931 | 6,085,956 | 59.6 |
| 1948 | 6,905,155 | 67.6 |
| 1953 | 7,399,027 | 72.4 |
| 1961 | 8,114,121 | 79.4 |
| 1971 | 8,976,195 | 87.9 |
| 1981 | 9,897,986 | 96.9 |
| 1991 | 10,337,504 | 101.2 |

Source: *Statistical Yearbook of Yugoslavia 1994.* Belgrade: Savezni zavod za statistiku, 1994.

Table 4. Gross Domestic Product and National Income Trends in the Federal Republic of Yugoslavia, 1987–1993 (1990=100)

| | 1987 | 1988 | 1989 | 1990 | 1991 | 1992 | 1993 |
|---|---|---|---|---|---|---|---|
| Montenegro | 116.2 | 112.1 | 110.2 | 100 | 90.5 | 66.4 | 43.8 |
| Serbia | 107.7 | 105.6 | 106.9 | 100 | 91.9 | 67.9 | 49.3 |
| –Central Serbia | 104.6 | 102.8 | 105.6 | 100 | 90.3 | 67.2 | 48.4 |
| –Vojvodina | 109.8 | 107.5 | 106.9 | 100 | 94.4 | 67.7 | 49.0 |
| –Kosovo and Metohija | 132.2 | 129.6 | 123.4 | 100 | 98.0 | 76.6 | 60.5 |
| FRY | 108.1 | 105.9 | 107.1 | 100 | 91.8 | 67.8 | 49.0 |

Source: *Statistical Yearbook of Yugoslavia 1994.* Belgrade: Savezni zavod za statistiku, 1994.

Table 8. The Domestic Product of the Federal Republic of Yugoslavia by Republic, 1976–1990*

| Year | FR Yugoslavia | Montenegro | Serbia (all) | Vojvodina | Kosovo & Metohija |
|---|---|---|---|---|---|
| 1976 | 1189.3 | 55.5 | 1133.8 | 323.1 | 65.0 |
| 1977 | 1284.7 | 61.6 | 1223.1 | 352.1 | 68.1 |
| 1978 | 1356.3 | 65.2 | 1291.1 | 366.0 | 69.5 |
| 1979 | 1454.8 | 65.3 | 1389.5 | 389.5 | 74.2 |
| 1980 | 1502 | 78.7 | 1426.3 | 393.8 | 75.9 |
| 1981 | 1530.8 | 79.0 | 1451.8 | 412.2 | 80.4 |
| 1982 | 1549.7 | 77.7 | 1472 | 419.5 | 80.1 |
| 1983 | 1524.6 | 77.7 | 1446.9 | 413.4 | 78.7 |
| 1984 | 1548.7 | 80.7 | 1468 | 422.7 | 76.9 |
| 1985 | 1553 | 81.7 | 1471.6 | 410.9 | 83.1 |
| 1986 | 1610.3 | 84.5 | 1525.8 | 424 | 890. |
| 1987 | 1583.8 | 80.8 | 1503 | 419.2 | 87.2 |
| 1988 | 1563.2 | 78.6 | 1484.6 | 411.7 | 85.9 |
| 1989 | 1592.8 | 79.1 | 1513.7 | 411.7 | 83.7 |
| 1990 | 1459.1 | 70.8 | 1388.3 | 382.3 | 66.4 |

* Figures in thousands of 1972 dinars

Source: *Statistički godišnjak Jugoslavije 1991*. Belgrade: Savezni zavod za statistiku, 1992.

Table 9. Inflation Rate in the Federal Republic of Yugoslavia, February 1992–January 1994

| Month | Monthly Inflation rate | Daily Inflation rate | Hourly inflation rate |
|---|---|---|---|
| 02/92 | 50.6% | 1.33% | 0.06% |
| 03/92 | 42.0% | 1.26% | 0.05% |
| 04/92 | 77.5% | 1.87% | 0.08% |
| 05/92 | 80.8% | 1.99% | 0.08% |
| 06/92 | 102.2% | 2.30% | 0.09% |
| 07/92 | 62.0% | 1.62% | 0.07% |
| 08/92 | 42.4% | 1.15% | 0.05% |
| 09/92 | 64.4% | 1.62% | 0.07% |
| 10/92 | 49.8% | 1.36% | 0.06% |
| 11/92 | 33.3% | 0.93% | 0.04% |
| 12/92 | 46.6% | 1.28% | 0.05% |
| 01/93 | 100.6% | 2.27% | 0.09% |
| 02/93 | 211.8% | 3.74% | 0.15% |
| 03/93 | 225.8% | 4.31% | 0.18% |
| 04/93 | 114.1% | 2.49% | 0.10% |
| 05/93 | 205.2% | 3.79% | 0.16% |
| 06/93 | 366.7% | 5.09% | 0.21% |
| 07/93 | 431.6% | 5.73% | 0.23% |
| 08/93 | 1880.6% | 10.11% | 0.40% |
| 09/93 | 643.2% | 6.68% | 0.27% |
| 10/93 | 1895.6% | 10.49% | 0.42% |
| 11/93 | 20190.1% | 18.69% | 0.72% |
| 12/93 | 178882.0% | 28.36% | 1.05% |
| 01/94 | 313563558.0% | 62.02% | 2.03% |

Source: Dinkić, M. *Ekonomija destrukcije—velika pljačka naroda.* Belgrade: VIN, 1995.

Table 10. Population of Bosnia and Hercegovina by Religion (Census from 1879 to 1910)

| Year | Total | Orthodox | | Muslim | | Catholic | | Other | |
|---|---|---|---|---|---|---|---|---|---|
| | | Count | % | Count | % | Count | % | Count | % |
| 1879 | 1,158,164 | 496,485 | 42.88 | 448,613 | 38.75 | 209,391 | 18.08 | 3,675 | 0.31 |
| 1885 | 1,336,091 | 571,250 | 42.76 | 492,710 | 38.88 | 265,788 | 19.88 | 6,343 | 0.47 |
| 1895 | 1,568,092 | 673,246 | 42.94 | 548,632 | 34.99 | 334,142 | 21.31 | 12,072 | 0.76 |
| 1910 | 1,898,044 | 825,918 | 43.49 | 612,137 | 32.25 | 434,061 | 22.87 | 26,428 | 1.39 |

Source: Bataković T. Dušan: *Serbs of Bosnia & Herzegovina: History and Politics*. Paris: Dialogue, 1996.

Table 11. Ethnic Structure of the Population of Bosnia and Hercegovina, 1948–1991

| | 1948 | 1953 | 1961 | 1971 | 1981 | 1991 |
|---|---|---|---|---|---|---|
| Montenegrins | 3,094 (0.12%) | 7,336 (0.25%) | 12,828 (0.39%) | 13,021 (0.34%) | 114,114 (0.34%) | 0 |
| Croats | 614,123 (23.9%) | 654,229 (22.9%) | 711,665 (21.7%) | 772,491 (20.6%) | 758,136 (18.3%) | 755,895 (17.3%) |
| Macedonians | 675 (0.02%) | 1,884 (0.06%) | 2,391 (0.09%) | 1,773 (0.04%) | 1,892 (0.04%) | 0 |
| Muslims | 788,403 (30.7%) | 891,800 (31.3%) | 842,248 (25.6%) | 1,482,430 (39.5%) | 1,629,924 (39.5%) | 1,905,829 (43.6%) |
| Slovenes | 4,338 (0.16%) | 6,300 (0.22%) | 5,939 (0.18%) | 4,053 (0.1%) | 2,753 (0.06%) | 0 |
| Serbs | 1,136,116 (44.2%) | 1,264,372 (44.3%) | 1,406,057 (42.8%) | 1,393,148 (37.8%) | 1,320,644 (32.8%) | 1,369,258 (31.3%) |
| Yugoslavs | 0 | 0 | 275,883 (8.4%) | 43,796 (1.1%) | 326,280 (7.9%) | 239,845 (5.4%) |
| Other | 18,528 (0.72%) | 21,869 (0.76%) | 20,937 (0.64%) | 35,399 (0.94%) | 67,265 (1.6%) | 93,747 (2.1%) |
| TOTAL | 2,565,277 | 2,847,790 | 3,277,948 | 3,746,111 | 4,121,008 | 4,364,574 |

Source: *Statistički godišnjak Jugoslavije 1991*. Belgrade: Savezni zavod za statistiku, 1992.

Table 12. The Serbian Population on the Territory of Contemporary Croatia, 1910–1991

| Year | Total Population | Serbs | | Yugoslavs | |
|---|---|---|---|---|---|
| | | Count | Percent | Count | Percent |
| 1910 | 3,460,584 | 611,257 | 17.70 | - | - |
| 1921 | 3,443,375 | 606,252 | 17.60 | - | - |
| 1931 | 3,785,455 | 636,284 | 16.80 | - | - |
| 1948 | 3,779,858 | 543,795 | 14.40 | - | - |
| 1953 | 3,936,022 | 588,756 | 15.00 | 16,694 | 0.40 |
| 1961 | 4,159,696 | 624,991 | 15.00 | 15,560 | 0.40 |
| 1971 | 4,426,221 | 626,789 | 14.20 | 84,118 | 1.90 |
| 1981 | 4,601,469 | 531,502 | 11.60 | 379,057 | 8.20 |
| 1991 | 4,784,265 | 581,653 | 12.20 | 106,041 | 2.20 |

Source: *The Serbian Question in the Balkans*. Belgrade: University of Belgrade, 1995.

Table 13. Ethnic Structure of the Population of Montenegro, 1948–1991

| | 1948 | 1953 | 1961 | 1971 | 1981 | 1991 |
|---|---|---|---|---|---|---|
| Montenegrins | 342,009 (90.6%) | 363,686 (86.6%) | 383,978 (81.3%) | 355,632 (67.1%) | 400,488 (68.5%) | 380,664 (61.8%) |
| Serbs | 6,707 (1.1%) | 13,864 (3.3%) | 14,087 (2.9%) | 39,512 (7.4%) | 19,407 (3.3%) | 57,176 (9.2%) |
| Muslims | 387 | - | 30,665 (6.4%) | 70,236 (13.2%) | 78,080 (13.3%) | 89,909 (14.6%) |
| Albanians | 19,425 (5.1%) | 23,460 (5.5%) | 25,794 (5.4%) | 35,634 (6.7%) | 37,735 (6.4%) | 40,880 (6.6%) |
| Croats | 6,801 (1.1%) | 9,814 (2.3%) | 10,664 (2.2%) | 9,192 (1.7%) | 6,904 (1.1%) | 6,249 (1.0%) |
| Gypsies | - | - | - | 397 | 1,471 | - |
| Yugoslavs | - | - | 1,559 (0.3%) | 10,930 (2.0%) | 33,146 (5.6%) | 25,854 (4.2%) |
| Turks | - | - | 2,392 (0.5%) | 397 | - | - |
| Others | 1,860 (0.4%) | 2,625 (0.6%) | 2,755 (0.5%) | 7,662 (1.4%) | 7,079 (1.2%) | 14,715 (2.3%) |
| TOTAL | 377,189 | 413,873 | 471,894 | 529,592 | 584,310 | 615,447 |

Source: *The Serbian Question in the Balkans*. Belgrade: University of Belgrade,1995.

Table 14. Deputies to the Federal Parliament by Political Party, December 1992

| | Chamber of Citizens | Chamber of Republics |
|---|---|---|
| Federal Parliament of the FRY | 138 | 40 |
| Political Parties of Montenegro: | | |
| Democratic Party of Socialists | 17 | 15 |
| Socialist Party | 5 | - |
| Serbian Radical Party | 4 | 2 |
| Peoples' Party | 4 | 3 |
| Political Parties of Serbia: | | |
| Socialist Party | 46 | 12 |
| Serbian Radical Party | 30 | 8 |
| Democratic Movement of Serbia | 20 | - |
| Democratic Party | 7 | - |
| Democratic Association of Hungarians in Vojvodina | 3 | - |
| Does not belong to a political party | 2 | - |

Source: *Statistical Yearbook of Yugoslavia 1994*. Belgrade: Savezni zavod za statistiku, 1994.

Table 15. Deputies to the Federal Parliament of the Federal Republic of Yugoslavia and Parliaments of Republics

| | |
|---|---|
| Federal Assembly | 178 |
| Chamber of Citizens | 138 |
| Chamber of Republics | 40 |
| Assembly of the Republic of Montenegro | 85 |
| National Assembly of the Republic of Serbia | 250 |

Source : *Statistical Yearbook of Yugoslavia 1994.* Belgrade: Savezni zavod za statistiku, 1994.

Table 16. Ethnic Structure of the Population in Sandžak*, 1961–1991

| Ethnic group | 1961 | 1971 | 1981 | 1991 |
|---|---|---|---|---|
| Serbs | 119,385 (32.3%) | 125,239 (31.6%) | 105,915 (25.3%) | 112,807 (26.6%) |
| Montenegrins | 119,029 (32.2%) | 95,247 (24.0%) | 103,903 (24.8%) | 81,215 (19.2%) |
| Muslims | 107,265 (29.0%) | 160,712 (40.5%) | 192,525 (46.0%) | 215,291 (51%) |
| Tuks | 15,440 (4.1%) | 4,614 (1.1%) | - | 46 |
| Others | 6,514 (1.7%) | 8,307 (2.0%) | 13,582 (3.2%) | 11,503 (2.7%) |
| TOTAL | 367,594 | 394,119 | 415,925 | 420,862 |

* The population of municipalities Berane and Rožaje included (70,000 people)

Source: *The Serbian Question in the Balkans*. Belgrade: University of Belgrade, 1995.

Table 17. Ethnic Structure of the Population in Vojvodina, 1910–1991

| Ethnic Structure | 1910 | 1921 | 1952 | 1971 | 1991 |
|---|---|---|---|---|---|
| Serbs | 510,186 (33.7%) | 526,134 (34.6%) | 865,538 (50.8%) | 1,089,132 (55.7%) | 1,1143,723 (57.1%) |
| Hungarians | 424,555 (28.0%) | 370,040 (24.5%) | 435,179 (25.5%) | 423,866 (21.7%) | 339,491 (16.9%) |
| Germans | 323,779 (21.4%) | 333,272 (21.9%) | | 7,243 (0.3%) | |
| Croats | 34,089 (2.2%) | 122,684 (8.0%) | 127,027 (7.4%) | 138,561 (7.0%) | 101,607 (3.6%) |
| Slovaks | 56,689 (3.7%) | 58,273 (3.8%) | 71,153 (4.1%) | 72,795 (3.7%) | 63,545 (3.1%) |
| Romanians | 75,223 (4.9%) | 65,197 (4.2%) | 57,218 (3.3%) | 52,987 (2.7%) | 38,832 (1.9%) |
| Montenegrins | | | 30,516 (1.7%) | 34,416 (1.7%) | 44,838 (2.2%) |
| Ruthenians | 13,479 (0.9%) | 13,664 (0.9%) | 23,038 (1.3%) | 20,109 (1.0%) | 17,889 (0.8%) |
| Macedonians | | | 11,622 (0.6%) | 16,527 (0.8%) | 16,641 (0.8%) |
| Others | 72,804 (4.8%) | 25,182 (1.6%) | 78,254 (4.5%) | 94,897 (4.8%) | 247,323 (13.1%) |
| TOTAL | 1,510,804 00 | 1,545,446 00 | 1,701,498 00 | 1,950,533 00 | 2,030,419 00 |

Source: *The Serbian Question in the Balkans*. Belgrade: University of Belgrade, 1995.

Table 18. Distribution of Persons Declaring as Yugoslavs by Republic, 1961–1991

| Republics & Regions | 1961 | 1971 | 1981 | 1991 |
|---|---|---|---|---|
| Bosnia & Hercegovina | 275,883 | 43,796 | 326,316 | 239,845 |
| Montenegro | 1,559 | 10,943 | 31,243 | 25,854 |
| Croatia | 15,559 | 84,118 | 379,057 | 104,728 |
| Macedonia | 1,260 | 3,652 | 14,225 | |
| Slovenia | 2,784 | 6,784 | 26,263 | 12,237 |
| Serbia - total | 20,079 | 123,824 | 441,941 | 317,739 |
| Central Serbia | 11,699 | 75,976 | 272,050 | 145,810 |
| Vojvodina | 3,174 | 46,928 | 167,215 | 168,859 |
| Kosovo & Metohija | 5,206 | 920 | 2,676 | 3,070 |

Source: *Statistički godišnjak Jugoslavije 1991*. Belgrade: Savezni zavod az statistiku, 1992.

Table 19. Distribution of Yugoslavs in Socialist Federal Republic of Yugoslavia (Percentage Share in the Population)

| Republics & Regions | 1961 | 1971 | 1981 | 1991 |
|---|---|---|---|---|
| Bosnia & Hercegovina | 8.4 | 1.2 | 7.9 | 5.5 |
| Montenegro | 3.3 | 2.0 | 5.3 | 4.2 |
| Croatia | 0.4 | 1.9 | 8.2 | 2.2 |
| Macedonia | 0.1 | 0.2 | 0.7 | |
| Slovenia | 0.1 | 0.4 | 1.4 | 0.6 |
| Serbia - total | 0.3 | 1.5 | 4.7 | 3.2 |
| Central Serbia | 0.2 | 1.4 | 4.8 | 2.5 |
| Vojvodina | 0.2 | 2.4 | 8.2 | 8.4 |
| Kosovo & Metohija | 0.5 | 0.1 | 0.2 | 0.2 |

Source: *The Serbian Question in the Balkans*. Belgrade: University of Belgrade, 1995.

# Appendix

## UNITED NATIONS SECURITY COUNCIL RESOLUTIONS ON YUGOSLAVIA

It is not within the scope of this book to analyze, or provide in full, the United Nations Security Council Resolutions on the situation in the former Yugoslavia. Instead, the aim is to provide the reader with an indication of the subject areas covered by the resolutions and also the importance that the Security Council has given to the conflicts in the former Yugoslavia. From the first resolution on the subject, Resolution 713, 128 resolutions have so far been issued. In the same period, on other subjects, the Security Council has issued 260 resolutions. Since 1945, the former Yugoslavia accounts for 10% of all resolutions issued. It is not feasible to summarize every aspect of the resolutions; the aim has been to summarize the most important elements. Measures imposed under Chapter VII of the United Nations Charter are mandatory on all member states, so resolutions or individual measures under Chapter VII are so indicated. Chapter VIII measures are nonmandatory. All measures not specifically under Chapter VII and not referring to previous Chapter VII measures are nonmandatory.

The mnemonics, in the right-hand column of the table, have the following meanings: AE = Arms Embargo; PK = Peace-keeping; HA = Humanitarian Aid; HR = Human Rights; UN = United Nations Business; TE = Trade Embargo; NF = No-fly Zone; IL = International Humanitarian Law; SA = Safe Areas; WC = War Crimes; AP = Air Power; B-H = Bosnia and Hercegovina; CRO = Croatia; FRY = Federal Republic of Yugoslavia; MAK = Macedonia; KOS = Kosovo.

The full text of the resolutions can be found at UN Depository Libraries and UN Information Centers around the world or at the United Nations site on the World Wide Web (URL = http://www.un.org).

| YEAR / RES. | DATE | BRIEF DESCRIPTION | MNEMONIC KEY |
|---|---|---|---|
| 1991 | | | |
| 713 | 9/25 | Invoking Chapter VII of the UN Charter, specifically to "establish peace and stability," institutes a mandatory arms embargo against Yugoslavia. | AE |
| 721 | 11/27 | Ponders the establishment of a UN peace-keeping force for Yugoslavia, if the agreement signed in Geneva (11/23) is adhered to. | PK, CRO |
| 724 | 12/15 | Authorizes a limited military observer deployment as part of the mission of the secretary-general's personal envoy to consider preparations for a peacekeeping force. Also, under Chapter VII, requests all states to report on measures to impede arms deliveries and establishes a Committee of the Security Council to seek information from states; consider the information with the aim of increasing the effectiveness of the embargo, recommend appropriate measures in response to violations of the embargo, and provide regular information to the secretary-general to distribute to member states. Calls upon all states to cooperate fully with the committee. (This last call, mandatory due to the invocation of Chapter VII, was ignored by the United States from 1994 onwards when Iranian weapons shipments were known of but not reported). | AE, PK, CRO |
| 1992 | | | |
| 727 | 1/8 | Welcomes the "Implementation Accord" signed in Sarajevo on January 2 relating to the November 23 Geneva cease-fire. Endorses the sending of 50 military liaison personnel to promote maintenance of the cease-fire. Reaffirms the arms embargo and decides that the embargo applies in accordance with the secretary-general's Report S/23363, paragraph 33 (to any states that arise out of the dissolution of Yugoslavia). | AE, PK, CRO |

| | | | |
|---|---|---|---|
| 740 | 2/7 | Reaffirms the approval of the UN peace-keeping plan. Calls for full acceptance of the secretary-general's 11 December plan (S/23280). Calls on all states to cooperate fully with the committee established by Resolution 724, including reporting information of violations of the embargo. | PK, AE, CRO |
| 742 | 2/21 | Establishes the United Nations Protection Force (UNPROFOR). Initiates biannual reporting by the secretary-general on progress towards a peaceful settlement. Decides that the arms embargo does not apply to UNPROFOR. | PK, AE, CRO |
| 749 | 4/7 | Approves the secretary-general's first report on UNPROFOR (S/23777). Authorizes the full deployment of UNPROFOR. Appeals for all parties in Bosnia-Hercegovina to cooperate with the European Community to bring about a cease-fire and a negotiated political solution. | PK, CRO |
| 752 | 5/15 | Demands an end to fighting and respect of the 12 April cease-fire. Welcomes the efforts of the European Community. Demands that all interference from outside, by the JNA and element of the Croatian army, cease immediately. Such military forces to be withdrawn, put under the authority of the government of B-H, or disbanded with arms under effective international monitoring. Requests the secretary-general to consider assistance in this connection. Demands all irregular forces be disbanded. Calls for an end to forcible expulsions and any attempts to change the ethnic composition anywhere in SFRY. Emphasizes the need for humanitarian assistance. Welcomes the deployment of UNPROFOR in Eastern Slavonia. | PK, HA, HR |
| 752 | 5/18 | Acceptance of Croatia into the United Nations. | UN |
| 754 | 5/18 | Acceptance of Slovenia into the United Nations. | UN |
| 755 | 5/18 | Acceptance of Bosnia and Hercegovina into the United Nations. | UN |

| | | | |
|---|---|---|---|
| 757 | 5/30 | Acting under Chapter VII, condemns the Federal Republic of Yugoslavia, including the JNA, for failing to comply with the full requirements of Resolution 752. Demands that elements of the Croatian army in B-H act in accordance with paragraph 4 of Resolution 752. Decides that states will adopt the following measures until the Security Council decides that the FRY has taken measures to fulfil the requirements of Resolution 752. Bans trade, funding, flights, servicing or maintenance of aircraft, participation in sporting events, scientific and technical cooperation, and cultural exchanges. Reduces diplomatic representation in the FRY. Excludes transshipment of equipment and prevents legal action against the FRY for contracts affected by the resolution. Excludes UNPROFOR from any measures. All states must report measures instituted to the Security Council. The committee established under Resolution 724 will also be used to monitor progress on the trade embargo. Demands unimpeded humanitarian aid in B-H. | TE, HA, FRY |
| 758 | 6/8 | Enlarges mandate and strength of UNPROFOR, allowing deployment in B-H. Demands unimpeded aid to Sarajevo and other parts of B-H, including the security zone around Sarajevo and its airport agreed to in Geneva on May 22. | PK, B-H |
| 760 | 6/18 | Acting under Chapter VII, decides that, with the approval of the committee established under Resolution 724, funds or commodities and products are exempt from the trade embargo, paragraph 4(c), if they are for "essential humanitarian need." | TE |
| 761 | 6/29 | Authorizes the deployment of UNPROFOR to Sarajevo airport. | PK, HA |
| 762 | 6/30 | Urges the government of Croatia to withdraw behind the front-lines prior to its June 21 offensive. Authorizes a further 60 military observers as part of UNPROFOR. Reaffirms the arms embargo. | PK, AE, HA |

| | | | |
|---|---|---|---|
| 764 | 7/13 | Authorizes additional UNPROFOR units for the security and functioning of Sarajevo airport. Reaffirms that all parties are bound by the obligations of international humanitarian law, in particular the Geneva Convention of 1949. | PK, HR, HA |
| 769 | 8/7 | Authorizes enlargement of UNPROFOR's mandate and strength. Condemns abuses of civilians. | PK, HR |
| 770 | 8/13 | Acting under Chapter VII, calls on states, nationally or through regional organizations, to use all measures necessary to facilitate, in coordination with the United Nations, the delivery of United Nations humanitarian assistance. Demands unimpeded access for the ICRC to camps, prisons, and detention centers. | HA, HR |
| 771 | 8/13 | Reaffirms that international humanitarian law is binding on all parties to the conflict. Strongly condemns such violations, including those involved in the practice of "ethnic cleansing." Demands that relevant international humanitarian organizations, in particular the international Committee of the Red Cross, have full access to camps, prisons, and detentions centers within the territory of the former Yugoslavia. Calls upon states and international organizations to collate substantiated information in their possession relating to violations of international humanitarian law, including grave breaches of the Geneva Conventions, and to make this information available to the Security Council. Requests the secretary-general to collate such information and report to the Security Council. Under Chapter VII, all parties must comply with the current resolution, failing which the council will need to take further measures under the Charter. | HR |
| 776 | 9/14 | Authorizes the enlargement of UNPROFOR's mandate and strength in B-H, to include the protection of convoys of released detainees if requested by the ICRC. | PK, HR |

| | | | |
|---|---|---|---|
| 777 | 9/19 | Considers that the FRY cannot continue the SFRY's membership of the UN. Recommends to the General Assembly that the FRY should apply for membership and be excluded from the General Assembly. (General Assembly Resolution 47/1 implemented this decision). | FRY |
| 779 | 10/6 | Under Chapter VIII (nonmandatory), authorizes UNPROFOR monitoring of the withdrawal of the JNA from Croatia, the demilitarization of the Prevlaka Peninsula, and the removal of heavy weapons from neighboring areas of Croatia and Montenegro. Calls for increased cooperation with UNPROFOR. | CRO |
| 780 | 10/6 | Establishes an impartial commission of experts to examine and analyze information submitted pursuant to Resolution 721, the present resolution, and such further information as is supplied to the commission, with a view to reporting to the secretary-general on the evidence of grave breaches of the Geneva Conventions and other violations of international humanitarian law in the former Yugoslavia. | HR, WC |
| 781 | 10/9 | Acting pursuant to the provisions of Resolution 770 (under Chapter VII). Bans military flights in the airspace of B-H, except for UNPROFOR or flights in support of United Nations operations. Requests UNPROFOR to monitor the ban, including placing observers at airfields in the former Yugoslavia. Requests UNPROFOR approval and inspection of nonbanned flights to ensure that they comply with Security Council resolutions. Requests all States to provide national or regional assistance in monitoring the ban. | NF, PK |

| | | | |
|---|---|---|---|
| 786 | 11/10 | Welcomes the deployment of UNPROFOR and the European Union Monitoring Mission (ECMM) to airfields in Croatia, B-H, and the FRY. Reaffirms the ban on fixed-wing and rotary flights and that all parties concerned must comply with the ban. Calls on all parties to direct flight authorizations to UNPROFOR. Approves the further expansion of UNPROFOR for duties associated with the flight bans. | NR, PK |
| 787 | 11/16 | Reaffirms that the taking of territory by force or any practice of "ethnic cleansing" is unlawful. Demands all outside interference cease, including infiltration by paramilitaries. In particular, elements of the Croatian army are to be withdrawn or subject to the B-H government, disbanded, or disarmed. Condemns all violations of international humanitarian law. Under Chapter VII, transshipment of major raw materials through the FRY is banned unless authorized by the UN committee. Also bans vessels not wholly owned, but with a controlling interested deemed to be held by a person or undertaking in or operating from the FRY. Under Chapters VII and VIII, authorizes the halt for inspection of all inward and outward maritime shipping to ensure compliance with resolutions 713 and 757. Considers that observers should be stationed on the borders of B-H. Calls upon all parties to allow unimpeded delivery of humanitarian aid. Invites consultation on the establishment of safe areas for humanitarian purposes. | IL, TE, HA, SA |
| 795 | 12/11 | Authorizes an UNPROFOR presence in the former Yugoslav Republic of Macedonia. | MAK |
| 798 | 12/18 | Appalled by reports of massive, organized, and systematic detention and rape of women, in particular Muslim women, in B-H. Strongly condemns these acts, requests the secretary-general provide means of support for the European Community delegation to have free and secure access to the places of detention. | IL |

| 1993 | | | |
|---|---|---|---|
| 802 | 1/25 | Demands the immediate cessation of hostile activity by Croatian armed forces within or adjacent to the United Nations Protected Areas. Strongly condemns attacks by these forces against UNPROFOR and demands their immediate cessation. Demands that heavy weapons seized (by RSK forces) from UNPROFOR-controlled storage areas be returned. Demands compliance with cease-fire arrangements, including disbanding of Serb territorial defence units or others of similar function. | PK, CRO |
| 807 | 2/19 | Acting under Chapter VII, demands all parties comply with UN peace-keeping plan in Croatia. Demands forces not be sited near UNPROFOR in Croatia. Demands observance of UN resolutions relating to UNPROFOR in B-H. Extends UNPROFOR's mandate to March 31. | PK, CRO, B-H |
| 808 | 2/22 | Decides to establish an international tribunal for the prosecution of persons responsible for serious violations of international humanitarian law committed in the territory of the former Yugoslavia since 1991. | WC |
| 815 | 3/30 | Acting under Chapter VII, extend UNPROFOR mandate until June 30, 1993. Demands full respect for international humanitarian law in the UNPA's. | PK, IL, CRO |
| 816 | 3/31 | Acting under Chapter VII, authorizes the enforcement of the banning of fixed- and rotary wing military flights in B-H airspace seven days after the passing of the resolution. UNPROFOR to modify mechanisms of Paragraph 3 of Resolution 781 to allow humanitarian flights and other flights consistent with relevant resolutions of the Security Council. | PK, NF |
| 817 | 4/7 | Admits Macedonia to the UN, under the provisional name of the Former Yugoslav Republic of Macedonia (FYROM). | MAK |

| | | | |
|---|---|---|---|
| 819 | 4/16 | Acting under Chapter VII, demands that all parties concerned treat Srebrenica and its surroundings as a safe area that should be free from any armed attack or any other hostile act. Demands the cessation of attacks by Bosnian Serb paramilitary units and their withdrawal from surrounding areas. Demands that the FRY immediately cease the supply of military arms, equipment, and services to the Bosnia Serb paramilitary units in B-H. Demands cooperation with UNPROFOR. Condemns and rejects the deliberate actions of the Bosnian Serb party to force the evacuation of the civilian population of Srebrenica, as well as from other parts of B-H, as part of its overall abhorrent campaign of "ethnic cleansing." Reaffirms condemnation of violations of international humanitarian law. Demands unimpeded delivery of aid and the safety and freedom of movement of UNPROFOR. | SA, PK, HA, IL |
| 820 | 4/17 | Recalling the provisions of Chapter VIII, commends the peace plan for B-H and its acceptance by two of the parties. Expresses concern at the refusal of the Bosnian Serb party to accept. Demands observation of the cease-fire. Demands free movement for UNPROFOR and international humanitarian agencies. Condemns violations of international humanitarian law. Under Chapter VII, includes UNPAs and Bosnian Serb-held areas of B-H in the trade embargo. Limits Danube traffic transshipments. Confirms the banning of FRY-controlled or owned ships on the Danube. Freezes FRY-controlled or owned funds. Bans the transshipment of goods by road. Impounds all FRY-controlled or owned vehicles, ships, and aircraft currently outside the FRY. Allows the detention of all such vessels, which may be forfeited to the detaining State. Expenses for impounding such vehicles may be charged to the owners. Prohibits all services, financial or non-financial, with the FRY. Prohibits commercial maritime traffic in FRY waters. Authorizes force for any measures of the current resolution and other relevant resolutions. Exempts UNPROFOR, ICFY, and ECMM. Measures to be reviewed on verified acceptance and compliance by the Bosnian Serb party with the peace plan. | TE |

| | | | |
|---|---|---|---|
| 821 | 4/28 | Bans the FRY from the work of ECOSOC (the UN Economic and Social Council). | UN |
| 824 | 5/6 | Acting under Chapter VII, declares Sarajevo, Tuzla, Žepa, Goražde, Bihać, as well as Srebrenica, and their surroundings to be treated as safe areas by all parties concerned. Authorizes the strengthening of UNPROFOR. | SA, PK |
| 827 | 5/25 | Acting under Chapter VII, establishes an international tribunal for the sole purpose of prosecuting persons responsible for serious violations of international humanitarian law committed in the territory of the former Yugoslavia between January 1, 1991 and a date to be determined by the Security Council upon the restoration of peace. The Statute of the Tribunal is adopted (S/25274). Decides that all states shall cooperate fully with the International Tribunal and its organs in accordance with the present resolution and the statute of the International Tribunal. States shall take any measures necessary under their domestic law to implement the provisions of the present resolution and the statute. Urges states to contribute funds and resources to the International Tribunal. | SA, PK, AP |
| 836 | 6/4 | Acting under Chapter VII, calls for the full and immediate implementation of all its relevant resolutions. Commends the peace plan (S/25479). Decides to ensure full respect for the safe areas. Extends the UNPROFOR mandate to allow it to deter attacks against the safe areas, to monitor the cease-fire, to promote the withdrawal of military or paramilitary units other than those of the government of B-H, and to occupy some key points on the ground. Affirms the safe areas are a temporary measure. Authorizes UNPROFOR to use force to carry out its new mandate, acting in self-defence, including replying to bombardments or armed incursion or the freedom of movement of UNPROFOR or protected convoys. Authorizes States, nationally or through regional organizations, to supply close air support to UNPROFOR. | SA, PK, AP |
| 838 | 6/10 | Requests a report on options for the deployment of international observers on the borders of B-H and on the measures relating to the trade embargo. | TE |

| | | | |
|---|---|---|---|
| 842 | 6/18 | Expands the UNPROFOR deployment in FYROM. | PK, MAK |
| 843 | 6/18 | Confirms that the committee established under Resolution 724 is entrusted with the task of examining requests under Article 50 of the Charter of the United Nations. | TE |
| 844 | 6/18 | Acting under Chapter VII, authorizes the reinforcement of UNPROFOR for the safe area policy. Reaffirms the availability of close air support for the safe areas and encourages member states, acting nationally or through regional organizations, to coordinate with the secretary-general on that matter. | PK, AP |
| 845 | 6/18 | Commends the ICFY proposal on the name of FYROM to both Greece and FYROM. Urges a speedy settlement of remaining issues. | MAK |
| 847 | 6/30 | Requests a report on the progress of the peacekeeping plan for Croatia. Authorizes an extension to UNPROFOR's mandate to September 30. | PK, CRO |
| 855 | 8/9 | Calls on the FRY to again allow CSCE monitors on their territory. | FRY |
| 857 | 8/20 | Establishes a list of 23 nominated judges for the UN Tribunal, 11 of whom will be selected by vote in the General Assembly. | WC |
| 859 | 8/24 | Acting under Chapter VII, calls for an immediate cease-fire. Demands unhindered humanitarian aid, in particular to the "safe areas." Demands the safety and free movement of UNPROFOR and UNHCR. Affirms sovereignty, territorial integrity and political independence of B-H, and the principles set out in the London Conference (August 1992). Recalls the individual responsibility for war crimes. | SA, PK, WC, AP |
| 869 | 9/30 | Acting under Chapter VII, extends UNPROFOR mandate until October 1. | PK |
| 870 | 10/1 | Acting under Chapter VII, extends UNPROFOR mandate until October 5. | PK |

| | | | |
|---|---|---|---|
| 871 | 10/4 | Acting under Chapter VII, extends UNPROFOR mandate until March 31, 1994. Decides to review the question of close air support for UNPROFOR in Croatia. (With the Croatian army launching an attack on the Medak Pocket in September, which included heavy fighting with UNPROFOR units, the UNPROFOR mandate, which was due to end on September 30, became a "hot potato," leading to the two short extensions above while a compromise was sought. This resolution reiterated the territorial integrity, sovereignty, and independence of those States where UNPROFOR was based [Croatia, B-H, FYROM] and that the peace-plan for Croatia includes the demilitarization of the UNPAs, where Croatia claimed UNPROFOR was blocking progress). | PK |
| 877 | 10/21 | Appoints Ramon Escovar-Salom as prosecutor of the International Tribunal. (Shortly afterwards he resigned to take up a senior post in his own government). | WC |
| 1994 | | | |
| 900 | 3/4 | Acting under Chapter VII, calls for cooperation with UNPROFOR to consolidate the Sarajevo cease-fire. Calls for complete freedom of movement. Requests that a special representative be appointed by the secretary-general to draw up a plan of action in conjunction with the Bosnian government and local UN representatives. Invites the establishment of a voluntary trust fund for the restoration of essential public services in Sarajevo. | PK, BOS |
| 908 | 3/31 | Acting under Chapter VII, extends UNPROFOR mandate until September 30. Authorizes reinforcement of UNPROFOR in B-H by 3,500 personnel. Decides that close air support may be provided to UNPROFOR in Croatia. Urges compliance with the March 29, 1994 cease-fire agreement for the UNPAs in Croatia. Demands the cessation of hostilities against Maglaj and that the feasibility of extending the safe area concept be investigated. | PK |

| | | | |
|---|---|---|---|
| 913 | 4/22 | Acting under Chapter VII, demands an immediate cease-fire in Goražde and throughout B-H. Invites the secretary-general to ensure UNPROFOR is ready to monitor cease-fire and take heavy weapons under control in Goražde. Condemns the Bosnian Serb attack and demands withdrawal of these forces to a distance specified by UNPROFOR. Calls for an end to provocative action by whomsoever committed in and around the safe areas. | PK, SA |
| 914 | 4/27 | Acting under Chapter VII, authorizes an increase of up to 6,550 additional troops for UNPROFOR, 150 military observers, and 275 civilian police monitors. | PK |
| 936 | 7/8 | Appoints Judge Richard Goldstone as prosecutor of the International Tribunal. | WC |
| 941 | 9/23 | Acting under Chapter VII, reaffirms that all parties are bound by international humanitarian law. Strongly condemns all violations, in particular "ethnic cleansing" in Banja Luka, Bijeljina, and other areas under control of Bosnian Serb forces. Demands unimpeded access to areas of concern by UNPROFOR, UNHCR, ICRC, and the special representative. Requests the deployment of UNPROFOR troops in Banja Luka, Bijeljina, and other areas of concern. | PK, IL, HR |
| 942 | 9/23 | Acting under Chapter VII, approves the overall peace settlement (Contact Group plan). Strongly condemns the Bosnian Serbs for failing to agree to the plan unconditionally and in full. Requires all parties to continue to observe the cease-fire agreed on 8 June and refrain from new acts of hostility. Bans states from talking with the Bosnian Serb leadership as long as that party has not accepted the settlement in full. Further tightens economic sanctions against the Bosnian Serb areas with extensive new measures. | TE |

| | | | |
|---|---|---|---|
| 943 | 9/23 | Acting under Chapter VII, permits passenger flights of non-impounded aircraft to and from Belgrade airport. Permits the running of the passenger ferry service between Bar and the FRY. Suspends the cultural, sporting, and scientific bans, Paragraphs 8 (b) and (c) of Resolution 757, for 100 days. Streamlines the procedures of the sanctions committee concerning "legitimate humanitarian assistance" in particular for UNHCR and ICRC. Requests a report every 30 days on the closure of the border between the FRY and Bosnian Serb areas. Decides that if the closure is not enforced, the suspensions will be cancelled. | TE, FRY |
| 947 | 9/30 | Acting under Chapter VII, extends UNPROFOR's mandate to March 31, 1995. Urges the Bosnian Serbs to respect the territorial integrity of Croatia. | PK |
| 958 | 11/19 | Acting under Chapter VII, decides that all measures relating to the use of air power in B-H safe areas also apply in Croatia and the UNPROFOR mandate of Resolution 836, Paragraphs 5 and 9. | PK, AP, CRO |
| 959 | 11/19 | Condemns violation of international borders by the forces of the RSK. Expresses full support to UNPROFOR in the implementation of safe areas. Requests an update by the secretary-general on the safe area policy. Calls for an intensification of efforts to demilitarize Sarajevo. | PK, SA |
| 967 | 12/14 | Acting under Chapter VII, permits the export, otherwise banned, for a period of 30 days of 12,000 vials of diphtheria vaccine to counter an outbreak outside the territory of the former Yugoslavia at the request of UNICEF. Any payment for such serum, the only stocks available in the world, must be made from bank accounts that are already frozen under previous measures. | HA |

| 1995 | | | |
|---|---|---|---|
| 970 | 1/12 | Acting under Chapter VII, increases by another 100 days the suspension of some sanctions against the FRY. Further tightens measures against the Bosnian Serbs to prevent transshipment via the UNPAs. Requests the sanctions committee to expedite its procedures for the UNHCR and ICRC and UN organizations. | TE, FRY |
| 981 | 3/31 | Acting under Chapter VII, establishes the United Nations Confidence Restoration Operation in Croatia (UNCRO), for a period terminating November 30. As well as other tasks, it will monitor some border-crossings between Croatia and B-H and the FRY. Demands that all parties refrain from any acts of intimidation or violence against UNCRO. Urges the Croatian government to provide radio frequencies and television slots at no cost to the United Nations. | PK, CRO |
| 982 | 3/31 | Acting under Chapter VII, extends UNPROFOR's mandate in B-H to November 30. Authorizes the redeployment of any redundant UNPROFOR forces in Croatia to B-H. UNPROFOR HQ in Croatia will remain. Demands that all parties refrain from intimidation or violence against UNPROFOR. Calls for UNPROFOR to aid an extension of the current cease-fire beyond April 30. Notes progress with B-H government on the question of radio frequencies and television slots. | PK |
| 983 | 3/31 | Renames the UNPROFOR operation in FYROM the United Nations Preventive Deployment Force (UNPREDEP), terminating on November 30. | PK, MAK |
| 987 | 4/19 | Acting under Chapter VII, demands parties refrain from any act of intimidation or violence against UNPROFOR and its personnel. Invites the secretary-general to consider proposals to improve the safety of UNPROFOR. Calls for an extension of the cease-fire beyond April 30. Urges all parties to resume negotiations on the basis of the acceptance of the Contact Group plan as a starting-point. | PK |

| | | | |
|---|---|---|---|
| 988 | 4/21 | Acting under Chapter VII, further suspends measures of the embargo against the FRY to 5 July. Requests member states to reinforce the ICFY border monitors. Encourages the FRY to reinstate the removal of telecommunications links originally established in August 1994 between the FRY and Bosnian Serb areas. Requests the sanctions committee to urgently conclude its streamlining procedures. | TE, FRY |
| 990 | 4/28 | Acting under Chapter VII, authorizes the deployment of UNCRO. | PK |
| 992 | 5/11 | Acting under Chapter VII, exempts activities related to the repair of locks on the Danube from the trade embargo. | TE, FRY |
| 994 | 5/17 | Acting under Chapter VII, stresses the need for the reestablishment of the authority of UNCRO (following the seizure of the UNPA Sector West by the Croatian army on and after May 1). Demands the status, mandate, safety, and security of UNCRO be respected. Demands that parties refrain from taking any further military measures and warns that failure to comply with this demand may lead to the Security Council's considering further steps. | PK, CRO |
| 998 | 6/16 | Acting under Chapter VII, demands that Bosnian Serb forces release immediately and unconditionally all UNPROFOR personnel. Calls for a cease-fire. Demands free humanitarian access to all parts, in particular the safe areas. Demands that the parties respect fully the status of the safe areas. Underlines the need for a mutually agreed demilitarization of the safe areas, in terms of the cessation of attacks on the safe areas and of launching military attacks therefrom. Decides on a reinforcement of UNPROFOR by up to 12,500 troops. Welcomes the establishment of a rapid reaction capacity. | PK |
| 1003 | 7/5 | Acting under Chapter VII, Suspension of sanctions on FRY to continue until 18 September. Renews call for early mutual recognition between the states of the former Yugoslavia within their internationally recognized borders. | TE, FRY |

| | | | |
|---|---|---|---|
| 1004 | 7/12 | Acting under Chapter VII, demands that the Bosnian Serb forces cease their offensive and withdraw from the safe area of Srebrenica immediately. Demands also that the parties respect fully the status of the safe area of Srebrenica in accordance with the agreement of April 18, 1993. Demands that the parties respect fully the safety of UNPROFOR. Demands that the Bosnian Serb forces immediately and unconditionally release all detained UNPROFOR personnel. Demands that all parties allow unimpeded access to the United Nations high commissioner for refugees and other international humanitarian agencies. | SA, PK |
| 1009 | 8/10 | Acting under Chapter VII, demands that Croatia cease all military actions and that there be full compliance with all council resolutions, including resolution 994 (1995), to respect fully the rights of the local Serb population including their rights to remain, leave, or return in safety, allow access to this population by international humanitarian organizations, and create conditions conducive to return. Reminds Croatia of its responsibility to allow access to the ICRC. Reiterates that all those who commit violations of international humanitarian law will be held individually responsible in respect of such acts. Demands that the government of the Republic of Croatia fully respect the status of United Nations personnel, refrain from any attacks against them, bring to justice those responsible for any such attacks, and ensure the safety and freedom of movement of United Nations personnel at all times, and requests the secretary-general to keep the council informed of steps taken and decisions rendered in this regard. | CRO, IL |
| 1010 | 10/8 | Demands that the Bosnian Serbs give immediate access to the UNHCR, the ICRC, and other international agencies to persons displaced from Srebrenica and Žepa. Reiterates that all those who commit violations of international humanitarian law will be held individually responsible in respect of such acts. | IL |
| 1015 | 9/15 | Acting under Chapter VII, extends the suspension of sanctions until March 18, 1996. | TE, FRY |

| | | | |
|---|---|---|---|
| 1016 | 9/21 | Deplores the casualties suffered by the Danish peacekeepers and demands that all parties fully respect the safety of United Nations personnel. Calls upon all parties and others concerned to refrain from violence and hostile acts and to reach immediately a cease-fire. Calls upon member states involved in promoting an overall peaceful settlement in the region to intensify their efforts to this end with the parties to ensure that they take no advantage of the current situation and show utmost restraint. Requests the secretary-general to provide to the council as soon as possible information on the humanitarian situation, including information available through the UNHCR and other sources. | PK |
| 1019 | 11/9 | Condemns all violations of international humanitarian law. Reaffirms demand that the Bosnian Serbs give immediate access to the UNHCR, the ICRC, and other international agencies to persons from Srebrenica, Žepa, and the regions of Banja Luka and Sanski Most. Reaffirms further the freedom of movement the United Nations and other relevant international organizations. Demands that all detention camps throughout B-H be immediately closed. Reaffirms its demand that Croatia end violations of international humanitarian law and investigate all reports of such violations. Reiterates its demand that Croatia respect fully the rights of the local Serb population. Demands that all states and all parties to the conflict in the former Yugoslavia comply fully and in good faith with the obligations contained in Paragraph 4 of Resolution 827 (1993) to cooperate fully with the International Tribunal. Demands that all parties, and in particular the Bosnian Serb party, refrain from any action intended to destroy, alter, conceal, or damage any evidence. Requests the secretary-general to submit to the council a report based on all information available to the United Nations concerning recent violations of international humanitarian law in the areas of Srebrenica, Žepa, Banja Luka, and Sanski Most. Requests the secretary-general continue to inform the council on a regular basis of measures taken by the government of the Republic of Croatia to implement Resolution 1009 (1995) and the present resolution. | IL, WC, B-H, CRO |

| | | | |
|---|---|---|---|
| 1021 | 11/22 | Acting under Chapter VII, sets out the means of lifting the arms embargo initiated by Resolution 713. | AE |
| 1022 | 11/22 | Indefinite suspension of the various trade embargo measures, excluding those applied to the Bosnian Serbs, until military withdrawal is confirmed to the Security Council. The suspension can be revoked by the international force commander or the high representative for Bosnia. Provides that measures will be terminated on the tenth day following the occurrence of the first free and fair elections in B-H. | TE, FRY |
| 1023 | 11/22 | Welcomes the Basic Agreement on the Region of Eastern Slavonia, Baranja, and Western Sirmium. Recognizes the request to establish a transitional administration and authorize an appropriate international force. | PK, CRO |
| 1025 | 11/30 | Acting under Chapter VII, requests the secretary-general to submit a report on all aspects of the establishment by the council of an operation consisting of a transitional administration and a transitional peace-keeping force. In order to allow for the orderly establishment of the operation referred to in paragraph 2 above, the mandate of UNCRO shall terminate after an interim period ending on January 15, 1996 or when the council has decided on the deployment transitional peace-keeping force, whichever is sooner. | PK, CRO |
| 1026 | 11/30 | Acting under Chapter VII, decides to extend the mandate of UNPROFOR for a period terminating on January 31, 1996, pending further action by the council with regard to the implementation of the peace agreement. | PK |
| 1027 | 11/30 | Decides to extend the mandate of UNPREDEP for a period terminating on May 30, 1996. | PK |

| | | | |
|---|---|---|---|
| 1031 | 12/15 | Acting under Chapter VII, all States shall cooperate fully with the International Tribunal. Welcomes the OSCE to adopt and put in place elections for B-H. Welcomes the securing to all persons within their jurisdiction the highest level of internationally recognized human rights and fundamental freedoms in B-H. Welcomes the commitment to the right return. Notes the invitation to the international community to send a multinational implementation force for the period of approximately one year. Authorizes the member states acting through or in cooperation with the organization referred to in Annex 1-A of the peace agreement to establish a multinational implementation force (IFOR). Demands that the parties respect the security and freedom of movement of IFOR and other international personnel. Decides the arms embargo does not apply to weapons and military equipment destined for the sole use of IFOR or of international police forces. Stresses the need for early action in Sarajevo to create confidence between the communities and to this end requests the secretary-general to ensure the early redeployment of elements of United Nations civilian police from the Republic of Croatia to Sarajevo. Decides that the mandate of UNPROFOR shall terminate on the date on which the secretary-general reports to the council that the transfer of authority from UNPROFOR to IFOR has taken place. | WC, PK, PP |
| 1034 | 12/212 | Strongly condemns all violations of international humanitarian law by Bosnian Serb forces in Srebrenica, Žepa, Banja Luka, and Sanski Most. Supports the efforts of ICRC to trace missing persons. Affirms that such violations must be fully investigated. Notes the further indictment of Radovan Karadžic and Ratko Mladić by the International Tribunal. Demands immediate access to areas in question. Demands closure of detention camps. Condemns looting and destruction by HVO (Bosnian Croat) forces in Mrkonjić Grad and Šipovo. | IL, WC |

| | | | |
|---|---|---|---|
| 1035 | 12/21 | Decides to establish, for a period of one year from the IFOR takeover, a United Nations civilian police force to be known as the International Police Task Force (IPTF) to be entrusted with the tasks set out in Annex 11 of the peace agreement and a United Nations civilian office with the responsibilities set out in the report of the secretary-general. | POL |
| 1996 | | | |
| 1037 | 1/15 | Acting under Chapter VII, establishes UNTAES for an initial 12 month period. Demilitarization to take place within 30 days of the deployment of UNTAES. Consists of an initial deployment of 5,000 troops. States may take all measures necessary in the support of UNTAES. Reaffirms that all states must cooperate with the International Tribunal. UNTAES is to cooperate with the International Tribunal. | PK, WC |
| 1038 | 1/15 | Authorizes the United Nations military observers to continue monitoring the demilitarization of the Prevlaka Peninsula for a period of three months. Requests the United Nations military observers and (IFOR) to cooperate fully with each other. | PK |
| 1043 | 1/31 | Authorizes, as part of UNTAES, the deployment of 100 military observers for a period of six months. | PK |
| 1046 | 2/13 | Authorizes a further 50 personnel for UNPREDEP, approves the establishment of the position of force commander of UNPREDEP. | PK |
| 1047 | 2/29 | Appoints Mrs. Loiuse Arbour as prosecutor of the International Tribunal on the effective date of Richard Goldstone's resignation. | WC |
| 1058 | 5/30 | Extends the mandate of UNPREDEP until November 30. | PK |
| 1066 | 7/15 | Authorizes the United Nations military observers to continue monitoring the demilitarization of the Prevlaka Peninsula until January 15, 1997. Requests the United Nations military observers and IFOR to continue to cooperate fully. | PK |

| | | | |
|---|---|---|---|
| 1069 | 7/30 | As part of UNTAES, the deployment of 100 military observers for an additional period of six months, ending on January 15, 1997. | PK |
| 1074 | 10/1 | Acting under Chapter VII. Notes elections took place on September 14, 1996, in B-H. Decides, in accordance with resolution 1022 to terminate, with immediate effect, the measures referred to in that resolution. Decides to consider the imposition of measures if any party fails significantly to meet its obligations under the peace agreement. Decides to dissolve the committee established by its Resolution 724 once its report has been finalized and expresses its gratitude for the work of the committee. | TE |
| 1079 | 11/15 | Acting under Chapter VII, expresses its full support for UNTAES and calls upon Croatia and the local Serb community to cooperate fully with UNTAES, including the holding of local elections in the region. Urges Croatia and the local Serb community to avoid actions that could lead to refugee movements and in the context of the right of all refugees and displaced persons to return to their homes of origin, reaffirms the right of all persons originating from Croatia to return to their homes of origin throughout Croatia. Decides to maintain the United Nations presence in the region until the end of the extended transitional period as provided for in the basic agreement and decides to extend the mandate of UNTAES until July 15, 1997, and requests that as soon as possible after the successful holding of elections, and in no case later than July 1, 1997, the secretary-general provide to the Council for its immediate action his recommendations, in the light of the parties' progress towards fulfilling the basic agreement, for the further United Nations presence, possibly a restructured UNTAES, consistent with the fulfillment of the basic agreement, for the six-month period beginning from July 16, 1997. | PK, CRO |
| 1082 | 11/27 | Decides to extend the mandate of UNPREDEP for a period terminating on May 31, 1997, with a reduction of its military component by 300 all ranks by April 30, 1997, with a view to concluding the mandate as and when circumstances permit. | PK, MAK |

| | | | |
|---|---|---|---|
| 1088 | 12/12 | Acting under Chapter VII, deals with the extension of overt international intervention in B-H beyond the original one year envisioned by the Dayton Agreement. The NATO-led Implementation Force (IFOR) is to be replaced by a NATO-led Stabilisation Force (SFOR), which is authorised to run for 18 months. The International Police Task Force (IPTF) is authorised for a further one year (to 21 December 21, 1997) and is given increased powers, including the ability to command dismissal of local police personnel, and to train local forces in democratic and human rights policing. The authority of the civilian high representative is reiterated and strengthened. The mandate of the OSCE (already extended by the OSCE themselves) to "prepare and conduct" the municipal elections (previously postponed by the OSCE) is rubber-stamped. International financial support for rebuilding is linked to adherence to the Dayton Peace Agreement, specifically to cooperation with the war crimes tribunal. In something of a contradiction to this, the resolution "Emphasizes the importance of the creation of conditions conducive to the reconstruction and development of Bosnia and Hercegovina, encourages Member States to provide assistance for the programme of reconstruction in that country." In case this causes the parties to forget about the war crimes issue, they are later further, separately, reminded that they have to cooperate with the International Tribunal. | PK, WC, HR |
| 1997 | | | |
| 1093 | 1/14 | Authorizes the United Nations military observers to continue monitoring the demilitarization of the Prevlaka peninsula until July 15, 1997. Requests that the United Nations military observers and SFOR cooperate. | CRO, PK |
| 1103 | 3/31 | Decides to authorise an increase in personnel for UNMIBH, by 186 police (for UN-IPTF) and 11 civilians, required by the extension of control over the disputed town of Brčko. | B-H |

| | | | |
|---|---|---|---|
| 1104 | 4/8 | Establishes a list of 19 nominated judges for the UN Tribunal, 11 of whom will be selected by vote in the General Assembly. The list includes judges standing for a second four-year term. | WC |
| 1105 | 4/9 | Suspends the reduction of military component of UNPREDEP prior to the end of its mandate on 31 May, welcomes the redeployment of UNPREDEP in the light of the situation in Albania and encourages the Secretary-General to continue redeployment of UNPREDEP taking into consideration the situation in the region. | MAC, PK |
| 1107 | 5/16 | Decides to authorise an increase in personnel for UNMIBH, by 120 police (for UN-IPTF), due to the extension of powers at the London Peace Implementation Council meeting of 4-5 December 1996. | B-H |
| 1110 | 5/28 | Extends the deployment of UNPREDEP until 31 November, with a phased two-month reduction of 300 personnel starting 1 October. Redeployment relating to the situation in Albania is welcomed, with the Secretary-General to report on the situation in the region, especially Albania, by 15 August. | MAC, PK |
| 1112 | 6/12 | Confirms the appointment of Carlos Westendorp as replacement to Carl Bildt as the UN High Representative for Bosnia, as decided at the Steering Board meeting of the Peace Implementation Council held at Sintra, Portugal, on 30 May. Thanks Mr. Bildt for his work. Reaffirms that the High Representative is the final authority relating to Annex 10 of the Dayton Peace Agreement. | B-H |
| 1119 | 7/14 | Authorizes the United Nations military observers to continue monitoring the demilitarization of the Prevlaka peninsula until January 15, 1998. | CRO, PK |

| | | | |
|---|---|---|---|
| 1120 | 7/14 | Acting under Chapter VII, supports UNTAES, and calls upon the Government of the Republic of Croatia and the local Serb community to cooperate fully with UNTAES and other international bodies. Reaffirms in particular the importance of full compliance by the parties, in particular by the Government of the Republic of Croatia to respect the highest standards of human rights and fundamental freedoms. Reaffirms the right of all refugees and displaced persons originating from the Republic of Croatia to return to their homes of origin. Strongly urges the Government of the Republic of Croatia to eliminate promptly the administrative and legal obstacles to the return of refugees and displaced persons. Reminds the local Serb population of the importance of continuing to demonstrate a constructive attitude towards the reintegration of the region. Reiterates its previous calls on all the States in the region, including the Government of the Republic of Croatia, to cooperate fully with the International Tribunal for the Former Yugoslavia; urges the Government of the Republic of Croatia to eliminate ambiguities in implementation of the Amnesty Law. Extends the mandate of UNTAES until 15 January 1998. | CRO, PK |
| 1126 | 8/27 | Temporarily extends the presence of three judges at the International Tribunal who were not re-elected, but who are sitting on a current case. It is hoped the case will be finished before November 1998. | WC |
| 1140 | 11/28 | Extends the mandate of UNPREDEP until 4 December. | MAC, PK |
| 1142 | 12/4 | Extends the mandate of UNPREDEP until 31 August, 1998. | MAC, PK |
| 1144 | 12/19 | Extends the mandate of UNMIBH, which includes the IPTF, to 21 June, 1998, to be further extended unless there are significant changes in security arrangements in the country. | B-H |

| | | | |
|---|---|---|---|
| 1145 | 12/19 | Reiterates the continuing obligation of the Government of the Republic of Croatia to respect the highest standards of human rights and fundamental freedoms. Underlines that it is the Government of the Republic of Croatia and the Croatian police and judicial authorities who bear full responsibility for the security and safeguarding of the civil rights of all residents of the Republic of Croatia, regardless of ethnicity, urges the Republic of Croatia and the Federal Republic of Yugoslavia to pursue further normalization of their relations, especially in the areas of cross-border confidence-building measures, demilitarization and dual nationality. Decides to establish, with effect from 16 January 1998, a support group of 180 civilian police monitors, for a single period of up to nine months as recommended by the secretary-general, to continue to monitor the performance of the Croatian police in the Danube region. | CRO, PK |
| 1998 | | | |
| 1147 | 1/13 | Authorizes the United Nations military observers to continue monitoring the demilitarization of the Prevlaka peninsula until July 15, 1998. | CRO, PK |

| | | | |
|---|---|---|---|
| 1160 | 3/31 | Acting under Chapter VII, Calls upon the Federal Republic of Yugoslavia immediately to take the further necessary steps to achieve a political solution to the issue of Kosovo through dialogue, calls also upon the Kosovar Albanian leadership to condemn all terrorist action, and emphasizes that all elements in the Kosovar Albanian community should pursue their goals by peaceful means only. Agrees, without prejudging the outcome of that dialogue, with the proposal in the Contact Group statements of 9 and 25 March 1998 that the principles for a solution of the Kosovo problem should be based on the territorial integrity of the Federal Republic of Yugoslavia and must also take into account the rights of the Kosovar Albanians applies an arms ban and establishes an oversight comittee. Decides to review the situation on the basis of whether the Government of the Federal Republic of Yugoslavia, cooperating in a constructive manner with the Contact Group, have:<br><br>(a) begun a substantive dialogue; (b) withdrawn the special police units and ceased action by the security forces; (c) allowed access to Kosovo by humanitarian organizations as well as representatives of Contact Group and other embassies; (d) accepted a mission by the Personal Representative of the OSCE Chairman-in-Office for the Federal Republic of Yugoslavia that would include a new and specific mandate for addressing the probems in Kosovo, as well as the return of the OSCE long-term missions;<br>(e) facilitated a mission to Kosovo by the United Nations High Commissioner for Human Rights;<br><br>Urges the Office of the Prosecutor of the International Tribunal established pursuant to resolution 827 (1993) of 25 May 1993 to begin gathering information related to the violence in Kosovo. | KOS, WC |

| | | | |
|---|---|---|---|
| 1166 | 5/13 | Acting under Chapter VII, decides to establish a third Trial Chamber of the International Tribunal, with an additional three judges shall be elected as soon as possible to serve in the additional Trial Chamber, and decides also, without prejudice to article 13.4 of the Statute of the International Tribunal, that once elected they shall serve until the date of the expiry of the terms of office of the existing judges, and that for the purpose of that election the Security Council shall, notwithstanding article 13.2 (c) of the Statute, establish a list from the nominations received of not less than six and not more than nine candidates. | WC |
| 1168 | 5/28 | Increases the IPTF by a further 30 personnel. | B-H |
| 1174 | 6/15 | Acting under Chapter VII, extends SFOR for a further 12 months and extends the mandate of IPTF to June 21, 1999. | B-H, PK |
| 1183 | 7/15 | Authorizes the United Nations military observers to continue monitoring the demilitarization of the Prevlaka peninsula until January 15, 1999. | CRO, PK |
| 1184 | 7/16 | Extends the authority of UNMIBH to oversee the legal system in B-H. | B-H |
| 1186 | 7/21 | Extends the mandate of UNPREDEP to February 28, 1999, increases force to 1,050 troops. | MAC, PK |
| 1191 | 8/28 | Forwards nine nominated judges for the additional three positions opened by the new trial chamber for the International Tribunal. | WC |

| | | | |
|---|---|---|---|
| 1199 | 9/23 | Acting under Chapter VII, demands that all parties, groups and individuals immediately cease hostilities and maintain a ceasefire in Kosovo, also that the authorities of the Federal Republic of Yugoslavia and the Kosovo Albanian leadership take immediate steps to improve the humanitarian situation, calls upon the authorities in the Federal Republic of Yugoslavia and the Kosovo Albanian leadership to enter immediately into a meaningful dialogue without preconditions and with international involvement, demands further that the Federal Republic of Yugoslavia implement immediately the following concrete measures towards achieving a political solution<br><br>(a) cease all action by the security forces affecting the civilian population; (b) enable effective and continuous international monitoring in Kosovo; (c) facilitate, in agreement with the UNHCR and the International Committee of the Red Cross (ICRC), the safe return of refugees and displaced persons to their homes; (d) make rapid progress to a clear timetable, in the dialogue with the aim of agreeing upon confidence-building measures and finding a political solution to the problems of Kosovo;<br><br>Requests States to pursue all means consistent with their domestic legislation and relevant international law to prevent funds collected on their territory being used to contravene the arms embargo. Calls upon the authorities of the Federal Republic of Yugoslavia, the leaders of the Kosovo Albanian community and all others concerned to cooperate fully with the Prosecutor of the International Tribunal for the Former Yugoslavia. Decides, should the concrete measures demanded in this resolution and resolution 1160 (1998) not be taken, to consider further action and additional measures to maintain or restore peace and stability in the region. | KOS |

# About the Author

Željan E. Šuster, professor of economics and the associate dean of the School of Business at the University of New Haven, was born in Split, then Yugoslavia, in 1958. He received a Ph.D. in Economics from the University of Belgrade in 1988. From 1983 to 1989 he was a research associate of the Institute of Economic Sciences in Belgrade. In 1989 he moved to the United States and after teaching appointments at the University of Connecticut and Wesleyan University joined the University of New Haven (1990). He has published extensively in the area of international political economy, economic history, and international finance. He is currently researching the liberalization of the financial sector in the Federal Republic of Yugoslavia.